THE DEMON CROWN TRILOGY

"Die, swine!" cried the rebel. The man's sword rose and fell. Blood spattered from the constable's wound. The remaining constable proved easy prey. The six who survived the ambush stood over the bodies, gloating. Again Vered tried to attack, and again his blade passed through his target as if traveling through smoke.

Vered jumped back to reassess his actions. The rebels paid him no heed. It was as if he did not exist for them. But he *saw* and *heard* so clearly!

Movement behind drew him around. He faced the leader of this small group. He *felt* power exuding from this man.

The wizard halted and cocked his head to one side. He yelled, "Search the area! There is another lurking nearby! Another wizard!"

Vered spun and used his *sight* to look for the other wizard. He *saw* no one. It took several seconds for him to realize that this sorcerer did not mean another. He meant Vered.

THE DEMON CROWN TRILOGY

The Glass Warrior
Phantoms on the Wind
A Symphony of Storms

Robert E. Vardeman

NEW ENGLISH LIBRARY
Hodder and Stoughton

First published in the United States of
America as three separate volumes:

THE GLASS WARRIOR
© 1989 by Robert E. Vardeman
Published by Tor Books in 1989

PHANTOMS ON THE WIND
© 1989 by Robert E. Vardeman
Published by Tor Books in 1989

A SYMPHONY OF STORMS
© 1990 by Robert E. Vardeman
Published by Tor Books in 1990

New English Library paperback
edition 1990

British Library C.I.P.

Vardeman, Robert E.
  The demon crown trilogy.
  I. Title
  813.54 [F]

ISBN 0 450 53170 8

Printed and bound in Great Britain
for Hodder and Stoughton Paper-
backs, a division of Hodder and
Stoughton Ltd., Mill Road, Dunton
Green, Sevenoaks, Kent TN13 2YA.
(Editorial Office: 47 Bedford Square,
London WC1B 3DP) by Cox & Wyman
Ltd., Reading, Berks.

CHAPTER ONE

"Betrayed! Lord Dews, we've been betrayed! Everywhere! Their soldiers surround us!"

"Calm yourself, Jiskko. They come to join us, not to fight us." Dews Gaemock leaned back, feeling the bones in his spine separate. Jabs of pain made him think for the hundredth time this day that he had grown too old for insurrection. No matter that the rulers in Porotane were despots and that the royal line had died with King Lamost. Gaemock slowly straightened a war-weary arm. More joints cracked, like corn thrown into a campfire.

"But Lord, look at them! They do not carry the black and gold banner of Ionia's ruffians. The only war pennants in sight are pure green."

Gaemock forced himself upright, then got to his feet. It took him only seconds to see that his adviser had spoken the truth. "Whose banners are those?" he demanded. His dark eyes scanned the circle of his silent commanders. They shook their heads and averted their eyes.

Again, his intelligence had failed, perhaps fatally. Gaemock cursed. "This never happened when Efran rode at my side."

1

"Lord," said Jiskko, "your brother is long the traitor."

"Never say that!" raged Gaemock. His dark eyes burned like coals. Jiskko wilted under the look. "My brother is no traitor. He has chosen to support the royals. That is all."

"But Lord, we *fight* the royals. We march on Porotane to take it from Duke Freow and his sycophant dogs."

Dews Gaemock forced down his seething anger. His younger brother had always acted independently. Sometimes Efran had been independent of good sense, but Gaemock could not fault him for that. Sometimes *he* acted stupidly.

As he did now. The green banners were not those of Lady Ionia, his temporary ally in this siege of Porotane's castle. Had she betrayed him already? Ionia was a treacherous bitch, and he had allowed Jiskko and the others to convince him against his instincts that alliance with her would prove the turning point in the civil war. Too long they had battled, faction against faction, brother against brother, Gaemock thought bitterly. If only King Lamost had not died so suddenly. Assassinated some said.

The cause of the king's death mattered little. The kidnapping of his twin children, Lokenna and Lorens, did. Without a successor to ascend the throne, without a true heir to don the Demon Crown, the entire kingdom had disintegrated over the past twenty sorrow-and-death-filled years. Duke Freow claimed to hunt for the children. Gaemock could not believe it. Even if the duke's claim that Lorens and lovely little Lokenna had been stolen away by a wizard were true, some trace of them would have been found over *twenty* years.

"Sire," called Jiskko. "A runner from the front lines." Gaemock's adviser motioned. A youngling, hardly more than eight summers, dashed up and fell to his knees, head bowed.

"What have you seen, son?" asked Gaemock, holding back the tears as he spoke. So young. The boy was so young. His spies had been reduced to children. Not two years ago his intelligence network had been the strongest in all Porotane. Not even Duke Freow matched it. But that had been before Efran left to side with the royals. Gaemock hoped that the duke appreciated his brother's tactical brilliance and unerringly strategic instincts.

"Lord Dews, they are commanded by a wizard. I was unable to learn his name."

"That is all right. Wizards are not known for their loquacity when it comes to naming themselves in public."

"Lord, I was close enough!" the boy cried. "If I had learned his name, I could have slain him!"

"The wizard's name means little. Another trader in magicks entering the battle does not matter. We have many who chevy our steps for their own gain. What did you see of their battle strength? This is of true importance."

"Lord, I believe the wizard entered into treacherous alliance with the Lady Ionia. He mentioned her often, laughing as he did so. At his command are a full five hundred armed soldiers. They have fanned out along the valley to our right flank, and move steadily forward to put themselves between Porotane's castle and our escape route."

Gaemock nodded. "Continue your report, son." The boy rattled on but Gaemock did not listen. His mind worked over the tactical considerations of continuing the siege against Duke Freow and the castle of Porotane. He had to consider that Ionia had either been destroyed or had betrayed him. Gaemock's eyes rose and scanned the two hills his troops occupied—and the valley below. If he ordered the attack on Porotane's castle, the wizard would be in good position to push through that valley and cut Gaemock's rebel forces in half.

If he did not advance, Gaemock controlled the high ground and might be able to trap the other's forces should the wizard prove impatient.

"Lord, we should retreat. Leave Porotane for another day. Without Ionia's assistance, we stand little chance for success in battle." Jiskko shifted nervously from foot to foot, his fingers drumming on his sword hilt.

"The River Ty," said Gaemock. "Have our sappers readied the dams?"

Another commander spoke to this. "Lord, they are ready. The flow can be diverted in less than an hour, leaving the castle without water."

Gaemock brushed this aside. "That is of no consequence now. Freow has cisterns filled with water. He has tuns in the cellars of the castle, enough to supply his defenders for a month or more. When we planned this attack, we saw it as a lengthy siege. We would cut off their water, burn their fields, and force as many to take shelter within the castle walls as possible."

"Lord, the wizard's troops begin to advance," said Jiskko, his attention focused on a semaphore signaler on a distant hill. Even as he watched, the signalman burst into flame.

"The wizard's doing," Gaemock said tiredly. "I can fight with sword and bow, but not their demon-damned magic! How I hate them all!" Dews Gaemock waved his fist at the sky, cursing all sorcerers.

The earliest battles in the civil war had been feeble when compared with more recent ones. Only a month previous, Gaemock had seen an entire field ripped asunder by a wizard's lightning bolt. Not only the crops in the field but a score of peasant farmers had perished. The wizard had misdirected his blast and missed the rebel soldiers.

Seldom did such wanton and senseless killing occur when sword was in hand. The warrior's code held, even among the fighting segments of Porotane, and only those armed and in battle were slain. Surrender might come too slow, but was observed more often than not when soldiers could fight no more. Gaemock had gained his most valued commanders through surrender. Jiskko had roamed the countryside with his own band of mercenaries for over three years before meeting Gaemock's forces and being vanquished.

Jiskko had given his solemn oath of allegiance, and Gaemock valued him above all others on his small staff. And never had Jiskko given him reason to doubt that loyalty.

But wizards? Gaemock scoffed at them and openly shouted obscenities when he saw one. They had no honor. Random slaughter meant nothing to them. A field filled with peasant farmers, women, and children? The wizard had no doubt felt only passing scorn for them. Perhaps anger at his intended victims for not being where he directed his magical blast, but remorse for the innocent dead? Never.

How the wizard he now faced had subverted Ionia, he couldn't say. The woman had given her word, but Gaemock had extracted it from her under less than honorable circumstances. A smile slipped across his lips, vanishing as quickly as it had appeared. The night in Ionia's camp had been interesting. Seldom had Gaemock found a bed companion as skilled and exciting. She had vowed her undying love for him. This Gaemock had thought exaggeration generated by the throes of passion, but she had also pledged support for his thrust into Porotane's belly.

"Damn her, too," he said.

"Lord?"

"Nothing, Jiskko. You are correct in your appraisal. We cannot attack the castle successfully. Not now, not with a rival force in the field threatening us."

"We do not believe Freow will sally forth from the castle," said another commander. "We can deal with this wizard and . . ."

Gaemock shook his head. The commander's voice trailed off when he saw the disapproval on his leader's face. "No," said Gaemock, "this battle must wait for another day. We seek only escape now, escape with as little damage done to our soldiers as possible."

"Lord!" protested Jiskko. "We have spent vast sums on this attack. To stop now, why, that would set us back six months or longer. We could not hope to mount another force before autumn, if then."

"I will not see my brave fighters killed senselessly," Gaemock said firmly. "There will be more gold." He laughed harshly. "We have lived as brigands for years. Another few months should do nothing but enhance our cutthroat reputation."

"I'll order the sappers to destroy the dikes, Lord," said the commander of the battle engineers.

"No!"

"But why not? Diverting the River Ty was intended to break the spirit of the castle's defenders. Why—"

"No. Bring me a map and I'll show you what I have in mind."

The boy dashed away, returning in a few minutes with a large parchment scroll. Gaemock took it and spread out the illuminated map, ignoring the dragons and other wivern frolicking around the borders. Gaemock stared at the map, then thrust his finger onto it.

"Here. This is the point where the sappers have prepared the temporary dams. If they move them less than a hundred paces upstream and place them thusly, the Ty will flow past our position. Otherwise, the river is diverted into the southern swamps past the castle."

"The valley between our forces will be flooded if they move upstream," said Jiskko. "But such a move is not possible without an additional week of hard work. The sappers sought only to divert the river from supplying the castle, not bring its course down this valley."

"A pity, isn't it?" mused Gaemock. "We need the valley flooded, if we are to rout the other forces."

"That prevents the wizard from attacking," said Jiskko. "But even if such a flooding were possible, his purpose is still served. Our strength will be halved. He can choose which side to attack and we shall be unable to reinforce because of the river."

Gaemock nodded, a lock of lank black hair falling forward to dangle before his eyes. "It would appear so, wouldn't it?" He smiled broadly. "We shall have a surprise for our backstabbing wizard."

"And Ionia?" urged Jiskko. He alone had cautioned Gaemock repeatedly against any alliance with the woman.

"We might seek her out at leisure, after our troops are secure. I would have words with her. Curt ones." Gaemock moved his finger on the map around the sappers' position, then stabbed down hard. "Abandon the dikes along the Ty. Since the engineers cannot serve us in time, remove them immediately. We will need them in the autumn for our new campaign."

"As my lord commands," said Jiskko.

Dews Gaemock dismissed his commanders to begin their new assignments, turning attention from the Porotane castle to the wizard's forces. He reached out and collared the boy who had acted as messenger.

"A word with you," Gaemock said.

The boy dropped again to his knees, head bowed. "I am yours to command, Lord Dews."

"Rubbish. Stand up straight, proud. Why do you think we fight?"

"To gain power over all Porotane."

"And then?" Gaemock prompted. "What do we do then, once we have won this war?"

"Why, you become king. I do not understand what you seek of me, Lord." The confusion on the boy's face showed that he had no firm knowledge of why Gaemock fought this bloody war. But then, the boy was only eight years of age. How many of Gaemock's adult advisers understood the purpose? Simple power? To throw Duke Freow out and sit upon the throne in his stead?

"I fight for freedom, son. I do not wish to replace the regent only to rule. I wish to restore order, to give Porotane a sense of security. Without any of royal blood on the throne, without the Demon Crown on the head of the true ruler, upstarts like Baron Theoll will force brutal laws on all our heads. I do not wish to overthrow royal authority, I fight to restore it—with freedom."

"But there are many others besides the baron," protested the boy.

"Most roam the countryside, setting up their own fiefdoms, enslaving rather than freeing. Yes, I know, oh, how I know. I fight them, also. That makes the war all the more brutal. Not only do I fight those who have usurped the throne, I fight those who *want* to usurp it."

The boy grinned shyly. "I never thought Duke Freow was a bad man."

"He isn't. But he is old and infirm and has been unable to restore either Lorens or Lokenna to the throne."

"Have you worn the Demon Crown?" asked the boy.

"No, and if I should triumph against the duke, I would not. Although royal blood flows in my veins, there is not enough to protect me against the ill effects of its magic. The crown is a symbol; it is also a two-edged weapon. It can be used for good, as King Lamost used it. It can also slay mercilessly, both the wearer and those unfortunate enough to reside within its range."

"Does the duke wear the Demon Crown?"

Gaemock shook his head. He had no idea what had become of the fabled, demon-given circlet. Duke Freow had never worn it in public. Spies told of Baron Theoll's attempts to steal it—and his failures to find it. Duke Freow had been a resourceful, if flawed regent. He had not kept order in the kingdom, but neither had he allowed ambitious men such as Theoll of Brandon to take full control.

"When we depose the duke and the baron and the others now in the castle, we will not wear the Demon Crown. That is only for full-blooded royalty. Unlike Freow, we will find the twins and place one on the throne."

"Which one, Lord Dews?"

"I cannot say. Either will do, if the kingdom can be united."

Gaemock shook himself free of the daydreaming. His power waxed and waned. He must now retreat and conserve his strength, prepare to again launch a siege of the castle. In the autumn, next spring, sometime. To do that, he must win free this day.

"I am entrusting you with a singular mission, son. You will run as fast as you can and tell the old woman who lives at the edge of the river that I need her immediately."

"But Lord, there are so many old women living on the River Ty. Which shall I fetch?"

Gaemock laughed. "You go. Which old woman I want will become apparent to you. And you shall not fetch her. You will be polite, do as she says, and make it plain to her that I am in dire need of her skills. If she will not aid me, get her to tell you outright and return immediately with the message. Do you understand?"

"No," the boy said slowly. "I might choose the wrong woman. Please, Lord Dews, describe her to me more fully."

"Trust me in this. You won't miss her. And I cannot tell you what she looks like, because her appearance changes often. Go now. Be swift of foot. She must respond before the sun sets this evening or half my troops will be lost."

The child bowed deeply, backed off a pair of steps, then turned and ran, his bare, callused feet pounding hard on the grassy slopes. Gaemock watched the boy leave and wondered if this fight was worth the death and suffering it caused. The boy obeyed so eagerly, not knowing his errand would mean the deaths of dozens or even scores of valiant men. Or perhaps the boy *did* know and that added speed to his step.

That thought appalled Dews Gaemock. The young learning the ways of death and dying and reveling in it. And why not? For an entire generation, war had been a constant, unvarying companion.

"The war," he wondered aloud. "Do I seek to overthrow Freow for good reasons or foul?" He shook his head. Gaemock knew he did not want to rule. He wanted only to install a rightful heir on the throne. Let another carry the heavy burden of the Demon Crown. But one of the royal blood would rule! He would see that the duke and his followers were deposed! The fight was worth it, if only to stop the tyranny that had grown, if only to put to rest the Inquisition that Archbishop Nosto fostered in Freow's name.

"Lord, the signals have been sent, but already the enemy marches on our position." Jiskko shook him gently, bringing him out of the latest round of endless worry about the righteousness of this war.

"Sorry, Jiskko. You say they have us boxed already?"

"Split, Lord. Each band can flee."

"Can we lure them into pursuit of one group, then attack their rear?" Even as he spoke, Gaemock saw that this would not be possible. The wizard they opposed might be venal and conniving, but he was no fool. The magical ward spells would alert him to any such plan in time to break off the engagement and retreat up the valley.

"If the wizard retreats, can we reform in the valley and pursue?" Gaemock asked.

"Yes, of course, but the wizard must know this. He will have prepared a surprise for us, I am sure."

"I am, also, Jiskko. Just a thought, not an order. Continue. Let the wizard divide our forces. But also alert each band to the chance to drive the swine's troops back into the valley. We do hold the high ground."

Gaemock's eyes turned toward the castle. It pained him to put away the siege until another day, but survival demanded this course. Duke Freow could not maintain his flimsy grip on Porotane forever. If Gaemock failed to dislodge the regent today, then autumn would see another attack. Let that fail, and another could be mounted in a year's time. Eventually the defenders had to tire and relent.

"They attack, Lord!" cried Jiskko.

"So I see." Gaemock watched as a thready line of his troops began falling back under the uphill charge on the far side of the valley. The range proved too much for the archers arrayed around him, but those on the other hill took a fearsome toll on the enemy.

"They waste lives with their attack. Their commander throws troops against the strongest parts of our line." Jiskko shook his head.

"They die, yes," said Gaemock, "but they have diverted us from Porotane's castle. No matter the outcome this day, Duke Freow has won a small victory."

"And Lady Ionia," Jiskko said bitterly.

"And lovely Ionia," agreed Gaemock. He settled down on his haunches to watch the progress of the battle. When the wizard's troops reached a spot two-thirds of the way up the hill, the boy Gaemock had sent as messenger came back, breathless from the long run.

"Quick, boy. Did you find her?"

"Yes!" The boy's eyes opened wider than saucers. "It was as you said. I had no trouble locating the old woman. I gave her your orders—"

"My *suggestions*," corrected Gaemock. "I do not order one such as she." He had not wanted to use the witch at all, but now he was obligated to her. So be it.

"Aye, that I found, Lord Dews." The boy swallowed hard. "In spite of my error, she has agreed."

"Good!" Gaemock rose and motioned. The signaler to his right passed the message across the field. The distant troops mounted a savage counterattack that drove the wizard's fighters back toward the valley floor. In concert, Gaemock ordered those arrayed around him to plunge downward, down into the valley, down to attack the enemy's rear.

The response from the enemy's line, although

expected, still stunned Gaemock and sent him reeling. The wizard had placed more than a simple ward spell along the bottom of the valley. Huge sheets of flame rose more than a hundred feet into the air to cut off any possible attack.

"We can't fight this!" cried Jiskko.

"We won't have to," said Gaemock, recovering. The heat boiling up from below made him think he stared into the opened gate of hell. "The wizard is not powerful enough to maintain this spell for more than a few seconds." Even as he spoke, Gaemock worried. The flames continued to rage long past the point where a sorcerer should have collapsed in exhaustion. A well-trained warrior might march all day and fight for an hour before tiring to the point of insensibility. Gaemock had never encountered a wizard able to maintain a potent spell for more than a minute.

But still the flames clawed upward, preventing him from reinforcing his troops on the other hillside.

"Lord," said the boy suddenly. "Mayhap we face more than one sorcerer."

"The boy speaks the truth," said Jiskko. "We need more information about who oppose us."

"The only possibility is that Duke Freow has formed an alliance with several wandering wizards. I do not believe this is possible. We would have heard of the duke's intent to recruit. No, we face only one wizard. He will tire."

Gaemock smiled when he saw the outer fringes of the flame wall begin to cool. The sheets of fire flickered, died, and soon only charred land remained—land and more than a few skeletons of those unfortunate enough to be caught in the blaze.

"Are those ours or the wizard's?" asked Gaemock of his adviser.

Jiskko said, "Evenly divided, I fear, Lord. We took as good as we gave."

"Signal the assault on the other hill," said Gaemock. The sight of the burned bones of valiant soldiers sickened him. Damn all wizards!

"Should I also order your personal troops to retreat?"

"Yes. Do it now. The enemy will remain in confusion for a few minutes due to the wizard's spell. He did not warn them before casting. I can see the signs of their disarray."

Dews Gaemock watched as his tactic unfolded. The soldiers who had borne the brunt of conflict thus far responded well, driving the wizard's troops back to the valley floor. Only when the enemy began retreating up the valley did Gaemock signal for full attack. His two halves met, then pursued.

"Jiskko!" called Gaemock after they had gone less than a hundred paces after the fleeing enemy. "To the high ground. Both sides of the valley. Signal it now. Break off pursuit and run for the high ground!"

"But Lord, why?"

"Do it, damn your miserable hide!"

Jiskko ordered the signalers, but the formation proved too drawn out for effective communication. Two trumpeters came to the fore, their mournful blasts producing instant obedience by Gaemock's troops. None had the heart for this battle. They all sought the downfall of Duke Freow, not some wandering wizard intent on looting and random destruction.

The soldiers racing for the high ground

brought a change in the enemy troops. They wheeled and attacked.

The pounding of their horses' hooves, the triumphant shouts of their pikemen and bowmen drowned out the deep, resonant sounds from high up the valley.

"Keep the trumpeters a-blowing," ordered Gaemock. "Get the troops to even higher ground."

"The sound, Lord," murmured the boy. "It . . . it's a flood!"

Before the words had blossomed from his lips, the ten-foot-high wall of water swept through the valley, caught up horses and soldiers and rocks and trees, and carried them away. The roar of the watery battering ram silenced the trumpets, and a sheet of spray blasted into the air higher than the flame wall the wizard had constructed.

Gaemock leaned against a tree, his arms circling it. He watched the carnage below. The old woman might be a minor sorceress, scorned by those more powerful, but she controlled the dikes along the River Ty with her petty spells. A simple pass of her hand had opened flood gates and washed away all challenge to Gaemock's army.

And now he owed her. Damn!

"Get the semaphores working, Jiskko. Signal the far side of the valley. Rendezvous in one week at our training site."

"We abandon the siege of the castle?"

"For now Duke Freow and Porotane are safe from us. But only for the moment," said Gaemock. "I will not stop until the kingdom is wrested from him." With that Dews Gaemock spun and stalked off. The attack had been blunted by that meddling wizard, but his forces remained intact. For that, he gave thanks.

But so many deaths this day. And for what?

The only thing sadder than not knowing the name of the wizard he had slain this day was not caring.

CHAPTER TWO

The black cloak whispered softly around the man's small, wiry frame as he pulled it closer about his shoulders. With the cloak in place, he vanished from sight in deep shadows. Softer than the shadows he mimicked, he drifted down the castle's main corridors, found secondary routes, stopped to look to see if anyone followed, then reached out and tugged at a rocky protrusion high on the wall. Silently, a section of wall slid back. The ebony-cloaked man entered. The door closed behind and plunged the secret passage into utter darkness save for seven tiny pinpoints of light in the distance.

On feet quieter than velvet moving over velvet, he went to the first spyhole and peered into the room beyond. Nothing. The next afforded a sight hardly more interesting. Two serving wenches sat about gossiping. Their wild rumors and obscene comments about the lords in the castle of Porotane might have interested him at another time. Not now. He drifted on, choosing the fifth spyhole.

Eye pressed hard against the hole, he looked into lavishly appointed sleeping chambers. Tiny moans of pleasure came to his straining ears. He turned until he saw the large bed piled with silks and furs. Atop the bed lay a nude couple, their bodies intricately intertwined in the passion of lovemaking.

He held down his own excitement as he watched the act proceed as surely as any play in the castle's yearly drama pageant. Licking dried lips, he moved away, then placed his other eye to the spyhole. His right had become blurred from the tension of the position.

If he had designed these secret ways, the spyholes would have been placed lower to better accommodate one of his stature.

"Oh, Johanna," came the soft cries from the room. The watching man smiled. This confirmed all he had heard. Lady Johanna and the lieutenant of the night guard. For this dalliance the guard could be put to death. His post was along the castle battlements watching for rebel attacks, not locked in the passionate arms of a noble lady.

"Seen enough, Baron?" came a low voice. The dark-clad figure sprang from the spyhole, his hand flashing to a dagger sheathed at his belt. He blinked rapidly, trying to readjust his eyes from the light of the sleeping chamber and the amorously locked pair to the inky darkness of the passageway.

"Who's there?" Baron Theoll demanded. "Speak or I'll slice your tongue from your head!"

"It is a sin to spy on others," came the disembodied voice. Although Theoll could not see his accuser, he recognized the voice now.

"Archbishop Nosto, you startled me. I only spied on those disloyal to the throne."

"You get strange pleasure from this act of 'patriotism,' Baron. It is not natural. Is the scrying power granted by the Demon Crown the reason you desire it so?"

"Do not think to anger me, Nosto," snapped
Theoll. He sheathed his dagger. His eyes had found
the dim figure of the prelate. The floppy headgear,
the tight-fitting red suit of a cleric, the tall, thin
body, all these identified Archbishop Nosto.

The Archbishop brushed past Theoll and
peered through the spyhole, then pulled away.
Theoll saw the cleric shaking his head in bewilder-
ment. What did a cleric know of intelligence-
gathering? The entire castle ran rampant with
plots, allegiances forming and disintegrating hour
to hour, second to second. Without such current
information, how was Theoll to survive?

How was he to ever find the accursed Demon
Crown? And don it?

"Let us adjourn to my chambers, Archbishop.
It is quieter there." The crescendo of sobs and
moans from Lady Johanna's chambers emphasized the baron's words.

They walked down the secret passageway and
out into a main castle corridor. At this late hour,
no one stirred in these halls. Baron Theoll made
an impatient gesture to the cleric and strode off,
his short legs trying and failing to outdistance the
taller man's. Theoll stopped in front of the door
leading to his quarters, glanced along the corridor
in both directions, and then entered.

"Always so suspicious, Baron. You should
learn to trust those within the castle. We all oppose
the rebel forces."

"That is true," said Theoll, "but it does not
mean that we do not also oppose each other.
Enemy of my enemy does not make my friend."

Archbishop Nosto settled onto a simple footstool and looked up at the baron. The man's quick
movements betrayed nervousness. Or excitement?

Had he been so stimulated by spying on the Lady Johanna? Nosto shook his head sadly. For all the instruction he had given Theoll, this seemed one lesson that had been ignored. Privacy meant nothing to the Baron of Brandon—except his own, which he guarded with a jealousy approaching fanaticism.

"The Demon Crown is once more within the castle walls," Theoll said. "That fool Freow has sent for it. I must obtain it! I must!"

"What is the source of this information?" asked Archbishop Nosto. "No one has come forward and told me."

"You mean you haven't been able to torture the information from anyone," Theoll said, sneering. "You prattle on about me peering through a spyhole at traitors while you break bones and burn out eyes in the name of the Inquisition. Which method obtains the better intelligence?"

"I do not enjoy my work as Inquisitor," said the cleric. He sighed. "But sinfulness is everywhere. So many stray from the True Path." He straightened on the stool, his face almost glowing with his righteousness. "The tortures are not to squeeze out information but to instill godliness in the miscreants."

"It's fortuitous that your heretics and my enemies happen to be in league," said Baron Theoll.

"Who can say where a lamb blunders when it leaves the True Path?"

Theoll laughed harshly. "This lamb will never stray, will it, Nosto? I see that it won't." Theoll settled into the heavily padded chair on a dais. From this vantage, he towered over anyone who sought an audience with him. Theoll had long since stopped noticing that the Archbishop always sat on this footstool to maintain a "proper" elevation. They needed one another, the baron and archbishop, and neither fully admitted it.

"You have sought the Demon Crown since King Lamost died. Why do you think the duke has become so careless to reveal it to you now? Although he is gravely ill, Freow retains much of his former cunning."

Theoll smirked. Direct assassination had proven impossible with the regent, unlike the unlamented King Lamost. Duke Freow had deftly avoided every attempt. Even the judicious use of wizardry had proven ineffective. But Theoll had found the way through Freow's defenses. For over a year he had been slowly poisoning the duke with a potion prepared by a sorcerer sequestered in the upper reaches of the Yorral Mountains. Not magical in nature, the potion worked by accumulation over the years. Theoll often waited weeks or even months before adding new doses of the potion to the duke's food. Even a taster with a sensitive palate could not detect the poison in such small amounts.

"Now that the duke lies near death, he has summoned the keeper of the Demon Crown."

"Have you learned who this mysterious keeper is?" asked Archbishop Nosto. "I have heard only rumors."

"We thrive on rumors in Porotane," said Theoll. "I *know* the keeper." He paused to build the proper amount of anticipation in the cleric. Nosto enjoyed these revelations and Theoll delivered the words dramatically and well. "It is the Glass Warrior."

Archbishop Nosto made a rude noise and

waved his hand, as if dismissing the baron. "Do not waste my time, Theoll. She is legend and nothing more. The Glass Warrior." He snorted and pushed to his feet. Even with Theoll's raised chair, Nosto stared directly into the baron's cold eyes.

"I do not jest," snapped Theoll. "She exists. She has been entrusted with the Demon Crown until the twins are found."

"Does that search progress any better than your other schemes?"

"Duke Freow has not pressed the search; he has enjoyed rule in Porotane for too long."

"And you seek out Lokenna and Lorens to slay them, to establish yourself as heir to the throne."

"Would such an occurence displease my lord archbishop?"

"The twins have been missing for too long. What would they know of ruling a kingdom the size of Porotane? I feel you are a better choice, Baron. You know that."

"They would certainly never honor the leading cleric in the realm as I would, I who know your true merit," taunted Theoll.

"If you seize the Demon Crown from this mythical warrior woman, what would you do with it first?"

Theoll studied the tall, thin man intently. The question seemed innocuous. Theoll knew otherwise. "There are two problems of paramount importance to unifying Porotane," he replied. "The Inquisition must be brought to an end by the elimination of the heretics, and the rebels must be routed. Dews Gaemock and his ruffians must not continue to rob and pillage as the duke has allowed for too long." Theoll saw the fervor return to

Archbishop Nosto's face. The death of all heretics lay near to the cleric's heart. For all his protests, Nosto enjoyed the sight of tortured bodies as much as Theoll enjoyed the stolen sight of women with their lovers.

"After these matters are resolved," Theoll continued, "I would don the Demon Crown and seek out Lokenna and Lorens."

"They are of the blood. They are the true heirs," pointed out Nosto.

"I would take care in how I eliminated them." Theoll smiled wickedly. "Perhaps the sight granted by the Demon Crown would show that the children have become heretics."

This line of thinking appealed to Archbishop Nosto. He nodded. "They have been gone from the grace of my services for almost twenty years."

"They were stolen away the year following King Lamost's death."

"Nineteen years then," mused Nosto. "A time long enough to be seduced from the True Path."

"They would be of twenty-four summers now," said Theoll.

"If they live."

Baron Theoll said nothing. As he had learned that the Glass Warrior had been entrusted with the Demon Crown, so had he learned that both twins survived. All that he needed was to locate the pair.

Locate and kill the offspring of Lamost—and take the Demon Crown for his own. Success that had stretched out of reach for years now dropped into his lap.

The jester shook his head and sent his lank dark hair flying in wild disarray around his face, turning him into something less than human. Harhar bounced up and down on legs that seemed to have steel springs instead of flesh and blood muscle, then he slipped and fell heavily to the floor.

Sheepishly, the jester looked up and smiled weakly. He rubbed himself where he had fallen. Those he tried to entertain ignored him. Their full attention focused on Duke Freow, lying pale and emaciated on his bed.

"Has she come yet? I must see her," the ancient duke said.

"Please," said the court physician. "Rest. Do not speak, my duke. You are too weak."

"Let me tell a joke. Let me make him better." Harhar bounced up and perched on the end of the duke's bed. "O Mighty Duke, once there was a sweet young lass of sixteen summers who—"

Harhar crashed to the floor when the physician cuffed him. "Leave us, fool. The duke requires rest, not your madness."

"No, wait," said Freow, a skeletal hand clutching at the physician's sleeve. "Let Harhar stay. He . . . he amuses me."

With ill grace, the physician nodded. The jester moved to a corner of the room and stood quietly, ebony eyes darting around, seeking out any opportunity to amuse the failing monarch.

"I must see the Glass Warrior," said Freow. "Bring her to me at once."

"Sire, she was summoned. She travels as she pleases. The messenger told her that you . . . that the matter was of utmost urgency."

"I have been so selfish," moaned Duke Freow. "So selfish. I thought to rule Porotane."

"You tire yourself, Duke," said the physician.

"You have done what you thought best for the kingdom. None fault you for that."

The old man made a gesture. The physician said nothing. The duke was dying by slow inches and he had been unable to discover the reason. The best wizards had checked for ensorcellments and found naught. Physically, the duke seemed healthy. But he died, slowly, painfully. The physician guessed at a slow poison, but had been unable to detect it.

The physician cursed his own failure to discover the reason for the infirmity even as he secretly considered the potential of the poison. To possess this for his own use would enhance his power in the court a hundredfold!

"Leave me for the moment," ordered Freow. "No, Harhar can stay. He still amuses me."

The physician left the jester to do what he could to brighten the old man's flagging spirits. It seemed little enough for a man who might not see another sunrise.

The castle walls rose into the darkness of the night until they blocked even the stars. The snow-white-haired woman walked her steed at the base of those walls until the postern gate appeared behind a tall, leafy shrub of indeterminate variety. The Glass Warrior drew her strangely shining blade and slowly pushed away the bush. No trip wires had been attached since last she entered the castle of Porotane.

Careful examination of the door lock betrayed no bright, recent scratches. She drew a key of glass from a pouch and inserted it in the lock. A quick twist and the narrow, low door opened. She hurried down the long, dark passageway between the walls and emerged to glance about the deserted courtyard beyond, then ducked back to tie her horse to the bush.

"I'll return before dawn," she said, patting the animal on its powerful neck. The mare nickered and tried to pull away. The Glass Warrior stayed until the horse quieted. Only then did she slip back into the castle and make her way through silent passages to the uppermost levels of the castle where Duke Freow lay dying.

Tall, confident, she walked along the deserted halls of power. Only when she reached the branching, empty corridor leading to Duke Freow's bed chambers did she pause. A frown marred the perfection of her ageless face. She took off her cape and wrapped it around her left arm. A guard always stood at this juncture.

The lack of a guard meant danger.

She sucked in a deep breath, settled herself, and drew her sword. The faint light from candles along the corridor caught the glass blade and reflected rainbows. Along the back side of the blade gleamed a thin tube of purplish liquid. The Glass Warrior adjusted the tube in such a fashion that it would not break if she slashed or thrust with the blade. Only then did she advance.

Her quick gray eyes darted back and forth, studying every entryway. But only her quick reflexes saved her from the attack from above. A dark clad assassin dropped from a niche in the roof.

He shrieked in pain and death as she took a quick step away and dropped to brace the sword hilt against the floor. The falling killer impaled himself on her blade. She rolled him over and carefully drew the now-bloody blade from his chest. His open eyes stared sightlessly at the ceiling from which he had jumped.

She spun in time to meet the silent, vicious attack of another. Her glass blade deflected shining steel. A quick whipping motion brought her cape around and tangled the man's feet. The Glass Warrior jerked hard, sending him to his back. He hit hard, rolled, and tried to escape her vengeance. She lunged, the tip of the long glass sword driving through his back and penetrating his heart.

She swung about and faced a third assassin. The Glass Warrior deflected the first thrust with her cape. She flicked her sword wrist in a curious fashion. The action forced the thin-walled tube of liquid along the back blood gutter and to the tip of her sword. She danced away from the wall, parried, backed, then riposted. The tube broke and liquid sprayed forth.

The soul-tearing scream torn from the assassin as the burning acid melted his face died when she lunged and drove the tip of her blade into his throat. Coughs, gurgles, thwarted shrieks of pain, then silence. The final assassin lay at her feet.

The Glass Warrior flicked her wrist once more, sending the now-empty tube to the floor. She drew another tube of the purplish acid from the hilt of her sword and fitted it carefully onto the tip of her blade. If three had ventured out to kill her this night, more might await her.

Armed and ready for any new ambush, she went to the door of the duke's chamber and pressed her ear against the heavy wood panels. From inside came muffled words and a weak chuckle. She opened the door a fraction and peered in. She smiled. Harhar entertained his dying master.

"Duke?" she called softly. "I have come, as you commanded."

The jester swung about, eyes narrowed, hand clutching his rattle as if it were a weapon.

"Harhar, no!" cried the duke. "She is a friend."

The Glass Warrior bowed deeply. "And I will always remain a friend to whoever attempts to restore King Lamost's line to the throne of Porotane."

She stiffened when she saw tears forming in the old man's eyes. How he had aged in the four years since last she had seen him. It might have been a hundred passing for all the ravages time had brought to him.

"I am unworthy of such loyal followers," the old man sobbed.

"You have done well, my duke."

"No!" he protested. He reached out his bony hand and clutched at her cape, drawing her closer. "I have not. I have betrayed the trust placed in me by Lamost."

"How is this? Have you not sought out Lokenna and Lorens? Have you not given into my protection the birthright of the Porotane rulers?" His stricken look put her on guard.

He shook his head and cried openly now. "I have made no such attempt to find Lamost's kidnapped children. I have done nothing! I sought only to rule Porotane myself. The power, oh, how I loved the power!"

"But, my duke, you could not love only power. Why entrust me with the Demon Crown when wearing it would allow you the ultimate power in the kingdom? No place would be closed to you, no action hidden, no thought too well guarded."

"You know of the crown's power," Freow said, his voice faltering. Both the Glass Warrior and Harhar moved closer. She reached out and squeezed the jester's arm to reassure him.

"I do," she said.

"Then you know that, when the last demon bestowed it as tribute and reparation on the rulers of Porotane, a condition went with it."

"Yes, only those of the blood royal may wear it. But Freow, you are a *duke*. You are Lamost's brother."

The wizened old man shook his head. The tears pouring from his eyes soaked the bedclothes. "I am a pretender, a fraud. Harhar is more a duke than I."

"You are a changeling? But Lamost—"

"Lamost never knew. The true Duke Freow ruled the lands along the sea. None in the castle had seen him in many years."

"There had been some dispute between Lamost and you."

"Between Lamost and his true brother. When the king was assassinated, Freow began a solitary journey of penitence and mourning. I . . . I slew him on the road and assumed his role."

"You are not of the royal line," said the Glass Warrior. "You cannot wear the Demon Crown!"

"Nor could I relinquish the power I found following the king's death. I was weak. Never had I seen such wealth, such riches. Freow was a cruel lord. I considered this a way of regaining what had been taken from me."

Harhar moved about nervously, looking from the frail old man to the Glass Warrior.

"You also killed the duchess when she came to Porotane," accused the woman.

"I did. She would have exposed me. I was so weak, so weak." The man's voice told of weakness beyond that of morality.

"You have ruled well, however," the Glass Warrior said. "And you did entrust the Demon Crown to me when others might have destroyed it."

"Again, weakness. I sought only to keep it from those with true claim to the throne. But now I am dying."

The Glass Warrior stared at him. Her emotions raged. She had believed Freow—the man posing as Duke Freow—to be honorable and honest. Now she discovered his venality overshadowed even that of Baron Theoll. Did this erase all the good he *had* done? She needed time to consider.

"Please, I wish to repent my sins. You have the Demon Crown?"

Silently, the Glass Warrior pushed back her cape and pulled forth a small backpack of the purest midnight velvet. She opened it. Within rode a crystalline box. Within the box rested a plain circlet of gold. A few runes crossed the brow. Other than this, the crown lacked ornamentation of any kind.

"So simple-looking, yet so powerful a tool for good or evil," Freow said.

"You wish to don it?" She thrust the glass box toward the man. He recoiled.

"No! I wished only to gaze upon what can never be mine."

"Why did you summon me?" The Glass Warrior wondered if Freow had sent the assassins after her. She doubted it. Whatever troubled the old man, it was not her caretaking of the Demon Crown. He had only to ask for it without baring his soul.

"I want you to perform the task I should have carried out nineteen years ago. After Lamost died, I was appointed regent for the twins."

"Did you have them kidnapped?" demanded the woman. Dying or not, he would suffer the dire consequences if he had made craven war on young children.

"No, not I. A wizard. Never have I learned his name."

"How will I locate the heirs?" she asked.

"Never have I revealed this to another. The wizard responsible for Lamost's death is Tahir d'mar. Seek him out. He knows what has become of Lorens and Lokenna. He must!"

The Glass Warrior frowned. Tahir had vanished long ago. She had never suspected him of complicity in King Lamost's death, but then she avoided political intrigues and idle speculation on them.

"Tahir acted on orders from another. Who, I have never learned. Baron Theoll of Brandon perhaps. Almost certainly," the old man said. "But he is both cautious and powerful, and I have never openly challenged him."

The Glass Warrior wondered how many assassination attempts had been made. This man who posed as Duke Freow might be of common birth but he possessed a royal's knack for court machinations.

"Go, find the children, restore one to the throne—it matters little which one. Let one wear

the Demon Crown and end the war wracking
Porotane. I want the kingdom to find the peace I so
ardently seek for myself."

Harhar tugged on the woman's cape. "He
fades quickly."

"Yes, he does, but within is a core of steel.
Duke Freow might recover enough to maintain
order until I have completed the mission he has
given me."

"But he isn't—" The Glass Warrior's hand
covered the jester's mouth and silenced him.

"You are not to repeat this to anyone. Do you
understand?" He bobbed his head in assent.
"Good. Look after him as if he were the true duke.
Keep his spirits up with your antics."

"And you'll return with a new king or queen?"
The jester's eagerness amused her.

"I will try. Finding Tahir after so many years
will be difficult. He might have had nothing to do
with the kidnapping." She abruptly cut off her flow
of words.

"I will find the true heirs and give them their
heritage."

The Glass Warrior held the crystalline box
containing the Demon Crown at arm's length, as if
it contained only death and destruction.

CHAPTER THREE

Baron Theoll drifted along the castle corridors like a phantom, his dark cape making the only sound as he moved. He stood stock still when he saw the first assassin laying face down in the hall. Burning eyes lifted and found the second killer. Theoll knew that the third assassin had also been slain. Although the trio had not been his best, they represented a new school of mercenaries in whom he had placed great trust.

They had not proven adequate for the task of slaying a lone woman.

Theoll experienced a polar chill racing up his back at the thought of the Glass Warrior. For so many years he had tried to kill her. Each attempt had been thwarted. Theoll had no evidence that he had done more than irritate her. Never had even one of his carefully trained assassins seriously wounded her. Theoll worried that she had not even been bloodied.

He paid no heed to the corpses. He rushed to a panel in the hall and ran his nimble fingers along the horns of a ram trapped forever in the ornately carved hunting scene. The secret door swung inward. Theoll paused for a moment before entering. He controlled so little in this portion of the castle. High risk meant more than mere discovery. If Duke Freow caught him, no amount of influence-bartering would save him from the castle executioner.

Theoll closed the secret panel and moved quickly along the narrow passageway, climbed a short flight of stone steps, and then crawled on his belly for another fifty feet. The spyhole into the duke's chambers had been drilled at the juncture between ceiling and wall. The view was obstructed by furniture in the room and overhearing what transpired within proved impossible. But any knowledge gained might mean his salvation.

Theoll squinted and scooted closer, his eye hurting as he strained to see through solid furniture and the gauzy curtains veiling the duke's deathbed.

He saw only the duke's feeble hand—and the Demon Crown beside the duke on the bed.

Theoll caught his breath and held it. The Glass Warrior had brought the Demon Crown to Freow!

The baron almost turned and wiggled back to summon a full platoon of his guards. Seizing the Demon Crown now might allow him to assume the throne. Then reason settled and he continued his uneasy vigil.

The Glass Warrior might be capable of fighting even a brigade of his best soldiers. She was rumored to be a sorceress, a fighter second to none, a phantom returned to the world, a goddess. The first might be possible, the second had proven true on many occasions, and the other two rumors Theoll doubted. But capable of defending Freow she was—at least long enough for those still loyal to the failing duke to aid him.

". . . entrust you with this mission," Theoll heard Duke Freow say. Moving about, almost injuring his eye, Theoll spotted the Glass Warrior. She stood quietly beside the bed, hand resting on the hilt of her glass sword.

The woman's words rang clearer than the dying duke's. "You may depend on me, Duke."

Theoll saw the Demon Crown vanish from the bed. A sharp click as of a latch closing echoed through the silent chamber. Two quick, hollow bootsteps and the sound of the door closing.

The Glass Warrior had departed!

Theoll knew he could never get back to the corridor in time to stop her. The coldness he had experienced on realizing that she had slain three of his better assassins poured like cold water over him once more. His fighting prowess on a good day equaled that of many in Porotane. But those that he could consistently best were few. To attempt to stop the Glass Warrior alone would be suicidal.

He watched as the jester cavorted about, uttering silly noises, trying to make the dying duke's last minutes less painful. Theoll wished that he could poison both duke and jester. Harhar always made him the butt of his cruel jokes, but who could discipline a lowly jester? To do so would show weakness that others vying for power in the castle might exploit.

When he became king of Porotane the jester's ugly head would grace a pike outside the gates.

Theoll worked his way backward in the tight crawl space and descended the stairs. He pressed his ear against the secret panel leading into the corridor, listening intently for a hint that the Glass Warrior lay in wait for him. Theoll finally opened the panel a fraction of an inch and peered out. He saw only one corpse. Slipping out, he glanced back and forth.

As he had thought, the woman had not lingered. Freow had given her a mission, and the baron had a good idea what it might be. For almost twenty years Duke Freow had told the council of nobles that he sought the heirs to the throne of Porotane. Theoll knew that he lied. No emissaries visited neighboring lands to inquire of the missing twins. No soldiers scoured the countryside, save to do war against the rebel bands. No wizards cast scrying spells. The duke ruled and did not want to find the children.

Until now. Until he felt the life holding him to this world slipping from weak, poisoned fingers. He had dispatched the Glass Warrior, with the Demon Crown, to find Lokenna or Lorens.

The baron threw caution to the winds as he raced along the deserted corridors. His heavy bootsteps echoed until the sound threatened to deafen him. He skidded on the slick floor and spun about to enter a tiny dormitory on the level below his own quarters.

A dozen men slept on pallets. His entry brought them awake, daggers in hand. Theoll paused to smile at their alertness. They would need that and all the training he had lavished on them for the past two years to equal the Glass Warrior.

And equal her—best her!—they must.

"You, you, you," Baron Theoll barked, pointing out the soldiers he wanted. "Come with me immediately. The rest of you, prepare to ride at the first light of dawn."

He stood by impatiently as the trio donned

their uniforms and settled their sword belts around their waists.

The baron spun and hurried from the barracks room, the three following close behind. He hastened to the battlements and studied the stars above. The constellations twisted in preparation for sliding below the curtain of blue that drew across when the dawn broke. The Box of Gems had closed for the night and the Thief's grasping hand had almost vanished, too. There would be enough time for his soldiers to pursue the Glass Warrior, Theoll decided. The darkness would hinder her.

"Scan the countryside for a lone rider," he ordered. These three had the sharpest night vision of any in his small platoon. "Be alert for any glint of light off a glass weapon."

"Glass?" asked one. "The only one carrying a glass sword is—"

"Look!" snapped Theoll. "You need not make comments."

The trio began their scrutiny of shadows and movement across the broad fields surrounding the castle of Porotane's ruler. Theoll paced along the battlements, hands clasped behind his back, a dark scowl marring his regular features. As he walked, he thought hard of what must be done. The duke's condition worsened daily. It was only a matter of time—perhaps hours—before the potion worked its fatal duty and left Porotane without a ruler.

Duke Freow was only regent for the twins, or so went the thread of law. Freow had ruled in their stead, but the children were children no longer, if they lived. The Glass Warrior had been sent to locate Lokenna and Lorens. It took only one twin to don the Demon Crown and become undisputed ruler of Porotane.

The baron growled deep in his throat. A soldier looked fearfully at him, then turned back to his duty of searching for traces of the Glass Warrior. Possession of the Demon Crown was pivotal to ruling Porotane. With it on his head, Theoll could project his image anywhere in the realm. His phantom image might spy on enemies in their most secret councils, no matter how near or distant. Theoll's fists closed so tightly that his fingernails cut into his flesh. How he needed the Demon Crown now with everyone possessing even a drop of royal blood in their veins conspiring to succeed Freow!

The Demon Crown would allow him to root out Dews Gaemock and the other rebel bands. No one would dare stand against him within the castle walls—or without. He would rule with an iron hand because he would know his enemies' cleverest schemes!

The baron pondered Freow's failure to use the Demon Crown. It had to be for a reason other than the fiction that the Demon Crown rested only on the brow of Porotane's rightful ruler. Theoll *knew* Freow had not pursued the search for the twins. Why had the duke not used the Demon Crown to cement his power over the years? That failure had plunged the kingdom into civil war. A wise man, even one truly acting only as regent for one awaiting majority to assume the throne, would have used the Demon Crown to quell the rebellious factions.

Theoll knew that the Demon Crown tried to possess the wearer, but the knowing of its evil kept the wearer pure. Theoll did not foresee any possibility of being seduced by the power of that crown.

Why had Duke Freow chosen not to wear it during his two decades of rule?

The secret lay with the Glass Warrior. Theoll's curiosity on this point was great, but not as great as the need to possess the Demon Crown for his own.

"There, Baron, there. See?" The soldier who had gone to the north side of the castle battlements called. Theoll raced to his side. "Beyond the line of trees. A spot of darkness against darkness."

Starlight flashed against a glass sword, or so Theoll imagined.

"Yes!" he cried. "She rides north to the Uvain Plateau!" Theoll rested his hands against the cold stone walls. But why? How did the Glass Warrior know where the twins would be, if they still lived? The Uvain Plateau seemed a poor choice, too.

"She might turn to the east, Baron," said the sharp-eyed soldier. "The River Ty affords access to many points in the kingdom to the northeast."

"She might think to confuse pursuit," said another.

"Mark that spot," ordered Theoll. "Mark it well. You will lead the others after her at first light."

"Do we follow only or should we slay, Baron Theoll?" asked the third soldier, just arriving from his position along the western castle wall.

Theoll considered. All twelve would ride after the Glass Warrior. She had bested three hidden assassins. How would she fare against a dozen making no secret of their pursuit?

He came to a decision quickly. For all the information carried within the warrior woman's head, he desired above all else what she carried in trust for Duke Freow. "Kill her. And bring me everything in her possession."

"The Demon Crown?"

Theoll sucked in his breath. Secrets were difficult to keep in Porotane. Everyone bartered information for gain. "For a commoner to don the crown means instant death," he said. "Do not think to gain advantage for yourself or any of the others with you. Only through me can you prosper."

"That is why you chose our platoon so carefully," said the guardsman.

Theoll laughed harshly. "I know your pedigrees and talents better than you know them yourself. You are all of the basest peasant stock. Nary a drop of royal blood flows through your scurvy veins. Touch the Demon Crown and you will have visited upon you the full wrath of the last demon to walk this world."

"Only nobles of royal blood can wear the Demon Crown," muttered one.

"Aye, only nobles. Such as the Baron of Brandon." Theoll executed a mocking bow. "Bring me the Demon Crown and each of you will be rewarded beyond your wildest imaginings." Theoll let their avarice run unchecked. He smiled sardonically. He had chosen them well, and trained them well, too. They would not betray him.

They would not dare.

"Off with you. Rouse the others, mount, and ride after the Glass Warrior." They rushed to obey.

Baron Theoll leaned against the wall and peered into the false dawn beginning to turn the night sky into a glowing pearl. What information drove the Glass Warrior toward the Uvain Plateau? Or did she seek passage on the River Ty? Theoll had been careful in his quest for supreme power in Porotane, but a nagging thought returned to bother him. Should he have pursued the search for the twins when it became apparent so many years ago that Duke Freow had not?

To *know* they were dead would let him rest easier.

Theoll had been engaged in constant intrigue to maintain his position in Porotane. He had done all he could. The time to act was now.

Resolution surging through him, the small man straightened and turned. The barely audible scrape of boot leather against stone gave him scant warning. Thoughts flashed through his head. His men had left. They would not return until they had the Demon Crown. The guard officer posted on the walls this night had been locked in the Lady Johanna's arms. His sentries had no doubt drifted off to sleep in some warm corner. Who walked the battlements?

Theoll threw himself forward as a small missile sang a deadly song and smashed into the wall. The stone's passage had ripped a piece of scalp and hair from his head. Theoll landed heavily, rolled and came to his knees, dagger in hand.

A second stone whistled through the gathering light of dawn, catching him in the upper arm. He yelped in pain. His dagger fell from a numbed hand. Theoll fought to get to his feet. He opened his mouth to cry out, to alert the sleeping guard, to get his personal guardsmen to return.

A heavy stone caught him squarely in the center of the chest. He felt himself lifted up and thrown backward over the battlement. Dazed, he lay on his back, staring up at the stars fading in the new light of day.

Strong hands grabbed his ankles and heaved. Theoll threw out his arms as he fell through the air, his cape trailing like the broken wings of a bat. He tried to scream but the stone's impact had driven the air from his lungs.

The baron plunged toward the ground from the highest point of the castle's battlements.

CHAPTER FOUR

Baron Theoll gasped for air as he turned slowly in midair. For a brief instant, his head spun about so that he could see where he fell. He saw only death rushing up at him, but the stone had driven the wind from his lungs and he could not scream in fear.

He crashed into the ground—hard. The pink and gray blossoms of dawn vanished in a blackness filled with pain.

Theoll groaned when he felt hands on his shoulders, lifting, shaking, bruising his already battered body. His eyes popped open and a cry of surprise escaped his lips.

"I still live!" He fought to get free of the clutching hands and look around.

"Quiet, Baron. You are sorely injured."

"I'm still alive, damn your eyes! What happened?"

"You fell from the battlements."

"I know that, fool. What saved me?" Theoll forced his head up and got a chance to look around. He had crashed through the thatched roof of a chicken coop. The slender poles supporting the roof had taken the force from his fall; landing in the soft muck on the floor had also cushioned his landing. Everywhere he looked he saw frightened chickens, feathers suspended in the air, and a uniform grime of chicken shit. Theoll tried to pull entirely free of the hands supporting him.

He failed. To his horror, he found that his legs refused to obey his wishes. He tried to reach down and lift them. His right hand twitched weakly. His left gave only throbbing pain.

"Baron, you are severely injured. I have called the court physician, but he can only tell you what I already have. Both your legs are broken, as is your left arm. If you have no other injuries, count yourself as fortunate. Few survive such clumsiness."

"Clumsy!" Theoll bellowed. The air came smoothly to his lungs now. His legs and arms might be fractured but he felt nothing but power within his chest and loins.

For an instant, he wondered at this. Death had been close and now he felt . . . aroused.

"How else could you fall from behind such tall battlements?" demanded his benefactor.

"I was thrown over the wall!"

No answer came. The man dressed in the dingy, tattered clothing was obviously a peasant. Equally as obvious was his disbelief that such a thing might happen in Porotane. In his tiny world only carelessness produced such unfortunate results.

In Theoll's world, the carelessness lay in not completing an assassination. Someone had foolishly allowed him to live. He would discover the villain's identity—and he would not be as inept with his swift, killing blade.

Pain began to mount within his small frame, driving knives of agony into his brain from all quarters. He allowed the shock to take him to a land unvisited by the red-hot pain.

"Your personal saint watches over you well, Baron," said Archbishop Nosto. The tall man stood over Theoll's bed, staring down at him. Theoll tried to guess at the thoughts within the cleric's mind. He failed. Theoll saw no hint that Nosto had been the one trying to kill him, although the idea had certain merit.

"For that I give thanks," said Theoll. "My legs were unbroken, for all the damage they sustained."

"But your left arm is definitely broken." Nosto stared openly at it, his face curious. "It does not appear that you will have the use of it again."

"The physician claims it will not heal properly. Although it might be bent permanently, I will have some use of it." Theoll flexed his right hand. The only damage he had sustained to his right side had been the stone striking the fleshy portion of his upper arm. The large bruise remained tender to the touch, but Theoll was in no condition to be stroking it.

"The saints are bountiful indeed. You are beloved by all, Baron," intoned Archbishop Nosto.

"All save one of this world," Theoll said bitterly. "I will find the person responsible for throwing me over the wall, Archbishop. And when I do . . ." Theoll's right hand gripped down so hard on the edge of the bed that mattress stuffing escaped through the rents he opened.

"I have made discreet inquiries but have found no one willing to accept blame for this."

"Had they killed me, no one would," said the baron. "They maneuver into position, waiting for

Duke Freow to die. They all realize I am the leading contender for the throne when he dies. Remove me before his death and it does not appear to be a self-serving assassination."

"Your mind walks curious paths," said Archbishop Nosto.

"I sinned, Nosto. I had the sin of pride thinking none would harm me because of my power in Porotane. I see the error of such pride. They would harm me *because of* that power."

"This is the reason for the armed guards outside your chambers?"

"It is. While I lie abed, my agents circulate throughout the castle hunting those responsible. If they tried to kill me, they might be bold enough to injure the duke—or even you, my dear Archbishop." The expression on the cleric's face told Theoll nothing. Nosto appeared startled at this notion of being harmed for some abstract, secular gain, yet Theoll knew that the cleric played the power game as well as anyone in Porotane.

"You should forgive the person responsible, and apply your energies toward the betterment of Porotane. The civil war rages on."

"You refer to Gaemock's attempted siege?"

"Only a wandering wizard more interested in booty saved the castle from this siege," said Archbishop Nosto. "Gaemock had to decide between holding position or retreating in the face of this new menace. He retreated."

"For the time, yes," said Theoll. His mind raced. Could Dews Gaemock have sent the assassin to remove the true power within the castle? Theoll decided that Gaemock had worries other than assassination. Also, it behooved a lord bringing a castle to siege to allow the leaders to surrender.

Assassination created turmoil, not opportunity from without.

"Only from within," Theoll said aloud.

"How is this, Baron?"

"Nothing, Archbishop. I require your cooperation in finding the assassin."

"But, Baron, I have told you that my inquiries have proven fruitless. There is nothing more that I can do."

"I need the power of the Inquisition to—"

"No!" The answer came sharp and emphatic. "The Inquisition is not a political tool. It is a religious quest to find and remove heretics from our midst."

Theoll saw no difference. Any opposing him had to be a heretic. But Archbishop Nosto saw his holy tortures in a different light. Theoll shifted in bed and raised himself slightly on his good arm. The time had come to firm the tenuous alliance with the archbishop.

"Nosto, I *must* move against those opposing me."

"Do so," the archbishop said primly. "But do not think your affairs are those of a cleric."

"Our interests cross. The heretics are responsible for my condition."

Archbishop Nosto's skepticism did not have to be put into words. His thin face radiated doubt and even contempt that Theoll stooped so low in his accusations.

"I have not spoken of this before. I am compelled to do so now."

"Of what?"

"I trust you, Nosto. You will not reveal what I say to anyone, will you?" He peered at the tall man and read only confusion on the cleric's face.

"I cannot make such a promise, Theoll. If this matter is of importance to the Inquisition, it is my sworn duty to reveal it."

The baron nodded solemnly. "I understand this. I leave it to you to decide if this is truly a matter for Church investigation."

"Speak."

Theoll forced away the grin of triumph. The archbishop had taken the bait and now found himself trapped with a cage of words. Not until Theoll had finished would Nosto be released.

"There are those in the castle who summon a demon for counsel."

"Impossible!"

"So I thought, but with my own eyes I have witnessed such a meeting of supernatural with . . . those of this world."

"Who? I demand that you reveal their names. Such obscene and blasphemous congress is forbidden!"

Archbishop Nosto calmed himself and continued in a quieter voice. "There can be no such congress. The Demon Crown is proof of that. Kalob, the last demon to walk this world, made reparation for the misery it had caused. The crown given to Porotane's ruler signified total demonic surrender."

"So I thought. Perhaps the Demon Crown remains as a gateway for the demons' return," said Theoll, playing on a theme that unnerved Nosto. "Or perhaps there is more to the pact than we have been told. So much of the gift of the Demon Crown is shrouded in mystery."

"There has been no demon in the land for over three hundred years."

"Yet the Inquisition finds traces of demonic influence," said Theoll. "Why else seek those who have strayed from the True Path?"

"You make light of the testing," accused Archbishop Nosto.

"No! Not I!" protested Theoll. The baron pulled himself to a sitting position. "I tell you that I have witnessed a meeting between a guard officer and a demon."

"Before the Inquisition you would swear to this?"

"Archbishop, I am sorely wounded. Better that a cleric—such as yourself—also witness it and assess the truth or falsity of my claim. You are trained in such matters. I might have been an unwilling dupe, though I doubt it. On my soul and the blessing of my personal saint, I so swear."

"I can witness a meeting of mortal and demon? When? Where?"

The baron could not hold back the smile twisting the corners of his lips. How the cleric believed!

"This very night. Do you know the unused pantry behind the castle kitchens? You do? If you enter through the kitchen and hide behind the furniture stored there, you will see a meeting such as I have described."

"Who is the heretic?"

"Archbishop Nosto," Theoll said seriously. "I may have erred. See for yourself if this guard lieutenant is not also a traitor and heretic."

"Yes, yes, I will."

"At midnight, Nosto. The demon will come at midnight."

The archbishop left Theoll's chambers, muttering to himself and invoking the succor of a dozen different saints. Theoll sagged, the strain of the meeting wearing on him. Still, he called out.

A guard appeared instantly, hand on sword. "How may I serve you, Baron?" the guard asked. His quick eyes circled the room to check for danger, then returned to lock boldly with Theoll's.

"The jester. Harhar. Bring him. I feel the need of amusement."

"The physician has ordered rest."

"Damn the physician! Obey me! I need the jester's wit. Fetch him immediately."

The guard saluted and left. Theoll let the grin spread broadly now. Victory edged ever closer. He had no idea who had tried to kill him on the battlements, but with Archbishop Nosto's unwitting help, he would remove one cabal plotting against him. If they were not responsible for the assassination attempt, at least the effort would not be wasted on hapless innocents.

As if anyone in the castle of Porotane was truly innocent. All had blood on their hands from a score of years under Duke Freow.

"Baron?" came a tremulous voice.

Theoll jerked around to see Harhar standing in the doorway, a rattle in one hand and a battered rag cap in the other. The sudden movement sent waves of pain throughout Theoll's body. He fought to keep from fainting.

"If you wish, Baron, I will leave. The guard said . . ."

Theoll gestured the fool to silence. "I require your services, Harhar. Will you perform for me?"

"Baron, yes!" Harhar stuck the cap on his head and put the rattle in his mouth. With an agility that defied joints and muscles, Harhar be-

gan a series of leaps and aerial twists. Each movement allowed him to snap his head about, causing
the rattle to whine and purr and whistle and
produce sounds Theoll could not identify.

"Harhar, wait, stop. No more. You make me
tired watching this display."

"It does not please you, Baron?" Harhar sank
to the floor, his forehead on the rug beside the
baron's bed. "A joke?" the jester asked hopefully.

"No, no, not here, not now. But a joke, yes. A
fine jest. The best you have ever done. Will you do
this for me?"

"Oh, Baron, yes, of course!" The jester's eagerness to perform disgusted Theoll, but he
needed this simpleminded acquiescence to his
scheme. For over a fortnight he had prepared the
pantry for Archbishop Nosto. He had intended to
be the primary actor in the drama but his condition prevented it now. Letting Harhar perform
struck Theoll as ironic and appropriate retribution
for Nosto's pomposity.

"You will be costumed by the guard who will
accompany us."

"Us? But Baron Theoll, your condition!"

"That is not your concern, fool," he snapped.
"You will dress and speak loudly the words I
whisper in your ear. Is that understood?"

A frown crossed Harhar's handsome face.

"You will repeat what I tell you," Theoll
explained, impatient with the jester's lack of un-
derstanding. "If you please me, I shall give you a
gold coin. Displease me and I shall see you
whipped through the streets like a dog!"

The jester cringed again, head banging on the
rug. "I will please you, Baron, I will, I will!"

Theoll summoned the guard to aid him. Al-

though fully three hours remained until midnight,
Theoll thought the journey to the pantry would
prove slow and tedious. He endured the pain, but
had to stop even more often than anticipated. A
scant hour remained by the time the trio—baron,
jester, and guard—reached the deserted pantry.

"Guard, remain hidden in the kitchens. No
matter what you see or hear, do not reveal your
presence. Only on my command will you attend
me. Do you understand?"

The guard nodded. To Harhar, Theoll said,
"Help me into the pantry storage room."

The jester helped the disabled noble. Theoll
pointed out a hidden panel. "There. We go in
there."

"Why, it is like a small stage," marveled
Harhar. "The door closes, but a window opens to
reveal us."

"To reveal you," corrected Theoll. "Put on
this costume. Can you use makeup?" He drew
forth a large box of paints and colored greases.

"It is second nature to me, Baron. But what
character do I perform this night? Punctilious? Or
perhaps Wobbles?"

"Nothing of the sort. No characters from a
children's play. A demon. You must look like a
demon." Theoll snorted in disgust when the jester
cringed away. The baron grabbed the fool's collar
and dragged him into the small box built into the
wall. He settled down on the floor. Harhar had to
stand with legs spread to avoid stepping on the
noble. When the window in the secret door
opened, Harhar would be visible only from the
waist up, allowing Theoll to remain seated and
coach him. The baron saw that this might prove

more difficult than he had thought because of the fool's reaction.

"Put on this snakeskin jerkin." Theoll watched as Harhar stripped off his rags and donned the sleek, gleaming garment that transformed a human into a reptilian creature. The baron guided Harhar in applying the makeup. In less than twenty minutes, the jester had become a convincing serpentlike demon.

"Do I please you, Baron?" asked Harhar.

"Even this close, you look the part," said Theoll. "From the room, you will seem to *be* a demon."

Harhar stirred uneasily at the notion but said nothing. Theoll painfully worked his way into the secret box again and motioned for Harhar to enter also.

"Stand and wait. Do not open the window until I order you to do so."

Theoll drew a dagger and bored a small spyhole with the tip so that he could peer out into the dusty pantry. He had intended to look through a crack between window and shade but his injuries changed that plan. He looked at Harhar and decided that this might be even better. Nosto would never believe the jester capable of such perfidy.

"What do I say, Baron?"

"Remain silent. I shall whisper to you. Repeat exactly what I say or I will cut out your tongue."

The jester bobbed his head like a crane fishing in shallow waters but said nothing. Harhar entered the box on the baron's order and closed the secret panel. Within the box it was dark, stuffy, and for the jester, terrifying. For the baron, it proved only cramped and increasingly painful. He used his spyhole to look out into the pantry. He hoped that Archbishop Nosto proved prompt. It had to be within a few minutes of midnight.

"Baron!" cried Harhar. "Someone is coming!"

"Silence, fool!"

Theoll squinted hard at the spyhole, a rising excitement within his breast. He needed Archbishop Nosto's influence if he was to stop the Lady Johanna in her drive to depose him. Whether she had been responsible for his brush with death, Theoll neither knew nor cared. Eliminating her from power within the castle meant one less opponent when the ancient duke finally succumbed.

"Good," murmured Theoll. "That's the way, Nosto. Hide there. Yes, yes!" To Harhar he said, "Scream as loudly as you can. I want his heart to explode with fear."

Harhar responded. Even expecting it, Theoll started. He smiled. Harhar was beginning to enjoy his role and it showed.

Theoll began feeding the lines to his willing fool.

"Archbishop Nosto," called Harhar. "You are not the one I chose to meet this evening. Come forth!"

Theoll watched as Nosto crept from hiding. The baron reached up and opened the curtain. Harhar, in his demon's colored makeup, was dimly revealed to the cleric. Theoll had tested this effect; it appeared as if the demon was inside the solid wall, making it all the more frightening.

Archbishop Nosto made protective signs in the air in front of him. "What demon are you?" he demanded.

"You do not fear me?" Harhar asked, on Theoll's prompting.

"The saints protect me from all evil."

Theoll had to admire the cleric's courage—or his fanaticism.

"You would serve me as the lieutenant of the guard does?" asked Harhar, his voice rumbling in a deep bass.

"What guardsman is this who strays from the True Path?"

"You know the one," said Harhar. "The Lady Johanna fornicates with him nightly. You know the one. I have given him the object of his lusty desires because of his faithful service."

"Lieutenant Oprezzi?"

"That is his mortal name," agreed Harhar. The jester chanced to look down as Theoll worked on a candle. The baron motioned him back to the task. Archbishop Nosto must not suspect trickery.

"You are not a demon. The last demon was banished more than three hundred years ago."

"Aye," said Harhar. "When Kalob the Fierce made reparation to you puny humans, he left the trinket you call the Demon Crown. Kalob was banished, but others of considerably more power have returned. Oprezzi and those of his ilk appease us with their bodies and souls. They do our bidding. We will triumph over you, Archbishop Nosto. Demonic power returns to this world!"

To emphasize the words, Theoll lit the candle and cupped his hands about the flame to focus the light upward. From the pantry, it appeared as if the disembodied demon had opened a trapdoor to hell and the hellfire shone upward on his face.

Archbishop Nosto made another ward gesture.

"You will aid me, Archbishop?" demanded Harhar.

"I order you back to the depths of the hell from which you come!"

"You cannot order me. Not when there are those among you who do my bidding!"

"Then they shall be put to the Question. They shall never stray from the True Path!"

Harhar laughed until his voice began to turn hoarse. Theoll snuffed out the candle flame, almost choking on the sudden plume of smoke rising from the wick. He turned back to the spyhole and peered at Nosto. The cleric turned and bolted from the room.

Baron Theoll wanted to laugh and cry out loud at his victory. Nosto would not stop with his Inquisition of Oprezzi until the feckless lieutenant confessed everything—truth or not. And through the guardsman, Nosto had to come to the Lady Johanna.

Theoll did not care if Nosto put her to the Question. The cleric's suspicion would keep the woman busy and allow Theoll a free hand in his own dealings.

Duke Freow would die soon. Theoll would see to that. And when the duke passed on, the power would come to Baron Theoll of Brandon.

CHAPTER FIVE

The Glass Warrior rode slowly from the castle, knowing that she had seen Duke Freow for the last time. Success or failure, her mission marked the ruler's last significant command.

She reined in and looked at the dawn-lit castle walls. She shook her head, soft white hair floating like a nimbus around her face. It seemed an eternity since Freow—or the man posing as King Lamost's reclusive brother for all these years—had entrusted her with the Demon Crown. She reached behind, her fingers lightly touching the velvet sack in which rested the magical crown. As always, a tiny thrill passed through her. Although she had no royal blood and could never don the crown without risking instant and total madness, some of its magic inspired her.

"To rule all this," she said, her keen gray eyes looking around the farms surrounding the castle. Good land, rich and productive. And the workers strove to bring in bountiful harvests. "A shame the wars have raged so long. What might Porotane have accomplished as a whole instead of fractured into a dozen warring pieces?"

Again she shook her head. She tried to stay above politics, to remain aloof from the machinations of those in the Porotane court. But as long as she held the Demon Crown, she knew she would be the center of a vortex of death and intrigue.

"The scurvy son of a bitch wasn't even Lamost's kin," she said aloud. Freow had completely fooled her. She had believed him an honorable, decent fellow intent only on locating the twins and returning them to power. For almost twenty years she had believed this. It was for the best that she had not partaken of the feuds and power games being played out in Porotane. She was too easily duped.

But the man who had assumed Freow's identity had chosen her with uncanny skill. For twenty years she had fought off legions of thieves, both lowborn and noble, seeking to steal the Demon Crown. She had kept the crown as a trust for Lokenna and Lorens and never thought for an instant of betraying it.

The Glass Warrior stretched, her joints popping. She was no longer the young warrior woman who had accepted this task. It was for the good of all that she now do what Freow had promised for so many years. She had done her duty in protecting the crown for the twins. Now she must find them to hand over their heritage.

"Mayhap then I can rest," she said, patting her horse on the neck. The mare whinnied and tried to rear. "Whoa, now. What's the trouble? Do we have company on our ride this fine morning?"

The horse bobbed her head up and down, as if she understood. Sometimes, it seemed to the woman, the horse truly foresaw the future and tried to tell of it.

The Glass Warrior reached into her pouch and pulled out a short string of wildcat gut with a small

cut-glass spike tied to it. She held it at arm's length
and closed her eyes. Soft chants rose from her lips,
the weak magic turning the glass into something
more than a convenient device for finding her way.
Vibrations from the crystal raced up the gut string
and into her fingers, down her arm and into her
shoulder.

Her entire body began to quiver under the
impact of her scrying spell. A darkness fell over
her mind as if a box of purest ebony encased her.
With sight went sound and smell. She floated in the
magical void, the only sense being the shivering
gut string in her fingers.

"Come," she coaxed. "Show me who follows."

A vivid picture formed, as if before her eyes.
But the Glass Warrior's eyes were screwed shut in
concentration. The image came magically and
from a distance beyond sight.

Twelve riders rode from the Porotane castle,
circled to where she had tied her mare, then
followed her spoor with uncanny skill.

The image intensified. She now heard the
leader speaking. "I sighted her along the trail.
Make good speed, men, for we ride under the
baron's strictest orders."

"The baron," she murmured. "Baron Theoll.
Who else could command such resources within
Porotane?"

The riders galloped along her trail. She
watched and listened magically until their leader
reined in and slowed his band of fighters with their
clanking swords and rattling armor. "Here," he
said. "Here is where I sighted her. Dismount and
find the trail. We must not lose her—or the Demon
Crown!"

The Glass Warrior's concentration began to

slip. The pure blackness of the box in which her senses were encased developed cracks. Wind blew across her face, carrying soft scents and the promise of rain before nightfall. The light of a new day pried its way under her lids and she saw instead of *saw*. The chirping of a songbird broke the spell completely, and she again saw only the world around her. Her fingers tightened on the gut string and she drew the glass crystal into her hand. She squeezed so tightly that blood dripped onto it, renewing its power for her next use.

"So, Baron, you think it this easy to steal the crown?" The Glass Warrior threw back her head and laughed, her mockery of the diminutive noble frightening the wildlife into silence. She controlled her scorn, and slowly the birds again sang and the crepuscular animals moved through the low brush around the trail.

She put her heels to the mare's flanks and started off at a good pace. Let her pursuers tire their steeds. She had an unknown distance to travel before she found the heirs to the throne— and she had all day in which to lay a false trail for the baron's men.

They were soldiers, fighters trained in the ways of killing. She knew the forests and plains and all the ways of eluding pursuers.

The Glass Warrior used her full knowledge. By midday, another scrying showed the soldiers racing directly north to the Uvain Plateau. She turned east and then south, circling wide around the castle, and by late afternoon, was heading in the opposite direction from her pursuers.

The small cooking fire drove back the dampness of the night. The Glass Warrior hunched forward to warm her hands. The rabbit she had hunted and eaten for dinner had been too small, its taste doing little more than supplementing the dry trail rations she carried. But the tiny fire did more to raise her spirits than anything else. She could stare for long hours into the dancing orange and blue flames, studying the ever-changing patterns and trying to impose sense on them.

One childhood story she remembered well was that fire had been given to mankind by a demon repentant for all the woe it had visited on the world. The Glass Warrior smiled wanly. So many myths sounded similar. The Demon Crown had been given to King Waellkin by the demon Kalob in reparation for the destruction brought by demonic acts. It mattered little to her. The sight of fire carried its own magic, soothing and warming.

Her hand flashed to her dagger when distant clanking echoed through the copse where she camped for the night. She strained, listening intently. Then she dropped to the ground, pressing her ear into the dirt. She straightened quickly. The ground had been soaked by the afternoon rains and carried sound poorly.

The sound of a wagon grew louder. She sighed and stood, buckling the sword belt around her trim waist. Returning her glass dagger to its sheath, she drew her sword. In the firelight, its glass surface reflected rainbows. Moving like the wind, she vanished into the thicket around her campfire and crouched, waiting.

Those in the wagon made no attempt to hide their arrival. Boisterous shouts, curses, and laughter preceded the pair.

"I tell you, Vered, you cannot hope to escape the wheel if you keep doing such things."

"You're getting old, Santon, old and frightened!"

"Courage has nothing to do with it. You stole from the village elder."

"He was the only one with money. Why bother picking empty purses? Hot air I can get from you. Gold I get only from the rich!"

The one called Santon grabbed his companion's sleeve when he spotted the campfire. "Looks as if we've another traveler along the road this evening, Vered. But where has he gotten off to?"

"Your odor sends even the strong-stomached running. If my nose wasn't clogged constantly, I couldn't stand you either."

"Bathing gives me the vapors. I need all my strength."

"Not of smell, Santon, not of smell." Vered made a gagging noise. The sound of a strong blow silenced his antics.

"That's better," came Santon's words. "Since our fellow traveler has seen fit to rush off, mayhap a quick examination is in order. Just to be sure that nothing untoward has happened, mind you."

"And you declare me to be a ruthless, impatient thief. Ha!" The wagon came to a clanking, creaking halt and the pair dismounted.

From her hiding spot in the bushes, the Glass Warrior saw two tall men of good build separate and advance cautiously on the campfire from different directions. The one named Vered was young, hardly twenty summers, and carried himself with the assurance and arrogance of youth. From his quick movements and easy way of handling his sword, she thought him a dangerous adversary. But the other, Santon, held her attention. Older by ten or more summers, he carried the scars of devastating warfare. His left hand clutched powerfully around the handle of a battle-ax; his right arm dangled helplessly, a withered remnant of former strength. He moved like a soldier, his eyes seeing more than the superficial.

It took Santon only seconds to find the trail she had left in leaving the camp. The Glass Warrior rose and walked into the light of her campfire when Santon peered at the very bush behind which she had tried to hide.

"Good evening, sirs," she said.

"And to you, fair lady," answered the brasher Vered. Santon took a step to the side, his heavy ax held away from his body and ready for action.

"There is no need to rob me," she said. "I have little worthy of your attention."

"Rob?" protested Vered. "Gracious one, how can you think such a nasty thing of us? We are but traveling jugglers."

Her quick glance at Santon's crippled arm brought a laugh from Vered. The young man said, "*I* juggle for coins. My dear friend only assists, sometimes acting the fool."

"Quiet, Vered. She knows your honeyed lies for what they are."

"Lies? Really, Santon, we—" The man reached out, as if to protest. But as quick as he was in bringing up his sword, the Glass Warrior proved faster. She caught the edge of his steel blade and deflected it with her glass one. Vered recovered swiftly and tried to lunge, to drive the razor tip of his sword past her guard and cut a hamstring.

She stepped into the thrust, disengaged, and spiraled around his blade. She took it from his hand and sent the weapon flying into the night. Before Vered could recover, the glass point rested at the hollow of his throat.

"Stay your blade, dear lady. I meant nothing! Honest!"

"I doubt you've ever been honest in your life. Is this not true, warrior?" she asked of Santon. From behind she saw the man beginning to come at her. This pair worked well together, for all their insults and bickering.

"If his lips are moving, you can be sure Vered is lying."

"A vile canard!" cried Vered. He did not seem to notice the point menacing his throat. The Glass Warrior had to admire his courage. She lowered her blade and stepped away so that she could see them both.

"We've met our match," said Santon. "Can we call a truce? Or do you wish us to travel on?"

"Travel in this miserable, inky night?" protested Vered. "We'll become irretrievably lost. None will find us for a hundred years! Our bones will be gnawed by wild animals, then bleach in the sun for the rest of eternity. We—"

"Quiet, Vered. Do you not recognize her?"

Vered fell silent as he studied the Glass Warrior more carefully. "She is truly beautiful. Never have I seen such lovely hair and so fine a figure. And she is adept with her sword. A peculiar brand of weapon it is, too. Glass? Yes, I thought so. I've never seen one, though I've heard the legends."

"He thinks you a legend, Lady," said Santon.

"No legend," she assured him.

Vered frowned. "I do not understand." He brightened. "I do understand that we have been incredibly rude. Allow me to introduce ourselves.

I am Vered, and my friend who cannot juggle is Birtle Santon. We are—"

"Traveling entertainers," she finished, with a laugh. "Traveling thieves appears to be a better description."

"And you, dear lady, who are you?"

"She's the Glass Warrior, Vered," said Birtle Santon.

"That's ridiculous. She's only a legend." Vered's words trailed off as he looked at the glass sword held so easily in her hand and at the glass dagger sheathed at her belt.

"The cape is spun from glass, also," she said, seeing his interest. "I seldom wear it unless I require protection. Your dagger. Draw it and try to thrust through the cape." She spun about, sending the cape swinging from her body. She held out an arm and let the cape dangle.

Vered whipped out his slim-bladed dagger and slashed with all the power locked within his strong arm. The tip danced along the cape and skittered away.

"It can be cut, but it requires luck as well as skill and a sharp dagger," she told him. "Go retrieve your sword. You look lost without it."

"What would I do with it?" Vered asked, making a helpless gesture. "Never have I found a cape that resists my sharpest blade." He backed away, then went in search of his lost sword.

She turned to Santon and motioned for him to sit by the fire. "It is not much, but it helps hold back some of the night's chill."

"Vered can get more wood," said Santon. He settled down warily.

"No." The Glass Warrior's order came out sharper than she had wanted.

"So you are followed," mused Santon. "No, let me guess. I have heard the legends, but the reality must be something less. No woman, even one as handsome as you, could live up to the tales told over a tankard or two of ale."

He poked at the fire and urged the flames higher. "Do not worry," he said. "The flames are hidden and the smoke can't be seen. Vered and I both keep a sharp watch. We were almost upon you before we saw the fire."

"You run, too?" she asked.

"Let's say that we've had our share of disagreement," said Vered, returning with his sword. He dropped to the ground, legs thrust out and propping himself up on one elbow. In the firelight his brown eyes danced with mischief.

"Thieves," she said.

"Some have called us that," admitted Birtle Santon. "We think of ourselves as two lost souls seeking a bit of adventure wherever we can."

"Thieves."

"Yes," said Vered. "But you. What of you? We are an ex-soldier and a youngling unable to cope with a bad case of wanderlust. You are a legend."

"You flatter me, but I see that is part of your charm. Flattery and a quick slice with the knife to remove the money pouch."

"You have nothing to worry from us," said Santon.

"No," agreed Vered. "We can see by the way your pouch swings that it is as empty as ours." He reached out with the tip of his sword and bounced her money pouch. "I am more interested in how your blade survives real combat. Steel against glass? Surely, the glass must shatter."

"I am skilled at its preparation. At times, I wish it to shatter. At others, it is stronger than your blade."

They traded banter and odd stories for a time, edging around one another while they decided if trust was merited. The Glass Warrior decided long before either Santon or Vered.

"You are not actively sought by the authorities?" she asked. Their expressions, guarded though they were, showed that they were. "That is no concern of mine. What is of importance is a sacred vow I have taken."

"Sacred vows tend to be written in blood—others' blood," said Santon.

"You have seen combat too often. You grow cynical," she accused.

"I have, and that is a fact. For long years I rode Porotane trying to maintain order. Too many demon-damned brigands for that. Kill one and two spring up. I decided to make a path for myself through the world."

"Would you see an end to the civil war?" she asked.

"Who wouldn't? But the duke is too feeble. The others in the castle . . . by the saints, I wouldn't trust a one of them!" declared Santon.

"You would support a true king or queen?"

"One of royal blood?" asked Vered. He shrugged. "For all my life, there's been naught on the throne but Duke Freow. Santon remembers old King Lamost."

"Aye, and his children," said Santon, almost dreamily. "They'd be older than young Vered by now, had they lived."

Both men stiffened when Santon uttered

those words. Santon paused for a moment, studying the Glass Warrior's face, then asked, "They are dead, aren't they? It's been too many years for them to still live."

"This I do not know," said the Glass Warrior. "But Duke Freow has entrusted me with the task of finding Lokenna and Lorens. He is dying. One twin must assume the throne soon or Porotane's wars will intensify and permanently divide the kingdom."

"Where there's strife, there's opportunity," quoted Vered.

"For the likes of us, aye," said Santon. "For the likes of Baron Theoll, too."

The Glass Warrior saw the men's dislike for the small baron. "I seek the twins. I hope to find both, but either will be able to succeed to the throne. We must hurry, though. Freow is dying and the baron is becoming bolder."

"We? You think to count us into this madness? Oh, no, dear lady, not us. No," said Vered. "We're honest thieves, not heroes bent on dying nobly."

"He has a good point. This is not our worry. Theoll is a swine, but the likes of Dews Gaemock oppose him, not that he is that much better. I say, any who seek the throne should be denied it."

"Spoken like a former soldier," she said. "But I do need help. The baron has sent a squad after me. No, do not fear. I have eluded them for the moment, but they are determined. His threats drive them faster than any promise of reward."

"We want nothing to do with it," said Vered, his tone firm and his gaze unswerving.

"And you?" she asked of Birtle Santon. "What of you?"

"Vered's right. We have no stake in this.

Gaemock would make no different a ruler than Theoll—or either of the twins."

"You are wrong. There is good reason for once more seating royalty on the throne. Too few follow Gaemock or any of the hundred other would-be rulers of Porotane who are little more than brigands. No one wants Theoll on the throne. No one, I assure you."

"No," said Santon.

"I cannot coerce you," she said. "Come morning, we'll ride our separate ways."

Santon nodded, then asked, "Would you like a small drink of brandy? I've saved it for a special occasion. Meeting the famed Glass Warrior on a mission for the duke is as special as I'm likely to find."

"I'd be pleased."

Santon fetched the bottle and two battered metal cups. He poured her some and took one for himself. "What of Vered?" she asked. The young man had already drawn his cloak tightly around himself and lay sleeping by the low fire.

"Vered doesn't drink such swill. Slows the reflexes, he says. Burns out the brain, he says. He drinks only the finest of wines from the Uvain Plateau wineries."

"In that, he may be right."

"He is," said Santon. "It burns out both brain and memory. It's the only relief I get from the past." He tossed back the full cup, coughed, then poured himself another.

The Glass Warrior sipped slowly and considered the two men carefully. "I am sorry you will not aid me," she said.

"If it's true you're a wizard you might put a spell on us," suggested Santon.

"I command a few spells," she admitted. "But I would not force you to help. Such would only work against me."

The Glass Warrior took a long drink from the cup, the brandy burning her gullet and belly. She put the cup down and said, "You know that a wizard seldom reveals a personal name."

"The name can be used against them in spells and in battle," said Santon.

"It is a sign of trust."

Their eyes locked.

"My name is Alarice," the Glass Warrior said.

CHAPTER SIX

Vered stirred and turned, wrapping himself so tightly in his cloak that his arms tingled from lack of circulation. He sneezed, his nose clogged. Still more asleep than awake, he opened one eye and tried to remember his dreams.

Pleasant ones, he knew. The saucy wench chasing him had been gorgeous. And the commotion when she insisted that they . . .

Vered sneezed again and came fully awake, the dream remnant finally fleeing from conscious thought. He sat up and looked around. The fire lay cold and black between him and Birtle Santon. For a few seconds, Vered puzzled over the curious lump where his friend lay.

Vered then realized that Santon had not slept alone this past night. The Glass Warrior had curled up close by, whether to share only warmth or more, Vered didn't know or really care. She was an attractive one, he thought, but not his type. More Santon's, with her sturdy build and obvious fighting prowess. Vered preferred his women less combative and more curvaceous. Like the one in his dimly remembered dreams.

He shook free of his cloak and stood, stretching. The cold morning air caused his breath to come out in silvery plumes, but it invigorated him and convinced him that this day might be better than the last. He strolled off into the bushes to relieve himself, then returned to the cold campsite.

Santon and the Glass Warrior lay spoon-fashion, sleeping deeply. It might be another hour before they roused. What harm could there be in aiding this handsome woman by giving her some of his expertise in packing? She carried a lush-looking knapsack, but the lumpiness must tax her sorely, Vered thought. The harsh edges of whatever lay within had to cut into her softer curves as she walked.

Fingers nimble from practice, Vered opened the ties on the black velvet knapsack. The only sounds were those of the forest animals and wind blowing softly through the spring leaves. The sounds of velvet slipping across velvet were drowned out even by the distant brook burbling on its way to the River Ty.

He drew forth a crystal box and ran his fingers along the edges, seeking a possible trap. Some of the less enlightened booby-trapped their prize possessions with poisoned needles that leapt out at the wrong touch. Vered had even found one or two who installed spring-driven catapults within to kill the unwary.

No such trap had been laid by the Glass Warrior. He held the box at arm's length and peered through its crystalline sides. A simple gold circlet rested within.

"Not worth more than a few days' lodging in a good city," he decided aloud. He looked at the sleeping pair. Santon stirred now, unconsciously considering rising. In another few minutes, he would awaken.

Vered knew that it would be a churlish thing to do to steal this simple gold ornament from a woman who might have been Santon's lover the past night. He knew it. Still, he opened the crystalline lid and withdrew the circlet.

A tingling passed through him, electric and startling. Vered rocked back on his heels and laid the crown on the ground until he regained his senses.

"Too little food," he decided. "Weak from starvation. Imagine me, master thief the length and breadth of Porotane, being unable to lift a light gold circlet without fainting dead away! A travesty of honorable thievery!"

On feet quieter than a stalking cat, Vered went to the wagon and searched through the littered interior until he found a coil of wire. He balanced out an amount equal in weight to the gold circlet and placed the wire into the crystal box. The tricks light played as it went through the cut glass box walls made it appear as if he had left the circlet untouched. Pleased with his petty deception, Vered took the box with its wire crown back to the velvet knapsack. With care equal to that he had shown in removing the box, he replaced it and retied the velvet bindings, duplicating the Glass Warrior's simple knots.

Birtle Santon made an inarticulate sound that Vered knew to mean that his friend awoke.

"Good morning, Santon," Vered greeted brightly. "And how did you sleep? Better than I, from all appearances." He inclined his head in the direction of the still-sleeping Glass Warrior.

"Aye, for once you've hit on the truth of the

matter." Santon disengaged himself from the woman's arms and stood.

"What do we do about her?" asked Vered. "I have no desire to be broken on the wheel because of her mission for the duke."

"Nor I, but she pleads her case well."

"How well?" asked Vered, a grin on his face.

Santon grunted and threw a stone at him. Vered dodged easily. "We can let her ride along with us for a time," said Vered. He smoothed out his rumpled clothing and ran his fingers through light brown hair hanging in greasy strings. "If she can stand the odor, that is."

"You worry too much about appearances. You should consider the inner soul, that which cannot be scrubbed clean with only soap and water."

"And you, Santon, worry too much about your soul and not enough about how you smell!"

Alarice rolled over, awakened by their banter. Her eyes blinked open, gray orbs holding Santon and Vered pinned as firmly as if she had driven pins through them.

"Good morning, Lady," said Vered.

"It is, isn't it?" she said.

"And it will be even more of a good morning when we've eaten. I could eat a horse."

"Touch that nag pulling our wagon and I'll cut off your ears," growled Santon. To Alarice he said, "His belly often gets the better of him. No discipline."

"Santon wants us to march on no rations for a month, though he is a less than harsh taskmaster at times," said Vered. "He might let me drink a thimbleful of water once a week." The younger man began preparing a cooking fire, then jumped up when he saw Santon heading toward their dilapidated wagon.

"Here, Santon, you do the fire. I'll get the rations." He pushed past his friend and blocked the view into the wagon. He had forgotten to hide the pilfered circlet properly. Deft movements drew forth small portions of their food and hid the gold band where neither Santon nor the Glass Warrior was likely to see it without much searching.

"You hate to cook," said Santon. "Why the change of heart?"

"There is no constant in the world but change. Perhaps I've tired of your flavorless, tough concoctions. Perhaps I seek a cook who washes his hands."

"Perhaps I can get some peace," grumbled Birtle Santon.

Vered worked quickly and well to fix breakfast. The trio ate in silence, cleaned their plates, and stared challengingly at one another, almost daring the other to speak first. Vered broke the deadlock.

"I'll tend to the wagon. We can be on our way in an hour or less."

"May I have a word with you, Birtle?" asked the Glass Warrior.

"Let's walk," Santon said. He heaved his bulk up and forward and got his feet under him. His immensely powerful left arm showed no strain when he helped Alarice to her feet. Together, they vanished into the dense undergrowth.

This suited Vered. He hastily packed their equipment, tended the swayback horse, and then climbed into the wagon, its rear door slightly ajar so that he could keep watch for the Glass Warrior's return.

He reached under the sacks where he had hidden the gold circlet. He drew it forth and stared at it.

The electric tingle returned and set his heart racing faster. Hands trembling slightly, Vered lifted the Demon Crown and placed it upon his head.

Santon and Alarice found a small game trail and followed it until they came to the brook wending its way into larger waters. Santon paused and stared at the churning surface, then picked up a stone and dropped it into the stream. The rapid current robbed him of the pleasure of seeing ripples expand outward.

"Have you come to a conclusion, Birtle?" Alarice asked. "This is not something to be taken lightly. The fate of Porotane rests on your decision."

"What can I do to help? Or Vered and me? We're not soldiers. We're certainly no heroes."

"You are adept with a blade and, in spite of all you say, I see the goodness within you both. And courage. More than you think."

He stared into her slate gray eyes and felt as if he fell a hundred miles. More stirred within this woman than he could guess. So like the stream she was! The surface carried one message, while others lurked beneath frothy waters. Santon felt as if he would step into her eyes and vanish forever into a world beyond his wildest imagining.

"We cannot. Despite all that you say, this isn't our fight."

"I understand," she said. "But I had hoped for

more from you. It was wrong of me to impose, even asking this of you. Duke Freow has given me the mission and no one else. I sought only to lighten my burden."

"Alarice," he began. He bit back words ill considered. Santon almost agreed to abandon Vered and travel with her.

"Friendships are precious," she said, supplying him with an excuse.

"Vered and I have traveled far," Santon said. "He's saved my life well nigh as many times as I have saved his." He smiled as he remembered. "We met on the coast. I had been mustered out of the King's Guard over fifteen years when I came on this ruffian trying to steal from a sailor. The old salt had caught him and wanted to cut off Vered's ears. The boy lacked a summer of being fifteen."

"You rescued him?"

"Of course. I pretended to buy him from the sailor. I paid five gold pieces. Oh, that Vered's quick on the uptake. He saw what I did. He had the sailor's money pouch long before I grabbed him by the ear and led him from the tavern. He tried to rob me when we got free! After we settled that, we got along well. His skills are great."

"As are yours," Alarice said, her fingers moving along the sinews on Santon's powerful arm. "I remember last night."

"It's been a long time," he said, embarrassed.

"For me, too. Perhaps that made it the sweeter. I choose to think otherwise."

"We can't go with you. There's too many on our trail," Santon said, coming to a firm conclusion now. "We would only hold you back from wherever you go."

"I seek the wizard Tahir d'mar."

"A wizard, is it? That's too risky for the likes of a pair of sneak thieves. Neither Vered nor I are adept at even simple fire spells."

"I feel more in Vered," she said. "Are you sure he is not hiding spell-casting abilities from you?"

"We've been together five years. He's a sly one, but not even Vered could pretend for that length of time. He's as lacking in magic skills as I."

Santon stared at her and said, "I wish it could be otherwise, Alarice. If for nothing more than to guard your back."

"Companions can mean life or death." She saw the conflict still raging within his mind, but Birtle Santon had decided. The Glass Warrior would not ask him to recant. "Let's return to camp. I . . . I have an uneasy feeling."

"Theoll's men?" he asked.

"No, something . . . more."

Alarice spun and started back to camp at a pace Santon worked hard to equal.

Vered lowered the crown, then jerked back when biting sparks exploded from the circlet and burned his scalp. But the Demon Crown remained on his head—and he *saw*.

He had always thought his vision good and his hearing acute. Vered knew the truth now. He had been as one aged and infirm, seeing half the world and hearing nothing. But no longer! The world sharpened and brightened and the sounds blasted into his ears.

He saw the songbird in the tree a mile distant, heard the faint quavers in its mating call, understood all, and found the golden bird's mate four miles away. Vered listened to her answer, saw her take wing and fly directly toward the tree branch.

A shiver possessed him. His *sight* extended farther along the road he and Santon had traveled. His hand flashed for his sword when he *saw* the rebel band stalking the four local constables. Vered did not know which side he should support with his fighting prowess.

He had no love for the constables; they insisted on foolishly enforcing laws that Vered chose to break or ignore. But the rebels! These were of a band led by a minor wizard. How Vered knew this, he could not say.

He knew. He *knew*!

The rebels ambushed the four constables, killing two instantly. The two survivors stood back to back to defend themselves. Vered chose. He rushed forward to aid them against the rebels. Politics meant nothing to him. Helping those against whom the odds fell appealed to him. For all his life, he had been the longshot, the poor bet, the one no one expected to survive.

Vered rushed forward, sword swinging. The blade drove down on a carelessly exposed wrist . . . and passed through.

He gasped and stared in disbelief at his blade. Every detail of the blade was his to examine minutely. The tiny nicks he thought he had honed out, the imperfections in the metal, small islands of carbon in the steel, Vered *saw* all this and more.

"Die, swine!" cried a rebel. The man's sword rose and fell. Blood spattered from the constable's wound. A second slash ended the man's life. The remaining constable proved easy prey for the rebel band. The six who survived the ambush stood over the bodies, gloating openly. Again Vered tried to attack and again his blade passed through his target as if traveling through smoke.

Vered jumped back to reassess his actions. The rebels paid him no heed. It was as if he did not exist for them. But he *saw* and *heard* so clearly!

Movement behind drew him around. He faced the leader of this small group. He *felt* power exuding from this man.

The wizard halted and cocked his head to one side. He yelled, "Search the area! There is another lurking nearby. Another wizard!"

Vered spun and used his *sight* to look for this other wizard. He *saw* no one. It took several seconds for him to realize that this sorcerer did not mean another. He meant Vered.

The thief blinked and moved away from the wizard. The speed of retreat took away his breath. Never in his life had he run this fast. Vered *looked* beyond the rebel wizard and saw other men and women, in a village, beyond the village, beyond the River Ty, all the way to Porotane's castle.

And within the strong stone walls stirred hundreds of people. Vered found it increasingly easy to follow an individual. Freow lay dying. The court jester, called Harhar by a nobleman, cavorted and pranced and tried to cheer the duke.

Vered's head spun. Dizziness assailed him. He *saw* even farther away than the castle, to the coast, to a swamp, to the Yorral Mountains, across the Uvain Plateau. The world swung in wide circles, twisting him around, turning him inside out, forcing sensations on him he could not put into words.

Vered cried out for Santon to help him, but no words formed. He spun and gyrated and tumbled and surged endlessly. Trapped. Unable to right himself. Trapped and helpless. Helpless. Helpless!

CHAPTER SEVEN

Vered tried to cry out in panic. The words clogged in his throat—but he *heard* them. He *heard* everything. The pounding of his own heart, the sweat breaking out from his skin, the creaking as his hair grew, the rush of blood through his veins, everything.

He *heard*!

He gagged when a heavy fist drove into his gut. Vered tried to double over and vomit. The Demon Crown held him in thrall. The more he struggled, the worse became his disorientation. Spinning colors filled his eyes. He *saw* too much. His eyes refused to separate the details, the riot of hues, the lightning-intense blasts that seared his brain.

Again came the blow. He tried to reach out to defend himself. He failed. No matter what course of action he tried, he failed. The blows increased in severity until he thought a giant wielding a sledgehammer was breaking his bones.

Vered felt himself rising up, even as the kaleidoscope around him robbed his senses of direction. The impact as he struck the ground stunned him—and the senses-wrecking assault stopped.

Gasping for breath, unable to move, he stared up from the ground at Birtle Santon. The man towered over him, his single arm bulging from the exertion of lifting his friend into the air and then flinging him down.

"You?" asked Vered, the air painful in his lungs. He choked. A gentler hand slapped him on the back to help him regain control. He looked over his shoulder and saw the Glass Warrior, concern etched on her fine face.

"Who else would save you from yourself, you stupid lout," grumbled Santon.

"What happened? I . . . I remember what I experienced, but what was it? I mean, my head, oh, it feels like some vile forge and a smithy is banging away at his anvil—my head!"

"You are adept at thievery," said Alarice. "I never noticed that you had stolen the crown."

"Crown? Ah, the gold circlet, that paltry bauble of insignificant value. There it is." Vered reached out to recapture the fallen crown. He yelped in pain. The Glass Warrior's boot crushed his hand into the dirt, preventing him from again touching the Demon Crown.

"It will kill if you touch it again."

"That?" Vered's amazement was echoed by Birtle Santon.

"What manner of magical device is this?" Santon asked, peering at the fallen crown. "It seems no different than any other crown for a minor noble."

Alarice said, "You forget the legend. How Kalob gave over the Demon Crown as a token of restitution, how only those of royal blood can wear the crown."

"That's the Demon Crown?" asked Vered, his eyes widening.

"What of your parents?" Alarice asked. "What can you tell me of them?"

"Nothing. I am an orphan. The unrest after King Lamost died caused many such as me. My entire village died as rebels pillaged and burned. Or so I was led to believe."

"Royal blood runs in your veins," Alarice said. "To touch the Demon Crown without that blood means instant death."

"I felt as if I had died. But not at first. On fitting the crown to my head—ouch!" Vered had touched his brow. A charred band of flesh circled his skull. He touched the burn gingerly. "The Demon Crown did *that*?"

"And more, unless they have lied to me about its effects," said the Glass Warrior. "Your vision became perfect, and not only for things within normal sight. You saw events at a great distance, as if you stood nearby."

"I did," Vered said, his fingers still probing the extent of his physical injuries.

"All your senses became heightened. You saw, you heard, you felt—"

"Wait! No, I did not experience anything of the sort." He sneezed. "And my sense of smell did not improve. I am still cursed with nose drip."

"The blood in your veins is not pure enough," said Alarice. "You have some touch of royal blood, but not enough, not enough." She sighed. "If you had donned the crown and controlled it, there would have been no need to find Lorens or Lokenna."

"You would have installed Vered as ruler of Porotane?" Santon made a rude noise.

"Why not? As it turns out, he is not pure enough of the blood. My guess is that his mother might have been raped by a soldier carrying as much as one-eighth royalty in his veins. Many pretenders to the throne existed at the beginning of the war. Time and intentional extermination have eliminated most over the past years."

"That makes me one-sixteenth noble," said Vered. He made a face. "I do not like the idea. I wish to be nothing more than a mongrel. Like Santon."

"You've had your taste of power, Vered. How did you like it?" Alarice asked.

"I didn't," he admitted. "Can you tend my wound? It is beginning to burn."

"First, a favor of you," said the Glass Warrior. "Pick up the crown and replace it in the crystal box. No, it won't kill you if your fingers move swiftly enough."

Vered moved the Demon Crown from where it had fallen back into the glass box Alarice carried inside the velvet bag.

"See how the metal glows a dull green?" she asked. "The crown would have blazed with blinding light had he been of pure blood."

"My blood's pure, as is my heart," said Vered. "It's just not pure royal blood."

"The crown's back in place," said Santon. "What do you need to tend his wound?"

"Very little. The wound, although magical in origin, is only physical. There might be a scar but it does not extend down into his brain." The Glass Warrior began working on the deep burn on the man's scalp.

"What happened to me?" asked Vered. "I wore the crown and found myself spinning out of control. How did I chance to again return to this fine world?"

"Santon's doing," said Alarice. "I ordered him to get the Demon Crown from your brow without touching it. He hit you in the belly several times. Now *there* will be a bruise, on the soft part of your stomach."

"Soft part!" protested Vered.

"Birtle forced you to bend over. The crown fell from your head and the spell it cast on you was broken. For either Birtle or me to have removed the crown in any other way would have meant both our deaths."

"But you're a sorceress. Surely, a spell or—"

"Only in this way. Kalob's coronet possesses a magic far beyond my control." Alarice finished doctoring Vered and stepped back to survey her handiwork. The bulky white bandages made him appear to carry a cloud for a hat.

"What was it like?" asked Santon. "To be a king, if only for a few minutes?"

"Santon, you can't believe what I saw. How I saw! Every detail of my blade, of a songbird miles distant, of a quartet of constables ambushed by a rebel band led by a wizard. I saw it all. No, I *saw* it. Description of the experience is beyond my powers."

"Speechless," muttered Santon. "For the first time, he's speechless. It must be magic."

"A moment," cut in Alarice. "A wizard? Where? Did he sense your presence?"

"He ordered his troops to seek out another wizard, but I *saw* no one else in the area." Vered's face went slack with shock. "He meant me!"

"He sensed the Demon Crown. We should leave immediately. The value of so much power to a wizard would be incalculable. Vered, direct us away from this wizard and his armed men."

"Why, I saw them over . . ." Vered's words trailed off as he stood and turned in a full circle. "I saw them, but I cannot say where. My head spun so that I've become confused. One instant I looked at the haze-purpled peaks of the Yorral Mountains, and the next I saw only the dusty flatness of Uvain Plateau."

"We were proceeding to the south," said Santon. "Let's continue in that direction. We stand as good a chance of avoiding this marauding sorcerer by this tactic as by trying to scout him out."

"I agree," said Alarice. "Staying here only invites disaster." She looked at Santon for a moment, then said, "May I accompany you? Our paths need not continue together, but for now it might be for the best."

"Is Vered in any danger?"

Alarice laughed. "He's in constant danger— from his thieving impulses. The crown has done all it can, unless he wears it once more. Are you willing to do this, Vered? To don the Demon Crown again?"

"No!"

"So I thought. There is no permanent harm. Even the burns will heal without scarring."

"Let's be on our way. We've let that worthless swayback nag of ours rest long enough. It's time to be a-pulling, beast," called out Santon. He hitched the balky horse to their wagon and climbed into the wagon box. Vered pulled himself up beside his friend and waved to the Glass Warrior.

"Ride," she ordered. Alarice swung her mare

about and trotted to the south, following the faint woodland trail. Two doughty fighters accompanied her, but she did not know for how long.

Long enough, she hoped, for long enough!

"It's past midday and I'm starving," protested Vered.

"You're always hungry," said Birtle Santon. "Either that or complaining about the sanitary inconvenience of living away from the big cities."

"A bath doesn't hurt anyone," said Vered. "In your case, it might reveal a lighter shade of skin, should you clean off the caked outer layers."

Before his friend answered, they saw Alarice galloping back from scouting the dusty trail ahead. She reined in and said, "We've trouble. The wizard drawn by your use of the crown has laid his men in ambush not a mile down the road."

"Hard to retreat now," said Santon. "We could cut through the forest, though the trees are growing more sparse now. The rolling hills might hide us, even if the sounds of this creaking wagon carry from here all the way north to the Yorral Mountains."

"The wizard knows we approach," said Alarice. "His scrying spells are similiar to those that I use. If we do not appear soon, he will know that we try to evade him."

"So he comes after us later, rather than sooner," said Vered. "Does this give us a chance to prepare a trap for him? I feel more comfortable attacking than being attacked, especially if I can choose the battlefield."

"What you say has merit," Alarice said. "But I see nothing in the terrain that we can turn to our advantage. The wizard has positioned his men on either side of a narrow draw. We are too few to duplicate such a plan."

"What good does it do for us to run?" asked Vered. "This wizard watches us with his infernal spells and knows everything we do." He turned to face Alarice. "He does watch, doesn't he?"

"The use of magic is tiring," she said. "He might know we are here, but watch us constantly?" She shook her head. "That I doubt."

"So he uses the spell and drains himself until he is bedridden," scoffed Vered. "What matters this to him? He has a score of armed ruffians at his service."

"Magic is not the answer," said Alarice. Her cold gray eyes scanned the rolling hills. No opportunity for ambush suggested itself. Nor did it seem likely that they could tumble boulders off tall cliffs and crush the rebel band.

"Cast a spell and mask our path," said Vered. "But no, you said this is tiring. We will need to fight soon."

"Premonition?" asked Santon.

"Good eyes."

Clouds of dust rose. The wizard's fighters had tired of waiting and rode along the narrow, rutted road to seek them out.

"There are not a score," said Alarice, her face vacant and her eyes glazed with concentration. "Only ten."

"Three against ten," said Vered. "Why, these ruffians have no chance against us! You, Santon, you take the first three and a third. I'll take the next third, and Alarice can finish them off. Unless that does not include the wizard."

"It does. There are only ten. But the wizard is

more likely to use sword and shield than spells for this attack. Spells work too slowly, unless you are a master wizard."

"He isn't? You aren't?" Santon sounded disappointed.

Alarice smiled sadly and shook her head. "Never have I controlled more than a few simple spells. This is my weapon."

She drew forth her long glass sword. In the bright sunlight it shone like a solidified rainbow. She wheeled her mare about and said, "They come. Soon."

Vered heaved a sigh and climbed to the roof of the wagon. He drew his sword and a wicked basket-hilt dagger, spread his legs for a better stance, and began settling himself for the fight. Birtle Santon dropped to the ground and pulled his battle-ax from the wagon box. His left arm bulged as he swung the heavy ax about, getting the feel of it.

"Three and a third apiece," called Vered when the first rider came into view. "No slackers!"

The first wave of horsemen surged forward, lance tips shining in the sun and multicolored ribbon banners flapping from the shafts. Santon roared and took two steps forward to build momentum for his swing. The heavy ax passed through the leading horse's front leg and sent the rider sailing through the air to land hard near the wagon.

Vered shouted a warning to Alarice, but it was not needed. The Glass Warrior swung about, her fragile-appearing sword deflecting a lance. She put spurs to her mare and edged forward to lunge and impale the rider, her lethal glass tip penetrating leather armor and chest with equal ease.

Then Vered no longer saw what happened. Two riders had circled the wagon and he found himself engaged from two directions simultaneously. The young thief vaulted one sweeping blow with a lance shaft. He ignored that rider. His attention turned fully on the lancer charging from the far side. Vered used his dagger to parry; the lance tip drove into the top of the wagon. The shock brought the lancer up in his stirrups.

Vered's sword ended the man's life.

Vered twisted about and again parried a lance thrust. He took the opportunity presented when the other horseman foolishly turned away from the wagon. Vered leaped and landed behind the lancer. A quick slash with the dagger sent a fountain of crimson spewing forth. The horse reared and threw Vered off.

He hit, rolled, and came to his feet beside Birtle Santon.

"Some fight, eh?" he shouted. "How many?"

"Just the one," said Santon.

"I need only one and a third to go!" Vered rushed forward, a lance tip almost opening his skull. He thrust his dagger into the horse's flank even as his sword reached upward to gut the rider. If either attack had failed, the other would have proven effective. As it was, Vered scored easily with both. Horse and rider died in a pool of blood.

Santon had unseated another lancer. A powerful overhead swing with the ax shattered an upraised shaft. A return swing ended the life of the lancer.

"I still need a third of a rider. You need one and a third," called Vered. "But where are they? Have the cravens run? What manner of ruffian is this, to attack in overwhelming numbers, then flee?"

Vered turned in a full circle. He hardly believed his eyes. The fight had gone well, he thought, but how could it be over? It had barely begun, yet the corpses he counted totaled ten. He had accounted for three and Santon two.

His brown eyes rose to stare in surprise at the Glass Warrior. Her long blade dripped gore. "You have vanquished fully half the force," he said. Then, angrily, "How dare you! You took more than your fair share!"

"Calm yourself, Vered. She did us both a favor."

"The wizard?" Vered walked to a fallen man whose throat had been neatly slit. Only a thin line of red appeared beneath his chin, but he had died from the wound.

"A minor one," said Alarice. "I have seen him before in the southlands. Never have I heard a name."

"Too bad. I wouldn't mind it if you cursed him and sent him and the entire pack of ruffians to the hottest depths of demon-infested hell." Vered knelt down and used his dagger tip to lift the sorcerer's pouch. He opened it cautiously, spreading the contents on the ground.

"I see nothing of interest," said Alarice. "Take what you will, Vered. There's no magic potion hidden there."

"To hell and gone with magic potions," he cried. "I want gold! The wizard is as poverty-stricken as we are. What kind of brigand was he? Imagine, dying without a full purse. The impudence of it all!"

Santon and Vered searched the bodies and found fewer than a dozen coins, mostly silver and copper. No gold. Even the equipment carried by the rebel band proved worthless to them.

"We should only allow better-quality rebels to attack us. This is ridiculous. No booty. Pah!" Vered dropped down beside the wagon, his back against a wheel.

"We've gained a few horses. The ones you didn't gut in your clumsy attempts to kill the riders," said Santon.

"Horses. We can't hitch them to the wagon. These are saddle mounts, not work horses. They'd be more trouble than they're worth. What a wasted fight." His eyes turned back to Alarice. In a lower voice, he said, "But it was an honor seeing her fight. By the saints, what a warrior!"

"She's that and more," agreed Santon, emotions Vered had seldom seen in him rippling across the man's weathered face.

The pair sat in silence for some time. Then both spoke at the same time. They quieted, and Santon said, "What do you think of her quest to find the twins? A worthy one?"

"It would eliminate scenes such as this. No rebel bands. The countryside would be quieter, more peaceful, less suspicious."

"Our trade would be the easier for that," said Santon.

"What else do we have to occupy our time?" asked Vered. "We're wanted by too many local constables to travel freely. I had demurred originally because I thought she was no true warrior. But she equaled our combined best."

"Better than that," said Santon. "She hardly seemed tired from the exertion."

"Neither of us worked up a sweat," Vered pointed out. "She is quite a woman. One fine warrior. And the season is good for exploring. Who's to say that we wouldn't find the twins—and a sizable reward?"

"There is that," Santon said.

They sat in silence for another few minutes, then stood and began stowing their weapons so that they would come easily to hand. Wherever the Glass Warrior led them, they knew those weapons would be needed.

CHAPTER EIGHT

"There's no need to keep looking for the wizard's fighters," said Vered. "We finished them off." He sneezed, wiped his nose, then said, "Or perhaps it is not the wizard you seek. Could it be that your heart reaches out to Alarice?"

Birtle Santon glared at his friend, then turned his eyes squarely ahead to the double ruts they followed across the countryside. Rains had washed away much of what had been a road, and with the minor battles raging constantly, no one had the will or time to repair it.

"What's wrong with me looking at her? She's a fine-looking woman."

"She is," Vered agreed.

"You go whoring about whenever we find a town large enough."

"Most are large enough," said Vered.

"Who are you to pass judgment on what I think or feel?"

"We all need a vice or two. Makes life more interesting." Vered leaned back and put his feet over the edge of the wagon box. "It seems that you have more than a few vices, though, Santon my friend. If you add Alarice to the list, why, you might spend all your time trying to remember what to indulge in next."

"You mock me."

"Of course I do! It's all in good fun. You take yourself much too seriously. Loosen up. There is nothing wrong with lusting after a wench so comely."

"She's no wench."

Vered quickly apologized. "She's even better with that strange sword of hers than I am with mine. And I have grown accustomed to the balance of mine. Best weapon I ever stole."

They rode along in silence until Alarice reined in and waited for them to catch up. "Pull over," she said. "We need to discuss our course. The land is turning against us."

"But the day is beautiful," protested Vered. "As far as the eye can see, it is lovely. No storms, although the muddy road suggests we might be in for more rain this evening."

"We go to the southlands," she said patiently. "The way is dangerous and we must discuss how we are to proceed."

Santon pulled on the reins and the horse gratefully slowed and stopped. The animal bent forward in its harness, straining to graze at a patch of verdant grass. Vered swung down and released the horse to graze freely. He doubted the horse would run off. Its running days were long past.

"Here is the castle," Alarice said, her finger marking a spot in the damp dirt. "The River Ty runs along this course, then empties into the delta swamps."

"I've never been there, but others who have report only insects and disease. Why do we go there?" Birtle Santon settled down on his haunches to await the answer.

"Tahir d'mar killed King Lamost."

"I'd heard of Lamost's death," said Vered. "Never has it even been hinted that foul play helped him along to his grave."

"Tahir is a powerful wizard and adept at traceless potions carrying a hundred deaths in every drop."

"What did he hope to gain from killing the king? He certainly hasn't been active over the past decades," said Santon. "If he sought power, he failed miserably."

"These are matters I hope to explore with Tahir. I am sure that he killed Lamost *and* kidnapped the twins."

"He might have exploited that and gained a small part of Porotane as his own. Yet we go into the filthy bowels of the swamps. This Tahir could not have chosen such a spot for his domain."

"This is something else to discover, Vered. Tahir lives. My best scrying shows that. Why does he hide in a swamp laced with death and disease? Even a sorcerer cannot avoid all enemies. If I sought to harm Tahir, I would choose an insect carrying a deadly poison as my weapon. Should the victim swat it, another could be a-wing in seconds. This is opinion and not magic, but I feel that Tahir did not choose this retreat willingly."

"The twins are with him?" asked Santon.

The Glass Warrior shook her head. "I detect no sign of them, but Tahir must know. It is possible that both Lokenna and Lorens died soon after the kidnapping. Tahir might have decided they, too, had to die in some scheme that failed later. These are things we must learn."

"Is it wise to carry the Demon Crown into a wizard's stronghold, even if the stronghold is hidden by swarms of gnats and sucking swampland?" Vered worked over lines of approach and liked none of them. Alarice had picked the worst section of Porotane for attack. Who can charge properly through scummy swamp water? At best, he would look ludicrous. At worst?

Vered turned his thoughts from this sorry picture. That which worried a soul the most always came to pass. Better to consider only successful ventures.

"My scrying shows only that Tahir lives within the confines of the swamp. I have no clear idea where he is."

"How do we track within such muck? Better to simply stand on the fringe of the swamp and yell for him to come out. A challenge always provokes response." Santon sank back into silence.

"Not this wizard. Tahir scorns society. He thinks little of violating sanctions simply because it causes discord. Of all the wizards I have known, Tahir was the one most likely to have assassinated a king and stolen away the heirs to the throne."

"Might he have done it out of spite? He might not have sought power," suggested Vered.

"His motives are obscure, but Tahir wanted something more tangible than discord," said Santon. "This sorcerer isn't driven by insane urges. He seeks gain. All men do."

"But Alarice says he is irrational." Vered tried again to formulate a plan and failed. The Glass Warrior's quest took on disturbing aspects that he could not cope with.

Alarice made a motion that quieted the men. "This swamp lies many days' travel to the south and west," she said. "The land between here and the edges of the swamp is dangerous. Rebel bands roam freely."

"We've been across it a few months ago," said Santon. "You speak the truth about the land. The people are left homeless and many have taken to wandering. Some are even joining rebel bands, although they have no sympathy for the leader's cause."

"They join only to have food and protection," said Vered, cutting in. "It is a sorry state for any country's citizenry to be in. Possibly the worst in all Porotane."

"We can reach the swamp in a week, if we travel swiftly," she said. "Are you up to it?"

"Are the horses up to it," corrected Vered. "Mayhap the wagon has outlived its usefulness. What do you say, Santon? Leave it and ride our captured horses?"

"The roads get worse with every passing mile. If we want to reach this Tahir before he dies of old age, we'd be well advised to do just that. Let's ride."

The men chose horses from those taken from the soldiers and used two extra ones as pack animals. Their swayback horse that had served them so well they let roam free.

"Dinner," said Vered. "That scrawny animal will end up as dinner for someone. Mark my words."

"Why not?" Santon said. "You mark your cards."

But he, too, hated to set free their trusty

swayback horse. The Glass Warrior called, and he wheeled his horse about and trotted off, willing himself not to look back.

"This is our destination?" asked Vered, horror in his voice. "We have endured all manner of deprivation these past ten days. Starvation, no sleep, the saints take them—cannibals! And for what? So we can arrive at a place like *this*?"

The swamp extended in a noisome fan before them. Heavy-limbed mangroves appeared to sway and move, as if alive. The clouds of insects around these trees were more than Vered wanted to consider. The green slime-covered waters circling the thick tree trunks rippled with unseen life. When an unblinking amber eye rose and fixed on Vered, his hand flashed to his sword.

"I know not what it is, but it sizes me up for dinner."

"A swamp swimmer," said Alarice. "Nothing to fear."

Vered tried to outstare the eye that began moving slowly along the scummy surface. He failed. When he looked back, the eye had vanished beneath the water.

"What should we fear? I like nothing about this place." Vered swatted at a hungry insect working its way past his collar. His hand came away sticky with blood.

"We cannot ride aimlessly," said Santon. "Alarice, how do we find your murderous wizard in this slop?" His horse bucked and protested. Standing at the edge of the slime-covered pond, the horse had begun sinking into the muck. Santon got the horse moving and pulled free of the sucking mud.

The Glass Warrior stood in her stirrups and slowly scanned the swampland. Vered and Santon exchanged glances. They had no idea what she sought. The banyan trees, with their long armlike branches, dangled mosses to form feathery green curtains preventing anyone from seeing into the swamp. Of dry land, there was none in sight.

"There is much power locked within this land," Alarice said. "It is stunted, though. A power once great but now on the wane. This has to be Tahir d'mar."

"So much for the notion that wizards live lavishly. Why does he hide in such a place, unless another pursues him? Could this have something to do with the twins?" asked Vered.

"That direction," Alarice said. "We ride to the center of the swamp. I see a small island. Dry land. Tahir is there."

"How far?" Santon had increasing difficulty controlling his horse. The animal did not enjoy the sucking yellow mud around its hooves.

"Distance means nothing. Time? Two days', travel. Longer. I cannot say. There is more than swamp swimmers and catamounts."

"Catamounts!" Vered turned to Alarice. "The last of that species died before I was born. From all accounts, they fought fiercely and loathed humans."

"Many hundreds survive in the swamp," she said. "Otherwise, you are correct. They will not like being disturbed by our passage through their breeding grounds."

"Santon," Vered said in disgust. "Seldom will you hear this escape my lips. I have made a mistake. We should not have accompanied her. Not only will we be eaten alive by bugs, we disturb fornicating cats able to tear our guts out with the single swipe of a paw. And for what? So we can find a king-killer wizard who, in all probability, will be only too happy to slay us, also."

"True," said Santon.."There is one thing you can say about this, however. It's not dull."

Alarice put spurs to her mare and splashed off through the shallow swamp. Santon convinced his steed to follow. Vered coughed, wiped his nose, swatted two more marauding bloodsucker insects, then urged his horse after Santon's. As he rode he stared down into the murky water for hint of swamp swimmers, whatever they were. He had never seen one and had no desire to see more than the eye that had watched him.

"Take a care," Santon called back. "The path is narrow. A step to either side will cast you into deeper water."

"To think, we could be enjoying ourselves in a brothel," Vered grumbled. "Or lounging at the seaside, watching the beautiful blue waves crash against the shore. Or we could even be socializing with cannibals." A sudden splashing caused Vered to jerk about. Except for the expanding rings of ripples, he saw nothing.

Even dinner with cannibals seemed less objectionable.

An hour's ride brought them to drier land surrounded by stagnant ponds. Alarice dismounted and tended her mare. Santon heaved himself to the ground, too, but Vered remained in his saddle.

"Aren't you going to rest? This is the first solid ground we've found all day," said Santon.

"Solid? Does this muck look solid to you. See? You sink to your ankles in it." He dropped to the ground and moved around, stomping in small puddles. "What are we doing? The Demon Crown must have addled my wits. This is no fit place for me."

Vered stopped. Neither Alarice nor Santon paid him any heed. He fumbled in his pack and found a brush to curry his horse. As he pulled the brush free from the pack, he stared over the horse's back. The movement in tangled, low shrubs drew his attention. He stiffened, thinking this to be another "harmless" creature like the swamp swimmer.

When he saw the powerful, hairy arms, the immense shoulders, the tiny furred head, and the savage yellow fangs, he knew otherwise.

"Trouble!" he called, dropping the brush and drawing his sword. Vered slipped and fell to one knee in the mud. In the span of one frenzied heartbeat, the yowling creature had crossed the intervening distance and attacked.

Vered looked up into tiny red eyes filled with hatred and a mouthful of teeth capable of ripping him apart. He had no time to properly thrust. Instead, he braced the hilt of his sword on the ground, aimed the point in the creature's direction, and fell backward.

The beast launched itself and came down on the sword point, impaling itself. Sizzling hot yellow blood erupted from the gash in its chest. A few drops spattered onto Vered's boots and breeches; the acid blood burned through the clothing and into his flesh.

He yelped in pain and began kicking against the yielding ground to get away. Only Birtle Santon's quick reflexes saved Vered. The heavy battle-ax swung parallel to the ground and struck the beast's collarbone. The sickening crunch of the collision echoed through the swamp.

For an instant, the hairy monster stood and stared at the ax buried in it. Then the scream of agony drowned out all other sounds. The creature reached up and plucked the heavy ax from its body and cast it aside as if it were made of splinters.

Vered avoided the shower of yellow blood and drew his dagger. Gripping the hilt firmly, he thrust upward, seeking the creature's foul heart. The blade sizzled and hissed as the acid chewed away metal along the razor-sharp edge. Vered drove the blade up but found no secure berth. He pulled away and rolled, coming to his feet beside Santon.

"You've lost your ax, old friend," observed Vered.

"You've lost your sword."

Alarice pushed past them, her glass sword extended *en garde*. "It does little good to attack with steel," she told them. "Let me see how I fare with this beast."

The creature bellowed and beat its chest with heavy fists. Alarice did not let the challenge go unanswered. She stepped forward with a move-ment more like a dance step than a battle move and lunged.

The glass sword tip drove directly into the hollow of the creature's throat. It gurgled and choked on its own blood. The burning flow of acid blood had no effect on the Glass Warrior's sword. She twisted it savagely, drew back, and lunged again.

The thrust went straight to the creature's heart. It groped at empty air with its paws, then fell forward, dead before it struck the ground. Alarice wiped off her blade on the beast's matted fur back.

The deadly blood burned a small band where her sword had touched, then quieted as it ate into the corpse.

"What *is* that thing?" demanded Vered. He held up his dagger. The dull pits along the once-sharp edge made it almost worthless as a weapon. The acidic blood had eaten huge chunks from the metal.

"Who can say?" answered Alarice. "The swamplands are filled with creatures real and magical. This is an example of the latter. Tahir might have set it to protect his little kingdom."

"Let him keep his saints-damned kingdom," exclaimed Vered. "Why risk our lives against *things* like that? And look! I am filthy from rolling about on the ground."

"A true disgrace to your clan and your country," Santon said sarcastically. He hefted his battle-ax and swung it. "Balance is off. The beast ruined the temper of the blade. Look!"

"Forget the blade," said Vered.

"Vered, Alarice, look!"

The burly man's tone brought both of the others around to face a scaly monster wobbling up onto dry land from the pond. Scum clung to its back, giving it a curious color in the fading sunlight. But Vered did not concentrate on colors or texture.

"The teeth! Damn me if they all don't have twice the number of teeth they should!"

Eyes on the knee-high beast, he picked up his sword and tested the blade. It had suffered the same fate that his dagger had. He might be better off using it as a club. For slashing or stabbing the sword had outlived its usefulness.

Vered and Santon worked together well as a

team. They split, one making distracting noises while the other advanced. When the long-jawed monster turned to attack, the other began the noise. Back and forth they worked the dim-witted monster.

But neither could make a clean kill. Vered's blade glanced off a thick, armored back. Santon's battle-ax fared little better as he swung it down as hard as he could atop the flat head. Even attacking simultaneously, they failed to stop the monster's advance.

"This one is stronger than the both of us," panted Santon. "Not for the first time do I wish I had the use of both arms."

"Let's hope that wish is not for the last time," muttered Vered.

"Can you stop it with a spell?" Santon asked of Alarice. The Glass Warrior stood, staring off into the distance, as if listening hard for sounds no human could hear. His question shook her from the reverie.

"No, it's natural. Unlike the ape-thing, no spell drives it."

"Let me guess," said Vered as he dodged a savage snap of powerful jaws. "This is a swamp swimmer. The harmless animal you said not to worry over."

"It is." Alarice avoided the closing jaws and moved behind the swamp creature. "Dealing with them is simple. They are protected too well for ordinary attack. No!" she called to Vered. "Don't thrust into its mouth. It can break your blade."

Vered glowered at her and moved back.

"You have to distract it," Alarice continued, "then attack from the rear." The beast moved sluggishly toward Santon. As it did so, Alarice grabbed its tail and grunted as she lifted. The swamp swimmer's legs proved too weak to support it; it flipped over onto its back, exposing bone-white belly.

"Do we gut it?" asked Vered, not daring to advance on it, even in this helpless condition.

"No. It is formidable even now. As a hunter might try such a shot on a deer, so we must work on the swimmer."

Alarice's glass sword drove down toward the beast's anus. The swamp swimmer made a strangely soft noise as the glass blade vanished into its bowels. It kicked weakly, then slumped, head lolling to one side.

"Now?" asked Vered.

"It is dead," the Glass Warrior said. "But our problems are only beginning."

"What?" Vered and Santon said as one. They moved to stand back to back, ready for still more dangers.

"We are a long distance from Tahir. There is no way we can hope to fight through a legion of such creatures."

"You're not giving up," protested Santon.

"You can't! We've gotten dirty and bloody and gone hungry to get this far. We cannot surrender. We've yet to do battle with the murderer of our beloved King Lamost. And what of the twins?" Vered's face gained color as his indignation rose.

Alarice did not answer. She had not expected them to come this far, yet they had and she appreciated their loyalty. But the Glass Warrior knew that the most dangerous part of the journey lay ahead. Could she ask even more of these two adventurers?

CHAPTER NINE

Baron Theoll drew himself up to his full height and barely came to the guard lieutenant's shoulder. He glared at Oprezzi and, when this disapproval went unnoticed, pushed his way past to stand unsteadily beside the duke's bed.

Freow's eyelids fluttered and he stirred. Unfocused eyes opened and a parchment-like hand reached out. To whom Theoll couldn't tell. Nor did it matter. Circling the bed were the powers in Porotane's castle. The physician tending the failing duke mattered little to Theoll. The others, however, held his full attention.

The Lady Johanna he considered something of an interloper. Almost a year ago, she had arrived from a distant province a few minutes ahead of Gaemock's band of ruffians. The castle guard had fought off the rebels, and Dews Gaemock had retreated. Johanna had given proof of noble birth —she was the bastard child of Lamost's youngest nephew. The way she had declared this dubious lineage rankled. Theoll did not call her a liar openly, but the scheming she had engaged in warned him that her ambitions knew the same bounds as his own: none.

Johanna had begun bedding each of the

111

guardsmen until she found Lieutenant Oprezzi.
The man had the power Johanna sought and was
willing to trade it for a few minutes of fornication.
Theoll looked from Oprezzi to the cool, calm
Johanna. Those were damned few minutes the
guardsmen had had with her. He had watched
often enough to know.

He studied the woman closely. Her gown
proved demure for someone with such well-known
flamboyant tastes in clothing. Perhaps she thought
it improper to come to a death bed in party
clothing, yet the smile trying to force up the
corners of her mouth showed her true feelings.
Freow's death meant opportunity for her.

A castle coup? Theoll thought it possible.
Oprezzi had the loyalty of more guardsmen than
the captain of guards. The duke dies, Johanna
ascends the throne and takes Oprezzi as consort.
That seemed the most likely plot she would have
held out to the young and ambitious lieutenant.

Theoll pushed them from his mind. Others
gathered about the duke like vultures waiting for
their dinner to die. A few royal second cousins
who had no chance for the throne nonetheless
hoped for suitable recompense. A small estate. A
castle. A lifetime stipend.

A swift blade slid through the ribs and into
their black hearts would be their reward, if Theoll
triumphed.

That would remove those of distant claim to
the throne. Theoll followed this line of thinking
and frowned. What of Freow's family? His wife had
been killed on her way to the castle after Lamost's
death. No children? Not even a bastard? Theoll
wondered about Freow's manhood, yet he had

spied on the duke with numerous women, sometimes many at a time. Still, he thought it strange that the duke had no family in the distant province. He and his brother had not been close. Rumors of discord—even a blood feud—between him and Lamost had run the circle of Porotane society.

But no family? Strange.

"Excuse me, Baron." Theoll stepped to one side and allowed Archbishop Nosto to stand beside Freow. The cleric took the old man's hand in his and held it gently. Theoll wished he could see the archbishop's eyes. Despite his sincere-sounding words and loving caresses, Nosto's eyes held nothing but polar ice. The cleric had begun his Inquisition, and it now ruled him totally.

Theoll could not decide if Archbishop Nosto used it as a means to gain the throne for himself, or only desired to choose the next ruler of Porotane. Either way, Theoll had to cultivate the cleric's friendship and loyalty. The meeting with the "demon" had done much to convince Nosto of the existence of evil within the castle walls.

It would soon be time for the Question to be put to Oprezzi. That would snap the backbone of Lady Johanna's power, Theoll decided. She would have no chance to forge new bonds with another guard officer of sufficient standing in time to oppose him.

Theoll winced at the pain in his legs as he stood on tiptoe and peered past Nosto's shoulder at the duke. The amount of poison had been increased to accelerate the old man's decline. It worked well. How he hung onto the thin strand of life that kept him from the Eternal Abyss, Theoll did not know. But soon, very soon Duke Freow would die, and he would replace the old regent as king.

"Yeow!" Theoll cried. Someone had come up behind him and driven something hard and round into his posterior. He spun, hand on dagger. Harhar stood there, an idiotic grin on his face. The jester held up his rattle and shook it at Theoll. In other company, the fool would have died. Instead of driving his dagger into Harhar's gut, Theoll grabbed him by the collar and sent him tumbling across the room.

The jester hit and rolled and came to his feet, the rattle making odd sounds as he shook it vigorously.

"Why so sad?" Harhar called. "Duke Freow is stronger than ever. He will live, if you permit a jest or two to brighten his outlook."

"Get him out of here," Theoll ordered Oprezzi. To his surprise, the lieutenant glanced over at Johanna. He obeyed the tiny shake of her head and not Theoll's command.

"He harms nothing," said the physician. "The duke responds well to him. Let him stay. For a time, at least."

To Theoll's disgust, the jester's cavortings and salacious japes *did* help Freow rally. Color returned to the translucent cheeks and the eyes focused.

"I would rest," came a weak voice, but one lacking the edge of death that Theoll expected. The duke's gaze went around those at his bedside. He looked like a death's head when he smiled. "I am not dead yet, my dear friends. When I go, rejoice, for there will be a new ruler, a true ruler. I have sent for the royal twins."

"You know their location?" cried Johanna, obviously startled.

"I do, I do." Freow's eyes closed and he drifted into sleep, his chest rising and dropping slightly the only indication that life remained within his withered frame.

"All away, go, go," ordered the physician. He pushed the expectant onlookers away. Theoll allowed the physician to start him for the door. To his considerable irritation, the physician did not treat Harhar equally. The jester stayed behind.

In the corridor outside Duke Freow's chambers, Theoll tugged at Archbishop Nosto's sleeve with his good hand and pulled the man's ear down where he could whisper without being overheard.

"Oprezzi. See how he and Lady Johanna talk to one another?"

The archbishop said nothing, but his thin frame stiffened and his hands clenched. Even more revealing for Theoll was the way Nosto's jaw muscles tightened. The cleric had taken seriously the "demon's" condemnation of Oprezzi.

"He is a heretic, as you must know. He has strayed from the True Path."

"What?" Theoll cried, feigning astonishment. "I did not hear wrong then? I know that he and Johanna plot against Freow, but a heretic? That is a serious charge, Archbishop. I had hoped I was wrong. Your, uh, assignation proved fruitful?"

"I have the proof."

"He must be put to the Question. The full extent of his treachery must be learned." Theoll's voice dropped even lower. "Or do you already know facts I do not?"

"He has congress with demons."

"That is no way to speak of Johanna, although in bed she seems possessed." Theoll allowed himself a chuckle.

"Do not speak heresy, Theoll," snapped Archbishop Nosto. "These are matters of the utmost gravity."

"I beg your forgiveness, Nosto. I meant no disrespect."

"No, of course not. How could anyone following the True Path know of this swine's obscene behavior?"

"Tell me more," Theoll said. "I need to know more. I cannot accuse Johanna of poisoning Freow, but the thought refuses to leave my brain. She has come from a distant province with the flimsiest of claims to the blood royal, and yet she is now a pretender to the throne. She might assume the throne, should her royal line be verified."

"She is of no importance. It is Oprezzi who occupies my thoughts and prayers. I seek guidance in that matter," said Archbishop Nosto, "and the saints have failed to answer. I drift on a sea of heresy and know not how to proceed."

"Truly, a serious concern for everyone in Porotane. This lieutenant must not contaminate Johanna, should her claims to the throne prove valid."

"He must be put to the Question immediately. There is no other way to know his involvement with demonic forces."

"No!" Theoll said, too abruptly, too forcefully. He wanted Oprezzi in the hands of Nosto's Inquisition, but not yet, not until Freow died. Only in that way could he indict Johanna and remove her. A premature questioning of the young lieutenant would allow her time to respond and sway others to her favor.

"I have no choice, Theoll. None. By the saints, I shall find out about his involvement with demons!"

Archbishop Nosto pulled free of Theoll's grip and stalked off. Theoll controlled his anger. This precipitous questioning would remove Oprezzi, but not when the baron desired. Freow's death and Oprezzi's torture must come within hours if Johanna was to be discredited.

"Damn you, Nosto, damn you and all your fornicating saints!" Theoll bit his tongue and looked around to be sure that no one overheard his outburst. Still seething, he stormed off. New plans had to be made. He had to profit from Oprezzi's death. But how?

Baron Theoll slipped from the secret passages, his heart pounding furiously from his spying. This night proved exceptionally active in the castle's bedchambers. His eye hurt from being forced against too many spyholes and his legs throbbed mercilessly. Only his left arm gave him true difficulty, however; it hung useless and twisted at his side. He emerged into the corridor outside Nosto's quarters. For a moment, he considered slipping back into the secret panel before the red-clad Inquisitors in the corridor challenged him.

Too late. The one at the far end of the hall tugged his blood-red hood down so that the eyeholes were in place and pointed a ceremonial dagger at Theoll. "Halt!" the Inquisitor cried. "Halt and be identified to the Inquisition!"

"Baron Theoll of Brandon," the small noble said. "I come to speak with the archbishop on a personal matter."

"He is occupied with clerical matters."

"Does it have to do with a guardsman being put to the Question?"

Both Inquisitors adjusted their hoods and shuffled nervously from one foot to the other. A silent decision was made. The one closest to Theoll grabbed his good arm and swung him toward the door leading to Nosto's chambers. "Inside," ordered one. Theoll did not resist. Both Inquisitors had drawn their daggers and were ready to use them should he protest. He shrugged off this lack of respect and pushed through the heavy door and into Nosto's sitting room.

"Archbishop?" he called. "I'd speak with you."

Nosto emerged from an inner room wearing a hood similar to those of the guards outside, except his had the bone-white sigil of the True Path imprinted on the face. Theoll blinked in surprise, not at this but at Nosto's muscular development. The archbishop was naked to the waist, displaying power Theoll had not even guessed at. Tightly cinched around the cleric's waist was a hair belt.

Human hair, Theoll saw. He did not doubt that Nosto had taken it from previous victims— heretics—of the Inquisition who had confessed their heresy before dying.

Skintight breeches the same color as the hood disappeared into the tops of soft leather boots, also adorned with the white sigil of the True Path. In the top of the left boot was thrust a dagger like the ceremonial implements carried by those outside.

"You come at a bad time, Theoll. The work of

the Inquisition requires my full attention. Come back tomorrow. Tomorrow afternoon."

"Nosto, wait. Does the Inquisition go to put the Question to Oprezzi?"

"Yours is a secular realm, mine is religious. My duties as Inquisitor do not concern you, Baron."

Theoll's mind raced. He saw that nothing would dissuade Nosto from torturing the lieutenant. He had to turn this to his own benefit.

"Do you know the questions to ask?" he demanded of the archbishop. "Not the religious ones, but the secular. Who seduced Oprezzi? I have reason to believe that Lady Johanna is a demon in human form."

"Ridiculous, even I—" Archbishop Nosto cut off his words. Theoll stared at the tall, thin cleric. Had even Nosto succumbed to Johanna's influence? The vision he had of this whipsaw-muscled cleric and the lovely, lush-figured, frosty blonde Johanna together turned his gut to jelly. What a powerful alliance those two would make if he did not stop them!

"These are matters to investigate," said Theoll.

"What is the source of your accusation?"

"A dying messenger," Theoll lied. "He crossed a strife-torn Porotane from the lady's province to tell of demonic deeds before her departure. Many died, some horribly with boils disfiguring them. Each had been touched by Johanna." Theoll said no more. To do so would prejudice Archbishop Nosto against him. If Johanna and the archbishop shared a bed, it was better to let Nosto's imagination fill in any discrepancies. Because of his work as Inquisitor, he did a fine job of jumping to conclusions based on the flimsiest of evidence.

"Perhaps you speak the truth. You have always walked the True Path, and often revelation is given to the faithful."

Theoll bowed his head.

"Stay here. The Inquisition seeks Oprezzi. He will be put to the Question this night and truth will flow from the heretic's lips!"

"May I . . ." Theoll cut off his request and bowed his head again when he saw the determined set of Nosto's lean body. Religious matters brooked no interference by a mere baron. Theoll bowed even lower as Nosto left abruptly, the loose fabric of his hood snapping as if in a high wind.

Theoll released a pent-up breath, then counted slowly to one hundred. He peered into the corridor and saw that Nosto and the two Inquisitors had left on their mission of righteous interrogation. Even if Oprezzi sat surrounded by his fellows, none would dare defend him against the Inquisition.

Theoll almost laughed when he thought of the possibility that Oprezzi lay with Johanna. The notion of Nosto plucking the lieutenant from the blonde's bed amused the baron greatly. But he knew such was fantasy only. The guardsman patrolled the battlements, as was his duty. All day long Dews Gaemock's rebels had been sighted riding across the burned-out farmland surrounding the castle. What this scouting on the rebels' part portended, no one knew. Another siege? Doubtful. Trouble? All agreed on this point and vigilance rather than dalliance ruled the guardsmen this night.

He considered going to the battlements and waiting for Nosto and his Inquisitors to take Oprezzi into custody. He reconsidered. It would appear that he maneuvered the archbishop into the action. Theoll wanted no hint that he *had* been responsible. He turned to his secret ways in the castle walls and found a spiraling staircase leading four levels lower into the dungeons.

He went quietly along a passage so narrow that his shoulders brushed the walls. Occasionally he dallied to peer through a spyhole. Nothing caught his fancy. Theoll finally stopped behind a large wooden panel with a dozen different cutouts. He slid back several and peered through, finding the few that gave him the best view of the dungeons used by the Inquisition.

Theoll waited only a few minutes before loud shouts and the scrape of metal against stone alerted him to Nosto's entrance. He bent forward, eager eyes pressed against the wood panel. With a vantage point better than if he'd been in the room, Theoll saw Oprezzi being dragged between the two hooded Inquisitors, Archbishop Nosto following closely behind.

"There," ordered Nosto. "Place him there."

"I am a guardsman," protested Oprezzi. 'You cannot take me from my post without imperiling the entire castle! What if the rebels attack? Who would command?"

"What if a lieutenant of the guard strays from the True Path and has congress with demons?" Nosto parried.

"I am no heretic!" cried Oprezzi. "I know nothing of demons. Praise be to the saints!"

"Blasphemer!" Archbishop Nosto struck the

helpless soldier with the back of his hand. Oprezzi's head jerked back and a tiny trickle of blood ran down his chin.

The Inquisitors heaved the guardsman onto a wooden platform and fastened him spread-eagled on it to stare in fright at the cold stone ceiling. While Nosto watched, his eyes gleaming through the eyeholes of his hood, the other two stripped Oprezzi of his uniform. The naked man struggled futilely.

"What do you want of me?" he asked, fear tingeing his words. "I am no heretic."

"The Question will be put to you later. Now we need know of your involvement with demons."

"There isn't any. I know nothing of . . . aiee!"

One of the hooded clerics used the tip of his blade on the man's bare chest, inscribing the sigil of the True Path.

"What of Lady Johanna?" came Nosto's query.

"What of her? She's a lady of the realm. She's of royal blood. What do you want from me?" Again Oprezzi shrieked in pain as the Inquisitors drew their knife-points over his flesh and duplicated the sigil on his trembling arms and legs.

"She is a demon. Admit it."

"I know nothing of that. She does not seem to be."

"Beneath you," said Archbishop Nosto, "are cages of famished weasels. The blood from your wounds drives them wild. Small panels in the wooden platform on which you lie slide back." Nosto gestured. An Inquisitor pulled a thin wooden sheet away, leaving no protection between helpless flesh and savage fangs.

Oprezzi shrieked in true agony now as the

weasels ripped his flesh. He surged and strained, trying to break the bonds holding him to the table. He stood a better chance of pulling his arms from their sockets. Nosto nodded. The panel was slammed back into the platform, denying the weasels their meal of human flesh.

"The doors open the entire length of your body. We can open them singly or in concert with others. No portion of your body will be denied them if you refuse to speak truthfully." To emphasize his determination, Archbishop Nosto drove his dagger between Oprezzi's legs. The lieutenant tried to move; his bonds prevented it. "The dagger sticks in the last door we shall open—unless you speak now."

Baron Theoll moved to other spyholes to get a better view of the torture. He hoped that the lieutenant did not die of fear before he confessed. So many of those facing the Question expired from sheer fright. Theoll needed Oprezzi to curse the Lady Johanna, to condemn her, to declare her a demon.

After that, Theoll was willing to let the archbishop have his heretic.

"Anything," Oprezzi said. "I'll confess to anything you want."

Theoll was disappointed in the young lieutenant. He had hoped the man would show more courage. He could have at least tried to protect his lover's honor. But no, the presence of voracious rodents beneath him produced a torrent of words.

Before Oprezzi stopped to catch a breath, he had condemned Johanna as both a demon and a poor lover. Theoll smiled wickedly when he saw Nosto begin to twitch in anger. The archbishop *had* shared Johanna's bed! Oprezzi's denunciation on that score did nothing to gain him mercy from the cleric.

"You have spoken enough of these matters," Nosto said to his victim. "What of your congress with demons?"

"I know nothing of it. I swear!"

Theoll's heart raced as one door after another opened. Bloody strings of flesh remained before Archbishop Nosto ordered the doors closed.

"Are you a heretic? This is the Question. Are you a heretic? Answer truthfully and beg forgiveness."

"No!"

Theoll knew the guardsman had had no demonic contact. But Archbishop Nosto had seen with his own eyes the demon in the wall of the pantry, heard the naming of Oprezzi, seen heretical activity.

Oprezzi denied it, blaming all on the Lady Johanna.

"Roll him over on the table," ordered the cleric. The hooded Inquisitors did as they were ordered, falling to their task with a will. Face down, Oprezzi was dangerously exposed to the weasels and their ripping teeth.

One by one the doors were opened, Nosto saving the one at Oprezzi's groin for last, as he had promised. Oprezzi confessed everything, but he never provided the details Nosto knew to be true.

Lieutenant Oprezzi died a heretic.

CHAPTER TEN

Vered cursed to himself as he tried to put the fine edge back on his sword. The whetstone seemed less the tool to use than a coarse rasp. The acid blood from the apelike creature had permanently ruined the cutting edge and the temper of the blade. Vered did not even look at his dagger. Most of the hilt had vanished because of the sizzling yellow blood.

"What do you mean you won't turn back?" Alarice demanded. The Glass Warrior stood and stared in disbelief at Birtle Santon. The man rubbed his withered arm with his left hand. A slight smile danced on his lips.

"Life's never been easy for me and Vered," he said. "That hasn't meant it's been interesting. Fact is, of late life has been dull."

"That's not what you told me before," she said, exasperated. "You said the constables track you mercilessly—"

"They do," cut in Vered.

"And that more nobles want to break you on the wheel than there are fiefdoms in all Porotane!"

"A sorry state when you have so many pretenders to minor posts," said Vered. He thrust his

125

sword into the muddy ground and drew it back, as if this would produce a new edge. It only left the blade more nicked and dirty than before.

"You owe me nothing," cried Alarice. "You shouldn't have come this far. This is my duty, not yours."

"We go where we choose," said Santon. "That's the kind of life we *want* to lead. We've been fleeing. That's no fit existence for anyone. Even us."

"I don't understand this. Not at all," the woman said. "You have only savage death to look forward to in this saints-abandoned swamp. How does this allow you to lead a 'fit existence'?"

"Because we'd be doing what we want, not what some scurvy ruffian of a rebel leader or a petty baron or count wants us to do. They chase, we run. What life is that? We'd rather stay in one place and . . . ply our trade in that fashion."

"You want to steal without being punished?" Alarice shook her head. This made no sense to her.

"A notion worthy of consideration," said Vered.

"But . . ."

"We go where you go, Alarice," said Santon. His eyes locked with her steel-gray ones.

"There is nothing binding you to me," she said, not sure she truly meant this. Birtle Santon pretended to be old and tired, he had an arm withered by war, he stank of animals and dirt and sweat, his manners were crude—and she found herself liking him. And more.

The Glass Warrior dared not believe the feelings she felt for him were returned. Yet this seemed to be what the man implied.

"You mistake our wandering thoughts for real

logic," said Vered. "Consider: We return one twin to the throne. A reward? Possibly. Certainly, we would gain a royal pardon for past crimes. Even better, Porotane would be united, freeing us from the warlords and annoying rebels."

"You seek only to rob and plunder without interference from other thieves?" Alarice asked, amused now. She heard the steel under Vered's bantering tone. He desired a peace for Porotane as much as she. Commitment to a cause lay within this one's breast, no matter how he tried to hide it with ignoble reasons.

"Of course," Vered said. "Looting, robbing, a bit of purse-cutting. That keeps Santon and me alive. Why shouldn't we want free rein to continue?"

"No reason, save that the course through the swamp will be infinitely more dangerous than Dews Gaemock and his band of rebels or your petty barons threatening to put you on the rack."

"This Tahir d'mar," said Santon. "Are these his magical creatures?"

"The ape is not of this world. I can only surmise that Tahir conjured and sent it. The swamp swimmer is a harmless resident in these ponds."

"Harmless," snorted Vered, staring at the ass-stabbed monster. "Crowds of whacking big oafs would part in front of me when e'er I passed if I were half that harmless."

"The spells," said Santon, drowning out his friend's complaints. "Can you counter them or must we suffer their full impact?"

"I can use my own limited sorcery," Alarice answered. "It might not work as well as a quick blade, though. It takes time and preparation to cast most spells powerful enough to benefit us. I have neither the ability nor the strength to cast those able to win us free of the swamplands and their magical protectors."

"This blade is better used to pry open doors," said Vered. His work had availed him little. The sword was useless as a precision fighting tool.

"You begin to understand my fondness for glass weapons," she said. "Here, Vered. Take this short sword." She handed him a weapon drawn from a sheath on her saddle. "Use it as you would a regular blade, except in hammering nails with the flat."

Vered made a face as he swung the short sword. To be of use, he would have to crawl within the arms of the ape creature before lunging. Vered did not think this was a proper use—or a decent way to die.

"And you, Santon," she said. "Your battle-ax is still useful. Its edge hasn't corroded as badly as Vered's sword and the heavy spiked ball is still formidable, but your infirmity works against you. We must change that."

"You can fashion a glass arm?" Santon lifted his right arm. "Truly, you would be a sorceress second to none if you do that for me."

"That lies beyond the power of any wizard," she said. "However, I have something which might serve you well." She pulled a small round woven glass-fiber shield from her saddle and motioned to the man. Alarice worked to fasten the straps around his upper right arm so that he could twist and turn the shimmering glass shield.

"This is comfortable," Santon said in amazement. "I had seen yours and thought it would be difficult to use."

"It might not withstand the blow of a battle-ax such as yours, but it will turn aside a sword thrust—and resist the burning blood from the swamp creatures."

"I hardly feel whole again," Santon said, waving the shield about, "but I feel more secure. Let's not allow Tahir to rally his noisome beasts. Let's attack!"

"A noble sentiment," said Vered. "But where do we go? What do we attack? We must *find* the wizard before we fight him."

Vered fell silent when Alarice drew the glass rod on the gut string from her pouch. She closed her eyes. Lips moving in silent spell, she held the clear crystal far from her body. The swings became less random, and soon aligned with what Vered saw as due south.

"That path leads directly into the bowels of this foul-smelling swamp. Why are we cursed with the smell and texture of viscera all about us?" Even as he grumbled, Vered stood and brandished the glass short sword. He shrugged and smiled at Santon, then made a mocking bow and indicated that his friend should mount.

"How much distance can we make in this muck before sunset?" Santon asked of Alarice. The sorceress opened her eyes and stared up at the two mounted men.

"Enough," she said. Alarice held out her hand, first to Vered and then to Santon, in silent thanks for their courage and faith in her.

The Glass Warrior swung into her saddle and pointed out the path through the swamp.

Hardly had they ridden a hundred yards when Vered protested loudly. He swatted at the insects buzzing over his head and caught one between thumb and forefinger. "See!" he called. "See the menace we fight? I can battle beasts that don't belong in the miserable quagmire, but bugs? Never!" Vered's fingers closed. The insect let out a screech that sounded almost human. It died amid a flow of sticky red blood. With some distaste, Vered wiped his fingers on his tunic. The new stain mingled with the old and vanished instantly, much to the fussy man's disgust.

Riding alongside the Glass Warrior, Santon said, "Is it safe to camp when it gets dark? Should we ride directly for Tahir's palace?"

Alarice shook her head, fine white hair flying in a halo around her. "We must rest soon. There is no way to tell how far off Tahir is. And I do not think he lives in any palace."

"But he is a wizard," protested Santon. "All wizards live like royalty."

"I don't," she said. "I never have, but then I have little power when compared to the likes of Tahir." She sighed deeply. "I remember him as a decent fellow. Odd, but all wizards are strange in some respect, or we would not be able to cast spells. I rather liked him before . . ." Her voice trailed off.

"There is no doubt he murdered King Lamost?"

"None. I have received this information from Freow."

"Why didn't the duke do something about it before now? He's been searching for the heirs for over nineteen years."

Alarice told Santon the story of Duke Freow's perfidy—or that of the man posing for all these years as the duke.

"So," said Santon, sucking on his teeth as he

thought. "We have put up with two decades of civil war because of a man's quest for power. It always seems this way."

"Do you still want to find Lokenna and Lorens?"

"All the more!" he exclaimed. "The fake duke must be replaced quickly with true members of the royal family."

"Santon, Alarice," called Vered from the rear. "Something follows. I hear its heavy breathing. I swear by all the saints, I hear its belly rumbling in anticipation of a fine meal—of three fine meals!"

Alarice turned in the saddle. She wobbled as dizziness hit her like a solid blow. Only Santon's good hand reaching out saved her from a tumble into the filthy swamp.

"What is it?"

"Magic," the Glass Warrior said. "It swirls about us. Something is wrong. I feel so . . . disoriented."

"You can feel dizzy later," called Vered. "The thing comes up quickly!"

Santon scanned the area in front and to the sides. Too often an enemy launched a diversionary attack to mask the true thrust. And so it proved this time. From ahead came a huge man, one tall enough to stare Santon squarely in the eye when the adventurer sat upright in his saddle.

"Ahead! A warrior of immense size!" he cried. Beside him, he felt Alarice straighten. The way she wobbled told of continuing problems with balance. Santon hefted his ax and prodded his horse forward, being careful to remain on the solid portion of ground.

Vered whipped out the glass sword and wheeled about to face the challenge from behind.

But even as he prepared for the fight, all sounds stopped. He no longer heard the sucking of feet pulling free of the swamp muck. The snuffling and snorts faded away. And all wildlife ceased to howl and buzz and sing. It was as if he had been struck deaf.

Panicked, Vered fought his horse to turn around and join Santon. But his friend sat astride his steed, the man's confusion obvious.

"Where's this giant foe?" called Vered. He got his horse under control and joined Birtle Santon.

"I . . . he's gone. As surely as I sit here, though, Vered, I saw a gargantuan man. His arms were thicker than my thighs. He—"

"Wait, a moment, please," gasped out Alarice. Vered and Santon turned to her. She wobbled but maintained her seat. "Something has happened. A spell was cast—or we entered a spell."

"What do you mean 'we entered a spell'?"

"Powerful magic held a bubble around this portion of the swamp. We somehow penetrated it."

"Tahir!"

"I fear this is so," she said. "We blundered into a ward spell."

"But the giant. Whatever it was Vered heard. What of them? Where did they go?" Santon's head swiveled back and forth so fast, Vered feared it might come unscrewed.

"We are not in the swamp. Not the one we entered," said Alarice. "Stop, wait. Extend your senses and tell me what lies around us now."

"No insects," said Vered. "No sound. No bugs buzzing or biting. The wind still blows, though. I hear its soft sighing through the banyan limbs."

"The time of day has not changed," said Santon. "The sun remains just over the treetops.

But the odor of the swamp is . . . different. The decay is subtly changed from what it was."

"How can you tell?" demanded Vered. "Rot and decay are all the same."

"This is not the same. Alarice is right. Superficially, it looks the same but other things have changed."

"The ground!" Vered urged his horse forward. "Look! Solid." The horse pranced on dry dirt. "The pathway is clear."

He considered the implications of this discovery. He looked from Alarice to Santon.

"It leads to Tahir's 'palace'," the Glass Warrior said. "We have entered another realm—and this is the road to the one we seek."

"What of the giant?" Santon continued to crane his head about looking for the monster.

"A magical manifestation. A warning, perhaps, or a sentry placed to keep out unwanted visitors," she said. "We will find out for certain at the end of this path." Alarice put the spurs to her horse. It reluctantly obeyed, tossing its head and shying away repeatedly.

They rode in the eerie silence until Vered said, "I liked the bugs better. They gave something more than Santon's curses to listen to."

Then Vered cursed. The swamp opened into a lake. In the center of the lake rose a pitiful mound of black dirt that beggared the glorious title of "island." Built in the center of the lump rising from the lake sat a rude hut with thatched roof and no windows.

"Who lives in that?" Santon wondered.

"You spoke of immense castles and palatial estates where we wizards live," said Alarice. "That is Tahir's domain."

"That?" Santon and Vered spoke simultaneously, amazed and bemused.

"Tahir is a powerful wizard, but I begin to think that the spell we penetrated is not of his casting. Another, more powerful sorcerer might have bound Tahir to this swamp."

"But why? For killing Lamost?"

"Ah," said Vered. "Consider a more devious plot to ruin Porotane. What if Tahir only carried out the orders of another wizard? What if he were a mercenary and failed in his mission?"

"But he didn't," said Santon. "Until meeting Alarice, we both thought King Lamost died of natural causes. The kidnapping of the heirs, of course, might have been a failure. No claims for ransom were made—or none I heard about."

"None was made," confirmed Alarice. "That always seemed suspect to me. It made me believe the two had been killed, either by design or accident."

"If our thinking turns even more devious," said Vered, "it is not stretching possibility to say that Tahir might have succeeded in snatching away the twins and that he killed them. Accidentally or otherwise would not matter to a more powerful wizard."

"Another wizard who imprisoned Tahir in this wretched swamp for his misdeed," finished Alarice. "Aye, that is possible. Tahir loved his comforts. He would never stay here without good reason."

"I do not like the idea that our quest has ended, that Lokenna and Lorens perished nineteen years ago." Santon coughed and spat. The gobbet went into the water. Ripples appeared, then raced in concentric circles to infinity.

"Creatures too dangerous for description reside in the water. There'll be no wading across for us," said Vered, relieved. He had not liked the idea of getting wet. The lake water on his grimy clothing would produce a stench that would gag the very saints.

"A boat." Santon rode to the small craft. Oars rested within the frail shell. "Looks sturdy enough for the three of us."

"Mayhap we should consider leaving someone behind to guard the horses," suggested Vered. He eyed the boat with growing skepticism. "It doesn't appear strong enough for three, but for two . . ."

"All or none," said Alarice. "The horses will not be harmed. The land seems scoured clean of life."

"But not the water." Vered dismounted and tossed a stone into the lake. Again came the racing ripples indicating beasts just below the surface.

They tethered the horses and entered the boat. Santon pushed off, then jumped aboard before his feet entered the water. Grunting and straining, Vered rowed while Alarice sat in the prow studying the island and Santon crouched in the stern, his withered arm restlessly moving the glass shield as if readying it for combat.

Vered hazarded a glance over the side of the rowboat. He felt faint at the sight of human faces peering back at him—but attached to those all-too-human faces were piscine bodies. He jerked back and bent to the task of rowing. The sudden surge in speed almost tumbled Alarice from the boat's bow.

She laid a gentling hand on his shoulder and said, "They are those who have entered the water and were magically transformed. We do not want to join their ranks. Magic beyond my imagining plays around this island."

"And it is not of Tahir's doing?" asked Santon.

"Another. There are only a few wizards living able to cast such spells and Tahir is not one." She shook her head, white hair going in all directions. "Tahir was always too careless. Did I not learn his name many years ago?" She peered over the side at the swimming creatures and shuddered. "I do not relish the thought of meeting any of them, should they have control of the heirs."

"But you will," said Vered.

"I must. My word has been given to restore one of the royal blood to the throne." Both men heard the pain in Alarice's words. She wished to recant her promise but couldn't. Once given, honor demanded that her promise be fulfilled.

For the first time, Vered found himself wishing that the twins both lay dead. He cast a glance over the side of the boat again and caught sight of a leering face. He gulped. "If only they have not become fish," he prayed.

He stroked powerfully, putting his back into the effort. A sudden crunch and pressure told him that the rowboat had beached on the island. Vered reluctantly climbed out. As frightening as the journey had been, the boat provided a safety that wasn't likely to be found on the island. Even the crumbling black dirt beneath his boots felt odd.

Vered walked a few paces behind the others, trying to decide how this soil differed from that in the rest of the swamp. It occurred to him that he felt lighter, more nimble. Every step was into a spring that gently pushed back at him.

"It's as if the souls of the dead and buried try to rise up," said Santon. Vered almost bolted at this thought. But fear seized him and held the man firmly in place. His knuckles closed around the hilt of his glass sword until they turned white with strain.

"I shouldn't have doubted you, Santon," he choked out. "He *is* a giant!"

An immense man, easily twice as tall as Santon, came from the pitiful hut. The giant peered at them, as if not believing its eyes. Then it bellowed and charged.

All three readied for a fight that could end only in their deaths.

CHAPTER ELEVEN

Vered bellowed and whined and protested—
except during battle. He fell into a deadly silence.
His nerves calmed. His heart rate picked up and
blood rushed through his body, heightening his
senses, putting an edge to his reflexes. His keen
eyes studied the charging giant for weaknesses.
Through his mind flashed the chances of using the
glass short sword, of pounding at the giant with his
acid-blunted dagger, of a dozen different attacks.

When he moved, Vered didn't even realize he
had reached a decision. Three steps forward, a
quick drop, and his legs entangled those of the
lumbering Gargantua.

The monster man shrieked and threw out his
arms to catch himself. Even as Vered had executed
the perfect attack, so did Birtle Santon launch one
of his own. He stepped to one side and let the giant
topple past. He turned, batted away a huge hand
with the glass shield, then used the same motion to
power the up-and-down arc of his battle-ax. Santon
aimed well. The ax drove directly into the base of
the giant's skull.

Such a horrendous blow should have severed
any beast's head from its torso. Santon staggered
away as the shock of the blow vibrated all the way

up his left arm and into his body. He stared stupidly at the cutting edge of his ax. It had skittered off the giant's neck as if flesh had turned to steel.

"The edge," Santon muttered. "The acid blood dulled my ax!"

Vered untangled his legs and scrambled to his feet. The giant kicked about and almost sent Vered flying. The man twisted and drew the tip of his glass sword across the giant's hamstrings, trying to disable him. A screeching of metal on metal sounded.

Both glass sword and giant's flesh remained untouched.

"I should have cut his leg in half with that slash," protested Vered. He danced back and fell into *en garde*. As the giant rose to a sitting position, Vered lunged. The tip snaked in past a clumsy hand and struck the giant's left cheek. Vered jerked upward and guided his blade directly for the creature's eye.

Again he failed. The blade refused to thrust home into the giant's brain.

"What manner of creature is this?" Vered cried. "I refuse to be thwarted. How dare you deny me your death!" Vered launched a flurry of thrusts, none intended to do harm. He distracted the slow-witted giant while Santon sneaked into position behind the sitting monster.

Santon put all his strength behind the blow. The muscles along his left arm rippled with the power of the stroke aimed at the giant's spine. Again Santon staggered back, his killing blow turned away harmlessly.

The giant moaned and bent forward to rise to his feet. Vered kicked a supporting hand out from under the giant and sent him tumbling back to the ground, but again this diversion did not help Santon get in a killing stroke with his ax. When the monster stood, he towered over either man. Santon and Vered parted to keep the giant distracted, then attacked. Santon came in with his glass shield raised high to protect his head; his ax swung at waist level, aimed at the giant's thigh. Simultaneously, Vered attacked the tendons behind the giant's vulnerable right ankle.

The giant roared and grabbed. Both men were lifted into the air and hung, feet kicking. They might have been rats caught by a terrier for all the good their strength did them.

The giant cast them away, as if he considered them nothing more than debris. Vered hit the ground and rolled easily to his feet. Birtle Santon had the wind knocked from his lungs and lay gasping for breath.

Before Vered could renew his attack, Alarice held up a hand. Her gray eyes never left the giant. "Hold, Vered. Your efforts will only fail."

"If he's of flesh and blood, he is vulnerable. No spell can protect him indefinitely."

"He might not be human," Alarice said. She circled to place her body between that of the giant and the fallen Santon. "Tend to Santon. I would have words with Tahir d'mar."

Vered frowned. A huge tear formed at the corner of the giant's eye. It rolled like an ocean's wave down a grimy cheek and dripped to the ground. Where it landed a small plant sprouted and grew with astonishing speed. The giant knelt and gently plucked the plant from the ground, roots and all.

"It will die soon," the giant said, his voice

rumbling deep in his barrel chest. The action and words struck Vered and Santon as incongruous, but Alarice accepted them easily. The Glass Warrior waved back both men.

"So will all things, Tahir," she said. Vered and Santon exchanged glances. It hardly seemed likely that this mountain of impervious gristle and bulk was the wizard they sought. But Alarice had addressed him as such.

"You recognize me, woman of glass. After all these years, you still remember poor Tahir d'mar." The giant dropped the withered plant. It fell to dust within seconds.

"So, Tahir, you remember me, too."

"Of those remaining, I always thought you would be the one sent to find me." The giant collapsed to a cross-legged sitting position, hands resting on his knees. Even so, he almost looked them squarely in the eye.

"It has taken me all these years to learn you were the one who killed Lamost."

Tahir vented a sigh that sounded like gas escaping from a volcanic fumarole. "That spell was pernicious, devious, a glory to cast! He wasted away, with none in Porotane the wiser."

"You also kidnapped his children."

"I did," the wizard agreed.

Vered and Santon moved closer to each other, Vered letting Santon keep the glass shield between them and Tahir. Vered whispered, "He acknowledges the crime too readily. I fear a trap."

"No trap, short one," boomed Tahir. "It is no sorcery I use to overhear. Since my exile to this pathetic island, I have come to know loneliness. I spend my nights awake, straining to hear another's voice. Seldom do I hear even wind. This island is at the vortex of a spell so powerful I cannot escape it."

"The royal twins," urged Alarice. "What of them? They are not with you?"

Tahir laughed, the echoes dying in the distance. The wizard shook his head. "I am alone. I have been alone for nineteen years. See?" He indicated the hut. "Go, look, tell the Glass Warrior what you find there."

Santon looked to Alarice. She made no effort to stop him. Santon trotted up the slope and peered into the hut. The simple thatched hut was bare inside, save for a straw sleeping pallet. On a long wood pole Tahir had carved a line of notches, one for each day of his imprisonment. Santon reported this to the Glass Warrior.

"So, Tahir," she said. "You cannot leave. I take that at face value. There is no reason to deceive me with mere physical evidence. You always used spells to do your bidding. What happened after you took the heirs?"

"I do not remember you as being this anxious. Spend time with me. You still have a few minutes."

"What do you mean by that?" demanded Vered.

"Who cast the spell binding you to this island?" asked Alarice.

"What did he mean that we have only a few minutes?" shouted Vered. "Demons take the wizard forcing him to stay here. We're in danger!"

"Aye, that is so, noisy one," said Tahir. "Exactly at sunset, I must kill everyone on this island. That is part of my curse."

"Who?" Alarice asked gently. "The sorcerer must be of exceptional power."

"The strongest. I angered the Wizard of

Storms. It was he who cast me here, he whose spell binds me more firmly than life itself."

"The Wizard of Storms never leaves the Yorral Mountains," said Alarice. "What is his interest in Lokenna and Lorens?"

The giant shrugged. "Who can say? I dickered with him for the children. I slew Lamost and then . . ."

"You could not give over the twins," supplied Santon. "Why not?"

The laugh issuing from Tahir's lips carried pure evil. "False pride. I thought myself invincible —with the spells promised me by the Wizard of Storms, I *would* be invincible. I fell into another's trap."

"Another wizard has the children?"

Tahir's lips pulled back in a sneer. "He stole the children and forced me into this odious body. Then the Wizard of Storms exacted his toll for my failure. He sentenced me to this island forever."

"Then it was his spell we crossed in arriving in the swamps."

"Space is contorted. Long distances are short, short are long. I saw you and tried to approach, but the movement produced by his spell pulled you away. But you found me anyway." The giant stood, flexing powerful muscles. "Now that it is sundown, I am compelled to slay you. No hard feelings, Warrior. It is required by the curse."

"Why? What is the nature of the spell? Perhaps I can lift it—in exchange for information."

"You would do that for me?" Tahir shook all over. "No, I see that you would not. It is for the royal heirs that you would risk it." The giant laughed at her naiveté. "I cannot leave this island, I cannot entertain visitors during the hours of darkness—and I am immortal. Forever must I endure my solitude."

"The creatures surrounding this island," noted Vered. "The ones with human faces. What of them?"

Tahir shrugged. "The waters are cursed, also. Should you become totally immersed, that is what you become." With a bull-throated roar, Tahir charged. He picked up Vered in his powerful hands and lifted him off the ground. "That is what you *will* become, you chattering magpie!"

Tahir's muscles bunched as he rocked back to heave Vered into the lake. Santon attacked. He ran forward at full speed, the glass shield smashing into Tahir's kneecaps. He bowled over the giant. Although Vered rolled out of the wizard's grasp, Santon had not injured Tahir.

"Back," ordered Alarice. "There is nothing you can do to him. This is my fight." She drew her glass sword and moved forward.

"We can take him if we work together," said Santon.

"Stay back. Do not interfere." Even as she spoke, Alarice lifted her glass sword and held its tip pointed at the twilight sky. Green fire danced along its length.

"He uses sorcery against her," whispered Vered. "How can we fight that?"

"We can't." Santon swallowed hard and pushed his friend back. "We must let her fight this battle. It is not for us to triumph in this. We could not. Ever."

"You cannot be immortal, Tahir," Alarice said. "Your energies are too weak. You expend more than you absorb. You *must* die." Again the glass sword glowed with the vivid green glow as she sucked strength from the giant with her spell.

Tahir stumbled but did not fall. "You are clever, Warrior. But the same spell can be turned against you. I know your name! You are Alarice!"

Vered and Santon did not understand the sorcery dancing about them, but they saw its effect on the Glass Warrior. She stood her ground, but she seemed diminished. Her lips moved to cast counters, to renew her own assault on Tahir, but she weakened visibly as she worked.

"She turns to glass before our eyes!" cried Vered.

Santon moved forward, the glass shield riding high on his withered arm. He placed himself between the battling wizards. He shrieked and fell backward, but the ploy worked. Alarice regained her substance. The transparency developing in her body misted over and solidity replaced it.

She lowered the tip of her sword and ran forward. The lunge started from a distance and snaked toward Tahir with deceptive slowness. The tip of the blade nicked the giant's upper arm. Blood spurted.

"You are *not* immortal," Alarice called as Tahir jerked back and ran to his hut. She moved to follow, but got no farther than halfway before Tahir reappeared. In his brawny hands he held a great sword so massive that even the giant wizard had difficulty balancing it.

When he began swinging it, the men saw that no human could stand before the deadly arc. Tahir advanced, forcing Alarice to retreat. She made no attempt to parry with her glass weapon. Against this battering ram of edged steel it would shatter.

"Beneath your feet, Tahir. Look at your feet."

The giant yelped and danced away from some menace only he saw. Vered and Santon saw nothing; this spell Alarice cast only for Tahir. As the wizard backed in fright, Alarice again attacked. Her glass sword shone in the dusk. Another pink to Tahir's leg; more blood. Nothing serious, but Tahir had received two wounds and given none in return.

"You anger me, Alarice."

"Fight, don't talk," she chided. She slashed viciously for the giant's midriff and opened a long gash that bled profusely. Any ordinary man would have been disabled by this gutting cut. Not the wizard. Tahir fought on, his massive sword singing through the air. Alarice dodged easily, but dared not get too close. A single cut from that mighty weapon would behead her.

"Who did you give the children to, Tahir?" she asked. "Surely, you can tell me this small thing."

"Defeat me and I will tell you."

"How can I defeat you if you are immortal?"

Tahir roared with laughter. "That's the curse! I cannot be killed—and slaying me is the only way to learn the name that dances on the tip of my tongue." Tahir thrust out his tongue. The tip glowed a bright pink, shimmered, and vanished.

"Always the jape," Alarice said. She circled warily, studying the wizard for weakness. The instant before she lunged, a yawning pit opened at her feet. The Glass Warrior leaped over it in time to avoid falling face first into a pit seething with poisonous snakes. The vile stench from the poison dripping from their fangs rose and caused Vered to wrinkle his nose. He backed from the pit.

"She cannot defeat him alone. We must help." Santon started forward, but Vered held him back.

"We can do nothing in a battle fought with *that*." He used the tip of his glass sword to show the sinuously moving black mass at the bottom of the pit. Illusion it might be, but Vered would not chance it. Better to believe the snakes and death-giving poison fangs were real.

Swords he understood. Sorcery lay beyond his expertise.

"We must do something!" protested Santon.

"Think of it and I'll do it. Until that time, we stand and watch. If we interfere, we risk distracting Alarice."

Santon saw that his friend spoke truly. The Glass Warrior had begun to turn glass-transparent once more. Her hair vanished and bits of her flesh winked in and out of existence. But the glass sword she clutched so firmly remained solid and she used it well.

Tahir's body dripped blood from a half-dozen wounds.

"Alarice," called the giant wizard. "A trade. Do you agree to this?"

"What are your terms?" She continued to circle, not trusting her opponent.

"I sense that you carry the Demon Crown."

"How do you know this?"

"I may be imprisoned but I retain all my magical skills. The crown blazes within my brain, just as it must for you. Give it to me and I'll tell you the name of the sorcerer who stole away the royal twins."

They continued to fight as they negotiated. Even though every stroke threatened to divide Alarice in half, the great sword always missed by inches. Her ripostes lacked Tahir's power, but she had opened wounds all over his body.

"Ridiculous, Tahir, and you know it," she answered, beginning to strain. Her breath came in short gasps and her movements slowed. Tahir, for all the bloody cuts, seemed no weaker than when he had begun the fight. "What good would it do me to find even one twin but lose the Demon Crown? The crown is necessary to reunite Porotane. It must rest on a royal brow."

She weakened further. Vered had to restrain Birtle Santon. The man wanted to rush forward, but Vered saw the clever use Tahir made of the great sword. The wizard wove a curtain of steel around him that no ordinary mortal might pierce.

Just as it appeared that Alarice would fall victim to the wizard's sword, she moved with blinding speed. She lunged, the glass sword blazing so brightly that it might have been forged from a dazzling emerald. The tip found Tahir's navel. Alarice performed a quick skip and got her back leg repositioned for an even more powerful lunge. The scintillant glass weapon sank into the giant's gut.

Both Santon and Vered threw up their hands to protect their faces from the heat and light emanating from Alarice's sword.

Vered peered through his fingers. His heart turned to a lump of polar ice. Although Alarice's sword had pierced Tahir, it had not killed the giant.

"He must be immortal," moaned the man. "Not even a magical thrust stops him!"

The wizard bellowed in pain and grabbed the blade of Alarice's sword. Tahir jerked about and ripped the sword from the Glass Warrior's grip. Sobbing in agony, he pulled the sword from his body.

But Alarice had not stopped her attack. She leaped, acid-filled glass dagger lifted high above her head. She brought it down, its fragile tip penetrating Tahir's breast. Once in the wizard's body, she twisted the knife. Vered heard the *snap!* as the hollow blade broke.

Tahir's flesh sizzled as the acid raced through his heart.

"Look!" Santon bumped Vered with his shield to make certain the other man saw and confirmed the strange sight. The giant began shrinking, turning in on himself until a man slightly smaller than Vered struggled on the ground.

"The curse!" cried out Tahir. "You have broken the spell binding me to this pitiful island!"

"You are not immortal," said Alarice. She had retrieved her sword and stood over the body of her fallen opponent.

"No longer. Your spells and fine sword work defeated me. Oh, I tried to defeat you, I did. I could do nothing else because of the curse. But now I can die. Glorious day, I can die!"

"The children," urged Alarice. "What of Lorens and Lokenna? Which wizard took them from you?"

The laugh coming from Tahir mixed with a burbling sound. Blood dribbled down his chin; he turned his head to one side and spat. "It burns," Tahir said, almost in awe. "Your acid fills my veins already. I taste it on my tongue. It . . . it is strangely sweet, like a honey-filled pastry."

"The name of the wizard, damn you!" Alarice placed the tip of her glass sword at Tahir's throat, then leaned on it.

"You can no longer threaten me, dear Alarice.

Not as you did before. I am dying. Sweet oblivion is rushing up on me."

She pulled the sword away. "I can bind you, Tahir. I can bind your phantom to this island and be sure that you never see a proper burial. Would you allow your phantom to roam endlessly? Or will you trade the name for a consecrated grave?"

Tahir spat at her. "You evil bitch! I always hated you!" The wizard rolled into a fetal ball, arms clutching at his knees. "The pain grows. The acid no longer tastes so sweet."

He peered up at her, his eyes fogging over with death. "I . . . the name you seek is Patrin." Tahir jerked once, then relaxed. His face looked strangely serene.

"Alarice, is it true? Did he tell the truth?"

The Glass Warrior nodded. "Tahir spoke the truth. For that small favor I will not bind his phantom to this land. He will receive a formal burial."

"What's wrong?" asked Vered. "Your words convey a strange sorrow."

"He spoke the truth, damn him!" cried Alarice. She thrust her blade into the dirt beside Tahir's diminished corpse. "Of all the wizards, Patrin of the City of Stolen Dreams is the worst. Better I had never learned his name. Better I faced the Wizard of Storms himself!"

Vered and Birtle Santon exchanged worried looks. Of Patrin they had never heard, but dread began to build within them.

No one looked upon the City of Stolen Dreams and lived to tell of it. No one.

CHAPTER TWELVE

Birtle Santon rubbed his hand against dirty breeches and stepped back. Vered and Alarice rolled Tahir d'mar into the shallow grave. The wizard lay at the bottom of the grave, a serene expression on his handsome face.

"He knows nothing can happen to him now," grumbled Vered. He ran grimy fingers through his brown hair and looked up at Alarice. "What did you mean when you promised him you would not doom him to wander as a phantom?"

"Just that. Once the grave is consecrated, his soul is at rest." The Glass Warrior stared at the corpse, as if trying to come to a difficult decision. "No," she said at last, "I cannot do such a thing to him, although it lies within my power. He gave me the name I sought."

"How can you turn him into a ghost?" asked Santon. "Such power is reserved for saints—or demons."

Alarice smiled sadly. "Alas, it is a simple spell. Most wizards are able to conjure it."

"Why aren't we overrun with phantoms then?" Vered began scooping the loose dirt up in his hands and tossing it onto Tahir.

"In some parts of the country, the phantoms outnumber the living," she said. "The places where battles have raged are the worst. Who properly buries the dead after a major defeat?"

Vered looked over his shoulder, as if a ghost crept up on him. "Never seen one. Not sure I want to."

"Tahir did give you the name of this Patrin," said Santon. He saw the way Alarice reacted. "Is Patrin so evil?"

She shivered. "He is. Never have I encountered a man more evil. If any had conspired to steal away the twins and create a reign of confusion, it would be Patrin."

"What of this Wizard of Storms? The one who locked Tahir to this island. He must control vast power. He seems the true villain."

"Patrin I have met and know all too well. The Wizard of Storms is a recluse, content to weave his spells and avoid human contact. Unless Tahir lied, and I see no reason for him to have done so, there is more afoot than we understand. Porotane's rulers must play an important part. How, I can't say."

Vered finished moving the dirt back to the grave. He stood and brushed off his hands while Santon stamped down the rich black dirt with his boots.

"Why we do this is a mystery," he said. "There are no animals on this island. Save the one we've just buried."

"The spell is gone," said Alarice. "With Tahir's death, nature reasserts control."

As if to emphasize the truth of her statement, Vered yelped and swatted at an insect boring hungrily into his neck. His hand came away bloody.

"See?" she said. Taking a deep breath, the Glass Warrior started reciting the burial ceremony that would keep Tahir's phantom from rising to walk the world endlessly. Finished, she made a gesture over the grave as if dismissing a servant. "That takes care of Tahir."

"You sound skeptical," said Vered.

"Not skeptical. Tahir is gone for all time. Sad perhaps. The information I sought is mine—and the easy part of the quest is finished."

"The *easy* part is done?" exclaimed Vered. "How can you say that? We've fought magical ape creatures, a wizard turned into a grotesque giant, the damned insects, the sucking swamp, the . . . things in the lake. How can you *possibly* say the easy part is behind us?"

"Because it is. You and Santon are free to leave, should this please you." Alarice spun and stalked off. Santon and Vered followed quickly, going to the boat. The Glass Warrior sat in the boat, arms crossed over her chest, deep in thought.

"Let's both row," said Santon. "You take that side, I'll take this. And match my rhythm. I can't handle the oar with one hand as well as you can with two."

"Anything," Vered said, "if I don't have to look down into the lake." The thought of vanishing beneath the magical waves, then having his body transformed into a fish's, upset him more than words could tell.

They rowed across the lake. As they went, they both commented on the changes being wrought around them. Birds flew overhead, their dark forms visible in the dim light of the rising moon. Fish swam in the lake, occasionally breaking the surface in pursuit of a succulent bug. And from the shore toward which they rowed came the normal sounds of swamp creatures snuffling and screeching and hunting and dying.

"Do we ride on?" asked Vered, once they beached the boat. He started when he felt Santon's strong hand gripping his arm. Silently, they watched the boat dissolve like salt poured into water.

"What happened to it?" whispered Vered after several seconds, hardly daring to speak.

"Sorcery," said Santon. "The boat was part of the spell."

"Whose spell, Patrin's or the Wizard of Storms'?"

Santon didn't answer. He turned to Alarice, who worked to pull her bedroll from the saddle and spread it on the ground. She prepared for the night. The way she chose her sleeping site told Santon that she intended to sleep alone this night. She had been worrying deeply over something since leaving the island.

"Could this Patrin upset her so?" he asked Vered. "She has vanquished a giant, a wizard, the man responsible for the death of a king and the kidnapping of the twins. She can conquer anyone, warrior or wizard."

"She doesn't think so. See how she sits?" Vered prepared a small cooking fire and fixed a meal, though neither of them had much appetite. Alarice refused to even look in their direction.

The men spoke quietly after eating, then stretched out in their blankets. Vered lay flat on his back, staring at the stars and trying to work out the constellations. As always, he failed to find the patterns officially sanctioned by the royal astronomers, but he found constellations of his own making. Each was more lewd than the last.

He amused himself with the Negligent Whore and the Obedient Dog, invented a few more combinations, and finally sat up, tired of the pastime. Santon snored heavily, long since fast asleep. Vered turned to Alarice. The Glass Warrior sat tailor fashion, her gray eyes glinting with reflected starlight.

Before her on the ground rested the Demon Crown. It glowed a pale green, as if it had rested on the brow of royalty. She reached out; the glow intensified. As if succumbing to a fever, Alarice shivered and worked the crown into its crystalline box without touching it. She put the Demon Crown back into the velvet bag and leaned back, her arms circling the knapsack.

Vered wondered what thoughts coursed through her head. Did she desire the power the Demon Crown offered to the right person? Or did she desire only surcease, an end to this search for the heirs?

Vered turned over and lay down, momentarily worrying about snakes and insects crawling beneath the blankets with him. Better a willing woman. But such was not to be had. He drifted off to a sleep troubled by giant wizards and fish with men's faces.

Vered awoke with a start, not sure what disturbed him. He lay back, unmoving and straining to hear. It took several seconds for him to realize that he heard nothing—and this was what awoke him. He reached out and gently shook Santon. The man rumbled deep in his throat, stirred and tried to pull away.

"Santon, trouble. The animals have fallen silent."

"Spell," Birtle Santon mumbled, more asleep than awake. "The spell keeps them away."

"The spell died with Tahir."

Santon came to a sitting position in a movement so abrupt that Vered drew back, hand going to his worthless dagger. The man's eyes took on an inner light as he stared at Vered, then cocked his head to one side, listening intently.

Santon began buckling his shield onto his limp right arm. Vered reached for his glass short sword and opened his mouth to alert Alarice. The blow to the back of his head doubled him over. Vered rolled to the side, pain blasting through his entire body. The glass sword fell from his numbed fingers. An infinity away he heard Santon bellowing incoherently.

"Alarice, to the attack!" yelled Santon.

Vered struggled to hang onto the frayed thread of consciousness. The Glass Warrior did not respond. He tried to rise to aid his friend. His legs weighed like lead; his arms twitched feebly; the pain centered in his head blotted out the world and left only a red curtain.

Through the battle in his head came sounds of the battle without. Vered rolled onto his back. His blurry eyes caught glimpses of moving figures. The flash of light off a round shield might have been Santon. Vered blinked and cleared his vision. He could not let his friend down. To lie helpless on the ground spelled both their deaths.

But who dealt that fate? Vered did not know

or care. The attack might come from ruffians roving the countryside, Dews Gaemock's band of rebels, even remnants of the wizard's soldiers they had left unslain on their way to this miserable swamp.

Vered sucked in a lungful of air and gave voice to his battle cry. When he realized it came out as a kitten's mewling, anger forced away the last of the pain he felt. Vered came to his hands and knees, only to be knocked down again by a glancing blow. He rolled and used the momentum to get to his feet.

Somehow, he still clutched the glass short sword in his hand. His motion more falling forward than lunging, Vered thrust at the nearest moving shadow. A mortal man's cry of pain told of a direct hit. Vered fell to one knee but felt stronger from his minor triumph. He parried a thrust, disengaged, and rammed the tip of his blade into his opponent's armpit. From the spastic jerk he felt, he knew that their foes numbered one less.

Vered swung his sword and took the legs out from under another. Strength flowed into him like rainwater into a cistern. He drew his dagger and used it to parry. For stabbing it proved worthless. Repeatedly, he met solid armor. These were no starving farmers banded together to rob careless travelers. They fought with military precision and skill and their accoutrements were of the finest quality.

"Santon," he gasped out. "What happened to Alarice?"

"Don't know," came the reply. "Don't see her. But we need her. I count three in front of me."

"Another three here," said Vered. He rolled

his blade around his opponent's and carried it out
and away, to splash in the lake. "Go fish," he called
after his retreating foe. Vered hoped the man
immersed himself totally in the lake. Perhaps the
spell lingered.

The remaining two forced Vered back until he
fought with his spine pressing into a cypress. They
separated and engaged him from each side, one
attacking until he responded, then the other trying
to hamstring him.

"Santon, can't hold off these two much longer." Vered riposted, missed, and nearly lost his
head when the enemy behind swung his sword
two-handed in a powerful cut. "Santon? Santon!"

No response. Vered's heart missed a beat
when he saw that he no longer faced a pair of
swordsmen. Three more joined the battle. Santon
had fought his last.

"Aieee!" he shrieked, hoping to shock his foes
into temporary immobility. Vered tried to fight his
way through the ring of steel. A powerful blow sent
him tumbling face forward into the ground. Dirt
entered his mouth and nose, choking him. A
second knobbed hilt smashed into the base of his
skull.

Blackness settled over him like an old, familiar blanket.

Vered awoke to pain. Not since he had been
lost and starving after his village had been burned
had he felt this lost and miserable. His eyes fluttered open. A slow smile crossed his lips.

"Truly, I have died and am in the arms of the
saints."

"He's all right," said Alarice. She dropped his

head from her lap. He winced at the sudden pain. "I had feared the blow might have addled his wits permanently, but his skull is too thick for that."

"Being partially of royal blood helps," Vered said. He touched the back of his head. Alarice had bandaged him expertly once again.

"A sorry trio we are," the Glass Warrior said. "Not even posting a guard, being taken unawares, the theft." The bitterness in her voice hurt Vered worse than the wounds to his head.

"What theft?" he asked. He looked past the Glass Warrior to Birtle Santon. The man stood behind her, his expression baleful.

"The Demon Crown," said Santon. "The ruffians took it from her."

"That's all they wanted? Just the crown? How did they know we had it?"

"I fear that these are assassins sent by Baron Theoll. A squad followed me from the castle after Duke Freow entrusted this mission to me. I thought I had eluded them, sending them along a false trail to the Uvain Plateau."

"Assassins?" Vered tried to think. The effort hurt too much. "Why did they not kill us instead of taking only the crown?"

Alarice snorted derisively. "You are not the only one able to fight. When you woke Santon, I had already drawn my sword. You two did well, but I did better. At least, I drove them off."

"I accounted for two," said Santon. "And you, Vered, you killed one and wounded two others."

"I remember being backed into a tree. Santon, your attackers finished you and came for me!"

"Nothing of the sort. Where those extra ruffians came from, I'll never know. I fought well, but it was Alarice who drove them away."

"With the Demon Crown," she said in a tone lacking any emotion. "More important than finding the twins is recovering the crown. With it Theoll can rule Porotane."

"He is of royal blood, isn't he?" Vered tried to stand. Alarice had to help him remain on his feet.

"Just shows that some bastards can be legitimate."

Vered saw the bodies at the edge of their camp. Either Alarice or Santon had stacked them neatly. The cloud of insects on them caused Vered's nose to wrinkle in distaste. Death could be so messy.

"Which direction?" he asked. "They cannot have ridden far, not in this sucking swamp."

"It's that very swamp that makes it difficult to find them," observed Santon. "I've circled about, trying to find spoor. I can only guess that they head in that direction." He pointed north.

"They take the Demon Crown to Theoll." Vered stretched and tried to get some feeling that wasn't entirely pain back into his body. "We should start out immediately. No time to lose."

Vered looked from Alarice to Santon and back, hoping one of them would argue. When neither did, he vented a huge sigh and went to saddle his horse. The white agony in his skull had died down to a dull throb. He had felt better; he had also felt worse. To regain the crown—to keep it out of Theoll's grasping fingers—he could endure anything.

Ten minutes later, the three rode slowly north. Alarice had tried scrying with her gut string and crystal and found the results inconclusive. The residual magic from Patrin's binding spell muddled her responses.

"Is there another spell to home in on the crown?" asked Santon. "Such a powerful magical ornament must radiate energy."

"There might be," said Alarice. "I know nothing of it, though. I am a sorceress with little power. What spells I cast are elementary. Anyone with a modicum of ability can duplicate all I do."

"I doubt that," said Santon. His green eyes locked with her gray ones. A shadow of a smile crossed his lips. Then he spurred his horse and rode ahead to find Vered.

"What from the rear echelons?" asked Vered when his friend pulled up next to him.

"No hope of tracing the crown magically," Santon reported. "Have you found their trail yet? You're the best tracker in Porotane."

"Go on, make it difficult for me. Make me feel guilty if I can't locate it."

"Sorry."

"We ride less than an hour after them."

"What? You did find their spoor!" cried Santon.

"Of course. Hasn't it been said, even recently, that I am the best tracker in the kingdom?" Vered grinned broadly. It hadn't been easy finding the assassins' trail in the quagmire, but he had. A thread caught on a shrub. A bit of bark missing from a tree trunk. A stone with a fresh nick on it. Those were the clues that only a master hunter could observe.

Santon thrust out his shield and motioned Vered to silence. Ahead in a small, swampy clearing stood a horse. The animal tried to crop at a patch of grass but its tether proved too short.

"What do you make of that?" asked Santon.

"One thing only," said Vered. He turned in the saddle and motioned to Alarice.

"I fear you are right." Santon paused, then in concert with Vered, rode into the clearing, alert for danger.

They dismounted and went to the horse. Bloodstains on the saddle showed where the rider had been injured.

Neither man paid attention to the moans coming from behind a fallen tree trunk. They turned, backs together, and readied glass blade and battle ax.

"The trap is sprung," said Vered.

From three sides came armed soldiers. They advanced, anger shrouding their faces like dark storm clouds. They had expected Vered and Santon to fall completely into their trap.

"What would we have found by the trunk?" called out Santon.

The answer came from the man Santon had already guessed to be the leader. "Poisoned needles in the fallen man's clothing. But you insist on making our task difficult."

"Seems as if a few of you are shirking your duty," observed Vered. "Shouldn't there be a *solid* ring about us? Why let us have an escape path?"

The leader turned and looked over his line. His eyes widened. "By all the saints and demons, where are—" He never finished. Alarice had ridden around the perimeter, seeking out the ambushers. She had slain three and rode down hard on another. Her glass blade flashed. An assassin's throat exploded in a bloody welter as the tip drew along a line below his chin.

The leader feinted, then waited, hoping to draw out Vered or Santon. Both men stood their ground. As long as a friend remained at his back, the other knew a modicum of security.

"Get them!" cried the enemy leader. Those were his last words before Alarice's clever sword found a berth in the man's mouth. His sword fell from lifeless fingers. He tried to bat away the sword thrust down his gullet and failed, already being dead. The officer sagged away from Alarice, the sword pulling free.

The remaining five men tried to flee. Vered and Santon took quick steps forward. Santon's blade killed one man; Vered's short sword ended another's flight. Alarice engaged a third, making short work of him.

"The last two run," shouted Vered. He sprinted after one, diving and tackling the man before he could vanish into the tangled undergrowth around the clearing.

Vered struck the man twice, both blows landing squarely in the center of the man's face. He threw up his hands to prevent Vered from making further attacks.

"The Demon Crown," came Alarice's cold voice. "Where is it?" She shoved the point of her sword into the hollow at the captive's throat.

The soldier looked from Vered to Alarice and saw no mercy in either's face.

"Speak or die!"

"He . . . Vork . . . our leader. He has it. Had it!"

From across the clearing, Birtle Santon called, "I have it. It's untouched. Still in the velvet bag."

"Vered, check it," she said. Her steely gray eyes never left the man trembling under the point of her glass sword.

Vered rose and went to verify the crown. He place his hand on the crystalline box. The answering green glow showed that it responded to the royal blood sluggishly flowing through his veins. "It's no decoy," he told Alarice.

A strangled cry answered him. Both men were halfway across the clearing when Alarice emerged. She thrust her blade into the soft dirt to cleanse it.

"They were assassins. They deserved worse than a quick death, but that's all I could give them. It will do." She took the Demon Crown from Santon and stared at it. Her face became an unreadable mask. Vered wondered what thoughts fluttered through her mind. Did she see paradise or perdition in that crown fashioned by a demon's hand?

Vered shrugged it off. They had recovered the crown. He turned and surveyed the clearing, counting the dead bodies. He stopped, frowned, and counted again.

"There's one missing," he told Santon.

Santon counted. The two men cursed. To Alarice, Santon said, "One of the killers is missing. Vered caught one of two remaining after your attack. We must track down the last one or he will return to Theoll for reinforcements."

"Let him," she said, her bloodlust momentarily sated. "It is more important to find Lokenna and Lorens. We must seek out Patrin and the City of Stolen Dreams."

Vered shivered at the Glass Warrior's words. She made their goal sound like a death sentence.

CHAPTER THIRTEEN

Birtle Santon hitched the shield higher on his withered right arm. All day the arm had been hurting. The hot sun and the dry wind did nothing to soothe the pain building in his body. Nor did Alarice seem willing to slow their breakneck pace. They had left the swamps where Tahir had died and found firmer footing on rolling lands that pleased Santon. He had grown up in farmland much like this, and seeing it once again caused cherished memories to bubble to the surface of his mind. But the grassy lands had given way to more barren stretches within a week.

And still Alarice plunged on, driven by her quest. Santon tried not to stare at the woman as they rode. To do so would be intolerably rude, but she attracted him strangely. Pretty in a wild way, yes, but the Glass Warrior offered more than simple physical beauty. He smiled. The way the hot, dry wind whipped her white hair back into a never-resting banner highlighted the firm jaw and softened the sharp, hard lines of her cheekbones. But nothing softened her determination or the steel-gray hardness of those eyes.

Santon had seen action in the past twenty years that had toughened him, but he felt like a kitten mewling for milk in comparison to Alarice. They had shared the comforts and joys of one another's bodies. For Santon it had been more than physical. For Alarice, he could not say. He doubted that she felt any emotional attachment. But he could hope. The road had been long and lonely for him. Having someone as fine as Alarice to share it made the journey worthwhile.

Santon turned his eyes to the terrain ahead. He should not allow himself to feel more than simple gratification with her. The Glass Warrior's quest consumed her totally. He should keep matters between them on an impersonal plane. He closed his eyes and tried to settle the churning of his mind and emotions. He should. But he didn't. So much about Alarice attracted him—the quick mind, the devotion to duty, the loyalty, the independence tempered with need for another.

He opened his eyes and caught full in the face a blast of dust that caused watering in his eyes. He blinked the dirt free. What others had there been in the woman's life? He did not know, and Alarice never spoke of her past. For that, he felt some small thankfulness. His own past had been blighted, then lit with love and blighted anew too many times for the subject to be a comfortable one. To reveal that part of his life to Alarice would be giving away all he had.

"Santon, what do you see yonder?" Vered's insistent tug on his left sleeve caused him to jerk about, startled.

"What? Where? Can't see for all this dust."

"You need to show more care," said Vered. "Your eyes pour tears." Vered looked at him strangely, then lifted his arm and indicated a collection of low hills off to their right. "I caught the glint of sunlight on metal a few minutes ago, but have seen nothing since."

"It might be nothing more than debris long discarded. The weather seems dry enough to prevent rust for many a year."

"This time of season is deceptive," said Vered. "Dry winds now, wet and cold autumns. Still, you may be right in this. It might be nothing more than my fertile imagination since I see no dust rising from horses' hooves."

"We should investigate, though," he said. "It pays nothing but death to allow an enemy to come up on us from behind once we enter the mountains."

Santon peered into the distance and saw the ragged, torn black peaks of the Iron Range. Crossing them would be difficult. Getting into the narrow, torturously winding passes and finding armed men behind would be fatal. His eyes slipped from the mountains back to the prairie lands to the right of their travel.

"Let me scout. You stay with Alarice."

"Not good, Santon. Dividing our forces only weakens us, if you happen to find trouble."

Santon laughed. "You think I am so inexperienced that I'd take on an entire band of brigands without letting you in on the fun? I go only to spy, not to fight."

Alarice overheard their conversation and dropped back. Her mare tossed its head and looked sideways at the men, as if thanking them for this brief respite from the demanding pace her mistress set.

"Why stop?" she demanded. "We must reach

the foothills soon. The heat of spring melts the snows quickly. I have no desire to be caught in the Iron Range with floods cutting off the passes."

"Vered saw riders. I'll check them out. They might be nothing more than traders beginning to move from winter quarters to the south." Santon knew better than this. The nomadic traders who roved Porotane seldom appeared until midsummer, when the festivals began, with the plays and gatherings of musicians. The springtime carried too much work for farmers intent on getting seeds in tilled ground. Only after the saints blessed the ground and the first green shoots rose did many in Porotane think of frolicking.

Santon turned melancholy at the thought of the many festivals lost to the civil war. Even with crops growing, not many people had time for proper festivities.

"Or I might have seen nothing. A trick played on me by these accursed winds." Vered brushed dust from his cheeks.

Alarice stared at him. Vered shrugged. "All right. I *saw* something, and do not think it was a reflection from a harmless castoff."

"We dare not linger here. We must reach the mountains soon if we are to get through before summer."

Santon knew the true reason behind Alarice's concern. Although mountain flooding posed a problem, it mattered less than entering the Desert of Sazan on the far side of the Iron Range in summer. The desert heat melted metal, or so he had heard. Santon had no reason to doubt the tales told by others, fantastic though they seemed. He had witnessed stranger occurrences with his own eyes.

"How long will it take to find Patrin and the City of Stolen Dreams?" he asked.

Alarice shrugged. "I have no idea if my scrying spell works on the city. It is a place where intense magic dwells—and Patrin is its ruler. If he thinks to affect the politics of Porotane, he plays a game deeper than any he has chosen before."

"No wizard seeks out visitors," said Vered.

"Me least of all," added Alarice. "Patrin and I have never been on friendly terms. If he truly kidnapped Lokenna and Lorens, that dislike has become total enmity."

"Then there will be no surprises when we find this City of Stolen Dreams," said Santon, his mood darkening even more. "That does not resolve the dilemma of our distant watchers." From the corner of his eye, he, too, caught a glimpse of movement. A rider? An animal hunting late in the afternoon? With the sun at their backs and their shadows long on the ground, they would be ideal targets for ambush. An attacker might have the sun in his eyes, but they would be silhouetted as they rode.

And the wind! It switched direction constantly. What had been in their face a few minutes earlier now came from the rear. Somehow, this boon from the saints did not keep the grit from Santon's green eyes or pasty mouth.

"We should camp soon," said Alarice. "We can wait for them to come to us—if they mean us harm."

"Another night of watches," sighed Vered. "Before we find the twins, I shall be a hundred years short on sleep. When one ascends the throne, my first request of the monarch will be for a month of never being awakened!"

"Sounds like death to me," said Santon.

"Birtle, you are much too gloomy," said Alarice. "The reason we ride is serious, but you need not carry the full weight on your shoulders. We do this together." She reached over and laid a hand on his. The smile warmed him. He tried not to think of the eyes and the cold depths within them.

They rode for another hour, then camped. It took the men another hour to tend to the horses and prepare a simple meal. While they worked Alarice used her scrying spell to discover the identity of any who followed them into the Iron Range.

"I'd be tempted to say that we do the hard part," said Vered, staring at the Glass Warrior while she concentrated. "We tend the horses, we make the meal, we stand the watches, but this time I stand mute."

Alarice's face was drawn and white. Her eyes were closed and sweat beaded on her forehead in spite of the hot breezes still blowing. Finally, she sagged forward, her hands falling limp to her sides.

"Are you . . ." began Santon. He knelt. Alarice opened her eyes and smiled weakly.

"I am unharmed. This scrying proved more taxing than before. Someone counters me. I cannot tell who the wizard is, but it must be Patrin. Somehow, Tahir's death alerted him. Perhaps when the imprisoning spell vanished it triggered a magical alarm. I don't know."

"I've been to the top of yon tree," said Vered. "From the topmost branches I've watched for the past half hour and seen nothing. If we are being tracked, they have no desire to approach before complete darkness." He cocked his head to one side. "The moon rises in another two hours from behind the mountains. An attack would come from that direction. We would shine in moonlight and they would be invisible to us."

"So," mused Santon. "If they rode parallel to us all day, they would continue on, then circle back and come at us. When? We have a two hour period of grace before moonrise. Call it another three hours before the moon rose too high to afford them any benefit from the attack. One should keep watch, then, for two hours, all three of us until the moon is overhead, and the usual watch afterward?"

"Sounds good," said Vered. "Since I crawled up that damnable tree and got sap all over me, you can take the first watch while I clean off." Vered made a face as he pressed his hands together and started to pull them apart, only to find the sticky sap gluing them together. The expression on his face when he saw the sap on his clothing told of extreme contempt for any pursuit in which he would sully himself.

Santon prowled to the perimeter of their camp and began carefully studying the terrain. If attack came, he wanted to know the land better than the enemy. Less than a hundred paces along the route of his careful scouting, he got the eerie feeling of being watched. He did not turn; he moved onward slowly, adjusting his shield as he went. The feeling of being stalked increased.

Only when he had a large boulder to put at his back did he turn, his battle-ax singing as it whipped free of his leather sling. Santon held back his chagrin. He had been *sure* that someone stalked him. Try as he might, Birtle Santon saw no one.

But the feeling persisted—and grew.

He retraced his path, every sense straining. The wind had died down shortly after twilight. He scented nothing but cloying blossoms in the air. His ears picked up only faint sounds from Alarice and the muffled curses Vered uttered as he peeled the sticky juices from his hands. A horse neighed, then fell silent—one of their own. Santon's sharp eyes studied the dirt for signs of passage other than his. He had moved so carefully he had left only faint smudges marking his trail. Nothing else had passed this way.

Santon still *felt* eyes on him.

Heavy ax swinging restlessly, he walked on. A sudden gust of wind brought him spinning around, the blunted edge of his battle-ax slashing through a vicious arc. The ax went through empty air and his glass shield protected him from nothingness. But Santon jumped back in surprise when his attack produced an anguished cry.

"Who's there?" he demanded, seeing no one. His hand tightened on the handle of his weapon. "Come out and fight like a warrior. Your death will not be any less easy if you hide."

"My death was not easy the first time," came a moan that might have been wind in tall trees had it not formed true words.

"Where are you?" Santon lowered himself into a defensive crouch, his ax moving slowly from side to side, ready for instant use.

"Here." A tiny spiral of dust rose. Within the column of dancing brown motes appeared a faint glow. The glow intensified until it took on the vague form of a man. Santon felt as if he peered into another world—and, in a way, he did.

"A phantom!" he exclaimed.

"I roam these plains seeking my body. It is a lonely quest. Would you aid me?"

"I cannot," Santon said, relaxing his extreme posture. He lowered his battle-ax and moved the shield to one side for a better look at the ghostly figure. The phantom hovered two paces distant. The face glowed with an eerie pinkness and the body tapered off into the bottom of the swirl of dust; Santon could not tell where dust began and ghost-body ended. The features proved too indistinct for him to identify the phantom.

"I was lost in a battle on these plains over fourteen years ago. Since then I have sought aid from all who pass. You must help me. I've become so tired of roaming, neither alive nor truly dead. I have none of the bodily woes of the living but all the sorrows are mine to suffer. Forever! I cannot bear this burden much longer."

"What will happen if you can't?"

The phantom rippled like water in a pond filled with myriad fish beginning to feed. "I will surely go insane. Instead of knowing I should seek out my corpse, I will wander and embarrass myself completely, performing irrational acts. This behavior I have seen in others."

"Who were you? In life?"

"Dare I tell you?" the phantom wailed. "If I fought on the wrong side in the battle, you might think it a boon to let me suffer. I was only a petty soldier, a pikeman. Nothing more. I had nothing to do with the officer corps."

"Your allegiance does not interest me. I'll help, if I can."

"You will?" The phantom's excitement caused it to come apart. Bits of glowing substance flew in all directions, slowly coalescing as the ghost regained control. "How I have longed for one such as you."

"Where do you remember last?" asked Santon.

"Nearer the Iron Range. In a pass. Just going into a pass. We had ventured too far from the main body of our force. My squad started into the mountains when the enemy came from behind. We were trapped, unable to move forward quickly enough."

Santon nodded. These were the fears Vered had voiced about entering the Iron Range without being sure if any tracked them. He raised his eyes and studied the sky. The moon poked above the hills. The time for attack, if it came from their mysterious followers, if they even existed, would come soon.

"We enter the Iron Range on the morrow," Santon said, "and we have reason to believe we will be similarly attacked."

"By those camped a league toward the mountains?" asked the phantom.

"You've seen them? How many? Do they plan to attack us tonight?" He let his battle-ax drop and hang from its leather wrist strap and reached for the phantom, thinking to shake the information from the ghost. His hand passed through the ghostly substance. Santon experienced a momentarily tingling sensation in his fingers and nothing more.

"Sorry," apologized the phantom. "It is difficult for me. The ruffians yonder refused me aid. I became so enthused that I neglected to offer a trade of information when you so kindly agreed to help me find my corpse."

The phantom reformed after Santon's hand had sundered it.

"Come along. You must talk with Alarice."

"The Glass Warrior?" asked the phantom. "Many have spoken of her but so few have seen her. This is a signal honor for me."

"How do you know her name?" demanded Santon, instantly suspicious. He did not see how the phantom could be a spy for those following them. There was no need for the ghostly being to appear to him. Simply drifting disembodied around their camp would provide adequate intelligence for an attack.

"I . . . I know so many things and do not understand why. You are Santon. It is as if all living are known to me. In exchange for this worthless boon, I know naught of my body." The glowing column shook, as if the phantom cried ectoplasmic tears.

"Who follows us?"

"Do you want their names? Those I can give. But who orders them after you?" The phantom made a gesture Santon guessed to be a shrug of nonexistent shoulders. The man silently motioned for the phantom to follow. They returned to the camp. Alarice's cold eyes instantly locked onto the phantom.

"You found us a spy," she said with no enthusiasm.

"For us, against us, who can say?" Santon warmed his hand on the small cooking fire. Across from him Vered lay sleeping lightly. "I'll make a quick circuit of the perimeter and return. If they are to attack tonight, it will come soon."

"They will," said the phantom. It spun about, its substance agitated and glowing more brightly. "I don't want you hurt. Santon promised to help me find my body."

"I can help," said Alarice. "I might be able to scry your body."

"You are a wizard! But of course. The stories of the Glass Warrior say you are. It becomes so hard for me to think like this. Oh, thank you, thank you!"

Santon snorted and returned to his patrol. He had little liking for dealings with phantoms, yet this might prove to their benefit. If he had his way, entire battalions would be dispatched to scour Porotane to find the unburied bodies and properly consecrate graves for them. Leaving their shades to wander like this one did was needlessly cruel. Santon smiled without any humor. To die in battle was a risk all took. To drift aimlessly in search of your body after dying—that was a burden no one should bear.

Tiny sounds alerted him. He fell to his knees and hid behind a low tangle of shrubs. The moon had risen too high in the sky to cast good shadows on attackers from the east. Santon knew that the moon would illuminate him well for the enemy, though, if he ventured out into the open. He lay in wait, not daring to move. He wanted to shout, to alert Vered and Alarice. To do so would precipitate the attack and gain him nothing.

Three men skulked past him, not even noticing him. Santon kept his shield and battle-ax low to prevent vagrant moonbeams from reflecting and warning them.

Only when they had passed by and he had

assured himself a second wave did not follow did he turn and silently stalk the stalkers.

The one in the rear sensed him. Santon rushed forward, battle-ax raised. The man emitted a squeak more like a mouse than a human before the heavy spiked ball behind the ax blade crushed his skull. Santon's strong wrist flipped the ax around. The blade cut into the second brigand's leg. He fell to the ground, screaming in pain.

"Die, fool!" cried the man who had been in the lead. His sword flashed toward Santon's breast. A quick movement brought the glass shield into play. The blade deflected and Santon used the shield edge as a weapon, driving it into the man's arm. This caused the brigand to stumble off balance. Santon's ax assured that the assassin need never worry about his clumsiness again. Brains spattered over the moonlit ground to glow phosphorescently.

Panting with the exertion, Santon recovered. He stood and stared at the bodies. Death had come so quickly. It always did. Only now did he realize how it might have been his corpse cooling on the ground. His hand shook and sweat made the handle of the battle-ax slippery. No matter how many times he faced danger like this, he reacted strongly afterward, his stomach churning and threatening to regurgitate. Santon held down his gorge and concentrated on scouting. If three had come, there might be more.

He found no sign of other assassins creeping through the night. He returned to camp.

"You took your time returning. You got them?" asked Vered, casually lounging on his bedroll. For all the man's flippancy, Santon saw the tension in his body. Santon reacted physically to danger; Vered tried to laugh it off.

"Of course. Were there others?" The small movement of Vered's hand toward his sword showed that there had been. Vered had already cleaned the gore off his blade.

"Five," said Alarice. "Eight, all told."

"I got three. Does that end the madness for the night? I need sleep."

The phantom spoke up. "Five remain in camp."

Santon squatted down and stared into the embers of their fire. "Do we leave them be or take them out?"

"You promised the phantom that we'd find his body?" asked Alarice.

"I said that your magic might help us. I made no definite promise. But he can aid us. He died in an assault similar to the one we feared in the mountain passes."

"His body lies a hundred yards from their camp."

Santon sighed. Always it came to killing. For too many years he had been the best. He tired of it. "Let's go," he said, rising to his feet. "If I am to sleep this night there are five more who must die."

"Don't you even want to know whose men they are? Whether they are simple brigands or Theoll's soldiers?" asked Vered.

"What difference does it make? They want us dead. We must kill them first."

Vered rose like a feather on a summer breeze. "That's what I like about Santon. He's such a philosopher."

The five in the brigand camp died under ax and sword before the moon rose to zenith.

CHAPTER FOURTEEN

Baron Theoll pulled himself up to the greatest
height possible and still the assassin towered over
him. Trying not to be obvious about it, Theoll
moved around the table between them and
perched on one edge, a short leg swinging slowly,
to prove to himself that the pain had fled. He
glared at the man. He might be taller than the
baron but the assassin knew who was the more
powerful. His paleness had turned to a pasty white
before he had finished his sorry report.

"You let these two ruffians and a woman
defeat you?" Theoll asked in a voice both low and
menacing. "How is this possible? You were the
best in all Porotane. None came close to your skill
or stealth."

"They . . . it was magic, Baron. It had to be.
We could not fight them. They . . . they summoned
demons!"

Theoll snorted derisively. He knew better. The
Glass Warrior had proven more dangerous than
he'd thought possible. He had underestimated the
woman's abilities. Even though the assassins had
found her true path into the swamps after being
misled north, they had failed against her. And the
Demon Crown had slipped from his grasp!

"There is more," Theoll said. "Tell me."

"The two with her. They fight like a dozen warriors."

Theoll shook his head. Everything fell apart around him. His carefully built plans turned to ash. His assassins, the pick of all in the kingdom, proved ineffectual against a wizard and her two pets. His fists clenched so tightly that the fingernails cut into the flesh. Tiny crescents of blood formed. Theoll jumped to the floor, staggering slightly as his weakened legs yielded under his weight, and spun to prevent this worthless creation of his from seeing his infirmity.

Never let weakness show. Never. Especially to underlings.

Before Theoll formed the proper reprimand, a page burst through the door and stood breathless.

"What is it?" Theoll had little time for such intrusions. The boy would be punished.

"Baron, Dews Gaemock attacks the castle!"

"Impossible. Gaemock's forces withdrew. He can't reform his siege until fall." Theoll cocked his head to one side and listened hard. The pounding footsteps of hundreds of soldiers came to his ears. "Damn," he said, knowing that the page spoke truthfully. To the assassin, he said, "Wait here. Don't stir until I return."

It pleased him to see the man frozen to the spot by the command. Theoll motioned. The young page fled. Theoll followed closely, checking his dagger and making certain that the light leather armor he always wore covered the vital spots on his body. He burst into brilliant sunlight and squinted. By the time his vision cleared sufficiently, the battle raging below had progressed—too far.

"Who are they?" he demanded of the guard captain.

"Not Gaemock's troops as we first thought," the captain answered. "It might be a band of ruffians we found a few weeks ago. They headed to the sea and we ignored them."

"What do they hope to gain?" Theoll watched the flow of battle with a critical eye. Porotane's troops—he thought of them as his own—had been caught unawares. Their position proved poor for defense; the field commander showed a spark of intelligence. Unable to defend, he had attacked and split the rebel band in half.

"Lieutenant Squann's forces have been reduced by almost a hundred, with losses to the rebels of only a score," said the guardsman. "If Squann had not attacked when he did, they would have been wiped out."

"He should concentrate on the northern flank. Give him covering archery fire against their southern half."

The captain motioned and sent runners off to the far reaches of the castle's battlements. Flight after flight of feathered death arched into the air and fell in rebel ranks. The rebels had depended too heavily on surprise and too little on planning. Either an arrow had felled their leader or the leader failed to keep discipline in his ranks. The southern formation disintegrated, letting Lieutenant Squann commit his full force against the other half.

Theoll watched with little pleasure as the field commander killed every rebel that fell within sword range. No quarter was offered, although the rebels tried to surrender. Theoll wondered if this Squann knew he was being observed. Possibly. But the chance existed that Squann was vicious and offered no quarter under any circumstances. The baron made a small notation in a book he always carried with him to check out this commander. The assassins had done poorly. He needed new recruits for his personal guard.

"Why do they continue to attack?" he asked aloud.

"The rebels expect Duke Freow's death to weaken our resolve and crack our solidarity. They hope to assume the throne by a clever thrust at the proper instant. Yes, Baron, that's definitely the way I see their battle plans forming."

Theoll glared at the guard captain. This man was stupid. Oprezzi had been cunning, if not careful in his sexual liaisons with the Lady Johanna. But Oprezzi's replacement? Theoll suppressed the desire to throw the verbose fool over the battlements and to his death.

The baron spun and stalked off. Squann had turned the attack. The neighboring countryside would have to be scourged of all future threat. The spring and summer crops must not be allowed to suffer under the thousands of hooves of rebel cavalry. The food had to be used to supply the castle throughout the autumn and winter months. Theoll knew that Gaemock would never stop.

Kill him and perhaps end the single-minded drive for the throne. Maybe. Theoll had nightmares of Dews Gaemock's phantom ascending the throne, placing the Demon Crown on a vaporous skull, and ordering everyone put to death. The small baron shoved such nonsense away. Let it inhabit his dreams, not his waking moments. He hobbled back to his quarters, then paused.

An idea formed. The guards had abandoned

their posts in the castle corridors to protect the walls. Freow would be unattended. Theoll's fingers tapped along the hilt of his dagger. Making his decision, he hurried to the duke's quarters and burst inside.

One muscle strained against another as Theoll fought to keep from drawing his blade and plunging it into Freow's thin chest. The duke was not alone. Harhar capered and japed between baron and duke.

The jester turned and stared at the baron. "What is it, my lord? Do you come to help me entertain our duke?"

Theoll weighed the chance of killing the jester and the duke. Such would be for the best. Harhar carried in his dim-witted brain the knowledge of how Archbishop Nosto had been duped into putting Oprezzi to the Question. That little play had crushed Johanna's chance to ascend the throne. Her power gone, she had pulled back to defensive positions, trying vainly to reform her power base. With Nosto so firmly on Theoll's side, few would even talk to Johanna.

Harhar should die to protect the guilty knowledge of Nosto's deception. Theoll dared not have the archbishop turn the Inquisition against him.

But the jester was strong and young and the element of surprise had passed. In the corridor he heard the shuffling of guards returning. Theoll cursed his bad luck.

"I came to see how the duke is," he said lamely.

"Stronger. Stronger because he enjoys my jokes." Harhar did a handstand and began relating a preposterous story about two ducks and the king's handmaiden.

Theoll went to the duke's side and stared at him. Freow's eyelids quivered and then popped open. Theoll almost cried out in shock. For months the slow poison he administered had taken its toll on the duke. As if some horrid magic erased all that, Freow looked and acted stronger than ever.

"Theoll?" came a weak voice. "How nice of you to visit me."

"My . . . duke." Theoll bowed. "I am pleased to see you recovering from your grave illness." Theoll almost choked when Freow sat up in bed unassisted. The poison should have robbed the old man of every ounce of strength. He should have died by now!

"I recover too slowly," said Freow. "It is as if I have come through a veil of fog and the bright light of day has yet to burn all traces of the mist away from my tired old brain."

"You fare well, my duke." Theoll again cursed his missed chance. The poison had failed. He should have driven the dagger deep into Freow's putrid heart and seized the throne!

"My jests cheer him," declared Harhar. The lank-haired jester turned a set of powerful handsprings that brought him to the foot of the bed. He jumped straight up into the air and caught a bedpost. Harhar hung like a gigantic fly on the wall. Theoll wilted under the jester's hot, dark scrutiny.

Behind him he heard guards enter and resume their posts. Theoll bowed deeply and backed away, all thought of assassination passed. He would have to devise another scheme.

All the way back to his chambers, Theoll

stewed. When he finally entered his secure rooms, he boiled over. The lone assassin returning from the attempt to steal the Demon Crown from the Glass Warrior cowered.

"You," snapped Theoll, pointing at the assassin. "You failed once. Will you fail me again?"

"Never, my baron, never!"

"No, you wouldn't dare." Theoll slumped in his chair and stared at the frightened man. He had selected for courage as well as ability, yet this man almost burst into tears at the mere sight of his lord. Theoll rejoiced in this. It showed someone feared him. He had considered removing this abysmal failure permanently, executing him painfully as an example for others.

Theoll thought better of such a dire course now. The assassin would risk anything to serve him in return for his miserable life. If anything, that fear might make him all the more effective a tool to use against Duke Freow.

For a fleeting moment, Theoll worried over the failure of the poison. It had sapped the duke's strength for months. Why did it suddenly reverse itself when death should have been imminent? Could it be interference by the Lady Johanna? Theoll discarded that notion. Johanna's power had been broken with Oprezzi.

"Archbishop Nosto," he murmured.

"Baron?"

"Silence," he ordered. He had forgotten the assassin's presence in the room. His thoughts returned to the archbishop. Nosto might scheme against him. The Inquisition provided a convenient vehicle for obtaining information and exerting considerable power. Too many in Porotane feared heretics for the cleric's pogrom to be stopped. Had Nosto decided to save Freow and use him as a puppet?

Theoll shook his head. The notion was too preposterous. During the peak of Freow's rule, Nosto had been virtually exiled. Freow and Nosto had clashed constantly. Only when the duke took to his death bed had the archbishop again dared to return to the castle. The Inquisition had followed soon after.

An even more ridiculous idea was Nosto's assuming the throne. Never had a cleric become king of Porotane. The Demon Crown would destroy one so closely aligned with the saints. The tension between demon artifact and belief provided much of the power generated by the Demon Crown, or so Theoll believed. Archbishop Nosto could never surrender himself adequately to the immense demonic power of the crown to use it.

And without the Demon Crown on a true king's head, the civil wars in Porotane would continue. Should Archbishop Nosto assume the throne, the entire land would be split asunder in a matter of weeks.

Theoll pushed such nonsense from his mind. Nosto might lust after power but he found it by posing the Question, through the Inquisition, by acting the Inquisitor for the saints.

Some other power opposed him. But who might it be? Theoll had eliminated all the other players. He snorted. He had eliminated the strongest, but the factions against him still presented a difficult obstacle to overcome. If he killed Freow outright they would unite against him. Perhaps even Archbishop Nosto would turn on him. The cleric had lain with Johanna, of that he was sure. What other vices did Nosto have that he knew nothing about? The poison had been his best chance and its effect seemed blunted now.

Another sought the throne. If he could not decide who it was, he had only one clear choice. Freow must die quickly so that Theoll could immediately ascend the throne. Such a move would throw the opposition into disarray long enough for him to consolidate his power. Then none would dare oppose him!

"You will obey my commands?" he asked the assassin. The man's head bobbed up and down as if on springs. "Good. You will prepare for this mission carefully. You will make no mistakes. Is this understood?"

The man bowed his head.

Theoll tented his fingers and rested his chin on the peak. "Very good. You will assassinate Duke Freow in such a manner that it appears to have been done by, say, the Lady Johanna. Yes, she is a good choice."

"I am to kill the duke?"

"By the saints, you haven't turned deaf as well as stupid, have you? Yes, yes, *yes*! You will slay the old bastard. You will do it so that none can suspect me of the crime."

"When, my lord? It might take time so that none links us. I have been under your command for over a year."

"I understand that, fool. I'm not asking you to perform a suicide mission. I want you to kill Freow and leave subtle clues pointing to Johanna as the instigator. You are not to be caught or even suspected of the crime."

Theoll hesitated. He had the feeling that he

chose a weak tool for this task. The man had failed once. The Glass Warrior still had the Demon Crown—she still lived!

Theoll had no other choice. "You will do as ordered. I desire Freow's death within a fortnight."

"Yes, Baron." The assassin left quickly—and Theoll was left with a feeling of frustration.

Loud rapping came on the barred door of Theoll's sleeping chamber. The small man came awake instantly, hand on dagger, heart pounding and ready to face danger. He sat up and peered over at his bed—he never slept in the bed for fear of assassination. For weeks he had moved about the room, sleeping in chairs, under tables, even on the narrow, cold window ledge.

"Baron, come quickly. There is trouble. Duke Freow!"

Theoll wanted to laugh aloud. In only four days his assassin had done his job!

He pulled on clothing and went to the door. Outside stood a small squad of castle guards.

"What is it?" he asked, trying to keep the tone of his voice somber. "Am I needed?"

"At once, Baron. Hurry please."

Theoll almost ran to keep up with the escort's quick pace. He burst into Freow's chambers, ready to spout inane condolences. Instead, he choked.

Freow sat up in the bed, looking healthier than he had in over a year. Surrounding the bed were Archbishop Nosto, the physician, Johanna, a few minor nobles, and Harhar.

"We are glad you came so quickly, Baron," said Nosto. "There has been an attempt on the duke's life."

Theoll's eyes darted around the room. He saw feet sticking out from under a blanket on the floor. The lump under that blanket had to be the body of his killer.

"Yes, an assassin. He was slain before he could work his perfidy on the duke."

"But who . . ."

Nosto shook his head. "We do not know." The cleric stared straight at Theoll. Nosto knew but could not prove it.

"What happened?"

"I slept," Freow said. His voice cracked occasionally but came out strong otherwise. Too strong for Theoll's liking. "I heard noises, a struggle. The room was dark but I saw two dark figures. The killer was killed."

"How? By whom?" demanded Theoll.

Freow shrugged. "I did not see. The guards claim it was none of their rank." The old man smiled feebly. One parchment-skinned hand lay outside the coverlet as a tribute to the physician's skill in caring for the decrepit duke. "It would seem that I have an unknown protector in the castle."

"The saints smile on you, Duke," intoned Archbishop Nosto.

"Yes, I'm sure that is it." Theoll's mouth had turned drier than the Desert of Sazan. His poisons had failed. His assassin had failed. Who guarded Freow so well?

Who?

CHAPTER FIFTEEN

Vered put his hands over his ears to keep down the din from their horses' hooves echoing along the dark iron canyons. It muffled the sound a trifle but did nothing to diminish the pounding inside his skull.

"Not even rags stuffed in my ears help," Birtle Santon said in a too-loud voice.

"Is this the only pass?" complained Vered. "Surely other, quieter routes to the Desert of Sazan exist."

Alarice rode alongside. Her lips moved but Vered heard no words. She repeated; he caught the gist of her comment.

"Sorry," he said. "Santon and I never got used to silent communication. That's one reason we did so poorly in battle." Vered smiled as he remembered. "No commander dared send us on the dangerous missions. We chattered like birds quarreling over a tasty morsel. The others used sign language or semaphore. Not Santon and me."

The echoes from his voice rang from the iron walls of the canyon and returned to haunt him. He gazed up from the floor of the narrow canyon they followed. The walls had an ugly blackness to them, the only color being spots turning to rust from constant exposure to the elements. Truly, he knew why they called this sorry collection of rock the Iron Range. Such purity of ore he had never seen. Vered would have exchanged a fraction of the hematite for a grassy slope or a gently flowing stream.

They had encountered neither since entering the pass after slaying the brigands.

Alarice held up her hand. Vered reined in while Santon continued on to scout their path. In a voice low enough to be heard but not so loud that it triggered new echoes, Alarice said, "This is the spot where our phantom friend died."

Startled, Vered looked around. "So far away?" he said. "The remains were found not a league from where we slew the brigands. Your scrying proved remarkably accurate."

"Especially so since Patrin blocks my attempts to see into the City of Stolen Dreams."

Vered jerked nervously when the phantom appeared at his elbow. The sudden swirl of air caught up tiny bits of debris and dust laying on the floor and spun them in blinding circles.

"Is this truly the spot where I was slain?" asked the phantom. The intense longing in his voice communicated to Vered and touched the man's heart.

"Here you died. Your body was taken out of the pass, possibly for burial, possibly to prevent your enemy from learning the true numbers of your casualties." Alarice shook her head, sending a wild frizz of snowy white hair away from her eyes. She pointed. "There. You died there at the base of that hillock."

The phantom drifted toward the indicated spot and hovered. Vered knew it might have been his imagination but he thought the ghostly pillar took on added substance and became less transparent.

"Yes, I feel it. Here. I died here!"

Alarice whispered in Vered's stoppered ear. "The remains should be laid to rest on this spot. The digging will be difficult. The ground is extremely hard."

Vered kicked at the scattered rocks with his boot and found the layer of soil beneath. It looked as if they would have to blast through solid iron ore. Frowning at something he uncovered, he dropped to one knee and pawed through the rocks. A rusted corps insignia came to light. He lifted it for closer examination and saw that the medallion was brass, that the red splotch was dried blood. He sagged. Fourteen years, the phantom had said. For that long this bit of military uniform had lain exposed to the winds of winter and the searing heat of summer and still the blood remained.

"That was mine," said the phantom. "An insignia from the left shoulder of my uniform."

Vered nodded. He recognized it as such. "This is where you died," he said. He took out his dagger and scraped at the ground. It resisted. He worked until sweat poured down his face. The Glass Warrior added her blade to the chore. After Santon returned to report that the way ahead was clear for another day's travel, he added his nicked ax blade to the task. Hours later they had carved a shallow crypt in the stone.

Vered wiped the sweat from his face and sank back, the hard canyon wall supporting him.

"That's enough, is it not?" He had become increasingly disheartened as they dug, in spite of the phantom's enthusiastic encouragement for their task. Vered had found that the blood shed in this forgotten battle had seeped into the ground and turned the very soil rusty. The amount of life's blood needed to perform this transformation measured in gallons—and what distressed him the most was his ability to imagine such carnage. He and Santon had seen worse during their days together.

"Give me a hand," said Santon, struggling with the sack containing the remains.

"Then I'd be the one lacking a pair," said Vered. Santon glared at this tasteless joke at his expense and said nothing. Vered grunted as Santon pulled the sack containing the remains from the back of a packhorse and dropped it fully on Vered's shoulder. The smaller man staggered under the load, then turned and made his way to the grave. He tried to lower the sack as easily as he could. It landed with a *thunk*! loud enough to give birth to new echoes.

"I feel strange," the phantom said. "It . . . I cannot tell you what is happening."

"Rest easy," Alarice said. They piled rocks over the sack, then built a small arch above to mark the grave. She began the death litany.

"Peace," the phantom said. "I feel tranquility settling over me like a warm, comforting blanket. Thank you, my dear friends. For so many years I prayed for this. Thank you . . ."

The words vanished into echoes, drowned by the Glass Warrior's recitation. When she finished, all trace of the phantom had gone. For several minutes, the trio simply stared at the grave.

Vered broke the silence. "May we be as lucky to find peace in death."

Alarice looked at him sharply. "You don't have the second sight, do you?" she demanded.

"No. I have trouble predicting what I'm going to say and do next. The future is closed."

The Glass Warrior relaxed. "This quest has been difficult for me. It will become even more taxing before we . . . succeed."

Vered and Santon exchanged glances. Not for the first time, Vered wondered at the Glass Warrior's age. Alarice walked with a spring in her step and fought with reaction and strength that would be the envy of a new lieutenant of guards, but a miasma of age about her descended now and again. Vered thought she had come by the white hair honestly, by living through ages undreamed of by-ordinary men. She might match Santon's thirty summers or she might be three hundred. He could not tell.

"When do we leave these demon-damned passes?" asked Santon. "The echoes are driving me insane."

"Such torture is used by the Inquisitors," said Vered. "They place a bell over their victim's head, then ring it occasionally, when it is least expected. The sound is terrible, but the uncertainty is worse."

"There is no uncertainty to *these* echoes," said Santon. "We talk. Echoes. We ride. Echoes. Even the echoes spawn echoes."

"We must ride for another few days. How many, I cannot say."

"Our water runs low," Vered said. "We use more for the horses than I anticipated. The heat radiating off these accursed iron walls are cooking the water from our bodies, too." He tried to spit and couldn't form enough to clear the grit in his mouth.

"There is water," she said. Alarice closed her eyes and turned slowly. When she completed a full circle, she pointed to their left. "In that direction. A small spring. The lip of the basin is rusted but the water within is pure."

"Thank the saints for such a small favor," Santon said glumly. "It'd be my luck to find water poisoned by the heavy metals."

They mounted and rode until they found a crossing canyon. Vered swayed in the saddle, the heat putting him to sleep. The exertion from digging the shallow grave had also drained him, but putting to rest the shade of the fallen soldier had buoyed him. To become trapped between death and life, to wander endlessly seeking succor, was a fate he wished to avoid. To help another escape this limbo must give him a better chance. The Death Rota carried all acts good and ill performed while mortal and living. This day Vered had negated several of the reprehensible entries against his name.

"There," came Santon's booming voice. Vered struggled to open his eyes. The tiny puddle of water surrounded by the rust-brown iron shore looked more appealing to him than the coldest beer, the frothiest ale, the headiest brandy. He spurred his steed forward and dismounted.

"Should we sample the water first to be sure it won't harm the horses?" he asked. Better that one of them turn sick from unsuspected poison than to kill their mounts. No one could escape the Iron Range on foot. Not amid this sweltering heat and interminable twists and turns of rocky canyon.

"The water is pure," Alarice said. "I detect no spell placed on it. And my scrying shows nothing harmful within." She dangled a cord with a catamount's fang tied onto the end. The hot wind whipping along the canyon failed to stir the tooth. "If the water had been tainted, the tooth would point downward. It reacts only to my magic."

Vered knelt and cupped his hands. The water almost burned his lips. He spat it out. "It's almost boiling hot."

"Not that hot," said Santon. Although he sampled gingerly, the bigger man did drink. "The taste is peculiar."

"That comes from the iron. It is not harmful," Alarice said. She dipped her empty water skin into the pool and filled it. The wind caressed the exterior of the damp bag and evaporation cooled the contents. Only then did she drink. A satisfied smile crossed her lips.

"What can we do for the horses?" asked Vered.

Santon laughed. "They seem not to mind the temperature. Just be sure not to let them drink too much and begin to bloat."

Their three horses, plus the two captured animals they used as pack animals, shouldered one another to the side to stick their noses deep into the pool. They lapped noisily. The echoes annoyed Vered. He considered totally clogging his ears with mud to shut out the sounds.

Vered settled down and began to drift off to sleep. The heat soothed him, swaddled him, and took all burden of thought from his mind. His head swayed, then his chin dipped.

He awoke suddenly when he heard cackling laughter. Vered looked around, his brown eyes bloodshot from the heat. Shimmering curtains of heat waves danced from the walls and along the canyon they had traversed to reach this spot. But of others he saw naught. Again lethargy crept up on him and sleep controlled his mind.

—mine!

"No," Vered mumbled. "Can't have me." He stirred, wrapped his arms around himself, and noticed the sweat flowing copiously from his body. Too hot. He drifted into deeper sleep.

—you are my slave!

Vered experienced a moment of drowning, the fluids claiming his life being those that had given him life. Blood and sweat mingled and rose around him. He panicked. He fought, trying to escape. Ever higher rose the waters of death. Vered threw back his head, trying to keep his nose and mouth above the flood. The harder he tried, the more he sweat. The more he sweat, the higher the waters rose.

—surrender to me, my little one. you are mine!

"No," mumbled Vered. He thrashed from side to side. The lapping waves crested over his head. He felt himself sinking, a sailor on the seas of his own juices.

Sudden searing pain caused him to scream. His eyes popped open and he stared up into Alarice's concerned face. She held her glass dagger in one hand. A tiny drop of blood—his blood! —dripped from the tip.

"Do not go to sleep. You must not," she said. The concern in her voice frightened him.

"What's happening to me?"

"I had not expected to find any still alive. But one roams these mountains."

"What? A wizard?"

"A wizard's creation. A mind leech. It hunts only when its prey sleeps."

"I was drowning." Vered dragged his hand across his face. It came away drenched with sweat. He reached out and touched his shoulder; the hand found a bloody streak where Alarice had cut him to force him from his trance.

"I'm sorry. Pain is the only way to combat the lure of the mind leech."

"It made me think I was drowning," Vered said, his voice cracking from strain. He looked directly into the woman's cold gray eyes. "What would it have done to me?"

The shudder passing through the Glass Warrior's body made Vered not want to hear the answer —yet he had to. Alarice said, "It saps your will. Slowly, you become its slave, doing its bidding. The more you resist, the more ways it finds to break your resolve."

"When we're awake, can it get us then?"

"No, not as easily. I felt it tugging at the edges of my mind, but it sensed my control of magic. The mind leech is a cowardly beast, never risking physical contact. It hunts with its mind—and this is how it triumphs."

"It uses slaves to kill for it? The slaves tend it?"

Alarice nodded. "They hunt, they protect, they obey. Submit once, and its insidious mind probe slips into your will. Submit further and you are doomed."

"So it's a physical being," said Vered. "One that can die?"

"Vered, no. I know what you are thinking," said Alarice. She took a step away. "We dare not seek out the mind leech. There is no time. Patrin. The City of Stolen Dreams. We must not tarry."

"This creature might be sent by Patrin," said Santon. "To kill it is to weaken Patrin."

"To attempt to slay a mind leech is easy. To accomplish such a feat is almost impossible. Any fear you might have would be turned against you."

"We dare not let it rove the Iron Range," said Vered. He yawned. "Besides, we can never win free of this wretched, hot place before falling asleep."

"You are especially vulnerable to it now, Vered," she said. "It has almost taken you."

"Then we *must* find it. No other way exists for us to safely escape the mountain passes," said Santon.

"Is there *any* fear in your heart, armless one?" she asked.

"Fear?" Santon shook his head. "Bitterness? Yes."

"I think there is fear," Alarice said. She circled, her dagger point raised. "Is there not a small shred of fear that your left arm will wither like your right? To lose that arm in combat? To fall and break it and starve to death?"

"Don't be ridiculous." Santon's voice lacked confidence. Both Alarice and Vered heard the worry hidden by years of denial.

"How dangerous is it facing a mind leech— with real fear lurking inside you?" asked Vered. He hastily added, "I'm seething with fear myself. It wouldn't do for me to approach this matter without knowing the full extent of my danger."

Santon's heavy breathing slowed. Vered had lessened the tension the one-armed man felt. But what might happen if Birtle Santon confronted the mind leech and this gnawing, buried fear was turned against him?

"The creature is able to attack several at a time. Simply presenting a united front will not permit us to triumph," said Alarice.

"Are there spells you can cast to destroy it?"

"No, Vered, none. I am not a wizard of Patrin's class." She laughed without humor. "I am unable to magically defeat even a creation like the leech."

"We must try," said Vered. "The three of us. Can you predict success with this monster lying in wait for us? An unsuspecting moment, a drifting into sleep, an unrecognized fear, and we are victims, not rescuers."

Alarice's face contorted in anger. "By the saints, you are right. Damn you for that!"

"Where do we find the leech?" Santon asked. "Near, I trust. Watching Vered yawn and stretch is making me sleepy, too."

Alarice looked around, up the towering walls of iron. "High. It will have its lair high so that it can look down on its prey. And near. It is a living creature as we are and needs water."

"Since this is all the water we're likely to find in this miserable stretch of the Iron Range, let's go upslope," said Vered.

"It might lair near the snow line." The tallest peaks retained heavy white caps and only reluctantly allowed thin trickles of moisture to creep downward. In another few weeks or even days, the spring sun would send down torrents from the melting snow.

"Dangerous," said Alarice. "The mind leech is sensitive to temperature. Physically it is weak. Only through strength of mind and the mental weakness of its prey can it survive."

"Let's look for traces of its slaves obeying its

will. I've never known slaves to be particularly neat nor slave masters to care," said Santon.

They tethered their horses and went into the searing heat of the iron canyons in search of spoor. Only a few paces farther into the canyon Vered discovered a well-chewed carcass. He called, waited for the echoes to die, and then motioned to the others. He pointed silently.

Alarice closed her eyes. She turned slowly, trying to locate the mind leech. When she stopped and her face turned as white as her hair, both men acted. As one they started up the slope, the loose rock coming back downhill in dusty torrents. Vered reached the top first. His short sword swung as he yelled in attack. ·

"Boars! Three demon-damned boars!"

The rush of one tusker sent Vered back-pedaling too fast. He lost his balance and slid down the slope, enduring minor cuts and abrasions until he regained his feet at the bottom.

"Careful, Santon!" he called. Vered remembered what Alarice had said about the mind leech finding the festering sore of fear in a man's mind and using it against him.

"Careful be damned. Get your ass back here and help me!" The heavy battle-ax rose and fell. An anguished squeal told of porcine death. Vered and Alarice hurried back to the top of the slope. Santon held at bay the other two tuskers.

The yellowed fangs snapped and flashed at Vered, taking away part of his breeches. He avoided the filthy fang and the possible infection it offered by a hairsbreadth. Off balance again, stumbling forward, he lunged with his short sword. The glass tip penetrated the boar's flank. The ponderously heavy pig died without a sound; Vered's blade had found its heart.

Vered laughed joyously. The adrenaline flowed through his arteries. The fight brought him to full awareness of his world, gave him confidence —and allowed him to know his true enemy.

Birtle Santon stood over the last boar, his heavy ax lodged in the animal's thick skull. Santon was Vered's enemy. Santon would split his skull asunder as he had done to Vered's ally, the tusker.

Vered pulled his blade free and advanced. In the distance he heard the Glass Warrior calling to him. He ignored her. Santon must die. Kill or be killed!

The expression on Vered's face when he lunged and missed by a fraction of an inch told of his expertise. None bested Vered in battle! Not even a demon in human form like Santon.

"Vered, stop, don't!" Santon used his shield to deflect a lunge.

"Both of you, stop," came Alarice's harsh command.

Vered saw fear on Santon's face. He knew he could not fail. He redoubled the speed and power of his attack, working around, trying to pink Santon's good arm. Only by playing on his fear of losing his left arm might he slay this foe.

"I don't want to do this, Vered. Please, don't force me." Santon parried the blows with his heavy ax, but his protective glass shield accomplished more.

"The mind leech," pleaded Alarice. "It creates fear to gain control over you."

"It has Vered," Santon cried in anguish. "I don't want to harm him."

The Glass Warrior did not reply. Vered circled even faster. His heart almost exploded in fear when he saw the woman enter a shallow cave.

"No, stop, don't go in there!" he shouted. Vered broke off the attack he launched against Santon. He had to stop the Glass Warrior!

Santon used the edge of his shield to smash into the side of Vered's head. The smaller man went spinning, blood matting his brown hair. The impact jolted Vered and pain burned through his brain—and cleared it!

"The mind leech," he gasped. "It used me. Alarice is going after it. We must help her!"

Santon looked at him skeptically, then indicated that Vered should precede him into the cave. Vered wasted no time. He had not detected the leech's insidious presence in his mind. He had been too wrapped up in the heat of battle. But now he knew the sensations. The instant he entered the cool mouth of the cave, he felt the leech again trying to subvert him.

"Santon," he said. "It works on me. Help me!" Vered turned to his friend. Santon stood in silence, as immobile as a marble statue. The expression on his face told Vered that the leech had taken over the man's mind.

Without thinking, Vered dropped to the cave floor and kicked out, his legs scissoring. One foot went behind Santon's ankle. The other foot snapped into his kneecap. Like a giant tree felled in a forest, Santon crashed to the rocky ground. When he sat up, the dazed look had passed and one of chagrin replaced it.

"The demon-damned thing had me!" he exclaimed.

"Alarice. We must help her." Together the

men hurried into the depths of the cave. Less than ten paces into the low-ceilinged cave they found the Glass Warrior. She stood with sword drawn. Her entire body trembled, as if she fought against unseen bonds.

"There," she said between clenched teeth. "There it is. The mind leech!"

Vered almost laughed. The pitiful creature cowering against a cave wall could hardly be the magical beast capable of subverting his mind. It was smaller than a princess' lap dog, a sickly pink in color, and had eyes as round and wide as yellow spring flowers. A long, slender tongue probed constantly from between its lips. No teeth showed as its lips drew back in a grimace.

"We must kill it!" Alarice shrieked. The echoes down the iron cave assaulted Vered's ears and sent new waves of pain into his head. The surge of agony pulled him free once more of the mind leech's power.

A heavy hand tried to restrain him. Vered twisted, grabbed Santon's left wrist, and broke free. The fear on Santon's face came not from within but from the leech's fear for its own death. It had again taken over Birtle Santon.

Vered dodged to one side, tripped Santon, then used his dagger on the mind leech. The first prick produced a tiny spurt of thin, orange blood. Vered felt the lifting of mental pressure as the leech panicked, sensing its own death.

Vered had no chance for a second strike. Alarice's glass sword slashed past, barely gutting the mind leech before Santon's ax decapitated it.

The magical creature's death released them totally from its mental influence. The trio sank to the cave floor and shook in reaction. Alarice reached out and put her arms around both men's shoulders. For a long time, no one spoke.

Then Santon said, "See? I told you. I'm not afraid of losing my arm. I'm afraid of nothing!"

"At least one of us has kept his sense of humor," said Vered. It was all he could do to keep from staring at the dead mind leech and reliving the horror of its bondage.

Chapter Sixteen

Vered almost tumbled from the saddle. Exhaustion had taken its toll on him over the past three days. They had defeated the mind leech, but the heat, the constant pounding echoes, the hardship of traveling through the barren Iron Range had worn him down.

"There," came Alarice's quiet voice. For a moment, he thought he had gone deaf. No echo returned to torment him. He rubbed his bleary eyes and sat straighter in the saddle. Hot winds blew at his back. For a moment, this confused him. Then he realized that they had finally escaped the black mountains and had emerged on the side most distant from fair, green Porotane.

Shock rolled through him. He had never recovered fully from the encounter with the mind leech. Afraid to fall asleep because of the nagging fear of having his mind taken over, Vered had become increasingly tired. The heat radiating from the high walls of the iron canyons had also sapped his strength, but now he stared out across land presenting a true challenge.

Vered was not sure he had the strength for it.

"Never have I seen such desert," he said. The barren waste appeared stripped of all vegetation.

Huge dunes of ochre sand rose like waves in the ocean. The tireless winds had cut creases into the sides of the dunes in their quest to move the ponderous mounds from one location to another. Here and there Vered saw the grit whipping along the ridges. The winds caught it and sent it upward, sometimes over five hundred feet high in a miniature tornado. More often, the winds played sleight of hand and hid the airborne sand behind the dunes.

"The Desert of Sazan," said Santon. "Only once before have I seen it. Luckily, I skirted the edge on my way south to Rievane."

"We must cross it. Straight across. In that direction." Alarice stared into the heart of this sprawling, overheated monster.

"Water," said Vered. "Do we have enough? Just looking at it turns my mouth into a furnace."

"How far do we need to go before finding the City of Stolen Dreams?" Birtle Santon hooked one leg across the saddle pommel and bent forward. "Vered has a point. We could never find water if we begin wandering aimlessly."

Alarice silently held out her scrying cord and crystal. The sunlight caught the facets of the glass splinter and turned them into glittering rainbows. Santon raised his hand to hold back the blinding glare. Vered found himself drawn into the ever-changing pattern as Alarice spun her spells.

The crystal spun in circles, never stopping until the Glass Warrior's spell came to completion. Like a true compass needle, the crystal pointed in the direction Alarice had indicated.

"Perhaps it means we should follow the hind end and go back into the Iron Range," said Vered.

"The City of Stolen Dreams," she said. "I . . . I cannot see it. Patrin still prevents direct viewing through a scrying spell, but I can do this much. My power seems to grow."

"Enough to confront Patrin directly and challenge him for the twins?" asked Santon.

"We don't even know if this Patrin has them. All we truly know is what Tahir told us—and I brand him a liar. He might have been imprisoned, but what evidence do we have that it was Patrin's doing?"

"Ah, Vered, you doubt even the rising of the sun every morning." Alarice put away her scrying crystal.

"There's no way to know if the sun will rise until it does," he pointed out. "Simply saying it will because it always has before is to deny change."

"I'll wager that it does," said Santon. "How much on the rising of the morrow's sun?"

"Fifty gold pieces," said Vered.

"Do you want odds?"

"Fifty to one."

"You seek twenty-five hundred if it does not?" Santon laughed. "What a crazy bet! If the sun does not rise, what matters gold?"

"At least I'll die with money owed me. The saints might appreciate that and enter it in the Death Rota."

"We will not die. We will prevail." The Glass Warrior spurred her mare forward. The horse hesitated when the hard hematite of the Iron Range turned to shifting sands beneath her hooves, but Alarice's insistence kept the animal moving. Vered and Santon followed, silently agreeing with the mare that they should not venture forth.

Vered let the Glass Warrior ride ahead. In a low voice, he said, "We can stop this now. There's no need for us to continue with her. What use can we be against Patrin?"

"We've not been promised riches," agreed Santon. "Nor are we likely to find anything but death."

"The Demon Crown is a dangerous relic. The wearer might become perverted by its power. The war might worsen."

"Even with a strong ruler, the civil war might have raged overlong," said Santon. "There is nothing to suggest that a new ruler will put an end to the warring."

"You mentioned Rievane to the south. What sort of city is it?"

"A fine one," said Santon, remembering with relish. "Women come into the street and beg you to join them in their soft bed and share their soft flesh."

"What of their men?"

"Few. Most go into the desert to hunt artifacts. They are gone much of the time, leaving the women—and how fair and beautiful they are!—to pine away."

"My kind of place."

"Ah, yes, Vered. And mine. And the women. They are alone so much of the time, they seek out companionship in foolish ways. Gamble? They are worse than even you! Anyone who could not come away from Rievane with a pouch brimming with gold is a fool."

"And the women."

"Yes, and the lovely, lovely women."

The men fell silent, each lost in his own thoughts. But neither looked to the south toward Rievane. Both stared at Alarice's back, the proud set of her head, the straight back, the determination in her mount. Vered's mind turned over and over as he wrestled with the problems of following the Glass Warrior. She offered hope to Porotane.

For Vered and Santon, she offered hardship and pain and probable death. Vered forced his body to forget some of the tiredness. He saw how Santon responded to the woman. Alarice had a quality about her that he found appealing—for Santon it had been irresistible. He could not deny his friend Alarice's companionship and love.

He forced such a notion from his mind. He had no designs on Alarice, and Santon's attachment to her had no bearing on his own decisions. He and Birtle Santon had gone their separate ways often enough in the past, only to rejoin and rediscover their friendship. If he let Alarice and Santon continue and headed for Rievane or some other spot to while away the time, neither would object. Vered had to admit that he stayed with Alarice because of the adventure it afforded. Life had not been dull, but it had become routine.

Brigands and rebel bands and renegade wizards and constables. Dodging them and trying to live the best he could took on a deadly sameness. Danger followed by flight and a seeking of new territory. Alarice offered something different and, as much as it wore him down physically, Vered had never been more excited about the future.

"Baron Vered," he said to himself, letting the title roll from his tongue like a honey lozenge.

"Rogue Vered," Santon said gruffly, interrupting his fine daydream. "We'll be lucky to escape this alive, much less with fine and fancy titles."

"One can hope," Vered said. "Restoring a monarch to the throne ought to be worth something."

"A title is little enough. What would you be like as a ruler of a small barony?" asked Santon. He answered his own query. "Miserable, that's how you'd be. So would I. What do we know of rule?"

"More than Freow, if Alarice's tale is even half true."

"He has done well enough, for a common ruffian," said Santon. "But would you want to live as he does?"

Vered's face tightened as a breath of hot desert wind brushed by. Pillars of dust rose on either side as cyclonic winds pulled aloft huge amounts of sand. He laughed aloud. Even if he had to live in a miserable place like the Desert of Sazan, Vered would not trade places with Duke Freow.

"My feelings, too," said Santon. "We have a freedom to roam."

"A freedom to do!"

Alarice had reined in. They came even with her. She said in a voice carrying a steel edge, "We also have the freedom to die. There. The City of Stolen Dreams."

"So soon?" Vered peered into a haze of dust blowing across the dunes. He saw nothing.

"Patrin's magical city is in the center of the Desert of Sazan."

"But," protested Santon, "we've ridden less than an hour!"

"We could ride for eternity and never find the city—if Patrin desired it."

The woman's words caused Vered to shiver, in spite of the furnace winds gusting around him.

"You say that Patrin *wants* us to enter this phantom city of his?" Vered did not like the implications. He felt like a bug being drawn into a spider's killing web.

"That is true," Alarice said.

Vered started to ask where this mysterious city was when he heard a deep rumbling. It built to a roar. He fought to keep his horse from bolting. The sound mounted, higher, deeper, until Vered felt his internal organs grinding against one another. And appearing through the brown haze came a city shimmering not with heat but with magic.

"The City of Stolen Dreams," Alarice said in a low voice. "The place where all your dreams can be snatched away and you are left hollow and haunted."

"Patrin steals dreams? Truly?" asked Santon.

"He tends the poisoned gardens of your mind, finding those weeds most likely to destroy you. The fine plants Patrin plucks and kills. What remains is vile."

"He drives his victims insane?"

"Worse, Vered," said Alarice. "He leaves them bitter and knowing that their lives were once better. Your fondest ambition, your greatest dream, *that* is Patrin's target."

"What are we to do? How do we fight him?" Birtle Santon looked uneasily at his withered arm. Vered read the concern in his friend's face. Recovering the use of that nerve-injured arm was Santon's dream. To lose that meant to lose much of the will to live.

"No sword can defeat Patrin. His weapons are magical. He is not the greatest of all wizards—the Wizard of Storms is that—but Patrin is powerful."

"More powerful than even the Glass Warrior?" came a rumbling voice. "Such humility. I never thought to hear it from you, dear lady."

Vered looked about but saw no one. He had almost called out to Alarice, named her name. He did not know if Patrin held this power over her, but he would not be the one giving it inadvertently to Patrin.

"Come. We ride to the City of Stolen Dreams," she said. Slowly, the trio rode forward. Outwardly, they showed no fear, but Vered fought hard to keep his hands from shaking. His horse trembled, eyes wide and nostrils foaming. Alarice's mount reacted similarly. Of Santon and his horse he saw nothing. The man rode behind.

But the Glass Warrior gave him courage. She rode, back ramrod stiff, hand easy on the reins, and with a determination to her that outshone any possible fear. Courage lay not in having no fear but in overcoming it.

The hollow clicking of the horses' hooves against paved street startled him. Vered looked around, then spun in the saddle and peered behind. The Desert of Sazan had vanished totally. Everywhere he looked, he saw a fabulously rich city. Buildings constructed of jasper and jade and onyx. Fixtures of silver and precious stones. Windows of stained glass depicting valiant scenes of combat and courage, crystalline sheets with beveled edges opening into lavish suites and courtyards with delicately spraying fountains filled with subtle perfumes. Everywhere he looked he saw opulence and . . . emptiness.

"Where are the citizens of this fine city?" he asked.

"There are none. Who can live without dreams?" asked Alarice.

Again Vered shuddered. To Santon he said, "My aspirations are simple but they are *mine*. I have no wish to lose them."

"Speaking seems sacrilegious," said Santon. "Any sound in this dead city is wrong."

Vered looked along intersecting streets, some paved with gold and other precious metals, some homey and quiet and begging for the laughter of children and the soft sighs of lovers. No sound reached him. Only the muffled clicking of their horses' hooves interrupted the deathly silence.

"Where do we find Patrin?" he asked the Glass Warrior.

"We ride until we come to him. As before, it might be an hour or it might be eternity. This is Patrin's center of power. We do his bidding or die."

"Why doesn't he just kill us?" asked Vered. "We disturb him. Surely, a wizard who hides in a place such as this does not wish to waste time with our like."

"Patrin did not exile Tahir and steal away the twins for amusement. He has plans. Somehow, we must fit into the matrix of those schemes."

"She has a point," said Santon. The man looked around, his sharp eyes missing nothing. "Patrin's power is immense to maintain such a city. He wants more, and we can give it to him."

"Very observant, Birtle Santon," came the booming voice. The three halted. From a small, simple peasant's hut walked a man of medium height, age, and coloring. Of his clothing, Vered saw nothing out of the ordinary. In truth, the harder he tried to find something unique about this man, the more he failed.

"It is a trick of Patrin's," explained Alarice. "He manipulates his image. I am uncertain that any has looked upon his true visage."

"Always the skeptic, eh, Warrior?" The man held out his hand. A tiny sun appeared. Vered held up his own hands to shield his eyes from the intense glare. So bright did the miniature sun grow that Vered saw the bones within his hand as the light passed through his flesh. Then the burning orb winked out of existence, as if it had never been.

"Your dreams are common," said Patrin. "Hardly worth my time." The wizard sighed deeply. "So few have uncommon dreams these days. Do you have any idea why this is so, Glass Warrior?"

"You rob humanity of its best, Patrin."

"Hardly, my dear. I find *your* dreams of interest, but they are not out of the ordinary. In fact, they fall into a category that perplexes me. You do not seek personal gain or glory on this quest of yours."

"You were always able to discern truth in motive," said Alarice.

"I do more than detect it, I collect it," he said. Patrin turned to Santon. "Your dreams are painfully mundane. You seek her love." Before Santon could protest, the wizard pointed to Vered. "And yours. You have a different set of ambitions. You talk of baronies and titles. Those are not what you really seek. You dream of unending friendship. Fear of loneliness drives you more than attaining any other goal."

To this Vered said nothing.

"You begin to bore me, Patrin. You know why I have come."

"Ah, yes, the royal twins. I know that you've spoken with that fool Tahir."

"Your spell killed him."

"Hardly possible. I turned him into an immortal creature so hideous that he would cringe whenever he saw his own reflection. What other fate could I give to a wizard who thought so highly of his good looks? What held him in the swamp, that's another matter and one not of my doing."

"He died."

Patrin peered at Alarice, as if believing her a liar. Slowly, the expression turned neutral. "You speak the truth. Tahir is dead. You countered my spell? I had no idea you controlled such power, Warrior."

"Another wizard's spell chained him to the swamp?" asked Vered. "The Wizard of Storms?"

Vered saw a flash of fear cross Patrin's face. He hid it so quickly that Vered began to doubt he had seen any emotion.

For the first time since entering the City of Stolen Dreams, Vered felt that success might be possible. Alarice had made Patrin out to be incredibly powerful. That he might be, but there were others he feared. This Wizard of Storms produced definite anxiety. And what of Alarice? She had protested for so long that she possessed only tiny powers. What magical spells were hers to command? Vered had the feeling that she had told them very little about her true abilities.

"You must be tired after your travels," Patrin said, suavely moving from a topic that disturbed him. "Enjoy the hospitality of my city. The entire city. Sample the dreams I have placed about it. See what can be yours."

Patrin whirled and vanished through the doorway of the simple hut. Vered took two quick paces and followed. He peered into the hut; it was empty.

"He vanished," Vered reported.

"Patrin always had a flair for dramatic entrances and exits," said Alarice. She looked from one man to the other. "Thank you for not mentioning my name aloud. He may try to trick this knowledge from you. As you value your life, so should you value my name. None of us will leave the City of Stolen Dreams alive if Patrin learns it."

"But you know his name. Can't you use it against him?" asked Santon.

The expression on Alarice's face told them more than they desired to know. Vered felt the coldness in his belly spread until icy fingers clutched at his heart. Alarice had been using this against Patrin, in spells so subtle that they had not detected them. Without these magics, Patrin would have slain them instantly.

"Yes," she said softly. "I am your only defense against him."

"Can you overwhelm him?" asked Vered. "With either spell or sword?"

"It must be with magic. While he remains within the boundaries of this city, Patrin is invincible against physical force."

Vered frowned, a disturbing thought occurring to him. "If this is so, why did he leave to imprison Tahir?"

"Patrin's reasons must have been more important than life itself to him."

"Power," said Santon. "Only more power

would draw a wizard from such a fortress." He looked around the empty, haunted streets.

"And it has to do with the Demon Crown," concluded Vered. "Can Patrin wear it?"

"No more than I," said Alarice.

"There is more to this than a sage can unravel," declared Santon. "Certainly more than I can consider on an empty belly. Is Patrin's offer of hospitality to be taken as truth?"

Alarice's face had become pinched and drained of blood. She nodded slowly. "He can do nothing to us."

"Your spells?" Santon moved closer. His good hand rested on her shoulder.

"Yes." She leaned heavily on him. Vered led the way into the heart of the City of Stolen Dreams, letting Santon and Alarice follow at their own pace. He marveled at the richness of the place— and worried at the souls lost to afford Patrin this luxury.

"This seems a good spot to spend a few hours," he said. A magnificent structure rose in the architectural style of Lubraenian palaces. Filigreed arches rose over curtains beaded with precious gemstones. Buttresses lifted and met the soaring walls, supporting and adding an element of grace and delicate beauty. Vered went inside. There lay the true attraction for him.

"Nothing is lacking," he said. "Except a few servants."

The curtains rattled as a plainly dressed man pushed through. Vered smiled and motioned to the servant.

"We need food and drink. Some white wine. From the Uvain Plateau, of course." Vered hesitated when he saw the look of anger cross the servant's face. "You *are* a servant?" Vered demanded.

"I am ordered to serve you," the young man said with more than a hint of bitterness in his voice. "I am Lord Patrin's apprentice."

"A wizard's apprentice serving me. I like the idea."

Santon and Alarice had finally followed him inside. Alarice stopped and stared at the apprentice wizard. She said, "Well, Vered, you like the notion of a young sorcerer serving you, eh?"

"I do," Vered declared. But something in the woman's tone put him on guard.

"Then you must love the idea of a prince serving you." Alarice bowed deeply. "Prince Lorens, we have come to take you back to Porotane to assume the throne."

Vered's mouth opened and closed. No words came out. He stared at the apprentice wizard—and king of Porotane.

CHAPTER SEVENTEEN

Vered struggled to find words. Nothing came out.

"Prince Lorens," said Alarice. "We have come in search of you."

"I am not a prince. I am Lord Patrin's apprentice." He stiffened and took a step away from the Glass Warrior. "He warned me of your lies. I am a commoner, not of royal blood. He told me you would try to drive a wedge between us."

"No lies," said Alarice. She examined the young man carefully. Fully twenty-four summers, he resembled dead King Lamost enough to dispel any doubt about his paternity. "Your uncle, Duke Freow, has ruled as regent until you were found. The duke is dying. It is time for a true heir to regain the throne and put an end to the wars raging in Porotane."

"This is my home." The sullen expression on the young man's face angered Vered.

"Porotane is your home. You and your sister were kidnapped."

"Yes," cut in Santon. "What of Lokenna? Is she also in this dead city?"

"My sister?" Lorens almost spat out the name, as if it left an acid taste on his tongue. "She has gained what she sought. May the demons take her!"

Vered and Santon exchanged glances. There seemed little need in pursuing this line of questioning. Lorens had been found; Alarice was convinced of his blood. Why seek out the sister?

"You cannot turn your back on Porotane. Your people need you."

"My lord needs me. No one else." Lorens glared at her. "If you speak the truth, why has it taken so long for someone to locate me? I have not hidden. Why has the duke not summoned me previously? My lord does not prevent travelers from entering our city."

"You do not believe," said Alarice. "You must be convinced."

"That is not possible." Lorens crossed his arms and glowered.

Without another word, Alarice pulled out the black velvet bag cradling the Demon Crown. She tugged at the fabric and withdrew the crystalline box holding the crown. Inside, the demonic circlet glowed more brightly than when Vered had donned it.

"The Demon Crown," Lorens said. His arms dropped to his sides and he moved forward to stare at the crown. "I have read about the demon Kalob's gift in my lord's grimoires. I always doubted." Eager hands took the box and lifted it. Vered squinted to keep from being blinded by the green-glowing crown.

"Put it on," urged Alarice. "Wear the Demon Crown and know the truth. Patrin has lied to you. You, Lorens, are the true heir to the throne of Porotane."

Lorens opened the clear crystal lid and lightly

touched the crown. The blaze of glory did not strike the young man dead. Instead, the green deepened in hue, became less eye-searing. Lorens lifted the crown and placed it gingerly on his brow.

"I *see!*" he cried. "Beyond the city, I can *see!*"

"You are the rightful king of Porotane. This is your father's legacy. You must return with us and take your place in history."

Lorens spun around and around, his face contorted with insane rapture.

"Santon, Vered," the Glass Warrior said urgently. "Take the crown from him. He is like one drunk."

"Drunk with power," said Vered. Knowing that only he could touch the Demon Crown, he motioned for Santon to attack low. When the one-armed man hit Lorens behind the knees and sent him toppling, Vered snared the crown before it struck the floor. He recoiled in shock as the magic flowed through him, even in this brief contact. He *saw* again—and the lure of such power proved almost more than he could bear. If it had not been for Alarice lightly touching his arm and drawing him back, he would have followed the images blasting into his brain wherever they took him.

"Here, Vered," she said softly. Alarice held out the opened crystalline case. He dropped the Demon Crown into its receptacle. The instant it left his hand, he sagged to the floor, drained.

Vered blinked and saw that Lorens had experienced much the same enervation. But the royal heir recovered quicker.

"The Demon Crown," crowed Lorens. "Such a treasure! It surpasses any of the dreams my lord has hidden away in the city."

"It will be yours—when you ascend the throne." Alarice stashed the box back in the velvet bag.

"Mine. It's mine! I want it now!" Only Santon's powerful left arm circling Lorens' neck kept the young wizard from ripping it out of Alarice's grasp.

"He's king of Porotane," protested Vered. "Leave him be, Santon."

"He thinks he's a demon-damned commoner. I think he is—"

"Santon!" The Glass Warrior's sharp command silenced the man. He released Lorens, who returned to his sullen glaring and surly manner. The apprentice spun and stalked from the room.

"And he never did bring me food or the fine Uvain Plateau white wine," said Vered.

"He is Patrin's pawn. The wizard has molded Lorens to his will over the years." Alarice looked worried. "And what of his sister? What became of Lokenna?"

"What'll become of us?" demanded Santon. "He'll tell Patrin that we have the Demon Crown. Do you think the wizard will let us go free without leaving it behind?"

"A moment," said Vered. "If Patrin is so powerful, why did he not sense the presence of the crown? It is a potent artifact. Surely, a sorcerer of his acumen must be able to sense such power."

Alarice smiled faintly. "I am not without my own spells. But I am sure that Patrin knows that we carry the Demon Crown. I worry more about Lorens. He is heir to the throne, but he must *want* to rule. He has had no training, other than that given him by Patrin."

"We install Lorens as king and Patrin will

become the true power, no matter what the young-ling king does with the Demon Crown." Santon settled into a chair and rested his chin on his hand. "Was that the wizard's plan?"

"Patrin is powerful within the City of Stolen Dreams," said Alarice. "Controlling Lorens and the crown would make him even more of a force to be reckoned with. But it cannot be the full scope of his plan."

"This Wizard of Storms," said Vered. "Patrin is terrified of him. Could he use Lorens and the Demon Crown against him?"

"Ah," said Alarice. "There is more than a hint of truth to what you say, Vered. The crown might give Patrin the power to upset a delicate magical balance between two foes."

"Then Porotane means nothing to Patrin?" asked Santon.

Vered shook himself and rubbed circulation back into arms and legs. The effects of his fleeting contact with the Demon Crown passed. He left Alarice and Santon to their weighty discussion of Patrin's motives and their future plans. His belly grumbled and he could not spit because of the dryness in his mouth. More than reason, he re-quired food and wine.

The pair chattered away while Vered explored the room. He had picked well. The furnishings outshone anything he had seen in Porotane. A single gold-legged couch or a finely wrought chair would fetch a pile of coins big enough to keep him happy for months. Years!

He circled the room, half-listening to his friends. Vered stopped and looked at a small stoppered vase placed carefully in a wall niche. The vase had the look of a storage vessel. Thinking it might contain dried fruit or grain, Vered took it from its shelf. He turned it over in his hands, studying the patterns on its ceramic surface. Vered shrugged. The patterns meant nothing. He preferred his art to represent something.

With a flick of his thumb, he broke the wax seal.

Vered shrieked, dropped the vase, and grabbed his groin. He felt himself growing to monstrous proportions. Pain shot into his gonads and then turned to a pleasure even more intense. Women moved around him to stroke, to touch, to lewdly expose themselves.

He cried out again, whether in pain or joy he could not tell. Scores of women, beautiful creatures all, pawed him, begged him for his attention, pleaded for him to take them. He doubled over, sobbing.

A cool hand touched his forehead. He jerked away. A rougher, more forceful grip shook him.

"Please, no, I can't," he moaned. "I hurt! I cannot!"

"Vered." The hand on his collar lifted until his feet left the floor. Then waves of relief laved away the confusing sensations in his loins. He became aware of Santon straining to hold him aloft and of Alarice's soothing voice. Her words took form in his ears; he recognized a tranquilizing spell and gratefully succumbed to it.

Birtle Santon dropped him and stepped back, grumbling. "What foolish thing did you do this time?"

"Nothing. I was hungry. The jar. I opened it." Vered's recollections became jumbled after this. His eyes went wide when he remembered segments of all that had happened. "I grew. Oh, by the saints, how I grew!"

"You stayed the same size." Santon snorted derisively.

"No, not all of me. Just a part." Vered looked guiltily to his groin. "There. To proportions more than—"

"Enough," interrupted Alarice. "You have opened one of the dream traps."

Vered did not understand.

"Why do they call this the City of Stolen Dreams?" she asked. "Patrin strips away the dreams, the longings, the ambitions of those who venture into the city."

"Someone wanted to—" Vered blanched.

"You know now why Patrin considered your dreams to be paltry in comparison."

"But to—"

"Enough," Alarice insisted. "Do not open any more of the dream traps, unless you wish to experience the bizarre fantasies Patrin has stolen for his own amusement."

"I could have satisfied every whore in Porotane and still had enough energy left for all the ladies of the court," marveled Vered.

"Why do you need a jar for that kind of daydream?" asked Santon. "Haven't I listened enough times to such maunderings from you? How you'll—" Santon cut off his diatribe when Alarice pulled back from the pair of bickering men.

"What is it?" Vered asked of the woman.

"Patrin. Lorens must have reported to him. He comes for the Demon Crown."

"How?"

"He'll use Lorens as a pawn," she said. "We dare not harm the prince. Our quest would turn to dust, if we did. But we cannot allow him to seize the crown and use it for Patrin's gain either."

"A pity we didn't leave the crown hidden in the Iron Range, then lured Lorens out. That would keep the crown free of Patrin," said Vered.

"What keeps the wizard away from it is Alarice's spell," snapped Santon.

For an instant, it was as if time stopped. Birtle Santon knew instantly what he had said. The mocking laughter told that Patrin had been spying and had overheard.

"So?" came the wizard's voice. "The lovely white-haired lady's name is Alarice. My spells now carry your name, Alarice, and are magnified in their power tenfold. More!"

"I know your name, too, Patrin," she said, but the stricken look told that she had lost much of her leverage. Repeatedly, the Glass Warrior had said that Patrin was the superior sorcerer. She had held him at bay only through knowing his name—and his ignorance of hers. That advantage had vanished in an instant's carelessness.

"I am sorry," Santon said. "I did not think."

"No," mocked Patrin. "You did not. But I applaud you for the slip. In fact, should you give me the Demon Crown without further struggle, I will allow you and your friend to leave the City of Stolen Dreams unharmed."

"And the Glass Warrior?"

"You mean Alarice?" the wizard taunted. "She must remain behind. For her, I have special plans. She has dreams. No," he hurriedly corrected himself. "She has *dreams*. I want them for my own!"

"Santon, Vered, leave the city. At once," she said. "You can do nothing against him. This is my battle."

"No," they said as one. "We all leave or none does."

"Foolish bravery on your part," said Patrin. He entered the room. At his elbow stood Lorens. The apprentice wizard basked in his master's approval. "That was your only opportunity."

Patrin's lips began moving, but no audible sounds emerged. Vered felt himself being crushed to death. He saw Santon struggling in an unseen grip, too. The magical death coming at them from all sides could not be evaded. They stood struggling futilely, the weight of the world slowly pressing the life from them.

"Lord Patrin, the bitch!" warned Lorens.

Alarice drew her glass sword and walked forward, as if she had no care to occupy her. The glass tip rose and pointed at Patrin. Vered thought she would lunge. Instead, she paused. Red lightnings danced along the tip, growing in power.

"Patrin, die!" the Glass Warrior shrieked. The flaming crimson bolt leaped from the tip of her glass rod and smashed squarely into Patrin's chest. The wizard staggered. Vered gasped in relief when the pressure around his chest suddenly lifted. Alarice's attack had drawn Patrin's full attention.

Vered wiped sweat from his eyes and sucked in huge draughts of air to steady himself. But Vered saw nothing he could do to aid Alarice. She and Patrin stood less than a pace apart. The air between them turned silvery, then translucent, then flowed into a liquid carrying writhing, slippery beasts unseen on this or any other world. Their spells constituted an attack more powerful than any he could mount with his puny glass weapon.

"Santon, get him. The apprentice!" Even as he called to his friend, Vered dived forward, his body crossing in front of Lorens' legs. The apprentice went down in a heap.

"I curse you!" shrieked Lorens. "You are mine. You—" The young man's head snapped back when Santon's powerful fist struck him squarely on the jaw.

"You didn't have to break it," said Vered. He ran knowing fingers along the line of the fallen Lorens' jawbone.

"I broke my hand." Santon rubbed it against his chest.

"He'll be all right. He's just knocked out." Vered rolled out from the tangle of legs and came to his feet, ready once more to aid Alarice. Both he and Birtle Santon stood and stared.

The magics burned and froze, surged and waited. For any not dealing in the most esoteric of spells, this battle would mean instant death.

"She's losing," said Santon, anguish in his voice. "See how she looks? Her face, her lovely face!"

Alarice faded and lost opacity even as Patrin grew in stature.

"The Demon Crown will be mine!" cried Patrin. "You are yielding to me, Alarice. Yield and die miserably!"

"He uses her name as a weapon." The sound of Santon's pitying voice tore at Vered. He knew his friend blamed himself for this. If he had not carelessly uttered the woman's name, Patrin could not have used it against her in his spells.

"We must do something." Vered rocked from

side to side, indecision eating at him. He was no wizard. Neither was Santon. How could they fight magic when they controlled none?

"The City of Stolen Dreams," said Vered, almost in wonder. "That's it. It must be!"

He pushed Santon aside and ran to the wall. He quickly went along it until he found another niche containing a sealed dream trap. He seized the jar and ripped off the wax seal. In the same motion, Vered heaved it at Patrin.

"What are you doing?" cried Santon.

"The dreams. Let him deal with them *and* Alarice."

"See how he uses them?" raged Santon. "He grows more powerful!"

And so it seemed. The dream trap had broken at Patrin's feet. Whatever had been contained within fed the wizard's abilities. Alarice weakened even more, sinking to her knees, battling and losing.

"No!" cried Vered. "That is just one jar. Throw them all! Let him experience a hundred perverted dreams!" Vered began heaving the magical dream traps at Patrin. When Santon saw the effect on the wizard, he joined his friend. The pair tossed the fragile jars from two sides. Try as he might, Patrin could not dodge both. Vered had no idea what dreams—what nightmares—they released, but the effect on Patrin was dramatic.

The wizard's lips pulled back in a soundless shriek. He tore at his hair and jerked from side to side, as if they drove burning spikes into his belly.

"Alarice," whispered Santon. "She is destroying him with her magic!"

Vered dared to hope again. The Glass Warrior stood on shaky legs and turned her full attention to Patrin. The man clawed at his face now, gouging out bloody chunks. When he tore out his eyes, Vered knew the wizard posed no further threat. Patrin sank down and seemed to melt. Alarice's magics reduced him to a smoldering puddle of grease.

"Dead," she gasped out. She fell face forward onto the floor. Santon rushed to her and turned her over. He cradled her head in his lap. The eyes looking up had lost their gray coldness. Only love shone there now.

"Alarice, my darling," Santon said, holding her close.

"I love you, too," she said in a voice almost too faint to be heard.

"We've won."

"Yes, Santon, we've won. You've won."

Something in her tone caused Santon to stiffen. "You're going to be fine. You'll recover. You're just tired, drained. The battle . . ."

"The battle killed me. Patrin's spell burns on within my breast. No one can halt its slow progress."

"No!"

"Yes, my love." She swallowed. A frail hand reached up to touch Santon's cheek. "Promise me. Promise me you'll return Lorens to Porotane and see him crowned as king. The land must be united or my death is in vain."

"You won't die. You won't," Santon said.

Vered put his hand on his friend's shoulder and squeezed gently. Vered reached over and closed the Glass Warrior's eyelids. "She has succeeded, Santon," he said quietly. "She achieved her goal." In a lower voice, he added, "She loved you very much."

Birtle Santon held her while the building around them turned translucent, transparent, slowly vanished. Even when the streets and other buildings faded from sight, Birtle Santon held her.

Only when the harsh desert winds whipped around him did he lower her head to the sand.

CHAPTER EIGHTEEN

Birtle Santon stood and stared at Alarice, no expression on his face. But Vered saw the tear slowly rolling down one dusty cheek and leaving a muddy track. The hot winds whipping across the Desert of Sazan quickly sucked up the moisture and left only a dried trail to mark its passing.

"Patrin killed her," said Santon.

"She destroyed him," said Vered, hand on his friend's shoulder. "She destroyed his greatest work, too. The City of Stolen Dreams is no more." He gestured to take in the emptiness of the desert. "When the wizard died, his dreams died with him."

"Evil dreams. They were evil."

Vered felt the powerful muscles ripple under his grip. He tried to stop Birtle but the man was far too strong. Santon whirled and drew his battle-ax, intent clear. A few paces away lay Lorens. Patrin's young apprentice stirred, one hand exploring his jaw where Santon had hit him.

"You can't," pleaded Vered. "He's our king!"

"He's the demon-damned wizard's apprentice."

"Lorens is the heir to the throne. Alarice

wanted him on the throne. She risked her life—
she *gave* her life!—to put him there."

Santon had passed beyond reason. He
shrugged his powerful shoulder and sent Vered
reeling. The smaller man hit and rolled, somer-
saulting over and coming to his feet. Without
thinking, he charged like a rogue bull. Vered's
arms circled Santon's waist and the force of his
charge carried both men forward. Santon's ax fell
from his grip and dangled by the thick leather
thong. This prevented him from swinging it and
splitting Vered's skull.

"Stop, think, damn you. Think about why
we've come this far!" Vered fought a silent Santon,
but the life had gone from the man. He fought
without purpose. When Vered got behind him and
pinned him face down in the sand, Santon ceased
to fight.

"There," Vered said. "Will you behave?" He
rolled off and stayed on one knee, ready for
renewed wrestling. If Santon had the fire of old
Vered knew he would have been an easy victim.
Santon might lack an arm, but the left had overde-
veloped and was prodigiously strong. As a result of
this and his many hours of practice, few men with
normal strength and two arms could best him. The
exhaustion Vered felt welling inside him told that a
strong breeze might knock him over. A fight was
beyond his winning.

"He doesn't deserve to live. Patrin trained
him."

"Away from the wizard's influence, he might
be different."

"Normal?"

"What wizard is normal?" asked Vered. "Except Alarice," he added hastily.

"No," said Santon. "Even she was not of the common people. She was special—she was also a wizard."

Vered went to Lorens' side and helped the man sit up. A large bruise had formed on his chin, and a lump the size of a small egg made speaking difficult for him.

"Where's the city?" he asked, his bright blue eyes darting about. "And my lord? Where's Patrin?"

"Dead," Vered said with some enthusiasm. "The Glass Warrior perished in the battle, too. That was a magical fight about which legends are born and ballads sung."

"My master is dead?" Shock clouded Lorens' face.

"Does this bother you? He seemed a cruel and thoughtless master."

"But he was all the family I've ever known."

"What of your sister?" asked Santon. The man's intent seemed clear. If Lokenna lived, the apprentice could die for his master's sins.

"She is dead. Long dead. She betrayed me. Only Lord Patrin helped me."

Santon slumped. "Then you are the one and only true ruler of Porotane. We have come far to install you on the throne."

The shock began to fade as Lorens gathered his wits. "Is the City of Stolen Dreams truly gone?"

"Like that." Vered snapped his fingers.

"My master *and* my home have deserted me."

Vered refrained from pointing out that Patrin had not willingly left his apprentice. Had Alarice been less capable, Patrin would have killed them all and taken the Demon Crown.

"The crown," Vered said to Santon. "Where is it?"

"There." Santon picked it up. The black velvet bag seemed none the worse from dirt or wear. He peered inside. "It still glows its ghastly emerald color."

"The Demon Crown?" Lorens forced his way to his feet. He wobbled slightly, then reached for the bag. "Give it to me. It's mine!"

As if one brain powered three arms, both Santon and Vered shoved the bag holding the crown from the young man's grasp.

"Not until you ascend the throne," said Vered. "Those are the orders given us by Alarice."

"But the Demon Crown is rightfully mine! I am of the royal blood. You told me so."

"Patrin did lie to you on this point," Vered said cautiously.

"Whether my master did or not is meaningless. I can *use* the crown. Such power should not be wasted."

"Such power is for the good of the people of Porotane," Santon said gruffly. "As the Glass Warrior ordered, so shall it be. You will be crowned when you assume the throne and not one instant before."

"I can force you to relinquish it," Lorens said in a nasty tone.

"Of course you can," Vered said smoothly, before Santon could give a toss to his wrist strap that would put the handle of the battle-ax in his meaty grip. "But how are you going to survive? Simply wearing the Demon Crown does not provide you with the knowledge we possess."

"I am a wizard. Patrin taught me well."

"Then conjure me a drink. I am thirsty. You

promised a fine white wine from the Uvain Plateau. I never received it."

"I cannot do such magic."

"So reduce me to ash," snapped Vered. "And then let yourself die in this miserable desert. The Desert of Sazan is not known for its caring attitude, whether you wear a crown or not."

"How far is it to the edge of the desert?"

"A day's travel," said Santon. The smile crossing the wizard-king's face turned nasty. Santon added without pause, "To the Iron Range. Another week crossing it. I doubt if any this far north of Rievane know the waterholes as well as Vered and I."

"The Iron Range is hot and dry, drier than the desert."

"And on the other side of this mountain range?" asked Lorens.

"Brigands, warring rebel bands all too eager to slay any pretender to the throne and seize Porotane for themselves, others." Vered did not mention the legions of phantoms roaming the land. Let those come as a surprise to the would-be king. Vered slowly began to agree with Santon about removing this arrogant demon-spawn permanently.

If Alarice had lived, would she permit such as Lorens to rule Porotane?

Vered had no answer. He could only hope that Lorens became more civil and the lingering effects of Patrin's life-long education wore off.

"You have made your point," said Lorens. "Lead me to Porotane. Until then, we need one another."

"No," said Santon, dark rage barely masked. "You need us. We have no use for you."

Vered whispered to his friend. "We get off to a bad start with the next king of Porotane."

"Why change our ways now?" said Santon. He turned and lumbered off, finding their horses on the far side of a sand dune. Ten minutes later, they rode slowly for the edge of the Desert of Sazan.

"We needed Alarice and her scrying tools," said Santon. He turned in the saddle and peered at the towering black peaks of the Iron Range. It had taken three times as long for them to find their way back to Porotane as it had to traverse the passes originally.

"I miss her, too," said Vered. He sat astride his horse, feeling ready to die. He had not bathed in a month and smelled like a charnel pit. His skin itched constantly, his clothing hung in tatters, his belly grumbled from the pitiful food they were able to find, and for a taste of good wine he would have cheerfully wrestled Kalob and forty other demons.

"Is this all there is? I expected more." Lorens rode the strongest of the three horses. The other animals had died en route. "If I am to rule, I want Porotane to be exquisite, a gem, a work of art!"

"It's endured twenty years of civil war," said Vered. "Actually, this is a quieter section of the country."

"Quiet? With that howling?"

"What howling, Lorens?" demanded Santon. He cocked his head to one side and strained. Turning to Vered, he said, "It is a familiar sound. I think it is a phantom."

"We have too little time," said Vered. "We must ride for the castle. Duke Freow leaned against death's door when Alarice left. He might already be gone."

"That would mean Baron Theoll has assumed the throne," said Santon. He spat.

"Maybe not. The duke was a strong one," said Vered.

"It matters naught who is on the throne. The regent, this duke who is supposed to be my uncle, does not sound fit to rule. And the baron of whom you speak with such loathing, cannot stand against me. Not when I wear the Demon Crown."

"In that you are probably right," said Vered. He touched the saddlebag where he carried the crown in its crystalline case. "The mere sight of anyone wearing the crown will rally many to your banner."

"Will it bring you, Vered? Or you, Santon?" Those bright blue eyes fixed firmly on the men. "I know you hate me because my master killed the Glass Warrior. But they were enemies. She killed the only teacher I've known."

Vered saw a hint of the true and likable Lorens shine forth. "Hate you?" he said. "No. Distrust anyone who can use such power as is offered by the Demon Crown? Definitely."

"I can accept that. I must. But what of that horrid howling?"

"A phantom," said Santon. "No other cause presents itself."

"Let's ride. Due west, then to the north until we find a branch of the River Ty. We can follow it to the castle."

"What of this phantom? I have never encountered one."

"Ride and we can talk," said Vered.

Barely had they gone a hundred yards when a miniature whirlwind caught up leaves and debris from the trail in front of them and carried it high into the air. The familiar mistiness of the phantom's body took on substance.

"That is a phantom?" asked Lorens, fascinated. "All it needs is a proper burial to be put to rest?"

"Something like that," said Santon. "This one seems intent on blocking our way."

"You there, phantom," called out Vered. "Why do you stop us? We are simple travelers on our way to . . . the Uvain Plateau."

"Liars!" whined the phantom. "You are spies. You report back to those in the castle. You report to Theoll!"

"Not him," argued Vered. "We have no desire to see the baron grow more powerful."

"Spies! I will stop you from reporting."

"Reporting what?" asked Santon.

The phantom's torso darkened and the mistiness turned to opaque body. "You cannot pass me. You will die on this spot as I died."

"A trade," said Vered. "We'll find your body and—" His words were cut off by the phantom's attack. Vered had not appreciated the power locked up within the ghostly beings until this instant. The wispy arms reached out and then solidified around his throat. He choked. The phantom spun wildly about its central core and rose, taking Vered with it. The brown-haired man found himself being lifted high into the air.

Strangling, he fought to pry loose the phantom's fingers. Only the fingers choking him had substance. Cool, moist fog met his feet and hands as he strove to free himself.

The blood pounded like drums in his temples and his vision blurred. Vered's struggles diminished as his strength fled. He had been close to exhaustion before encountering the phantom. This battle gave promise of being his final one. He fought, but the struggles grew ever weaker.

The howling he heard he thought came from within his own mind. Did demons come to ferry him to hell? He knew that the saints could not make such a soul-rending noise. And what had he done to entice them when the final entry on the Death Rota had been made?

He gasped when he fell hard to the ground. It took several seconds for Vered to realize that the phantom shrieked in anguish, not demons. The ghost whirled around and around, stirring up a miniature cyclone with its body. With a tiny *pop*! it vanished.

"What happened?" he asked, rubbing his throat. He felt the weals circling the flesh. This had been all too real and wasn't the product of exhaustion delirium.

"I had never dealt with phantoms before. The spells are difficult to remember. It took several tries before I drove it off." Lorens sat on his horse, his expression one of awe. "The spell I used worked!"

"You're a wizard's apprentice. Why shouldn't your spells work?"

"But you don't understand. Patrin never allowed me to cast a spell. Oh, simple ones to start cooking fires, things like that. This was a powerful one."

"You destroyed the phantom?" asked Vered. He pulled himself back onto horseback.

"I can't. Only consecrating the phantom's

grave can do that. But I drove it off."

"Listen hard," said Santon.

"Not more phantoms," groaned Vered. "I've had enough of just one. If it's gone and found a dozen friends . . ."

"Hoofbeats. Many. The ground trembles under them."

"The phantom scouted for a band of ruffians," said Lorens, his eyes unfocused and his face slack. What he concentrated on, neither man knew or was willing to ask.

"Never heard of a phantom spying for rebels, but it might be possible. By the demons, why not?" Santon pointed. "Let's try to hide. In our condition, we'd never be able to outride or outfight them."

"A sage suggestion," Vered said.

They rode into a small copse and dismounted. It took long minutes to tether their steeds and build up a shielding wall of brush. Any rider chancing more than a casual glance in their direction would surely see them. But it was all they had time for. The riders pounded hard into view.

"Let's hope they keep riding," said Santon.

They did not. They reined in and milled about the spot where the phantom had originally appeared.

"Can you hear what they say?" asked Vered.

"Give me the Demon Crown," said Lorens. "With it I can learn much."

Vered felt himself torn by the request. Lorens' attitude had changed only slightly. Still self-centered, still obnoxious and demanding, he was the perfect apprentice for a demon-spawn like his unlamented master Patrin. But Vered could not deny that the wizard-king had saved his life. And occasionally sparks of humanity shone through the tough veneer of his arrogance.

Vered reached for the saddlebag containing the Demon Crown.

"Do you know what you are doing?" demanded Birtle Santon.

"We need information. With the crown, he can get it." Vered drew out the box containing the crown. To Lorens he said, "Remember what happened the first time you wore the Demon Crown."

"I did not know what to expect."

"It is like a powerful drug. It will become *your* master if you let it. Wear the crown for only a few seconds, then return it to the box."

"If I don't?"

Santon moved slightly, the heavy battle-ax in his hand. His intent was obvious. Lorens nodded and held out his hand to accept the crown.

The brilliant green glow faded to a more bearable emerald when the Demon Crown came into contact with Lorens' flesh. He quickly lifted the circlet to his head and placed it squarely on his own brow.

Vered watched in fascination. A shock went through Lorens' body. He stood rigidly, teeth grinding, eyes screwed shut. Sweat beaded his forehead and began to run down into his eyes. But it mattered little. Lorens did not see with eyes or hear with ears. The Demon Crown provided those senses for him.

And what else? Vered wished he knew, but such knowledge was barred from him.

"The leader," Lorens said in a low voice. "He rides for a rebel called Dews Gaemock. The phantom did spy for them. It was the brother of one in the band. Baron Theoll's troops killed him. No, not Theoll's. One close to him. The Archbishop Nosto might be the one doing it during the Inquisition."

"The Inquisition!" exclaimed Santon. "They put their own people to the Question!"

"Quiet," said Vered. "He does not dare wear the crown much longer. We must learn what we can."

"Farther. Oh, by the saints, I am traveling so far!" Lorens staggered. Vered supported him, then eased him to the ground where the wizard-king sat, eyes still closed. "I see Gaemock. I *see*!"

"What do you see?"

"He has many phantoms scouting for him. They cannot enter the castle. Spells bind them if they do. They suffer horribly, but Gaemock uses them well in the field."

"What of the company not a bowshot from us?" asked Santon. "Gaemock might be foremost among the rebels, but these are the ones most likely to gut us."

"Turmoil within the castle. Death. No, not death. But close. Theoll. I see him. Such a small man, so insignificant-looking." Lorens cackled evilly. "He is no worthy opponent. I can crush him beneath my boot heel as I would a desert scorpion."

"The rebels," insisted Santon.

Vered licked his lips nervously. He cast a glance over his shoulder in the direction of the rebel band still in the clearing where they had encountered the phantom. Had they summoned back the banished spirit? Or had they seen the hoofprints heading for this copse?

"Theoll engineers Freow's death. He places

poison in the duke's food. But another—who?—I cannot see who!—removes it. The duke has an unknown protector. Archbishop Nosto? Possibly."

"Damn the court intrigues!" raged Santon.

"You're right," said Vered. "He's too caught up in spying on Theoll." Vered sucked in his breath and held it. Quick hands grabbed the Demon Crown from Lorens' head. The explosions in his own body burned and froze, but Vered got the crown back to the crystalline box. He dropped the magical crown and shut the lid. For long seconds, visions fluttered before his eyes.

"Duke Freow will die within a few hours," said Lorens. "And Baron Theoll will ascend the throne of Porotane."

"For us, that means naught," said Santon.

"Why not?" asked Vered. "We might have to fight both rebels and the baron's soldiers to get Lorens into the castle if the duke dies before our return."

"Prepare to fight just the rebels. They've seen us!"

Vered peered through the screen of bushes and saw that his friend spoke truly. The rebels had found their hoofprints and were slowly following them directly to their hiding place.

CHAPTER NINETEEN

Vered pushed aside the branches and saw the rebels moving quicker now that they had a spoor. Some worked to free swords and battle-axes. Still others unlimbered bows.

"The archers won't be of any good in the forest," said Santon. "When they are mounted, we have a small advantage on the others."

"Damned small," muttered Vered. He drew the short sword of shining glass that Alarice had given him. Against so much steel it seemed a puny weapon. But something of the Glass Warrior's courage went with the blade. Vered felt himself forgetting his tiredness and surging with strength.

"Can you use a sword, Lorens?" asked Santon. "If so, take the one sheathed on my horse."

"Alarice's blade?" asked Vered, startled. "You'd let him use her weapon?"

"We need all the fighting prowess we can muster," said Santon. "They are upon us!"

With that, the burly man lunged through the thin wall of bushes and swung his battle-ax. He grunted as it cut into a rider's fleshy thigh. The rebel shrieked in agony and toppled from his mount. He landed heavily and tried to wiggle away. The blood fountaining from his thigh weakened him quickly. Vered saw him die before the next rider knew what was happening.

Santon's ax swung again, this time the heavy spiked ball on the back of the ax head crushing a horse's leg and sending its rider tumbling. Vered pushed through the gap in the bushes left by his bigger companion. The short sword lacked the reach needed, but the dense trees and tangle of underbrush aided Vered. The rebels could not get into position quickly enough to launch a concerted attack.

Vered batted aside a steel blade and leaped upward, the tip of the glass blade working under leather armor. He felt an instant's resistance, then the blade sank into the rebel's side. Vered doubted he punctured any vital organs, but the rider fell from his horse. Just eliminating one of the score against them counted heavily.

Santon fought like a madman, felling two more. Vered fought but had less success. His opponent proved more wary and retreated quickly.

"They fight like a legion!" cried one rebel. "But there are only two."

This bit of information filtered along the rebel ranks. They withdrew to the edge of the forest and formed a ragged battle line. Santon and Vered caught their breath as the ruffians prepared to attack.

"We're dead men," said Vered. "They know our number."

"And surprise is lost to us."

"Even worse," moaned Vered, "they stopped using their muscles and started using their heads.

They'll flow over us in one rush like the River Ty overflows its bank every spring."

Santon sucked in a deep breath, then exhaled slowly. "Our lives mean naught—"

"Speak for yourself!" cried Vered, incensed.

"—in comparison to Lorens. We must see that he gets to the castle. If Freow is dying, Lorens must ascend the throne."

"You've changed your tune greatly from wanting to slit the royal bastard's throat."

"Alarice died finding him. For her memory, I'll see Lorens on the throne."

"We're not likely to see anything but our own deaths," said Vered. "Look."

"The phantom that Lorens banished. It has returned." Santon sagged slightly. "So much for our apprentice wizard's spell-casting."

"It is another phantom," Lorens said from behind. "The rebels use a dozen or more of the ghosts to scout for them. This one is recently appeared. I can banish it, too, but other spells occupy me."

"Be sure to compose the last verse of your death song. You want the saints to look favorably on you when they come for your soul."

"I will not die this day. Nor will you."

Vered ducked as an arrow winged toward him. The broad head slipped with liquid ease into a tree trunk to his side. He tried to imagine what that arrow would have done to his body. He shuddered at the thought.

"They stand back and think to pick us off," said Santon. "Stay behind the trees and—Lorens! Stop, wait, don't!"

Santon dropped his ax and tried to grab the

wizard-king. A dozen arrows drove him back to cover.

"He goes to his own death so willingly," Vered said in wonder.

Arrows flew until the air whistled with their passage. Strangely, however, none touched Lorens. He floated in a bubble amid the feathered flights of death.

The rebel leader held up a sword, motioning for the archers to cease. Lorens stopped a dozen paces from the mounted man.

"I go to the castle," said Lorens. "It is not wise to hinder me. I go there to accept the monarchy of Porotane."

"Oh," scoffed the rebel. "So you're another pretender to the throne? The woods are filled with them. But in you I detect something of the wizard. Well, good Sir Wizard, the woods are full of sorcerers aspiring to the throne, too."

Lorens said nothing. The fifteen men in the rebel party spread out slightly, without being ordered to do so. Vered saw the tension mounting in their ranks. Their leader would order Lorens' death at any instant.

"I am of the royal blood," said Lorens.

"Aren't they all?"

A dozen archers loosed arrows. None arrived at their target. Lorens held out his hands, now glowing a pale red. From each finger flew a crackling red spark that intercepted an arrow. The arrows stopped in mid-flight, turned, and wobbled off in unexpected directions.

"A nice trick, wizard," said the rebel leader. "I have seen better, though." Without another word, the rebel whipped his sword around and urged his horse forward. He rode Lorens down.

Vered winced. The apprentice wizard's spell failed him at the last instant; the rebel's sword slashed through the upper portion of Lorens' arm producing a cut bloodier than it was dangerous. The rebel turned his horse and prepared to gallop back for the killing stroke.

Vered felt the sudden tension in the air. Even Santon, who professed no magical abilities at all, stiffened in expectation. In the distance a phantom howled, "The spell. He casts a powerful spell!"

The flames that engulfed the rebel band produced no heat, but the searing light dazzled Vered. He turned away. The light reflecting off the leaves and trunks of the trees proved almost as blinding. Then it vanished as suddenly as it had appeared. He turned back to see Lorens standing alone in the small clearing.

"What magic is that?" wondered Santon. "I've never heard of a wizard able to command such force."

Vered rushed out to Lorens' side. The man stood stock still, his blue eyes glazed over. Vered touched him. Lorens toppled forward, as rigid as any tree felled in the forest. Vered tried to break the wizard's fall and failed. Together, they went down in a heap.

"Whatever he did, it drained him completely," said Santon. He rolled Lorens over and examined him. "I've seen men look like this—after a week-long debauch."

Vered scrambled to his feet and looked at the tiny piles of gray ash that marked where the rebels and their horses had been. "And that is how I feel after a week-long binge." Vered ran his fingers through the gray ash. He brushed it off and moved away, trying not to shake too hard. "I'll get the horses. You get Lorens into shape for travel. We've a long journey ahead if we are to arrive at the castle before Duke Freow dies."

Vered stumbled off, avoiding walking on the ash as he returned to the grove where their horses pawed the ground nervously. He soothed the animals, then led them back to the clearing. Santon had Lorens sitting upright, but the wizard-king showed no signs of life.

"Is he all right?" asked Vered.

"He lives. The spell-casting took everything out of him. How long this shock will last is beyond my knowing."

They heaved Lorens over the saddle and tied him down. The ride would be uncomfortable, but in his present condition, he would not notice. Vered climbed into the saddle and found this almost more than he could do. His body rebelled at any strain he placed on it.

"No more fights," he told Santon. "I have no reserve strength to draw upon."

Santon's shaggy head nodded. He rode with shoulders sagging.

"What a fine trio we make. All hail the conquerors returning to install the rightful king! Why, I am so exhausted, even the promise of a coronation orgy does nothing to perk me up."

"You're not exhausted," Santon said. "You must be dead."

Vered saved his strength and did not answer. But he wondered at the truth in his friend's words. How would he know when he died? Vered glanced about and found a pair of shimmering columns marking the spots where phantoms stalked the land. Would he end up like them? Or was death something else? He was too tired to ponder such philosophical notions. Vered let his horse go where it wanted. His head rocked forward and he slept.

"More trouble," moaned Vered. "I'll never get to bathe or change into decent clothing." He leaned forward in the saddle, hands spasmodically clutching at the pommel. Arrayed around the castle were rebel troops.

"I thought Alarice said that Dews Gaemock had retreated for the year," said Santon. "She scryed constantly to learn of Freow's fate."

"It seems that Freow's impending death—perhaps actual death, by this late time—has brought out the vultures."

"Gaemock's not that bad," said Santon. "Truth to tell, I have more sympathy for him than I do for Theoll."

"And I," agreed Vered, "but it is difficult to join a band of rebels when all they seem to do is waylay honest travelers and rob them."

Vered glanced over at Lorens. The wizard-king's head lolled forward, bobbing as his horse walked. Since he had reduced the rebel band to ash blowing away in the breeze, he had not spoken. Vered worried that the strain of casting such a potent spell had burned out Lorens' brain. His blue eyes stayed open as he rode, but no intelligence shone through. Vered had not liked Lorens much, but for Alarice he would tolerate the heir to the throne of Porotane.

Now he only felt pity for him.

"Find a way in?" he asked of Birtle Santon.

"We must. Getting through the lines might prove easy, even with him in such a condition." Santon's critical gaze appraised Lorens' physical set and judged the young man wanting. "But getting into the castle will prove even more difficult."

"Who under siege would let in scragglylooking travelers such as us, eh?" said Vered.

"We might enter under a flag of truce."

"More likely they would fill us with arrows or pour burning amber on our heads. No, Santon, my good friend, stealth will win us entry quicker than honesty."

"I leave that to you, Vered. You always were the . . . craftier."

"You chose your word well. I do not tolerate being called a thief and a liar."

"Even if those are truer descriptions?" taunted Santon.

"You never complained before. In fact, you always joined in. For the adventure, you said."

"Only for the adventure. You keep life from becoming too tedious."

Vered subsided and studied the dispersal of Gaemock's rebel troops. No matter how much he thought Dews Gaemock an unrepentant ruffian and thief, Vered had to acknowledge the man's tactical ability. With a handful of troops, Gaemock prevented easy entry—and exit.

"Twilight," he decided aloud. "We try when the sun begins to set. Shadows dance then and make less clear a man's intentions."

"And thoughts turn to a warm supper and a night's sleep," finished Santon. "I agree to that, but how do we enter the castle once past Gaemock's lines?"

"Alarice mentioned a postern gate. I think the key of glass is the one she used for entry. If we cross the River Ty and go directly for the western wall of the castle, do you think we can find it?"

"The wall is long and her description was vague." Santon stared directly at the castle, but Vered saw the moisture beading in the corners of the man's eyes at the mention of the Glass Warrior. Santon had cared deeply for Alarice, and still mourned.

"There is one last matter to consider," said Vered. "When we enter the castle, what then?"

Santon looked again at Lorens. He shook his head and indicated that he had no idea. They might succeed, only to find they presented a brainless husk as king of Porotane.

They rode slowly well behind Gaemock's battle lines. Occasional arrows arched from the castle battlements, but always fell short of the lines. Vered estimated that the royal archers intentionally fired short by a hundred yards—and that Gaemock's men stayed back twice that for safety. The antagonists played a deadly game, daring, taunting, moving, always challenging. He had to be certain that Lorens stayed beyond the range of both sides until the young king consolidated power within the castle.

Vered snorted. With Lorens in this trance, it might all go for naught.

But they could only try.

"It's later than I intended," said Vered.

"The patrols could not be hastened along their routes," said Santon. "We have done well avoiding Gaemock's rebels."

"Half-dragging *him* is slowing us," complained Vered. Lorens sat docilely, staring into their cooking fire. He had eaten with deliberate mechanical jaw movements, showing neither approval nor disdain for their simple repast. When Lorens moved, he moved only in a straight line. To dodge and hide or to change his direction required considerable effort on the parts of Vered and Santon.

"We wouldn't have gotten this far if he hadn't stopped the rebels," Santon pointed out.

"Better to have died out there than to be caught between Gaemock and Theoll." Vered grumbled under his breath, then said, "That's not so. We still live. We can finish what we started."

"For Alarice," Santon said quietly.

"And for ourselves. We've never been quitters. We need not begin now."

The dusk cloaked the River Ty in soft light and a buzzing cloud of insects. Bats swooped low to gorge themselves on their aerial meals, and the water rippled as fish surfaced to dine. Vered spent a considerable time swatting at the bugs trying to suck his blood. He cursed constantly as they forded a tributary to the river.

Halfway across, they sighted a sentry on the bank in front of them.

"Gaemock's?" Vered asked Santon.

"Without a doubt." Santon lifted his good arm and waved. He called out, "Hello! Ready for the shift change?"

Vered saw the sentry's confusion. He might have several hours remaining on his watch before relief came. But he dared hope and did not shout warnings to other sentries. He stood and waited for them to ride up on the muddy banks.

"You come from the main camp?" the sentry asked.

Vered felt sorry for the youngling. Hardly fifteen summers had passed since this one's birth. He had not yet had time to learn suspicion. Vered only hoped that it would not prove necessary to end the young guard's life before he could learn.

"From the other side," said Santon, his gruff, military bearing quelling any fears on the sentry's part. "You are Grogan's brother, aren't you?" Santon tipped his head to one side. Before the youth could answer, Santon said, "By all the saints, he's not the one!"

The sentry's confusion mounted. He had forgotten totally about passwords or security. "What do you mean? I have no brothers. No living brothers," he added sadly.

Santon cursed volubly. "They sent us to the wrong post. For that, give praise to the saints. Grogan died this afternoon, an arrow in his gullet."

The youth relaxed even more. "I don't even know this Grogan."

"An officer in the main camp."

Whether Santon had said too much and given them away or the youth's wits had returned and he realized that proper procedure had not been followed, Vered couldn't say. The expression altered on the boy's face. Before he could issue the challenge, Vered slipped his foot free of his stirrup cup, gauged the distance, and kicked hard. The toe of his boot crashed into the youth's head, knocking him back. The guard staggered and fell flat on his back, arms outstretched.

"He looks comfortable," observed Vered. "Just as if he's sleeping."

Santon fingered his battle-ax, then relaxed, his decision made. "We can reach the castle walls before he regains his senses. He won't even mention this little foray."

"Not unless he wants the hide stripped off his back by his officer's whips. Stupidity is never appreciated, whether the army be rebel or royal."

The trio rode on into the gathering night. By Santon's estimate, it lacked only an hour before midnight when they reached the castle wall. Most of the growth had been stripped away from the walls to give better vision, but they found an ill-traveled path that led them through a patch of trees and past a tangle of shrubs.

"There," said Vered. "I feel it in my bones."

Santon craned his neck back and studied the battlements above, seeking evidence of a trap. He saw nothing unusual. Shrugging, he silently indicated that Vered should investigate.

Vered slipped through the bushes, thorns tearing away clothing and skin. He winced but kept on. He could not contain his cry of happiness when he found the hidden door.

"Santon, hurry! I have it!"

The bushes rustled and Santon pushed through, leading Lorens. The young man had not regained a hint of his senses. For a moment, Vered considered whether they should continue or not. They might survive well outside the castle. Within the walls, they would be on unfamiliar ground, surrounded by enemies intent on slaying any intruder.

Should Baron Theoll find that their charge was Prince Lorens, their lives would end swiftly.

"We go in," decided Vered.

"Where else?" Santon shoved Lorens forward. For a fleeting instant, it seemed as if he emerged from his daze. The consciousness fled as quickly as it appeared.

Vered fumbled at his pouch and withdrew the glass key that had been Alarice's, fitted it into the lock, and turned. The lock snapped open easily. Vered lifted the latch and shouldered the door open. A dark corridor led through the wall. He pulled Lorens after him. Santon closed the door and said softly, "Lead the way, Vered."

"But it's as dark as a whale's gut!"

"Just pretend you're seeking out a married woman's boudoir and you want to avoid her husband."

"That I can do," said Vered. "I've done it enough times before."

"But how many times were successful?"

"All," Vered answered.

"All save this time," came a booming voice magnified by the narrow corridor walls. A torch flared, momentarily blinding Vered and Santon. "Do not reach for your weapons."

They stood in the shoulder-wide passageway, blinded and unable to retreat.

CHAPTER TWENTY

Vered tried to pull out his sword, but even the short length of the glass weapon proved too long for the narrow corridor. Behind him Lorens bumped against his elbow and Santon bellowed for them to retreat.

"Wait," Vered said. His eyes adjusted to the flickering light of the torch held by the man blocking their path. "Who are you?" Vered asked. He had detected no animosity in the man's original challenge.

"I, good sirs, am Harhar, Duke Freow's jester. Would you hear an amusing story?" Harhar spun about; bells tinkled lightly with his every movement. "Or would you prefer a dirty limerick?"

Harhar launched himself straight into the air, twisted nimbly, and landed on his head. Vered took an involuntary step forward to aid the dark-haired man. He stopped when he saw that Harhar had cunningly turned at the last possible instant and had rolled safely.

"Does that bring a smile to your lips? Or should I do something more?"

"How did you happen to be in this corridor?" demanded Birtle Santon. "Are you guarding the entryway?"

"Guard? Me?" Harhar laughed uproariously. "The baron would never trust me with such a role. Even that fount of kindness, Archbishop Nosto, ignores me. But I help Duke Freow."

"How?"

"I make him laugh. I have brought him back repeatedly from the edge of his grave with my jokes." Harhar pulled his legs up tightly against his chest and hugged his knees, his rattle by his side. The torch fell from his grip and landed on the floor. Vered scooped it up and peered at the jester. Harhar cried.

"What's wrong?"

"Duke Freow has died. Even my amusing capers could not save him."

"When? When did he die?"

"Early this morning, just before sunrise. He left me. He left us all."

"Has Theoll crowned himself ruler of Porotane?" Vered's sharp question brought the jester's wide, dark eyes up.

"An odd question. Who else? The Lady Johanna was unable to sleep with enough nobles to insure her ascendancy, though I am sure she got many in the castle to rise to her schemes."

"Just what we need," grumbled Santon. "A jester and a gossip."

"Who is this with you? He speaks little. Is he depressed? May I amuse him?"

"We need to get out of this corridor," said Vered. "A small room where we could go? Do you know of one, jester?"

"Harhar will show you! I know every room in the castle. I do!" The jester somersaulted off, heels kicking in the air with every rotation. He stopped, spun, and kicked open a door. The dusty room he rolled into served Vered's purposes well.

"Where does this door lead?" asked Santon, pressing his ear against a heavy panel. "There is a rhythmic hollow sound outside. Guards patrolling?"

"Verily, yes, that. But they are so easily distracted. That is how I came to this secret passage."

"Tell us about it," said Vered. He moved Lorens around and shoved the wizard-king into a chair. Some small flickering of interest shone behind those blue eyes, but Lorens did not speak.

"I saw you from above. From the battlements. I practice my jokes nightly to keep the guards amused. I happened to lean out to relieve myself when I saw you."

"May the saints be praised. We were quick enough to miss the yellow rain," said Santon. To Vered, he said, "I like this less and less. If Theoll has gained power, we are doomed. And if the likes of this crackbrained jester watch us entering, what chance do we have? All in the castle may know of our presence."

Vered nodded. He hated to admit defeat, but all that Santon said paralleled his own thoughts.

"Is he in need of cheering?" asked Harhar. He danced about in front of Lorens. "Who is he?"

"Quiet, fool," snapped Santon.

"Let him do his best—or worst," said Vered. "It can't hurt." He stared at Lorens. The young man had never recovered from casting the spell. He had said that Patrin had not allowed him to use the more potent spells. Had the casting somehow affected his mind? Or had it merely drained him? It mattered little to Vered. With Lorens in this condition, he could not challenge Theoll for the throne. Who would believe this mute, glassy-eyed man was the true heir?

"What are we going to do?" asked Santon.

Vered had no answer. "The jester does as good a job as we've done with Lorens."

"How do we prove him to be of the royal blood?" Santon slammed his fist against a table and exclaimed, "Damn you, Alarice! Why did you put such a burden on us?"

The jester turned and stared at him curiously, then returned to his capering.

"Santon," said Vered. "We agree that there is no hope with Lorens in his present condition. What do you think would happen if we put the Demon Crown upon his brow?"

"All it could do is kill him. At the moment, that might be preferable to this damnable uncertainty."

"Demon Crown?" croaked Harhar. "You have the Demon Crown? You know the Glass Warrior?"

"She is dead," Santon said with more than a hint of bitterness in his voice. "And yes, we have the crown. Get it, Vered. Put it on Lorens."

"Lorens?" cried the jester. "This is one of the royal twins? But how can this be?"

"The Glass Warrior entrusted us with returning Lorens to Porotane and seeing that he ascended the throne," said Vered. He carefully drew the Demon Crown from its velvet bag. The box within glowed brilliantly with the green from the Demon Crown. Vered flipped open the lid and moved as close to Lorens as he could get. He had to push the curious jester back.

"Is it safe for you to handle it?" asked Santon.

"For a moment. I cannot but wonder who in the family tree gave me the drop of royal blood."

"Start naming the outcasts," grumbled Santon.

Vered moved quickly. He picked up the crown and hastily transfered it to Lorens' head. The young wizard stiffened as the effect of the crown's magics worked on his brain. He smiled almost benignly.

"I am home," he said in a soft voice. "I have returned to my home!"

Lorens rose and turned slowly. His eyes focused past the cobweb-ridden stone walls in the small storage room. He used the powers of the Demon Crown to see *beyond*.

"Truly, he *is* King Lorens!" cried Harhar.

"It is our belief," said Vered. "At least, he's come out of his trance."

"Trance?" asked Lorens. "Yes, I was in a trance. The strain of casting the spell proved more than I had anticipated. But the Demon Crown gives power."

"It also demands a price for it," said Vered. But Lorens did not hear. He pushed past Santon and went into the corridor.

"Wait, Lorens, you dare not let Theoll learn of your presence." Vered's warning went unheeded. Lorens walked confidently past the patrolling guards. Vered and Santon exchanged glances. Vered smiled and shrugged, then hurried after Lorens. It seemed safer to be with the wizard-king than to be left behind.

Vered heard Harhar cackling to himself as they raced along the stony corridors, went up spiral staircases, and eventually emerged in the main audience chamber.

"Now there'll be trouble," whispered Santon. "Theoll is on the throne."

They stopped just inside the massive wooden doors of the chamber and watched. Vered looked around, trying to find the best escape route when Theoll ordered Lorens killed for his impertinence.

"What is this? We are discussing affairs of state!" bellowed Theoll from the throne.

"You discuss Gaemock's forces knocking at the castle gates," Lorens said with great confidence. "You ignore the ten other rebel bands, not aligned with Dews Gaemock, who march toward the castle. You should turn them against Gaemock. That would lift his siege."

"Who is this?" cried Theoll. "Guards! Remove this fool!"

Lorens walked slowly up the steps to the throne. Each step he took caused the Demon Crown to glow more brightly. By the time he reached the top step, no one in the room could look directly at Lorens. The wizard-king reached out, plucked Theoll from the throne, and cast him down the steps. Lorens turned and seated himself. The glow moderated; Lorens wore a shimmering curtain of light born in the Demon Crown.

"I am Lorens, son of Lamost. The Demon Crown is mine by right and by birth. I claim it—and the kingdom of Porotane."

"At least he no longer speaks of himself as a commoner," said Santon.

"How much else of Patrin's spurious education will he deny?" Vered wondered aloud. "He seems able to fend for himself."

"The Demon Crown has done that for him," said Santon.

"More," croaked Harhar. "It takes more to rule." The jester's eyes were wide at the sight of the wizard-king on the throne.

"Well said, fool," agreed Santon. "And we have no idea if he is capable."

"Baron Theoll," came Lorens' rumbling voice. "Order Captain Squann to attack Gaemock's main force immediately."

"What? That is suicidal!" Theoll pulled himself up to his full height. "You can't walk in and declare yourself king. You—"

Archbishop Nosto took Theoll by the elbow and spun the smaller man around. The two talked for several minutes, their argument heated. All the while, Lorens sat on the throne, his concentration elsewhere.

When Nosto made the final gesture of dismissal to Theoll, the cleric called out, "The Church supports King Lorens, true heir and wearer of Kalob's gift!"

"Send messengers immediately," said Lorens. "The fighting will be over in days if the other rebel bands learn that the true king has ascended the throne."

"It can't be that easy," muttered Santon.

Lorens turned toward Birtle Santon and shouted, "Yes, Santon, it is. I know what lies in their hearts and minds. The Demon Crown allows me that, just as I see and hear all that happens nearby."

"He couldn't have heard me," protested Santon.

"Not with his ears," agreed Vered. "You cannot know the power of the Demon Crown unless you've sampled it yourself. He *hears*. He *sees*."

"I am king of Porotane!" shouted Lorens.

Those assembled in the room fell to one knee and bowed their heads. Vered followed their lead, but from one corner of his eye he saw that Baron Theoll's obeisance to the new king came slower than that of the others. To most, Lorens might be king. But not to the diminutive baron.

"The burial should have been more," observed Santon. "After all, Freow ruled Porotane for twenty years."

"Only as regent," said Vered. "But I agree. It was as if Lorens denied all connection with those who have come before." Vered wondered if Lorens knew that the dead duke had not been his uncle, had been nothing more than an opportunistic pretender. Even if he did, Vered puzzled over why the young king did not acknowledge Freow's contribution for so many years.

The wars might have been worse.

"There," said Santon, nudging Vered in the ribs. "There're the first representatives from the rebel bands."

"Only three? Lorens spoke of ten."

"A start," said Santon.

Vered watched as the three marched across the vast expanse between the chamber door and the foot of the steps leading to the throne. Harhar cavorted and rolled about at one side of the throne, oblivious to the pomp and ceremony of the occasion. For the first time in two decades, rebels met to discuss a truce.

"At last we meet in the flesh," Lorens said in a voice an octave deeper than usual. Vered noted how the young king had grown in stature while wearing the Demon Crown; it affected his voice, also.

"We have never met, even in spirit," declared one rebel leader.

"Not so, Tuvonne. I have visited your secret councils and listened to your schemes. You do not bargain in good faith, not when your soldiers march against the castle under the banner of truce." Lorens gestured to the guards lining the walls of the immense audience chamber.

"Wait, stop!" cried Tuvonne. "You violate the terms of the truce!"

"You violated them before entering." The rest of Lorens' words died in the whistle of arrows flying. Tuvonne screamed as a dozen—more— pierced his flesh.

"Uh, King Lorens," ventured another rebel.

"You declare allegiance to me, Belmorgan? Or do you allow yourself to be seduced by Tember of Farreach's sister, Oturra?" Lorens pointed to another rebel.

"No, my king, no!" protested Belmorgan. The man fell to his knee and cried, "I am ecstatic that one of the true royal blood again sits on the throne."

"Good. Then divert your troops against those of Tuvonne. Destroy that traitor's force totally."

"Your Majesty!"

"Destroy them and you will become First Duke of Porotane. And," Lorens said, sarcasm coloring his words, "if you still want her, Oturra will be your consort."

"You are most generous, Majesty."

"Only to those who serve me well." Lorens turned his attention to the remaining rebel leader.

"You, Tember of Farreach, have one chance only of declaring allegiance to the throne of Porotane. How say you? Loyalty to me or death?"

Tember dropped and pledged his unswerving loyalty to King Lorens of Porotane.

"The others who refused to attend. I know the most intimate details of their battle plans, of their lives. In your service to the throne, this information will be given you. None dare oppose the one who wears the Demon Crown!"

Blazing green swathed his body as Lorens stood and shoved a shaking fist into the air.

Lorens swirled around and vanished through a door immediately behind the throne. Harhar followed Belmorgan and Tember from the chamber, shaking a rattle at them and making lewd comments about Tember's sister and Belmorgan's mistress. The men strained to keep their blades firmly in sheath. But Harhar's intimate knowledge of Oturra's affairs stayed them. The jester could have learned such matters only from King Lorens —and the Demon Crown.

"The countryside is more awash in blood now than it was when Freow lived," said Santon. "There seems no end to the double-dealing and merciless battles."

The two men walked to the battlements. Some distance away Theoll spoke in guarded tones with Captain Squann. Squann's arm rode high in a sling and bloody bandages attested to his wound sustained in battle for the new king.

"What do they discuss?" wondered Santon.

Vered did not even glance in the baron's direction. "Plots to overthrow Lorens. Theoll is not the kind to take defeat easily. He has been on the throne, however briefly, and tasted the heady wine of kingly power."

"Power," snorted Santon. "What power can mere men bring to bear against the Demon Crown? Lorens sees and hears everything, no matter where in the kingdom."

"There," said Vered, pointing. "See how the troops line up along the River Ty? A good tactic. Gaemock must either retreat or sustain massive damage to his flank."

"The siege was ill-conceived."

"He had no choice after Duke Freow died." Vered smiled weakly. "Dews Gaemock might have been king if we had not returned with Lorens. Theoll's iron grip would have spawned more dissension within the castle than twenty years of civil war had."

"Nosto could have controlled them with his Inquisition," countered Santon.

"But the Inquisitor is not totally under Theoll's power. Not yet. Archbishop Nosto works for his own ends. He might even believe in what he is doing."

"The saints help us all, if that be true," said Santon. "Forty-three have been put to the Question and died just since we've been in the castle."

"Forty-three in only nine days," mused Vered. "Bloody times. Look! Gaemock retreats, as I thought."

"Even with Belmorgan and Tember supporting Lorens' soldiers, they cannot score a clean victory over Gaemock. See how he slips away to the north?"

"The Uvain Plateau is a difficult spot to hide in," said Vered. "Especially when Lorens magically spies on everyone." A shudder raced up his spine. He fell silent and lost himself in thought.

"Did we do right?" asked Santon. "Bringing Lorens back? Even if it was what Alarice wanted, did we do the proper thing for Porotane?"

"The civil war comes to an end," said Vered. "More death must precede peace, but it comes. Lorens slowly unites the scattered rebel bands— or annihilates them."

"Gaemock's followers are too loyal. He will not be denied the throne."

Vered said nothing to this. He agreed. Had fate turned in different ways, he might have been a supporter of Dews Gaemock, rebel and thief though the man was.

"We know so little about Lorens."

"He works swiftly to consolidate his rule," said Santon.

"But he kills when a better, if slower, way would be through negotiation. He knows the innermost secrets of everyone confronting him. He could use that rather than force of arms. There's been so much killing. Too much."

"He changes, even as we watch."

Both Santon and Vered jumped in surprise at the newcomer. Vered turned to see the court jester behind them. They had been so engrossed in their discussion that neither had heard Harhar approach.

"What are you saying, fool?" demanded Santon.

Harhar shrugged and cut a caper. "He turns cruel. The Demon Crown does it to him. It might do it to anyone enduring its magics night and day."

"He never removes it?" asked Vered, startled at this revelation. He remembered the way it had affected Lorens when he had donned the crown for the first time.

"Never. And he changes, always he changes. Who's to say that this is bad? Or good? Not I, not I!" Harhar jumped to the battlements and started walking on his hands along the precipice.

"Porotane will be at peace one day soon," said Santon. "That is good."

"Good," echoed Vered. "Yes, I suppose it is. It is what Alarice sought for the kingdom."

"The Glass Warrior!" called Harhar. "Such beauty, such courage. Yes, yes, it is what she sought for Porotane. But is it all that she sought?"

For that neither Vered nor Birtle Santon had an answer.

PHANTOMS ON THE WIND

ONE

"The screams," said Birtle Santon. "It's their awful screams that I cannot tolerate." Even as he spoke, another shriek of pure agony echoed through the corridors of the Castle Porotane, center of power for the kingdom and new residence of King Lorens.

"I think it lends an air of distinction to these miserable, dismal stone corridors," said Vered. The young man lounged languidly on the black velvet-covered fainting couch, nibbling almost daintily at a slice of cheese impaled on the tip of his needle-pointed dirk. "Any castle can be home. I get so tired of simple dripping walls and dungeons that beg for that certain touch of humanity."

"That certain drop of blood, you mean," snapped Santon.

"A drop, a bucket, what matters this?" asked Vered, enjoying his friend's anger. "As long as it is not *our* precious blood being spilled by those butchers of the Inquisition."

Birtle Santon snorted and moved to the narrow window. The view of Porotane's farmlands and the gently flowing, green-hued River Ty from this castle aerie proved deceptive. All seemed tranquil in the land.

Another hideous scream, louder than before, made Santon cringe.

"Is it the Inquisition or merely another of dear King Lorens' interrogations?" he asked of Vered. Santon tapped his withered left arm against the outer stone wall nervously, knowing that it might soon be their screams tormenting the peace of the castle.

For all Vered's apparent ease, Santon saw subtle signs of tension in his friend. The brown eyes darted to and fro at the slightest of sounds. Muscles tensed along his powerful shoulders. The way he ran his hands through the shock of light brown hair dangling into his eyes gave more proof, as if Santon needed it, that Vered grew increasingly apprehensive about their safety. He taunted his friend only to break the boredom—and to relieve the strain they both felt so keenly.

"Lorens owes us much," said Vered, as if trying to convince himself. "Did we not seek him out in the City of Stolen Dreams and pluck him from his cruel master's bondage?"

"I think our young king approved of Patrin."

"Impossible. The wizard was a despot. He ruled the city with an iron hand. He badgered his apprentice. Lorens *must* consider us his saviours. And if that's not enough, we—"

"Gave him the Demon Crown," finished Santon.

They both fell silent at mention of the crown. The simple circlet of gold had been given to King Waellkin three centuries ago by the demon Kalob as restitution for the evil demons had visited upon humans. Only those of the royal line could wear the crown. And therein had been planted the seeds of even more demonic evil.

Civil wars had split the kingdom for years after King Lamost had died mysteriously. Lamost's brother, Duke Freow, had assumed the regency until the twin children of the king could be rescued from a kidnapping wizard.

Freow had proven to be a commoner, a usurping impostor intent on maintaining his own rule over the kingdom. Not until he lay on his deathbed had he sent Alarice, the Glass Warrior, to find an heir to the throne and to restore the Demon Crown to the proper royal brow.

"Alarice," Birtle Santon said in a whisper so low that Vered could not hear. How he had loved her! And how he had wept bitter tears when she had perished rescuing Lorens from the City of Stolen Dreams. Her body had vanished in the sands of the Sazan Desert and they had been unable to pay her the homage due a true hero.

"Very well," said Vered. "Lorens may not approve of our past lives. Who can say that being itinerant thieves is a proper life? But he cannot gainsay our help in restoring him to the throne."

"Was that such a triumph on our part?" asked Santon.

"Quiet, fool!" hissed Vered. His brown eyes grew wide with fear. This startled Santon more than anything Vered might have said. The young warrior feared nothing, and now he showed every sign of outright terror. "Lorens might be wearing the Demon Crown and overhear us!"

Santon sighed. Such was the power of the demonic crown. The wearer could project his senses anywhere in the kingdom, hearing and seeing every word and deed. The intelligence so gathered proved a boon to Lorens in his fight against the rebel factions striving for supremacy in the countryside. It also gave the monarch the perfect method for ferreting out traitors in his own rank.

New screams, higher, shriller, more feminine, raked across Santon's consciousness. He tried to shut out the cries of agony generated in the dungeons and failed. It required no major leap of imagination to picture himself thrust into the wire coffin and having a hooded torturer begin heating the wires. Santon tried not to think of the stench of burned flesh or the pain it would give.

"You think too much, Santon," Vered said. "You dwell on the dark rather than seeking the light."

"You may be right. But there is one point on which we both must ponder. What is to be our destiny? Simply sitting and idly eating until we grow fat and dull, or should we be doing something more?"

"What do you suggest?" Vered had tried to show himself impervious to the agonies being dealt out below them in the dungeons. The new screams visibly wracked him. His face paled and his quick, steady hands developed a tremor.

"Not joining the rebels," Santon said. "There is no profit in being a soldier for even an enlightened commander like Dews Gaemock."

"The name," Vered whispered urgently. "Do not mention it! *He* might be listening!"

"Such fear," scoffed Santon. "Do you think Lorens needs *any* reason for cruelty? Listen well. Let your ears give testimony to the king's generosity with wanton pain."

"He needs no reason to send the innocent

to the dungeons," agreed Vered. The young man sagged in the couch's softness, all pretense of ease gone. A tiny facial tic jerked under his left eye. His nimble fingers stroked up and down the blade of his dirk and one long leg hooked over the couch arm swung constantly. "He needs no reason to send us into the uncaring arms of a torturer, does he?"

"My thoughts match yours, it seems. We have done what Alarice asked of us. We have delivered the true king to the throne and given him the Demon Crown. There is nothing more for us to do here. Let us find safety elsewhere." Again his green eyes turned to the narrow slit in the castle wall and focused on the purpled summits of the Yorral Mountains.

"It has been some time since we travelled across the Uvain Plateau," said Vered. "The wines there are second to none. I can drink no other. The swill they serve in this miserable heap of stone and mortar is certainly not to my liking. And the food tastes of month-old mold and inexpert preparation. Better to endure your trail cooking than this cuisine."

Santon listened to his friend work up trivial reasons for departing the Castle Porotane. The only reason to leave lay in their desire for continued life. Along with the ability to magically cast his senses across the kingdom using the Demon Crown, King Lorens also accepted the penalty: creeping madness.

A sudden rap on the heavy wood door brought both Birtle Santon and Vered to their feet, weapons ready for the fight that would end their lives.

"Vered?" came a muffled voice. "Are you in there? Please. It is Kerin."

"Ah, such a lovely lass. She should not be

kept waiting in the drafty hallways." Vered spoke bravely but his caution in opening the door was not lost on Santon. Vered kept one booted boot planted securely on the floor to prevent the door from being kicked open and his dagger poised for a killing thrust. "It is Kerin!" Vered exclaimed, almost surprised at not finding deception.

The flame-tressed serving maid slipped into the room. Vered closed the door and bolted it, only to find Kerin's slender white arms thrown around his neck. She buried her face in his shoulder and sobbed.

"There, there," he said, trying to still her unbridled sorrow. "What makes one so lovely weep so? Have I not been good to you? Surely, you did not find fault with anything happening last night." He glanced over at Santon and shrugged, as if saying, "Are they never satisfied?"

"Kerin," spoke up Birtle Santon. "What is wrong?"

"It's awful. Th-they came and took her. Rogina."

"Her sister," explained Vered. "Who has taken Rogina? And for what reason? She is only fifteen."

"In the night when I was with you. The king's guard took her. They gave no reason for it. I . . . I just found that they took her to the dungeons."

Another long, high-pitched shriek rose and rattled the foundations of their nerve.

"Can it be Rogina's cries we hear?" Vered asked.

"No," Santon said quickly. "No, it is another's."

Vered knew his friend lied; Santon could not know whose pain they listened to. But Kerin accepted even this small white lie because she wanted to believe.

"There are factions at war within the castle as well as without," said Santon. "Baron Theoll has never accepted Lorens' return. The baron saw the chance to sit on the throne uncontested and did not willingly step down."

"A cruel man, the baron," said Kerin. "But he is not as cruel as Archbishop Nosto."

"Ah, yes, the follower of the True Path with the fanatic's fire in his eyes." Santon had heard the gut-wrenching tales of Nosto's Inquisition against impiety and the holy Inquisitor who tortured until those straying from the path of righteousness confessed—or died before confessing. Luckily, neither Santon nor Vered had occasion to cross paths with the archbishop after Lorens' had been crowned King of Porotane.

"Can you find her? Can you save her?" Kerin's plea almost choked in her throat. "I know it's much to ask. After all, we only shared a bed a few nights."

"But those were the best nights of my life!" exclaimed Vered. He shot a glance at Santon to keep his friend silent.

"Then you will find Rogina and save her?"

"Save her?" asked Vered. "From what? We know that a girl so young cannot be a rebel or a conspirator against the king. And what crime could she possibly commit that would require her imprisonment? No, we must look elsewhere."

"Archbishop Nosto?" asked Santon.

Kerin shook her head. Strands of the fiery

hair fell into her eyes. Vered gently pushed them back to stare into her gold-flaked green eyes. For the first time he noticed a tiny island of carmine in her right eye and a circle of black around the iris.

"My sister is devout. She never strays from the True Path."

"Theoll has perverse tastes. Could he have whisked her off to his bed?" Vered clutched Kerin tightly. "There, there," he soothed. "I merely think aloud. This might not have happened at all."

"It might be a better fate than being sent to the king's dungeons," said Santon, not trying to temper the bitterness in his words. He cared nothing for the politics within the castle's walls. He preferred the open countryside with wind in his hair and sun burning his face.

"We need information," said Vered. "And I know the source for all wisdom."

"Harhar?" asked Santon.

"Who else?"

"But he's the court jester! He's a halfwit. Listen to him. And he drools!" Kerin was shocked by the notion that the court fool could provide any information.

"He has astounding moments of lucidity," said Santon. "He listened long to Duke Freow and aided him in his last hours."

"His philosophy is what you would expect of a fool," cut in Vered, "but his eyes and ears are the match of any hunter's."

Kerin stared at Vered in disbelief, but she had no one else to go to for help. Vered seemed competent enough, even if he did think the fool might be of some help.

"You stay in our quarters, my dear," said Vered, "and let Santon and me make a few discreet inquiries. Harhar is easy to find but hard to talk with. He is always near the king."

"Or the baron," said Santon. "He and Baron Theoll spend a considerable amount of time together, or so it's rumored among the house guard."

The two adventurers left the serving maid in their suite and ventured forth. Santon carried his shield of spun glass given to him by Alarice, and Vered sported her short glass sword. They stalked the castle's corridors more like hunters than guests.

"There. The throne room," said Vered. "I hear his silly jape."

Santon pushed aside a hanging curtain of gold beads and peered into the long, narrow throne room. He blinked. How it had changed —and not for the better. The brief time Theoll had occupied the tall-backed ebony throne he had brought in jeweled ornaments for the cold stone walls, fancy carved wood chairs for the court retainers, tapestries both rich and intricate to soften the cold walls, and a magic lantern that emitted a soft, diffuse golden light on everything within the room. It shone on Theoll, when seated on the throne, a single shaft of pure white light.

All that had changed. Gone were the censers burning sandalwood and pine. The heavy, cloying scent from the room reminded Santon of a charnel house. Death was everywhere. Over the jeweled coats of arms on the walls were hung the shriveled bodies of traitors. The tapestries and rugs had been spattered with blood as executions took place at the foot of the throne. Worst of all from Santon's view was the change in the magical light source.

Gone was the golden hue it had once cast.

The single ray of light centered on the throne had turned from virgin white to a sickly green that hinted at corruption and unholy decay.

And King Lorens seemed not to notice—or care.

"The king is in court again," Vered said. He made no attempt to keep his voice down. With the Demon Crown settled upon his temples, the monarch could hear and see anywhere in the kingdom. Those closest garnered the majority of his attention, though, because of several abortive assassination attempts.

Santon tried to hold back the shudder that wracked his body. His distaste for Lorens knew no bounds. The youngling had been apprenticed to the wizard Patrin for too long. He had never learned how to diplomatically deal with others. He had been a slave suddenly released from his bondage and had responded with the same savagery that Patrin had shown him. He knew only master and servant. The word "peer" was lacking in both his vocabulary and experience.

"The crown," said Vered. "See how it glows?"

"I have never seen it radiate that putrid color before. It must be the magic lantern's doing."

"You have it ass backwards, Santon, my friend. The magic from the Demon Crown affects the lantern."

"Infects is a better word," Santon said. The bladder green halo around the crown surged and contracted like a giant muscle flexing. Lorens sat rigidly on the throne, fists clenched and his glassy eyes peering directly ahead.

"He sees nothing," said Vered. "Nothing within this room. He casts forth for traitors in other parts of the kingdom. This is our chance to speak with Harhar."

The two men tried to moderate their pace across the empty throne room but soon found themselves running. The court jester rolled and bounced and shook his rattle at the foot of the dais, as if performing for an audience of thousands.

"Harhar, a word with you," said Vered.

"Ho! My good friends! You have come to see my new act! Listen to my japes. They are ever so much better than the others." Harhar looked around as if imparting court secrets. "I have hired two soldiers to write the jokes for me."

"Fine, yes," said Santon, glancing upward at King Lorens. The monarch's expression had not changed. He might have been one of those impaled along the walls for all the life he showed. Santon knew they were as safe talking in the presence of the king as they were meeting clandestinely—perhaps safer. Secrecy drew the suspicious ruler's attention. But to so openly oppose the young king worried Santon.

"A curious thing happened in the night," said Vered.

"Oh, I've heard this one. It's a joke, isn't it? About the chambermaid and the duke's prize stallion?"

"No, no, not exactly," said Vered, trying to keep his temper. "Rogina, the younger sister of Kerin. You know who I mean?"

"Rogina? Such a brat, but her sister is nice. Fine hair so red that it appears to burn in the sunlight. She has given me food from the royal table. I know Kerin."

"She loves her sister very much and would like to know what has happened to her," continued Vered. "Rogina was taken by guards in the middle of the night."

Santon moved slightly, his shield coming up to protect his side. The motion was pure reflex. The flash of intelligence that had crossed Harhar's face made him doubt the jester's apparent idiocy.

"No reason for Lorens to take her," said Harhar. "He has the pick of any lady in the kingdom."

Santon could not resist asking, "Who does he sleep with? What lady?"

"Or lord. He might sleep with a lord," said Harhar. "But he doesn't."

"Sleep with men?" asked Vered, frowning.

"Sleep with anyone. He might be a cleric for all his escapades."

"Living in the City of Stolen Dreams as a wizard's apprentice might have . . . done things to him," suggested Vered.

"Oh, no, I think not. I think he is frightened. So much power and he is frightened. That is a fine jape, isn't it? More power than any king in our memory and he is afraid." Harhar laughed maniacally and somersaulted to the foot of the throne and peered up.

"Is that it, my liege? Are you scared shitless of the little people like me? Is my wit so barbed that it pierces your lion's heart?" Harhar laughed again and did a double handspring to return to Vered's side.

Santon lowered his shield. The brief flash of intelligence Harhar displayed had passed, the old crackbrained behavior returning. No man taunted a king, much less one as powerful as Lorens.

"What, then, do you make of the serving

maid's disappearance?" asked Vered. "A man of your standing hears all."

"My standing?" Harhar leaped into the air, turned adroitly, and landed on his belly. He began wiggling about like a *poulten* lizard trapped in the Desert of Sazan's midday sun. "I never stand. I lie!" Harhar rolled onto his back and laughed hysterically.

"This is not as good an idea as I thought," said Santon. He stared at Lorens. The king moved slightly, as if shifting his attention from one distant spot to another. Sweat beaded his forehead as if he strained. The obscene pulsations of the green halo from the Demon Crown accentuated the high cheekbones and cast a pallor on Lorens that made him seem sickly.

"We should explore other avenues for our information," said Santon. "Others that take us away from this room." He was not a squeamish man. Being surrounded by the impaled, mummifying remains of so many nobles robbed him of any desire to linger.

The sight of what Lorens had become sickened him even further.

"Harhar, are you sure you cannot tell us who stole the lovely young girl?" Vered tried to coax the information from the jester.

"I lie, I die, I cry, I sigh. It is all too fey for me to say nay or yea."

"Leave him," said Santon. He tugged at Vered's sleeve with his good hand. "Even if he knows, it doesn't seem that he is going to tell us."

"Good day to you, sir jester," said Vered. He performed a courtly bow and backed away, treating the fool as nobility.

Once past the golden beaded curtains,

Vered heaved a deep sigh. "It is difficult dealing with one such as Harhar. I feel the currents of deep thought in him, yet only bubbles of noxious gases rise to the surface."

"The lieutenant of guards who cheated you out of the ten gold pieces," said Santon. "Do you think you might get him to talk of Rogina?"

"Cheated me!" cried Vered. "He did no such thing. I let him take the money in what appeared to be less than fair circumstances. I cultivate him as one cultivates a sickly plant. One day he will bloom and give forth the tempting fruits of information."

Santon started to tell his friend what he thought of such an approach when he stopped and stared. Ahead of them in the hall stood three burly soldiers with swords drawn. Santon glanced over his shoulder. Three more soldiers blocked their retreat.

"We seem to have found the ruffians responsible for poor Rogina's kidnapping," said Vered, drawing his glass sword. "Let us hope they can be convinced to tell us where they've taken her."

"Let's hope we can fight our way out of this!"

Santon lifted his shield in time to deflect a thrust from the soldier in front of him. He whipped a length of chain from around his waist and flailed away with it.

Whoever had stolen away Rogina did not intend for them to find her. Ever.

TWO

Baron Theoll paced the length of his sleeping chambers, one leg dragging slightly from an old wound. He cradled his left arm protectively; that assassin's injury had yet to heal fully. The small, dark, intense man spun suddenly and pointed at Harhar.

"That is all you can tell me?" he demanded of the court fool.

Harhar's head bobbed up and down as if it had been placed on a spring. "Truly, Baron, I know nothing more. How can I when he sits on his throne and stares at . . . places no ordinary mortal can see or hear?"

"He checks on the rebel forces," said Theoll. "That is the only reason he would be so preoccupied."

"Dews Gaemock is a fine man," said Harhar. "I have met him. He gave me sweets and an entire piece of silver for my capers."

Theoll scowled. At times he wondered if anything but maggots infested the fool's brain. At other times, Harhar's observations proved astute. "What of Lorens? His condition. His words. I need to know everything. He has barred me from the throne room."

"A grim place now, Baron Theoll," Harhar

said solemnly. "I can hardly get into the mood for joking with the corpses strewn about. You would think that a king could be neater."

Theoll stared at the jester. Did he mock Lorens—and Theoll—or were the words without sarcasm? Theoll could not tell.

"I need to know everything about our newly crowned king. Tell me of the Demon Crown and how it affects him."

"The ugly green nimbus around his head," Harhar said, as if reciting a litany, "billows and boils. The more he concentrates, the uglier it becomes. It is hard to tell whether he controls it—or it controls our beloved king."

"The crown is dangerous. It is no mere legend that it can seize the mind of a weakling."

"Not like you, O my Lord Theoll?"

Theoll's right hand lashed out. He slapped the jester and sent him tumbling. His hand stung but the jester's face remained untouched. Theoll thought his blow had been robbed of real strength by the fool's quick reflexes.

"Do not taunt me," Theoll said in an icy tone. "I am not of the direct line and could never wear the Demon Crown for the lengths of time Lorens does. But it would sit well on my head for a few minutes a day."

"How goes the spying on the serving wenches? Do you still peer through the holes in the walls at them as they disrobe for their toilet?" The jester scuttled like a beetle to avoid Theoll's weak kick. The baron's injuries prevented him from catching the mocking fool and giving him the thrashing he had so richly earned with that remark.

"I need to know what happens within these walls. Only my constant surveillance can put down dissent."

"Against King Lorens?"

"Against the kingdom. Porotane desperately needs a strong leader. That old fool Freow managed to let the civil war rage for decades." Theoll spun about, pulling his purple silk cape about his small frame. "Lorens is not the leader his beloved father was."

"He's not the leader Duke Freow was," muttered Harhar.

"Even with the crown," Theoll went on, "he is unable to crush the rebels. If anything their power grows. Lorens' coronation has united the strongest rebel bands."

"Dews Gaemock and Dalziel Sef join forces on the other side of the River Ty."

"How did you know that?" snapped Theoll. "Only this morning did my scouts return with that information." Theoll's dark eyes narrowed as he looked at the jester. "Lorens *saw* their alliance using the Demon Crown. Is that how you discovered it?"

"Oh, yes, Lord, yes, yes, of course it is." Harhar hunkered down behind a low table and put up an arm to fend off any further blows directed at him by the baron.

Theoll ignored the fool. The jester had his uses. He overheard tidbits of valuable information because no one considered it necessary to stay their tongue in his presence. Only Theoll had learned to tap this geyser of knowledge. But such an unreliable fount Harhar was!

"Lorens' power extends beyond the crown," Theoll said. "He was not apprenticed to Patrin those long years for naught. But what does he know? What spells does he cast?"

"How badly has he angered the Wizard of Storms?" asked Harhar.

"What?" Theoll swung around, almost losing his balance. His good hand reached out for support. He blanched at the mere mention of the powerful wizard. "What do you know of the Wizard of Storms?"

Harhar shrugged. The fool moved out from behind the table. "I heard Lorens mention him, mayhaps. Or perhaps it was Archbishop Nosto. Someone did. The storms march down the valleys in the far mountains and assault the Uvain Plateau. The Wizard of Storms is upset. That is all that is known."

"For more years than I have been alive, no one has heard from the Wizard of Storms. Why does he choose now to make his power felt?" Theoll sagged into a chair. His rise to power had seemed so simple when he learned that Freow had not been the true brother of King Lamost. Kill the impostor, assume the throne. Simple. Easy. But Freow had clung tenaciously to life. Too tenaciously. The subtle poisons that Theoll had fed him had been neutralized. But who in Castle Porotane had both knowledge and opportunity? Why save the old faker?

Theoll's teeth ground together as he thought of Freow sending the Glass Warrior to find the royal twins.

"They had been gone for so long. Who would have thought either lived?" he said aloud.

"The twins? Everyone, Lord, everyone knew they lived. Even old Duke Freow."

Theoll glared at the jester. "Lorens lived. His ability to wear the crown as he does proves his royal blood. But nothing has been shown of his leadership. He spies endlessly using the Demon Crown and allows underlings free rein within the castle walls."

"You mean others instead of you, Baron?"

"Is the Glass Warrior truly dead?"

"Alarice perished," Harhar said in a sad tone. "She laughed at my jests. She was a good person. She brought me sweets and gave me money, too."

Theoll reached across the table to cuff the jester. Again his blow missed its target, but Harhar tumbled across the room and crashed into the wall as if it had landed with full force.

"The two who returned with Lorens and the Demon Crown. I need to know their part. I have tried to spy upon them and received—" Theoll abruptly stopped speaking. He had been reaching for the small puncture wound under his right eye. The night after Lorens' coronation Theoll had slipped along his secret passages to open a spyhole into Birtle Santon and Vered's quarters. For his trouble he had received a poke with a pointed stick that nearly put out his eye. Each subsequent attempt to spy on them had resulted in failure. The two petty thieves proved more careful than others inside the castle in both word and deed.

"They are prisoners," said Harhar.

"What?" Again Theoll tried to hide his shock at the jester's words. The baron felt his threads of power breaking. Harhar knew more about movement in the castle than he did.

"The Inquisition, the Inquisition, no one knows when Archbishop Nosto brings his Inquisition!" Harhar turned his words into a shrill chant that set Theoll's nerves on edge.

"Silence!" the baron roared. "How dare Nosto meddle like this!"

"The Archbishop dares to dream. He is a fanatic with a dream. When was the last cleric king in Porotane?"

"There has never been one. Don't be absurd. The people would never tolerate it."

Theoll spoke one way even as his thoughts turned another. Nosto *might* have such aspirations hidden in his putrid heart. With the kingdom torn asunder by the warring factions, who could say that a strong religious leader might not unite Porotane?

"Yes, Baron, the Inquisition is a potent tool," said Harhar. "Are you going to let him keep Santon and Vered?"

"Why not? They are insignificant characters in this passion play." Theoll watched the fool's reaction. Forbidden knowledge, guilty knowledge, revealed knowledge. It all flashed across Harhar's face. "What do they know that can harm me?"

"They travelled with Alarice. She spoke of many things. Maybe they know that the demon Kalob has been banished permanently. To reveal this to Archbishop Nosto might mean . . ." Harhar's words trailed off.

Theoll wiped sweat from his brow. He had used the jester to dupe Nosto into thinking that the demon had returned. It had been a clever piece of stage acting, or so he had thought at the time. Archbishop Nosto had responded in exactly the way Theoll had hoped.

"They cannot know. There is no way that the Glass Warrior could know. Only you and I know, Harhar." From the folds of his cape Theoll drew forth a wicked dagger. He rose and went to where the jester cowered. If Harhar thought to threaten him with this damning information, he could stem the source with a single slice across the fool's throat.

To his surprise, the fool rolled over onto his back like a dog and exposed his privates. When he began barking like a dog, Theoll put the dagger away and turned away in disgust. Harhar was not merely simpleminded. He was demented.

"The guards took them to the dungeons for the Inquisitor," called out Harhar. Theoll looked at the jester and again wondered if insanity or cunning drove him.

"Come along. We must find Archbishop Nosto and get to the prisoners. There might be a way to use them against the Archbishop *and* Lorens."

"Dangerous ploys, my Lord."

"Of course it is dangerous," said Theoll, his mind already exploring possible avenues of intrigue. "Do you think that ruling Porotane is a simple game?"

Theoll started off, his game leg dragging slightly and making a sliding noise along the corridor. At a discreet distance his guards followed. Harhar bobbed and bounced and danced around, showing himself for the fool that he was. Theoll motioned for his guards to hold station when they arrived at Castle Porotane's lowest levels. The Inquisition allowed only a few into the dungeons.

Most departed with neither life nor soul.

The crimson-clad guard at the door opened it and admitted Theoll but tried to slam the heavy wood portal in Harhar's face. The jester began to cry like a small child deprived of his favorite toy.

"Let the fool in," Theoll said distractedly. "He will harm nothing."

"Archbishop Nosto's command—"

"Such an order is meaningless when it comes to a fool. Look at him. He has no soul to contaminate. He has no mind to be swayed from the True Path."

The guard reluctantly allowed Harhar inside the torture chambers. The jester cut capers and danced about until the guard got dizzy watching. He returned to his post at the door to keep unbelievers out—and in.

"Do you come to cleanse your soul, Baron?" asked Nosto. The archbishop had stripped to the waist and wore only tight-fitting red silk breeches and red and black armbands with mystical signs on them. Blood smeared the man's flat, well-muscled belly. Theoll saw no indication that it was Nosto's blood. The archbishop had been converting heretics with knives and branding irons.

"My soul treads the True Path," Theoll said, speaking carefully. "It is yours that worries me, my good friend."

"Mine?" This oblique accusation of impiety affected Archbishop Nosto as Theoll had hoped it would. "I spend so much of my time and effort in this dreary place with heretics. Have they infected me with their evil thoughts? How have I strayed from the Path? My devotions last long into the night."

"The Demon Crown touches us all," said Theoll.

"Yes, the crown. King Lorens refuses my visits." Nosto closed his eyes and muttered what might have been a ward spell. "I feel him not in my presence."

"You sense his scrying spells?" asked Harhar.

"As a higher ranked cleric I wield certain small spells permitted by the saints. The crown's magic does not intrude on my work."

"What of the Wizard of Storms?" asked Harhar. "What of him? Do you sense his magic trundling down from the Castle of the Winds?"

"No." The denial came sharply. The archbishop spun and glared at the jester. "Do not even speak of that one in my presence. He opposes all I attempt."

"How do you know this, Nosto?" asked Theoll. "The Wizard of Storms has not been seen or heard from in decades."

"In my meditations he comes to me with obscene proposals. He sows the seeds of revolt in the land. His storm warriors again do battle with humans."

Theoll reached out and supported himself using the heavy wood table laden with torture instruments. Porotane teetered on the brink of complete war if the archbishop spoke the truth. Few armies were the match for a single magical storm warrior—or so went the legend. Theoll had never seen one of the mythical fighters. He barely believed that the Wizard of Storms existed.

But now? A chill raced up Theoll's spine and embraced his neck. He tried not to choke. Not only did Gaemock and Dalziel Sef disrupt the order of the kingdom, a wizard worked his way into the intricate equations of power. The baron began to doubt his chance for deposing Lorens and assuming the throne once more.

"We have wizards and rebels and a king turned from the True Path. A sorry state for Porotane," the baron said. "What is it that I can do to aid you in restoring order and piety, Archbishop Nosto?"

"Your words assure me that goodness has not fled the people of Porotane, Theoll. I attempt to find the root of festering evil within the walls of our castle. Only when this putrid heart is ripped out and the wound cleansed can we look farther afield and work on those warring beyond the walls."

Theoll slowly scanned the cells and re-straints used by the Inquisitors. He held back the shiver of distaste. His methods were more subtle. He preferred the slow poison to the branding iron. Many dangled from wrist chains fastened to hooks driven into the wood ceiling beams. Others had no chains; the hooks pierced their bodies. Still others were secured by form-fitting wire cages awaiting the heat that would burn the holy wire's imprint into heretical flesh.

"What of her, Nosto?" Theoll pointed out a red-haired girl chained into a contorted position across a barrel-shaped torture machine. Theoll wondered what had been done to her—what would be done—but did not ask to satisfy his curiosity. "She seems too young to be seduced from the True Path."

"She is a special case. Knowledge has fallen into her hands and she refuses to yield it to me. The Inquisition must know of every heretic if we are to succeed. Aiding those opposing me is the same as opposing me." Archbishop Nosto walked past a burning brazier. For a brief in-stant, Theoll fancied that the cleric had turned into the very demons he opposed. Light shone upward and gave an inhuman cast to Nosto's face. Sweat gleamed on his arms and chest, and the skin-tight breeches showed how excited Nosto became with his work.

Harhar gestured wildly from the far end of the dungeon. He pointed to a row of wooden coffins with holes cut for arms, legs, and heads. Two of the coffins were occupied. Theoll nodded slightly to indicate that he understood. These two were Vered and Birtle Santon.

Theoll tried to put together a plan that would benefit him the most. Archbishop Nosto wanted the two freebooters for interrogation.

What did they know that the cleric wanted? What did the serving wench know? Theoll had to believe that the young girl knew nothing. Nosto's reaction when he went to the wheels and barrels over which the redheaded girl was chained convinced Theoll of that.

"It is good that you hear it from another's lips," said Theoll, staring at the girl. He felt a moment of pity for her. Then the emotion faded. He could use her to his own ends without remorse. He had to consider her a victim of Archbishop Nosto's techniques and better off dead, as a result.

"What? Do you know?"

"That King Lorens is . . ." Theoll let his words trail off and entice Archbishop Nosto.

"The king is possessed by a demon!" the cleric roared. The echo throughout the dungeon drowned out the moans of the Inquisition's victims in various stages of dying.

"The Demon Crown has proven too strong for him. This must be the bait attracting the Wizard of Storms." Theoll threw out the name to evoke response. He was not disappointed.

"I knew it! This is proof of my vision! The kingdom has been handed over to demons once again! Heretics rush in to assume secular command and the spiritual is being stolen away by demons. Demons!"

Theoll started to add fuel to the fires of Nosto's fanaticism when he saw Harhar working on the coffins holding Santon and Vered. The baron started to gesture to the fool not to release them.

Too late. Both adventurers rose from their coffins and rubbed swollen and cramped arms and legs. Theoll's mind raced. He dared not bring this to Nosto's attention. The cleric would think him a part of the rescue and brand him a heretic.

The sight of so many lords and ladies dangling from chains and hooks convinced Theoll that his high position in the kingdom would mean nothing to Nosto. Even worse, if Harhar were caught, the fool would reveal the earlier hoax Theoll had engineered convincing Archbishop Nosto that the demon Kalob had returned to Porotane.

Baron Theoll had no choice but to hope that Santon and Vered escaped cleanly. Afterward, he would kill Harhar for putting him in such a dangerous position.

"Archbishop, a word," he said, drawing the cleric away from the serving wench. Theoll had no idea what he said. His lips worked to fabricate lies that would engage Nosto's attention while the two thieves escaped the dungeons. Theoll swallowed hard and almost babbled when he saw that Vered was not leaving.

The man worked his way along the dungeon floor on his belly, obviously intending to release the young girl.

"Tell me of the Wizard of Storms," Theoll said. "I have heard his name mentioned by Lorens several times. Are they truly allies?" Theoll did not listen to the liturgy delivered by the cleric. He had most of his attention focused on Vered cleverly picking the locks on the girl's chains.

She sagged forward and fell to the floor, bent in an arc from being pulled over the wheel for such a long time. Vered urged her to stand. The girl moved painfully, slowly, noisily. Theoll thanked his personal saints for the death sounds from so many others in the dungeon.

"How many Inquisitors do you have working here, Nosto?" he asked loudly. "At this moment there seems to be no one else."

"There is only the Inquisitor at the door and myself. The work must proceed cautiously. When the Question is put to a heretic, those with any doubt about their own belief in following the True Path might suffer."

"Understandable," said Theoll. Harhar and Santon had circled the dungeon and approached the exit from one direction while Vered and the girl approached from the opposite side.

Archbishop Nosto started to turn back to where he thought the girl had been securely chained. Theoll took the cleric's sweaty upper arm and maneuvered him about. "I must confess, Archbishop. I . . ." Theoll's mind refused to produce an appropriate sin for confession. Grasping at threads, he almost babbled, "Dreams. I have dreams inhabited by this Wizard of Storms."

"An evil sign, Baron, but not one to be concerned over unduly. Unless these dreams carry over to your waking moments."

Theoll dared to look over his shoulder. Santon and Vered had taken the girl out of the dungeon. The Inquisitor lay to one side of the door. Theoll felt a small surge of relief at this. His personal guards would capture the trio outside. All that remained was to escape Archbishop Nosto's clutches himself.

"Do your dreams affect you?" demanded Archbishop Nosto.

Harhar came to his rescue. The jester rolled over and over and began to sputter and shout and carry on.

"Him," said Theoll, inspiration upon him. "I dream of the jester being inhabited by demons. He is being seized even as we stare at him!"

Harhar gibbered and danced and ducked under Archbishop Nosto's arms as the cleric tried to restrain him. "Demons everywhere!" the jester cried. "I can see them. Big ones, little ones, they are everywhere! They enter the dungeons and come after me. But Harhar is too fast. He gets away from them before they can harm him!"

"Demons!" Archbishop Nosto reached for his holy book. "Demons have entered these sanctified chambers. Truly, this is the Wizard of Storms' doing!"

"Your Inquisitor," said Theoll, turning Nosto's attention from Harhar. "He is taken by demons!"

"By the saints!" Archbishop Nosto hurried to his assistant's side and knelt, beginning the exorcism rites.

"I will leave you, Nosto. If there is anything I can do to aid you—" Theoll knew that the cleric would deny help from a secular lord. He did. Theoll motioned to Harhar to leave the dungeons. To his relief, the fool did not hesitate.

Theoll closed the heavy dungeon door behind him, shutting off both death moans and Archbishop Nosto's rapid exorcism of nonexistent demons from his Inquisitor.

He had done well planting seeds of doubt about King Lorens and this Wizard of Storms in Nosto's mind. And he had escaped with his life!

Luck went with Theoll. By month's end he would again assume the throne and rule Porotane.

He strode off, his limp hardly hindering him. He wanted to interrogate Vered and Santon. By now his guards would have them safely hidden away in the wing of the castle where even the archbishop's Inquisition could not find them.

THREE

"Guards!" yelled Birtle Santon as the trio escaped into the corridor beyond the Inquisition's dungeons.

His cry alerted Theoll's soldiers. The four men had been relaxing, paying little heed to the ghastly noises coming from the depths of the infernal chamber. When Santon and Vered saw what was happening, they charged.

Bare-handed they fought the soldiers—and drove hard fists into throats and poked fingers into eyes and lifted knees into crotches. The skirmish lasted for less time than four beats of a frenzied heart.

"I'm all cut and bloody," complained Vered. He tried to smooth the wrinkles from his once elegant clothing and failed. Most of his finery hung in tatters from being imprisoned in Archbishop Nosto's coffin for long hours and having nails driven into his flesh.

"Good sirs, this way," Rogina urged. She motioned to a back passage.

"Where does it go?"

"What difference does it make?" asked Birtle Santon. "As long as it is away from the dungeons."

Vered scooped up a fallen sword and tossed

a dagger across to Santon, who deftly caught it in his good hand. Armed again, they felt more confident but neither wanted a fight with armed troopers. Both men found themselves hard pressed to keep up with the fleet Rogina as she climbed the narrow flagstone steps three at a time.

"She was a captive for how long?" panted Vered. "She was drawn on the wheel and stretched backwards over barrels? She's more nimble than any forest fox."

"The resiliency of youth," Santon gasped out, feeling the effect of the hard pace, too.

"You're an old man. Look at you. Arthritic and creaking and always complaining. But me?" Vered wiped sweat from his forehead. "I am hardly a half dozen summers older."

"Hurry!" Rogina was fully two flights of steps ahead of them now.

"It is the distance travelled in life that matters, not the age," said Santon. He sucked in a deep breath and grimly plowed on, refusing to slow or rest even though his body demanded it.

Both men collapsed when they reached the landing where Rogina awaited them. "Here," she said. "In here. No one will search for us if we stay hidden."

Vered's eyes widened in surprise when he saw the glass short sword Alarice had given him. To his right he heard Santon crowing when he retrieved his glass shield.

"You've brought us to the armory," said Vered, eyeing the racks of ready weapons.

"Aye," Rogina said, face flushed. "This is the archbishop's wing. They will seek everywhere for us, but not here. Who would think we would be foolish enough to crawl back into the jaws of the trap?"

"Good point," said Santon, "but then who would have thought we were stupid enough to do it the first time?"

Rogina went to Santon and shyly reached out and took his good hand. "If what you did is stupid, then thank you for being so stupid. You saved my life. The archbishop would have killed me." The young woman shuddered and wrapped her arms around herself.

"If we get word to your sister, can she find a way for us to escape the castle?" asked Vered. "It seems that Kerin is our only hope for leaving these stony walls."

"The walls have eyes," said Rogina. "Baron Theoll spies on everyone. That is well known."

Vered laughed. "He does it cleverly, but I was the smarter. I found his peephole in our quarters. A pity I did not put out his eye with my pointed stick." He made poking motions that produced first a smile, then a laugh from the girl.

"There is another watcher in Castle Porotane," said Santon. His green eyes locked with Vered's brown ones and silent communication passed. King Lorens might use the Demon Crown at any time to find them. If he did, what action would the monarch take? Neither man thought that Lorens supported Archbishop Nosto or Theoll. Both would have his throne. But his own plots and desires became serpentine as he cast his senses out across the kingdom.

"There are many," spoke up Rogina. "The king, aye, he watches." She shivered again at the thought of how the Demon Crown worked its evil magic on the king. "But Harhar sees all."

"And apparently tells anyone who asks in the proper fashion," said Santon. "He might have freed us but I am not certain that the jester wasn't also responsible for our capture."

"The time element is wrong, friend Santon," said Vered. "We had barely left the throne room when Nosto's soldiers captured us. From the looks on their faces, we took them by surprise. They might have thought to find us in our quarters instead of marching along so boldly in the halls outside the throne room."

"Too many seek to oust Lorens and place their own behinds on the throne," said Santon. "It is definitely time we faded into the woodlands and sought the serenity of nature."

"And the fat money pouch of a careless travelling merchant," chimed in Vered. "For all that the war has kept down the number of travellers, there are many who still dare us to rob them."

"You are thieves?" Rogina's eyes grew round. One tiny hand covered her mouth and she stepped back from Vered as if seeing him for the first time.

"It's a living," Vered said nonchalantly. "And it is what attracts your sister to me."

"Kerin prefers a thief to an honest man?"

"Who is honest within these walls?" asked Santon. "Theoll poisons. Nosto tortures. Who can say what Lorens does?"

"But her other lovers. They were all honest men."

"Soldiers, eh?" asked Vered, beginning to become irritated. "Have you ever seen a soldier in an honest game of chance? Or a merchant, mayhaps? Can anyone get an honest measure of grain from a merchant or assurance of not being shortchanged?"

"But—"

"Enough," interrupted Santon. "This is getting us nowhere—and we need to be long gone before the guards begin a systematic search for us. Even such a fine hiding place will come under scrutiny if the full force of the Inquisition is put behind the search."

"Find us or suffer for all eternity," muttered Vered. "A fine problem for the soldiers. We cannot be caught and Archbishop Nosto will damn them for all eternity if they don't find us."

"Let's make sure we are unfindable. Rogina, how do we contact your sister? We must be out of here before midnight."

"Why midnight?" asked the girl. "Oh, the guard changes then and more men patrol the walls."

"Giving Nosto and Theoll more guards to put into the search for us. There is no way we can get down the castle walls from the parapet."

"Not unless we want to end up in the thorny brambles surrounding the base of the castle. We need a special way out, an exit known only to a handful."

"Alarice knew of such," said Santon. Although his tone was neutral, his heart skipped a beat when he mentioned the Glass Warrior.

"She is not with us, except in spirit, old friend," said Vered, laying a hand on Santon's shoulder. "Finding the gate she used would do us little good. We lack the glass key that opens it."

"The postern on the north side?" asked Rogina. "When I was a child I used to play there. A long passage through the wall that opens into the castle? I know it. Not well, but enough to get you there."

"We can force the lock," said Santon. "Or your clever lock picking might again benefit us. Should we try?"

"I have no desire to spend the rest of my life in Archbishop Nosto's armory."

"Then Rogina, go and find Kerin. Bring her here and we will all leave. The Castle Porotane is no safe place for either of you after this day's deeds."

"But it's our home!" The girl almost cried at the idea of abandoning the castle.

"There will be better places," said Vered. "This pile of stone is drafty and rat-infested and reeking of magic."

"I'll find Kerin," Rogina said. "But it might be better if we met near the postern gate."

"She learns quickly," said Santon. "If she is followed, then we are almost free of the castle. Otherwise, she leads the guards back to this hidey-hole and we have to fight across the entire keep."

"The well marked with the statue of the farting cat is near the gate. Let's meet there," said Vered.

"It is a lion rampant," corrected Rogina.

Vered shrugged. To him most statuary looked obscene. The girl ducked through the armory door and vanished.

"It will take us only a few minutes to get to the well," said Vered. "Rogina must find Kerin and go there. We have a goodly hour to waste. Wake me when it is time to go." With that, Vered slid down the wall, pulled up his knees, and rested his head on them. Within seconds he snored loudly.

Santon shook his head. For all the battles he had survived, for all the times he would have given anything to rest for even an instant, he lacked his friend's ability to sleep in the midst of danger.

Birtle Santon stood watch, waiting for the proper time for them to make their escape.

"They betray us, Lord Dews," said Jiskko. "They surround us while we sit on our thumbs doing nothing."

"Calm yourself, Jiskko," said Dews Gaemock. "The meeting is carried out under a peace flag."

"No one but you honors the peace flag, Lord," grumbled the rebel lieutenant. "Remember how the black and gold banners of Ionia worked to cut us off during *those* peace talks?"

"I remember. But I feel that Sef is more honorable. And we knew about the trap in plenty of time."

"Dalziel Sef might be better at springing his traps."

"He might also want to parley."

"I do, Gaemock," came a gruff voice. Striding into the circle defined by the small campfire's light came a burly man with a great sword resting on his shoulder. He twitched a massive wrist and brought the heavy weapon about as if it were nothing heavier than a dirk. Sef drove the point into the dirt beside Gaemock's sword.

"Peace between us," Gaemock said.

"Peace," Dalziel Sef said reluctantly. "My advisors tell me this is a trap."

"You think to murder us!" protested Jiskko.

Sef and Gaemock stared at each other for a moment, then both burst out laughing. Gaemock said, "It seems we have some things in common."

"Untrusting advisors," said Sef. He motioned. A smaller man drifted in from beyond the fire's wan illumination, a nocked arrow ready to fire. "Enough, Asaway." He waited for the man to relax and put the powerful war bow aside.

"Can we get down to discussing an alliance or is there something more we have to endure?" asked Gaemock.

"A spot of brandy?" asked Sef, pulling a flask from his rucksack. He popped the cork and held up the bottle of amber liquid.

"Lord, wait!" Jiskko caught Gaemock's wrist and stopped him. "Poison!"

"Do you want me to drink first?" asked Sef, amused.

"The antidote," Jiskko whispered fiercely. "He may have taken it already."

Gaemock glared at his overly suspicious advisor and took the bottle. He tipped it back and almost choked on the powerful liquor.

"Good, isn't it?" asked Sef. He took the bottle and matched every drop Gaemock had swallowed and more. "The best there is from the shore provinces on the Uvain Plateau. It will be good when this war is behind us and I can return and tend my grapes."

"You're a vintner?"

"Aye. And it's hard for me to believe that you are a dirt farmer, Gaemock."

"Grain. Before Lamost was murdered, the Gaemock clan held the largest farms along the River Ty."

"So I've heard."

The two rebel warlords sat quietly for several minutes, each lost in memory of what had been lost.

Gaemock broke the silence. "Do you wish to ascend the throne?"

"Me? Hardly. I want only peace." Dalziel Sef scowled and peered across the fire at

Gaemock. "What of you? Do you hope to warm your ass on that high throne?"

"I wish to see a monarch able to keep peace in Porotane and nothing more."

"I heard tell that your brother Efran's a royalist."

"He seeks the same end as we, but in other ways."

Sef looked at Jiskko. "I read your lips easily. You think Efran is a traitor, eh?"

"My opinions do not concern scum like you," snapped Jiskko.

Sef rose, his muscles bulging. Asaway came up to stand beside him, hand on dagger.

"Peace. We are not here to discuss the failings of others in my family. Efran thinks Porotane is better off if one of royal blood is on the throne."

"King Lorens puts that theory to the test—and it fails!" Asaway almost shouted this into the night.

"I agree. Jiskko agrees, too," said Gaemock. "My brother is brilliant, but sometimes with brilliance goes a touch of insanity."

"Your battles have been harder fought since he defected to the royalists," observed Sef.

"He is the outstanding tactician of this country," said Gaemock. "I must do his work as well as my own until I can find another to replace him." Gaemock watched Sef carefully, then added, "Your style is much like Efran's. Daring, yet not rash."

"Your grasp of strategy is lacking in my campaign. Even Asaway has commented on this." Sef smiled, showing cracked, yellowed teeth.

"Another reason to join forces. If we, representing the two largest rebel factions, united, the other bands might also add the force of their swords to our cause."

"Possible," said Sef. "We must stand against a powerful wizard, no matter how many join us. The Wizard of Storms will never bend his knee to another."

"It is true, then?" asked Jiskko.

"That the Wizard of Storms has ended his long absence and returned from the Castle of the Winds? Aye, that it is. I have seen one of his storm warriors with my own eyes."

"Lies!" Jiskko sat with his arms crossed. "The Wizard of Storms is a myth, a tale meant to frighten children. What do you take us for?"

Sef shook his shaggy head sadly. "What else do I call a soldier standing half again as tall as you and throwing lightning bolts from his right hand and casting a tornado with his left? Formless he was and within the boiling cloud that made up his body I saw the stuff of storms. No guard from Castle Porotane this one, no. It was a storm warrior—and that can only mean the Wizard of Storms returns to meddle in our war-torn land."

"This is a spell cast by one of the wizards who bedevil us so," said Jiskko. "The wizard befuddled your senses."

"There are those among my rank who can counter spells." Sef glanced at Asaway.

"A sorceror!" cried Jiskko. The man jumped to his feet, his hand reaching beneath his jerkin to pull forth a throwing knife. The leaf-bladed knife flashed twice as it cartwheeled through the air. Asaway's head jerked back at a crazy angle as the knife tip penetrated his eye and sank deep into his brain. Dalziel Sef's lieutenant was dead before he struck the ground.

"Betrayed!" cried Sef. He jumped the fire and pulled his great sword from the ground.

"Wait!" cried Gaemock. "This is all a mistake. Jiskko, why did you strike?"

"He went to place a spell on us. Lord Dews, this maggot admitted that his toady was a wizard. He began the hand motions that would have paralyzed us!"

Dews Gaemock had pulled his own sword from the ground. He stood staring at the burly Dalziel Sef and then at his lieutenant. "Lord Dalziel, I am sorry for this."

"Sorry! This treacherous worm has killed my best spell-sniffer."

"Asaway was no wizard?"

"He had not the power within him, but he had the gift for scenting magic and alerting us to it. Many's the time he warned us of Lorens' probing with the Demon Crown. And now he lies on the ground, foully murdered!"

"*Wait!*" Gaemock lifted his sword. "If we are ever to have peace in Porotane, we cannot continue to war among ourselves. We must unite against our real enemy—King Lorens."

"I agree with you, but honor demands that I avenge Asaway's blood."

"Do so and I must avenge Jiskko's," said Gaemock. "There will be no end of the bloodshed between us."

The two men glared at one another. "So be it," said Sef.

"No, there is another way," said Dews Gaemock.

"I must have Jiskko's blood to appease Asaway's phantom. In no other way can he rest in peace."

"Then my duty is clear." Dews Gaemock

swung around, sword flashing in the night. Jiskko's eyes widened a split second before his lord's sharp blade sank halfway through his neck. Gaemock jerked and swung again. This time he finished the stroke. Jiskko's head rolled to the ground and came to rest next to Asaway.

"You would kill your own lieutenant to forge an alliance with me?" Sef asked in surprise.

"I would. The war has raged too long. If the Wizard of Storms again walks Porotane's fair ground, we must be united against two formidable enemies."

Dalziel Sef stared down at the slain advisors. "We must give them a proper funeral. I won't have their phantoms following us into battle. I could not bear it."

"Nor I. They deserve a long and peaceful eternity. They were good and loyal soldiers."

The two warlords began digging the graves that marked the beginning of their truce.

"Where are they?" Vered asked irritably. "They should have been here hours ago."

"We've only just arrived," said Birtle Santon. "Kerin and Rogina might be taking a more circuitous route to avoid being followed."

"There is that," Vered said, "but my gut churns. I never ignore that."

"You need food." Even as Santon spoke, he, too, experienced the uneasiness his friend mentioned. They lived by their wits and relied heavily on instinct. They had forged a fast friendship because of these shared feelings.

"The postern must lie in that direction. Let's explore and see if we can't find its entrance before they arrive."

Vered's nimble fingers worked over the

stone wall seeking evidence of a secret portal. Santon walked a pace behind, trying to see any release that Vered might have missed.

"This is the place. I remember that grotesque piece of statuary." Vered pointed to what he called a farting cat.

"Perhaps the release isn't on the wall but is some distance away."

"It would give reason for the sculptor to display such bad taste in his art," agreed Vered. The pair went to the well and examined the stonework carefully. But it was Vered who found the release. "As I thought. All in Castle Porotane show bad taste, but the locksmith designing this one wins the prize."

Vered reached over to the lion's posterior and ran his finger upward. Behind them a loud *snick*! signalled the opening of the hidden passage that led outside the castle walls.

"That is solved," said Santon, "but where are Kerin and Rogina?"

"There. There they are." Vered waved. To Santon he asked, "Why do they move so slowly? You would think they didn't want to leave."

"Rogina seemed reluctant," said Santon. "But she is a young girl and this life is all she has ever known. Change can be frightening to one so young."

"Hurry, you two," Vered urged. He pointed to the dark opening to the passageway.

The two girls exchanged glances, then Rogina bolted and ran—away from Vered.

"Rogina, this way!" shouted Vered.

"Vered, please forgive us," pleaded Kerin. "We do not belong outside these walls. This is our *home!*" She put her hands to her mouth, then turned and ran after her sister.

"They've betrayed us," said Santon.

"They've exchanged us for indulgences from Archbishop Nosto."

"Preposterous. The girl loves me." Only Santon grabbing Vered by the collar and yanking him aside saved him from being impaled by a dozen war arrows.

The clank of armored guards told Vered the truth of Santon's words. He got to his feet inside the passage and fumbled along the door's stony edges.

"What are you doing?"

"There's got to be a release for the door. If we close it, their pursuit will be the slower."

Santon deflected a sword thrust with his glass shield and kicked another soldier in the groin. A flick of his wrist brought his heavy battle-ax around and cracked a third guardsman's helm open.

"Hurry up. I can't hold off the entire castle guard all night."

"There!" Vered found the release and the door slid slowly closed. But one quick-thinking soldier shoved his shield into the narrowing gap between door and wall. The secret portal ground to a stop a handbreadth short of securely closing.

"Come on," cried Santon. "We've got to outrun them now. It'll be only minutes before they lever open that door."

In the dark passage the two freebooters ran, searching for the locked door that Alarice had once used. Sounds of pursuit behind them grew louder.

The soldiers had opened the secret portal and now flooded into the passage.

FOUR

"It's got to be here. It's got to!" Vered fumbled along in the dark passage trying to find the postern gate leading to freedom. The heavy footsteps of the guardsmen came closer through the darkness behind him. He heard the guardsmen's cursing and saw the sputtering light from a poorly burning torch.

"I'll keep them back," said Birtle Santon. Vered felt the man turning to face the guards. He ignored the sound of Santon's ax singing through the air and cracking still another incautious guardsman's helm. His full attention centered on the cold stone wall moving so slowly under his fingers.

"It's got to be here. This is the proper passage. I know it," he muttered to himself. Before the words left his lips, the stone turned to wood.

"What progress?" asked Santon in a tone appropriate for inquiring about the weather. But Vered knew his friend fought a losing battle from the sounds of sword tips slipping along the glass shield and the louder pounding of more soldiers pouring into the passage now.

"I've found the gate." Vered dropped to his

knees. A sliver of steel slipped from beneath his floppy collar; he applied this flexible metal strip to the lock. The tumblers within worked smoothly but he failed to open the door.

Santon grunted and almost fell over Vered. Vered turned, his knees grinding into the rough, rocky floor. He jerked his dagger free and blindly drove it upward. The point found human flesh; he was rewarded with a cry of anguish.

"Thanks," said Santon, recovering. "But do hurry. I can't hold them back any longer."

Vered's knowing fingers worked across the surface of the door. The lock had opened. Something still held the door.

"A bolt!" he cried. "There is a bolt on the inside. Newly installed, from the feel."

Vered gripped the metal handle and jerked it back. The door opened and a cold autumn wind gusted through. Vered inhaled and felt power returning to his enervated limbs. He jerked harder on the door and slammed it into a charging guardsman. The soldier bellowed and retreated, causing enough confusion among the men behind him to allow Vered and Santon to slip through the door.

"Help me hold it closed," Vered shouted. Birtle Santon pulled on the door, his bulk and the immense strength in his right arm adequate to keep the door closed while Vered's lock pick worked its magic on the tumblers. The lock fastened. Vered dropped back, sitting on the cold ground. He wiped sweat from his forehead.

"That will hold them for a while," said Santon. "They can't have the glass key Alarice used and I'm sure none have your expertise at opening locked doors without a key."

"Let's not tarry," said Vered, getting to his

feet. He looked around. The heavy brambles that protected the base of the castle wall formed a neat arch and provided a passageway out. "I'll feel safer when we have a day's travel and more behind us."

Santon nodded. Together they started through the brambles. Vered cursed volubly every time one of the dagger-long thorns ripped at his clothing. "I spent a month's salary to buy this fine tunic and here it is being ripped to threads."

"You never received a salary in your life. I remember how you stole this from the merchant in the castle courtyard not a week ago."

"Such finery deserves to be worn by someone who can appreciate it. Is it not fit for any prince of the realm?" Vered stuck out one arm and showed the puffed, verdant green sleeve woven with gold threads. Picks and tears in the cloth showed skin equally as battered. Vered bled from a dozen small thorn scratches.

"The end of our safety," said Santon, halting when he came to the mouth of the bramble tunnel. Beyond lay flat lands long since denuded by the tramp of soldiers and the hungry fire of magics misdirected.

Vered walked a few paces beyond and turned to stare at the Castle Porotane. He let out a gusty sigh. "Ah, Kerin. I know you loved me. What a terrible thing having a sister like Rogina."

Vered shook his head and let Santon know that this was not a matter for friendly debate.

"The woods are some distance to the north. Or should we head for the River Ty?" asked Santon, skirting the issue of their abrupt departure from the castle.

"Travel might prove easier on the river," answered Vered, "and I care little for having to walk. But the rebel forces will also seek out water passage. Dews Gaemock's siege last spring failed. The wiser among King Lorens' advisors mumbled about a new siege being laid this fall."

"War engines move more easily on a barge," agreed Santon.

"There must be someone hereabout with a pair of horses he hasn't counted recently," Vered went on. "Even bareback is a superior mode of travel to getting blisters on one's tender feet."

"The night is cloudy. That benefits us and hinders, too."

"Aye, that it does," said Vered. "My eyes are the keener. Let me see if I cannot penetrate the clouds and find the guiding stars." As they walked briskly from the tangle of thorny brambles, Vered craned his head back and studied the occasional clear patches of sky.

"There," he said at last. "There is a constellation I recognize. The Mider Lizard. The three stars forming its tail points a handbreadth from true north."

"We might cross a tributary to the Ty in a day or two," said Santon. "Mayhaps we should change to the north and west and seek the uplift of the Uvain Plateau."

"What we need more than anything else," said Vered, "is a notion of what we intend to do. That will dictate a destination."

Vered fell silent as he trooped along beside his friend. Life had never been easy for him. While still a child, his parents and family had been killed in a rebel raid. He had never discovered which rebel band was responsible; it might have been Duke Freow's troops, for all he knew.

If it had not been for the chance appearance of Birtle Santon, he would have perished.

The older man had taken him along on his aimless wanderings not as an apprentice or son but as an equal. For that Vered owed Birtle Santon much—more than simple coins could ever repay.

He mourned the loss of Alarice in the Desert of Sazan almost as much as his friend. He had loved Alarice in his way, but not as Santon had. The Glass Warrior had given Vered a hint of something more than love. Through her and her quest to find an heir to the throne, he had found purpose. With her dead, with King Lorens on the throne, with the condition in Porotane no better than it had been for all the years of his short life, Vered again lacked purpose. No progress had been made. Or so it seemed to him.

Porotane's wars still dragged on, rebel factions fighting the royalists. Worst of all, King Lorens was rightful heir and proved to be worse for the kingdom than the impostor-duke. Even as the thought crossed his mind, Vered looked around anxiously. He carried a drop of royal blood in his veins, perhaps the result of a long-forgotten foray into his mother's coastal village. He could don the Demon Crown for brief seconds, but the magical gold circlet's effect on him was too potent to bear any longer.

This touch of royal blood allowed him to sense the use of the Demon Crown, however. Hairs rose on the back of his neck and he knew that Lorens cast forth his phantomlike image to spy.

"The crown," he whispered to Santon. Chiding himself for such foolishness, he said louder, "Lorens is exploring magically. I sense the spells controlling the crown."

"Do you think he hunts for us to send troops?" asked Santon.

"The soldiers in the courtyard sported red armbands. They were Archbishop Nosto's guardsmen. What reprieve could Lorens give when Rogina's trouble lay with the Inquisition?"

"He is king."

"The Demon Crown makes him so, but Lorens does not handle the internal affairs of the castle well. He is too busy looking further afield, finding rebels and trying to crush the resistance."

"He might still want us," said Santon.

Vered agreed. They had brought him back to Porotane and they had carried the crown. Lorens might think they possessed power to oppose him. Had they not been with the sorceress who killed his master? The king's suspicions knew no bounds—and grew daily.

What a dangerous dilemma the Demon Crown posed for a ruler. Vered had felt its power and brushed madness as a result. Those of the blood royal who could wear it for long periods would fall under its influence unless they were possessed of a singularly strong will. From all Vered had seen, Lorens lacked such strength of character. His wizard master had not felt it appropriate to develop anything but servility in his pupil. Now that the apprentice became the master, he had few guidelines to aid him.

"What I could do with that crown," Vered said. He ducked, as if a low-flying bird threatened to rake his head with outstretched talons.

"Lorens?"

"Yes. He explores this night. But I sense his probing goes past us and heads to the north."

Vered took a deep breath to steady himself, and inhaled a familiar scent. He turned and homed in on the pungent odor of animals. Pointing, he said, "Horses. Transportation!"

Santon followed as Vered made his way across the rutted plain. Vered came to a corral with a score of horses inside its rough-hewn rails.

"So many horses," mused Santon. "This bodes ill."

"Rebels," said Vered. "But I saw no sentry."

"They might have grown careless."

Neither man believed that. Vered stood outside the corral and stared at the horses. His feet hurt and it offended his dignity to continue walking. If no rebel guard had been posted—and why should not at least one armed guard protect such fine animals?—that meant only one thing.

"Magic," Vered said. "A ward spell protects the horses. We have stumbled across a rebel band led by a wizard."

"Perhaps we would do better to continue without such fine animals," Santon said. Vered heard the longing in his friend's words. Neither of them would easily abandon a remuda waiting to have plucked from it such strong, handsome horses.

Vered walked around the corral trying to get some hint of the spell's power. He leaned against the rail and felt nothing. Cautiously, he reached across the top rail and extended his hand toward a curious mare. Before his hand touched the mare's head a powerful invisible force picked him up and cast him back. Vered landed on his rear.

"So much for that approach," said Santon. "We can dig under and enter the corral in that way."

"Why bother unless you intend to dig a hole large enough for the horses to exit? No, Santon, we need another approach." Vered paced around the corral a second time, keen eyes alert for any weakness. He rejoined Santon.

"Well? How does the master thief intend to pluck the prize steeds from the corral?"

"Above," said Vered. "We can enter from above."

"Insanity."

"Of course. Who else but a master thief would attempt such a foolhardy course?" Vered laughed as he moved closer to the corral. He overturned a bucket and placed it next to the tallest post. He pointed. Santon silently stepped onto the bucket, balanced precariously for a moment, then steadied. He curled his powerful right hand into a hook and waited.

Excitement surged through Vered. This was living. The challenge of entering the corral brought his every sense alive. He backed off a dozen paces, then ran for Santon. He jumped, got his foot in Santon's cupped hand, and launched himself upward. Santon added impetus with a powerful heave.

As he became airborne, Vered heard Santon's grunt. He also heard the air come alive with the hum of magic. Vered soared, gauged his progress, then somersaulted. A new sensation blasted through him: pain.

He crossed the invisible top of the ward spell and came down feet first inside the corral. Horses protested his sudden entry, neighing and pawing at the air.

"Down, old girl, down, easy, yes, it's only

Vered the master thief come to spirit you away!"
He approached one powerful dappled gray, his
voice soothing and his hands outstretched.
When the mare reared, Vered moved to one side
and dashed around. His arms circled the horse's
neck. Buck as she would, she could not dislodge
him. His voice soothed and cajoled as if he spoke
to a new lover. The horse quieted and Vered
relaxed his grip.

"That's all there is to it," Vered said, patting
his new conquest on the neck.

"There is another element to this little play
that has escaped you," said Santon. "How do
you get out? The spell still binds you within the
corral."

"A minor problem for one of my daring and
skill," said Vered. But he had no idea how to get
out with his prize. He mounted the horse and
gentled her once more, patting her frequently
and assuring her that she was the finest horse in
all the world. As Vered rode her around, a
thought came to him.

"Santon," he called out. "Would anyone,
even a wizard, wish to harm a noble steed such
as this one?"

"No. I fail to see what that has to do with
getting out of the corral with your prize."

"The horses don't need the corral fence if
the spell keeps them inside. A touch of pain here
and there and the horses would huddle together
in the center of the spell zone."

"Do horses huddle?"

"Don't cloud the issue." Vered looked up
and saw that the sky cleared. A pale crescent
moon shone down to give him courage. "The
rails hold the horses in, the spell keeps our kind
out."

"So?"

"So I can remove the horse with no trouble. It is only my own skin I need worry about."

"Test your theory. Send out that roan for me."

Vered tugged at the hide thong holding the corral gate shut, then herded what he already thought of as Santon's roan to the gate. A quick swat on the hindquarters startled the roan. It leaped forward, passing the magic barrier with no ill effect.

"I won't say you're a genius," said Santon, capturing the roan as it tried to bolt into the night, "but the word does come to my lips. Only good sense holds it back."

"Luck, skill, what's the difference?" Vered asked. He turned the gray's head toward the gate, then dug his heels into her side. He had sampled the power of the wizard's spell. Only speed would get him free of the corral.

Vered's eyes blinked open. Every part of his body screamed in agony and movement was out of the question.

"The stars?" he asked weakly. "Why are they in front of me?"

"You're flat on your back. The mare got you free but the spell still seized you. Only by hanging on to the horse did you get past its boundaries."

"It knocked me out?"

"And more, from the way you groan. Come along now. Let's ride these stolen creatures for all they're worth. The wizard might have felt some disturbance in his spell when you broke free."

"I can't move!" Vered tried to raise his arms and was greeted with intense pain. When he tried again, the pain diminished. A third attempt, while agonizing, proved possible.

Groaning like an old man, he climbed onto his mare and urged her forward. Every bounce, every change in gait, rattled his teeth and sent lances of white fire into his brain.

"Ride, master thief," came Santon's mocking words.

"Easy for you to say. You had the lesser role in that theft." They rode fast and hard and camped only when pink and gray fingers appeared in the east.

"I feel like death," said Vered. He sank to the ground. "Nay, it is worse. Death is surcease. This is continual misery. There is not a bone or muscle that does not ache abominably."

"Remember the pains, then," said Santon, as he tended their horses, "and become a chirurgeon. It'll save having to cut open your patients to find where all the parts are."

Santon finished his chore and dropped beside his friend. "We have done well this night. Not only did we escape the castle ahead of the Inquisition, we found horses worthy of us."

"We did all that," agreed Vered, "but what now? More of the same? Do we return to the ways that served us well before we met Alarice?"

"Weren't those times good?"

"Yes, but they pale now. I want more."

"Remember how we travelled up and down the coast? We left not a single wine cask untapped or wench untupped."

"The constable of that hamlet—what was it?"

"Landine," said Santon.

"Yes, Landine. The constable followed us for a fortnight before we sneaked into his camp one night and stole his clothing. I swear, he would still be after us if he hadn't been such a modest man."

They fell silent. Vered's thoughts carried on, after the constable, after the brief stint aboard a coastal hugger and being shipwrecked. Their life had been full.

Why did it seem so hollow now?

They had been together long enough for Santon to know Vered's moods. In his uncanny way, he answered the question Vered had only thought. "We know that there can be nothing worthwhile in the kingdom until the war is at an end. Alarice showed us that."

"Alarice," mused Vered. "Would she have accepted Lorens as king?"

"No. Any fool can see that his reign worsens the conditions in Porotane, not betters them."

"What would she have done?" asked Vered. "What would she have us do?"

Silence fell until Vered heard, "There is another heir."

"Of course there is," he said. "There were twins, Lorens and his sister Lokenna."

"What?" came Santon's startled voice. "You awoke me."

"Then you're talking in your sleep. You should stay awake and listen to yourself some night. You speak wisely and well."

"Lokenna can be found to the north. Claymore Pass."

Both men sat stiffly upright. Neither had spoken. And the voice was one they remembered well.

As one, they cried, "Alarice!"

FIVE

Raindrops the size of watery fists beat at the rock and bounced knee-high on impact. Above the barren plateau lightning danced and weaved and formed vivid eye-searing patterns. The actinic glare from the bolts cast an eerie illumination on the land, sending the small animals scurrying for cover from the sudden downpour. On the edge of a sheer precipice towered the Castle of the Winds.

Wind whipped across the plateau and worked airy fingers through the lofty, lacelike spires of crystalline diamond and jade. Aeolian harps sang, their haunting song challenging that of the elements. And on the tallest tower in the center of the castle stood a windswept figure dressed in a robe of grays and soft greens.

Kaga'kalb, the Wizard of Storms, raised his arms and called down lightning from the sky. The mighty lightning strikes touched his fingers and died. He threw back his sleeves and bared his arms and returned the prodigious power to the heavens with a single mumbled spell.

The Wizard of Storms' lightning bolt rivalled anything created naturally. Clouds boiled away and left the sky naked to his gaze. Kaga'kalb reached out with another spell and touched the exposed azure sky. The ring of jet-dark storm clouds he formed began to swirl, trying to close in on the intruding fairness. Faster and faster he let the clouds spin until they formed a tornado with a vortex larger than the Castle of the Winds.

Only when he was satisfied with the intensity of the rotary pattern did Kaga'kalb release his spell. A deafening roar that shook the very mountain on which the castle was built rumbled away. Behind the bull-throated roar of angry elements went the tornado.

Kaga'kalb smiled. He so enjoyed playing with his toys. He dropped his hands and let the long sleeves cover his hands. He rubbed them against his robe to bring back circulation. He was growing old. Frostbite set in more quickly now whenever he commanded the storms. Many years ago he had been able to summon blizzards and never feel their wintry bite. No longer.

And tiredness turned his sprightly step into one less energetic. Kaga'kalb cared little about this. The power he controlled from the Castle of the Winds was so immense that no wizard in Porotane could withstand his full attack.

Or so it had been for many decades. Kaga'kalb went inside the tower and walked slowly down the spiral staircase fashioned from huge blood rubies to the comfortable living quarters in the center of the keep. Porotane had changed after Duke Freow died.

Kaga'kalb settled into a well-cushioned chair and lifted his feet to a table. "I would view the kingdom and the petty warlords," he said aloud. Tiny white clouds formed in the corners of the room, hardly more than misty patches. They swirled and hardened and became dark balls of water vapor stretching out tendrils that touched in the center of one wall. At first all Kaga'kalb saw was water droplets trickling down the wall. Then a tiny lightning bolt crossed the wall. Following quickly came smudges that solidified into figures of men and women.

"The warlords, not the castle," ordered Kaga'kalb. The spells controlling his scrying wavered from time to time. He might have to recast. He noted some lessening of clarity and blurring of detail in the lifelike picture growing on his wall.

As if they shared the room with him, Dews Gaemock and Dalziel Sef popped into view. Their mouths moved but no sound came out.

"Full scrying," Kaga'kalb ordered. A flash of purple produced a sharper image of the rebels and their voices. Sef turned as if someone had tapped him on the shoulder, then frowned and returned to his discussion with Gaemock. The Wizard of Storms listened to the two rebel leaders forge their alliance. He shook his head. He had seen such unification in the past end with bloody murder. He doubted Dalziel Sef and Dews Gaemock would avoid that fate.

"Give me Lorens," he ordered. The small clouds expanded and turned mistier. Kaga'kalb frowned. He pulled back his sleeves and began the chant to intensify his spell. When this did not work the Wizard of Storms started making small gestures in the air before him. Tiny purple streamers of magical energy flowed from his thumbs. Each finger left a red and green trail in the air that shot sparks in all directions before dying. As quickly as the aerial trail vanished, Kaga'kalb replaced it.

Over and over, faster and faster the Wizard of Storms wove his potent scrying spell. The air in the room cooled and clouds formed along the ceiling beams. Kaga'kalb began directing the clouds like a general marshalling his forces. In precise ranks, the miniature thunderclouds floated across the room as if driven by unseen winds, merged, parted, and retraced their storm track.

"Damn him!" cried Kaga'kalb. "Damn Lorens!" The wizard worked even more intricate magic spells and found it impossible to penetrate the barrier the new monarch built around himself.

Kaga'kalb settled back, a pass of his hand dismissing the potent magic clouds he had summoned. "So Lorens dares block my view of him. The Demon Crown gives him false confidence."

The Wizard of Storms scowled and pondered the subject of the wizard-king on the throne of Porotane. He had not meddled unduly in Porotane's internal affairs when the Demon Crown had been inactive. Freow's death and Alarice finding Lorens upset the careful balance of nature that gave Kaga'kalb his power. With the crown becoming a force to be reckoned with in the kingdom, Kaga'kalb sensed his own power diminishing.

Not much, not yet. He scowled so hard that deep furrows creased his forehead and turned his handsome visage into something hideous. Lorens knew so little of the powers locked within the Demon Crown. His continued and constant use would only result in disaster for wizard and peasant alike.

Kaga'kalb shoved down hard on the arms of the chair. He shot to his feet as angry with his own inability as he was with Lorens' magical blocking. The crown's gift of knowledge had already pushed Lorens past all reasoning. The young wizard-king would never relinquish his magical aid now. The lure of seeing and hearing and tasting and feeling anywhere in the kingdom had proven too great a freedom for a youth imprisoned by a harsh master most of his life.

Steps long and sure, he walked outside the keep and into the empty courtyard. A single gesture of his hand blew open the ponderous opalescent gates of the Castle of the Winds. Onto the barren plain he strode, the natural storm raging around his mountaintop.

Kaga'kalb stopped and stared at the underbelly of the clouds. His left hand pointed. Searing white lightning shot to the cloud. Riding down this scintillant trail came a puff of cloud, swirling and uncertain of form. With his right hand, Kaga'kalb gestured at another cloud. A second misty patch detached itself and came sliding down the jerking rope of pure energy.

The two cloud segments stopped just above Kaga'kalb's head. He clapped his hands. A peal of thunder louder than anything produced naturally by the storm rolled across the windswept plateau. With it, the two clouds merged into one huge pillar.

Swirling tendrils shot forth. Within the dark cloud a dull red core formed that began a slow, rhythmic pulsation. The wisps of tendril hardened into arms and legs. A head without a neck formed. Twin beacons of red formed where human eyes would be had this cloud creature been born of woman.

Kaga'kalb stepped back and watched the final stages of transformation of his storm warrior.

"Pass in review!" bellowed Kaga'kalb, his voice almost lost in the violent winds whipping across the plains.

Lightning sizzled at the fingertips of the

huge storm warrior. Each spark produced a smaller version of the towering magical creature. Ten storm warriors taller than Kaga'kalb fell into step. From each of their misty fingers came a new warrior equal to Kaga'kalb in height. The hundred saluted as they passed their master.

They reached the precipice, wheeled, and came back. Each storm warrior in this legion reached out and produced ten. A thousand storm warriors reaching almost to Kaga'kalb's shoulder marched by, the impact of their misty feet on the rock sounding like a fierce rainstorm. Kaga'kalb smiled. The ten thousand waist-high warriors who returned from across the plains filled his vision.

"An army to be reckoned with," Kaga'kalb said. "No ragtag rebel band can oppose them!"

The Wizard of Storms uttered the magical command of release. His vaporous army marched in step over the edge of the cliff. They did not fall. Their substance dispersed, then whipped around and got caught in an updraft. Long columns of mist soared to rejoin the lightning-wracked cloud above.

Kaga'kalb turned to his giant storm warrior and smiled. No human army could fight his warriors. Rebels meant nothing. The full might of a kingdom dwarfed next to his cloudy minions. And neither could any wizard hope to defeat him, not even a wizard-king possessing the potent magic locked within the Demon Crown!

SIX

Birtle Santon and Vered turned and stared at one another in disbelief. Both opened their mouths to speak, then clamped them shut, as if doubting their senses.

Finally, Santon took the initiative and said, "It was Alarice. I know it."

"No," said Vered, shaking his head, "not Alarice—but it was her phantom."

"We never found the body in the Desert of Sazan to give her a proper burial. We should have searched harder."

"Patrin's magic and the destruction of the City of Stolen Dreams kept us from doing many things," said Vered. "How I would have loved to loot that city. The fine dreams, all locked away in tightly sealed jars. The price those would have fetched in a decent market!"

"She died and we didn't bury her. Alarice's phantom now walks the land."

"It was a faint and misty phantom. I barely heard her. At first, I thought it was you."

"And I thought it was you who spoke." Santon smiled slightly. "I knew it could not be, though. The words I heard made sense."

"You're saying I never make sense?" Vered snorted indignantly and settled down, his arms pulling in his legs and his chin resting on his knees as he stared into the campfire. "The other twin. Lokenna. We can find her and replace Lorens on the throne."

"Just like that?" asked Santon. He snapped his fingers. The sound was that of dried twigs breaking—or dreams falling apart. "Lorens has the Demon Crown. He is a wizard of small ability, true, but a wizard nonetheless."

"His sister might reason with him. She might moderate his wild swings of mood. She might introduce some humanity to his purges."

Santon shook his head. "You no more believe that than I. The crown is as much at fault as what Patrin did to the youngling in the name of apprenticeship."

"But Alarice spoke of the twin sister. Can we deny her shade?"

Santon had no answer for that. He had not been swift enough to look around at the sound of his beloved's voice. If he had, he might have caught a shifting form of white gauzy air, a small disturbance and nothing more. Would this brief glimpse of her phantom have assuaged his heartache—or made it worse?

They should not have left the Desert of Sazan until her body had been located and properly buried. One so valiant should not have to endure the uncertain fate of being a phantom, trapped between worlds, communicating only with difficulty to the living and not at all with the other dead who roamed as spirits.

"What do you know of Claymore Pass?" asked Vered. "Alarice said that Lokenna was there."

"The pass," Santon said with no enthusiasm. "That stretch through the Yorral Mountains has cost more men their lives than any other. The pass is deadly, even during high summer. The battles fought there have been even worse."

"I remember none."

"They were before your time. I was barely your age when I served with King Lamost's troops. We were attacked front and rear while we marched through Claymore Pass. Brutal. Slaughter. Five hundred entered the pass on patrol. Only fifty left."

"Rebels?"

"Not in those times. Not while Lamost reigned. No, Vered, those were brigands."

"Some band of petty cutpurses," Vered said. "I cannot believe you would march with troops ill-equipped or untrained."

"They called them brigands. Although I never knew for certain, I believed the rumors that they were mercenaries outfitted by a wizard living far to the north and desiring Porotane for his private domain. Whoever they fought for, it was a war of blood and iron and not of magic."

"This Wizard of Storms everyone is abuzz over? Was he the one?"

"No name was ever placed on him. It is possible. All that matters is the large graveyard in the pass. I cannot even guess how many bodies were never buried. On any given night you can hear the moans of the phantoms as they desperately seek their bodies and beg and cajole mortals for proper consecration."

Vered shuddered. "An unlikely place to find the heir to the throne of Porotane. Mayhaps we mistook a casual gust of wind for Alarice? We might have imagined hearing the name Claymore Pass."

"I imagined nothing. It was Alarice's phantom. We must do something."

"I agree," said Vered, "but am at a loss to decide what. We were going to the Uvain Plateau to sample their fine wines and . . . other delicacies. Should we delay this small holiday to the wine country and join with a rebel band?"

"To what end? I am not convinced that any want a true heir on the throne. Gaemock might. There have been rumors about him. But Dalziel Sef? He seeks power for himself."

"But he is a strong leader and his cavalry is second to none. Gaemock is an able strategist but he fails to carry out his fine plans."

"And Dalziel Sef executes well and gets nowhere because his reach is too short for his ambition. No, Vered, we began this mission with Alarice. We must finish it."

"For her?"

"For ourselves," Santon snapped.

"And I worried about purpose to life," said Vered, sighing. "Now I worry about dying for a cause." He let out a gusty sigh. "We ride north for Claymore Pass in the morning?"

Santon fell silent, his mind turning over the complex problem facing them. Rebel bands cared little what mission sent riders across Porotane—if they did not pay allegiance to the particular rebel leader, they were fair game. A temporary truce with Gaemock might give Vered and him safe passage to the north.

Or they might run afoul of other rebel bands. He had heard of the small but vicious groups headed by wizards. Most were rumored to be roving along the River Ty in the northlands and across to where the upthrust of the Uvain Plateau relieved the flatness of the river flood plains.

Santon's mind worked on, dismissing the

obvious. The rebels would be under continual observation by Lorens. The Demon Crown allowed the monarch to look and hear anywhere within the realm. As a pair of travellers, he and Vered posed no threat. They might never even come to Lorens' attention as he scanned the countryside. If they rode as emissaries of Dews Gaemock, they would definitely attract unwanted notice. Since their hasty departure from Castle Porotane he did not relish the prospect of once more falling into the clutches of those nobles.

Santon's green eyes locked with Vered's brown ones. The older man shook his head to deny that they both had come up with the same ridiculous, insanely dangerous idea at the same time.

"What other course is open to us?" asked Vered. "You see it, just as I do. We cannot move through Porotane in search of Lokenna without pulling Lorens' spying onto ourselves like a decaying carcass draws flies."

"If we return to the castle, Archbishop Nosto will seize us."

"If Baron Theoll doesn't find us first."

"Or," Santon went on, "the king himself. There is nothing Lorens wouldn't do to keep us from such a mad venture."

"Ah," said Vered, smiling broadly. "Therein lies the genius of such a plan. Who in their right minds would *ever* return, much less return to steal away with the most potent tidbit of magic in all Porotane?"

Birtle Santon leaned back and stared at the sky, trying to find a flaw in what Vered proposed. He couldn't. The same thoughts had taken a different road in his own mind but had

still arrived at the same destination. They could
never find Lokenna and place her in a position
of power while the Demon Crown allowed her
brother free access anywhere in Porotane.

"She might not be any better than what
we've got as king," said Santon.

"True. But can she be worse?" Vered countered.

"There is always room for things to grow
worse. Such is the nature of the universe."

"Pah!" snorted Vered. "You always look at
the dark side. You should consider—" The two
argued the proper philosophy of the world as
they mounted their horses and retraced their
path to Castle Porotane.

They had a crown to steal.

"Guards!" hissed Vered. "They will have
thousands of guardsmen waiting for us if we try
to reenter the castle through the same postern
gate."

"How else can we get inside?" demanded
Birtle Santon. "This is the only secret way we
know. We can hardly go riding up to the main
gate and proclaim that we have returned to steal
the Demon Crown and to please let us in."

The two stood at the entrance to the tunnel
through the thicket of brambles. Vered looked
around nervously, sure that a scouting patrol
would see them and bring the full armed wrath
of the castle guard down on their heads.

"What a time to die," he moaned. "My
clothing hangs in tatters and it's been forever
since I've had a decent bath."

"You won't die. Not even from the stench of
your journey."

"The horses should never have run through
the golden velvet stinkweed. Lorens need not

use the magic of the crown to find us. He need only sniff the air."

Santon had long since grown used to the odor. They had crossed a tributary to the River Ty and had washed off most of the lingering scent, but Vered needed something more than his sorry apparel to complain about to feel right.

"We go in here. If we find guardsmen, then we fight. If we don't, we press on to the throne room and steal the Demon Crown."

"You make it sound simple."

"Aren't we the greatest thieves in all Porotane? For us it *will* be easy."

Vered shook his head, wanting to believe the high praise but having to weigh it against common sense. The castle contained factions warring politically. No one slept with both eyes closed. Constant danger of assassination produced a society of fitful sleepers—and swift daggers.

"We may be the greatest thieves in the kingdom," said Vered, "but I fear that the Demon Crown might prove to be the greatest thief catcher."

"You chide me for being negative. Come and let's explore. Let's see if Kerin awaits you with open arms."

"That one?" Vered sniffed haughtily. "I had forgotten her until you mentioned her traitorous name. By now she has been in the bed of a dozen others—and not a one as good as I!"

"She'd been in the beds of a dozen before you," taunted Santon, trying to get his friend's mind off the thorns clawing at their flesh as they made their way toward the hidden gate.

"But I was the best. She told me so. What good is it finding a virgin? How can one with no experience know you are the best? Kerin compared me with the most famous lovers who have ever tramped the halls of the castle and named me best!"

As he bragged, Vered worked with his steel slivers on the lock. Tumblers fell into place with a well-oiled *snick*! and the door opened to darkness.

Santon strained for traces of guardsmen waiting in ambush. Vision gave him only blackness deeper than any moonless midnight. Smell was out of the question. His and Vered's pungent aroma overwhelmed this fragile sense. But Santon listened intently, for breathing, for movement, for the clank of swords against armor. Only the frightened scurrying of a rat came to his ears.

He motioned for Vered to follow. Glass shield on his withered arm and battle-ax ready for an overhead stroke, Santon walked the length of the unlighted passage.

"Here," said Vered. "Here's the doorway out into the courtyard and that hideous statue." The door slid open as he leaned against it. Vered stuck his head out and looked around. The courtyard was empty. "When we return, *you* have to open the door. I am tired of being humiliated by that farting feline."

"Whatever is necessary for our escape," Santon answered. He followed Vered. They had chosen the time of their assault well. They had waited until four hours past midnight when most of the castle's residents slept their uneasy sleep and the guards had begun to flag in their attention after having assumed their posts at midnight.

"What now? Do we just walk into the king's chambers and rip it from his head?"

"He cannot keep it on his head forever. When he removes it, we strike."

"I've known you most of my life, or so it seems, Santon, and never have I heard you spout such nonsense. Lorens is a *wizard*. Do you not think he protects the crown with a ward spell when he isn't wearing it?"

"Then we will have to be crafty."

Vered shook his head. A quick smile curled Santon's lips. He had no idea how they would steal the Demon Crown, but he knew that his taunts would put a dozen wild schemes into Vered's head. One would work. All he had to do was listen to the young thief and pick the one with the best chance of succeeding.

"He knows all his personal guards," Vered complained. "We cannot impersonate them and hope to get away."

"But Theoll's soldiers. They patrol everywhere," Santon said. They entered a long corridor that led back toward the wing where their quarters had been. Santon briefly wondered if others had moved in or if superstition kept out squatters. To occupy the sleeping chambers of those executed or otherwise in disfavor and in the dungeons was seen by some as bad luck.

"We dare not impersonate them, either. Lorens' guard would question them instantly. But consider Archbishop Nosto's holy soldiers!" Vered stopped talking for a moment as they crept past a sleeping guardsman. Once past, Vered picked up his thought. "The Inquisition is feared by all. I doubt even King Lorens challenges the archbishop openly."

"Then we get Inquisitors' uniforms to steal the crown," said Santon.

"If we are seen, who would dare to look us

in the eye? They all drop to their pitiful knees and beg not to be taken away and put to the Question."

"A good plan," said Santon. They stopped outside their former quarters. Santon pressed his ear against the panel and heard nothing. As thick as the door was, he had not expected to overhear anyone talking unless they shouted at one another.

"Here," said Vered. "This must be the entrance to the secret passage where Theoll spied on us." The young man ran his knowing fingers along the sides of a mahogany cabinet until he found the door catch. No sound went along with the cabinet swinging away from the wall and revealing a crawl space.

Santon quickly looked up and down the hall and followed Vered into the secret passage. They went only a few feet before finding the spy holes looking into their chambers. Both men squinted through the tiny slits.

"Empty," said Santon.

"No, not so. I see someone moving. It . . . it's Kerin! She is robbing me!"

"Quiet, you fool, or she'll hear you. Let her take what she wants. We will not need it."

"What could she possibly want with my fine clothing?" Vered scooted around and found another spy hole. "Ah, she's left that. She's taken only that which might be of worth if she sells it in the market."

Santon almost laughed. Vered did not understand that he'd just proclaimed all his supposedly stylish clothing worthless.

"She's gone now."

"Then let us enter and change clothing and bathe," said Santon. "I see the tub is still filled from when we left."

"The water will be cold."

Santon grabbed Vered's leg and dragged him back to the corridor. They waited until Kerin vanished around the corner before slipping out and going into their chambers. A half hour of bathing made them feel better. A change of clothing turned them into intrepids thinking they could challenge the world.

"We cannot stay here forever," said Vered, eyeing his remaining wardrobe with regret. He did not want to leave such finery. "What do we do? Go hunting for Inquisitors?"

Santon smiled without humor as he looked through the partially opened door. "No need. Luck is with us. A pair of the red-dressed ruffians are coming by. Get ready."

Archbishop Nosto's two guardsmen had just passed the door when Santon and Vered jumped out behind them. Vered used his dagger, driving it directly into one Inquisitor's kidney. Santon took aim and swung the glass shield, catching his victim on the back of the neck with the rounded edge. The impact knocked the Inquisitor's head forward. The crunch told that Santon had broken the man's neck.

Within minutes they had the pair dragged within the sleeping rooms and stripped. Vered's red uniform, even worn over his clothing, hung in folds. Santon had taken the larger and his was almost skin-tight, restricting movement as he swung the glass shield to and fro.

"Cut the seams under my left arm," he told Vered. "I might be able to fight then."

"The need for personal combat will not arise," Vered said with renewed bravado. "We have come this far. We will finish this job and none will be the wiser."

It was Santon's turn to worry. How long would it be before Archbishop Nosto missed his two Inquisitors? An hour? Five minutes? There was no way of telling. He felt the need for haste. Together, they almost ran to the king's chambers.

Santon lifted his shield and restrained Vered. In the corridor stood a pair of indolent guards. One looked as if he slept on his feet. The other stared out a window toward the rapidly flowing River Ty.

"We dare not attack them," said Santon. "There might be another pair inside the king's chamber."

"Doubtful. What monarch would want such ruffians watching him sleep? But you are right. They must be distracted."

"What is it?" demanded Santon. "I know that tone in your voice. What are you planning?"

"I'll be back in a few minutes. Stay here." Vered reached up and flipped forward the crimson hood on Santon's uniform so that it hid the man's face. He pulled his own up and forward so that his face vanished into shadows and soft folds.

Santon almost cried out when Vered returned in ten minutes. Dutifully following two paces behind him was an almost naked Kerin. She wore only the flimsiest of nightgowns and looked upset.

"There, my daughter," Vered said, his voice almost an octave lower than usual. "Those are the guards you must cause to stray from grace. Do as Archbishop Nosto commands."

"Must I?" she said, her voice almost breaking with fear.

"How long can you resist the pincers—or the Inquisition's branding iron on your fine body?" Vered reached out a crooked finger and pulled away what little cloth veiled the woman's body. He let it drop back into place. "Go!"

She scuttled into the hall, looked back, then cast her eyes down before going to the guards.

"What did you tell her?" asked Santon.

"She'll keep the guards busy—and happy —for an hour. It eludes me why this charity toward such uncouth guardsmen is ordered, but the archbishop feels this is penance for her sins." Vered shrugged. "You were the one who said that she'd bed a dozen others after me. Now she need find only ten."

Santon motioned to Vered. Kerin and the two soldiers had vanished into another room. Santon stopped before the door leading into the king's quarters. Vered gingerly touched the door latch. It moved easily. He pulled it back and ducked into the room. Santon followed, his heart beating wildly.

Lorens sprawled across the massive bed, still clothed except for one boot, which had been kicked off. Santon's nose wrinkled. The king smelled as bad as they had after going through the stinkweed patch. He had not bathed in many days—or weeks. The haggard look on his face even while sleeping showed the strain he endured.

"Can it be this simple?" Vered asked in surprise. Lorens had tumbled face forward onto the bed while wearing the Demon Crown. It had fallen off and lay near the monarch's head.

Santon gestured for Vered to carefully lift it from the soft bed. He saw the glass box in which Alarice had carried the dangerous magical artifact for so many years and picked it up. When he turned Vered had already scooped up the crown.

"My drop of royal blood stands me in good stead," Vered whispered. The crown glowed green between his fingertips. He dropped it into the glass box. Santon quickly closed the jewel-hinged transparent lid and glanced back to where Lorens stirred restlessly on the bed.

His hand held the box with the Demon Crown. He could use the edge of his glass shield to kill Lorens as he had killed the Inquisitor. It would be so easy and would solve so many problems for Porotane.

"Out. Hurry!" Vered stood at the door and gestured. Santon quickly joined his friend and saw the problem. Four of Baron Theoll's soldiers marched down the hall toward the king's sleeping chambers.

"Leave him," said Vered. "We must get out of the castle with all our parts in working condition." Before Santon could say a word, Vered slipped back through the door and into the corridor in front of Theoll's approaching guardsmen.

Santon joined him, keeping the glass box hidden behind his shield. He stretched slightly and felt the tight fabric give way.

"Give way for soldiers of the Inquisition!" boomed Vered. He strode forward, head high and hands hidden in the voluminous folds of the Inquisitor's uniform.

As he passed the leading guard, his dagger flashed out and up, entering under the man's lowest rib and cutting upward to pierce the heart. Before the man had fallen forward, dead, Vered slashed viciously and cut the second guard's throat.

Santon dropped to the floor and kicked out, his feet engaging the third guard's legs, one foot behind the guard's heel and the other snapping hard into the kneecap. The man went down in a jumble, too surprised at this sudden attack to do more than croak weakly. Santon rolled over and brought the shield down squarely on the man's throat, almost decapitating him.

The final guard made the mistake of attempting to draw his sword. Vered moved inside the arc of the man's arm and drove the hilt of his dagger into the guard's sternum. He let out a sick gasp and fell retching to the floor.

"Leave him be," said Vered when Santon started to kill him. Santon stared in surprise at his friend. Vered said loudly, "We have accomplished what Archbishop Nosto sent us to do. Let us hurry to his chambers with our prize."

Santon understood then. Confusion to their enemies! Let Theoll accuse Archbishop Nosto and Lorens suspect them both.

SEVEN

Lorens, King of Porotane, former apprentice to the wizard Patrin, son of Lamost and blood heir of Waellkin thrashed about on the bed and moaned loudly. His dreams had grown steadily worse. His eyelids fluttered but did not open as unseen terrors rose from the quagmire of his mind to torment him.

"No," he muttered, arms waving about to chase away the dark and unsettling dream figures. "Not me. You want someone else. Take my sister. Get away."

Lorens shrieked as the dream turned into nightmare. Talons raked at his face and eyes. Pits opened under his feet, threatening to plunge him into pools of burning sulphur. Boils sprouted on his arms and leaked yellow pus. And no one came to aid him. No one.

That was the worst punishment of all. Around him in a circle stood his advisors and none offered any help. No one grabbed his outstretched hand. No one cautioned him. No one even looked in his direction as the nightmare figures began their ghoulish tortures.

Lorens gasped and sat upright in the soft bed, drenched in sweat and heart pounding at twice its natural rate. A shaking hand wiped the perspiration from his face. He missed a few drops; the sweat got into his eyes and stung. Lorens leaned forward, head sagging. The nightmare had been so real. He had been tortured, yes, but worse than this was the betrayal of his closest advisors.

"I need to be more wary. Trust no one. That's the lesson Patrin taught. He was right. By the saints, he was right!" Lorens' throat constricted as he thought of his dead master. The wizard had been a harsh taskmaster and required every lesson to be learned exactly, but the discipline now stood the lonely king in good stead. He overlooked no detail. He suspected everyone. They all plotted against him. All of them.

Lorens' head came up and he straightened his shoulders. This was no condition for the ruler of the strongest kingdom to be in. He had to look regal and command with authority. A king needed a crown. Lorens' lips twisted back in a feral smile. His crown was enough to guarantee loyalty of his treacherous subjects.

Lorens reached out for the crown. His groping hand found only the soft down comforter on the bed. He spun around, bunching up the fabric under his legs. Panic again surged within him. He pawed frantically at the comforter as he searched for the Demon Crown.

He kicked himself free of the bed and dropped to hands and knees. "It must have fallen onto the floor. Under the bed. Somewhere!"

King Lorens sought the magical crown and failed to find it. He sagged, his back against a stone wall.

"It's here. Don't show fear. Weakness like

that will kill me. They'll all come swooping in like carrion hawks. I need the crown. I *need* it!"

Another feverish search failed to reveal the Demon Crown. On shaky legs Lorens stood. He quickly found that he had to lean against a table for support. The thought of losing the only protection he had against rebels outside the castle walls and insurrectionists within robbed him of his strength.

"Guards!" he shrieked. He swallowed hard and tried to compose himself. No weakness. Don't show fear, especially to guards. They were in the pay of others and would report his lapse to their true masters. "Guards," he called in a lower, more controlled voice. When neither of the men posted outside his chamber entered, Lorens flung back the door and peered into the corridor.

No guards. As if winter had come early to Porotane, Lorens felt a cold wind blow across his spine. He had no experience with palace politics, but he needed little to know that assassinations occurred in situations like this. The guards were either traitors or paid to leave at the proper time. The assassin quietly walked in, dagger drawn, sword ready, garrote looped for dropping over an unsuspecting head.

Lorens' hand touched his throat. Would the assassin try to choke him to death? He could not bear that thought. Better a slow poison or a foot of cold steel through his guts. To die slowly, the air gusting from his lungs and nothing coming in to replace it. The pressure in his chest. Encroaching blackness at the edges of his vision. His heart threatening to explode.

Lorens shrieked again in fear, hands tearing at the hair on his temples.

"King," came one guard's voice. The man

hurried down the corridor from the direction of a suite of empty bedchambers. The dead duke's whores had lived in those chambers. Lorens had ordered them all from the castle after his coronation. He need not share the bed with a woman who would slit his throat when he slept after making love to her.

"King Lorens, what's wrong?" The guard fastened his breeches as he ran clumsily. He dropped his sword, bent and retrieved it. By this time the second guard emerged, more unclad than in uniform. He held his dagger poised for an attack.

Was he the one? The thought blasted across Lorens' mind and exploded like Spring Festival fireworks.

"Him," he said, pointing a shaky finger at the guard with the dagger. "He wants to kill me!"

"Lader? But he's completely loyal to you, Majesty, as I am." The guard dropped to his knee, head bowed. Lorens sucked in several deep breaths in an effort to calm himself. The guard paid this small obeisance only to cover the act of fastening his sword belt and keeping his trousers from falling down.

"Where were you? Both of you?"

"We . . . I . . . we heard strange noises and went to explore. It was nothing, Majesty."

Lorens had lived an isolated existence but he was no fool. Patrin had tried to school him in human foibles that a wizard might exploit. He had learned of these from books and grimoires, not from experience. It took Lorens several seconds to piece together what he saw.

"Are you two lovers?" he asked, incredulous at the idea.

"Majesty, no!" both men protested in unison.

"It's as Deprry said," explained the one called Lader. "A noise. We went to investigate a strange sound."

Lorens pushed past the two guards and went to the door where they had emerged. Inside, cowering on the bed, was a redheaded serving wench. Lorens' hands clenched into fists. Power rose within him, magical power fostered and schooled by Patrin. But the proper spells to form the searing death bolt did not come to his lips. His anger blotted out the skills needed.

"Emotion has no place in wizardry," he said over and over to himself. Patrin had tried to teach him this and had failed. A simple spell would have boiled the blood of the serving wench who had seduced his guards—and he could not remember it.

A headache grew to torment him. A dull pulsation began at the back of his neck and worked up to fragment on the top of his head and send fiery knives deep into his skull from all sides. Lorens spun away from the naked woman. He stalked back to the guards, who had finished readjusting their uniforms.

"You abandoned your posts."

"Majesty," started Lader. He glanced at Deprry, then lowered his head. "Majesty, it is true. We were weak and throw ourselves on your mercy."

Lorens could barely stand. The headache turned the world red with pain. To Lader, he said, "Get me the jester. Harhar. Roust him from bed and get him here immediately."

"Th-that's all, Majesty?" asked Deprry, worried about his punishment for abandoning his duty post.

"Do it now!" he roared. Lorens went into his sleeping chambers and slammed the heavy door. He leaned against it, again wiping the sweat from his face.

Lorens yelped when a faint rap came at the door. He jerked open the door. Standing in the light cast by the guttering torch at the end of the hall was a strangely dressed figure. Lorens backed away, fear clamping icy fingers around his throat. He struggled to breathe and could not.

"You sent for me, King Lorens," said the court fool. Harhar dropped to his hands and knees, then kicked into a headstand. From this, he pushed to a handstand and flopped over, rolling easily and coming to his feet. He shook his rattle at the frightened monarch.

"Oh, this is wonderful!" crowed Harhar. "You are such a good actor, my king. You are doing such a *fine* job of looking scared at my pitiful act!"

"Yes, of course, that's all. Just an act. An act. Come in."

"I am in, Majesty. All of me," Harhar said, using both hands to check his backside.

"Close the door."

Lorens used this brief instant when Harhar's back was to him to stumble to a chair and drop heavily into it. The jester turned to see his king seated in a sedate pose, apparently at ease with himself and his world.

"What can I do to make your burden easier, Majesty?" Harhar made a mocking bow that ended with him unbalanced and teetering precariously. He bumped into a table and fell over it, coming to his feet on the far side as if nothing had happened.

In spite of himself, Lorens smiled. "What crushing burden is this, jester?"

"The burden of rule. Duke Freow spent long, sleepless nights worrying over this and that in Porotane. Do you do less?"

"Of course not. I am content." Lorens held back the tension that made his nerves twitch like the strings of a bull fiddle.

"Yet you desire my company in the middle of the night. Better the serving wench down the hall, eh, Majesty?"

"What of her?" Lorens demanded sharply. "What do you know of her and the guards?"

"Only that Kerin is lovely and would make a fine consort. A drop or two of royal blood flows in her, methinks."

"No." Lorens dismissed the idea with a pass of his hand. He dared not share his bed with a woman capable of cutting his throat. That this red-haired witch sported a drop of royal blood was something Lorens had not known. That made such a dangerous coupling even less likely. He dared have no one challenge his rule. They all conspired against him now. To have one that close to him would only make their schemes the more likely to succeed.

"A joke then, Majesty. How do you keep a barrister from drowning?"

"What?" Lorens asked, startled at the sudden turn in the conversation. "I don't know."

"You take your foot off his head!"

"That's not funny."

"It's not funny, if you are a barrister," said Harhar. "For the rest of us, it is a fine jest." Harhar did a cartwheel across the room, smashed into the wall, and then did a hand-spring to show that his clumsiness was all part of his act.

"You hear much in the castle," said Lorens. He wiped the sweat from his upper lip. The harder he tried to control his emotions, the more obvious his distress became. Would the fool notice?

"Ah, it's gossip you desire, then. I know much. Did you know that the second assistant chef is . . ." Harhar's voice trailed off. Lorens' anger mounted.

"I need information about those who conspire against me!" the monarch roared.

"Your power is supreme, Majesty," said the jester, his ebony eyes locking with Lorens'. "Use the Demon Crown to spy on your enemies. Such fine magic will show more than a simpleton such as I could."

Lorens wiped another river of perspiration from his face and neck. He had revealed the secret he wished kept—and he had done it to the court jester. He cursed himself for such carelessness.

"Unless," Harhar said slowly, "unless you no longer possess the Demon Crown. Could this be the heart of your melancholy this night?"

"I'll cut your tongue out and cram it up your nose if you tell anyone. *Anyone*! Is this clear?"

"Majesty, I am your humble and obedient servant." Harhar fell and began banging his forehead against the floor. "I would never betray your best interests."

"The crown is gone. Stolen. The guards were lured away and the Demon Crown was stolen from my very chambers. Who in the castle has committed this foul deed?"

"Not I, Majesty!" declared Harhar. "I am as innocent as a newborn babe in arms suckling at its mother's fine, shapely, firm breast. I am even *more* innocent. I—"

"Silence, fool. I am not accusing you. I am asking advice."

"From a fool?"

The headache blasted white-hot needles into Lorens' skull. He could barely focus his eyes. Never had such headaches assailed him— not until he wore the Demon Crown. But its power! The lure of knowing every spoken word in the kingdom, seeing every covert action, being anywhere his magical senses could reach. How could he relinquish the crown for even a few minutes when so many plotted against him?

Harhar rocked back onto his heels and stared up at the King of Porotane. "Majesty," Harhar said, "if your guards are innocent, then others must be guilty. Who can walk the halls of the castle unchallenged at this hour?"

A pounding on the door kept Lorens from answering. Harhar tumbled backward and came to his feet. He opened the door. The guard pushed him aside and hurried into the room.

"Majesty, we have information you must hear," Lader said. He motioned. Deprry dragged in a soldier clad in the uniform of Baron Theoll's service.

"What can he know?" Lorens asked. The headache had become a steady throb worse than the shooting pains. He could not concentrate.

"He and three others attempted to stop two men coming from your quarters."

Lorens blasted to his feet. He wobbled slightly and recovered. Of Theoll's guardsman he asked, "What men? Describe them."

"Majesty," the guard choked out. "They attacked me. I am in pain."

"Add to his pain. Get him to speak." Lader and Deprry twisted the poor wight's arms into a double hammerlock and applied pressure. The guard went white and stammered incoherently.

"Less pressure, more talk," suggested Harhar. Lorens motioned for his guardsmen to relax their grips.

"Majesty, they were Archbishop Nosto's Inquisitors," the captive gasped out.

"You recognized them? Their names. Be quick about it."

"I . . . do not know them, Majesty." The guard turned even paler. Lader and Deprry now supported him as he weakened. "They were dressed as Inquisitors."

"What did they look like? Describe their faces. Were they tall or short? Heavy or thin?"

"They . . . were Inquisitors."

Lorens motioned for his guards to again apply their grip. Theoll's soldier gasped and fainted from pain.

"No," said Lorens when his men started to drag out the unconscious soldier. "Revive him. I must know more of this. Can it be true that Nosto plots against me?"

"It is rumored that he is of the royal blood," said Harhar.

"What?"

"All rumors, only rumors, some rumors. Who can say what is true and what is only jest?" Harhar shook his rattle and smiled as if his wits had left him.

Lader shook the soldier awake again. "No more," the guardsman moaned. "I hurt so. They broke something within me. I cannot breathe without pain."

"They killed the other three, Majesty," said Deprry. "This one is in sorry shape. They might have thought him dead."

Lorens sat on the edge of his chair. He leaned forward so that his face was only inches from the guardsman's. "These red-clad Inquisitors killed your comrades."

"Yes," the soldier gasped out.

"They carried something with them. What was it?"

"I saw nothing, but . . ."

"But what?" roared Lorens, spittle running down his chin. Spells swirled in his head. He tried to sort out the proper words of magic and summoning chants, to find the invocation that would drag the truth from this dying soldier.

"Th-they said that Nosto awaited them. That they carried something to him. I saw nothing, but . . ." Again his words drifted away as pain worked its debilitating magic on his body.

Lorens gestured to his guardsmen. They broke one of the soldier's arms in their attempt to force the truth from him.

"A box. I saw a glass box. That's all. I—"

"What else?" Lorens reached out and grabbed the soldier by the throat and shook. The guard's head flopped loosely.

"Majesty, he is dead," said Lader. "We didn't mean to kill him."

"Get him out of here. Bury him in the gardens. Let no one see you."

"Sire," spoke up Harhar, "should both of your guards leave your side at this hour?"

"What are you saying?"

"Why did the good baron have a squad of men patrolling the corridor in front of your living quarters? Is he empowered to protect you in such a fashion?"

"The fool thinks more clearly than my personal guardsmen!" Lorens leaned back, hands on his head as if this would hold back the pain. It didn't.

Archbishop Nosto's Inquisitors had stolen the Demon Crown. Baron Theoll had a squad of soldiers in the hallway outside his quarters— while his own men dallied with a serving wench. Nosto had royal blood in his veins; he could wear the Demon Crown he had stolen. The Inquisition's brutal power spread and Theoll sent men in the middle of the night and his own were away from their post and he knew nothing about it because the crown had been taken. Lorens could no longer keep his emotions in check and broke down, weeping uncontrollably.

Life had been so much simpler in the City of Stolen Dreams under his master's tutelage.

Lorens turned and buried his face in Harhar's tunic and cried. The jester gently patted him on the head, as if he were a small child instead of king of a powerful and rich kingdom.

EIGHT

Birtle Santon watched silently as Vered drew the dagger and slipped it between his own clothing and the tightly fitting red Inquisitor's uniform. A quick motion parted the fabric and Santon wiggled out of it like a snake shedding an unwanted skin.

"I feel better," he said. "It cut off my circulation."

"And I feel better for being out of Castle Porotane once again," said Vered. He glanced over his shoulder at the bramble-arched tunnel leading to the postern gate they had used so many times. "When will Lorens post a guard there?"

"Does it matter if he ever does? Neither of us will be returning by this route. If the saints are with us, we go in the main gates or we never return."

Vered nodded. What his friend said was true. They might find Lokenna. If so, putting her on the throne in place of the demented Lorens might prove impossible. If they succeeded, it would not be by riding through the huge southern gate at the head of an army.

And if Lorens caught them before they found the royal twin sister, the monarch would never return them to the castle for trial. He would behead them on the spot.

Santon awkwardly shucked off the remaining sleeve of the crimson uniform and kicked the tatters under a rock and out of sight of a casual searcher. He moved so that starlight shone off the glass box tucked under his arm. Santon saw Vered's sharp interest. He used his good hand to hold the box at arm's length.

Resting within the container lay the Demon Crown. Starlight caught on the points of the crown and magnified so much that Santon had to look away. When they had carried the crown before, it had glowed a subtle shade of green. Now the verdant radiance was more insistent— and the blazing white tips of the metallic gold circlet showed that the magic once dormant within the crown had been awakened.

"It has changed," said Vered. "The brief moment I touched it, I felt the new power."

Santon's attention turned fully to Vered. Something in the way the man spoke seemed different.

"Isn't it lovely?" asked Vered. The young thief moved closer, his eyes on nothing but the crown. "It offers so much. A touch is hardly enough."

"What did you see when you put it in the box?" asked Santon. He moved away so that Vered had to trail along. He looked around, thinking that they were still too close to the castle. They had to find their horses and ride once more. Lorens would send out every soldier in Castle Porotane when he awoke and learned of the theft. Their small deception might put the monarch on the wrong scent, but he dared not count on it. Let Archbishop Nosto and Baron Theoll try to explain their doings this night.

How long this diversion would work, San- ton could not say. Not long. A day? A pair of days? He doubted that. Even if Lorens believed the Demon Crown was still within the castle walls, Archbishop Nosto and Theoll would know that it wasn't. If Theoll did not send forth men to capture them, Nosto would.

The crown was a prize to each of them.

"I saw nothing unusual," Vered said. "Only hints of what might be. There are so many people in the castle worthy of my attention. Rogina? She is cunning. More so than her sister. And what of Nosto? His Inquisition makes corpses and enemies. Who? We can find them with the crown and turn them to our side."

"Why do we need them?" asked Santon. His worry over Vered's behavior increased. It was as if the Demon Crown had infected him with the disease devouring Lorens' mind.

"We know little of Claymore Pass," said Vered. "Such ignorance means danger. If I just touch the crown to my head, I can send out a reconnaissance unmatched by rebel or royal. We can learn the location of every rebel trooper, every ruffian, every cow in all Porotane!"

"Lokenna," said Santon. He used the box containing the crown like bait to draw Vered on. Their horses neighed and pawed the ground nervously. Santon caught the box between shield and body and used his good arm to swing up onto the horse's back. He almost slid off the other side. They needed saddles for proper mounting and riding if they were to make good time.

"Yes," hissed Vered. "What a fine thought! I can use the Demon Crown to find Lokenna. Why spend fruitless days hunting her when I can spend only minutes with the crown and locate her?"

"Do you remember what Alarice said?" Santon used his knees to turn his horse. The roan tossed its head and sniffed the air. Finding the crisp autumn night to its liking, the roan trotted off. Behind, Santon heard Vered curse and get his own dappled gray mare onto the trail. It took only seconds for Vered to catch up and ride apace. His face shone in the pale moonlight with his enthusiasm for once more donning the Demon Crown.

"You lack enough strong arms to carry it easily," said Vered. "Let me tend to the box. I have two good arms and my balance on bareback is better."

"The Glass Warrior warned us of the insidious pull exerted by the crown. She had to use her magical abilities for over twenty years to keep from succumbing."

"What do we care of Alarice?" Vered snapped.

Santon jerked around, eyes blazing. He said nothing. Vered's expression changed from one of lust to utter confusion. The man touched his forehead, then stared at both hands as if he had never seen them before.

"Birtle, what did I say?"

"You know."

"I . . . yes, I know. But I did not mean it. I couldn't help myself. The words just slipped out because of—"

"The Demon Crown spoke for you," interrupted Santon. "Alarice warned us of its evil. If I don it, I die. Your fate would be even worse. You would become its slave."

"As Lorens is." Vered rubbed his eyes and said, "How our king must be suffering without it. I only brushed my fingertips across it and it almost possessed me. How diabolical the demon Kalob was, giving this to King Waellkin."

"For three hundred years the Demon Crown has been the focus of conflict. Porotane might be better off if we rode to the ocean and cast it in."

"No!" Vered's denial worried Santon anew.

"Please, Santon, it's not like that. I . . . I know its power over me now. I am warned. But we cannot destroy it."

"Why not?"

"This is a powerful legacy, a relic of our empire. It can be evil, yes, but if the monarch is aware and strong, it can be an even greater tool for peace and prosperity."

"The ruler's burden would be too great."

"That is not for you to decide," said Vered. "Nor is it for me, although I carry a drop of royal blood in my arteries. Think for a moment. If destroying the crown is a proper solution, why didn't Alarice do it in the two decades she was custodian?"

"She gave her promise to King Lamost—and to Duke Freow."

"A promise balanced against the peace of a kingdom? Do you think a decent, caring woman like Alarice would hesitate to dishonor herself for the good of uncounted millions of people? She would not consider only those caught up in our paltry civil war—she would think of unborn generations."

"She didn't destroy this demon device, did she?" Santon pulled his shield around and balanced the glass box containing the Demon Crown on its rounded surface. The magical brilliance of the crown shone undimmed and reflected like starlight from the glass shield.

Birtle Santon stared at it, and his thoughts turned to lovely Alarice, her white hair flowing as she rode, her trim figure that of a young maiden and not a woman years older than he.

She had ample reason to destroy it. And Alarice was a sorceress with power enough to deal with the crown's magical component. She had kept it for twenty years and had not destroyed it. Had she tried? Santon could not answer.

Perhaps she had. Perhaps she had tried and failed. If this were true, Santon knew they had no chance to destroy it. Both his and Vered's talents did not turn to magic. A strong arm in battle, a deft move resulting in a stolen money pouch, those were their talents.

"Do you think pursuit has begun?" asked Vered.

"We have an ample lead, if it has. They have to find our trail, though you might be right in thinking we should begin confusing pursuers. The River Ty lies a few leagues to the east."

"Why divert from our path north if I could just touch the crown and *see* if there is any pursuit?"

Santon's left arm had withered after being struck in battle. Over the years his right arm had grown immeasurably strong to compensate for the infirmity. He turned and put the full power of his shoulder and upper body behind the blow that landed on Vered's chest. The younger man was lifted up and off his horse by the force. He landed heavily beside the trail in a pile of leaves.

"Does that clear your head or should I bash it in and see if anything oozes out?" Santon hefted his battle-ax and spun it in a circle that could easily end at Vered's skull.

"You didn't have to knock me off my horse,"

complained Vered. He shook his head and winced at the pain. "My whole body hurts."

"What of this?" Santon tapped the glass box holding the crown.

"You keep it. I don't want to risk another fall. You could have crushed my chest." Vered rolled onto hands and knees, then forced himself up to his knees, breathing as difficult as standing. From this way station he got to his feet. His gray mare pawed at the ground impatiently. He remounted.

"I fear this journey might be our undoing unless you can control your urge to wear the Demon Crown," said Santon. "I cannot watch over you night and day."

"Mayhaps a change of clothing and some decent food will change my perspective on life. Why do I need to spy on others if I am content with my lot?"

"We have no money, we have no tack, an army might be following us, and everywhere across the land there are bands of rebels willing to slay us without even inquiring of our names. You think that a fine meal and fancy clothes are *all* you need?"

"They are a start," said Vered. "And you must admit that it's better than crowning myself."

"You carry it for a while," said Santon, handing over the glass box. He studied Vered's face as the man's eyes glowed with anticipation. But the look died as reason prevailed. Vered knew the danger of even a brief touch. That knowledge replaced the eagerness for the supreme power offered by the Demon Crown.

"Let's ride as if we meant it instead of dawdling. The stream feeding the River Ty is a good place to start losing any pursuit," Vered said. He put his heels into the gray's flanks. Santon had to gallop to catch up with his friend.

A war arrow whistled through the air and stuck into a tree trunk just beyond Birtle Santon. Reflexes caused the man to duck long after the arrow had sunk into the wood.

"You're slowing down," accused Vered. The young man's quick eyes scanned the terrain behind. They had ridden out of a thin forest and onto a plain, only to find themselves ringed by Lorens' troops. A clever retreat had gained them a few minutes and the cover of the forest once more. But the arrows arching into the air from the plain fell into the forest and drove them like cattle.

"They'll close in on us again unless we do something," Santon said. He shifted his weight in the saddle. They had stolen tack and food a day out of Castle Porotane. He wished that they had stolen a better quality of leather goods. The saddle's seat peeled and resulted in chafing after more than a week of perilous riding. All that faded into insignificance. They had eluded Lorens' soldiers until today.

"The Yorral Mountains are pretty this time of year," said Vered, his eyes focused on the horizon to the north. "The purple haze is offset so well by the first winter snows. See how the tallest mountains are capped with snow lit by the dawn's light? And is that a new storm forming around yon peak?"

"The soldiers, dammit!" flared Santon. "They will have our heads if we don't do something besides mooning over nature's beauty and the damned mountains."

"You anger so easily these days," said Vered. "Is the trip wearing you down?"

"Yes, it is," Santon said from between clenched teeth. "And if you had a whit of good sense, it'd be reducing you to the same condition."

"You want me to get mad?"

Santon sucked in cold air and exhaled, silvery plumes from his breath hanging in the chilly morning. He knew what drove Vered to this extreme. On the trip they had learned of the Demon Crown's power over the man, even though his royal blood was slight. By refusing to acknowledge his emotions, Vered had kept the crown's fatal attraction at bay.

"Claymore Pass is another two days' travel," said Santon. "We dare not let the troops know that is our destination. They can block our way too easily since they are between us and the mountains."

"Then let us go west, as if we are trying to reach the river. They might think we seek a barge to take us down the River Ty and back into the relative warmth of the southlands."

"Fine plan," said Santon. "But there are hundreds of them. How they got ahead of us I'll never know."

"They might have been on patrol," said Vered, hooking one leg across the saddle pommel and leaning forward. "A wizard's message might have alerted them about us. Or even something more common. The semaphore towers might be working once more."

Santon snorted derisively. "The rebels haven't allowed them to operate for more years than I can remember. They know the power of the royal army. The rebels' most potent weapons are speed and keeping the king in ignorance of their movements."

"All the more reason for our desperate

King Lorens to want to recover his precious crown," said Vered. Without another word, he pointed into the distance.

Santon shook his head. Attempting a ride west was out of the question. A thin column of cavalry trotted from the north, effectively cutting off travel in that direction. The flights of arrows had stopped, but the archers maintained their position to the north. They had no idea about the east and they had just ridden from the south. For all the need to succeed, Santon disliked the notion of retreating.

"No, friend, we need not backtrack," said Vered. "I have seen what your blurred vision has missed."

"My eyesight is fine." He stood in his stirrups and carefully surveyed the land gently rolling toward the river. It took several seconds before he made out a second longer column of cavalry, between the king's and the Ty.

"Rebels, aye," said Vered. "The horsemen cannot last long against the rebel troops. Unless I miss my count, they outnumber the royalist troops five to one."

"There's no way you can tell that from this distance. You're guessing."

"Perhaps," Vered said smugly. Santon cared little whether his friend knew the exact composition of the rebel band. As long as they drew the royalists' attention, that was all that counted.

"There, smoke," said Santon. The rebel forces touched the leading edge of the battle line formed by the king's men. "And dust. The archers are turning to join the battle."

"That is the only way they will drive off the rebels. It is time for us to be off for Claymore

Pass. We must slip past before anyone notices us."

"The rebels are as likely to kill us as the royalists," agreed Santon. They had been lucky in their forced ride to the north. Although they had seen several companies of rebel troops, they had avoided them easily. Most seemed intent on gathering materiel for the renewed siege of the castle and not on individual riders.

"Do you think they are Dews Gaemock's men?"

"They ride under a green and black banner," said Santon.

"Ionia again meddles in the northlands. If Gaemock learns of this, there might well be a three-way battle on those plains." Vered pulled his leg off the pommel and settled down. They rode out of the woods and onto the plain once more. Santon instinctively found the path through low, rolling hills that would shield them from prying eyes. Even though the soldiers fought on the west, they might have sentries watching for a flank attack.

"How do you stand on the rebel forces?" asked Santon. "If we are unable to find Lokenna, who would you see on the throne?"

Vered shrugged. "I never paid attention to politics. What matters it to me who collects the taxes when I pay none? Any trying to separate me from my hard-won coin is my enemy."

"We've seen how poorly Lorens has ruled."

"The crown has added to his woe. Without it, he might have been a weak but decent monarch." Vered rose in his stirrups again. "Be quick about it, Santon. Ride like the wind. The battle is nearing an end and I fear the rebel troops are withdrawing!"

Santon did not ask how Vered knew. His ears were keener and, as much as Santon hated to admit it, the young man's eyesight was better than his own. He had lived many summers and the penalties mounted, gathering like barnacles on the hull of a ship. His joints cracked and his senses failed. Santon tried not to think of the time when his strength would slip away like sand through an hourglass.

Better to die in battle.

"Ho, friend Santon, we have outdistanced any possible pursuit!" crowed Vered. But neither slackened their breakneck pace. They knew that the royalist troops might not have been hunting for them specifically—but they would hunt for them as rebel scouts now that Lady Ionia's forces had given them battle.

Birtle Santon stared ahead as his roan picked its way along the partially frozen plain. The Yorral Mountains rose as majestically as Vered had described them. And in Claymore Pass had been a battle the likes of which had not been fought in over thirty years, even in the worst years of the civil war. Hundreds, perhaps thousands, had died there and he had almost been one of that number.

The pass held bad memories for him, but what lay beyond? Where would they find Lokenna? To that he had no answer.

NINE

"The horses can't go on much longer," said Vered. The young man leaned forward in his saddle to relieve the pressure on his behind. The cold wind blowing off the steep, jagged slopes of the Yorral Mountains chapped their lips and burned their cheeks, but it was the steepness of the poor road that took its toll on their strength.

"We've got to," said Birtle Santon. "Lorens' guardsmen have found our trail again."

"Too bad Ionia's rebels couldn't have occupied them longer. I never cared much for that woman. All brag and no do."

"She's kept this section of Porotane in an uproar for over six years," said Santon. He stretched to get the kinks out of his tired, knotted muscles. His left arm throbbed dully, more annoying than painful. The withered hand flopped bonelessly and above his wrist along his forearm the tight straps on the glass shield Alarice had given him cut brutally into swollen, numb flesh.

"An alliance with Dews Gaemock might suit her. But there were rumors around the castle that she had approached him under a truce and attempted to kill him."

"I heard similar rumors," said Santon. "She was partly responsible for him lifting his siege of the castle in the spring." Santon's thoughts turned to those turbulent days. During Gaemock's siege Alarice had crept into Castle Porotane and left on Duke Freow's mission to find the royal twins. It had been shortly after that he and Vered had come across the Glass Warrior in the forest.

Santon slipped from the saddle and landed heavily on the loose stone in the roadway. He led his roan to give the noble steed a rest. The going got harder when the road appeared to climb straight up the side of a cliff. But such was road building in the Yorral Mountains.

"Where do we go? Claymore Pass is long, if I remember my geography aright," said Vered.

"It goes through to Ionia's fiefdom on the far side of the mountains," said Santon. "But we need to find villages, towns where someone might have heard of Lokenna."

"She might not be known by that name," said Vered. "We have a long and difficult search ahead of us. Damn all wizards!"

"Tahir stole the twins, but it was Patrin whom we should blame."

"I blame them all." Vered turned up the collar of his jacket as cold winds whipped down from the highest peaks. To the north and west gathered storm clouds of prodigious size and impenetrable blackness.

Santon had noticed those clouds as soon as they reached the foothills. No normal storm formed in that fashion—or no storm he had ever seen. The Wizard of Storms hid somewhere to the north of the Uvain Plateau. Santon had a feeling in his gut that the reclusive wizard was responsible for the towering columns of jet black clouds and the turbulence that overflowed into the Yorral Mountains.

"It is cold for this time of year. Cold for any time of year," complained Vered, lowering his head even more to shield himself from the wind.

Santon said nothing about his suspicions regarding the source of the fiercely biting wind. It might be the harbinger of an unusually early winter—or it might be wizardry.

"Hold for a moment. Let an old man rest." Santon watched Vered sink to the hard ground for a precious minute of not walking uphill. Santon did not sit. He looked back along their path for signs of pursuit. No dust cloud could rise from that rocky road, but he saw suspicious glints off shiny metal. Estimating distances in the clear, cold mountain air was difficult but Santon thought that Lorens' troopers were several hours behind them. Weighed down with armor and battle gear, the guardsmen made slower progress through the foothills and lower mountain slopes.

He considered several courses of action. They might take the time to lay an ambush. Rocks rolled down from the heights were devastating and easy to find, but he didn't want to use this ploy. Not unless there was no other way. Although a few large boulders might eliminate the entire force, if they didn't, he and Vered would face angry survivors. Better to keep ahead and tire out the soldiers.

"We can hide and let them go past," spoke up Vered, again uncannily reading his friend's thoughts.

"I don't think that would work. Our trail is faint on rock, but there are too few good places to hide. The steep walls keep us bottled up like cattle in a chute."

"So we ride ahead of them like corks bobbing on a tidal wave."

"Something like that," Santon admitted. He surveyed their route ahead. For an hour they would be going downhill but Santon saw that this was the last such stretch they would find for days. Only when they reached Claymore Pass would the terrain level out, and even this was small help for their straining lungs and aching muscles. The floor of the pass was several thousand feet above the level of the castle. Any exertion would tire them quickly. Riding would help but their horses would weaken without frequent rests.

Trying to cross the Yorral Mountains and not using Claymore Pass was impossible for a man on horseback.

"When do we encounter the checkpoints?" asked Vered. "I cannot believe Ionia allows anyone through the mountains without a fight."

"She knows that Porotane is ill-equipped to attack, even through the pass. She might not guard the way well."

"It wouldn't take many men. A few companies would make her fiefdom invincible."

"That's Ionia's trouble. She has no population on which to draw for her army. The few farmers working their poor, rocky lands protest losing their sons to Ionia's army. Her constant forays into Porotane do not please many at home. She must watch not only Lorens but those in her own country."

"Why bother, then?" asked Vered. "She could stay at home and tend to her vassals."

Santon laughed. "Vered, Vered, I'm surprised at you. What does lust for power have to do with practicality? Ionia desires control of

Porotane even though she has no reasonable chance to conquer a country ten times the size of her own and with a population a hundred times greater. But the lure of power and wealth has infected her, and *that* drives her on, not good sense."

"She would have done well to ally herself with Gaemock," Vered said. "She could have carved out a moderate kingdom on the far side of Claymore Pass and defended it well. From there she could have turned against Gaemock and sallied forth against him when he least expected it.

"Again, that is reasonable. I do not think she is any saner than Lorens—and he has the excuse of wearing the Demon Crown."

"Is there any way we could enlist her aid in finding Lokenna?" asked Vered. "Even if she has only a few hundred soldiers in the area, that magnifies our chance of finding her by a few hundred."

"We do not want to alert Ionia of our search." Santon started down the long incline, leading his roan. Ionia was treacherous, of that there could be no doubt. What would the mercenary would-be queen do if she found Lokenna before they did? Kidnapping? Murder? Santon didn't know. Whatever course benefited Ionia most would be followed. And did Ionia carry royal blood in her veins? Santon knew little of countries beyond Porotane and how their rulers were related, if at all, to those in Porotane.

The lure of the Demon Crown would be too great for a power-hungry ruler to refuse. Ionia would subjugate Lokenna, if possible, kill her if necessary—and she would try the crown for herself no matter how great the warnings.

"Secrecy serves us best in our search," Santon said as they reached the bottom of the incline and faced the steady climb up to the floor of Claymore Pass.

"Why do I always feel abandoned?" asked Vered.

Santon had to laugh at this. "It's because you always have been. The bastard offspring of some noble, rebels burning your village and killing your mother, constables in a hundred villages longing to cut off your ears and nail them to their punishment posts—where in all that is anything but abandonment?"

"I can always count on you to cheer me up," Vered said sourly. He, too, looked up the steep slope ahead and asked, "Can we ride? For a while?"

Santon answered by remaining afoot. The horses would be needed later. He knew. He had been in Claymore Pass before.

"With so many deep ravines, it's a wonder that water is so hard to find," said Vered.

"With so much rock, you wonder?" responded Santon. They had found a small, scraggly stand of trees in a level spot and had camped here. It took some digging before Santon had found a tiny trickle of water. "Rain runs directly off. It can't soak into the ground."

Vered swung his glass sword and scraped the ground, revealing nothing but solid stone beneath a thin layer of dirt. "I see your point." He looked around and shook his head. "Is there nowhere else to camp? I don't like this place."

"There's nothing wrong with it. We have a good view of the road. Should Lorens' men begin to narrow the distance between us we will have ample warning. And there is even some small game to be had around here trying to find water."

"Fresh meat is worth the risk," admitted Vered.

"What risk? Other than being in the Yorral Mountains?"

"You said that battles were fought throughout Claymore Pass. This is the mouth of the pass, isn't it? I feel a lingering *presence* that bothers me."

"There will be phantoms," admitted Santon. "We cannot do anything about them. But I did not know you were so sensitive to their presence." He frowned as he looked from his friend to the glass box containing the Demon Crown. Had such a brief encounter with the potent magical device imparted some measure of sorcerous power to Vered? As far as he could tell, the Demon Crown had lain quiescent in its beveled-glass case since being taken from the king's chambers. The brilliance of the crown's points remained but the putrescent green glow had subsided and returned to the more familiar verdant green before Lorens had donned it.

"We'll keep a sharp lookout," Santon said. "We don't want the king's troops sending a scout ahead to find us."

"It would take only a few to do us in," said Vered. He danced from foot to foot to keep warm, rubbing his hands together and then slapping himself on the shoulders. "I might have been more exhausted in my life but I cannot remember when."

"It's the altitude," said Santon. "And the cold. And the idea of being constantly chased."

"All that," said Vered. "And more."

He did not go into detail and Santon did not press the issue. They prepared a small meal from their trail rations. Santon vowed to hunt for game in the morning, but now, like his friend, he was too tired to do more than unroll a blanket and sleep.

Vered took the first watch. Two hours into the night he shook Santon awake. The older man shivered in the cold and wrapped the blanket more tightly around his shoulders. He found a rough-barked tree trunk to rest against and drew up his knees. The smaller the target for the biting wind, the better.

Santon strained to hear sounds in the night. Vered snored. He ignored that. The wind blowing through trees mostly shorn of their summer foliage produced an eerie whining. No animal sounds came to him. More important for his peace of mind, no sounds of approaching soldiers could be heard.

Santon walked around their tiny camp occasionally to keep awake, but he began to think the effort wasn't worth it. He craned his neck back and studied the constellations in the pure black sky. By their slow wheeling he kept track of the time.

He nodded, jerked awake, and began to nod off again when a distinct voice said, "I need your aid, fellow soldier."

"Are you dreaming, Vered?" Santon mumbled. "You were never a soldier." It took several seconds for Santon to come fully awake. Vered had not spoken. Across their low campfire he still snored away contentedly.

"I am a soldier. I was," the voice came again. "Sergeant of Scouts Ruirik Kulattian begging for your aid."

Santon's hand flew to his dagger but he did not draw. He had heard no one approaching camp. He got to his feet and turned about slowly. Nothing.

The voice came again.

"Please help me. It is so lonely in this terrible cold nothingness. I cannot even talk to my own kind. They drift just beyond the range of my voice and hearing."

"A phantom!" Santon saw a misty white patch weaving in and out of the wind-bent tree limbs above him. The mist took on a form he almost recognized as human before the strong, gusty wind carried thin tendrils downslope.

"Wait!" Santon called. "Ruirik Kulattian, wait!"

The phantom's torso became more substantial. Santon swallowed hard. There were no arms or legs—or head.

"Will you aid me? After all these years, are you the one who can deliver me to my deserved rest?"

"How long have you roamed these hills?" Santon asked. "Did you fall in Claymore Pass?"

"I did. For King Lamost I gave my life."

"I was a private in the army. Only fifty escaped Claymore Pass alive."

"Many still roam these mountainous trails," said Ruirik Kulattian. "Before I joined them, I pitied them. Then I died." The torso firmed until it glowed an eerie white. No legs touched the ground but faint hints of long, thin arms and a head appeared until a sudden gust of wind whipped them away.

"It's been more than twenty years," said Santon.

"So many," the phantom said sorrowfully.

"I guessed but did not know. There is no way to measure the passage of time. The seasons change but often confuse me since I am without sensation other than the coldness that invades my ectoplasm. Without true form or sensation, the world around me is all so vague."

"What's going on?" came Vered's sleepy voice.

"A visitor. A phantom late of King Lamost's army. A comrade in arms of mine, though I never met him."

Ruirik Kulattian solidified even more. Santon thought that the spirit forced himself to materialize. The set of the body and the determined expression on the indistinct face showed the importance of being seen to Kulattian.

"I tire of endless roaming. There is no death for me, only half life. Take me from this nothingness. I beseech you, as a comrade in arms, as a warrior, as a man, I beg you!"

Santon and Vered exchanged glances. Vered said, "How many other phantoms drift through Claymore Pass?"

"I do not know," said Kulattian's ghost. "I cannot talk to other phantoms. It is my curse to be trapped between worlds, neither alive nor dead. Others such as I are beyond my reach."

"What can you tell us of our world?" asked Vered, hunkering down and pulling his blanket around his shoulders.

"Do we barter?" asked Kulattian. "Have you no humanity and make me beg for release? Find my body and bury it properly!"

"Tell us of other humans in the area. King Lorens sends his soldiers after us."

"King Lorens? But Lamost is ruler of Porotane. There is no King Lorens."

"His son."

"Lamost has no children."

"You died before the birth of his children—twins," said Vered. "We seek his daughter Lokenna."

"A queen on the throne of Porotane," murmured Ruirik Kulattian, as if the concept lay far beyond his credulity. Santon had difficulty remembering that the phantom had been born in a different time and had died before the civil war wracked the country. When so many died, ability replaced consideration of gender.

"Lamost was foully murdered. A poison, though it was never proven. We have his crown and seek his daughter. We would crown her as Queen of Porotane."

"The Demon Crown," Ruirik said, his voice thin and reedy like the wind in high branches. "That is what draws me to you. Such power. I . . . I feel it. I actually *feel* it. It gives me warmth."

"The demon power is strong," said Vered. "We must be wary that wizards might sense it and be drawn to us."

Santon glanced into the dark night toward the distant peaks to the northwest. He was unable to see the gathering thunderstorm but knew the Wizard of Storms summoned his forces. Did the wizard know where they travelled? Did the Demon Crown serve as a beacon for those able to use—or misuse—its power? Birtle Santon had no easy answers.

"You cannot see other phantoms," said Vered, "but you can detect other humans. What of those following us?"

Ruirik Kulattian's substance thinned to a white streamer that twisted skyward and became so transparent that stars shone through. As quickly as the phantom had left, he returned, his appearance subtly different. Santon saw more character in the face now. Sergeant Kulattian gained in ability every time he reformed his body.

"A squad. Clumsy men. They know little of mountain warfare. They are burdened by useless armor. They sleep two leagues behind you, downslope and in a dry camp."

"That will slow them even more on the morrow," said Santon. "Their horses need water as much as the men." He straightened. "Thank you, Ruirik. This is important to us."

"Service for service," the phantom said, his tone pleading. "Find my body and bury it in a consecrated grave. Take me away from this senseless half-existence."

"You helped us, but there is no way we can aid you," said Vered. "Claymore Pass is long and the battles you speak of were fought long ago. Unless you can pinpoint your corpse, we have no way of finding or identifying it."

"I cannot locate my own body. Such power is denied me."

"I am truly sorry," Santon said, trying to lay his hand on the phantom's shoulder. His good hand passed through thin white fog and disrupted Ruirik Kulattian's body for several seconds. The phantom reshaped himself.

"I cannot locate my own body," Ruirik said. "Such is denied to a phantom. But you seek another."

"Lokenna, daughter of Lamost," said Vered. "Do you know of her?"

"Find my corpse and properly bury it," said Ruirik Kulattian, "and I will tell you where to find the royal heir. *I know where she lives in these hills.*"

TEN

"He might be lying," said Vered. "He might say what we want to hear simply to be free of his half-world existence."

"That is so," said Birtle Santon. To the phantom, he said, "How do you answer such a challenge? Do you lie only to win free of your current condition?"

"I would, if it benefited me. You cannot know the pain I feel. Not physical," Ruirik Kulattian hastened to add, pieces of his insubstantial body getting caught up in small eddies as the wind curled around the mountaintops and gusted downward into the Ty Valley. "I suffer psychic pain. I can talk only to those who still live."

"Other phantoms ignore you?" asked Santon.

"There is a barrier between the others and myself. I do not know if I have been singled out for this punishment or if it is universal. I can talk to those who live, not to those who are in transition—or beyond."

"Do you know what lies . . . beyond?" asked Vered.

"No. If it is total oblivion, I will greet it with

gladness. If it is more or less than I endure now, that will be its own reward. There is no change in this state. None. And it is so lonely."

"Most mortals want nothing to do with phantoms," observed Santon. "With good reason, too. Why should we be reminded of the slow march of days toward our own death?"

"Although I lack substance, I can drift from village to village much faster than you can travel. My search will be tireless. I have nothing else to fill my days."

"So you really don't know where Lokenna is," accused Vered.

"I can find her. I know of a village where one with this name lives."

"But?" urged Vered. "There is more. What is it?"

"I do not know how long ago she lived there. It might be a moment, or it might be a decade. In my phantom's existence, time is meaningless." Ruirik spread his vaporous hands in a gesture of helplessness.

"You'll do this searching in exchange for our finding your body and burying it?" Vered shook his head. "It seems our mission changes. We hunt for Ruirik's corpse while he looks for Lokenna. One search is as difficult as the other. If anything, our finding Lokenna might be the easier. She is alive and must have contact with others. If those others speak with still more, we can trace back the threads until we find the tapestry, if you get my meaning."

"What he says is true, Ruirik. It will be simpler for us to hunt for Lokenna on our own."

"Speed," the phantom said. "I can move more quickly. You have little time before the soldiers overtake you."

"They have followed us for long days. We can continue to elude them," said Santon.

"Claymore Pass is narrow and treacherously rocky. Dodging an enemy between those stone walls is impossible. If you were there as you claim, you remember."

Santon nodded. He remembered too well. They had tried to outflank the brigands and had failed. That move cost them fully half their fighting force. Any maneuver other than outright retreat or frontal assault had been thwarted easily.

"The soldiers follow us whether we hunt for Lokenna or your body," said Vered. "We gain nothing by adding this new complication."

"Not so," argued the spirit. "I can find Lokenna and lead you directly to her. If they dog your steps, you take them to her even as you search. The longer you hunt, the closer they get to you."

"A good point," said Santon.

"And if the soldiers overtake us when we find your body," continued Vered, "you can plead with them to bury you in a proper grave. They might take pity on you."

"That is so. They have no quarrel with Sergeant Ruirik Kulattian who died before many of them were born and who served the same throne."

"That poses a dilemma for us," said Santon. "Your honesty. We carry out our part of the bargain—but what keeps you from leading Lorens' guardsmen to Lokenna?"

"Why should I do this?"

"Our only hold over you is not burying your corpse. You might find a better deal with the soldiers."

"In all my dealings, I was honest."

"But you've admitted you would do anything to escape your current fate. Lying is a small price to pay."

Ruirik Kulattian said nothing. And Santon had little else to add. They either trusted one another or they didn't. The spirit's argument about their search leading the troopers directly to Lokenna carried much weight. The barren mountains did not offer much in the way of shelter. After only a few inquiries, the officer in charge of the squad would be on their trail.

"Where did you fall in battle?" Santon asked.

Kulattian's phantom asked, "We have an agreement?"

"We need more information. If we are to search these saints-deserted hills, we need a starting point."

"I am sorry. I cannot tell you. I was struck in the back by a war arrow. The poisons on the barbed head put me into a coma. I have the impression of being carried for hours—perhaps days or even weeks—before dying. All I know is that I died in Claymore Pass."

"A long stretch of rock," muttered Santon. The task appeared impossible. Louder, he said, "Very well. We will seek out the bones of all those fallen and bury the ones we can identify. You realize that if we cannot properly identify your body among the others, we cannot consecrate the grave and release you?"

"I will take that risk. Do what you can and I will find Lokenna for you."

"Agreed," said Santon, holding out his hand. A tendril of white vapor curled out and placed itself atop the man's good hand. Vered inched closer and placed his hand over the misty patch of phantom flesh.

"Agreed," Vered said.

"For all eternity will I search to carry out my promise. Agreed!" Ruirik Kulattian spun about his glowing core so rapidly that pieces of his substance spun off into the night. Within seconds nothing remained of the phantom.

"I hope we're doing the right thing," said Vered. "How can we trust a spirit?"

"You must," came a low voice.

"Easy for you to say," said Vered. Then he stared at Santon. "Your lips didn't move."

"That's because I didn't speak." They turned, hands on weapons. Less than a dozen paces away another phantom hung in a vaporous column.

"Finding you has been hard," the phantom said in a voice that brought a tear to Santon's eye.

"Alarice!" he cried.

"There is so little time." Santon paid no attention. He rushed forward, arm reaching for her. His mighty forearm passed through the phantom, scattering its gauzy substance. The ghostly figure reformed more quickly than Ruirik's had. "I must not waste energy," Alarice chided gently. "You must listen."

Vered gripped Santon's shoulders and held him in place. "Go on," Vered said. "You sent us here. Where is Lokenna? You can find her. We don't need the other phantom now."

"You do. I must not linger. I cannot. There is a magic coming alive in Porotane unlike any in my experience. The Wizard of Storms meddles once again. He is drawn to the power of my phantom."

"Your body," asked Santon. "Where is it? Still in the Desert of Sazan? We'll find it and give it a proper burial. I swear on my sacred honor!"

"That is nice but unnecessary. Let Ruirik find Lokenna. You must avoid Lorens' soldiers. They are almost upon you."

"We can outrun them."

"Take care!" Alarice warned. "Claymore Pass holds more than memories. Dalziel Sef's troops return from parley with Ionia."

"They're ahead of us in the pass?" Vered turned and looked, as if he could see them in the darkness. "That means we're caught between two war parties!"

"Alarice, there's so much you must tell me." Santon reached again for the Glass Warrior's phantom but she had dissipated, another victim of the strong wind blowing across the rocky slopes. He stood, his good arm futilely reaching out for her.

"She's gone again," said Vered in a soft voice. "She'll return."

"How she must suffer. You heard what Ruirik said. What must the existence be like for one as vital as Alarice?"

"She has powers Ruirik doesn't. She must have heard him tell us his tale of woe. She might be able to communicate with other phantoms. If not, she can at least eavesdrop on them. She was more than a doughty warrior, Santon old friend, she was also a sorceress of considerable ability."

"She fought Patrin to the death and he was supposed to be the strongest wizard in the kingdom."

"No longer," said Vered. "She fears the Wizard of Storms. We should, also."

"We should fear what the soldiers will do to us if they catch us. Let's get our gear ready. We must ride like the demon-cursed wind or we'll be trapped between them!"

"Wait, Santon. You're always telling me to make haste slowly. We should consider our next move with great care, or we might end up like Ruirik."

Santon said nothing to this, but the thought crossed his mind that it might not be a sorry fate. He might be able to again touch Alarice. No matter that they would both be phantoms. Just to be together with the lovely woman once more. . . .

"They ride early. Dawn has barely ignited the eastern sky." Vered shifted in the saddle as he peered down the valley at a single-file line of riders.

"Morning comes late in the mountains. The peaks block the sun until almost midday," said Birtle Santon. "A good commander would have had his men ready for the trail long before first light."

"Definitely Dalziel Sef's troops. Even though I see no banner, look at the way they stagger their line. No one is going to drop rocks on them from above and do much damage."

Santon studied the formation that Vered commented on. The rebel commander had his men spaced so that rock slides might kill a few but most fighting men would escape. He had either fought before in Claymore Pass or he had imagination.

Santon hoped it was the former. Any show of intelligence on the part of their enemies might mean their deaths.

"Lorens' troopers are less than an hour's travel behind us," said Vered, turning in his saddle to look backward.

Santon didn't listen to his friend's description of troop placements and their relative strengths. He concentrated on the jagged terrain. It had been many years—decades!—since he had been here, but the memory refused to fade. It had been brutal slaughter along that narrow trail. For weeks his troops had dealt bloody death to the brigands, only to have it returned when they encountered a force too strong to break with a frontal assault.

Somewhere in that valley lay Ruirik Kulattian's body. But where? The elements would have bleached the bones after the insects and mountain hawks had stripped the flesh from the skeleton. Or had Ruirik been left in the pass at all? He had said he was injured. The wounded men had been carried until suitable shelters could be found.

He began scanning the sheer cliffs for signs of caves. If his commander had discovered a small cave, he would have dispatched the medical team there with the wounded. Ruirik might have died in a cave. Santon shuddered. He could deal with chalky bones left twenty years in the sun and wind. A body placed in a protected cave might have mummified. He chided himself for such morbid thoughts. He had no fear of the dead. Phantoms did little more than annoy the living; they had no substance to do real harm. But the soldier's ancient fear of the dead and dying came back fully to him.

"Both sides have sighted us," said Vered. "We are in for a busy day."

"What? Already?" Birtle Santon snapped out of his reverie. A lone scout raced back along Claymore Pass to alert the rebel captain. He craned his neck and saw that a royalist soldier also galloped to inform his leader. Whatever they had planned was now past changing.

"Are you ready to lead them into one another's arms?"

"Neither has seen the other side?"

"How can they? Both scouts ran like the wind to report our presence. If they had waited even a minute before reporting, both would know. But not now."

"Let's hope that is so," said Santon. He had no stomach for deadly games such as this.

He urged his roan down the stony slope of the hill and into the valley that was Claymore Pass. He waited for Vered to join him. The younger man seemed to be enjoying his ruse.

"Which side do you want?" asked Vered. "Rebel or royalist?"

"What does it matter?" Since Santon's horse faced the rebels, he put his heels to the animal's bony flanks and shot forward. Behind him he heard Vered laugh. Then only the echoing clatter of the gray's hooves against flint could be heard.

Santon adjusted his shield and jerked at the thong around his wrist holding his battle-ax. It would not do to lose his most deadly weapon in the heat of combat.

His heart rose and clogged his throat when he saw that he faced not a lone scout but three. He had come too far to rein in and turn his horse. He continued to urge the steed forward. Attack might mean survival. Retreat meant only death.

A battlecry rose in his throat as he charged. A flick of his wrist brought the heavy ax up and into his grip. The thick shaft reassured him. The *thunk*! as an arrow glanced off his shield reassured him. The fear on the scouts' faces reassured him. He was again in battle!

His ax flowed in an arc level with his shoulders. He felt the impact as the well-honed blade struck the first scout's sword blade and snapped it off at the hilt. The scout tumbled backward from his saddle, falling heavily to the ground.

Well past him, Santon ignored the fallen rebel and turned to the second and third. Between them he rode, shield protecting him on one side and his ax finding a fleshy berth on the other. The wounded scout doubled over but stayed in the saddle. He turned and trotted back toward the main force.

Santon let him go. That was part of the plan.

And he found himself fully engaged with the remaining scout. The man did not fight well but fear and desperation gave him added strength. The tip of his sword raked along Santon's forehead and opened a shallow, bloody gash. Santon spurred his horse into a full gallop.

He had been wounded like this before and knew the danger. Blood gushed from the scratch and blinded him. The world turned red as the blood worked its way beneath his tightly shut eyelids. Santon dropped his ax and let it dangle from the wrist thong while he wiped away the blood.

He blinked rapidly and cleared his vision. As he had hoped, the scout had not pursued. The man had been so surprised that his feeble attack had driven off the warrior who had severely wounded one and downed another that he had failed to take advantage of his lucky sword stroke.

Ahead Santon saw Vered waving his arms.

Santon lifted his shield in acknowledgment. His friend had not found it difficult chasing the royalist scout.

"What happened?" Vered demanded.

"A lucky cut, nothing more. Let's ride. We don't want to tarry. There are three scouts behind."

"Only one on my side. I had to work to let him escape. What a fool!"

Santon and Vered rode hard back up the hill from which they had sighted the two opposing forces. By the time they reached the summit, their horses gasped and stumbled. There would be no more running—for a time.

"Let me tend that cut. It's leaking again."

Santon winced as Vered plucked a weed from the ground and applied its astringent to the wound. It took several seconds before the sides of the cut began to pucker and close.

"Hurts like a demon spitting on it," said Santon.

"Be glad that lucky cut didn't land a bit lower. You might be grinning from a new mouth." Vered touched Santon's neck to show where such a slash would have been.

They turned to see how their plan progressed. Santon forgot about his minor cut. Dalziel Sef's rebel force charged forward in a fan-shaped battle formation. Lorens' troops moved more slowly. They had already fought their way up steep slopes from the valley of the River Ty. Their horses and men were tired.

"This is like watching a boulder plunge from a cliff. It seems to move in the air so slowly," said Vered with some glee. "No real motion at first, then it picks up speed and goes faster and faster." He smiled broadly when the two forces spotted each other.

"Then the rock hits the ground and shatters," finished Santon. The rebels had the advantage of position and formation and used it. He watched with no real pleasure as the rebel forces let out a battlecry and charged. The royalist troops had an inferior position, lesser numbers, and the disadvantage of exhaustion.

But still they fought well. To the last man they fought well. Birtle Santon watched, thinking how similar this had been to the slaughter he remembered so vividly from more than twenty years ago.

ELEVEN

"A rider just reported sighting Lorens' troops in Claymore Pass," said Dalziel Sef. "I am at a loss to understand why the king would have such a large force there."

"A better question," said Dews Gaemock, "is why you had troops in the pass when we concentrate our forces in the south for another siege of the castle."

"It wasn't a *large* company," Dalziel Sef said, smiling broadly and holding out his hands to show his innocence. "They merely returned from negotiations with Ionia. They had been sent before our, umm, agreement to join forces for this new attack on Lorens."

Gaemock said nothing to this. The timing was poor. Dalziel Sef might have sent his representative to Ionia before the parley began, but Gaemock doubted it. Sef played his own game and thought to align himself with Ionia to control the northern reaches of Porotane. Cut off Claymore Pass and an important escape route could be denied to the rebels. It took little effort to get a fleeing army aboard barges and take them up the River Ty. From shallow-water ports near the foothills of the Yorral Mountains it was only a short journey into the pass and to freedom—in Ionia's fiefdom.

Cut off the pass, and such an interdiction would take only a handful of men, made a retreating army fair game for royalist troopers.

"How are preparations going for the siege?" asked Gaemock.

"Well. We have the design for a new siege engine that can throw boulders so large that five men cannot reach around them."

"Getting ammunition for this mighty catapult will prove chancy, won't it?"

"The basket is large for such a boulder. However, we think to throw in burning debris. Perhaps lighted pitch torches. We can burn them out." Sef smiled even more. "If nothing else, we can burn away the brambles surrounding the castle and give ourselves good ground for lifting ladders to their battlements."

"Such an assault will fail. It always has. We must break their will. Only surrender works, not attrition."

"With Lorens able to observe our every movement the siege might last a long time. We must show great strength and determination if we are to cow him."

"The Demon Crown gives him courage," said Gaemock. "We must break the will of those on the battlements."

"We will." Sef's confidence proved contagious and Gaemock felt himself believing such an attack could work. Gaemock watched the other rebel warlord saunter off to inspect his troops. Gaemock waited until Dalziel Sef vanished from sight, then slipped past the inner ring of sentries and started walking toward the distant castle.

Darkness enveloped him like a shroud. The

northern winter winds came early and their siege would be costly in lives if it did not end soon. They had been unable to find adequate food for their troops; it would not do having his freezing, starving men staring at the warm, well-fed royalists patrolling the castle's battlements. Gaemock felt an obligation to try the siege now but would lift it within a month in favor of a new siege before spring planting. If he could prevent foodstuffs from reaching the castle next year, he had a good chance to win by attrition.

His only hope for ending this attack was a poor harvest and lack of larder to feed those within Castle Porotane.

Gaemock stopped, turned to his left, walked a few paces, then retraced his path, every sense alert for anyone tracking him from the rebel encampment. Satisfied that he was alone, he continued toward the castle. The sound of the rushing river died behind him and the land turned loamy beneath his boots. An hour's walk brought him to the edge of a large field.

Castle Porotane loomed large and menacing, deep black against the lesser black of the nighttime sky. Again Dews Gaemock checked to be sure that he was not followed from the rebel camp. He dared not let anyone see who he met this night. They would brand him a traitor, in spite of his fine record against the royalists.

Gaemock grinned without humor when he thought of Sef's reaction if he blundered on this nocturnal meeting. He did not trust the other rebel leader, and he was sure Dalziel Sef did not trust him. This would be proof of duplicity.

No one followed—or if someone did, they were a better woodsman than Gaemock. He doubted this was possible. Much of his life, after leaving his fine grain farm to royalist tax collectors, had been spent in the forests as a hunter and scout. With a sureness in his stride, he went directly to the edge of the farm where a stump had been blasted by lightning. He settled on the blackened seat and waited.

Ten minutes later he heard a faint jingling noise.

"Bells? You have bells announcing your entrance? You have truly spent too much time in the castle. You have been seduced by their decadent ways."

From the direction of the faint jingling bells came a booming voice. "Dear brother, you are never suspicious enough. You have vision but no fear."

"I leave that to tacticians such as yourself. I can plan grand, sweeping campaigns. Only the details bog me down."

Gaemock rose and turned. Before him stood Harhar in his jester's costume. The two embraced, then held one another at arm's length.

"It's been too long since I saw you, Dews."

"Nonsense. It's been less than a month."

"Much has happened in that time," said the jester. He stripped off his peaked hat and tossed it aside. He carefully removed the threads from his fingers. The bells behind them jingled as he tugged on the invisible cords.

"Efran, leave this playacting. Return to camp with me. We don't need you risking your life inside the castle. We know all there is to know of those fools."

"You don't include me with the fools? I play the fool, yes, but like me none within Castle

Porotane really *are* fools. Ambitious, cunning, dangerous—but no fools. Those who were slow to learn have long since been executed."

"Lorens continues his purges?"

"Lorens has run out of people to put to death, but Archbishop Nosto finds new heretics to put to the Question every day."

"Can we use this to create a rebellion from within?"

Efran Gaemock—Harhar—shook his head. "Nosto blends faith and fear too well. Many go to their death praising him."

"Theoll? What of the baron?"

"He tasted a moment on the throne after Freow died and before Lorens came from the Desert of Sazan with the crown. He has become addicted to that high position, but he is not careless in his pursuit to regain it. Even after it became apparent that I was giving Duke Freow an antidote to his poison, Theoll did not panic."

"Does he know you were aiding the old duke?"

"He might suspect, though I doubt it. I have become confessor to both Theoll and Lorens." Efran Gaemock laughed a deep, rich laugh. "What a position! Both consider me an idiot—and safe."

"A dangerous position. Take care, my brother." Dews Gaemock settled down on the lightning-struck stump. "But I must know of the castle supplies. Can they withstand a siege if we begin immediately?"

"The larder is full. Theoll and Nosto have seen to that. Lorens spent all his days wearing the Demon Crown and spying on other parts of the realm. Without the baron and archbishop, the castle would be ripe for the plucking."

"There is something in your words that tells me you hide an important fact. What do you hold back, Efran?"

"There might be much to gain by restraining your soldiers for a few days. Perhaps a week would suffice."

"Why? Does Theoll plan to assassinate the king?"

"I am sure he has such a scheme brewing, and if he knew the truth he would strike immediately. King Lorens no longer wears the Demon Crown."

"Its magic has finally worn him down?" Dews Gaemock considered what his brother had said. His dark eyes widened. "The crown is stolen! Is that what you're telling me?"

"I cannot be sure who stole it. The pair who accompanied Lorens back from the Desert of Sazan, perhaps."

"Why would they steal it? They installed him on the throne."

"These two, Vered and Santon, play their own game—or that of the Glass Warrior."

"She is dead? Truly?"

"She is. Or Santon and Vered so believe. They are not good enough posers to feign such sorrow. I was unable to discover what happened when they found Lorens, but the battle must have been awesome and left the Glass Warrior a casualty."

"So they have no loyalty to Lorens?"

"None. I have watched them carefully and their disgust at him and his purges has grown. It is for this reason I feel they are responsible for the crown's theft."

"We can attack immediately. Why should we hesitate now that Lorens is not able to watch our every move?"

"He has confided to me that his forces in the north have located the pair. He is contemplating leading a few companies of men personally. He is desperate to regain the crown and does not trust any underling with the mission."

"We can capture or kill him on the way! Where have his men bottled up Santon and Vered?"

"Claymore Pass."

Efran's words shocked Dews Gaemock.

"What is wrong, brother?"

"Perhaps it is only coincidence, though I doubt it." Dews explained succinctly how Dalziel Sef had patrols roaming in the Yorral Mountains and along Claymore Pass.

"This alliance might end quickly, Dews. Be on guard."

The rebel leader pushed such problems aside for the moment. "When Lorens leaves, who will be in command of the castle? Theoll?"

"Whoever Lorens puts in control will quickly fall to the baron, so, yes, let us assume he will be in charge. However, he will be robbed of full control by Archbishop Nosto and the power of his saints-cursed Inquisition."

"Turmoil," said Dews Gaemock. "They will rot from within. Castle Porotane will be ours very soon!"

"And with it the power base to control the kingdom. Even with the Demon Crown, Lorens cannot retain power without the riches and safety offered by the castle."

"He would still be a thorn in the side—a dangerous one. We must capture him as he goes to retrieve the crown."

"Good. I will signal when he leaves. A thin red banner from the northwestern tower battlements."

"Be careful, Efran," Dews said. "The castle becomes more dangerous for you with every passing day."

"How? The baron loves to tell me everything. Lorens has no other confidant. And I am beneath notice for the Inquisition. I come and go and who listens to a fool?"

"Who cares if a fool is killed?" countered Dews.

"You worry too much. You must admit that this little spy mission of mine has given us the edge in the rebellion. Without me inside the castle, Lorens and the Demon Crown would have been too powerful a combination to overcome."

"It is a shame that he hasn't proven to be the ruler his father was. I would gladly bend my knee to one such as King Lamost."

"We will see a good ruler on the throne, dear brother." Efran clamped his hand firmly on Dews' shoulder. "Wait for my signal."

"I will." The two again embraced. And Efran Gaemock vanished when he put on his peaked cap and smoothed his motley; in his place stood Harhar, the royal jester.

Dews Gaemock watched his younger brother slip back into the night, a feeling of loss overcoming his excitement at the information Efran had given him.

TWELVE

The hard blow to the center of Birtle Santon's forehead opened the sword gash once more. Blood ran down, dammed on his eyebrows, and then flooded into his eyes. The world turned red around him as he blinked and fought to wipe off the blood. He found it hard to use his shield against his attacker and let his heavy ax swing free on the thong to do so. He backpedalled and almost lost his balance.

"Vered!" he called. "Lend a hand!"

Santon's vision vanished entirely when a fresh spurt of blood came gushing down from his wound. He lifted his glass shield and cowered behind it to ward off unseen blows.

None came.

He dared to use his right hand to wipe away the blood, then dabbed gently with his sleeve to clear his eyes. He blinked. The salty burn of the blood caused a flow of hot tears that washed away the last of it.

Vered stood over the fallen rebel soldier, his glass short sword dripping gore. The thief bent over and wiped the weapon on his fallen foe's tunic.

"Have you had enough or can we find shelter? They will follow us all the way into the jaws of a demon. Never have I seen such mindless enthusiasm for dying."

"They have a gusto for fighting that the royalist soldiers lack," admitted Santon. "But I would not want to meet with either at this moment."

He stood on shaky legs. Vered helped him back up the slope to where their horses were tethered. The animals cropped at the sparse, dry grass. When their masters settled for a rest, both horses glared at them, as if accusing them of being responsible for such a lean meal.

"How many of the royalists survived Sef's attack?" asked Vered. "Everywhere we turn, we find another pocket of them. Searching these mountains is becoming hazardous."

"Time works against us," said Santon. He carefully smeared a paste made from several plant stalks and roots along his cut. It puckered shut, but Santon began to worry about it ever healing properly. Twice since he had been cut it had opened to blind him. The first time had been during the night. He had rolled over and the wound had ruptured. This time was more understandable. The rebel had stuck him in the forehead with the butt end of his sword hilt.

"We do not want to be trapped in these miserable, barren passes when winter begins to cover the ground with snow," said Vered. "Why doesn't Ruirik Kulattian report back of his success? That demon-cursed phantom has been lying to us. I know it! He has no intention of finding Lokenna. He might be unable to."

"It does appear that all he wants is for us to find his corpse and give it a burial."

"There's nothing wrong with such charitable work," said Vered. "It's just that we have so little time to do it. Rebels and royalists everywhere! Why won't they leave us alone?"

Santon glanced toward the rucksack containing the Demon Crown. That single magical ornament drove the troops from Porotane. The rebel forces had other goads—unless the word had spread that Lorens had lost the crown. Santon shuddered at the idea of being the target for every petty rebel warlord and wizard in Porotane.

"Alarice said that we could trust Ruirik. What other choice do we have?"

"There is always another option," said Vered. "At the moment, the one I desire above all others is peace and quiet. To sleep undisturbed for an entire day, to have enough food to fill my belly, to find enough water to keep my mouth from feeling like desert sands—those are worthy goals for us to attain."

"I share them," said Santon. "How do we realize any of them? Game is sparse in the autumn. Water is always a problem in mountainous areas, and sleep? That is something I have long since given up on."

Vered mounted his gray mare and peered downslope. "Lorens' troopers march up to meet the tiny knot of resistance we stumbled across. The rebels will retreat, but that doesn't help us." He slowly scanned the countryside. He pointed to a narrow canyon leading westward. "There. Let's seek a spot there to rest."

"These side canyons were the sites of many massacres," said Santon. "Troop elements entered, only to find themselves boxed in. We don't wish to repeat previous mistakes."

"The royalist forces keep the rebels busy enough for the time being so that they forget all

about us. We will never find Ruirik's body if we
don't explore side canyons. There is little
chance of discovering his carcass in well-
travelled areas."

Santon sighed. His friend spoke the truth.
But it made him uneasy to ride into canyons
such as the one Vered indicated.

Santon climbed into the saddle. His roan
protested and tried to shy. His strong legs
guided the animal downslope and to the canyon
entrance. Again his horse protested. Santon had
come to depend on the horse's instincts. More
than once the roan had alerted him to an
ambush set by one side or the other.

"Vered, my horse is skittish."

"Mine is, also. That might mean anything.
We haven't seen troop movement in this direction."

Santon paused just inside the canyon
mouth, head cocked to one side. The sound that
had spooked his horse now became audible.
Santon settled his shield into a more comfortable position on his left arm and then swung his
ax up and into his hand.

"Birtle, wait," said Vered. The young man
frowned. "That isn't the sound of an army."

"But . . ." Santon's voice trailed off. His
friend's keener hearing had properly identified
the noise. And it was more chilling than if they
did face Lorens' entire army.

Phantoms.

"The entire valley must be filled with
them," Vered said, almost whispering.

"We seek Ruirik's body. What better place
than this?"

"We seek bodies, not more phantoms. None
of those can help us. Let us choose another

canyon to search. There are more promising ones to the north. I saw them from the hill."

"No, Vered. We look here." Santon put his heels into his roan's flanks. The horse reared and then settled down. The animal did not want to enter the canyon filled with the spirits of dozens—hundreds—of fallen warriors.

They rode forward slowly. Santon's head turned from side to side, studying the steep canyon walls. He tried to shut out the eerie, soul-searing wails that came from deeper within the canyon. He could not. Santon found himself shivering, in spite of the increased temperature in the valley.

"The rocks still hold summer warmth," said Vered. "That feels good after enduring so many chilly gusts coming down Claymore Pass. But that is all that feels good."

Santon lifted his shield and indicated a sparsely forested area ahead. He had seen low, long-limbed trees in swamps burdened with heavy hanging mosses. These tree limbs appeared to be infested with white moss—but the moss shifted position constantly. The lack of wind in the canyon contributed to lifeless heat.

"What moves the moss?" asked Vered.

"It is not moss. Those are phantoms."

Santon's guess proved correct. As they neared the stand of trees, they saw the gauzy white, insubstantial forms of scores of phantoms tirelessly shifting position, flowing upward and then collapsing back through the limbs and surging toward the ground. The ever-shifting array of spirits made Santon blink. He tried to focus on them and failed.

"They whine so," said Vered. "Never have I heard such a forlorn sound."

"They cry out for surcease," said Santon. "They might not even realize that they do."

He rode closer, keeping his horse under tight control. The animal jerked and tried to buck. Santon soothed it. He forced himself to remain calm when a thin sheet of white mist rose up from the ground and fell toward him.

He closed his eyes as the phantom passed through him. A tiny tingling at his fingertips and the end of his nose gave the only sign that the phantom even existed.

"They like you," Vered said uncomfortably. "They move toward you."

"I hope they don't sense that I will soon join their rank."

"Don't joke," Vered snapped. His discomfort was etched on every line of his wind-burned face. He sat stiffly on his horse, hand clenched on his sword hilt.

"You are the one with the flippant attitude. Come now, Vered. Don't you see any humor in this?"

"None."

Santon pulled his horse around and skirted the edge of the small forest. He halted at one point and dismounted. Santon silently motioned for Vered to remain mounted and on guard. He did not have to plead with his friend. Vered's tenseness showed that he was poised for instant flight at the slightest sound.

Santon walked slowly into the copse. The phantoms rose around him, like mist from the ground. The swirling obscured his vision but Santon pressed on. He stood and stared when he rounded a small pile of rocks. In the small depression lay a jumble of bones. He tried to restrain himself but failed. He began counting skulls as a way of estimating how many valiant men had died here.

Santon stopped at thirty.

"Please," came a soft plea. "Bury me. I was Hoaslare."

Other voices rose in chorus, each begging for surcease. "I was corporal of sentries. Wobare was my name."

"Imblade. Bury Imblade."

"Seek the body of Lespage."

"Give me grace. By the saints, bury Nicuner."

Santon backed away. The phantoms billowed around him. He stepped as if they might trip him. His substance proved more than enough to dissipate the ghostly spirits and tear them into tiny streamers. Some coalesced once more. The weaker ones vanished.

But there was no lack of new phantoms to replace them.

Vered swallowed hard and blanched when he saw Santon. "What did you find?"

"More than we can bury. At least thirty died here. My estimate is twice that number."

"So many," Vered said in a low voice. "Is there nothing we can do for them?"

"We do not even know if they were brigands or royalists."

"Does it matter? They were men. They deserve better than this damned, endless existence, if you can call drifting forever without body or companionship an existence."

"We cannot help them. We must identify and bury each. The consecration frees them from this . . . nothingness."

"Were there no nametags?" asked Vered. "Any way of identifying them would help."

"The phantoms we see might not even belong to those bleached bones. The spirits might be attracted to this spot out of hope that their bodies are here."

"Ruirik said he cannot tell which is his corpse. They are unable to identify themselves in death?"

Santon nodded sadly. "After all these years of exposure to winter cold and summer heat, there is no way we can be certain of their identity, either. Even if they carried engraved plates, who is to say we would get the proper arm bone with the skull? Such a mistake would doom them forever."

"They are already cursed," said Vered. "Can we do worse for them?"

"They give names."

"I hear their pleas." Vered shivered. "If we can do nothing, let us continue on our way. But how can we be sure that Ruirik is not among these?"

"We can't, but small deduction hints that he is not. King Lamost did not approve of leaving his dead in the open. He was not a gentle man, but he cared deeply about his troops and maintained a high level of morale. If possible, bodies would not be left in the open. Such a pit as the one I saw was the trademark of one particular brigand captain." Santon took a deep breath. "Bechadror was a beast."

"Why did he not care for those under him?" Vered's question was as sincere as it was shocked.

"Why did he doom them?" Santon laughed without humor. "Fight and win for Bechadror, or die and be forgotten. That gave a powerful incentive to his followers. I had seen his men crawl into our ranks and beg for clean death and burial."

"Did you give it to them?"

Santon laughed, this time with bitterness. "Seldom. But those we could save, we did. We found in them dedicated recruits."

"What happened to Bechadror? I remember hearing nothing of him as a power in this region."

"Who can say? My personal belief—and this was rumored widely—is that one of his own men killed him. Those were not days of mercy and justice."

"What days of war ever are?"

"Let us look along the cliff faces for caves. If Ruirik Kulattian's body is to be found, it might be there." Santon mounted and stared back toward the open pit with the bones of so many in it.

Phantoms weaved in and out of the trees, making their plaintive presence known to any of the living who passed. What had sounded like the wind whining through an Aeolian harp had been the massed cries of the phantoms.

Birtle Santon wished he could help them, give them the release from the trap between worlds in which they found themselves. But he could not. If Alarice had been here, with her special sorcerous powers, she might have aided the phantoms.

But Santon did not think so. These were the lost and nothing could be done for them except offer a moment of pity.

He prayed to the saints that he and Vered did not join these sorry ranks of floating, gauzy white, lost phantoms.

THIRTEEN

Rain pelted down and parted just before touching Kaga'kalb's face. The Wizard of Storms stood on the tallest tower of the Castle of the Winds and stared intently into the tempest raging around him. Eye-searing bolts of green and blue lightning crashed and sent waves of thunder rolling down the slopes of the mountain and across the Uvain Plateau. Winds whipped his garments and caused them to outline his thin, strong body. But Kaga'kalb paid no attention to the wind or the raging storm that had been his most recent creation.

He had played with it, orchestrating its progress across the Yorral Mountains. It had grown in intensity, then died down. A glissando, a softening, a gradual building to full-blown storm. The elements of nature became his musical instrument and he played them well.

Kaga'kalb ignored his creation to peer into a cloud overhead. Its lead-colored belly lit with an inner glow not of natural lightning but of sorcerous fire. The Wizard of Storms enticed the tiny glow, made it grow, watched intently.

Pictures appeared. Men moved. The cloudy frame of his potent scrying spell billowed and boiled with the storm feeding his wizardry. Kaga'kalb studied his larger-than-life picture and saw Dews Gaemock and another speaking. He could not hear their words over the rumble of his storm. It mattered little. Kaga'kalb knew the players in this little drama well. He had seen Efran Gaemock leave the rebel camp to become the court jester for Duke Freow. Kaga'kalb nodded in approval. Efran had courage and intelligence.

That made him more dangerous than his brother, Dews. The elder Gaemock led men well but lacked the ambition to rule. That drive burned like an ember inside Efran Gaemock. The slightest fanning of those smoldering coals would cause a conflagration that would envelop all Porotane.

Kaga'kalb watched and waited and followed Efran's winding path back to Castle Porotane, noting his secret entrance and the hidden ways built into the massive stone walls. Kaga'kalb shifted his magical focus a small amount and spied on Baron Theoll, who continued to plot against Archbishop Nosto and Lorens.

The thought of the new king caused the wizard to seek him out—but cautiously. Lorens lacked the developed sorcerous power of his former master, but Kaga'kalb still respected the bits and pieces of magic under the king's control.

Most of all he respected the awesome power locked in the Demon Crown.

Kaga'kalb frowned when he failed to find Lorens easily. The Demon Crown should have provided a pivot point around which everything in the castle revolved. The axle was gone. The Wizard of Storms summoned more power, gave himself a refreshing blast of cold rainwater in

the face, and then cut off the torrential downpour before it drowned him. He stared into the
underside of the cloud, watching the movement
of those within the castle—and still not locating
Lorens.

Kaga'kalb worried that the wizard-king had
found a way of blocking out even this potent
scrying spell. With the full force of a thunderstorm powering his spell, Kaga'kalb knew that
he would be unable to summon any more
energy. He had reached the limit of his ability.
And Lorens blocked him.

Or did he?

Kaga'kalb spread his magical search out,
looking not for the Demon Crown but for the
spark of Lorens' magical ability. He found it, a
tiny, wavering speck hardly worthy of his notice.
But the crown was not on the king's brow. Nor
was it in his chamber. Kaga'kalb searched further. No cranny in Castle Porotane went unchecked.

"The crown is gone! He has allowed it to be
stolen!" The shock of this knowledge rocked
Kaga'kalb. How could any wizard allow such a
prize as the Demon Crown to be taken?

Kaga'kalb threw out his arms and caused
the storm above him to expand. As the dark
cloud billowed and boiled, the scrying picture
also changed scope. No longer content to view
only the castle, the Wizard of Storms studied the
countryside around the castle. He saw Dews
Gaemock and Dalziel Sef in camp. Further. He
cast further afield.

The Yorral Mountains rushed past him. The
Iron Range grew in his magic picture on the
churning underbelly of the cloud. The ocean
beat against its shoreline and the swamp where
Tahir had been imprisoned showed its scummy

water and strange beats. But he failed to detect the Demon Crown.

Panic gripped him. What had happened to the most powerful relic of this empire? Kaga'kalb again magnified the range he viewed. This time the bright dot of the Demon Crown appeared.

"Them again," he said. "What power do they possess that they can so easily make off with the crown when it is protected by Lorens so well?" Kaga'kalb reduced the energy outpouring and concentrated only on Birtle Santon and Vered. They carried the crown in the same case that the Glass Warrior had used. Kaga'kalb's fingertips danced with electrical discharges from the lightning held prisoner within the dark storm clouds. He longed to direct just one searing blast at the pair of freebooters to see what their response would be.

He did not believe that they were wizards, yet they bested those capable of intricate major spells. They carried a demonic artifact that meant death to any not of the royal line.

"They must know its power. They *do*. Then where do they take the Demon Crown? Why do they rush to Claymore Pass?"

Wild thoughts rushed through Kaga'kalb's head. Ionia? He doubted the petty tyrant commanded the resources to make use of the crown. She had no chance of even touching the Demon Crown. She was not a descendant of King Waellkin, no matter what claims she made publicly. Only her own death would result if the crown fell into her hands.

"Another," muttered Kaga'kalb. "They seek another. Why give the crown to Lorens, though, and then steal it back to seek another?"

The Wizard of Storms did not understand

all that happened. But he would. His magic controlled the storms and through them he could watch any spot in Porotane afflicted by rain.

When he learned as much as he needed to know, he would finally put things right in the kingdom. No more would petty rebel warlords disturb the serenity. No more would inept wizards vie for power that was not theirs for the taking.

But how did those two adventurers fit into the storm track of Porotane's history?

FOURTEEN

Birtle Santon shifted suddenly in the saddle, the movement almost throwing him off his roan.

"What's wrong?" asked Vered. The younger man rode up beside his friend and eyed him critically. The wound on Santon's head had not begun to heal, and this worried Vered. He was no wizard and produced no magical healing potions, but the herbs and roots he had blended into a paste should have worked. They hadn't. The ugly red gash across Santon's forehead did not bleed; it oozed constantly.

Something about the way Santon moved also bothered Vered. It looked as if Santon grew increasingly stiff. For a man as powerful as Santon, that could mean more than physical problems. He might begin to doubt his own ability, and when he did, that spelled death.

"Pain in my joints. Comes from the altitude and being too long asaddle."

"You're getting old," Vered taunted, but he hoped that Santon's explanation struck closer to the truth than his own worry about magic-induced diseases. "Any head pain?"

"What? None." Santon reached up and lightly touched the gash on his head. "You fear the soldier poisoned his sword blade? No one's done that for many a year. No reason for him to start now."

"But it was done before, back when Claymore Pass was patrolled constantly. You just said so, even though I had not known it. We should look for a potion that counters poisons."

"What poison? If he did it intentionally, there are thousands of assassin's brews to select from. More likely, he had failed to keep a clean edge. See the jagged edges of the wound? He hadn't sharpened his weapon in many a day. You worry too much, Vered."

The man snorted and shook his head. It was not his way to worry needlessly. This did not seem to fall into that bin, however. Reason for concern existed. He did not want to lose his good friend to an insidious drug. There were too many phantoms loose in these mountains without adding another to their rank.

"See the rock structure?" spoke up Santon, trying to change the topic. "Wind whips along and cuts through the softer orange and yellow rock. Like cheese, that stone. Treacherous to climb. We tried. It crumbles under your fingers."

"Still, it forms interesting statues to the saints," said Vered. "See that one? It looks like a face."

"It looks more like a knob sitting on top of a pyramid."

"You lack imagination, Santon," exclaimed Vered, warming to his topic. "Turn your head to one side and peer at it. See? Doesn't it change and become the face of King Lorens?"

He watched Santon carefully as the grizzled man canted his head to one side. The brief flash of pain mirrored on his features told Vered that the wound bothered Santon more than he admitted.

"Let's rest for a bit," Vered suggested. "My rear end feels as if all the king's chefs have been hacking and slashing at it for their ground meat specials."

"A rest would do me. I feel tired after so many hours travelling." Santon climbed down wearily and looked around. "And I must admit it, the sight of so many phantoms wears on me, too."

Vered glanced back up the sheer canyon wall at the softstone formations Santon had pointed out. Through the smaller apertures soared gauzy white streams, like water forced from a drinking bag. The phantoms rose until strong updrafts caught their substance and pulled them skyward in long, thin streamers.

"The sight of even one phantom bothers me," said Vered. "So many make me wonder if there will ever be peace in the kingdom. So many souls lost and never redeemed. So many more who will be."

"Where's the old cheerful Vered?" asked Santon. "You are becoming much too morose."

"It comes from being around you too much. We should find ourselves a nice-sized city. Not too large, but large enough. Too large, they tax their citizenry unmercifully and spend overmuch on constabulary. Too small and there isn't enough diversity."

"What do we do when we find this mythical city?"

"Ah, then we begin to enjoy ourselves. I remember a woman with hair like spun sunlight and the scent of spring. She knew tricks that amazed even me. We should hunt for her."

"After we've finished our mission," said

Santon. He gathered up the rucksack containing the Demon Crown and tucked it under his withered arm. The glass shield he had gotten from Alarice protected it and helped hold it firmly. The way he sat so forlorn and defensive made Vered sorry he had tried to shift topics to something lighter.

Santon was obsessed with duty—and the Glass Warrior. Vered had seen his friend's love for Alarice. It could not be denied, even though Alarice lay dead in the Desert of Sazan.

"Is there any hope of finding Ruirik's body in this canyon?" asked Vered, giving up on banter.

"Some. I wish he could have given more information about his company. I remember several squads splitting off and seeking out positions in side canyons. They sought areas that might be fortified and held against the brigands."

Vered looked around. "They should have built a shoulder-high wall across the mouth of this canyon. A handful of bowmen could hold back a major assault."

"Or a few archers could bottle up an entire force in this place," countered Santon. "That is the treachery of the Yorral Mountains. What is a good position suddenly turns into a death trap when a commander a tad cleverer enters the fray."

"That is always the way."

"Not so. I have been in battles where a position was defensible by any fool—and just about any fool commanded to a victory. No, Vered, the king lost his best in these canyons."

"What's that?" Vered shot to his feet, head slowly turning to locate the source of the mysterious noise.

"Another phantom wailing out his misery. Think nothing of it."

"No, it was something more. I've almost gotten used to the phantoms and their incessant wailing." Before the words left Vered's mouth, the deep rumble of thunder rolled down the canyon and echoed off the softstone walls.

"A storm."

"The sky is clear. That was thunder but there is not a single cloud to be seen." Vered's hands shook slightly. "Look to the Demon Crown. Tell me what you see."

"I . . . I don't have to look," said Santon. "The sack glows. The crown responds strongly. But to what?"

"Magic plays along these rocks." Vered turned slowly, eyes closed. A soft, warm, secure feeling came to him. He spun until he faced in the opposite direction. He groaned. His heart missed a beat and his mouth turned to desert sand.

"What do you sense?"

"Tremendous magic is at work in the direction of the canyon mouth. We might be trapped, though the spell does not seem to be directed against us. It . . . it is directed against another."

"Do you know this for sure?"

Vered nodded. "My brief moments with the Demon Crown awakened something within me. I sense magic around us now, even if I am unable to do anything about it." He smiled slightly. "If I could cast a spell, I'd lift us out of here and all the way to Blisoic."

"Why to a smelly seaport like Blisoic?"

"That's where the girl with golden hair and delicate scent lived. I remembered even as I nattered on about decent-sized cities."

"Blisoic," muttered Santon, shaking his

head. He touched the wound on his brow, winced slightly, then stood. "We must ride. If the magic envelops the canyon mouth, we might be trapped, no matter who the spell is against."

The pair rode deliberately, retracing their path. Vered grew more and more nervous as they neared the canyon entrance. The phantoms who had once swirled about through the wormholes in the rocks had vanished, as if this magic threatened even their tenuous existence.

Santon cried out, "Look yonder. Lorens' troops. A full company of them."

"Your eyes grow old and weak, Santon," his companion said, studying the more than one hundred riders on the Claymore Pass trail. "Those are Lorens' personal guardsmen. See the golden fringe on the royal banner?"

"The king rides after us personally? He wouldn't dare leave Castle Porotane with Gaemock readying a siege."

"What is the castle to him without the crown? He gambles everything to regain his legacy." Vered glanced over at Santon. The man had stowed the Demon Crown in a sling that jostled behind him as he rode. Desire rose within his breast. How easy to reach over and pluck the magic crown from his friend.

Vered closed his eyes and forced down the feeling of emptiness. How filled with power he was when wearing the Demon Crown—how fulfilled. He transcended his petty existence. No longer a vagabond wandering aimlessly, he became the single most powerful man in Porotane. In the world! With the gold circlet around his head, he aspired to godhood. He rivalled the saints and demons in power. And more.

Nothing would escape him. His senses

would sharpen and his power would be absolute.

Vered bit his lower lip until blood flowed. The pain prevented desire from becoming fact.

He wiped sweat from his forehead, even though the cold wind whipping through Claymore Pass threatened to freeze him in the saddle. The Demon Crown's pull was great, and he had to keep fighting it.

"What's wrong?" asked Santon.

"The magic. Someone uses a potent spell against Lorens."

"Are you sure he's not using it to track us?"

"Look at his troops. They are milling around like small children at play. Lorens' commander is trying to form them into a defensive position. If he knew we watched him from less than five minutes' gallop, he would have every single soldier in full flight after us."

Another thunderclap left their ears ringing. Vered's eyes rose to the sky. A single dark cloud formed above Lorens' position. Streamers of mist flickered with lightning and drooped until they dragged foggy fingers along the ground.

"Lorens is a wizard of small power and no judgment. He had not finished his apprenticeship under Patrin. Mayhaps he practices his conjurations."

Vered turned cold inside when he saw the truth before his eyes. King Lorens did not summon these clouds. Not when red-eyed warriors of swirling fog and lightning-tipped fingers marched toward his battle array with destruction their obvious goal.

The yowls of fear from the king's personal guard drowned out the thunder. Vered turned even colder inside. The king's guard prided itself on fearless defense of their monarch. Now they whimpered like frightened children.

Vered did not blame them. The magical warriors that had descended from the clouds began to move inexorably toward the front rank of Lorens' personal guard. A flight of arrows arched up and over the heads of the leading guardsmen and dropped with startling accuracy into the storm warriors.

The poison-tipped missiles passed harmlessly through the lightning-wracked warriors.

"The Wizard of Storms sends *his* personal guardsmen," whispered Santon.

"They are not human. They are not even flesh," said Vered, in a voice hardly louder. He patted his gray's neck to keep the horse from rearing. The frightened animal sensed the powerful magic behind the storm warriors and wanted nothing more than to be away from it.

Vered's eyes widened in astonishment as the five pillars of dark cloud began to swirl and take on even more human form. The red eyes blazed. The lightning began to jump from finger to finger—and into the ranks of the human guards. Five mist-shrouded legs stepped out in unison. The storm warriors marched forward into battle.

"Look, Vered. See how it rains around them?"

"They aren't human. They are clouds. The Wizard of Storms has called down pieces of cloud to fight soldiers."

"To kill soldiers," corrected Santon.

The five storm warriors walked into the front rank of Lorens' guards. To their credit the men did not turn and flee. Vered knew his courage would not have withstood such an ominous assault. With every pointed finger a soldier died in the blaze of a cast lightning bolt. Sword cuts meant nothing to those inhuman warriors. Lances passed through their torsos, emerging damp with rainwater and not blood. Horses reared and kicked out war-spurred hooves. The horses died, their guts blown from their bodies by billowing gray cloud parodies of humans.

"There is Lorens," cried Vered. "See? In the rear rank?"

"It is. The rebels might find themselves in control of the kingdom sooner than they thought if the Wizard of Storms' cloud demons kill him now."

"Gaemock and the others might find themselves facing an adversary even worse than Lorens," said Vered. "Why should a wizard remain hidden away for so many years and then suddenly appear?"

Vered swallowed hard when he silently answered his own question. The reason had to lie hidden in Santon's rucksack. The Demon Crown had brought forth the storm warriors and the Wizard of Storms and magic unlike anything that had embraced Porotane for all the years of his life. Could he prevent untold deaths and suffering for the men and women of Porotane by grabbing the sack and throwing it downhill to the storm warriors? Would the Wizard of Storms accept the Demon Crown as a peace offering?

"No!"

The sharp word startled Vered. "I said nothing."

"You," accused Santon, "considered turning over the crown to those *things*." He lifted his withered arm and indicated the storm warriors. Even at this distance the magical beings' red eyes glowed with inhuman lust. The storm warriors killed because of the spell powering them, giving them form and substance—and because it was a basic part of their infernal magical existence. Like the mindless storms that wrecked incautious ships against the rocky shoreline, the cyclonic winds that blew away entire villages, the high waters that flooded farmlands, these warriors were implacable and uncaring.

And, Vered feared, they were invincible. How could anyone fight against the elements? Especially if they carried within their stormy heads the spark of intelligence?

"They are looking in our direction," said Vered, beginning to tremble. "See how they turn and point?"

"It's your imagination," Santon said uneasily.

"No, no, see?" Vered watched the storm warriors break off their attack on Lorens' soldiers and begin to wheel about slowly, as if listening—or seeking.

"They might sense the presence of the Demon Crown," said Santon.

"We can't get past them. They're blocking the mouth of the canyon."

Santon jerked at the reins and got his horse headed back into the canyon. Vered wasted no time in following.

"What can we hope to accomplish?" asked Vered, fear clogging his throat now. "We cannot outrun the wind. Better that we try to stop the rains from pouring out of the sky."

"They might not be after us. The Wizard of Storms might have sent his minions after Lorens alone."

Vered did not believe that. The now-ineffectual king had lost his power. The reclusive wizard could want only one thing. And Birtle Santon carried it.

Vered looked at the Demon Crown's sack. It glowed the same ugly green that it had when Lorens wore it.

FIFTEEN

Baron Theoll flexed his leg and twisted it around. The stiffness had passed and he might be able to walk without a limp. He stood and put his weight on it. The assassin had been careless and had missed his target, but Theoll was not sure that maiming him had not been worse than an outright kill. Who would follow a deformed ruler?

He practiced walking without the limp or slight hesitation that had developed. As he strutted back and forth in his chambers, he studied himself in a full-length mirror of polished steel. Posture. He had to work on posture to make himself seem taller. Boots. Thicker soled boots would elevate him, too. And never let the leg drag along behind. Theoll smiled slightly at his success.

Only his left arm still bothered him, sometimes giving enough pain to make him wince visibly. He would have to exercise it, test it, perhaps even find someone who would practice swordsmanship with him and not rush out telling everyone of the baron's true infirmity.

Theoll stood for a moment beside a decorative panel of carved woods and inlaid pearls. Behind it lay the entrance to the secret ways that ran throughout the castle walls—his private kingdom. He had learned much from his spying.

He felt his heart beating faster at the thought of again watching Lady Anneshoria trying to seduce her way to power. Even if he had not watched her working her considerable wiles on the commander of the castle forces, Theoll would have known soon after. Commander Squann was a loyal supporter.

"As loyal as any gets in this madhouse," Theoll muttered aloud. He turned from the secret entrance and started for the door. There was so little time for pleasure now. He had work to do. Because of a sudden unexplained cooling by the king toward him and the Inquisition, Archbishop Nosto slackened his efforts to find heretics among the ranks of the castle lords and ladies. This encouraged them to renew their efforts to overthrow Lorens.

Before he reached the door, a hesitant rapping came. Theoll flung open the door. Harhar crouched in the hallway, weakly shaking his rattle and trying to smile. The effort looked more like a grimace.

"May the demons take him," grumbled Theoll. Louder, he asked, "What's wrong with you?"

"Oh, mighty Baron, it is a tragedy. It is, it is!"

Theoll grabbed Harhar by the collar—he used his left hand to test the strength in it—and yanked the jester into the room. Theoll slammed the door behind them.

"What are you blithering about, fool?"

"The king, it's terrible, the king, the poor king!"

Theoll puffed up and looked around, hating

himself even as he did so. King Lorens could spy on anyone in the castle at any time using the Demon Crown. Had the monarch sent Harhar to squeeze an unsuspecting confession from his lips? Theoll pushed the idea aside. Harhar had shown no true love for the ruler. If the jester's sympathies lay anywhere, it was with Theoll's attempts to sit once more on the throne.

"What are you saying about Lorens? Has an assassin's quick blade robbed us of our dear king?" Theoll did not try to keep the sarcasm from his voice. If the king eavesdropped, let Lorens impale him for his disloyal thoughts. He cared little at the moment.

"He suffers so. I cannot bear to see him like that. No matter how I try, I cannot cheer him. His loss is too great."

"What loss?" Theoll cuffed Harhar to loosen the knave's tongue.

"The crown. His precious crown is gone."

Theoll stood and stared at Harhar, wondering if the fool lied. Nothing about the simple face showed deception. Harhar believed that the Demon Crown was gone.

"Stolen?" Theoll did not wait to see Harhar's head bouncing up and down. He locked his hands behind his back and began pacing. The movement let him think better. So much that had occurred within the castle walls took on new meaning—better meaning.

His troops had been ambushed outside the king's quarters. They had patrolled this section of the castle for no good reason. He liked the intelligence they ofttimes stumbled across. But they had been put to death—or so Lorens had told him.

"The guards lost the other night. What of them?"

"Three were killed. The fourth died after torture."

"What did he reveal?"

"Archbishop Nosto sent thieves to steal the king's crown."

"Nosto?" Theoll was stunned at this revelation. He knew every move made by the archbishop and his Inquisitors—or so he had thought. How could the archbishop steal the Demon Crown without Theoll learning of it instantly? The baron went over his network of spies and informants and slowly shook his head. It was not possible. Therefore, Archbishop Nosto had not stolen the crown.

"The king believed this until he spoke with the archbishop. Our cleric convinced him of his innocence in the theft."

"The crown would be a magical beacon. Nosto could never hide it from the king. I don't see how anyone could."

"The crown was spirited out of the castle and is now . . . elsewhere."

"Damn you!" roared Theoll. "Stop giving me the information piecemeal. Tell me everything. Now!"

Harhar babbled. Through the torrent of words Theoll puzzled together the curious story. Thieves had stolen the Demon Crown and left Castle Porotane with it. The king believed them to be in the Yorral Mountains, travelling through Claymore Pass. Strangest of all, Theoll had not felt the slightest tremor in his spiderweb of agents posted throughout the castle.

He went to the door and called to the guard stationed at the junction of two corridors, "Summon Squann immediately."

He slammed the door. "There is more. Tell me."

"There is nothing else to say," said Harhar. "You already know that King Lorens has left the castle and is galloping to the Yorral Mountains to retrieve his crown."

Theoll's legs turned weak under him. He wobbled and sat down heavily in a nearby chair. How could this happen and he remained ignorant of it? The king's crown was stolen? Lorens had left the castle?

Commander Squann silently entered the chamber.

"When did Lorens leave?" demanded Theoll. The contemptuous expression on the officer's face started a slow fire of anger burning within Theoll. Harhar had lied! If Squann knew nothing of the king chasing after the thieves who had stolen the Demon Crown, then it was not true.

"Put him to death," Theoll said, his emotions barely under control.

"At once," said Squann. "I've never liked his jokes."

"That's because they were always at your expense," said Harhar. The jester rolled into a tight ball and eluded the commander's groping hands. "You are a joke, a big one, a tall one. Look at your big, fake medals dangling and banging against your thin chest. How many did you award to yourself?"

Squann roared and whipped out his sword.

"Stop that," ordered Theoll, leaping to his feet. "Do not kill him in my chambers. Do it elsewhere."

"Baron Theoll, the king is gone. The crown is stolen. Does the truth offend you so?"

"He is lying," said Squann. "I saw Lorens an hour ago at his dinner."

"What? Wait." Theoll held out his hand to stay Squann. "You saw Lorens eating?"

"Like the pig that he is."

Theoll sat down again, no strength remaining in his legs. "The fool is telling the truth. But how? Lorens hasn't done more than peck at his food since he began wearing the crown night and day. It robs him of all appetite."

"But who was it I saw?"

"The king has a double. Why let yourself be assassinated if you can let a double die in your stead?" asked Theoll.

"True, true," babbled Harhar. "The king's double sits on the throne with a fake crown. He brought him here from far-off Linder."

"Find out for certain," Theoll ordered. "And be quick about it."

Commander Squann sheathed his sword and glowered at the jester. The soldier spun and stormed from the room. Silence fell as Theoll stared into space, his mind working over all the possibilities.

Lorens would not alert many to his absence, not when Dews Gaemock prepared another siege of the castle. Lorens might find himself trapped outside if the siege lasted very long. Such a position would cut him off from his most powerful allies. Losing Castle Porotane might prove a blow that he could never recover from.

No, the young wizard-king would not advertise his departure. Theoll smiled thinly. He would not want even his few allies within the castle walls to know. Allegiances shifted daily. If the king and his powerful crown vanished, new treaties would be forged. Lorens would quickly find himself without a castle—or country—to rule.

How could he profit by the king's absence?

Lorens would take his personal guard. With Squann in control of the castle guard, Theoll might launch a coup. His rear warmed again to the thought of being on the throne.

Caution prevented the baron from ordering Squann into immediate rebellion. Dews Gaemock still threatened a siege, but something more made Theoll hold back. Archbishop Nosto had been used as scapegoat for the ruffians who stole away with the Demon Crown. Theoll had no desire to see his own execution order signed should a coup fail.

Let Nosto take the blame. Theoll smiled wickedly as a plan formed in his fertile brain.

Stride firm and confident, Theoll left his quarters. Behind him he heard Harhar scurrying along, trying to keep pace. Theoll gestured at his guards at the end of the corridor. They fell into step behind to protect him from assassins sent by his enemies. Lady Anneshoria might have learned of his spying on her most intimate and calculating moments. He had to protect himself from her.

Theoll almost laughed aloud. If his scheme worked as it should, he could take Anneshoria for his consort. But he would never take her as his wife. That would make the conniving bitch his queen and place her on the throne beside him. Better to keep her out of the line of succession but where he could benefit from her skills—all her skills, in bed and out. Theoll admitted reluctantly that Anneshoria's plotting had been elegant, even brilliant, and would have brought her considerable power had she but known Squann's true master and Lorens' absence.

"Harhar," he barked. "Who else knows of the matter discussed in my chambers?"

"Only Squann, Baron. And you told him."

"No one else knows. Good. Keep it that way."

"You're not going to have me put to death?"

"Not today. Tomorrow is another day, however. Be sure you keep on my good side."

"Is that your right side or are you still pretending your left is whole again?" asked the fool.

Theoll bit back an angry response. The halfwit had given him the key to ultimate power. He could be charitable and not beat him for his insolence.

"Hold your tongue while we are in Archbishop Nosto's presence or I'll have it cut out and feed it to you for supper. Do you understand?" Theoll sneered when he saw Harhar grab his tongue with both hands and pretend to tug at it.

The baron rapped loudly on the door leading to the archbishop's audience chamber. Several minutes passed before a crimson-clad Inquisitor opened the door. The man wore a long silk cape, tight black breeches, and no tunic. His hairy chest was dotted with beads of sweat. As Theoll turned he saw rivers of perspiration run down the cleric's torso. The Inquisitor had been hard at work. Theoll did not want to know the nature of the work.

"I seek Archbishop Nosto's blessing," he said. "I have come to report a heresy." Theoll ignored Harhar's frightened gasp.

"Wait here. The archbishop will attend you soon." The Inquisitor closed the door in Theoll's face.

The baron let out a deep breath he had not known he was holding. Dealing with fanatics always made him uneasy. Better to treat with the greedy or ambitious. He understood their motives. Never had he gotten a clear picture of Archbishop Nosto's motives. It might be just as the cleric so loudly proclaimed. A desire to rid the kingdom of demonically inspired heretics might blaze within his breast. But what man's faith ran so deep and pure?

Baron Theoll simply did not understand such altruism. He thought that Nosto used it only as a ploy to gain power. If he was right Nosto would be unable to turn his back on what Theoll told him.

"Where's Squann? Hasn't he returned yet? How long does it take the man to go to the king's chambers and back?"

"There, Baron, there he comes now. See how he runs?" Harhar did a handstand. Theoll pushed him over and hurried to the guard commander's side.

"Well, is it true?" he demanded of Squann.

"Baron, it is incredible. The man is an almost perfect likeness of King Lorens."

"So the king *has* left the castle." Theoll smiled broadly. Success lay within his grasp. So soon, so very soon, he would be the true power in Porotane.

"I also checked the guard barracks. All the king's personal guardsmen have departed. Not even the stablehands know where, but they left over two days ago."

"Two days!" exclaimed Theoll. How had Lorens maintained this secret for even two minutes? It had to be wizardry.

"The crown is not the real one, either," said Squann. "The double wearing it is no wizard."

"Better and better." Theoll spun when the door to Archbishop Nosto's audience chamber opened to reveal the archbishop. The man toweled off bloody hands and threw the rag back into his rooms.

"You wished an audience with me, Theoll?"

"I have found a heretic, Archbishop. This is not a matter to discuss openly. May I present my case inside?"

Archbishop Nosto bowed and ushered Theoll, Squann, and Harhar inside. The jester perched on the edge of a straight-backed chair in the corner of the sparsely decorated room while Squann and Theoll stood before the cleric.

"There is a great need for speed, Archbishop Nosto," Theoll said without preamble. "Our beloved monarch has been deposed and an impostor has taken his place."

Nosto stared at Theoll as if the small lord had lost his mind.

Theoll kept from grinning like a fool. Disbelief now, gradual belief later, and then unthinking obedience in the end. That was his route along which to lead Nosto.

"I believe that Lorens has been kidnapped. A military coup in the rank of his personal guard resulted in the imposter taking the throne."

"Commander Squann, is this so?"

"Sire, all the king's personal guard left mysteriously two days ago. I learned of this only minutes ago."

"You? The commandant of all castle guards?"

"This is the horror of it, Archbishop. The king's true supporters have been left in the dark. I do not know who has done this vile deed, but it must be demon-inspired." Theoll watched Nosto's reaction. He had duped the man once before into believing he spoke with the demon

Kalob. The cleric's thoughts had to return to that charade now.

"Why do you think this is a demonic matter?"

"I cannot find what has happened to the Demon Crown," said Theoll. "The imposter—the heretic occupying the throne—does not wear the magical symbol of our monarch."

"Both crown and king are missing?"

"Taken by the king's personal guard," repeated Theoll. "If you so deem, this is a matter for the church and you must investigate immediately. I fear the worst."

"Why is this? Granted, the matter is serious, but it might be purely secular."

"Harhar, tell Archbishop Nosto of what you saw."

"What?" The jester's dark eyes shot open in surprise. "But I saw nothing."

"Sire, he saw a demon conversing with the impostor on the throne," cut in Squann. "He is too frightened to speak. The fool fears for his soul."

"Well that he should," said Archbishop Nosto. The cleric made a vague protective gesture in the direction of the court jester. His thoughts were obviously on the Demon Crown's absence from Castle Porotane and the impostor on the throne.

"Is this not a matter for the Inquisition?" asked Theoll.

"Heretics must be put to the Question, no matter what their rank," said Nosto. "There is no error? Lorens has been kidnapped?"

"Spirited away. I believe the renegade soldiers have taken him to Claymore Pass," said Squann. He fell silent under Theoll's dark look.

The baron did not want his minion revealing too much to Nosto.

The archbishop would believe it all the more if he discovered the details for himself.

"Heretics must never rule Porotane. Such is blasphemous to those of us treading the True Path. We must purge this impostor of his demonic influences." Archbishop Nosto motioned to his silently waiting assistant. The Inquisitor drifted away like a phantom. "We will go immediately to interrogate this ersatz king. Thank you, Theoll."

"I wish only what is best for Porotane," said Theoll. He hastily added, "And those walking the True Path as I do."

Theoll tipped his head slightly, motioning Squann and Harhar from the archbishop's chamber. In the corridor the baron allowed himself a wicked smile that lit his features with evil intent.

"The machine is put into motion. There is no stopping it now," said Theoll.

"But, Baron, the archbishop will get credit for unearthing the impostor."

"He will torture the impostor. By the time the Question is put to him, the heretic will say whatever soothes Nosto and his fellow Inquisitors and prevents them from inflicting still more pain on his fragile body and tormented soul. After the heretic has repented, we might find that Porotane is riddled with demonic influences that only a cleric-king can root out."

"Nosto as king? But that's . . ." Squann's voice trailed off. The commander's grin matched that of the baron's.

"Yes, Commander, that would place unacceptable strain on any of the nobility supporting the throne. It has never happened—and will not last long."

Theoll spun and walked off, head high. Let Nosto assume the throne for a few days. If Lorens played some deeper game, the archbishop would receive the king's full wrath. If Lorens had fallen prey to a coup and had been kidnapped, let him rot in the Yorral Mountains.

Baron Theoll would be King Theoll and no one would have the power to depose him!

SIXTEEN

Lightning crackled overhead. Vered could not keep from ducking every time the sizzling strikes smashed into the softstone cliffs behind them and sent powdery orange rock showering onto their heads. He and Birtle Santon had ridden quickly and well to keep ahead of the slow-marching storm warriors. But if the magical warriors moved with ponderous steps, they never rested.

Even worse, Vered could not still the frenzied pounding of his heart. Just being pursued by the towering, misty, magical beings took its toll on his strength. Even worse, he worried about Santon's condition. The man's wound had opened twice on their headlong rush back into the canyon; the poorly healing gash also robbed Santon of his usual endurance. He wobbled in the saddle and almost fell. Only Vered's quickness had saved him from a nasty fall.

"You're turning pale," Vered said. "We'll have to find a place to rest."

"Rest? With the Wizard of Storms' entire cloud army nipping at our heels?"

"I wouldn't call it 'nipping,'" said Vered. "More like raining."

"Raining at our heels?" scoffed Santon, trying to present a brave front. "What a terrible thing to tell our grandchildren."

"Any children I have are bastards, just like me, and I'll tell them any damned story I please." Vered looked back over his shoulder. The storm warriors were at least an hour's travel behind. Dare they rest? "And I'd never be content with the simple truth. It's usually too dull to repeat."

"You embellish with the best," agreed Santon, "but there'll be no need for you to add to this tale."

"Caves," Vered said suddenly. "There must be caverns we can hide in. The softstone formations provide limitless reaches of caves."

"Dangerous caverns," said Santon. "The roof can collapse from even gentle movement of horses' hooves. I remember being trapped once when on patrol. We dashed into a cave to get out of a downpour. The echo of the horses brought down half a mountain on our heads. Ten of thirty never left our sanctuary."

Entombed. Vered shuddered at the idea. He did not like closed-in spaces. Darkness gave him no trouble, but when he could see the walls— touch them—and the ceiling was low and confining . . . He shuddered. He had been in jails only occasionally for petty crimes. Those few times had been too many for him.

Another blue-white jagged streak of lightning crashed into the stony wall above their head. A small avalanche of pebbles rained down on their heads.

"We can be buried outside or in one of them," he decided. "Pick one. This is your country, Santon."

"Mine? For a bent three-penny you can

keep it. I have no love for Claymore Pass or these cheeselike rocks."

Vered spurred his gray mare closer and got his arm around Santon once more. The older man tottered precariously in the saddle, and his complexion had turned a disturbing and ugly jaundiced yellow. Vered would have thought that the Wizard of Storms had ensorcelled his friend if he had not seen the slow progression of the disease from the cleanly bleeding sword cut to this sorry state.

"I've gotten turned around. Where's the sun? What direction are we heading?" Vered hesitated choosing an opening to enter.

"It makes no difference. There are no side canyons. We are trapped in this one as surely as cattle run down chutes to the slaughter."

"Stop trying to cheer me. I can stand only so much mirth at a time," said Vered. He urged his horse forward. The animal slipped on the pebbly slope leading to the cave mouth Vered had picked at random. He waited until Santon joined him before dismounting.

"Inside," said Santon. He clung to his horse, his good arm thrown around the roan's neck for support. Vered nodded and led the way inside. The only good he saw coming of this was the rock-strewn slope outside. It left no track for the storm warriors to follow and seemed to be of sharp-edged hard stone, unlike the cliffs above.

Vered scowled darkly and wondered if the storm warriors needed to track by sight. What awesome magic had the Wizard of Storms instilled in his creatures? Vered glanced at the sack containing the evilly glowing Demon Crown. Did the magical warriors sense this prize and follow no matter how they turned and dodged and hid?

"I still prefer to know where north is. It keeps me happy. A map and knowledge of north makes life safer."

"Safer?" scoffed Santon, settling down heavily just inside the entrance. "Not in these hills. The beasts living at higher altitudes keep it from being safe—as do the human warriors in the passes."

Vered said nothing about the cloud creatures flinging lightning as they stalked along the floor of the canyon outside. He stared out the opening, expecting them to appear at any instant. After a few minutes, he knew how ridiculous this was. What if he sighted them? He could do nothing. If the storm warriors passed by, fine. If not, they were no worse off than they had been fleeing before the deadly storm front.

"How do you feel?" he asked Santon.

"All right," Santon replied, his voice low. Vered knew his friend lied. He abandoned his sentry post at the mouth of the cave and rested his hand against Santon's forehead. The fever burned bright and stole away part of Santon's soul.

"I'll look deeper in the cave," said Vered. "We might have to retreat if they follow us."

"Storm clouds cannot exist inside a cave with such a low ceiling," Santon said, looking around. Vered had the feeling that Santon spoke without knowing what he said. If the Wizard of Storms' magical killers could exist under a clear blue sky, they could enter a cave.

He left his horse with Santon, more to keep the man occupied than for any other reason. Vered knew his dappled mare would not run away, not from inside a cave. He drew his short glass sword and ran the tip along the wall to mark his path. The cut caused fine dust to fall from the gash. The walls were more like chalk than granite, he noted with increasing uneasiness.

By the time he rounded a second bend in the wind-cut cavern system, Vered found himself in almost total darkness. He hesitated, holding back the irrational fear of cramped spaces that afflicted him. All he had to do was backtrack. He had marked the walls. It would not be difficult to trace his way back to light and Santon and the horses, even if he had to do so by feeling the walls. The cuts were obvious, even in the dark. Over and over he told himself this.

Vered stood for a moment, collecting his courage. His eyes adjusted to the blackness. He started to turn and retrace his footsteps when he saw a shimmering white ahead in the tunnel.

A soft voice beckoned to him. "I need you so. Come, my lover. Come to me!"

Vered's hand tightened around the hilt of his short sword. He needed to know everything about the cavern if he and Santon were to avoid the storm warriors outside and unsuspected unpleasantness within.

"Come to me," came the crooning, seductive voice. Vered's eyes had fully adapted to the darkness and the white patches moving ahead of him came into focus.

"Are there other phantoms in this cave?" he asked.

"Save me from this existence," the woman's voice pleaded. "I can do so much for you, if you will only help me. Help me!"

Vered stopped and stared. If the phantom had not shed gentle illumination on the cavern floor, Vered might have taken a fatal tumble into a deep pit. He tried to estimate the size of the pit and failed. Writhing about in it were scores of phantoms. The tenuous spirits intermingled their substance, parted, flowed upward like liquid, and then dissipated into showers of tiny white sparks. He tried to see if they reformed and could not do it.

"How many of you are there?" he asked his spirit guide.

"How many? I cannot say. Too many. As many as you want! For too long I have been trapped in the crevice between worlds. Free me. Free me!"

"I can't." Vered used his short sword to tap along the edge of the pit. "Are your bodies in this cave or have you just congregated here for some other reason?"

"I do not know. Something pulls me to this spot. How can I say when I cannot identify my own body?"

"You see the other phantoms?"

"Not really. I experience an edginess that I have assumed to mean others like myself are near."

Vered changed his estimate. Thousands of phantoms might be in the pit. The tension in the air might account for this phantom's feelings of nearness to others.

"There's nothing I can do. Believe me, I would if I could. There isn't!" Vered almost wanted to cry in frustration. He had been against aiding Ruirik Kulattian, even if that spirit helped them locate Lokenna, but seeing so many former humans in psychic pain had changed his mind. He *wanted* to help. His personal hell was being unable to.

"*Vered!*"

He spun at the sound of Santon's voice. Vered left behind the pit filled with its nebulous phantoms and hurried back along the tunnel.

For a brief instant he feared that he had gotten turned around and had lost his way, but the sight of the cave mouth reassured him that his sense of direction remained intact. Santon sat just inside the opening.

"What's wrong?" Vered knelt beside his friend. In the brighter light of day falling across Santon's face, Vered saw the progress of the disease. Santon had turned a jaundiced color that gave him more in common with the dead than the living.

"There. Look."

Vered gritted his teeth in anger. The storm warriors had found them. The five gray, puffy, billowing creatures stood in a battle formation at the foot of the slope. Lightning danced within their bodies and a trail of dampness leaking from their feet was their legacy to the barren, rocky countryside. What turned Vered liquid inside, though, were their red eyes. He saw the windows of hell in their eyes.

"We might be able to go deeper into the cave. I found a pit overflowing with phantoms."

"I am too weak to run. We must face them here."

Vered reached over and laid his hand on Santon's forehead. The wound burned with its own intense inner heat; fever took possession of the man's body.

"Can you even stand?"

Santon shook his head. "I tried. I can crawl. Meeting them in battle on my knees is not to my liking, but I will not surrender."

"They want the crown. We can give it to them. Will the Wizard of Storms be any worse a ruler than Lorens?"

"Alarice wouldn't want it that way."

"No," Vered said. Expediency might save

them—but what would happen to Porotane if they gave in this easily? Still, how could they hope to defeat magical warriors such as the five now facing them?

Vered gripped his sword and stepped forward. He threw up his hand to shield his face when a sheet of hot water rained down. Vered stumbled back and fell over Santon.

"What happened?" demanded Santon. "I cannot see the storm warriors. Is this a new attack?"

"There are only four. One has disappeared." Vered looked up into the cold azure autumn sky and saw a tiny storm cloud drifting over the far canyon wall. Between the mouth of the cave and the remaining magical creatures flowed a small freshet. He looked above onto the softstone cliffs to see where it originated. It began at his feet.

"The storm warrior exploded," he said, realization slowly coming to him. "Its body erupted and sent down a cascade of water."

"Hot water," corrected Santon. "I felt it."

Vered stared in mute amazement when another of the storm warriors exploded. The thick body of restless cloud seemed to harden just seconds before the body lost form. Arms, legs, and head vanished into an amorphous mass. The geyser of water spewing straight up into the air sent a second hot rain down on them.

The last thing that disappeared were the malevolent, glaring eyes.

The remaining three storm warriors began moving up the slope. The one in the center shared the fate of its two comrades.

"There are only a pair left," said Vered, not knowing what happened outside but taking heart in it. "You get the one on the right. I'll take the one on the left."

Before Santon could respond, the storm warrior on the right blew apart in a shower of hot water.

"You always were the lucky one. I've still got one to fight." Vered stepped just outside the cave, sword in hand and a curious calm on him. It always felt this way before battle. His nervousness vanished and he concentrated only on his opponent, ready to respond to any attack or react if his enemy gave an opening.

Lightning danced from one cloudy fingertip to another, then formed a blue ball and shot straight for Vered's head. He parried, as if his sword would defect such an attack. The impact of lightning against his glass sword knocked him back into the side of the cave. What astounded him most was that he still lived.

"The sword Alarice gave you," called out Santon. "The glass sword saved you."

Vered nodded. If he had carried a steel blade, he might have been reduced to a sizzling spot of grease on the rocks. But this did not give him a clue about how to fight the storm warrior.

"Here, use this." Santon cast his glass shield out to Vered. Never taking his eyes off the cloudy body of his opponent, Vered hefted the shield and settled it into place on his left arm. He deflected another powerful bolt of lightning with the glass shield, but the impact left him numb and dazed.

"What am I supposed to do?" he asked Santon.

"It's coming for you. Fight it!"

"How?"

Vered moved sluggishly, getting his feet set. He had the high ground but the storm warrior towered above him. A gust of wind blew him back, in spite of his firm stance. Lightning crackled around him. Water pelted his face and blinded him. He hid behind the shield and tried to use his sword on the storm warrior's legs. The blade passed through harmlessly, slicing only fog as it went.

As abruptly as the other four magical creatures had vanished, so did this one. The explosion sent Vered tumbling back into the cave, almost into Santon's lap.

"Your shield worked," Vered said, handing it back. Santon's grip proved too weak to hold it. Vered fastened it onto the man's left arm for him.

Vered got to his feet and stared at the wet patches dotting the rocky slope where the storm warriors had perished. It hardly seemed possible that minutes ago he had faced certain death and now all that remained were thin wisps of clouds in the sky.

"The shield helped," Vered said. "Something more worked against the Wizard of Storms' warriors."

Vered cocked his head to one side as the sound of horses' hooves echoed down the canyon. He moved back into the mouth of the cave and knelt beside Santon.

"Riders," he said. Santon nodded weakly. Sweat beaded his forehead and yellow pus seeped from the wound on his head. "Since we saw no one but Lorens' guard, it seems a safe guess that the royalists will soon be upon us."

"Lorens is a wizard," Santon managed to grate out between clenched teeth.

"You think he is responsible for destroying the storm warriors?"

Santon could do little more than nod. His

eyes had glazed over and he simply stared. No intelligence shone from his green eyes. Vered ran his arm around his friend and heaved, getting Santon into an upright sitting position. Santon was the heavier and Vered did not relish the task of getting him onto his horse.

Even if he did, where would they ride? Lorens had an entire company of guardsmen with him. A small smile flickered on Vered's lips. He had the remnants of a company. The storm warriors had reduced the wizard-king's ranks before coming after the Demon Crown.

Vered hoped that Lorens would ride past, continuing down the canyon in search of some trace of the crown. Those hopes were dashed when the king reined in at the foot of the slope where the storm warriors had formed their attack line. Vered watched in fascination as Lorens weaved about in the saddle. An officer reached over to support the monarch. Lorens impatiently waved off the officer.

Tiny patches of dirt began to glow. Like footsteps left by an unseen giant, the green-glowing spots moved up the rocky slope toward the cave. Vered heaved a deep sigh. Magic had found them. Only swords would get them free.

"Sword," he corrected, looking at his friend. Birtle Santon could not fight. He lay in a semicoma on the floor of the cave. Vered had never run from a fight in his life, but he would have now if an escape route had presented itself.

None did.

When the royalist troops began dismounting, Vered knew he was in for the fight of his life. The last fight.

SEVENTEEN

"Santon, get on your horse and ride deeper into
the cave. We might be able to hide." Vered saw
his companion slumped to one side, unable to
move. The fever possessed him totally and
robbed him of any strength. He had slipped into
a coma.

Vered estimated his chances of getting
Santon onto his horse and riding past Lorens'
guardsmen. He cast out such a wild notion
immediately. The battle array he faced would be
too difficult to breach with such a tactic. A wild
thought made him want to ride down the slope
and try to fight his way through. They might
overlook Santon or think that he had ridden on,
hurrying deeper into the canyon. They would
never consider a comrade in arms holding back.

The glowing spots moving up the slope like
footprints of an invisible tracker told Vered such
a ploy would never work. Lorens' magic sought
the Demon Crown. The thought of returning the
crown to the wizard-king came and went almost
instantly. Vered would die rather than allow
Porotane to return to Lorens' rule.

"Up there. Check the caves. They are near,"
came Lorens' voice. Vered stepped out and

looked down the slope at the king. Two guardsmen had to support him. Vered knew that the
young king had reached the limits of his own
endurance. Countering the Wizard of Storms'
magic warriors had drained him.

That worked for and against Vered and
Santon. The commander of the king's personal
guard would not be a fool. In a sortie such as
this, he would not make any mistakes. Lorens
could not direct him; he would not need it.

But with the king unable to command, that
gave some sort of edge that Vered had to exploit.
He looked from the exhausted king, along the
pebble-strewn slope, to the area around the
mouth of the cave—and higher.

The softstone showed dozens of holes
carved by the incessant wind and rain. Vered
saw huge cracks in the orange and yellow stone
where water had seeped in, frozen, and caused
even greater fissures to form. The cliff face
above seemed poised to come tumbling down.
All it needed was a little help—from him.

Vered sheathed his sword and scrambled
up the treacherous cliff face. The holes cut by
the elements provided ample foot and hand-
holds. But he dared not place his entire weight
on any one without first testing it. Too many
simply crumbled under him and sent down
betraying clouds of dust and rock.

"There!" came the cry. "On the cliff face.
Archers, fire!"

Vered groaned. He had trouble enough
climbing without poisoned and cruelly barbed
war arrows digging into his body. The freeboot-
er climbed faster, his grips slipping more often.
He reached a dusty, narrow ledge and slid over
the edge to lie flat as the first flight of arrows

arched up seeking targets in his torso. Some penetrated the softstone and stuck. Others bounced off, rattling back down to the canyon floor. No matter what he did, it would have to be soon. The archers pinned him to the ledge. It would take only minutes for the other guardsmen to reach the cave and find Santon slumped and unconscious.

Vered grunted as he took out his short sword and drove it into a crevice at the edge of the softstone ledge. Twisting and straining, he levered the blade back and forth, shoving it ever deeper as he worked. When he worried that he might break off the glass blade, he began using it as a pry bar.

At first nothing happened. The rock remained obdurate and new flights of arrows sought out his precious body. But a few more seconds of work using his sword produced a grating sound. The sudden release of a huge portion of the ledge took him by surprise. Vered yelped as he fell with the ledge. Only quick reflexes saved him. He grabbed a rock spire and clung to it.

As his legs kicked futilely in thin air, he was conscious of what a fine target he presented to the archers.

No poisoned arrow buried itself in his back. From below all he heard were cries of pain and confusion. Vered twisted around and looked down. The miniature avalanche had kicked up a cloud of dust and masked the bigger rocks in his landslide. Although the guardsmen had not broken off their attack, they milled around in disarray.

"No!" he cried. Vered's anger flared and died, replaced by a feeling of loss. He had thrown the soldiers into confusion as he'd hoped. He had not counted on sealing the cave with his avalanche.

Birtle Santon lay inside the cave, unable to move because of his wound. Or worse, and Vered tried not to think about this, the rock slide had set off a cave-in. Santon might have found his eternal resting place under tons of the softstone.

"Vered," came a voice.

"Santon!" Vered jerked upright and almost fell from his precarious perch. "Is that you?"

"It is I, Ruirik Kulattian."

"What do you want, phantom? I have to find Santon. The slide buried him in the cave."

"There are soldiers below. They will capture you. You must not let them."

"I have to get Santon out. If that's what it takes . . ." Vered's mouth turned dry at the thought of turning himself over to Lorens, yet there seemed no other chance to rescue Santon. It would take an entire company of men to dig him out—and only King Lorens had the manpower to do it.

"You cannot," insisted Ruirik. "I have found the one you seek. I know where you can find Lokenna."

"It doesn't matter," Vered said.

"But my corpse! You promised. I have fulfilled my part of the promise."

"That's not what I meant. Santon has the Demon Crown in the cave. Finding Lokenna is pointless unless we can also give her the crown. She needs it as proof of her lineage."

"The crown is not buried," said Ruirik. "Neither is Santon."

"What are you saying, you vaporous fool? I know they're buried. I caused it!"

"Santon and crown are deeper within the mountain. This entrance is closed but your friend still lives."

"What do you mean, 'this entrance'? Are there others? Show me!"

The swirling white column of Ruirik's phantom moved along the face of the cliff, then vanished into one of the wormholes cut by erosion. Vered leaned out and tried to see where the spirit had gone. For his boldness he made himself target for an archer below. The arrow missed him by the span of a hand but Vered ducked back, legs locked around the spire and body pressing close. He scrambled up and found a ledge too small for easy travel. With the archer shooting one arrow after another at him, the way turned more dangerous than it should have been, but when he ducked in, Vered saw what Ruirik had found.

A rock chimney led downward. Without hesitation, Vered dropped into the narrow tunnel feetfirst—and instantly regretted his impulsive decision. The shaft twisted twice and turned black. The walls closed in on him, pressing his shoulders. A surge of irrational panic seized him when he felt unseen hands crushing in on him.

He screamed when the pressure around his body vanished and he fell in the velvet darkness. Vered landed hard on the cave floor, coughed from the roiling cloud of dust, and tried to get his bearings. The chute had turned him around. He had no idea in which direction lay the clogged cave opening. For several seconds, he simply sat on the floor and got nose and eyes clear.

"Santon?" he called. "Where are you?" His words echoed. No human response came.

The sound that did reach him chilled him. It was not human. What evil mountain beasts made their lair in such caves he could not imagine, but Santon had mentioned many at higher levels that even well-armed men avoided. In the dark he had no chance.

"To your right lies Santon and your horses," came Ruirik Kulattian's voice. Vered jumped nervously.

"I heard strange sounds."

"Your horses are not pleased with being trapped inside the cave. The walls muffle and distort sound. I remember." Ruirik's voice trailed off, then came back, stronger. "I remember. When I was alive, I remember being in a cave such as this."

"But not this one?"

"How can I say?"

"Lead me to Santon." Vered stood and reached out, his hand against a wall. When the dancing white mist that was Ruirik Kulattian's shade appeared, Vered followed slowly. He did not trust the phantom to steer him away from pits and other potentially dangerous traps. For the phantom, such no longer posed a threat and twenty years of neglect dulled even inbred reflex.

Vered's hand touched something warm and round and alive. He held back his cry of shock, then explored further. A smile slowly crossed his lips. He patted a horse's rump. Whether it was his gray mare or Santon's steed, he could not say. Just finding a familiar form in the darkness relieved much of his fear.

"Santon? Where are you?"

"Here," came a weak voice. "Let Ruirik guide you."

The phantom led Vered to his friend's side.

In the dim light cast by the phantom, Vered saw Santon's gaunt face.

"He's found Lokenna," Santon said. "Our mission nears an end."

"We go nowhere while you're ill. I need to find some medicinal plants and make pastes and potions to get your fever down."

"Lokenna. Get to Lokenna and give her the crown."

"I'll not abandon you. Certainly not in here with phantoms floating everywhere."

"There are others here?" demanded Ruirik. "Is my corpse nearby? Please! I remember a place such as this. You must search the tunnels and find out!"

"Being with someone so single-minded can be boring," said Vered.

But he spoke only to himself. Santon had passed out.

To Ruirik, Vered said, "Is there another exit from these caves, other than the way we entered?" He did not want to abandon the horses and did not think he could get Santon up through the narrow rock chimneys and small air vents. They would leave together, or perish together.

"There are many."

"You're not being very helpful," Vered said. "Which one takes us out—and as far from the soldiers as possible?"

Ruirik Kulattian did not reply immediately. Agitation showed in the foggy cloud of his being. "I think you lied. You are not hunting for my body."

"We told the truth, but you knew our other problems. The Wizard of Storms sent his warriors after us. Lorens trailed us using magic. The guardsmen want the Demon Crown back. These

are complications which slowed us drastically."
He refrained from mentioning how close to
death Birtle Santon was. The phantom might
take this as retribution for their supposed slack-
ening of effort in finding his moldering corpse.

"This cave looks familiar. I remember it."

"Do you remember this one in particular or
one which looked similar?" demanded Vered.

"I cannot say."

"Santon can. He was one of your companions who survived. He knows these mountains
better than anyone else living," Vered lied. "We
need to heal him so we can get on with finding
your damned body."

"Without him the task is impossible?"

"Absolutely," said Vered. "I cannot touch
the Demon Crown without dire consequences
befalling me. Consequences worse than mere
death." He swallowed hard at the idea of being
left alone with the magical device. Its attraction
for him would prove fatal. Without Santon to
stand between crown and him, Vered knew he
would succumb and don the Demon Crown.

How long would he survive? A day? Vered
doubted it. Lorens was directly of the royal
blood line and it had wrecked him in the span of
a few months.

If he could not endure its silent cry for even
this short a time, Vered knew he could never
make use of the information Ruirik Kulattian
had about Lokenna's whereabouts.

"You remain my best hope for passing beyond this vile half-existence," said Ruirik. "I will
aid you this one last time. Then you must show
me your determination to complete your part of
our agreement."

"Done," said Vered.

Ruirik's phantom shimmered and turned as

insubstantial as the flickering polar lights that veiled nighttime winter skies. Vered cried out to the spirit. "Stop, wait. You . . . your substance mingles with that of other phantoms. I cannot tell which is you and which is . . . someone else."

"There are others here? I *felt* presences."

"One shade told me there is a powerful attraction to this cave. Do you feel it?"

"No," said Ruirik. He formed into a mockery of a human being. "I find it difficult to control my shape for very long at a time. The strongest places are those where I can become almost human again. This is not one of them."

Vered took this as proof that they needed to search further for Ruirik's mortal shell. The other phantoms came here sensing some link with their former life. For Ruirik that bond lay elsewhere.

Vered tied his friend belly-down over his horse and then walked through the dark cavern, believing he travelled through infinite night. The closed-in feelings came and went, and always he was wrong. When he was positive that the walls were just inches from his face, he tried reaching out and found only void. At other times, when he felt as if he strode through airy spaces vaster than all Porotane he bumped into the softstone walls.

And always he saw the fluttering forms of the phantoms. He had thought that there were hundreds in the cave. He tried counting and estimated thousands. They skirted the edge of the immense pit where the female phantom had tried to lure him into her service. Again he listened to the plaintive cries for release, and again his heart went out to the phantoms. But he could do nothing.

He was not even sure they could help Ruirik Kulattian.

Vered shouted with joy when he saw the faint light of day down a side corridor. "Ruirik, here. A way out!"

"The opening is small. The horses might not be able to squeeze through."

"But I can. I need to feel wind on my face and see sky. Blue sky!" Vered shoved his head through the small opening and inhaled deeply. The musty odor from the cave vanished as cool, fresh mountain air replaced it in his nostrils. Even more promising, Vered saw growing an arm's length away two of the plants he needed for Santon's poultice. He plucked the leaves from the lacy green plants and settled down just inside the tiny hole.

"We rest for a while," he said. "I need to attend to Santon."

"This will cure him?"

"Perhaps. I don't think he will recover quickly with only mend-leaf and wild grayberry, but it is better than nothing. These will bring down his fever, even if they do little for the other diseases rampaging through his body."

Vered carefully prepared the potion and applied it to Santon's wound. The man moaned softly, shaking his head as if to tell Vered to stop. Vered worried about Santon's breathing. Blood had rushed to head and feet and further impaired healing.

"He bleeds," said Ruirik.

"The poisons flow from the wound," said Vered. "That is not what I'd intended, but it is good." He crawled back to the tiny hole and pulled in more of the mend-leaf. Balling it up and crushing it, he applied a fresh wad of pulp to Santon's head.

When his supply was exhausted, Vered returned to the hole and wiggled as far through it as he could, hand groping for the plants growing nearby.

He yelled when a rough hand seized his wrist and pulled. "Captain, I got one of the bastards!" the soldier yelled.

Vered struggled to break free and get back into the cave, but the guardsman's grip was too strong.

EIGHTEEN

Vered struggled to pull himself free from the guardsman's grip. He was too tightly wedged into the small opening to do more than wiggle futilely like a fish on a hook.

"Here. I have one. Over here!" the soldier cried.

Vered's shoulder began to ache from the strain. With his left hand he fumbled for his dagger, but even if he drew it he would be unable to use it. His body blocked the hole.

Vered blinked, thinking that his eyes were deceiving him. The rock in front of him began to shimmer and move. The movement ceased but the commotion outside grew.

"A phantom!" came the soldier's angry cry. For a brief instant, the grip slackened. Vered twisted, his sweaty skin slipping from the soldier's hold. Getting his feet around to where he could brace himself against the rock helped. Using legs and shoulder, Vered pulled the soldier toward the small opening. When a scarred, ugly face appeared, Vered used his dagger. Blood gushed from the gash he opened just under the guardsman's left eye.

As suddenly as he had been seized, he was

released. Vered tumbled back into the cave, staring out at the angry, injured soldier.

Just beyond the soldier a pillar of shifting white gauze caught the light of day.

"It's all right, Ruirik," Vered called. "I'm free."

The phantom whirled around its vertical axis and reentered the cave to appear beside Vered. Ruirik had enough strength to appear almost solid and definitely human.

"Others come. He summoned no fewer than ten. You must hurry."

Vered drew his short sword and cut at the soldier's hands as the man tried to pull away rocks and debris around the small hole. Such a tactic delayed; Vered knew that when the others arrived they would soon open the hole and pour into the cave.

"I'll cut your liver out!" the guardsman promised. "You cannot get by me. You will join your vaporous friend, mark my words!"

"It appears that I have already marked your ugly face. That is enough good work for a day." Vered backed off when the soldier bellowed incoherently.

"Is it wise to anger him?" asked Ruirik Kulattian.

"Of course not, but it gives me some small satisfaction." Vered backed from the opening, rubbing his shoulder and glaring at the soldier. He turned and ran back to where Santon lay. The thick, yellow pus still drained from the head wound but the man's color had changed for the better. No longer the jaundiced yellow, his complexion was now a pasty, almost deathly white.

"Santon, can you ride? We have found trouble again."

Green eyes flickered open. Before, they had

been glazed and unfocused. Now they centered on Vered. "How can we be in trouble? There aren't any women in these parts."

Vered grinned. "Since I haven't found any, there are none. But we must ride. They might not be able to move enough rocks to get in through that small hole but there must be other ways out—and in."

"Ahead," said Ruirik. "That direction." A misty arm pointed down a side tunnel.

"Narrow," said Vered, not liking the tightness of the fit. "And the roof is low. We can't ride."

"I'll make it. I have to."

Vered helped Birtle Santon to his feet. The man was hardly able to stand, but by linking his immensely powerful right arm through the reins and over the saddle, he was able to stumble along, the roan supporting most of his weight.

"It is a shame you cannot simply move in a straight line," said Ruirik. "We could be out of the mountain within minutes."

"I prefer to do things slowly," said Vered. He winced at the grinding noises behind them. The soldiers worked with too much energy on that tiny hole. With Santon unable to move any faster, an able-bodied squad could overtake them in minutes.

"I do not recognize this cave," said Ruirik, "but the rock is familiar."

"It's everywhere in these demon-cursed mountains," said Vered. "No reason you shouldn't recognize it. Besides, you've been wandering the Yorrals for twenty years. I'd think everything would look familiar after a decade or two."

"It's not like that. Phantoms are drawn to

points of power. Some remain, fearing to leave, thinking their bodies are near. I always had the feeling that mine was hidden away, yet accessible."

"I don't see how you think we can find it when you haven't."

"Years vanish behind me unaccounted for," Ruirik said sadly. "Time means little when you are robbed of body and peace. Concentrating becomes more and more difficult, too. And always the cold seeps in and steals away something of your humanity."

"And you cannot see your own body," finished Vered. He was not impressed with the phantom's litany of woe. He had troubles of his own to cope with.

He halted to check Santon. The man nodded weakly. Vered urged his balking horse forward, toward a dim dot of light that grew until it became a jagged opening in the side of the mountain. With some trepidation, Vered peered out. He expected to see Lorens' troops arrayed for an ambush.

"This is on a different spur of the canyon than where the soldier grabbed your arm," said Ruirik. "They might find this spot, but only after a full day of travelling."

"We cut under—through—the mountain?" Vered shuddered. He was just as happy having done it without knowing tons of rock were poised above his head, ready to collapse. As long as he thought about other matters, he could survive. Comments like this brought back to him the perilous nature of their trip through the caverns.

"A new path, Santon. Sunlight. We can breathe the air. We can get away from Lorens' troops!"

"I recognize this valley," said Santon.

"We rest for a while. I see more mend-leaf. And there's a scrubby crackle bush with enough dry berries hanging on it to make my special poultice."

"I can use a break," said Santon, sinking down, back against the rocky mountainside and face turned to the sun. Vered worked quickly to make the healing poultice and applied it to Santon's head.

"That stings," complained Santon. "But it's moist and cool. I like that."

"Your fever's broken." Vered no longer worried about Santon's survival on this score, but he continued to worry about Lorens' soldiers scouring the Yorral Mountains. The king would not lightly give up the hunt for the Demon Crown.

Vered shivered as if he were the one with fever when he thought of the Wizard of Storms' magical warriors exploding. Lorens might not have received the full training of a wizard but he controlled spells potent enough to destroy the storm warriors.

"It's as if I had left this valley only yesterday," said Santon. "So beautiful and yet it proved so deadly."

"You're not just caught up in a fever dream?" Vered scanned the deceptively serene, phantom-infested valley. It appeared no different from a dozen others they had searched in their hunt for Ruirik Kulattian's corpse.

"Yon tall mountain peak. The one split into a rocky trident, though you cannot tell that from this angle. How can anyone forget that triple peak?"

"Easily," said Vered. Then he paused. Something in his friend's voice cautioned him that this was not a subject for joking. "What happened there?"

"The brigands impaled a captive a day on one of those peaks. Needle-sharp points at the top. They'd put their victim on a blanket, with hands tied behind the back, and begin tossing him twenty feet and more into the air. Eventually he would fail to come down on the blanket and would land on one of the trident points. It is difficult to tell from here, but the peaks are almost pure iron. The elements have forged them into weapons aimed at the sky." Santon closed his eyes and seemed to shrink in on himself as memories assailed him. "Weapons aimed at the sky and many of my former comrades in arms."

"A good reason to dread this place," said Vered.

"Dread? Hardly. I came to think of it as a haven. The brigands did that to let us know that they were beyond our reach. But we were beyond theirs, too."

"A fortress?" guessed Vered.

"We fortified an old abandoned mineshaft near here. The brigands never penetrated our outermost defense perimeter, though our losses were great."

"Did all your forces use it as a base?" asked Vered.

Santon turned and stared at Vered. "I know what you are thinking. It is possible that Ruirik would be taken there if he lay in a coma. But so many died in other places scattered throughout the Yorral Mountains."

"My body?" perked up the phantom. "Do you know where it is?"

"You said this cave looked familiar. The inside of one rock prison looks like any other to me. You wouldn't have been too alert, either," said Vered.

"You know where this fortress lies?" Ruirik's phantom spun and whirled in excitement and sent off tiny streamers of white mist.

"Less than a league down the valley, if my bearings are right," said Santon.

"There is another matter to attend to first," cut in Vered. "Where is Lokenna? You said you found her. We're trying to recover your body. You've got to trust us with your knowledge."

"No!" cried Ruirik. "If I tell you, then you'll never try to find this fortified mineshaft. This is my last and best hope of escaping my sorry existence!"

"We have come this far in your behalf," said Santon. "There is no way of knowing if you're lying to us. You might be luring us on."

"I have found Lokenna." Ruirik Kulattian dissolved into an amorphous shape of ever-changing tendrils and columns. Slowly, he tightened into a glowing white sphere and then reformed. "Very well. I take the risk of my life."

"Some risk," muttered Vered, "considering that you're already dead."

"Lokenna lives in a village known as Fron."

"Do you know where this is?" asked Vered of Santon.

The grizzled, pale man nodded slowly. "It is not more than a day's travel off the main track through Claymore Pass. I remember it as a miserable little town that got burned to the ground by brigands at least once a month. I never knew why any of the inhabitants stayed."

"She is in Fron," insisted Ruirik. The phantom lost shape once more, hovering over their heads, as if waiting to see what they would do next.

Santon heaved a deep sigh, then forced himself to his feet. "The air renews me as much as your fine potions. I might be up to riding for a few minutes."

"For Fron?" asked Vered.

"For the fortress. We promised Ruirik to continue our search."

"Thank you!" came the long, low sigh of gratitude from the phantom. "You are honorable men."

"Stupid ones, too," said Vered. "Lorens is not going to stop hunting us." He scanned the sky for suspicious cloud formations. "I doubt that the Wizard of Storms will leave us in peace, either. Too many people want that accursed crown."

"Then it behooves us to hurry," said Santon, trying to get into the saddle. He tried twice and failed. "Give me a hand. I'm still weak."

"Don't let the nag run away with you," Vered said, hoisting the heavy man into the saddle. Vered brushed off his hands and stared at the tatters flapping on his back. "What a descent from high fashion. Look at me. The cave dust, the fights, everything has reduced me to rags befitting a beggar."

"Are we any more than that?" asked Santon.

"No, more's the pity." Vered swung into his saddle and started in the direction Santon indicated.

They rode for ten minutes, rested, then rode for fifteen before Santon straightened in the saddle. The man's face flushed and looked almost normal.

"There," he said softly. "There is our haven. Let us hope that brigands haven't taken it for their own since the days King Lamost held the Yorral Mountains in his grip."

Vered and Santon rode slowly up a weed-overgrown path. Vered saw where battlements had been placed in earlier days. Weather and occasional landslides had erased much of the fortifications. He looked up and saw where snow formed during the long winter months. A spring thaw would bring avalanches that would sweep clean boulders larger than any used by the soldiers in that bygone era of King Lamost.

"The entrance," said Santon. "Some heavy rock fall, but not enough to seal it permanently, I think. You might be forced to do some hard excavation."

"A pleasure," Vered said sarcastically. "Who wouldn't want to dig open still another hole in the ground so we can bury ourselves alive?"

Vered explored the area and found the shoring on the tunnel mouth in surprisingly good condition. The rocks blocking the entrance were too large for him to move alone, but a brushy area farther north drew his attention.

"What did you find?" asked Santon.

"The bushes are blown away from the rock. Unusual." Vered explored and found a large fissure. "I think this has opened up since last you were here."

"There are quakes of some intensity. None struck when I was on patrol, but the older veterans had tall tales to spin around campfires of the mountains themselves moving."

Vered tugged and cut and toiled to clear the fissure of dense undergrowth. An hour later, he indicated that Santon should follow him inside with the horses.

"A tight fit again," observed the older man, "but the horses are getting used to it."

"I'm glad someone is." Vered closed his eyes and tried to think of open spaces, of clean air and blue skies—the very things he left behind to entomb himself under still another mountain.

Mind unsettled but resolve firm, Vered entered. He found the going easy. In less than a minute he stood in a wide gallery dimly lit through the fissure.

"The main chamber," said Santon, joining his friend. He tethered the animals near a stone trough filled with pure, clean water. "An artesian spring feeds it year round," Santon said. He bent and drank of it himself, then washed away some of the trail dirt. "Still as refreshing as I remember."

"What else do you remember of this mausoleum?" asked Vered. White patches of phantoms drifted through the tunnels. "This is another spot where the spirits congregate."

Santon walked slowly, getting his bearings. "There. Down that tunnel is where the infirmary used to be."

Vered preceded him, sword drawn. The darkness closed in around him until he was forced to stop.

"Too dark."

"Then we'll need light." The sudden flare dazzled him. Santon had found a torch that burned fitfully, even after so many years. "We'd make our recruits bundle together rushes from a lake an hour's travel up the valley. They never understood why we insisted on rushes from that particular lake."

"They've lasted."

"Aye. We knew quality then."

Vered turned to the low, keystone-arched entrance to a room and felt light-headed. "You knew quantity, also."

"A moment, if we are going exploring." Santon unslung the rucksack containing the Demon Crown and hoisted it over his good shoulder.

"Why take it? The horses won't run off with it."

Santon looked at him for a moment, then said, "We wouldn't want to be split up in the caves. These tunnels are extensive and confusing."

Vered started to protest. Santon doubted his resolve about denying the crown's lure and did not want to tempt him. Before the words formed on Vered's lips Santon pushed him aside, holding the guttering torch high. The almost-smokeless torch illuminated a room filled with tiers of crude beds hewn from the living rock. Hundreds had died on those beds.

And the bodies had not been removed for burial.

"Retreat must have come quickly," said Santon.

"Or death. What was the fate of this fortress?" Vered forgot about the crown when faced with such magnitude of death.

"Abandoned. I never learned why. I was on patrol when we got orders to return to Porotane." Santon walked forward. "We never learned the details of the rout. I always thought the brigands overwhelmed us."

"Could it have been an epidemic that caused Lamost's change of heart in maintaining power in the Yorrals?"

"Aye. Let's hope, if it was disease, that it has died out over the years." Santon walked along the tiers of rocky death beds, looking at the corpses. "They are well preserved. The temperature is right and the cave is dry."

"Most seem to have taken severe wounds," Vered said, almost in relief. If plague stalked these soldiers in a bygone day, it might still hunt the unwary. Proof of war injuries reassured him that some other explanation for Lamost's hasty withdrawal was the correct one.

"Have you found my corpse? I sense great power here. A . . . an ineffable sensation rising from the middle of the mountain. I cannot describe it."

"Describe yourself," ordered Vered. "What did you look like in life? Any armbands or bracelets or rings that might help us?"

"Such would be stolen," said Santon, shifting the pack holding the Demon Crown into a more comfortable position on his back. "Even among comrades, there is the feeling that the living are better off with wealth than the dead."

"That is something I can agree to," said Vered.

"The steel foot," said Ruirik Kulattian.

"What?" Both men turned and stared at the phantom. So much energy had infused the spirit that he appeared to be a living human being. Only the faint white glow betrayed the truth.

"I had a steel foot. My left foot was crushed by a wagon more than a year before I died. A bladesmaster fashioned a hollow foot for me. I strapped it on and could walk with scarcely a limp."

"Fine," said Vered. "Rise!" he called. "All you corpses, get up and walk around. We want to see who doesn't limp—much."

"Vered, hold your tongue." Santon settled

down, resting against a stone table. His hand shook as he held the torch. Vered took it and continued the inspection while his friend rested. Never had he seen such a variety of ways to die. He poked through the rags hanging on a few of the corpses, looking for signs of a steel foot or name tags or other identification.

"It appears that these were left since none could be identified," he decided. "Lamost might have ordered the retreat but none of these unfortunates could be named, so they were abandoned." He shivered again. This wasn't as much an infirmary, then, as it was a mortuary for the unknown.

Vered used the tip of his sword to push back a blanket. A sergeant's sigil still gleamed after thirty years in the torchlight. The glass sword poked down further. Vered couldn't tell the cause of death from the body. He ran the edge of the sword along the legs. Then he tapped and heard a hollow ringing.

"Sergeant Ruirik Kulattian," he called. The phantom whirled up and stood beside him, a misty apparition that added to the light cast on the body. "Is it likely you kicked ass with this steel foot?"

"What?" demanded Ruirik. "What are you saying?"

"Look well. Might this be your body?"

"I . . . I see nothing. Of others, I see them well enough, though many appear as if through a veil. But I see nothing where you're pointing. This isn't a cruel joke, is it?"

"Santon!" Vered waited until his friend joined them. "Look this one over. The steel foot might have proven all the clue we needed."

"A sergeant, from the insignia. There's no way to match phantom with facial features."

"A front tooth!" cried Ruirik. "I was missing a tooth in front."

"Left or right side? Upper or lower?"

"Lower. But I . . . I cannot remember which side."

"Right?" asked Vered. He had pried open the jaws and ruptured long-dried tendons. A single tooth was missing from the jawbone on the lower right side.

"It's been too long. I cannot remember. Pieces flood back but so much is missing. I am confused. The world turns vivid colors around me and swirls. There has never been a time like this for me."

Vered and Santon exchanged glances. Santon nodded slowly, then said, "We may have found your body, Ruirik."

For a long minute, the phantom said nothing. Then in a voice so low that neither man could listen without straining, "Dare I believe this? You do not torment me?"

"Did you speak truly when you said Lokenna resides in Fron?" demanded Vered.

"I did. There is nothing for me to gain by lying."

"We'll consecrate a grave for this body and name you in the burial ceremony, Ruirik. We might have found the wrong body. This might not be yours."

"I have nothing to lose by the ceremony," Ruirik said.

Vered said nothing. If they consecrated a grave and named the wrong man, some unknown soldier would be doomed forever to existence as a phantom. Vered took a deep breath and let it out slowly. But the risk was small. No one had sought surcease for those who had died in Claymore Pass twenty years ago. The future would not bring in others who would care, either. One unknown man might be doomed to walk the world as a phantom but Ruirik Kulattian might also be freed.

Vered and Santon began construction of a rock cairn at the far end of the room. An hour later, Vered said, "That's good enough for a prince. Let's begin."

He went to fetch a flask of water from the trough. Ruirik dogged his steps, the apparition fluttering around him like a swarm of misty white flies. Vered returned to find that Santon had bundled up the body in a saddle blanket, leaving only the hands and face exposed.

"I'll do it," said Santon. "Although I never knew him, he might have ridden beside me as a comrade."

Santon began the mumbled prayer of leave-taking, dropping water on each of the corpse's fingertips, finishing with single drops on each of the hollowed eyesockets and where lips would have been if they had not mummified over the years.

"The saints are merciful and will carry Ruirik Kulattian, Sergeant of Scouts for King Lamost, to a better existence." With that Santon stood and backed away.

Both men jerked around when a sudden shriek cut through the heavy silence in the mine-fortress. The cry started as one of pain and climbed in intensity . . . and altered as it went. It ended as a shout of sheer joy.

"I am free!" Ruirik Kulattian exulted.

Vered covered the corpse's face with the blanket and began stacking the rocks atop the body—Ruirik's body. That brief cry had proven that they had properly matched phantom with body.

"Rest well, friend," Vered said, backing from the grave.

"He will," came a soft whisper, more like the wind through tall trees than a human voice.

"Alarice!" cried Santon.

"Thank you. There is one less troubled phantom because of you. But you must hurry."

"Wait, Alarice, don't leave. I want to—" Birtle Santon reached out with his good hand but found only emptiness. The Glass Warrior's phantom had existed for the span of two heart-beats and no more. She had again appeared and left.

"She wants us to go to Fron," said Vered. "That's where Lokenna is and that's where we can get rid of the Demon Crown."

"She could have lingered a few minutes," Santon said, his voice weak and his back bowed.

Vered stopped and cocked his head to one side, listening intently. Santon heard the sounds, too, and stiffened.

"Lorens! He has again found us!"

Vered heard the clank of steel weapons rubbing against stone. Lorens' guardsmen forced their way through the narrow fissure. The soldiers' cheer when they found the horses chilled Santon to the bone.

They had come so far only to be trapped within the fortress!

NINETEEN

"No!" screamed the Wizard of Storms. Kaga'kalb fell back, hands to his head. Blood spurted from a tiny wound on his temple. He staggered and dropped to his knees, rain pounding the barren plain around him. His eyes lifted to the monstrous, black-bottomed cloud above him. From this thunder cloud had sprung his storm warriors.

Kaga'kalb wiped the blood from the wound and smeared it on his robe. Determination replaced the surprise he'd felt. It had been so many years since any opposed him.

It had been many years since he had strayed from the Castle of the Winds and meddled in the internal affairs of Porotane.

He rose on shaking legs. He thrust out his hands and concentrated. Killing Lorens' soldiers had proven more satisfying than he had thought. But this was not his only reason for conjuring the storm warriors. He had sensed the presence of the Demon Crown and had directed the five cloud creatures to retrieve it, but something had gone wrong. One of the warriors had . . . ceased to be.

Kaga'kalb shrieked again. A new wound appeared on his temple. Both spurted blood. He touched the wounds and uttered a healing spell, but the tiny punctures refused to stop bleeding.

"Who opposes me? Who dares?" he bellowed.

A third storm warrior was destroyed. Kaga'kalb closed his eyes and let his senses merge with that of a warrior. The world shimmered as if seen through a veil of desert heat, but the deadly green glow told him that the crown he sought was near. He directed his storm warrior toward it. A shale slope led up to the mouth of a cave—and within the cave the Demon Crown sent out its silent message of power.

A fourth wound exploded on his forehead. Wind whipped about the Wizard of Storms and caused him to rock to and fro. He struggled to keep his balance, to remember where he was. Part of him inhabited the remaining storm warrior and the part of his being that was *him* stood battered by a thunderstorm of his own creation.

"The crown," he moaned out. "I will have it! But who kills me?"

He turned, his eyes seeing the castle and its lofty spires of precious gemstones—and his eyes also seeing a rocky canyon in the Yorral Mountains, not far from the track that mortals called Claymore Pass.

"Lorens," he said, not sure which vision proved truer. Kaga'kalb blinked. The towers of his castle vanished and he saw clearly through the storm warrior's glowing red orbs. "Lorens, you have powers I did not recognize."

He lifted a cloudy arm and pointed. Lightning from five fingers lanced forth, cremating five of Lorens' guard. The others scattered, leaving an empty battleground. Kaga'kalb sneered. Such cowards! They dared not face the power of a storm!

He turned and began striding upslope, intent on the faint but distinctive power emanating from the Demon Crown. A mortal emerged from the cave and slashed at him.

Kaga'kalb yelped in surprise. No mere blade cut at his cloudy leg. A blade fashioned by the Glass Warrior caused a twinge. He stepped back and glowered at the impudent mortal. Could this be the thief who ripped the Demon Crown from Lorens' brow? It hardly seemed likely, yet he showed courage lacking in the royalist troops.

Power built throughout Kaga'kalb's arm. He pointed his hand. Lightning blasted out to remove this annoyance. Again the accursed glass blade protected the mortal. Kaga'kalb started to use a different form of magic when pain surged within his head.

He staggered and . . . dissipated.

Tumbling through space, Kaga'kalb held his head. Blood oozed between his fingers from five different cuts. He smashed hard into the barren plain stretching before his Castle of the Winds. The rain laved his face. Lightning blasted down to touch his fingers, renewing him, reassuring him of his power. Kaga'kalb blinked twice and saw only the spires of his domain.

Five storm warriors had been destroyed.

"Lorens, your power is far greater than I anticipated. Even without the Demon Crown you show promise." Kaga'kalb wiped the blood from his forehead and stood. "You show promise that must be snuffed out. You will destroy Porotane and that must never happen!"

The Wizard of Storms walked slowly into

his keep, thunder rumbling down the slopes and across the Uvain Plateau.

"Sire, you are pale. Let us summon a chirurgeon for you. There is one only a day's travel down the River Ty."

"Silence, fool." Lorens struggled to sit upright and failed. The sight of the Wizard of Storms' powerful magical warriors had unsettled him, but the spells had come to his lips unbidden. He had remembered his lessons well! Patrin would be pleased with his pupil, had he survived to see this day.

But the cost had been great. Destroying one storm warrior had been simple. The next had proven ten times harder, and the third ten times harder still. By the time he destroyed the fifth, Lorens had become so drained that he had fallen from his saddle. Only a lieutenant had prevented him from injuring himself severely.

"They are near. I feel them. What has happened?"

"Sire, we lost them in the maze of tunnels."

Lorens worried that he would be unable to conjure the Spell of the Ten Trackers that had proven so useful before. It was a difficult spell to control and he was so tired. So tired, so tired.

"Sire?"

Lorens awoke with a start. He had begun to drift. He dared not do that. The Demon Crown. He had to recover it before anyone learned of his secret and hasty departure from Castle Porotane. That fool of a double he had left behind would not convince many should he try to hold a royal audience. And Lorens did not trust him to remain in chambers as he had ordered.

A fake king wearing a fake crown. Lorens snorted in contempt.

"What's happened?" he repeated.

"We've lost them. The thieves exited the cavern and are in the next valley over. Our scout saw them from the summit."

Lorens glanced up the steep cliff face. The softstone had proven treacherous. Two of his scouts had tried climbing that slope and had fallen to their deaths. He had not held out any hope for the third—but his luck had to change. It had to. So much had gone wrong.

His hands rubbed the place where the Demon Crown had rested. How empty he felt without the magical crown. He needed it. Why send scouts to do work he could do magically in the wink of an eye? And what went on while he was away from the castle? Plots, to be sure. But who sought his death?

Theoll? The conniving little baron would stop at nothing. But how did he work his perfidy this time? Lorens almost burst into tears at the depth of his ignorance. He had to know. And Dews Gaemock and Dalziel Sef? Their siege might begin soon. Where were their troops? He needed to know it *all!*

"The crown. I need the crown." Tears leaked from his eyes and ran down his cheeks. He was too weak to wipe them before they left dirty streaks on his face.

"The valley is accessible through a narrow pass. We can ride all day and be there soon, Sire."

"It is awful being blind."

"Sire?"

"What?" Lorens tried to concentrate but his mind drifted. The dissipation spell used against the storm warriors had left him no reserve. His puffy eyelids drooped and his head sagged forward until his chin rested on his chest.

"Should we pursue? All of us?"

His heavy snores gave the officer the only command he was likely to get. The King of Porotane slept so deeply that he might have fallen into a coma. More than one in his guard touched dagger or sword, thinking how easily a tyrant could be removed.

Lorens awoke with a start. He looked around and tried to remember where he was. His dreams had taken him back to his simple quarters in the City of Stolen Dreams. Patrin had been disciplining him for an infraction. Storm warriors had closed in and he had destroyed them, but a woman's face had floated above and had mocked him.

Lorens shivered. She had worn the Demon Crown. He had tried to touch it, to force her to return it and she had mocked him. Lorens struggled to remember who she was. She had seemed familiar, yet a stranger.

His throbbing head felt as if it would split open at any instant.

"Sire, we have followed their spoor to an abandoned fortress."

"A fortress?" Lorens sat up, curiously weak. Separating dream from reality proved difficult for him. "The Castle of the Winds?"

"Sire?" The officer glanced around. The others with him shrugged and averted their eyes. "No, Sire, this is a mine that had been converted into a fortress. One of my sergeants claims it had been built when his grandfather patrolled these mountains for your father, King Lamost."

"What are you telling me?" Lorens could not puzzle out his guard commander's words.

"We believe that the two thieves we chase have entered the fortress. The main entrance is blocked by fallen stone, but our tracker has discovered where they entered. A crevice recently opened by a quake leads inside."

"They are within that mountain?" Lorens pointed. Some small spark of the tracking spell he had cast so long ago remained in force. Tiny phosphorescent footprints marched directly for the fissure his commander had mentioned.

"It might be an ambush, Sire."

"What do they want inside an ancient fortress?"

"We do not know, Sire. They cannot hope to stand off our full might, even inside such a fortress."

Lorens tried to think of all the chances he took entering this deserted fortress. His head hurt too much. His hands shook and he could not stand upright without becoming giddy. The use of his few powerful spells had taken much from him and he tried not to show it in front of his officers.

When he had used the Demon Crown he had seen how few in Porotane—and his army— were loyal to him. All spoke highly of his father and vowed loyalty to the throne. Therein lay the troubles Lorens saw brewing. The soldiers swore their loyalty to the throne and not to him personally. In an instant they would turn against him if they saw the chance to put another in power.

Lorens tried to conjure just a small spell and found that he could not. The tracking spell continued working on its own, as if it had become a thing alive.

"Follow the footprints inside," he ordered.

"And you, Sire?"

"Where do you think I'll be?" he said, a sneer curling his lip. "I'll be in the front with you."

The guard commander shook his head slightly, as if not believing his ears. "Very well, Your Majesty. So shall it be." The officer bowed low, backed away, and then went to pass the order along the ranks of men anxiously waiting beside their horses.

For several seconds Lorens fought down his rising gorge. Had he done the wrong thing? The soldier expected another order. What? Why shouldn't a king lead his men? Did the officer know this was an ambush and only sought to lure him in?

Again tears of rage and frustration formed in the corners of Lorens' eyes. He *needed* the crown. Now more than ever he needed it. And it had been stolen by the ruffians hiding in the fortress.

"Forward!" Lorens took up the officer's cry and rode to the fissure. The glowing footprints he had conjured led inside. He followed their track, the first into the dark crevice. Only the pressure of men behind him kept Lorens walking forward. He imagined swords thrusting at him from every cranny. Arrows launched from deep inside the cave. Creatures beyond his most tormented dreams lurching up to devour him.

But he walked on. He dared not show cowardice.

It came as a relief when he entered a large chamber and was able to wave his men on past to scout the area.

"Sire, we've found two horses," reported his lieutenant. "What do we do now?"

"Search. Find the rogues who rode them."
Lorens glanced at the dim magical footprints on
the floor and saw with no pleasure that they
faded away. The Spell of the Ten Trackers had
finally weakened and vanished. He made futile
passes with his hand to renew it. No spell
worked, even the simplest. He was too drained.
Destroying the Wizard of Storms' tiny army had
proven too taxing for his limited abilities.

"The dust is disturbed. Footprints lead
down this tunnel," came back the report.

Lorens watched as the guard officer effi-
ciently positioned his men if this proved to be a
trap. He knew so little of such things, yet he had
to issue a command. He was King of Porotane
and kings commanded.

His lot would be easier with the Demon
Crown set at a jaunty angle on his head. Lorens
rubbed his temples, almost feeling the crown
resting there again.

"Are there other exits?" he asked.

"Sire, we don't know without extensive
scouting. None of my soldiers has been here
before, although many repeat tales told them by
their fathers and grandfathers."

"Torches. Light torches and advance."

"The smoke might blind us."

"No light to see by will be your downfall."

"We can see by the light shed by the phantoms, Sire. There are hundreds flitting about
inside this mineshaft." The officer ran his hand
along a roughly hewn wall, his blunt fingers
tracing a played-out vein of gold ore.

Lorens started at this notion, not having
seen the hundreds of phantoms when he entered. He stared at them and heard faint, plaintive cries for mercy.

"Will any of the spirits offer us assistance?

They can find our quarry much easier than we can."

"Doubtful, Sire. They promise anything in exchange for release. We cannot trust them."

"No, we cannot trust them. Any of them," said Lorens. It came as a mild shock to him that he didn't even know this young lieutenant's name who commanded his company of personal guards. When he had worn the Demon Crown, there had been no need for attention to such details. He had been able to see everything, no matter where it lay in the kingdom. Plots were laid bare and each person in the castle revealed all, whether they knew it or not.

"No side tunnels. They went directly to the infirmary," came a shouted report that echoed along the broad rock corridors. "We can get them now."

"Do it, Commander," he ordered the officer. "I want them and what they carry."

A war cry from the throats of twenty men rose. Swords clanking, armor creaking, shields scraping along the walls, the soldiers began their attack.

Lorens followed as fast as his debilitated condition would allow. But strength poured into him. It would not be long now. The Demon Crown would return to his royal head where it belonged!

TWENTY

"Break another bone," ordered Archbishop Nosto. The cleric stood impassively, watching as a well-muscled, sweating Inquisitor applied more pressure to the arm of King Lorens' double. The ersatz king screamed in agony as the complicated iron rods and pulleys tightened and snapped the vulnerable bones in his forearm. Jagged white bone protruded through the flesh.

The pain did not loosen the impostor's tongue.

Baron Theoll knew that there was nothing to be gained from this brutality—as far as the Inquisitor was concerned. He looked not at the heretic impostor Nosto tortured but at the assembled lords and ladies of Porotane. They watched from galleries and the main floor of the royal audience chamber. Once orchestras had played here for the amusement of the gathered nobility. Now only pain from the Inquisitor played its ugly song down the narrow chamber.

None dared speak out against Archbishop Nosto, yet none supported him, either.

In that lay Theoll's road to the throne.

His dark eyes moved slowly, studying reactions, guessing at alliances and loyalties. When he stopped at a plain, almost mousy brown-haired woman with an intense expression on her face, he shivered slightly with expectation.

Lady Anneshoria lacked the qualities so many in the court possessed. None would single her out for beauty or grace, and only Theoll recognized in her the drive and ambition to seize the throne. Her quick mind worked on new and ever more devious plots.

Baron Theoll could use her. In a way, he even admired her. But never would he turn his back on her.

His attention came back to Nosto. The archbishop straightened his shoulders and glared at the captive dangling in chains. "You will now be put to the Question. Have you strayed from the True Path in deed or thought?"

"No!" shrieked the victim.

"Evidence points to this being a foul lie. Are you a heretic? Do you have intercourse with demons?" New pressures were applied to the kingly double's body. More important bones broke.

"It is the belief of the Inquisition that this impostor has usurped the throne from the true King Lorens. A search of Castle Porotane is now being conducted to determine the fate of our king."

"I am innocent. He came to me. I lived in a small seacoast town, and he sent his agents to me. He is our king!" the poor wight screamed. "He *ordered* me!"

"Who is this mysterious *he* of whom you speak?" Archbishop Nosto asked in a deceptively mild voice. Theoll saw the cleric's hands trembling with anticipation of another lie. "Is it a demon who summoned you? It was! Admit it!"

"No, no!" The impostor struggled feebly in his chains. "The king ordered me. I am his loyal servant. He ordered me to impersonate him while he ventured into Porotane on a vital mission. He goes among his subjects for reasons of his own!"

"What mission could this be? He spoke of no such trip to me." Archbishop Nosto's logic continued along its inexorable course. King Lorens had said nothing about leaving the castle, therefore he had not left voluntarily.

"I know nothing of our dear king's motives. I am loyal. I obeyed his command."

"You thought to usurp power. But you are not capable of such a thought, are you?"

"No!"

Theoll closed his eyes for a moment. The interrogation now took a familiar course. Nothing that Lorens' double said would exonerate him.

"Of course not. Then you admit that a demon commanded you?"

"No, it was King Lorens!"

"Lorens is no demon. You speak treason— or heresy. Which is it?"

The victim gave up all hope. His lips rippled as if they had an obscene life of their own. "Treason," he said in a weak voice.

Theoll nodded. The choice was good. Archbishop Nosto would never rest until a confession was pulled from the man. Admitting to treason presented the lesser of two painful deaths.

"Continue interrogation of the traitor," ordered Nosto. "Find what has happened to our rightful king."

"He's dead!" shrieked the impostor. "I killed him. I did it to seize the throne for myself!"

Theoll hoped that would end the farce.
Nosto made a small gesture of benediction and
the torturing Inquisitor dropped the knotted
cord around the man's neck. A quick tug sent
the man's tortured soul to be judged by the
saints—and, Theoll knew, Archbishop Nosto
thought that the lost soul would be found wanting and doomed forever.

The baron waited for the announcement he
knew would come. He tried not to smile when
Nosto called out in his booming bass voice,
"King Lorens is lost to us. The kingdom is rife
with heresy. Too many, even within these castle
walls, stray from the True Path."

Theoll jumped when Anneshoria sidled up
next to him. Her voice was low. "You have done
well, Baron. Nosto is going to announce himself
king."

"I? Surely, Lady Anneshoria, you cannot
think I had anything to do with this? The Inquisition is responsible for uncovering the impostor
and returning us all to the True Path."

"Whatever you say, Baron." Anneshoria
smiled slightly and moved away. Theoll appreciated her diplomacy, even if she stood a full head
taller and insisted on peering down at him.

". . . there is no other choice left me," said
Archbishop Nosto. "I am installing myself as
king-regent to help everyone seek the True Path
and remain on it."

This announcement took many in the audience chamber by surprise. Theoll noted those
who seemed shocked. They could be dismissed
totally from any future power struggle. Those
who seemed annoyed or those with expressions
of disgust or shock formed still another power
bloc he would have to court. They would be his

stepping stone to the throne—and Archbishop Nosto would be the bridge.

"By the saints, I now ascend the throne of Porotane to act as king until the true heir can be restored—and the kingdom is once again returned to the True Path."

That final condition made Theoll smile. Let Lorens return. Archbishop Nosto would not relinquish the throne because Porotane would never achieve the moral and religious purity the cleric demanded. Even a saint would be hard-pressed to live up to standards Nosto demanded of nobles and peasants.

Only an internal struggle would remove Nosto. Or a clever assassination. Baron Theoll wondered how long it would take before someone drove a blade into Nosto's back. It would be amusing, he thought, if it happened while Nosto was seated on the throne.

The new king began barking orders concerning the disposal of the traitor's body. A wistfulness came to Nosto's words. He would have preferred that Lorens' double had confessed as a heretic. Baron Theoll slipped away. He cared little for the preparations for a formal coronation or the insincere congratulations from the nobles assembled. He had work to do.

"Is this all you can tell me?" shouted Theoll. He rocked back to strike Harhar but the jester cringed away, feigning fear. Harhar—Efran Gaemock—had endured much at this sadistic noble's hand, and he would endure much more to learn of the intricate plots running rife in Castle Porotane.

"Truly, Baron, there is no more. None at all!"

"There must be opposition to Nosto. Look at the way the others cower when he walks by!"

"They fear him, Lord, just as they feared King Lorens."

"Lorens used the Demon Crown."

"And Archbishop Nosto uses the Inquisition."

Theoll fumed. Efran studied him closely. Theoll wrestled with the problem of which was the more powerful tool for maintaining position on the throne of Porotane. Efran had his own ideas. Efran thought that he, like Theoll, would have preferred the crown, but Nosto used his position as head of the church to good advantage.

"What of Anneshoria?" Theoll asked.

"I can find nothing about her to indicate opposition to Nosto."

"Lies!" Theoll paced restlessly, hands clenched behind his back. The diminutive baron worked through the possibilities open to him. He could risk assassinating Nosto himself, but that left him open to countercharges of being against the church. That created more problems than it solved. Better to allow another to kill Nosto, then step in to fill the power void before real struggle developed.

A rap on the door interrupted Theoll's scheming. He turned from the jester and flung open the door. Efran Gaemock expected to see Commander Squann or another of his personal guard.

Lady Anneshoria stood in the doorway, demurely dressed in a high-collared plain gown. A small smile crinkled the corners of her full-lipped mouth.

"Baron, how good of you to see me."

"He granted no audience for this evening,"

spoke up Efran, wondering if Theoll worked to trip him up—or if the baron had no dealings with Anneshoria.

"Ignore him, Lady. Do come in." Theoll bowed slightly, the angle indicating the difference in their ranks. He made the gesture for a minimum of politeness, not as deference to a superior. Efran saw Theoll tense and start to grab her by the throat when she returned the bow in exactly the same degree.

She afforded him equal rank.

Efran settled down in one corner of the room, eyes alert. Such a meeting meant that strong forces combined in the castle. With luck, he could negate both and leave the gates open to his brother. Dews still carried on the siege, even though the castle's supplies would take them through the long winter with ease. Only by continuing the siege into the planting season could the rebels hope to bring Theoll and the others to their knees.

Anneshoria glanced in the fool's direction. "Get rid of him."

"Permanently?" joked Theoll.

"As you see fit."

Theoll motioned Harhar from the room. Efran Gaemock did not want to leave but his playacting as a jester required him to obey. He somersaulted and cut capers and tried to force the woman to relent.

Efran saw nothing but iron in her brown eyes. He left Theoll's quarters without further argument. In the corridor outside, Efran frowned. None of Theoll's guards were present. He explored and found the entire section of the castle empty of patrols. Was Anneshoria going to kill Theoll?

He squatted in the hall and worked on the

problems of power. He decided that the woman sought an alliance, not a death. She had removed Theoll's guards as a precaution against being overheard. If it had been anything more, she would have brought guards of her own—and Efran would be dead, also.

He slipped along the deserted corridor as quiet as any phantom drifting in the dead of night. Efran found a secret passage favored by Theoll and slipped inside. Quick, knowing steps took him through the maze of narrow walkways and past peepholes until he came to a secret panel within the secret passage.

A spring lock yielded to his patient tinkering, and he crawled on hands and knees to a point where he could spy on Theoll and Anneshoria. Efran had labored for months building and concealing this spy hole but had not dared use it before this moment.

A single mistake now meant the siege would drag on—and new rulers might destroy Porotane even more quickly than if Archbishop Nosto remained seated on the throne.

Efran Gaemock pressed his eye to the hole and listened intently.

"You leave me no choice, Anneshoria," said Theoll.

"I intended nothing less than to force you into supporting me."

"The plan is a good one, but I wish you had been more circumspect in execution."

"Damn caution!" the woman flared. Efran tried to follow her restless movement around the room but the field of vision through the spy hole was too limited. She moved like Theoll, pacing and gesturing.

"I had considered an alliance with you."

"With yourself on the throne as undisputed monarch," she said.

"Of course," Theoll said, smiling.

"This way is better. We rule jointly. In no other fashion could I ascend the throne." Anneshoria paused. "I refuse to be your harlot."

"Consort was the term I had in mind," said Theoll.

"We rule as equals."

"Of course," Theoll agreed. Efran heard the undertones in both nobles' voices. Neither trusted the other and each would betray their temporary ally at the first chance. But whatever scheme Anneshoria had put into motion, Theoll had gone along with it.

Did the baron have to agree or did he merely find it expedient to do so? Efran wished that he had heard the details.

"Is it done?" asked Theoll.

"Where would the jester have gone after I chased him from the room?" Anneshoria's tone caused a cold lump to form in Efran's belly. The part of the plan he had missed was to be revealed anew—and he did not like the turn it took.

"Possibly to the throne room. Possibly he would have roamed the corridors trying to gather further intelligence for me."

"Intelligence from Harhar?" Anneshoria's bitterness and contempt burned Efran's ears.

"What better source? Many speak freely in front of a fool. How can he betray them?"

"Is that your secret to power, Theoll?"

"Harhar has had his uses."

This simple statement from the baron sent Efran scrambling away from the spy hole. A dozen different plans formed and died in his head before he got back to the empty corridor. Not even slowing to close the secret passage panel, Efran ran directly to the king's audience chamber.

The tight knot of guards immediately outside the door alerted Efran that Anneshoria's plan had been put into action already. He dodged before any of the guards saw him and ducked into a small room that opened into another directly behind the throne. Efran peered out at the few men and women assembled at the foot of the dais. Their expressions mingled horror with relief.

Efran slipped unnoticed into the chamber and edged around to one side, using the tattered, threadbare tapestry to conceal himself.

Seated serenely on the throne was Archbishop Nosto, his hands folded across his lap. A heavy lance protruded from his chest. Small rivulets of blood that had seeped around the barbed head had dried and no longer flowed. Nosto was well dead.

Efran Gaemock took a deep breath and strained to hear what those assembled at the foot of the throne were whispering among themselves. Repeatedly he heard his name.

"Harhar did it. The jester! Imagine!"

Others supported this wild claim. Efran began working his way back to the anteroom. Sweat ran from every pore in his body by the time he was again safe within the confines of the room. He had not murdered Nosto. Anneshoria had dressed someone in a jester's outfit and *he* had killed the archbishop-king.

But who would believe such a tale?

Efran shook his head and fastened a headband so that it kept both lank black hair and sweat from his eyes. He took his rattle and twisted the handle. A wicked short-bladed knife came free. Efran used the sharp-edged weapon to cut the bells from his costume. Where he headed he did not want to betray himself with a jingle or a ring.

More guards had entered the corridor. Efran's heart felt as if it would explode; he forced himself to calm. Waiting for the opportunity to grab a solitary guard almost caused him to go wild with frustration. But the chance came and he moved swiftly and well.

One hand reached around the guard's face and strong fingers pinched down on nostrils to shut off breathing and stretch the neck taut. His other hand—the one with the knife—worked across the throat. A tiny ribbon of scarlet appeared. Efran dragged the dying guardsman into the anteroom and quickly stripped him of his uniform.

Efran allowed himself a slight smile at the irony of the situation. The guardsman owed his loyalty to Anneshoria and wore her uniform. She had put him in an untenable position; it seemed fair that she might get him out of Castle Porotane alive.

Dressed in the ill-fitting uniform, Efran Gaemock strode into the corridor appearing more confident than he really was. It had been too long since he had fought knife to knife, hand to hand. His battles had used a more subtle weapon during the months since Duke Freow had lain dying, the victim of Theoll's insidious poisons.

Efran made his way to the courtyard and the stables. "Make way for the royal courier!" he cried. The stableboy jumped, awakened from a nap.

"What is it?" the youth demanded.

"A message is to be sent. I ride to the rebel camp with an ultimatum. Dews Gaemock surrenders or the full might of Porotane is brought against him."

"How's that going to make him surrender?" the boy asked, confused. "We already do what we can against the rebels."

"You dare question the King of Porotane?" bellowed Efran. The stableboy cringed back.

"No, no!"

"A horse. Get me your finest steed. I must ride like the wind this night!"

"You can't leave the castle till dawn," the youth said. "Orders from King Nosto."

Efran cursed under his breath. He had wondered if the accursed archbishop had sealed the castle to prevent a mass escape from his Inquisition. He had.

Efran decided against further argument. He half turned, then spun, the whiplike action of his body driving his fist with irresistible force against the stableboy's belly. The youth buckled. Efran brought up a knee and caught him under the chin. When the stableboy went down, he did not stir.

Efran saddled and rode to the massive gates. He knew no one would open them during the night—and especially not with orders from the new king to the contrary. He reined his steed around and guided the gelding to a side gate where a pair of soldiers dozed. One looked up, eyes still fogged with sleep.

"Urgent orders from the king," Efran said softly, not wanting to wake up the other soldier. "There is a fire burning just outside the wall. I'm to investigate."

"The only fires outside are rebel campfires," the soldier said. "And you know the standing orders."

Efran saw the insignia on the guardsman's uniform and smiled. He leaned down from the saddle and beckoned the soldier closer, showing him a matching sigil on his sleeve. "Lady Anneshoria sends me on a special mission— one unknown to the king. If you need to know more, you must ask her."

The guard swallowed hard, his head bobbing up and down as if it were on springs. "You should have said so. Remember me to the lady, and thank her for her charity to my poor family. Sergeant Disso is always willing to please."

"Sergeant Disso," repeated Efran. "The name will not be forgotten in my report. Keep a sharp watch. I'll return in an hour's time."

"Aye, and good luck to you."

Efran nodded and urged his gelding through the small gate and into the open. Let Disso wait the hour. In that time Efran would have ridden to his brother's camp and would be safely away from the intrigues of Castle Porotane.

The promise of hot food in his belly and the first safety he had known in months kept him warm as he rode through the chill autumn night.

TWENTY-ONE

"The horses!" cried Birtle Santon. "We've got to get to them."

"Too late for that," Vered said. "I can't see in the darkness but I can hear. There must be a dozen or more guardsmen working their way down this tunnel."

Santon cursed the demons, the saints, himself for his weakness, Lorens for following so tenaciously, then began anew missing no one for his cursing. He finally stopped when he realized it was doing no good. To escape, they would have to act.

"I'm not sure how long I can run," he told Vered. Every muscle in his body had turned to water. Standing gave him no difficulty but exertion robbed him of strength quickly. He swung the rucksack containing the Demon Crown into a more comfortable position for carrying. The only stroke of luck they'd had was his insistence on not leaving the accursed crown behind with the rest of their gear where Vered might be able to slip back and touch it.

"Your fever has broken," said Vered, "and the mend-leaf has had a chance to work."

"I can't swing my ax very well." He hefted the heavy battle-ax that had once seemed to weigh nothing in his powerful grip. Now it required effort to lift to eye-level.

"We can't ride because they have our horses," said Vered, "and we can't fight because you're still weak from infection and I'm bone-tired from piling stones and burying Ruirik. That leaves only one course for us."

"Hide?" asked Santon. This didn't strike him as a good solution to their problem. Someone had used powerful spells to destroy the storm warriors. Any wizard able to conjure and control such power would be able to find them quickly.

"Subterfuge."

"Be quick about it," said Santon. "I *feel* them getting closer." Tiny sounds of the soldiers moving through the mountain-fortress tunnels echoed and magnified. He knew the guardsmen walked carefully, trying to make no betraying noise. That so many pebbles were kicked and blades rattled meant a full squad—or more—came after them.

"I wish the elements had been kinder to the uniforms," complained Vered. He pulled the rags off one corpse and began donning it over his own dishevelment. "Hold the torch low so that shadows are cast on my cheeks and forehead."

Santon did as he was told. The sight before him was ghastly. Vered had transformed himself into something unreal—and possibly undead. The phantoms wailing and moaning and fluttering around the tunnels were unnerving. Vered produced outright panic when he spun into the tunnel and waved his arms.

"Aieeee!" he shrieked. Santon knew what to expect and still jumped. The gasps and pounding of heavy boots against the rock floor told that the charade had the desired effect on the soldiers.

"Now what?" asked Santon. "The lure of the Demon Crown is too strong to keep Lorens at bay with a bit of arm-waving and shouting."

"Now we run. Come along. Let's hope that we've bought more than a few seconds of time to hide in these tunnels."

Santon followed his friend through the rocky passages as quickly as he could. The torch cast an ever-shifting, shadow light that gave birth to illusions. Santon jumped nervously several times at nothing more than a rock formation limned strangely. As he walked he tried to remember what he could about these abandoned mines, of how King Lamost had turned them into a fortress.

"Vered, wait," he called out. "We'll find ourselves in a dead end if we continue along this tunnel. We want to go . . . north."

"Make it sound as if you know what you're saying. Confidence, even false, is what I need to bolster my spirits." Vered turned and pointed down a crossing tunnel. "That's north."

"How can you be so sure?"

"I'm not. But I take my own advice." Vered started off at a pace too fast for Santon to maintain.

Panting harshly, Santon did his best to keep up. Soon he had to rest. Sweating and tired, he sank down and let the cool tunnel wall support his back. Santon worried over how little he remembered of the fortress. There had been special features to keep the royalist troops from being trapped. But what were they? Escape routes, undoubtedly, but where did they start—and end?

"It's too bad we had to abandon the horses.

They served us well and deserved better than being given over to Lorens' soldiers," Santon said. "But it might be for the best. It doesn't appear as if we'd have been able to ride them." The ceilings in these tunnels had lowered considerably. When he walked he could lift his shield and drag it along the rocky juts from the roof.

"They mined extensively," said Vered. "I see evidence of it in the stoops leading to either side. This is the main tunnel and must lead somewhere."

"It would do little good to have escape routes that required you to crawl on your belly," agreed Santon. "At one time over five hundred soldiers were quartered here."

Vered laughed softly. "An interesting sight, five hundred armed and armored men wiggling about in the dust trying to get free of this giant tomb."

"Don't make it sound so final. The sappers would have designed exits for the soldiers to leave on horseback and on foot, not on crawling on their stomachs."

"Engineers always design to please themselves," said Vered. He stood and explored further along the tunnel. He called back, "This might be an exit tunnel, though. New cuts have been made in the rock."

"How new? The fortress has been abandoned, except by phantoms, for twenty years."

When Vered didn't answer, Santon heaved himself to his feet and went to look at his friend's discovery. Santon went cold inside when he saw the bright marks on the rock.

"Metallic," said Vered. "Can it be from picks and shovels?"

"Look at the spacing." Santon reached out.

With the fingers on his powerful hand outstretched, he barely covered the long gouge marks. "That is left by a mouth. Those cuts are made by iron teeth."

"Teeth? Absurd. What manner of creature . . ." Vered's words trailed off.

"Aye, a rock worm. From the height above the floor, the worm must be as tall as you, Vered."

"Don't joke."

Santon was not joking. Their problems had grown with this discovery. Lorens' soldiers wanted what Santon carried in the rucksack. The pale green glow had increased, even through the cloth sack. Santon looked at the torch Vered held and saw that its usefulness was reaching an end. It would soon burn to the handle. Santon took out the glass box containing the Demon Crown and opened the lid.

The glow illuminated their way in a manner even eerier than that of the flickering torch.

"We'll have to move on," said Santon. He hadn't rested adequately but the sight of rock-worm gnawings added urgency to their flight. Better to die from running than to be eaten by worms while he rested.

"Did rock worms live in the fortress when it was occupied?" asked Vered.

"I remember nothing of them, but I spent little time here. Mostly, I patrolled Claymore Pass and camped rather than returning to this base."

"Have you ever seen one?"

"Never just one. They live in nests. Chambers filled with huge numbers of them. They gnaw through rock getting what nutrition they can from it. Aye, I've seen them and wish that I had not. They move slowly but are difficult to kill." Santon shuddered. "Their strong jaws enable them to bite through even the strongest armor with a single snap of their jaws."

"Remind me to never invite a rock worm to any of my formal dinners. It wouldn't do having them eat the flatware—and never noticing it wasn't the appetizer. The other guests would surely complain."

Santon felt a growing uneasiness as they walked silently along the tunnels. His memory of the layout had failed him. The best they could hope for was not to become utterly lost or blunder back into Lorens' troops.

The worst Birtle Santon refused to consider.

"How long before Lorens whips his men into pursuit?" asked Vered.

"You gave them a fright, but they are the best he has in the castle. The king's personal guard isn't composed of cowards."

"I looked a sight, didn't I?" Vered chuckled. He stopped in the middle of the tunnel and performed a slow turn to show off the rags dangling from his body. "They must have thought I was a corpse come back to life."

"With so many phantoms around, the guardsmen were ready to run, whether they realized it or not."

Santon joined Vered in a laugh at the expense of Lorens' guard. The laugh cut off suddenly when they entered a junction with a larger tunnel. Not a hundred paces down the tunnel strode six of the soldiers they made light of.

Santon kept walking, then grabbed Vered and spun him around. Vered hadn't seen the guardsmen. In a low voice Santon said, "They'll be on us in seconds. What are we going to do?"

"The same thing as before. It worked once, didn't it."

"The torch is out. All we have is the crown." Santon held it at arm's length. The pale green glow wasn't strong enough to cast a shadow on Vered's face as the torch had done.

"Might not be a good idea using it, anyway," said Vered. "They know what they're looking for. When they see it, in the hand of an animated corpse or not, they'll come for it."

Santon looked down the corridor they traversed. Only darkness lay ahead. "They're coming slowly, checking each side tunnel. We might have time to escape down this one."

"Do we have any other choice?" Vered paused for a moment, dropping to hands and knees and smoothing the rock dust on the floor to erase any sign of their passage. He did not do a good job.

"Come on. There's no time to do it right. They'll be here before you can completely hide our trail."

Santon walked as fast as he could. His legs trembled with every step and he found it increasingly difficult to hold the glass box with the Demon Crown at arm's length to light their path. He even considered letting Vered hold the box, but discarded this wild notion. Vered could not fully control himself in the crown's presence. The addictive lure of the Demon Crown's magic had made itself apparent, not only in Vered but in Lorens' behavior.

"They've found our tunnel," said Vered. "I can feel the vibrations through the walls. They've stopped. They're discussing it. They'll be sending men after us any instant."

"You're imagining that," snapped Santon.

"You can't make out anything by a few rock vibrations."

"They have an army after us, Santon. Put your ear to the wall and listen."

Birtle Santon stopped and found a flat spot where he pressed his ear. "That's not the sound of footsteps," he said, his voice choked. "That's the noise a rock worm makes when it is eating."

"Ahead? Or off to one side?" demanded Vered.

"How can I know? But you may be right about the soldiers following us. There is another, sharper sound that drowns out the rock-worm munchings."

"Die on a sword tip or a rock-worm fang. What a choice," grumbled Vered. "I have no wish to die dressed like this. I had something better in mind. A stately robe of red silk with embroidered patterns in gold thread, perhaps. Certainly in bed. I had even thought to have a pair of nubile young ladies to help ease me from this world. And a few—"

"Enough!" Santon's temper flared. "We've got to get away from both rock worms and soldiers. How?"

"Keep going," suggested Vered. "What can we lose if we are in as deep trouble as you think."

Santon wondered about Vered. At times he was morose and pessimistic. At moments like this, he seemed flippant and even cheerful. It might be nothing more than a way of hiding his fear. Santon knew that Vered did not like closed-in spaces, yet his friend showed no hesitation in entering increasingly narrower tunnels.

Did one fear drown out another? And were they all hidden by his cheerfulness?

Santon decided he would ponder this later. After they escaped the tunnels and Lorens and the rock worms.

The greenish glow cast by the Demon Crown wavered and Santon almost missed the motion ahead of him on the rocky floor. He danced back, dropping his shield to protect himself from the fangs that ripped at his legs. Metallic teeth bit into the glass shield and slipped off, leaving only scratch marks.

Vered bumped into him. "What—" When Vered saw the rock worm on the floor, he pushed Santon to one side and swung his short sword with surprising accuracy in the narrow tunnel. The glass tip cut across the worm's throat and left a shallow gash. The worm reared like a snake and struck.

Santon gasped. The worm's speed was greater than he had remembered, but Vered was faster—or luckier. The rock worm impaled itself on the point of the man's sword, the entire end vanishing into the worm's gaping, tooth-filled mouth.

"Twist it," cried Santon. "Twist it and get it out of the worm's mouth. They use acid to dissolve the rock they eat."

Vered regained his balance and jerked his glass sword from the worm's mouth. The arm-thick, pebble-scaled creature fell to the floor, lifeless.

"How long is it?" Vered asked, crouching down. The worm's body vanished into the wall. A hole hardly larger than the creature's body had been carefully gnawed through solid stone.

"Who cares? The soldiers are gaining on us. And worms are not solitary creatures. There will be more around. Close."

Vered said, "Seldom do I admit that you are

right, Santon. This time is an exception." With an almost prissy step, Vered got around the dead rock worm.

Santon had gone ahead, advancing cautiously, the crown lighting his way. His caution kept them from plunging into a pit filled with wriggling rock worms. The pale light cast by the Demon Crown revealed thousands of the creatures. They had eaten away the tunnel and surrounding rock to form a hole fifty feet deep.

"No chance of crossing that," said Vered. He tapped the rocks in the wall as if this might betray a new worm hole.

"Don't," said Santon. "That might attract them."

Vered didn't question his friend. He edged away from the wall and stood in the center of the narrow passage. Santon saw the fear of enclosed spaces beginning to work on Vered. Gone was the joke from his lip and the sparkle in his eye.

"We can get around them. There is a ledge circling the pit. If we move slowly and keep quiet, we will make it."

"What's on the other side?" asked Vered, eyeing the ledge with increasing fear.

"Who knows?" said Santon. "But we do know what lies behind us." The echo of guardsmen's bootsteps emphasized his claim.

Santon began the dangerous circuit around the pit. The worms writhed, hidden in shadow and darkness, only occasional glints from the Demon Crown's glow casting back from metallic teeth. Santon wobbled slightly as he moved. His weakness told on him. Even worse, he had to hold the crown, balance his battle-ax, and carry his shield. With one hand useless, the right hand had to do the job of many.

"Are you all right?" he called out to Vered.

"Just fine," came the shaky answer. Vered looked as pale as he had when the fever was at its peak. Anyone blundering upon them at this instant would have been hard-pressed to tell who was recovering from a seriously infected wound and who had been healthy.

"There!" came the cry. "There they are! And they have the Demon Crown!"

"Soldiers," Vered warned needlessly.

"I'm moving as quickly as I can," said Santon, but the battle-ax impeded his progress. He stopped and tucked the glass box containing the crown under his left arm. A quick movement brought the ax up and into his grip. Santon slipped the leather thong from his wrist. He turned on the ledge and saw the first soldier groping with his sword in an attempt to reach Vered.

The soldiers hadn't seen the pit filled with rock worms. Their attention focused on the crown.

Santon changed that situation with an adroit toss of his ax. The heavy blade twisted over and over in darkness and appeared as if by magic in the guardsman's chest. By some quirk of luck, he did not topple into the pit. He sank to his knees.

"Hurry, Vered. Hurry, before the others get around him."

Even as he spoke, Santon saw the guardsman behind the one dying from the ax strike working his way along.

"Kick him off the ledge," ordered an officer, still in the tunnel. "He's dead."

"He still lives," protested the guardsman behind his comrade.

"Do as you are ordered! King Lorens must recover the Demon Crown!"

Santon reached the new tunnel mouth and slipped inside. He spun around and held out his good hand for Vered. He clamped on his friend's wrist and pulled the man into the tunnel with a single powerful tug.

Vered dropped to his knees, sweating and shaking.

Santon checked the ledge. They might have to make a defense here, unless his gamble had paid off.

It had. The commotion on the ledge drew the rock worms. They surged up from their nesting place in the pit and attacked the dying soldier. The one behind yelled in fear when he saw the worms. His abrupt reaction cost him his balance—and his life. He tumbled into the pit, screaming until an iron-fanged rock worm ripped out his throat.

The guardsmen were diverted. Santon put his good arm around Vered and pulled the man to his feet.

"Come on," he urged. "We've got to find a way out of here."

"But where? What direction are we going? The walls. The roof. It's all closing in on me."

Santon kicked Vered hard enough to make the man cry out in pain. "You've got our only weapon. You bring up the rear and keep a sharp lookout for the soldiers." Santon's stern tones forced Vered to concentrate on something other than his morbid fear. Vered nodded and swallowed hard, his eyes still wild but his body set and coming back under control.

Santon's exhaustion kept their pace slower than he would have liked, but he did not stop to rest. He knew he might never rise again if he succumbed. As important, he did not want to give Vered the chance to dread the ever-narrowing tunnel.

When he did not think he could go on another step, he saw a small pinpoint of light. Santon hurried on, almost stumbling as he went. A cave-in had blocked an exit. Only a hole the size of his fist remained at the top of the larger mouth.

"We're still trapped," said Vered, "but we can see where we're going. Let me by. You rest and I'll get us out."

Santon let his friend begin to work. Vered's panic now fueled his actions in a useful endeavor. Rock and debris flew back from the hole until Vered had a space almost as large as his shoulders cleared.

"I see sky outside. It . . . it's sunrise! How long have we been inside this accursed place?"

"Keep digging. Your shoulders might clear but mine never would," Santon said. His broad shoulders required another foot of space to clear.

"Wind. There's a hint of winter in the wind." Vered babbled as he dug.

The refreshing breath from the outside renewed Santon's strength.

"How much farther?" he called to Vered.

"Not far. Another few minutes of digging, that's all."

Santon turned when he heard a scraping noise. He barely lifted his shield to deflect the downward cut of a sword. The impact knocked him staggering, but he managed to keep the glass shield up and between him and the pounding, slashing weapon.

"What's going on back there?" came
Vered's querulous voice. "I'm killing myself and
you're—"

"Vered!" Santon's warning came in time.
The smaller man had pulled back through the
opening and had settled down on the rocky
slope. When he saw the troubles facing his
friend, he scooped up his sword in time to
deflect the thrust of a second guardsman.

"Where did they come from?" Vered demanded. He kicked out and caught his opponent squarely under the chin. The blow knocked
the soldier back and gave Vered time to get his
feet under him.

"I don't know!" Santon hid behind the
shield and bulled his way forward. The soldier
did what he had hoped he would; he tried to
come over the top of the shield with his sword.
This left his legs exposed. Santon's powerful
right arm circled the soldier's legs and pulled
them out from under him.

Shield pinning the sword arm down,
Santon drove his knee into the guardsman's
exposed midriff. A hard fist to the side of the
head crushed his temple and ended the battle.
Santon stood, seeing that Vered had gutted his
opponent.

"They came on me with no warning," he
explained.

"Just like the others?" asked Vered. Coming
down a side tunnel were at least four bouncing
torches and dozens of shadows. "How many do
you think?"

"Too many." Santon grabbed his opponent's sword and scrambled up the rocky slope
and began wiggling through the opening Vered
had enlarged. His shoulders scraped rock and

left skin behind but Lorens' approaching soldiers added speed to his flight.

Santon tumbled out into dawn.

Behind him came Vered, clawing and kicking to get free. They stood and stared at the opening. On the far side a soldier entered the small crawl space to come after them.

"You've got the crown?" asked Vered.

"It's never left my side," Santon said, patting the rucksack with the Demon Crown in it.

"Good."

Vered kicked a large stone and caused a minor landslide. He worked his way up the slope above the opening and began working in earnest. Within minutes rock tumbled down in a steady blanket.

Vered joined Santon at the base of the hill. Avalanches both small and large continued from his activity.

"That will plug them up for a time."

"And it'll cover us if we don't get out of here." Santon saw several ledges of rock that trembled as they were undercut by rock sliding down the hillside.

"We should be on horseback," complained Vered. "But we are alive. That's what matters."

"We're alive and we know where Lokenna is," added Santon. "Truly, it is *that* which matters most."

They started on foot to find the village of Fron and the other heir to the throne of Porotane.

TWENTY-TWO

"May all the demons eat you alive!" raged King Lorens. His guard commander tried not to show fear. He failed in the face of his monarch's towering wrath. "Losing them in the mine was foolish. Your squad almost had them."

"Sire, please. I have explained that. Part of the squad had been killed."

"Rock worms, or so you say."

"Worms," the lieutenant said, his face stony. The king might not believe the report, but it had happened. His best men had fallen to their deaths in a pit filled with metal-toothed monsters.

"The squad that found them hadn't run afoul of . . . rock worms." Lorens' tone was sarcastic. Nothing had gone right during the past two weeks. Nothing. He was surrounded by fools and worse. The incompetence of his troops turned in his gut like a rusty blade.

"They took my men by surprise. We expected only attack from the thieves, not from rock worms. Before reinforcements could arrive, the thieves had slipped through the hole and escaped."

"You've told me all this. They brought the

mountain down and crushed another four of your valiant men. Yes, yes, you've said all this. It does not explain why days have passed since these catastrophes and you have still not found their spoor."

"Winter winds blow off the Yorral Mountains, Sire," the lieutenant said. "Their trail is covered by thin snow. Even worse, my finest trackers perished within the mine."

"Excuses. All you offer is more reason for me to question your ability to lead my elite guards!" Lorens' voice almost cracked with strain.

"Sire, if you could again conjure for us. Your tracking spell—the phosphorescent footprints—could lead us to them quickly. You are a wizard without peer. Conjure for us and we will fight to the death!" The lieutenant wanted to spit out the bad taste forming in his mouth from these lying words, but he saw his king's anger and had to turn it aside. Lorens had become more vicious with every setback—and he took out his rage on innocent guardsmen.

Lorens did not answer immediately. He dared not tell the officer that he had tried to again conjure the Spell of the Ten Trackers. Each casting had been weaker than the prior one. Something or someone blocked his every attempt to cast *any* spell.

Lorens wondered if this was some subtle revenge brought down on his head by the Wizard of Storms. Destroying the five storm warriors had required both skill and daring, but he had not been able to properly form a spell since then. It was as if his powers drained daily, leaving him weaker both physically and emotionally.

Lorens hid the tears forming in his eyes. It

would not do to let his lieutenant see his weakness. The soldier already hated and feared him. This combination made for more efficient service—as long as the ruler was strong enough to use it. Lorens had begun to doubt himself and, as a result, felt his ability to command slipping away.

Everything would have been different if those two ruffians hadn't stolen the Demon Crown. His hands rubbed along his temples where the potent magical crown had once rested. How easy it would be for him to rule Porotane with it. Simply cast forth his senses and *know* what others did and said, even in their most private moments. That was the source of true power.

Lorens pulled his long, thin cloak around his body as the cold mountain wind tried to snap it away. Winter would soon blanket the upper peaks and begin creeping down. He had less than a month before even Claymore Pass closed with heavy wet snows drifted higher than the spires of his castle.

Lorens continued rubbing his temples, as if this would return the Demon Crown to its former resting place. Nothing had gone right. Nothing. His personal guard had been reduced by half. Those the storm warriors had not slaughtered had perished within the old fortified mine.

Rock worms. Superior fighters. Lorens believed none of it. His guard commander lied to cover his own incompetence.

If he only had the Demon Crown he would know!

A commotion from the camp perimeter brought Lorens around. He frowned when a figure bundled in rags was brought before him.

"Sire, he claims to be your servant."

"I have no servants with me." Lorens scowled at the groveling figure dressed in brown and black motley. The man did appear familiar, but Lorens did not recognize him. He had left all his servants in the castle.

Lorens' lips sneered. The double he had placed on the throne enjoyed all the benefits of the monarchy, while the true king suffered the elements and outrageous fortune in the field.

A grimy face tipped up. "Mighty King Lorens, how is it you cannot remember your jester Harhar?"

"Harhar?" Lorens stared in disbelief at the fool. "It is you. But how did you find me? Why did you leave the castle?"

"It is under siege, Májesty. Theoll sits half-assed on the throne after assassinating Archbishop Nosto. And Lady Anneshoria shares the other half of the throne with Theoll. Together they duel and rule, and they are cruel to this fool, O my king!"

"What are you saying? How did you know I was gone from the castle?" Lorens glanced over at his guard commander. The officer stood impassively but Lorens detected the undercurrent of interest. Had the officer betrayed him? Few had known that he placed a double on the throne. The commander of his personal guard had been one.

Harhar huddled against the wind, his tattered clothing doing little to protect his thin body. Lorens made no effort to help him. All he wanted was information.

"How did you learn that I had left Castle Porotane?"

Efran Gaemock, speaking once more as

Harhar, related all that had happened, leaving out only the part about Anneshoria making it appear as if he had murdered Archbishop Nosto.

"Those traitors," whined Lorens. "How dare they do this to me? It's not fair!"

"No, Sire, it isn't. But what has brought you so far into the Yorral Mountains? And why did you not know of these terrible things happening in the castle?" Efran studied the guard commander, not Lorens, for the truth. From the stiffness in the officer's posture and the fleeting emotions of disgust and fear, Efran guessed that they had been unable to recover the Demon Crown. If Vered and Birtle Santon had stolen it, they remained free with it.

Efran's opinion of the two rogues rose.

And a new plot formed in his fertile brain. His brother and Dalziel Sef had failed to intercept Lorens as the king raced north on the mission to find the crown. Sef had been unwilling to commit more than a handful of troops to a hunt of the Yorral Mountains when so many were needed to keep the siege of the castle in place against constant forays by cavalry. Dews had agreed and, reluctantly, Efran did, too. Now the situation had changed. Lorens' forces were decimated by . . . what?

Efran would have to find out what had reduced the ranks of the palace guard to such an extent. Two ruffians had not done it. With ample reinforcements, the rebels could seize Lorens and force him to abdicate. And the Demon Crown might even be found.

The two main symbols of power in Porotane would be under rebel control. Efran knew the effect on the populace and the nobility. The civil war would end.

Efran frowned. The war between rebels and royalists would end, but the war between Dalziel Sef and the Gaemocks would begin. Efran did not have to conjure a spell to know that Sef wanted the throne for himself. All either of the brothers desired was stable and just rule.

"Find them. Find them and get me back the crown!" whimpered Lorens.

Efran blinked. The tone used by the king showed him to be nearing the limits of his control. Defeating a man such as this would take even fewer troops than he'd anticipated.

"Find them," muttered Lorens, wandering off. The commander of his personal guard hurried off, leaving the jester huddled in the snow. A smile crept across Efran's lips. It would be only a matter of time before he sent a message to his brother.

Dews Gaemock would capture the King of Porotane and end the war that had ravaged the country for too many decades.

"What do you mean the patrol has not returned? Of course they will return." Lorens stood and shifted his weight from foot to foot. His expression was not that of a confident ruler. His indecision radiated like the warmth of a fire.

"They are more than two days overdue, Sire," said the commander of the guard.

"But it's been over a week since those ruffians eluded us in the mine. How can this be?"

"I fear the patrol has deserted, Sire."

Efran cocked his head to one side. He had been telling bad jokes to cheer Lorens when the commander had entered the drafty tent with his report. This news cheered Efran greatly. He had released a message-carrying spite-wren upon learning of Lorens' bad luck. A day of flight had gotten the message to Dews. Another day's preparation and three of hard riding would bring a fighting force to the perimeter of the king's camp.

Dews Gaemock might have encountered the patrol and dispatched them. Efran gloated. The end for this petty tyrant neared.

"Deserted? Impossible. No coward dares leave the service of his king!"

"There is another possibility, Sire. Brigands still roam these hills. Ionia's forces are reputedly aligned with the rebels. She might have joined battle with our men and defeated them."

"Defeat? Never!"

"Sire," the guard commander said tiredly, "Ionia sends armies through Claymore Pass. A small patrol could never stand against such overwhelming numbers."

"It might have been the doing of the Wizard of Storms," muttered Lorens. "He hates me. He sends his storm warriors against me."

Efran listened closely. He had not been able to get a decent report from any of the guardsmen about that day when the five cloud-bodied demons had attacked. He hardly believed that Lorens had driven such powerful magical creatures off with spells of his own conjuring, but none denied it. What would the reclusive Wizard of Storms want from a petty tyrant like Lorens?

Even as the thought crossed his mind, Efran knew. The Wizard of Storms sought the Demon Crown. No other bait could lure the wizard from his mountain fastness. Had the Wizard of Storms already captured the crown? If he had destroyed the patrol, why hadn't he also destroyed the main force? Efran Gaemock did not think the wizard was likely to toy with Lorens, especially if the young king had vanquished five storm warriors.

Efran decided that the Wizard of Storms did not move against Lorens—yet. The loss of the patrol had little to do with the wizard. Desertion was a distinct possibility. Sudden storms might have trapped them in the higher passes. Even Birtle Santon and Vered might have killed the soldiers. Did one of them wear the Demon Crown? Efran worried more and more about that.

He and his brother fought to keep one tyrant using the Demon Crown off the throne. Efran did not want to work against another.

"Sire, there is a signal from the mouth of the southernmost canyon."

"The patrol!"

"No, Sire," said the lieutenant. "They would return from the east. These are unidentified riders."

"Ionia's troops?"

Even as the question passed Lorens' lips, the cry from the most distant sentry rolled through the camp. "Rebel forces! Dews Gaemock's soldiers!"

King Lorens and his guard commander flew from the tent. Efran waited a few minutes to be sure that no one returned unexpectedly, then examined the detail maps the king had spread on a low table. The canyons were marked with tiny dots showing the positions of the sentries. Efran hastily duplicated the map on a sheet of thin paper, then folded it and put it into his pocket.

The officer knew his tactics well. Dews would fight long and hard, even against the few remaining soldiers in the camp, if he did not learn soon of the enemy disposition. Efran ducked outside the king's tent and caught the full bite of a winter gust in his face. Squinting, hot tears burning against his frostbitten cheeks, he made his way against the incipient blizzard to where he kept the pitiful bedroll they had given him.

In the center of the blanket something moved. He reached in and pulled out a second spite-wren. The small bird shivered against the wintry weather.

"You'll soon be warm and fed, my little friend," Efran soothed. He stroked the small brown bird's red-tinged topknot as he affixed the map to the bird's leg. "Fly quickly to your mate. She awaits you with my brother."

The bird seemed to stagger. As it took wing, a gust of wind caught it. The tiny brown spite-wren beat its wings faster and blended in with the blowing white snow.

Efran turned to pull the threadbare blanket around his shoulders and found a pair of boots. He looked up until he came to the lieutenant's glowering visage.

"A good day to you, Commander."

"I'd wondered about you, fool. At times you seemed too alert, but I never knew. Until now. What message did the bird carry to the rebels?"

"Why, nothing. I just lost my dinner. Such a tiny thing, but fresh fowl is—" Efran's hand reached into the folds of his motley and found the handle of a tiny dagger. As he spoke he moved so that his thrust would be accurate.

He used the full power of his legs to drive

upward, the dagger aimed for the officer's heart. The lieutenant jerked back and stumbled; Efran missed his target and the knife point skittered along the front of the man's uniform. A ragged gash appeared and turned bloody, but the officer began shouting for help from his comrades.

Efran's hand clamped over the man's mouth. The dagger struck downward, seeking a more deadly berth than it had found before. The commander fought but he had not expected Efran's strength, skill, or swiftness. He had faced a jester whom he had thought a spy.

He had found a warrior—and death.

Blood sizzled and hissed as it drained from the lieutenant's neck into the snow. Efran Gaemock rose, gore-covered blade in hand. No one had seen him kill the officer. He wiped off the dagger and went to find King Lorens.

The swirling snow blowing down off the heights obscured the battlefield. Efran tried to make out the struggling figures and finally gave up. He had to believe that the bird had faithfully carried its message to Dews and that his brother had used the information to get past the king's guard. There wasn't any other way the rebels could have penetrated this quickly into the heart of the camp.

"King Lorens, where are you?" Efran called. Only howling wind and death cries reached him. He blundered through the blinding wet snow, then recoiled when a phantom fluttered past. Was this from a recently slain soldier or had it lingered for years in the pass? Efran did not stop to inquire.

In the tent once more, he brushed off the snow and looked for the king.

"Not here." Efran started to go back into the increasingly inclement weather, then stopped. Let Lorens come to him. He could wait in relative warmth and comfort. He sat down, dagger in hand, and stared at the tent flap as it snapped in the wind.

A dark figure appeared, silhouetted against the blowing snow. Efran caught his breath and held it. His hand tightened on his dagger as he waited to confront Lorens.

The flap jerked back and the figure entered. Efran sank back into the chair and sighed. "You can get yourself killed doing that, Dews."

"Efran! I found you!"

"You make it sound as if I'd been lost."

"We've taken the camp. Your map led us past their strongest points. The flank commanders tell me that Lorens' soldiers are in rout. They're running for their lives."

"What of Lorens?"

"I'd hoped to find him here." Dews sat beside his brother. "We'll scour the camp. He can't get far in this weather."

"I want him alive. We can use him as a lever to force the castle's surrender."

"What? Why would Theoll surrender because we hold the king? Or Anneshoria? She is even worse than the baron. They'd drive a knife into his back faster than I would!"

"The countryside still lends some small support to a king of the royal line. If the people give up the fight, the castle will fall."

"Aye, convincing the people that I'm not just another power-hungry tyrant seeking the throne has been hard."

"Allying with Dalziel Sef has made it even more difficult, I'd wager," said Efran.

"The truth is, I had no desire to leave him in command of the siege, but I did not think that Theoll would surrender easily."

"I'm glad you came personally."

"The crown?" asked Dews. "Had Lorens recovered it?"

"No."

The brothers sank into silence. Occasional loud clanks of steel against steel died and were replaced by the howling wind off the Yorral Mountains.

Ten minutes later, a rebel forced his way into the tent, barely able to stand against the wind. "Dews, we're in control. Everyone has surrendered. Do we put them to death?"

"No!" both Efran and Dews shouted simultaneously. Dews motioned his brother to silence. "We need their support, not their death. Treat them well and try to see that they don't freeze—but don't coddle them, either. They're not the enemy, but they are our prisoners."

"What of Lorens?" asked Efran. "Did you find him?"

The rebel shook his head. "Nowhere to be found. We'll keep looking, but the storm's getting worse. Some of the men're saying that the Wizard of Storms sent it to bedevil us."

"Keep looking for Lorens," ordered Dews.

Efran stared into the white wall just beyond the tent opening. Were they right? Did the Wizard of Storms send this as a warning?

He shook off the notion. They had achieved a great victory this day. Lorens had been routed —and he would be found soon and put into chains. Dead or alive, it did not matter. The petty tyrant would never again sit on Porotane's throne.

Efran Gaemock just wished that he could feel more positive about this victory.

TWENTY-THREE

"I don't need to ride. I don't *want* to. My ass is getting sore. You ride for a while, Vered." Birtle Santon shifted on the horse and glared at his friend. Vered walked a dozen paces ahead. He stopped and turned, shaking his head.

"You still haven't fully recovered."

"It's been more than a week since we buried Lorens in the mine."

"Buried? Trapped is more likely. Inconvenienced is most likely of all."

Santon grumbled and cursed under his breath. Vered spoke the truth. Even if their small avalanche had buried one or two guardsmen, the rest remained unscathed within the mine-fortress. All they had done was force Lorens to retreat, find another way from the mine and continue the hunt for them.

In that, Santon reflected, they had been lucky. They had come out of the fortress in an inaccessible valley. Lorens would lose days finding them. Or perhaps he had lost them totally. Santon could hope, even if he did not truly believe this.

Finding the horse wandering riderless had been another stroke of fortune for them. But

Santon felt whole again. He need not be treated like an invalid and given special privileges when his friend was obviously tired of hiking. An occasional throbbing in his head was the only remaining trace of his infection. Even the gash had begun to heal, although it looked as if it would leave a ragged white scar.

"The wind's getting colder," complained Vered.

"All the more reason for you to ride and let me walk. Save yourself for the steep passes."

"Steeper than this one?" Vered shook his head in amazement. They had crossed Claymore Pass' main track and headed south by west down a miserable rut of a path. Every notch in the mountains had seemed higher than the last, especially to a man walking.

"I cannot remember the village Ruirik mentioned, but it may be a new one. Fron is not a name to forget."

"Nor is it one to remember," said Vered. He turned and pulled his cloak tighter around his body. The wind caught the rents and further destroyed the garment. He finally gave up and continued the slow climb into still another rocky pass.

"It will be if he spoke the truth. Lokenna awaits us. I feel it," said Santon.

"Your hot air doesn't reach this far. Come closer before gusting out your fantasies."

Santon chuckled. Vered had been in a morose mood of late, in spite of their good fortune. A week without sighting Lorens' guard, almost a week of travel with this fine horse carrying a considerable burden, the end of their quest known. What more could he want?

"The storms worsen. We should find shelter for the night," said Vered.

"Winter comes quickly in the Yorral Mountains."

"This is a strange storm. It centers on the peaks to either side of the road, if any dares call this stony rut a road."

Santon turned in the saddle and looked at the far-flung peaks in the mountain range. Vered's sharp eyes had again found what he had missed. A few of the loftiest purple-cloaked mountains sported a fluffy white crown of clouds. Most were sharp and clear in the pure autumn air. Only the two ahead of them drew the full wrath of a storm.

As Santon watched, the violence locked within the thunder clouds burst forth. Lightning shattered pieces of rock from either side of the pass and sent boulders tumbling down to block their path. Black tendrils began to dip from the underbelly of the storm, turbulent and billowing with unnatural life.

"We ought to take cover now," said Santon. "It might do us no good. That storm." He swallowed, his mouth suddenly dry. "That is another of the gifts sent us by the Wizard of Storms."

"May all the demons take him and devour his flesh!" cursed Vered. He reached out and caught the horse's reins as Santon passed him. Vered led the horse to the side of the road where a scrubby mountain copperwood grew. Santon swung from the saddle and landed heavily. His legs yielded under the strain and he began to doubt himself.

While he rode, he felt fine. The slight exertion of dismounting robbed him of his strength. As much as he hated to admit it, Vered was right. He had yet to recover fully from the fever.

"Tether the horse. We should go scouting,"

Santon said. He flexed his right arm and rejoiced in the power there. His left carried the glass shield as if it were nothing more than a feather. But his legs! They worked like lead weights, numb and ponderous.

He and Vered worked their way up the hillside, reaching the crest and peering down into a small ravine. The trailing wisps of dark cloud touched not a hundred paces from them.

"The saints have blessed us with luck," whispered Vered. "We would have ridden into them if we hadn't seen the storm cloud."

A half dozen of Lorens' guardsmen had prepared an ambush on the trail. Their trap turned against them. The pillar of cloud stuff began to swirl and turn and whip about, sending out small fist-sized clouds randomly. Each of the tiny clouds sprouted arms and legs and a head with eyes blazing red hate.

"Storm warriors. The Wizard of Storms has sent his minions after us!"

"Or against Lorens. The magical warriors attack the guardsmen, not us."

Santon watched in mute fascination as the storm warriors took form and moved to attack the human soldiers. The patrol leader had positioned his men to command the road; they were cut off from their horses. The men fought valiantly but the lightning bolts caught them if they attacked, cut them down if they ran, and blew apart their hiding places if they did not move.

In less than a minute only smoldering bodies remained. The individual storm warriors lifted their arms and sent down a torrential rain that diminished them. When only tiny puffs of cloud were left, these were sucked back up into the thunder cloud above. The only evidence of battle lay with the victims.

"Can the cloud sense us?" wondered Vered. He craned his head back and peered at the peaks above them.

"The Wizard of Storms directs his army in some fashion. That was not an accidental attack."

"A wizard never works by chance alone," agreed Vered. He shifted and looked around, waiting to see if more of Lorens' soldiers appeared.

"The Wizard of Storms must want the crown," said Santon. "But can he use scrying spells to find it?"

"Let's hope not or the cloud will rain down on us. What should we do? Continue or turn back? I'm not in favor of staying here—not with *that* over our heads."

Santon stared at the underside of the black cloud and had to admit his own rising fear of it. He could best any man in single combat. With shield and ax—or even the puny sword he still carried—he feared no one. But wizards fought with weapons both unseen and unstoppable and all the more fearsome because of that.

"We ride on. With luck, we can pick up spare horses and ride the faster."

"Agreed." Vered already dashed forth, intent on the small corral the soldiers had fashioned for their mounts. Vered took the three sturdiest and fashioned travel packs from the provisions the soldiers would no longer need. By the time he finished, Santon had ridden up on the rapidly tiring animal that had served them so well during the past week.

"We can't leave the mare," said Santon.

"Didn't intend to," answered his friend. "Dismount and ride this one. We'll use your mare as a spare. We ride till one tires, then switch. That ought to get us into Fron before *we* tire."

"Too late," said Santon.

"And you were the one who was all healed," said Vered as he swung up and settled into the saddle. "This is a fine mount. Only the best for the king's guard—and us!"

With that he put his heels into the horse's flanks and turned the gelding uphill toward the pass.

The rest of the day they rode, stopping only to change horses every hour. By nightfall, they came to the top of the pass and looked down into a small lushly green valley still protected from the winter gusts they had fought.

"A lovely place," said Santon. "But is it Fron?"

"There is no way to tell from here. Down to the village and inquire, though it must be Fron. How many villages can there be in this remote area?"

Vered turned, straightened in the saddle, and asked of Santon, "Do you feel it, too?"

Santon nodded. His heart beat more rapidly and he had the eerie feeling of being on the brink of a great and wondrous discovery. The only sensation comparable in his life was when he had seen Alarice for the first time. He had known there was something special about the white-haired Glass Warrior.

There was something special about Fron— and it came from goodness, not evil.

They rode slowly into the village. A few men, going home from a day preparing their fields for winter, waved and hailed them. They returned the greetings but did not stop until they came to a small inn.

"I need ale," said Vered. "I need more than

that, but I'll start with ale," he amended hastily as he dismounted.

Santon held the rucksack containing the Demon Crown. The green glow had changed subtly. Before, after Lorens had worn it, the green had been that of corrosion and corruption. The hue had become brighter, purer, and in some fashion he could not put words to, *cleaner*.

"We should find Lokenna."

"Santon, you'll be the death of me. She has lived here for almost twenty years. Do you think she will run off on the very day we arrive? A few minutes to relieve our trail-thirst is all I'm asking."

"Very well." Santon climbed down, stiff but not as weak as he had been earlier. He tucked the rucksack under his left arm and followed Vered into the small tavern.

A burly man scowled at them as they entered. He called from behind the small, well-kept, and polished bar, "What's your pleasure?"

"Ale. Four mugs to start."

"There's more of you coming?" the man asked, his scowl deepening.

"Only the pair of us," said Vered, "but our thirst is greater than any two men's!"

Santon dropped the rucksack behind him on the floor to concentrate on the ale brought over by the innkeeper. He drank deeply and savored its fine malty taste as it slid smoothly down his gullet. "Good ale," he complimented.

"Make it myself."

"Excellent," agreed Vered. He finished his first and began to drink the second when he stopped and slowly lowered the flagon.

Santon turned to see what caught his friend's interest. He smiled broadly. Vered had good taste in women. Neatly dressed in a simple peasant blouse and green skirt, she was tall, lithe, and lovely. A bit too tall for his taste and much too thin, but still possessed of an inner radiance that outshone mere physical considerations.

"My wife," the innkeeper said, as if daring them to dispute it. Under different circumstances, Vered might have. How an ugly ape of a man like the tavern owner could marry such a fine woman would have provoked hours of hot debate—and fights.

"Can we have two more?" called out Vered, more intent on his drinking than the apparent mismating.

"Bring the empties over," said the innkeeper. "And the wife'll get you some food. You have the look of being on the trail all day. Travel in autumn makes you hungrier than any other time of the year."

"And then some. Thank you, good sir."

Vered returned with the foamy flagons as the woman placed a platter of cold cuts and a small loaf of bread on the table.

"I hope you enjoy this as much as you have the ale," she said. Santon stared at her openly now, wondering at such beauty in this hidden mountain village.

"If you've prepared it, I'm sure it will be splendid," said Vered, his eyes bold on the firm swell of her blouse and the trimness of her waist.

"A flatterer. I've been warned about men like you," she said, her smile robbing it of any disapproval.

Santon reached for the meat and bread, deftly cutting a slice of bread with his dagger before using the tip to flip the meat onto it. He stuck the dagger in the wood table and picked up the bread and meat when the woman passed behind him.

"Hold there!" he ordered. "Don't—" His words cut off in mid-sentence as the woman opened the rucksack and took out the glass box containing the Demon Crown.

The green glow almost blinded him.

"So pretty. May I touch it?"

She took the crown from the box and held it. She wobbled slightly, then smiled. "It is unlike anything I've ever seen."

"It's yours, Lokenna."

"What?" She turned and stared at him in astonishment. "How did you know my name?"

Santon and Vered exchanged looks. Their quest had ended. They had found the second royal twin.

"The Demon Crown is the property of the rightful heir to the throne of Porotane."

"But I . . ."

"Let us be the first to pledge our fealty, Queen Lokenna."

Unbidden, Lokenna placed the Demon Crown on her head. The glow filled the room with gentle light and Birtle Santon's heart with gladness. With Lokenna he felt the crown had found its proper owner.

A SYMPHONY OF STORMS

*This one is for Patty and
double rainbows*

CHAPTER ONE

Birtle Santon rubbed his withered left arm with his good hand and then drew his cloak around his body. The cold wintery winds whipping through the passes of the Yorral Mountains and sneaking into the pub where he sat sucked the warmth from him and made his joints ache. He was getting too old for this kind of adventuring.

The sight of the young woman across the room warmed him more than the cloak or the feeble fire guttering in the fireplace. She glowed with a beauty that made his heart pound fiercely. Her every movement was draped in grace and doelike litheness. Most of all she held the Demon Crown in her long-fingered hands and caused the diabolical device to shine with an emerald green that invigorated rather than enervated.

"A lovely sight, isn't it?" asked Santon's young

1

friend, Vered. The man's light brown hair had been blown into disarray, giving him a wild and dangerous look. The reflected gleam of the Demon Crown in his brown eyes caused Santon to sit a little straighter on the hard wooden bench and worry that much more.

"What is lovely?" he asked softly. "The woman or the crown?"

"Both," came Vered's answer. He laughed and slapped Santon on his good right shoulder. "Fear naught, dear friend. The crown is not seducing me. Oh, yes, I wish I could wear it. Damn the drop of royal blood flowing in my veins!"

"You miss its power."

"Aye, that I do," admitted Vered. "But the crown has found its rightful owner. She is Lokenna, daughter of King Lamost and heir to the throne of Porotane. There can be no question of that." Santon did not miss the wistfulness in Vered's voice. He *did* want the crown for his own.

"Titles mean nothing when dealing with magic of this order. You were unable to keep the crown from twisting you about. Can she prevent it or will she fall prey to its insidious call?" Santon knew this was no simple question. Lokenna had proven royal blood flowed in her veins; any commoner touching the Demon Crown died instantly. Santon considered this merciful. A member of the royal family wearing the crown became the focus of imponderable magic, power beyond belief, a weight too great to bear if the wearer showed any weakness.

Lokenna's twin, Lorens, had donned the crown and been broken by it. Would sister prove stronger than brother? Santon did not know. On that answer lay the destiny of the kingdom.

"What is all this madness about?" bellowed
Bane Pandasso. "These two freebooters come
dancing in here sweet as you please and give you
this geegaw. Return it to them and get back to
work." The burly man reached out to touch the
Demon Crown. A sizzling spark of the purest green
arched over to his fingertips. He yelped and
backed off, sticking thick fingers in his mouth to
soothe the burn.

"Do not attempt to touch the crown," Santon
called. "It cannot be taken from your . . . wife."
The word caught in his throat. Seeing such a
lovely young woman married to a brute with
heavy eyebrows wiggling like woolly caterpillars
on bony ridges, a nose that had been broken too
many times, pig eyes, a perpetual scowl, and a disposition to match his facial ugliness offended Santon. From the nervous stirrings of his friend,
Santon knew that Vered's thoughts wandered
down a similar path.

"He is good to me," Lokenna said, as if reading their minds. She sat between them, cradling
the glowing crown in her hands. The ancient magical relic radiated a pure light unlike anything
they had seen before. On Lorens' brow, it had produced a green the color of corroded copper. A
mere glance had convinced anyone with sensibil-
ity that evil was afoot.

No longer. Santon relaxed in the light bathing
him and knew that the Demon Crown could be
turned to benefit rather than destruction. With the
young woman he felt more at peace than he had
at any other time since . . . Alarice had died.

Birtle Santon's thoughts turned to the Glass
Warrior, the woman with hair of spun moonbeams, a beauty without peer. Tears beaded at the

corners of his green eyes. He moved quickly to dab at the betraying droplets, but no one had seen this momentary weakness. Through the years of wandering Porotane he had found few women who affected him as strongly as Alarice.

She had been a warrior, a redoubtable wizard, a woman whose concern for the citizens of Porotane had led to her death. For almost two decades she had been entrusted with the Demon Crown. When Duke Freow lay dying, he had summoned her and sent her on a mission that would never be finished in the usurping noble's lifetime. Freow had been interred before Alarice had reached the Desert of Sazan to seek out the true heir to the throne.

Santon remembered her fighting the master wizard Patrin for Lorens' freedom. What a waste! Santon spat at the memory of Lorens. Lovely, courageous Alarice had died to place the youngling's worthless arse upon the throne of Porotane. He had misused the Demon Crown and plunged the kingdom into a civil war so intense that it beggared description.

"Do not mourn me, dear Birtle," came the whisper from outside. "I died so that the kingdom might prosper."

Santon jerked around, his withered left arm knocking the glass shield that Alarice had given him to the floor. The noise alerted Vered, whose hand shot to his dagger hilt.

"What's wrong?" Vered demanded.

Santon peered through the dirty pane of glass set into the wall. Outside a new winter storm raged, whipping up snow pellets and dirty rain.

"Nothing. Just the wind."

"There's more," pressed Vered. He moved

closer to his friend. "Did you see her again? Alarice?"

"I . . . I don't know. Perhaps."

"Does she approve of Lokenna?"

"It might have been a trick of the wind. Yes, a gust coming through the walls. Pandasso is not a good carpenter. Can you feel the draft, too?"

"Aye, that I can." Vered looked closely at Santon, then moved back to where he could talk quietly with Lokenna. Santon cast one last lingering look outside. Alarice's phantom had appeared to him several times before, but not now. Not this time.

He was not certain if that was good. He wanted to see her again, even if it was only her tortured phantom. The magics unleashed by Patrin in the battle of spells had prevented him and Vered from properly burying her. The Glass Warrior's body lay in the sand, her phantom roaming endlessly, seeking surcease and not finding it.

Selfishly, he wanted her to remain beside him, but his love—and pain—was greater. She had helped them find Lokenna. He would return to the Desert of Sazan, find her corpse, and give it the proper burial. It was the least he could do for a true heroine.

"I told you to get this pigsty cleaned up, woman!" Bane Pandasso stormed about, knocking over pewter goblets, breaking ceramic plates, spilling ale, and making twice the mess that had been this sorry inn's legacy when Santon and Vered had entered.

Santon motioned Vered to silence. The younger man's temper knew few bounds. Santon cleared his throat and said loud enough to be heard over the whine of the wind. "That is past. Lokenna must return immediately to the castle."

"What for?" Pandasso lumbered over, his long arms swinging like an arboreal animal's limbs. "She's my wife. She does what I say."

"She is Queen of Porotane."

"Please, I'll clean up. Bane is right. There is work to do." Lokenna gingerly placed the crown on the table. Its vibrant glow faded slightly but remained at a higher level than either of the adventurers had seen before.

Santon shook his head sadly. Things would change. He knew it by the way Lokenna touched the crown—and the way it responded favorably to her. Beside him, Vered heaved a deep sigh. He, too, understood what had yet to occur to Lokenna and her brutish husband.

"We should tend to the horses," said Santon. "The winds blow colder by the minute."

"I've had my fill of weather. How can anyone survive in this miserable place, much less prosper?" Vered looked around the shabby inn and added, "If this can be called prospering."

"The village of Fron is not the place one expects to find a queen," agreed Santon. "Only this isolation has kept her away from the madness gripping Porotane."

"We should ask how she eluded the wizard who kidnapped her. Lorens ended up the wizards's apprentice. What of Lokenna?"

"Is that to say you find this place less appealing than the City of Stolen Dreams?" Santon could not hold back a shudder of dread at the mention of Patrin's city and the horrors magically stored within its boundaries. Alarice had died there—and only her sacrifice had allowed him and Vered to continue their miserable lives.

"Fron has a certain charm. The war has left the village unscathed. There is no hint of starvation. Remember the coast?" Santon immediately regretted this riposte. Vered's handsome face turned to stone and a small muscle at the corner of his mouth began to twitch. The ebb and flow of the civil war had taken Vered's family—and had given him life, if Santon's suppositions were accurate. The drop of royal blood flowing in Vered's veins that allowed him to briefly touch the Demon Crown had not come from a common fisherman. Santon thought that a conquering noble had taken his pleasure with Vered's mother and left behind a bastard son.

"Lorens' soldiers might still haunt these passes," Vered said abruptly. "We should backtrack to be sure we have not been followed."

"We have left them behind. All that roam these mountains tonight are phantoms."

Santon stared out the filthy window once more in the wan hope of seeing Alarice's phantom fluttering past. He saw only swirls of white snow and a deepening storm.

He heaved himself to his feet and settled the glass shield on his withered arm before pulling the cloak tightly around him. He motioned to Vered and left the inn without a backward glance. Lokenna and her husband stood nose to nose in the kitchen arguing. It did not take a wizard of any ability to know what caused this disagreement. The woman had touched the Demon Crown. For her there could be no turning back.

Santon dropped chin to chest to keep out the cold fingers of winter trying to strangle him. His exposed skin rippled with gooseflesh, and the strong wind coming from the high peaks ripped at his cloak and made it seem inconsequential against the cold.

"There," came Vered's voice. "There are the horses. They've come loose from the hitching rail. Stupid animals should know better than to wander off in this storm."

Santon held out the shield and restrained the impetuous Vered. He had survived many years of conflict and treachery by listening to his inner voice. That voice now rose to a scream.

A deft flick of his wrist brought a heavy war ax swinging about on its thong. Vered bobbed his head in agreement. He drew the glass short sword Alarice had given him and slipped into the storm's white shroud. Santon waited a moment, then moved in the opposite direction. Lorens' soldiers had fought bitterly trying to regain the crown for their king. Lorens himself had arrived and shown startling magical ability. And what of others? Santon guessed that the bands of brigands preying on travellers in the Yorral Mountains came and went through Fron unhindered by the fearful locals.

Worst of all might be the rebels led by the likes of Dews Gaemock and Dalziel Sef. Although Santon's sentiments rode with Gaemock more than with Lorens, on a battlefield it was difficult to tell friend from foe—and with the Demon Crown as prize, betrayal would come all too easily.

Santon tossed his head and got his thinning hair out of his eyes. The snow pellets melted on his forehead and plastered down the hair where it lay. He ignored this. His every sense reached out. The crunch of heavy boots on the icy crust of snow alerted him to another's presence.

Crouching low, he moved with no more sound that a snowflake falling into a soft wet drift. Santon had barely recovered from an infected cut to his forehead and every joint in his body ached from the cold and travel. All that misery vanished and he became once more the deadly fighter of yore.

He came upon the man lying in ambush. Santon judged the distance, noted that he was attacking from behind, and, giving the man no chance to respond, then swung his ax in a short, vicious arc. The heavy, battle-nicked blade met the would-be ambusher's neck at the shoulder. He grunted, tried to stand and turn. Only then did he feel the full impact of the deadly cleaver. He turned slowly and sank into the snow. The hot blood gushing from the cut sizzled as it heated the frozen crust of the snowbank. Santon paid the fallen man no attention. One enemy lay dead.

He had no idea how many more would die before he could again rest easily.

A shout alerted him that Vered had found a worthy opponent. Santon hesitated, worrying about his impetuous friend. He shrugged it off. Let the youngling have his day. He had proven himself a staunch fighter over and over. Santon doubted they would find any in the Yorral Mountains who could stand against their skill and daring.

He circled, his clear green eyes roving, ever-watchful for attack. Even with such alertness, his ears gave warning before his eyes. He dropped to one knee, shoved out the glass shield, and deflected a sword slash from the rear. He pivoted on his knee, grinding it into the frozen ground as he brought his heavy ax around in a circle parallel to the ground and knee-high.

He grunted when the blade struck an armored thigh. Then the air was filled with screeches of pain as his adversary realized that his left leg had been cut to the bone. Santon gave the man no time to regain his wits. Lowering his shield, he shoved hard and bowled over the swordsman. The ax handle rose and fell, smashing the man's skull.

"Two," Santon said softly, panting, his breath turning to silvery plumes in the frigid air. "How many more?"

He continued his hunt and found three slain foe. He dropped the ax and let it dangle from its thong when he saw Vered sitting cross-legged on the hitching rail and daintily cleaning his glass sword.

"I do not understand the magic spells Alarice used to fashion this blade," Vered said, "but it has served me well this day."

"Three?" asked Santon.

"And two for you," answered Vered. "I have taken the liberty of examining the pouches of those I felled."

"And? What did you find besides a few paltry coins?" Santon joined his friend in cleaning his weapon. Now that the battle had ended, a heavy weight descended on his shoulders, turning him once more into a man pushed beyond his limits.

Vered looked at him in concern but said nothing about Santon's paleness. "A few gold coins among the lot, true," the brown-haired man said, "but also a strange document that authorizes these brigands to call themselves friend with Dalziel Sef's rebels."

Santon took the torn and heavily creased parchment and slowly read it. "A letter of marque granted by Sef," he said in astonishment. "I have never heard of such a thing."

"A license to steal, and to do it in the name of the rebels," said Vered. He pointed with the tip of his sword. "Actually, they are allowed to steal in the name of the future monarch of Porotane, good king Dalziel."

"He flatters himself."

Vered shrugged. "Who can say what happens in the land? Lorens' power is broken. We stole away the Demon Crown and robbed him of the only link he had to the throne. The pretender Duke Freow is dead. Between Dalziel Sef and Gaemock might lie bad blood. If they fight for the throne, who's to name the victor?"

"The true queen is there." Santon indicated the dilapidated inn with the edge of his shield.

"If unrest in the land extends even to pitiful Fron, we had better convince Lokenna to return quickly. Porotane cannot stand more of this vicious civil strife. What has raged for so long has almost broken the people's will to live."

A chilly blast of frigid wind blew down the pass and whipped Santon's cape like a garrison banner. He stared through the vee-notch of the pass and fancied he saw all the way to the Wizard of Storms' castle hidden away above the Uvain Plateau.

They found brigands and rebels with steel and glass. What weapons did a wizard use to conquer Porotane?

"Aye, let's see if Lokenna has convinced that

pig of a husband that she belongs on a throne and not in a scullery."

Santon threaded his way through the rapidly cooling corpses and caught the reins of their horses. The animals shied and tried to bolt, but the brigands had securely fastened the reins to a post hidden under the snow. Santon fumbled using his single good hand until Vered assisted him. They led the horses back to the inn and around to a small stable where they tended to grooming until their hands threatened to turn to ice.

"I'm for another mug of ale, even if it is thin and watery," said Vered. He tossed a small pouch into the air and caught it handily. "We have enough money to live on for some time, compliments of our clumsy ambushers."

"We were lucky. Less suspicious men would have gone directly after the horses and died in the snow."

"Not us, friend Santon. We will live forever!"

Vered threw open the door to the inn and was catapulted back into Santon. A heavy club had caught him squarely on the top of his skull. The pair tumbled into the snow, more brigands rushing from the inn. Flat on their backs and weapons useless, they stared at certain death.

CHAPTER TWO

Baron Theoll looked up and down the corridor before running his nimble fingers along the wood carving of an armored knight that graced the wall. A small click sounded and a secret passage through the thick stone walls of Castle Porotane opened for him. He darted inside, rat-quick, and pulled the panel shut behind him. His heart raced. The game he played this night was a deadly one, and the slightest mistake meant his death.

On boots with carefully padded soles, he walked gingerly along the narrow passage. Other nights he would have paused to peer through the dozens of spy holes. Theoll knew the value of intelligence and information gathering. Spying on the serving girls in their quarters often gave him insight into castle alliances and new treacheries.

But tonight he passed by such salacious plea-

sures. Only when he had reached a branching corridor and slipped into this musty, unused portion
of the secret ways did he pause. Theoll cautiously
pulled back a black piece of cloth and peered
through the spy hole into Lady Anneshoria's quarters.

The sight of her undressing did nothing to
arouse his lust. Her sleek limbs had opened for
too many other nobles as she methodically worked
her way to power for Theoll to care about her. He
needed more this night—he needed to know Anneshoria's plan to assassinate him.

Theoll had heard rumors flitting about the
castle; there were always rumors. This time,
though, he had to give them credence. Anneshoria
had seized equal power when he had killed Archbishop Nosto. The cleric had foolishly mixed re-
ligion and politics—and Theoll had foolishly
permitted Anneshoria to share the throne as vice
regent to hold back the tide of indignation rising
against him.

He had made it seem that the dim-witted
jester Harhar had committed the heinous crime.
Anneshoria would have revealed the fool's part
and betrayed Theoll if he had not agreed to her
demands.

But he no longer could keep from moving
against her. For weeks they had maneuvered for
total dominance of the castle. What did the demon-
cursed woman plot? He had to know!

Theoll pressed his eye closer to the spy hole
and moved about slowly to scan the room. Another joined Anneshoria!

"Captain Squann," the woman said, barely
loud enough for Theoll to overhear. "You do me a
great honor with your presence this night."

"Lady Anneshoria, I seek only what is best for Porotane. The division of power in the castle weakens us. If we continue to fight among ourselves, the rebels will wash over us like a foul black tide."

"True," the woman said. She continued to disrobe, as if the soldier were not present. "Why do you come to me? Your ties are with Theoll. He has promoted you. You are his man."

"I am my own man," snapped Squann. He straightened his dark blue uniform jacket and touched the row of medals pinned to his breast. Theoll watched as the captain fought for control against Anneshoria's clever manipulation. "I seek only the best for the castle and the people of Porotane."

"How patriotic of you," the woman said scornfully. "No one else within these walls is so altruistic. What do you hope to gain? Would you become my consort when I depose Theoll? Ah, yes, that must be it. You like what you see now." Anneshoria pirouetted for him, naked. "You would like me the better if I were queen, wouldn't you, *Captain?*" She bore down on his rank to put him in his place.

Theoll prayed for Squann to whip out his dagger and drive it into the woman's foul heart. That would solve all the baron's problems. He could execute Squann as a traitor and need never reveal the reason for the noble lady's murder.

"Question my reasons, if you will, Lady," Squann said through clenched teeth. "I make a better ally than foe."

"No doubt, Captain," she said, softening her tone. She drifted to him, a lovely white speck carried across the room on a light summer's breeze.

Her hand reached out. Squann flinched. She tensed and caught at his cheek, drawing him closer. They kissed.

For the spying baron, time stood still. He raged and yet dared not shout. His hands clenched so hard that blood formed in the palms where fingernails cut into flesh. A big vein in his temple began to throb and hundreds of plans for revenge formed.

Theoll pulled himself back from the spectacle in Anneshoria's room. He did not wish to see them in rut. His time could be better spent consolidating his power base, finding those in the guard who hated Squann, getting promises of support from the other nobles. If he did not end this dual reign soon, the rebels would have all their heads on pikes outside the castle walls.

The diminutive baron slipped from his secret passage and into the main corridor once again. He walked quickly to his quarters, his left leg dragging slightly as old wounds made their presence felt. He massaged his arm where a sword thrust had nearly ended his life, and smiled. His disability was more feigned than real now, but he knew the value of having an enemy underestimate his prowess.

Nosto had made that mistake and he now lay in a crypt in the castle's catacombs.

He dropped into a chair behind a table strewn with papers. Theoll shuffled through them and carefully pulled out a single sheet covered with names connected by lines. The best place to hide battle plans in the castle was in plain sight. He had merely glanced toward the wall hangings concealing a spell-locked chest. Anneshoria's wizard was as adept as any Theoll could find. Small indications showed that the ward spells had been breached.

That mattered little. Theoll knew how to keep his secrets from prying eyes. He scanned the list, debating the loyalty of some and discounting others entirely. When he finished with his appraisal he vented a tiny sigh of disgust.

Squann had been his most powerful ally. Deposing Anneshoria and retaining the throne for himself would be doubly difficult without the guard captain's aid.

A tiny rap came at the door. Startled, Theoll looked up and moved worthless paper over the one detailing his coup.

"Enter," he barked. Dark eyebrows rose in surprise when Squann entered.

"Baron, I must speak with you."

Theoll eyed the soldier critically. The immaculate dress uniform now carried telltale wrinkles where Anneshoria had been less than discreet in stripping it from his broad shoulders. If he had not been watching through the spy hole, he would have assumed Squann had been on night patrol along the battlements.

He had been sheathing his sword, but Theoll knew it had nothing to do with duty.

"What is it?" Theoll tried to keep his tone neutral but a hint of his anger seeped around his words. Squann's eyes narrowed slightly.

"You know of my visit to Anneshoria this night?"

"What visit is this, Squann? Get to the point. I have much to do."

"I sought information from her, Baron. She is evil and must never rule Porotane alone. She will be worse than Lorens, even with the Demon Crown turning him down the road of madness."

"Fine words, Captain, but what do they mean to me?"

"You were watching. I know it, Baron. Nothing of importance escapes your alert eye. Anneshoria revealed her assassination plot to me."

"In the heat of fornication?" Theoll snorted in contempt. "She never loses control of her senses. What she told you was only what she wished to tell you. You pried nothing from her."

"The plan is a good one, Baron." Squann perched on the edge of the table. Theoll's hand moved toward the dagger he had sheathed at his belt. If Squann attacked, he would be greeted by cold steel.

"Please, Baron, I mean you no harm. You have done much for me when others turned away. I owe you everything and would never betray you. What I did was for you—and for the good of Porotane."

"You again beat the drum of patriotism?"

"I believe Porotane *must* have a strong ruler— soon. The kingdom will shatter into a hundred fiefdoms unless the civil war is ended and a king of great power and ability assumes the throne." Squann paused, his cold ebony eyes fixed on Theoll's. "You are such a man, Baron. Only you can unite a divided nation."

"Anneshoria offered to let you be her consort. What do you want from me in return?"

"Your trust. I know you can be generous to those who serve you well."

"Anneshoria knows of our past dealings. Why do you think she told you anything important that you wouldn't immediately reveal to me?"

Squann laughed. "I don't doubt that she mistrusts me. Her plan is a good one, though, and makes me think it is one she considered long and well."

"And?" pressed Theoll, interested in spite of his misgivings.

"She had discarded this one in favor of another. We know one route she will *not* take. That is valuable, as is some indication of the way she thinks."

Theoll leaned back and moved his hand from the sheathed dagger. He looked hard at Squann, then smiled slowly. "Porotane will need a new Marshal of Armies when I am king. Do you know where I might find a man suitable for such an exalted position, Squann?"

CHAPTER THREE

A hunting hawk swooped low, its talons dragging along the white drifts of snow. Lorens, King of Porotane, fugitive from rebels, screeched in fear and threw himself over an embankment. Hot streaks of red appeared on his back as the hawk tried to get a firm hold and lift him into the air. Lorens thrashed and screamed and lay in the frozen ravine until it became apparent that the bird of prey had left to find another, less taxing dinner.

Lorens stared into the pure blue sky framed by the razor-sharp peaks of the Yorral Mountains and laughed out loud. He laughed harder and harder until tears ran down his cheeks.

"You can never get me. Never! I am king! I am lord of all Porotane!" The tears fell from his cheeks and dropped to the crusted snow. There they froze after a brief fight with the cold.

Lorens heaved himself erect, tottered on the slick streambed, and finally wobbled along as if drunk. No man should endure what he had been through. Rebels. He cursed Dalziel Sef. The rebel had splintered what remained of his personal guard. Lorens had no idea what had become of his loyal followers and valiant soldiers.

He spat. None of this would have happened if those two worms had not stolen the Demon Crown. Shaking fingers touched his forehead where the magic crown had rested and given him limitless power. With its demon-granted magic he had been able to see anywhere in the realm.

More! He had *been* wherever he turned his magical senses. He overheard plots against him, saw troop movements, tasted the rebel's dinner, felt Sef's vile lover's caress, smelled the pungent wood smoke from campfires a hundred leagues distant, saw vistas locked away for too many centuries.

The demon Kalob had given the crown to King Waellkin three hundred years earlier as reparation for the horrors wrought on Porotane by demonic infestations. Lorens chuckled and wiped spittle from his lips. What treasure! What a prize! And it had been his!

He did not see the Demon Crown as another source of discord cast by the banished demon. All Lorens knew was the magnificent change. His entire life had been one of tedium and obedience. The tall, white-haired woman—the Glass Warrior his master had called her—had told him that he had been kidnapped when only a small child. Lorens cared little for this. He was a dutiful apprentice to the wizard Patrin and did not want to leave the City of Stolen Dreams.

He had not wanted to leave his apprenticeship until he touched the Demon Crown. Worlds opened for him—and even without the burning band around his head, some still stretched before him.

Lorens fought his way up the slippery ravine embankment and threw back his head, his shrill voice rising to challenge the heavens. "I see other worlds!"

And he did. His ringing words echoed not from lofty mountaintops but from dark and dangerous twisting corridors filled with sulphur fumes and timid beasts. Yellow eyes peered at him from the black depths. An occasional pink forked tongue slithered out and wiggled sinuously and suggestively in his direction.

Lorens laughed at them. They were powerless before him. The wedge opening their fearsome world to him lay in the Demon Crown, but he had no need of that magical device now. His power had grown. He had grown and he would use the denizens of this lava-and-volcano world as his soldiers. He would order them forth and their mere presence would cause the rebels to quake.

"When I regain the crown," Lorens muttered. His thoughts became incoherent and he drooled. "Nothing will be beyond my power." He turned to the dark world with its red-glowing lava twistings and beckoned. "Come forth, my little ones. Join me in this world and we will conquer!"

The deformed, grotesque beasts shuffled forward, talons clicking on hard rock, eyes darting and nervous.

"Come, come with me. Follow my banner and you will be rewarded! I, King Lorens of Porotane, will let you live!" He laughed harshly as the beasts recoiled. Lorens gestured. The beasts again shuffled toward him, ready to enter his world.

Lorens jerked about when a thunderclap rolled down from the uppermost reaches of the mountains. The sky remained unsullied by clouds. As lodestone draws iron, Lorens turned slowly until he saw a single lofty peak far away, looking over the Uvain Plateau. Eyes were not enough to see what came to Lorens.

"No, no, you won't rob me of this! You won't. Damn you, you hell-spawned fiend!" Lorens tried to use his feeble magical power to fend off the Wizard of Storms' most potent spells. He failed. The reclusive wizard had no need of the Demon Crown to make him whole and powerful.

A lightning bolt vaporized a large boulder a dozen paces away. Lorens threw up his arms to protect his face. Peals of thunder sounded constantly as the Wizard of Storms directed his attack from the distant Castle of the Winds.

"Come, come to me. Hurry, my friends. You must obey me!" Lorens shrieked when the first of the black-scaled reptilian creatures slithered through the portal he had opened for them. Sulphur fumes caused his nose to wrinkle and his eyes to water. He stood straight and tall and pointed. "There is the enemy. Destroy him! Do it for your lord and master! Do it for *me!*"

Another lightning bolt lanced down from the empty sky. This one touched the shimmering door into the netherworld that Lorens had opened. When the debris from the resulting explosion settled, only a dozen of the black reptiles had reached this side safely.

"Do not rest. Kill him. Kill whoever opposes me!" His shrieks turned incoherent. Lorens babbled and pointed. The reptiles dropped to all fours, then rose up in a parody of soldiers on parade. They formed a ragged rank and began marching toward the distant peak.

Lorens cackled. It might take them a month or a year or ten thousand years, but they would find the Wizard of Storms and destroy him. He, Lorens, son of Lamost, had ordered it!

Lorens fell silent when thick clouds formed directly overhead. Their leaden bellies split with flashes of lightning but no strikes reached the ground. In fascination he watched as raindrops formed—heavy-bodied, cloud-dragging raindrops unlike anything he had ever seen. The tendrils of cloud dipped lower and lower, their watery cargo glistening in the sunlight.

A sudden explosion knocked Lorens off his feet. From the cloud he saw four immense writhing blobs of water tumbling to the ground. When they touched the earth they did not spatter.

They grew. Slowly at first, then with great rapidity they grew into humanoid forms. Watery fingers reached out for the black, sulphurous reptiles. And every touch produced a soul-searing agony that caused the afflicted reptile to jerk violently, snapping important bones and dying instantly.

The Wizard of Storms' water warriors moved ponderously but managed to cut off all retreat by the reptiles. Lorens dropped to all fours and watched his alien army being destroyed by one born of pure magic.

Lorens scuttled off like a dog, leaving behind the unholy carnage. A league away, he dropped to his belly and lay panting. All concept of time had fled him. He could not remember if the battle of magic had been an hour or a year before.

His fingers worked weakly in the frosty soil until he touched a tuber. He smiled weakly and began digging. He ate the bulbous brown stem with an appetite that knew no bounds. When he had finished, Lorens belched and rolled over to stare at the sky and wonder what had caused his panic. He couldn't remember.

Everything was as it should be. Soon, very soon, he would regain the Demon Crown and again sit on the throne and rule Porotane. Soon. Soon.

CHAPTER FOUR

"He's dead. There is no need to search out his rotten carcass." Dews Gaemock glared at his brother, wishing Efran would show some sense. "You have played the fool overlong," the rebel leader said. "You still think like a court jester."

"That's not what you said when we engaged Lorens' troops. Whose plan did you select from all the ones submitted by your officers?" Efran Gaemock pulled his cloak tighter around him, thinking fondly of the warm corridors of Castle Porotane. The two years he had spent pretending to be Duke Freow's fool had not dulled his tactical sense. Once more in command of a company of troops, he had shown his skills.

He sneezed and looked around, as if he would find warm woolens awaiting him. The jester's motley he still wore provided almost no protection against the early winter winds blowing down from the highest reaches of the Yorral Mountains.

"You've not lost a bit of your talent," said Dews, clapping his brother on the back. "But prancing about in the midst of those royalist swine has made you too cautious. Lorens is dead. We routed his troops and scattered them from here to Porotane. I doubt if they've stopped running yet!"

Efran did not share his brother's confidence in either the soldiers' cowardice or the death of their king. Lorens' power was immense when he wore the Demon Crown. Efran had seen this too many times to lightly dismiss the demented wizard's apprentice-turned-king.

"The crown. Where is it?"

"The officer we caught and interrogated," said Dews. "He said that Lorens had lost it and sought those two you mentioned. What were their names?"

"The ones who installed Lorens on the throne. The ones recruited by the Glass Warrior." Efran frowned and began to pace in the snow, as much to keep warm as from nervous energy. Where did those two brigands figure into the power structure? They had aided Alarice and she had been a minion of Freow. But they had not supported Lorens, although they had returned with the young king and watched him mount the throne.

"They are petty thieves. You said so yourself. Come, brother. We have much to do. The kingdom is in disarray and awaits our tender touch to put it in order."

"There is still much to do here," said Efran. "Vered and Santon their names are. They might have recovered the Demon Crown."

"So? Neither can use it. Neither is of the blood royal."

Efran continued his aimless pacing, his mind turning over endless possibilities. In one thing Dews was right. The two could not put the Demon Crown to use. Efran had seen what happened when one not of the blood attempted to wear the crown. Lorens had amused himself too often by putting the crown on hapless prisoners. The agony etched on their faces before they died told of awful demonic worlds. No, Santon and Vered could not use the crown.

But they had found Lorens after fourteen years when all thought King Lamost's offspring had died. What other miracle were those two likely to perform?

"There is more that bothers me," said Efran.

"Brother, you try my patience now. We must ride for the castle. The defenders will throw open the gates and welcome us with garlands of flowers for our victory. Claymore Pass had been the scene of terrible slaughter in the past. It is now the site of our victory!"

Efran Gaemock shuddered at this. The phantoms drifting in and out of his peripheral vision appeared to be part of the swirling snow kicked up by gusty winds, but he knew better. Hundreds, perhaps thousands, had died in Claymore Pass and still roamed begging for their bodies to be properly buried. Efran sometimes could not tell the difference between the howls of the wind and the eternal pain of the undead phantoms.

To escape this he would gratefully leave the Yorral Mountains and Claymore Pass. But the feeling of duty undone gnawed at his guts. "I want Lorens' head as an ikon of our victory," he declared. "The head that wore the Demon Crown must now rest on a pike outside the castle walls for all to see."

"In this weather you expect to find a corpse?" Dews Gaemock's arm swept in a wide circle indicating the white curtains of blowing snow around them. "Not till spring thaw are we likely to find Lorens—or what remains of him."

"His phantom, then," said Efran. "His phantom will suffice."

"Who can capture a phantom and bend it to his will? Oh, a wizard of some power might. It was even said that the Glass Warrior controlled such a spell, but you would know that better than I."

"I knew little of her." Efran's eyes turned to the distant peak where the Wizard of Storms led his reclusive existence. He strained to see the fabled Castle of the Winds and failed. The snowstorm had worsened and threatened them with frostbite if they remained in this sparse bivouac any longer.

"We ride," Efran said. "I do not like leaving Lorens—or his body—behind. Remember that advice when it comes back to haunt us both."

Dews shook his head at such nonsense. They had routed Lorens' personal guard. The best Castle Porotane had to offer had run before them. What did it matter that the Demon Crown was again lost?

They mounted their horses and rode slowly down the winding path, the wind at their backs. Within a league they had re-formed. Of the hundred rebel soldiers who had entered Claymore Pass Efran noted only forty left. The toll had been great. His head sagged when he considered how few of those fallen had received consecration of their graves.

New phantoms to roam the rocky ways of the Yorral Mountains. So it had always been. Efran Gaemock wondered if this would ever change. He doubted it.

He rode, more asleep than awake, until a sharp noise brought him upright in the saddle.

"What is it, Dews?" he demanded. He blinked sleep and snow from his pale eyes and squinted. The banks of the River Ty stretched southward toward the castle and wended northward into their Yorral Mountain headwaters. What held his attention was a banner fluttering over a barge landing.

"I've never seen the likes of that before. No lord flies a gold-and-blue war flag." Dews motioned to a lieutenant, who nodded curtly and put the spurs to his horse. He galloped ahead, as much as emissary as a spy.

"Damn," cried Efran when he saw a single arrow arcing upward. The deadly missile found their lieutenant. From the boneless way the man fell from horseback, Efran knew he had died instantly.

"That was an unprovoked attack!" cried Dews. "How dare this lord of gold and blue!"

"Gold and blue," mused Efran. "That *is* familiar. A western province. A coastal city-state?"

Dews settled down in his saddle, his face turning stony. "Dalziel Sef hails from the westerlands. He calls the port city of Lih his home."

"Yes, Lih. Could he have mistaken our rider for one of Lorens' accursed soldiers?" Even as he asked the question, Efran knew the answer.

"Hardly. This can only mean that Sef has decided that, with Lorens gone and the castle defenses lacking a leader, the time is ripe for treachery."

"Sef was never noted for loyalty," Efran said sourly.

"I needed his troops. If we had continued to fight one another as well as Lorens's soldiers, we—"

"Brother, please. I *know* your reasons. They were good ones. We have this new problem to solve."

"No," said Dews Gaemock, his face turning even colder. "We are not the ones with a problem. It is Dalziel Sef. He must face us. And all the demons who once roamed this land will seem feeble when that treacherous son of a pig tastes my vengeance!"

Efran Gaemock nodded, his agile mind already working out the proper approach to the barge landing. Even with their handful of troops, seizing it would not be difficult against Sef's defenders.

And then? Efran would worry about that later. They had a skirmish to fight and win. He began ordering the rebel troops into position, again in his element.

CHAPTER FIVE

Birtle Santon struggled to roll to his left but he had become too tangled up with Vered for that. His eyes grew round as he saw death rising above him. The brigand-turned-rebel-soldier could crush a skull with a single swipe of his massive spiked club.

"Lokenna, wait, no!" came the cry from the inn. Santon recognized the voice as Bane Pandasso's. But that mattered naught. Not with death poised above.

A flash of lambent green caught Santon's attention. His eyes followed the arc of the Demon Crown as it came down over the blunt head of the raised club. The circlet spun about its new axis and descended. The rebel screeched in agony when the innocuous-looking crown touched the fingers gripping the club.

The brigand dropped his weapon and tried to back away. The Demon Crown stuck to his flesh as if it had grown there.

Santon shoved Vered aside and sat upright in the snow and mud, watching in helpless fascination. The soldier fought to pull the crown free. The more he struggled, the deeper the crown sank into his wrist. The green color of rotted flesh began to spread up his arm. The man's cries of terror were choked off when the rising tide of gangrene reached his neck and mouth. Putrescence destroyed further struggles. The bulky man sank to the snow and melted away.

"Never have I seen the like," muttered Vered. "And to think I put the crown on my own brow."

"Be thankful you've that drop of royal blood," said Santon. Lorens had tortured his prisoners using the Demon Crown, or so Santon had heard it rumored about the castle, but no one had described such a horrific action. He turned to the doorway of the inn. Lokenna stood there, face pale and hands shaking. Behind her Santon saw Pandasso, even more distraught.

"What d-did you do?" stammered Pandasso. "He melted away!"

Lokenna put a hand to her mouth and shook her head. Santon saw resolve filling her and color coming back to pale cheeks. "I couldn't let him kill those men."

"What did you *do* to him?" asked Pandasso, his voice firming now. A cunning look replaced the fear. "This is a skill that can make us a great deal of money."

"It's not for making money," Vered said briskly. He brushed himself off and frowned at the new dirt and tears in his clothing. "The Demon Crown gives power."

"Power," muttered Pandasso, as if this thought was totally alien to him. Santon snorted and got to his feet. Any thought might be lonely in that brutish head.

"We must return to Porotane immediately," Santon said. "These brigands carried orders from Dalziel Sef. With the crown in your hands, all will seek you."

"You are saying that this Sef wishes me harm?" asked Lokenna. "Because I have this crown?" She lifted the emerald-glowing crown and ran her fingers along its unadorned golden sides. "We know little of politics in Fron."

"My queen, politics comes to you," said Vered. "The brigands might have stumbled upon us by accident, but Lorens' soldiers still roam Claymore Pass. They would slay you instantly."

"Lorens?"

"Your twin brother," said Santon. He watched her reaction carefully. She did not believe him. "You and he were kidnapped when you were only children."

"Yes," she said slowly. "I was kidnapped. I remember escaping from an evil man who wanted to take me into a swamp."

"Tahir," said Santon. "He was a wizard of no real power and did Patrin's bidding. Patrin exiled Tahir when you escaped and took your brother as his own apprentice."

Lokenna shook her head. "This is all too confusing for me. I must begin supper. Not many in Fron patronize our inn, but they are the more important for their loyalty."

"Queen Lokenna, please," pleaded Vered.

"You are no longer a scullery maid. You are a monarch and must assume those duties."

"She knows nothing of being a queen," said Pandasso. "She is my wife and is needed here."

"With power comes money," Santon said. A foul taste rested in his mouth when he saw the avarice flare once again on Pandasso's face. "To reign supreme in Porotane means more money than you could count in a lifetime."

"With such power also comes . . . them." Lokenna pointed at the dead brigands. "Fron is isolated and peaceful because of that. I do not wish to change my life. I like it here. With my husband," she added, as if it had been an afterthought.

"With the Demon Crown comes duty. You are no longer your own person, Majesty," said Vered. "You can deny it, but others will continue to seek you out because of the crown."

"They cannot wear it, or so goes the legend. Why do they want it?"

"To prevent those in the royal house from using it," cut in Santon. "Nobles not of the royal blood hunger for power."

"Then let them take it. And you can take this, too." She tossed the Demon Crown toward Santon. Santon recoiled—but Vered moved faster. The young man dived and caught the crown before it touched his friend. The hue of green changed subtly.

For a moment, Vered stood juggling it. His face went slack when the crown's power began to insinuate itself into his brain.

"Vered!" snapped Santon. "Put the crown down. Now! *Do it now!*"

Vered reluctantly obeyed. He grinned sheepishly. "It was so nice to know real power again," he said. "I saw into Porotane. The castle is in turmoil. Baron Theoll and another I do not know vie for power."

"My bet is on the baron. He is a shrewd and ruthless man," said Santon.

"Wait," said Lokenna. "You, Vered, you can use the crown."

"I am of the royal line, but distantly. I use the crown—or it uses me. That is a better way of putting it."

"It uses him," agreed Santon, "even as it destroys him."

"Then it would destroy me, too," said Lokenna with loathing.

"No. You are linked together, you and the crown. See how its color changes when you are near it? You control it, not the other way around."

"It seems that way. I have no sense of it taking me over when I wear it." Lokenna lifted the crown and placed it on her head. The glow turned to a brilliance that dazzled the eye.

"We must go, Majesty. Dalziel Sef or others even worse will seek you out." Santon looked into the gathering blizzard and regretted the need to travel.

"She is not leaving Fron—or me." Bane Pandasso's words cut like a knife. "She belongs here and it's here she stays."

Santon motioned Vered back. The younger man would have driven his blade into Pandasso's fat belly to quell such opposition. Pandasso never realized how close to death he had come, but Lokenna did.

"My husband is right. I belong here." Even as she spoke, her eyes glazed over as if she focused on events far distant. Lokenna shook her head, as if denying what she saw.

"What is it, Majesty? What do you see?" asked Vered.

"Sef. Does he have cracked yellow teeth and a smile so evil that your blood turns to ice?"

Santon and Vered exchanged glances. They had no idea what Sef looked like. Their acquaintance with him came through rumors and stories told to frighten children.

"He is in the pass between Fron and the Lesser Ty." Lokenna turned toward the lower elevations. Santon and Vered followed her movement but saw only white curtains of blowing snow.

"How large a band does he command?" asked Vered. "We might be able to slip past in the storm and get to the Ty. A barge downstream will see us at the castle gates within a week."

"He moves well," she said. "His rebels allow no one past. They sweep upward. They travel quickly in the storm and will be here within the hour."

"We *must* leave," said Santon. "Sef will use the crown as a bargaining lever."

"There is more," said Pandasso. "You hold back. What?"

"He will try to capture Lokenna and force her to his will."

"She can slay with that magical thing," said Pandasso, shuddering as he glanced toward the fallen brigand. The flesh had stopped peeling from the man's bones, but the moaning of his newly released phantom rivalled that of the storm wind.

"If he puts her in a cell and magically binds

the door, he might be able to coerce her," said Vered. "Who knows what his plans are?"

"He wants to imprison me," Lokenna said. "Just as you said, he wants to use me—no, not *me*. He know Lorens no longer has the crown. He wants whoever can use *it*."

"How do you know this?" demanded Pandasso. "Look at me when I speak to you!" He shook his wife harshly, the Demon Crown tipping at an angle on her head. He stopped when he felt the sharp bite of Vered's knife.

"She is queen," he said softly. "We have sworn to protect her."

"As you protected her twin?" Pandasso edged away, glowering.

"Bickering accomplishes nothing," said Birtle Santon. "Sef will be here within the hour, if Lokenna is correct."

"The crown sees with crystal clarity," Vered assured him.

"The Lesser Ty affords us no escape. We must go back into Claymore Pass."

"But Lorens' troops will be between us and the Upper Ty!" protested Vered. "What does that gain us, other than the chance to freeze to death?"

"Yes, other rebels are there," said Lokenna. "Dews Gaemock fights a rebel band dockside on the Ty."

"Wait. Gaemock fights a rebel band? But he leads the rebels!" Santon held his head. The old wound throbbed mightily. He could not keep the elements in this battle from jumbling together and confusing him. The alliances shifted constantly— and all because of desire for the Demon Crown.

"Gaemock and his soldiers go south to the castle, but Sef's army will hinder them," said Lokenna. "There are others in the Yorral Mountains. Other soldiers. Uniformed officers work to re-form their ranks."

"Lorens's men," sighed Vered. "Everywhere we look, new armies pop up to oppose us. How will we ever get back to the castle?"

"The tunnel," said Lokenna. "I see it. North by northeast to Claymore Pass, then to the mountain tunnel. It emerges on the Upper Ty."

Santon groaned. "That tunnel is maintained by Ionia."

"And she and Dalziel Sef have formed an alliance," finished Vered. "Damn. What are we to do?"

"My brother. We must go to my brother. I want to see him face-to-face." Lokenna gestured vaguely toward Claymore Pass. "He is there."

"He'll kill you for the crown. We don't want him on the throne. He's mad!"

Vered's pleading did nothing to convince the woman.

"This is all so much pissing into the wind," spoke up Pandasso. "My wife's not going anywhere. She belongs here with me."

The rattle of metal on metal echoed up from the direction of the lower meadows. Dalziel Sef neared Fron.

"What you want is of no consequence," Santon said. "The war has come to you." He raced for the stables to see if there were more horses he could use. Two other animals looked at him curiously. When Vered joined him, he pointed. "Saddle them, too."

"Both?"

"Lokenna's not likely to leave her husband behind—and he'll be following when we ride out."

"I have no desire to again face Lorens."

"He is her brother and she's not seen him for fourteen years."

"He's crazed," Vered said hotly. "She's got the crown. She can *see* that."

"He's still her twin brother." Santon cinched the saddle as tightly as he could, then kneed the horse so that it exhaled sharply. Two more notches on the strap showed the horse's attempt to throw off saddle and mounted rider.

They led the horses outside. Pandasso and Lokenna stood in the inn's doorway arguing. He started to shake her again, then glance guiltily toward Vered. Pandasso balled his fists and let them dangle futilely at his sides. His need to strike out showed on every corded muscle but he held his temper in check.

"We do not leave Fron. This is our home. It's been good enough for you all these years."

"My brother hides in Claymore Pass," Lokenna said. "He needs my help."

"You didn't even know you had a brother until these two told you!" raged Pandasso.

"They did not lie." Lokenna jerked around, fear growing on her face. "The rebels! They're at the outskirts of Fron. Th-they're burning every house to find me!"

Through the swirling snowstorm rose orange tongues of flame from homes, from barns, from small businesses. The angry shouts of Fron's citizens carried on the wind.

Their death cries followed quickly. Sef gave no quarter as he slaughtered indiscriminately.

"We cannot fight him," said Lokenna. "There are too many—and we cannot sneak past. He has posted sentries to prevent any escape to the Ty."

"Back to Claymore Pass then," grumbled Vered. "I'd thought we were well quit of the place."

"Too many phantoms?" asked Santon, swinging into the saddle and flicking his wrist to bring his battle-ax to hand. He pinioned the reins with the edge of his glass shield and settled down. He did not ride and fight well—his useless left arm made anything more than a trot difficult, but he could manage if it kept them all alive.

"I don't want to add to their ranks," declared Vered.

Lokenna quickly mounted. The trio looked down at Bane Pandasso. Santon hoped that the man would stand his ground and refuse to join them. A battle cry from one of Sef's rebels sent Pandasso scuttling for the horse.

"Let's ride," said Vered.

"Wait," cautioned Lokenna. Her warning came simultaneously with Santon seeing two rebel soldiers emerge from the whiteness ahead of them. Sef had sent a squad to circle Fron to cut off even this risky escape.

"We can fight our way through, if there's not too many of them." Santon looked at the woman. Her face was pinched and drawn. Already the Demon Crown took its toll on her.

"There are only the pair," she said. "But they will slow us until the main force overtakes us."

Vered laughed and spurred his horse forward. The short glass sword gleamed from the light of burning buildings. His sudden charge took the two rebels by surprise. They killed peasants on foot and did not expect a cavalry attack. Vered ducked under one's clumsy swing with a lance. He rode inside and stabbed with his short sword.

Santon heard the glass screeching along metal body armor. Vered had not injured the rebel but had unseated him. The soldier fell heavily, struggling to regain his feet.

Santon used his good hand to loop the reins around the saddle horn, then guided his own horse forward using his powerful knees. A quick jerk brought his ax to hand and his shield into defensive position. He attacked the other rebel.

The rebel's lance danced off Santon's shield. Using all the strength locked in his powerful shoulders, Santon swung his ax—and connected with the rebel's torso. When the ax lodged in rib bone and flesh and did not come free, Santon found himself pulled from his saddle.

He landed on his back, the wind knocked from him.

"They come!" cried Lokenna. "Sef's troops are upon us!"

Cold wind blew across Santon's face and brought back life. He coughed and gasped and got to his knees. His fall had freed his ax but the leather thong around his wrist had cut deeply into his flesh. Blood flowed freely and made the ax handle slippery. Santon let the weapon dangle as he used the shield to lever himself to his feet.

"Did you lose this?" called Vered. The young adventurer tossed down the reins to Santon's horse. "You must be more careful with your belongings. It's hard stealing another in this wasteland!"

Santon heard a deep rumbling as a war cry rose in another's throat. He turned in time to see the man Vered had felled lift a mace. The glass shield deflected the blow. Vered turned his horse about and put spurs viciously to the horse's flanks, causing it to rear and paw the air.

One hoof caught the rebel and sent him crashing back to the ground.

"Are you coming, Santon? Fron is not my idea of a vacation spot." Vered laughed as he fought to regain control of his horse.

Santon mounted and looked back to the inn. Sef's men worked more diligently on setting fire to the buildings than they did in checking those who rushed into the storm to escape.

"My inn," moaned Pandasso. "My life is in that inn!"

"Your life lies ahead," said Santon. He did not look back to see if Pandasso followed. Ahead rode Vered and Lokenna, the Demon Crown glowing brightly and providing a beacon through the blowing snow.

CHAPTER SIX

Kaga'kalb, the Wizard of Storms, stood on the highest tower in his sprawling Castle of the Winds. Before him stretched a rocky mesa that dropped abruptly to the Uvain Plateau. His keen eyes watched the progress of a thunderstorm as it worked its way across the lower elevations. He smiled slightly. Those storms were not of his birthing.

Above his head swirled leaden clouds. *Those* were his. A thin arm raised. Lightning danced from the wizard's fingertips and lit up the tower with an eerie glow. As sudden as natural lightning, a bolt erupted from his hand and blasted asunder the dark clouds.

Rain fell. Kaga'kalb ignored it, secure and dry in a bubble of magic. His spells grew in potency.

His lips moved constantly as newer and more complex magics powered the storm forming.

Thunder rolled off his mesa and down the mountain slopes until all the Uvain echoed. He clapped his hands. The storm brewing exploded in a fury unseen in a score of years. More and more lightning sizzled and popped and exploded, reaching into the dark clouds and building them into a towering thunderhead.

When it seemed that the storm cloud would leave the planet, it began to shift away from the Castle of the Winds. Kaga'kalb guided its progress. He smiled broadly when his storm met the naturally occurring one and devoured it. For a brief instant, he was more powerful than the forces of air and sky.

Kaga'kalb leaned forward, his hands numb with the cold and frost forming on his thinning hair. The intricate spells he had woven collapsed. He watched the normal progression of wind and cloud with awe, as he always did. No matter how good he became, nature bettered his best.

Kaga'kalb straightened, amused with his handiwork now. His arms lifted again and he began to fashion tiny storms that darted about the perimeter of his larger creation. Here and there he formed lightning of varying colors and intensity. The thunderclaps met in counterpoint. He began directing them, moving lightning flashes into eye-searing patterns, sending cloud formations of dark and light into artistic forms. Like a maestro conducting a group of master musicians at the spring fair, Kaga'kalb created a masterpiece of sight and sound and feel.

Desiring more, he began snowstorms in the Yorral Mountains. A toss of his head created a hurricane far out at sea. A small tornado rose and fell, bucking and twisting and lightly touching ground in the far south of Porotane.

Kaga'kalb laughed aloud now. The power flowing through him this day revitalized and gave him fresh purpose.

"They have not learned," he said to himself. His vision was sharp but not good enough to focus halfway across the mountains to where the Demon Crown made its unsettling presence known to him. The magical device caused a darkness that both drew and repelled him.

Kaga'kalb would have the crown, not for his own use—that was not possible—but to keep the petty tyrants from ruining the kingdom. While the pretender Duke Freow had ruled, Alarice had kept the Demon Crown in safety. Freow's death and the search for the true heirs to the throne had upset the balance and disturbed Kaga'kalb's lonely meditations.

Like a black chancre growing within, he felt the crown's repeated misuse as Lorens tried to seize power. Kaga'kalb dared not allow such power to ruin Porotane. He cared nothing for the pretentious nobles or the petty peasants.

The land stretched out as a canvas to his cloudy paintbrush. The air filled with his watery artwork. Movements of storms both grand and small, those were his legacy, his duty, his pride. No wizard had formed the elements more cleverly or better.

Kaga'kalb would not allow fools to ruin land and sky, to render it unsuitable for his work through misuse of the Demon Crown. He had thought it gone forever when Lamost had died and he had convinced Patrin to kidnap the twins.

"I should never have trusted Patrin. The man always was a clumsy oaf. Never could weave a spell properly, even his dream specialties." Kaga'kalb dropped his arms and let the storms run their course. This day's work was not a masterpiece, but it served to soothe him. A more tranquil mind allowed him to work better. Tomorrow.

Or perhaps this night. His most interesting storms were created in the night, with silver moonlight and lightning vying for attention, with cloud patterns turning the world a dull gray and pitch-black, with raindrops giving a silvery sheen to the artificial and a pleasing smell to the natural.

Kaga'kalb pulled down the sleeves of his robe and wiped the frost from his hair. His fingers tingled. He put cupped hands to his mouth and breathed hard to warm them. He was getting old, but he was not yet ready to die. The true masterwork of his life had yet to be created.

"Can't create with the crown disturbing me." He turned and stared at a blank stone wall. Even through the dampening stone he saw the black pit of the Demon Crown. Not for the first time he cursed Kalob and all the demons for the disorder they had brought to this world. Then he cursed Waellkin for so foolishly accepting the crown as reparation.

"What kind of leader was he, anyway?" Kaga'kalb shook his head as he remembered Waellkin. The man had been vain and ambitious. Too ambitious for his own good or the good of Porotane. The lure of the Demon Crown had been too great.

Kaga'kalb shuddered and not from the cold. Lorens had again been stripped of the crown, he saw. But the two points of darkness, one intense and the other weak but growing, told of the disaster preparing to befall Porotane.

"The young fool could not control the crown—it controlled him and now the gateway to hell is open." Kaga'kalb sniffed and continued down the winding stone staircase until he came to a comfortably furnished room. He dropped heavily into a chair in the center of the room and looked around the circular space.

Subtle finger movements activated quiescent spells. Tiny clouds formed along the northeast portion of the wall. They billowed and roiled and turned from puffy white to ominous black. A miniature flash of lightning erupted from the storm he had brought into being.

Kaga'kalb smiled. "Ionia, Ionia, you magnificent slut. You always amaze me. You make a petty alliance with Dalziel Sef and then seek to betray it." The lightning flash closed the distance between the Castle of the Winds and Ionia's fiefdom. Through the magical cloud window Kaga'kalb watched as the noble parlayed with Dews Gaemock's emissary. Before this meeting concluded, Dalziel Sef would be neutralized and Ionia promised full control of Claymore Pass.

Kaga'kalb turned in his chair. The storm cloud spraying rain and snow pellets against the wall moved to follow the direction of his gaze. The Yorral Mountains stretched upward, harsh and rocky-sharp. The wizard studied this scene carefully. Blackness and blackness. The Demon Crown and Lorens. He studied the deeper speck of jet.

"Those two freebooters have found the other twin," he said in amazement. "That can be the only explanation for such power. Damn! Damn Alarice!

Damn them all! They will ruin a perfectly good kingdom. I'm too old to find a new spot to work my magic. Why should I move my lovely Castle of the Winds simply because they destroyed Porotane through ignorance and greed? Pah!"

The scrying spell controlling his cloud window began to weaken—the action of the Demon Crown. Kaga'kalb renewed the spell and changed the view to another portion of the mountains. Gaemock's troops met and defeated Dalziel Sef's at the River Ty. Of Sef's troops, the wizard saw nothing until he found the village of Fron. Sef had retreated back to the Lesser Ty and floated toward Castle Porotane.

"He goes to stir up more trouble. He senses the weakness within the castle walls. Sef is a cunning whoreson, that I'll give him." Kaga'kalb shifted to the castle itself.

The petty posturings and assassinations within had long since ceased to interest him. Only the majesty of storm-building and the symphony of the elements crashing together held his attention long. He cared little if Theoll or Anneshoria triumphed. As long as the Demon Crown rested on a royal brow, neither would sit on the throne.

Kaga'kalb turned back in his chair, strengthening his scrying spell and once more looking to the northeast and fair Ionia. The woman had concluded her treaty with Gaemock's ambassador and had moved on to more amorous conquests. The ambassador was willing.

The Wizard of Storms settled down to watch. He enjoyed storm building more than Ionia's antics—but barely. The fiefdom's ruler had proven inventive and diverting in the past. This time was no exception.

CHAPTER SEVEN

"We're lost," moaned Vered. "We'll never find our way in this storm. And worst of all, my clothes are ruined!"

"Quit complaining," called Santon, homing in on his friend's voice. The thick curtain of falling snow deadened sound and made vision beyond a few paces impossible. He urged his straining steed forward and bumped into Vered. Side by side they rode so that they could speak. A long, thin length of twine fastened to Vered's saddle extended tracelessly into the storm and connected with Lokenna's saddle horn.

"I know, I know," said Vered. "*She* can see where we are going. That does me little good—and my horse even less."

"Look on the bright side of this," said Santon. "There's no one to see how scruffy you look."

Vered snorted and sent silvered plumes leaping from his nostrils. The cruel wind caught the twin jets and mingled them with snow and polar air, as if saying that the same would happen to the warm body generating such steam.

"Some bright side. At the moment, I would settle for a warm side." Vered shifted in the saddle and rubbed his rear. "Especially a warm backside."

The twine went limp and dragged the ground. They stopped beside Lokenna and her mount. Another string went off to the right and connected to Bane Pandasso's saddle. The fleeting thought passed through Santon's mind that a careless swing of his ax would doom Pandasso to a frigid death.

"We cannot return to Fron," she said without preamble. "Although Dalziel Sef has personally left, he stationed a score of men to wait for me—for the crown." Lokenna self-consciously touched the glowing band of metal around her head. "I listened in to a meeting he had with his lieutenants. They hope to capture the crown and barter it away to the Wizard of Storms for the throne."

"What does he want with it? Even a spell-thrower of such power cannot wear the crown. Even Alarice couldn't." At the mention of the Glass Warrior, Santon fell silent, lost in thought. The white shroud wrapping him in its cold embrace reminded him of the white-haired woman and her cold undead existence as a phantom.

"What lies ahead?" asked Vered. "I do not want to ride forever in this storm. They will find us standing like ice statues come spring thaw if we do not stop soon and go to shelter."

"We are trapped between two forces," Lokenna said. "I have been watching, listening." Her eyes rolled up in a vain attempt to see the crown on her head. She touched the Demon Crown to reassure herself that it still sat firmly on her brow. "Dews Gaemock had forged a secret alliance with Ionia, one countering Sef's with the woman."

"I have never met this Ionia," said Vered, "but she must be a double-dealing witch."

"Then she's the only double-dealing witch you've not met," said Santon, coming out of his self-pity.

"Neither met nor bedded," Vered finished. He huddled forward, his entire body shaking with the cold. "A touch of warmth would be nice. Even one such as Ionia who would likely drive a knife between my ribs when it suited her."

"Her troops patrol Claymore Pass," said Lokenna, ignoring the men. "Gaemock's troops protect the ways to the River Ty."

"And you said she controlled the tunnel leading through to the Upper Ty," said Vered. "How can we escape the rebels?"

"I must see my brother," said Lokenna. "He can get us out."

"Lorens?" scoffed Santon. "He was a petty wizard at best. Only with the Demon Crown did he have any power."

"He is united with his troops again. Almost twenty soldiers ride behind his banner."

Santon and Vered both cursed. Santon said, "It is death to join ranks with him, Lokenna. He will kill you for the crown. He is demented. The crown has twisted him permanently."

"I see how he is," she said in a distant voice. Santon knew that she *looked* far beyond the range of human vision. What the Demon Crown revealed to her in this new foray he did not know. "If he is not shown the crown, he will not try to kill me."

"She might be right. Nothing but the crown matters to her brother," said Vered.

"There is no reason to let him know that she has ever worn the crown, either," added Santon. "You can hide a ways back while we parlay, then you can follow close as we get to the river."

"Yes, that is a good plan," Lokenna said without any inflection in her voice. Without another word she began riding. Santon and Vered watched her disappear into the whiteness as Pandasso rode up.

"What's going on here?" the heavyset man demanded in his gruff voice. "You been harassing her again?"

Neither man answered. Santon silently rode on when the string attached to his saddle began to draw taunt. He wished he had cut Pandasso's string when the opportunity had afforded itself. But he knew that would have done no good. Using the Demon Crown Lokenna could have located her husband easily.

The thought crossed his mind that she might not bother. Santon pushed that aside. From what he had seen of Lokenna, her loyalty knew no bounds. She might not love Bane Pandasso—Santon wasn't sure how even a mother warthog could—but Lokenna would not abandon him like castoff clothing.

Together they rode into the teeth of the snowstorm, each silent and lost in his thoughts.

* * *

"We cannot fight our way through," insisted Lokenna. "We see only the front of the patrol. Six others back these two."

Santon wiped the melting snow from his eyebrows and glared at the two riders. Dews Gaemock had again shown his cunning in stationing his men. Santon began to have a grudging respect for the man's ability and wished that they were not on opposite sides. Gaemock opposed any of royal blood sitting on the throne—and Santon had promised Alarice that one twin would ascend and rule.

"Birtle, they've sighted us!" Lokenna's cold grip on his shoulder tightened until it felt as if ice talons cut into his flesh.

"Damnation. May all the demons—and Lorens, too—take them!" He slipped from the shallow depression that had given them paltry shelter during their rest and moved quickly downslope. He had to position himself to keep these two from reporting back to the main patrol.

He and Vered worked well together. Past skirmishes had honed their instinct to the point that they knew how the other thought, what the other did, if the other needed help. Santon skidded and slid down a rocky slope, banging his shield and shoulder into the rocks. By the time he regained a precarious footing on a muddy patch, he faced both riders.

"What have we here, Tannay? Could it be the one Lord Dews sent us to fetch?"

Santon worked his glass shield into place and swung the ax up and into his grip. He winced at the pain this simple, practiced motion caused. The chaffed skin on his wrist had not begun to heal.

"Yes, Sergeant, he has the look about him.

Notice the arm. Look Efran himself mentioned that."

Santon frowned. Who was Lord Efran? He had no time to consider. Living took precedence over curiosity. He lowered his head, lifted his shield, and charged, his shining ax blade singing as it moved in an arc parallel with the frozen ground. The nicked edge caught one horse's leg just above the knee. Although he did not sever the limb, Santon heard fragile bones breaking. As the horse neighed in fear and tried to shy away, it threw its rider. All the way to the ground the sergeant of rebels cursed.

Santon had no time to finish off his fallen victim. Tannay attacked. The flat of a sword blade struck him on the side of the head and sent him tumbling. In the glass-slick mud Santon skidded farther than he anticipated. He had to struggle frantically to keep from falling over an embankment and down to a partially frozen stream.

Such determination to remain out of the water should have given an opportunity to Tannay. It didn't. Vered had attacked from the side, driving his sword through the rebel's armpit as he raised his weapon to kill Santon.

"You should be more careful, Santon," Vered told his friend. "That one intended to spit you." He carefully cleaned his glass blade in a snowbank.

"What happened to the other one? The sergeant?" Santon climbed to his feet and looked around. The unseated rebel had vanished into the whiteness around them.

"He has retreated to alert the rest of the rebels," came Lokenna's clear voice.

"Damn! We'll never elude them now."

"There is a way," said Lokenna, her voice as distant as her gaze. "We press on quickly, to the north, toward Ionia's troop bivouac."

"We might be able to confuse them, get them attacking each other!" cried Vered.

"No, they won't. They have established recognition signals."

"You know them?" Santon shared Vered's eagerness to learn this.

"They have exchanged soldiers and the codes are in their battle languages. I can mimic but not duplicate. They would know instantly."

"Why seek out Ionia, then?" asked Santon.

"My brother is near. He heads for the tunnel to the river. We can join him before he begins his fight through Ionia's forces."

"Always Lorens," muttered Vered. "If he sees either of us, we're dead. He *has* to know we stole the crown."

"He . . . he thinks his court jester is responsible. Harhar. He speaks of him with great rancor."

"Lorens would execute us on sight, just to stay in practice," insisted Vered.

"You will have the crown and follow. He will never see you. If you are afraid, Birtle, you can remain with your friend."

"You'd trust us together with the Demon Crown?"

"You did not have to give it to me. This Alarice of whom you speak so highly trusted you. I feel that I can, also."

"We ought to take the crown and throw it into the river—or bury it or somehow get rid of it," said Vered.

"No," snapped Santon. "Alarice said that the

crown was Porotane's only chance for peace, for unification."

"She had not met Lorens when she said those fine things." Vered went to the fallen soldier and began pilfering the body for anything of value. He tossed most aside until he came to a metal tag.

"What do you have?" asked Santon.

"A name tag for identification."

"Lokenna," asked Santon, "how long before the rebels overtake us?"

"At least an hour. Why?"

"There is time," said Vered. He began piling rocks to make a crypt. As he worked, Santon joined him.

From above came Pandasso's querulous voice. "What are you doing? We must ride to save ourselves!"

"We're going to bury him," said Santon. "Vered and I have seen enough phantoms wandering the pass to add to their rank. It won't take long and we know the man's identity."

Lokenna smiled. "You risk your lives to save a fallen enemy from eternal anguish? Indeed, I can trust you two with the crown—and my life."

Vered grumbled as he worked. Under his breath, he said to Santon, "Little does our new queen know that we plied our trade as thieves for many a year."

"Does that matter to a woman able to see any pilfering, no matter how well concealed?" Santon heaved the last rock into place and let Vered lower the slain soldier into the crypt. They began the tedious chore of piling the rocks backs. The burial site would keep out all but the most determined of scavengers.

Vered said the service laying the rebel's phantom to rest. He finished quickly, putting the metal tag on a rock above the grave.

"Rest well," Vered said softly. He vaulted onto his horse and never looked back as he rode off after Lokenna and her husband. Santon brought up the rear, his ears straining for some indication of pursuit by the rebels. Within minutes the softly falling snow blanketed out every sound but the *click-click* of his own horse's hooves on the rocky road through Claymore Pass.

Santon drifted, feeling as if he had entered a land without dimension or form. Whiteness greeted him in every direction. He rode along, nodding off and coming awake with a start, unsure of the passage of time. It might have been an hour or a day when he overtook Lokenna. Vered and Pandasso had already stopped.

"Ahead," she said softly. "Ionia's troops have set up guard posts to block travel. A league beyond lies the tunnel."

"What else?" asked Santon, hearing the edge in her voice.

"What else could it be?" Vered said with some bitterness. "Lorens lies between us and Ionia's troopers."

Santon looked at the Demon Crown perched on Lokenna's brow. The green was still warm and cheery rather than the corrupted color when Lorens had possessed it. Santon was unsure how to take this omen. Lokenna had worn the crown constantly since leaving Fron, but how long had that been? A few days, he was sure. Tiredness and hunger gnawing at his belly robbed him of his normal measures. How long must the woman wear the crown before it began to infect her as it had her twin?

"I feel nothing unusual, Birtle," she said, reading his expression. "I have seen what my brother has become. I've never known him but from all you have said, he was not always like he is now."

"Would that the tyrant were dead," grumbled Vered.

"He is my brother and I truthfully cannot say I remember him. If you say that we were kidnapped as small children—"

"Not that small," cut in Vered. "Alarice said you were five or six at the time. You should remember Lorens."

"I should," Lokenna said, "but I do not. This is all the more reason to see him. So much of my early memory is . . . gone."

"Magic?" suggested Santon.

"Perhaps. If the kidnapping was as brutal as you suggest, I may have simply blocked it out. If so, meeting Lorens might help return this part of my past." Lokenna smiled and Santon felt his coldness vanish in its warmth. "I do remember wandering and being taken in by an elderly couple who lived outside Fron."

"She married me when she was about fifteen," Pandasso added. "We've been happy till now."

Santon watched the gentle smile turn to wry amusement. He saw that Lokenna was content but not happy. With a man like Bane Pandasso how could any whose birth had been noble be happy?

"Let me wear the crown for a few miles more until we approach where my brother prepares his men."

"They are going to attack Ionia's position? In this blizzard?"

Santon couldn't believe it but Lokenna nodded slowly. She turned her horse and got it walking. Santon followed blindly, one direction no different from another.

Santon heard Lorens haranguing his soldiers long before he sighted them. The snow flurries had lightened and gave visibility of almost a hundred yards. For the kind of travelling they had done, this seemed extraordinary. He reined in and waited for Lokenna to decide her course of action.

"There he is," said Vered. "Your brother readies his men for a suicide mission. Without the crown, there is no way he can know how Ionia's troops are deployed."

"He might be crazy but he is not stupid," she said. She shivered. Santon did not think it was from the cold. "He still possesses a modicum of magical power. I see it boiling around—or swarming about his head. It is difficult to describe. He appears to be surrounded by hundreds of black insects."

"Those reflect his ability?"

"Who can say?" Lokenna took off the crown and held it out for Vered to take. He recoiled. "I am sorry," she said. "It is incredible to me that others find this wondrous device so deadly." The woman fumbled in her pack and came out with the glass box and carrying pouch. She put the Demon Crown within, closed the box, and handed it to Vered, who gingerly accepted it.

"I can feel its power, even through the case," he said.

"Resist, friend," urged Santon. "Remember what it can do to you."

"Aye, I remember too well. You need have no

fear on that. There are other matters that concern me more." Vered cleared his throat before continuing. "My queen, it pains me to ask this. What happens if your brother does not greet you with open arms and sibling love?"

"Lorens is incapable of either, but still I must meet him. He suspects another's presence. The Demon Crown is potent and he is hungry for it. If necessary, I can use it as a bargaining point."

"No!" Santon and Vered cried at the same time. Santon motioned his friend to silence. "You dare not, Majesty. Better the crown is destroyed and Alarice's quest dies."

"Along with it all hope for peace in Porotane," added Vered.

"Lorens is cruel and capricious and not in his right mind. All that is true." Lokenna stared down the slope. "There is much I must learn from him. He has worn the crown longer than I. Questions rise in my mind and asking another lessens the danger to me should I be forced to find out the answers by experiment."

Santon shook his head. Lokenna had seemed a simple serving wench in Fron. Such a comment from that woman would have been out of place. But it fit well with the different Lokenna, Queen Lokenna of Porotane, wearer of the Demon Crown.

"You will do nicely on your own, Vered. I trust you. Come along," Lokenna said, a hint of steel in her voice.

Santon and Vered exchanged glances. Vered shrugged and motioned for his friend to ride on. Santon rode slowly, his horse picking out firm spots in the muddy hillside.

Lokenna played a dangerous game, but he had to trust her. She had used the Demon Crown and seen the troop deployments in Claymore Pass. And he could understand her need to speak with her long-lost brother. But what other motives drove her?

He had no idea, and that worried him.

CHAPTER EIGHT

Birtle Santon looked over his shoulder to see if Vered watched, also. He did not. The younger man had wasted no time in finding cover. Santon hoped that his friend withstood the lure of the crown. The last time Vered had worn it, he had been drawn into a maelstrom from which return had been difficult—and without Santon helping, Vered would have perished.

The Demon Crown gave immense power. It also extracted a great penalty from anyone wearing it.

"Let me do the talking," said Lokenna.

"This isn't right and proper," her husband protested. "I speak for the family."

"She is queen. She speaks for the kingdom," said Santon.

"Queen," sneered Pandasso. "There vou go

calling my Lokenna queen again. What does it mean? She puts on that fancy shining green crown and *that* makes her high royalty? Don't go giving me any of that. You been lying to me and her. I don't know what your scheme is, you petty cutpurse, but—"

"Silence." Lokenna's tone cut off her husband's tirade. Pandasso stared at her openmouthed with astonishment.

To the guard posted at the perimeter of the camp, Lokenna called, "We seek a truce. We have come to parlay with Lorens."

"Parlay?" came the skeptical reply to her request. "Who makes such a claim?"

"Let Lorens decide. I refuse to bandy words with a commoner."

The way she spoke startled Santon. Lokenna fell into the role of a monarch quickly. Too quickly, for his taste. Had the Demon Crown infected her as it already had her brother?

"Who causes such an uproar when quiet is needed?" Lorens came out of a crude tent and stood, hands on hips, glaring up at Lokenna.

All around the trio of riders the would-be king's soldiers fingered their weapons, unsure of what to do. But Santon saw—*felt*—that Lokenna and her brother were two poles of an immense energy. The others felt it, too, and this added to their uncertainty.

"Who are you?" asked Lorens. His face lost the rigidity and turned to a constantly flowing mass of conflicting emotion. Santon marvelled at the way Lorens' eyes finally bugged out and he exclaimed, "Sister! You are my sister! I feel the power in you!"

"I feel no kinship with you," Lokenna said

coldly. She sat stiffly in her saddle. "However, it seems that our paths have crossed and we travel side by side for a time."

"Kill her!" Lorens' face underwent another transformation, this time to stark hatred.

"Do so and you'll never recover the Demon Crown." Lokenna's voice was pitched so low that only Lorens and Santon heard. "What would you be then, brother? A nothing, as you are now." Lokenna spat. Beside her Pandasso protested this unladylike behavior. Santon silenced the woman's husband with a prod to the ribs with the edge of his shield.

"You have it?" Cunning came into Lorens' face, making him appear feral. "Yes, of course you do. You could never have found me this easily without it."

Lorens signalled his loyal guardsmen to close in. Santon allowed the soldiers to disarm him. Fighting a full score of them would accomplish nothing but a quick death—and he still thought that Lokenna had the upper hand.

"Do you think me foolish enough to ride into your camp with it? Hardly, brother. It seems that our parents birthed only one idiot—you."

Lorens held his madness in check through urgent need to again assume the supreme power offered by the Demon Crown. "Where is it? My torturers can make you tell."

"My name is Lokenna. And it will do you no good trying to force information from me that I cannot divulge. Another has the crown."

"Harhar!"

"You mean Lord Efran?" Lokenna asked. "Perhaps he has it. But that hardly seems likely, does it, brother? We must return to the castle. By the time we arrive, the crown will also be there. Other than this, I can tell you nothing about the crown's location."

"Who has it? If not Harhar, then it must be—"

"Lorens." Lokenna's voice cracked like a whip. "We share common goals at the moment. Both of us wish to return unharmed to the castle. To do so requires us to sneak past Ionia's troops. I know where they are posted."

"You've used the crown!"

"I have," she admitted. "Many days ago."

"You lie!" Spittle ran from the corners of Lorens' mouth. A lieutenant supported his liege. Santon saw how easily won over these fighting men would be. They had seen nothing but madness from their leader. Lokenna offered more than sanity—she offered safety and return to the protection granted by the castle walls.

"Officer," Lokenna said briskly. "Ionia has twelve men posted in the following locations. We must fight through her troops, but this is the weak spot."

"Yes, milady, it is," agreed the lieutenant, staring at the diagram Lokenna scratched in the snow with her boot. "What good does it do us to win through to the tunnel? Lady Ionia has hundreds of soldiers camped inside."

"Rumors, or lies. Take your pick. She is stretched thin. Her farmers refuse to give up their sons to be soldiers on winter patrol in Claymore Pass. We get past these paltry troops and the tunnel lies open before us."

"Why did you not bypass them and ignore us?" the lieutenant asked.

"She is a fool, that's why!" shouted Lorens.

"Consider," spoke up Santon. "For us to evade Ionia's guard positions is impossible, and we are too few to fight through. Together we *can* get to the tunnel."

"You are *my* officer," cried Lorens. "You will obey *me!*"

"Yes, Majesty." The office bowed low but his eyes remained on Lokenna and her serene acceptance of the situation. Santon knew that they had made an ally. The officer wanted only for his men to survive. Lokenna offered that and Lorens did not.

Lorens wiped the spittle from his lips and calmed. "Where is this weakness in the enemy line?"

Lokenna silently pointed out the posts once more, then erased it all with a quick stamping of her foot. She spun and mounted, not waiting to see if Lorens approved.

The former king did not but Santon did. Lokenna had handled both her brother and the situation with the skill of a diplomat. She had given away nothing, gotten much, and forged an alliance that would get them through the rebel lines. Santon hoped that Vered would be able to slip through the confusion unnoticed. Without him and the Demon Crown, Lokenna would find herself in dire straits at Castle Porotane.

"These posts. How many soldiers man each one?" asked the officer.

Lokenna quietly told him. Together they plotted, then the soldier nodded briskly and rode off to prepare his troops for battle.

"Your brother doesn't like you usurping his power. He might be crazy but he is not stupid. He knows what is going on," said Santon. Even as he spoke he watched Lokenna's husband. Bane Pandasso did not accept his wife's newfound power easily, either. Pandasso lacked Lorens' brilliance or magical ability and had nothing but jealousy to fuel him. That jealousy smoldering within Pandasso's breast would one day burst into flame.

Santon wasn't sure if Lorens' madness wasn't preferable—and safer.

They rode forward slowly, hugging one steep wall of rock until Lokenna lifted her hand as a signal for attack. Then all pretense of caution vanished. The lieutenant urged his troops on in a frontal assault on a small guard post positioned halfway up a gravel-strewn slope. The soldiers' horses slipped and stumbled but enough got through to overwhelm the post. Santon held back, watching carefully for sign that supporting troops came to regain the post.

"There!" he called to Lokenna. "One of them is escaping!" He didn't wait for Lorens' soldiers to give chase to the fleeing guard. Santon put his heels to his horse's flanks and sent the animal surging forward. He closed the distance between them quickly—almost too quickly.

The wily guard spun and put the butt end of his lance to the ground, thinking to impale Santon as he rode by. Santon swung the glass shield over and protected his right side. The steel tip of the lance bounded off the rounded surface and left him unharmed.

The impact also unseated him.

Hitting the ground would have knocked the breath from his lungs if he hadn't been screaming the entire distance from saddle to soil. Santon rolled and used his shield as a support to get to his feet. He immediately found strong arms circling him, carrying his backward, threatening to crush him.

Santon tried to get his ax into play. A powerful hand gripped his wrist. Santon's withered left arm proved no match for his opponent's right hand. Eye to eye they fought for supremacy.

If it had been a battle only of strength, Birtle Santon would have lost to his stronger, younger opponent. But over the years he had been in similar situations and knew brute strength was not the only way of winning.

Their faces pressed together, Santon strained to gain another fraction of an inch. When an ear came within reach of his mouth, he bit down hard. Gristle filled his mouth. The guardsman let out an agonized scream and momentarily faltered in his attack.

Blood flowing from his torn ear, the guardsman stumbled back half a pace. Santon judged distance and swung his shield. The edge caught the guard under the chin and knocked the man's head back. This put another pace between them. Santon's ax came to hand. The silvered downward arc ended in the guardsman's collarbone.

The impact rocked Santon—and killed his foe.

"Are you all right?" came Lokenna's worried call.

"Killing like this leaves a bad taste in my mouth." Santon spat again and wiped his lips on his sleeve. He needed a full quart of ale to wash away the taste. He wished Ionia would teach her troops simple hygiene like washing their ears.

"We must hurry. You have saved us from immediate battle with their reinforcements. It will take several minutes before they realize anything is awry," said Lokenna.

Santon got into the saddle but paused to look behind.

"I haven't seen Vered," the woman said softly. "We must trust to his skill."

"His skill isn't in question. He might beat us to the castle. It's that damned crown that worries me."

"It affects him as it did Lorens?" she asked, gazing at her demented brother. Lorens issued conflicting commands ignored by both officers and soldiers as they prepared to fight their way to the tunnel.

"Vered didn't wear it as long, but the effect was similar. He would have been driven crazy by the images crashing in on him."

"You must will them to slow and accept only the ones you desire," said Lokenna. "It . . . I don't know how I knew to do it. I just did. It surprises me that others don't have similar skill."

"Hurry, Majesty," cried the lieutenant. Santon wasn't sure to whom the officer called. Lorens thought it was to him and Lokenna didn't care. They rode quickly down a narrow ravine that opened onto a broad flood plain.

Deep canyons had been cut in the rock by spring runoff. Snowbanks piled head-high on either side of the plain turned it into an icy temple. Santon wanted nothing more than to worship within the dark circle he spied in the mountainside.

"The tunnel!"

"Aye, it is," said Pandasso, licking his lips apprehensively. "What do we want to go in there for? It looks dangerous."

"It's more dangerous staying here and waiting for Ionia to find that we've overrun a guard post."

"I don't like close places. I think me and Lokenna will go back to Fron. The brigands have left. We can rebuild the inn and everything will be fine again."

"You'll end up dead before you've ridden a single hour. Look." Santon pointed to steam rising from just inside the mouth of the tunnel.

"Soldiers," muttered Pandasso. "All the more reason to go home and forget this crazy scheme."

"Too late, too late," roared Santon. He swung his ax into his grip and kicked hard at his horse's sides. He led the assault directly into the tunnel, not knowing if the others followed. Santon saw no other course. If they hesitated now, they were lost. An all-out attack might take the guards posted within the tunnel by surprise, even if they outnumbered their attackers.

Santon's horse's hooves clattered on hard rock flooring and sent sparks skittering into the darkness. Santon's charge carried him deeper into the blackness, effectively blinding him until his eyes adjusted to the dimness. His ax swung to and fro but found no target. He reined back to wait for the others to catch up with him.

The bright circle of the tunnel mouth suddenly filled with soldiers—Lorens' soldiers!

"This way!" called out Santon. "There aren't any defenders."

He blinked and peered into the darkness, wondering at the source of the steam he had seen rising from the tunnel. In the distance he saw white, gauzy veils drifting along. Polar-cold fingers gripped at his heart. He hadn't seen steam or smoke from cooking fires; he had seen phantoms.

How many had died within these treacherous, rocky confines and had gone unburied? Santon counted no fewer than ten phantoms and more came and went untallied.

"Please help me," came one plaintive's cry. "My body is somewhere near. I know it. It must be . . ."

Santon did not answer. Phantoms could not detect their own corpses; they were souls cut adrift and lost between heaven and hell. Contact with those still living proved possible but they could not communicate with other phantoms. Santon had done his part in finding bodies and giving them the proper burial to put the shade to rest, but he dared not make that effort now.

Cocking his head to one side he heard the pounding of hooves—more hooves than Lorens' troops accounted for.

"Pursuit! Ionia sends her guardsmen after us!" He reined his horse around and plunged into the inky blackness, praying that Ionia had not littered her commerce tunnel with pits or booby traps.

The level floor proved slippery from seepage but otherwise safe. Still, Santon pulled back and let the others catch up with him. He strained to see if the guardsmen entered after them of if they considered pursuit futile. If they followed, Vered might never be able to get by them. They would form a plug that would effectively stopper him on the wrong side of the tunnel.

If that happened, the pressure to use the Demon Crown to see a way past would be overwhelming.

"Are they pursuing?" Santon asked of the lieutenant.

"They are moving slower but yes, they come after us." The officer frowned as he peered at Santon. The only illumination afforded them came from the feeble light of drifting phantoms. "You do not want them in the tunnel. Why?"

"I . . . Lokenna's husband is afraid of tight spaces. He likes to be able to see a way out." The lie came slowly to Santon. He did not prevaricate as easily as Vered. This sounded flat and both he and the lieutenant knew for what it was.

"Very well. We can send a small squad back to do what they can."

"Let me go with them."

"Lorens' orders are to see you and the woman through to the other end of the tunnel. I'll tend to this personally."

Santon watched the officer wheel around and go to the three nearest soldiers. The four rode back to do battle. Santon hoped that they succeeded in driving Ionia's men out of the tunnel. If they failed, Vered would never be able to get through. Santon wondered why Ionia had not placed a stronger guard at the tunnel mouth—but he knew she would after this.

"Come, we must hurry. There will be barges at the docks soon," said Lokenna.

"You saw this—before?"

"Yes. Cargo had gone upriver. The sudden winter storms prevented heavy loading on the return trip. We can get passage."

"And then?"

"Then we reach Castle Porotane and have other matters to cope with."

"How's your husband holding up?" Santon looked up and saw the arched vault of the tunnel coming lower and lower as they rode. The rocky roof soon brushed the top of his head, forcing him to ride hunched over. If it came any lower, he would have to dismount and lead his horse.

"Bane was trapped in a cave when he was a young boy. This must be frightening for him." Lokenna spoke in an offhand manner, no emotion tingeing her words. Santon wondered, not for the first time, how loyal she was to her husband. Love seemed to be lacking on both their parts; was devotion enough to hold Lokenna to him?

Santon didn't think it was, not when she had tasted the power granted by the Demon Crown.

Santon rode along in silence, trying not to hear the phantoms' wails or the steel-on-steel clanking from behind.

CHAPTER NINE

"I can't take more of this. I can't!" Bane Pandasso screamed and charged ahead wildly, leaving his protesting horse behind. Birtle Santon had seen the tension mounting in the man for the past mile. Pandasso's shoulders had hunched far more than needed to get through the low-ceilinged tunnel; it appeared that the innkeeper carried the weight of the entire mountain on his back.

The lieutenant, carrying a guttering torch that produced more noxious fumes than light, started after him. Lokenna held the officer back. "Let him go," she said. "He isn't going to run far, nor is he likely to hurt himself."

"Not in this tunnel," grumbled the lieutenant. "There's nothing in here except those bedamned phantoms."

Santon wiped the back of his neck to get off a

cold droplet of water that had dripped from above. Ahead he heard Pandasso running as if a horde of demons chased after him. He felt sorry for the man. Fearing tight spaces had to tell on his courage, and who was without some fear, but Santon scorned the man more. Others in the tiny band obviously disliked the low roof and tight fits through the tunnel with their horses, but they controlled themselves. Such weakness on Pandasso's part only shamed Lokenna.

Or so it seemed to Santon.

He paused and pressed his ear to the cold rock wall to detect any vibrations in the tunnel behind. The lieutenant had driven out Ionia's guard with a single frontal attack. Had this given enough opportunity for Vered to enter the tunnel? He could not tell. Between the noises made by the restless horses and the frightened, running Bane Pandasso, all hope of hearing a solitary man following vanished.

Without Vered, his and Lokenna's position became untenable when they reached the castle. Santon heaved a deep sigh and doggedly walked on. He estimated his chances for driving a dagger into Lorens' corrupted heart and did not like the odds for escape afterward. The mad king cavorted and bounced around like a child's toy, appearing boneless at times and then going stiff like a stone statue come to life.

The more Lokenna attempted to talk with her brother, the more Lorens spurned her.

Santon did not think there would be such difficulty in killing Lorens—except for the occasional cunning glint he caught in the wizard-king's eye. It was as if Lorens put on a small drama to keep the troops amused while his agile mind worked

on, considering matters great and small. Santon
ignored the antics. The problem Santon faced was
the loyalty of Lorens's soldiers. They had gone
through much with their king in the Yorral Mountains. Did this bond them strongly enough or could
they be swayed to Lokenna's side?

Santon had no easy answer for that. In the
officer he saw a chance for shifting allegiance to
Lokenna. The lesser ranks might follow their lieutenant, who was personable and fair as a commander. Santon shook his head and gave up such
speculation as a waste of time.

"It would not work," came Lokenna's soft
voice. Santon jumped at the unexpected answer to
a question he had not given voice to. The woman
laughed gently. "No, I do not pry into your mind
using some arcane magic spell. Your intentions
are obvious to everyone."

"He is your brother. I meant you no disrespect."

"No disrespect to me or death to him." Lokenna's eyes fixed on her brother. Lorens dangled
over the back of his horse, pretending to be a sack
of flour. "Look at him. Child or madman? Who
can say?"

"Madman. The Demon Crown did it to him."

"You've known him longer than anyone else
here. I must believe you."

"Have you learned what you need from him?"

"No. He is careful when he speaks of the
crown, not revealing enough to fill in the gaps in
my knowledge. Lorens is also far more adroit a
wizard than he lets on. The crown has brought out
skills even his master did not possess."

"Patrin was the most powerful wizard in the
kingdom, or so said Alarice."

"Alarice," mused Lokenna. "That is a name my brother refuses to mention. I have pointedly inquired after her and he turns the question to an insult."

"She died so that he could ascend the throne." Santon did not try to keep the bitterness from his voice.

"You loved her," stated Lokenna. "I see the way you examine each phantom as we pass. Do you think to find her among these poor abandoned souls?"

"She is—was—a wizard in her own right. She is not bound to the area where she died like these wights. She has spoken to me several times."

"I would like to meet her, even if it is only a dim shadow of her former self. There is so much I need to know that Lorens will not speak about." With a sudden animation, Lokenna asked, "What do you know of the Wizard of Storms?"

"Nothing more than that Alarice feared him—no, wait. Fear is too strong. She respected him but also strongly disapproved."

"He brings the storms to the mountains. These are not naturally occurring—you can sense that, can't you?"

Santon shook his head. "I guessed it."

"Magic," Lokenna sighed. "There is so much to learn and so little time."

Santon stopped and stared. Outlined in an arch of twilight stood Bane Pandasso. Tears of joy ran down the man's cheeks. He threw himself to the ground and dug his fingers into the rocky soil. "We have come to the end of Ionia's tunnel," said Santon.

"So it seems. The worst of the journey lies ahead of us," said Lokenna. She held her head up high and walked on, looking more like a queen by the instant.

"Too much. Too high," insisted Santon as he bargained for the use of the river barge.

"Then stay and freeze off your arses." The bargemaster stopped and inclined his head slightly in Lokenna's direction. "No offense meant to you, milady."

"So you think to insult the rest of us. Is that it?" demanded Santon, enjoying the haggling. Life pumped through his tired body and the argument gave him purpose once more. Lorens and the soldiers held back and let him ply his skills against those of the river man.

Santon took the bargemaster by the arm and led him to the side of the craft. "The soldiers I travel with—you know them?" The bargemaster shook his head. "They are King Lorens' personal guard."

The grizzled man laughed out loud. "You want me to think that *he* is our king? That's a rich one!" The bargemaster pointed at Lorens, then began to laugh even harder until tears ran down his ruddy cheeks.

"Do you deny we could seize this barge by force of arms?"

"You threaten me? Me? That's even funnier. I have Lord Dews' personal guarantee of safe passage."

"Indeed? Show it to me."

"Right here it is." The bargemaster fumbled beneath his heavy coat and pulled out a tattered slip of paper. He held it up for Santon to scan. "You see? I have the protection of Lord Dews himself."

"Alas, I do not see him or his sword here to aid you." Santon swung his shield around and caught the bargemaster's arm just above the elbow. The man yelped in pain as his arm went numb. With a deft grab, Santon took the pass.

"Here now, you can't do this!"

Santon swung the shield around once more, this time connecting just under the man's chin. The bargemaster's head snapped backward as he tumbled into the icy River Ty. He came to the surface sputtering and gasping for air.

"Best get into dry clothing before you catch your death," Santon said, unsmiling. Seeing the former bargemaster paddling for the far shore, Santon turned and signalled Lokenna and the others. "My liege, the craft is ours for the taking."

Santon showed the rebel pass to Lokenna, who handed it over to the lieutenant. She said, "Do with this what you must."

"Get us to the castle. Do it now, now, yes, do it now!" Lorens cut capers like a jester, trying a handspring that failed and left him upside-down against the rude shelter in the aft of the barge. Santon would have laughed save for the momentary impression of ugly black insects coming from Lorens's mouth. He remembered what Lokenna had said about her brother—darkness and evil surrounded him.

The expression on the king's face also bespoke of death. His lips moved and a spell formed.

"Brother, stop it!" snapped Lokenna. The sense of dread faded as Lorens righted himself and motioned imperiously to the officer and the few men remaining in his personal guard. They had already begun leading the horses aboard.

"You deny me my simple pleasures, sister. Do

not make that mistake again." His dark eyes blazed with hatred. Hardened though he was, Birtle Santon found himself moving away from the madman.

"Cast off the mooring lines," came the lieutenant's command. The movement of the barge into the sluggish flow of the river broke the tension. Lorens spun smartly and vanished into the bargemaster's rude quarters as his men started the tedious work of poling along.

The craft moved slowly at first, then gained speed as it neared the center of the current. Occasional ice floes banged hard against the hull. Each one startled Santon.

"You are no river man," said the lieutenant, laughing at his discomfort. "I grew up here. Makes me feel alive."

"Do you regret leaving to join the king's guard?" asked Lokenna.

"Of course. But the rebels must be put down." The lieutenant touched the rebel pass in his pocket. "Someone of royal blood must reign in Porotane." He issued a few more commands to keep the craft on a straight course in the flow, then asked Lokenna, "Is it true? Are you his sister? There is so little resemblance."

"We are twins." Lokenna stared at the distant, passing shoreline. "It is difficult for me to believe we are related, yet I know it is true. Even more than your word, Birtle," she added.

"She is a wizard, too?" the officer asked of Santon. Santon's voice failed him. All he could do was nod. The Demon Crown had awakened much in Lokenna—and it continued to grow. He looked to the land in hope of sighting Vered.

The young adventurer was nowhere to be

seen. Santon didn't know if this was for the good or not.

"Lieutenant," came an aggrieved cry from the stern. "There is a chain across the river ahead of us. Men with bows are positioned on either shore to keep us from cutting the barricade."

"Strip off your uniform insignia," the lieutenant ordered, obeying his own command. He heaved the betraying rank into the river, where it vanished tracelessly into a cold, watery grave. "We are filthy enough to hide the fact that the uniforms are of the same cut and color. Most of you, stay in the hold."

A tall man with a long red banner signalled them from the near shore. Santon waited anxiously as the lieutenant expertly guided the barge over, his soldiers poling slowly.

"Good day to you, Bargemaster," came the greeting. "You don't look to be laden with cargo this trip."

"We need drydocking. Sprung a leak in the hold, we did. Damn boat's going down on us slow," the lieutenant shouted back.

"You got the proper papers?"

The officer held up the pass issued by the rebel leader. Santon held his breath. He saw from the size of the garrison on the bank and the heavy stone fortifications that stretched around the river's bend that fighting their way free would be impossible. They had to bluff—and avoid a search.

"Can't see it from here. Pole closer." Behind the rebel moved archers. Santon saw one dip the arrow tip in pitch and wait beside a firepot. A single flaming arrow could send them to the bottom of the river.

"We can't get past the chain without using the

pass," the lieutenant said. "We'll be fine. Wait and see."

Two of his men worked a pole back and forth along the riverward side of the barge, complaining as they worked. When the barge was close enough, the lieutenant jumped across to the bank with the pass.

Santon waited impatiently, his barrel chest ready to explode from holding his breath. He panted harshly when the officer returned and signalled for his men to pole them back into the river.

"The pass was good?" asked Santon.

The lieutenant shook his head. "He never looked at it." The officer rubbed thumb and forefinger together to show what had convinced the rebel to let them pass.

Santon watched as the massive chain was pulled back from the river to let them by. He waved to one rebel on the shore, who waved back. The rebels weren't so much different, he decided.

How could the kingdom be any worse off in Dews Gaemock's hands when bribery still worked its own magic?

"There are the royal docks," said Santon, not sure if he was happy to see them. The barge had listed in a storm two days prior and the rocking motion had given him a continual case of seasickness. Even the lieutenant who professed to have been raised on the river had not fared well. Only Lokenna appeared untouched by the motion. But considerations other than his personal comfort nagged at him.

"You fear for me," said Lokenna, leaning against a thin pole and staring at the castle rising in the distance.

"I fear for my own life, too. Now that we have arrived, Lorens can tap into new reserves of troops. They still remember him as king, after all. Even without the crown, he is more formidable here than in the Yorral Mountains."

"What has happened in Castle Porotane in his absence?" Lokenna asked. Santon wasn't sure if she spoke to him or merely put voice to her inner thoughts. Changing subject abruptly, she said, "I remember it. The details aren't mine yet, but I remember the castle, but not in winter. In spring, with greenery surrounding the castle. An arbor?"

"Brambles for defense," supplied Santon.

"That the demon-damned place you been yearning for?" asked Pandasso. He had lost weight from his own bout with river sickness. Santon still considered him to be a pig.

"Her castle," Santon said pointedly. "It belongs to the ruler of Porotane."

"She's no ruler. She's my wife." Pandasso's tone had changed during the trip, though. He had seen Lokenna grow in stature until her regal bearing matched that of the proudest monarch. His words carried less belligerence even if he still protested the obvious.

"There is fighting on the shore," said Lokenna, interrupting the pointless squabble. "Rebels attack the royalist troops."

Santon did not need the woman to tell him this. The ragtag rabble attacking the uniformed ranks could be comprised only of rebels. They fought with the unity of a company, yet had the look of poor farmers and merchants. He found himself shaking his head in amazement. The rebels parted the approaching cavalry and began hacking the soldiers to bloody ribbons. For all their lack of military precision and beauty, they fought valiantly and well—and their officers knew tactics.

"We must make our own way to the castle," said the lieutenant. "We can expect no help from them. The fools! They ran into a trap as if they were led by the greenest recruit."

"They might be. Who can say what has—" Santon fell silent abruptly when he saw Lorens lightly jump from the barge to the dock. The man's eyes had glazed over. He held his arms in front of him as if blind and he had to feel his way along an unknown corridor. But the dancing sparks at his fingertips told of immense magic powers beyond an ordinary mortal's control.

"I feel it. The blackness rises within him," said Lokenna, her eyes clamped tightly shut. "How does he tolerate it? It . . . it makes my skin ripple with its evil."

The explosion knocked over those on the barge. Santon shook his head, trying to clear away the ringing in his ears. His vision had filled with dancing yellow and blue dots that only slowly faded. When his keen sight returned, his stomach turned over and over worse than it had during his bout of seasickness.

Wars had washed past him. He had seen destruction so bad that it dulled his mind. But this? Never had Birtle Santon seen such destruction of life. He wanted to vomit.

Lorens' spell had exploded *within* each of the rebel soldiers. As if a huge taloned beast had clawed its way free, their bellies and chests were left in mutilated, bloody strips. The snow-dusted landscape had turned an ugly red from their life's blood. Here and there spots sizzled as the super-heated fluid cooled.

"There," said Lorens with some satisfaction. "That will keep the rebels in their place."

Santon found it difficult to stand. Only Lo-kenna's aid made it possible for his rubbery legs to begin walking. When they reached the dock, he waved her off, preferring to be on his own. How could such a fiend possess so much power?

Lorens had slain with the pass of his hand—and showed no remorse at the ghastly deaths. He acted as if he had stepped on a *mor*roach and nothing more.

The ambushed soldiers re-formed their ranks. Santon looked around the countryside, hoping to see Vered. Lokenna needed the Demon Crown to counter such immense power on her brother's part.

Santon walked, but he did not see his friend. Every step closer to the castle caused dread to mount that much more.

"The castle," Lorens said with gusto. "And it is mine! I rule with absolute power within its walls. Soon enough, that power will enfold the entire kingdom!"

Darkness had fallen. Watchfires along the battlements sputtered and sent sparks and smoke into the clean, clean air. They had not encountered any more rebels on their march from the docks, but many spies had been eliminated. Lorens licked his lips at the thought of those fools sending small children to spy on him.

He cared naught if they were grown or babes in arms. Traitors were traitors and he would kill them all!

If only he had the Demon Crown . . .

His hard eyes turned back to the castle walls. Fear leaped and died inside him when he thought of what he might find. Archbishop Nosto had been so powerful. But what of Theoll? The small baron had coveted the throne. And others? Lorens had spied on dozens of plots and counterplots when he had worn the Demon Crown.

The crown. He needed it now!"

"Majesty?" came a timorous voice. For an instant Lorens thought the voices that sometimes spoke within his head had returned. Then he realized it was only the whoreson married to his sister.

"Yes, my dear brother-in-law," he said with mock civility. Lorens pondered the spell that would remove this odious piece of garbage. Patrin had not taught him many useful spells, but that small grounding in magic had served him well enough. What he had not been taught by his master, he had learned wearing the crown.

Where was that wondrous magical device? Torturing Lokenna might be enough, but he doubted it. She spoke with the ring of truth in her voice when she said she did not know where the golden crown was—but could recover it.

"King Lorens?" Pandasso licked dried lips and rubbed his pudgy hands together nervously, as if to cleanse them of guilt. "We're almost at the castle, aren't we?"

Lorens held back his acid retort. Of course they were at the castle. Any fool could see it rising before them.

"Yes. What can I do for you?" he asked, his voice silken.

"Majesty, you see, it's like this. Between me

and Lokenna, it was all just as good as fresh cream until those two showed up with that damned crown."

Lorens said nothing. New schemes formed. He might have found an unexpected ally in this oaf. Torture might not be required, after all.

"I want things to be like they was between us. I'm a good husband." Pandasso shuffled his feet and averted his eyes. Lorens knew the man lied. "I just want us to go back to Fron and forget all this. I don't need to go into the castle—and my wife's no queen."

"True," Lorens said. "But there are problems with restoring your former life."

"The rebels burned the town and my inn with it."

"The crown, dammit," flared Lorens. He quieted down and went on, carefully choosing his words with studied calm. "With the crown, I could aid you immensely."

"I saw what you did this afternoon. The rebels . . ." Pandasso's voice trailed off.

"The King of Porotane has powers far beyond those granted by the Demon Crown." Even as he spoke, coldness gripped Lorens' innards. The power came and went, as did the voices. Now he felt hollow and alone—and weak. So weak! No matter how superior he was to this ignorant peasant, he was deathly alone and vulnerable.

"What if I told you how to get this crown back? What would that mean to me? To me and Lokenna?"

"My sister is stubborn, but I am gracious in my rewards. The crown is hardly necessary, but it is a symbol of power in Porotane." Lorens tried to arc sparks between his fingers to impress Pandasso. He hastily hid his hands under his cloak when nothing happened.

"You give me a new pub and some money—and Lokenna back—and I'll tell you how she intends to get the crown."

"It has something to do with the missing thief, does it not?" Pandasso jumped as if stuck with a needle. Lorens laughed at his simplemindedness. "Of course it does. Why else would one accompany us and never mention the other?"

"She's to meet this Vered outside the castle. He was following us all the way from the Yorral Mountains."

"How is she to signal him?"

"They don't know I know, but I overheard them talking."

"Yes, yes." Lorens stilled his need to recover the crown. He laid a hand on Pandasso's arm. "It's what Lokenna needs, even if she does not realize it. You see more clearly than she does in this. What is the signal?"

Bane Pandasso told him.

CHAPTER TEN

·"The situation is critical, Baron." Commander of
the guard Squann did not have to make this report to Theoll. The small noble had eyes. All he
needed to do was gaze from the uppermost battlements at the gathering horde of rebels to know
the peril. They came like flies to decaying meat.
Getting rid of them would be harder than merely
brushing them off.

"Captain, I appreciate your concern about ex-
ternal matters. What concerns me more is internal—and political. Lady Anneshoria grows bolder
by the day."

"She has many believing her."

Theoll wondered if Squann played some du-
plicitous game. The captain had rushed from Anneshoria's arms to report that the woman plotted
against him—but had the officer known that Theoll

watched his every movement? Were Anneshoria and Squann engaged in triple-dealing?

In Castle Porotane those who merely worked plots within plots were novices—and usually perished for their inexperience. What game did Squann really play and whose pawn was he?

"She awaits you at dawn. The meeting is set so that the other nobles will appear minutes after you have been killed."

"What?" Theoll jerked his attention back from the ramifications of a traitorous guard commander to what the man really said about the plot. "Oh, yes, yes. I know this. I will not let her do away with me that easily."

"It might prove an excellent opportunity to remove Anneshoria," suggested Squann.

Again Theoll worried. Squann shared the woman's bed when she had pointedly refused such an offer from him. And he was regent king! That Squann played both sides to his own advantage, Theoll never doubted. What did he gain? What could Theoll lose?

"The rebels have infiltrated the castle," said Theoll.

"Who, Baron? Give me their names and I will have them beheaded!"

"Nonsense. We can use them. Anneshoria . . . has contacted them. She is a traitor in our ranks." Theoll watched slow realization dawn on the captain's face. The officer brightened at this lie that might rid the castle of Anneshoria permanently and with no chance of reprisal from her supporters.

"I had heard such rumors. I can find facts to verify this."

"Of course you can. Go and do so." Theoll dismissed Squann with a wave of his hand but called out before the captain had left, "A moment, Captain. Who commands the rebel forces at this moment?"

"We have been unable to find out, but from the deployment and tactics, I believe Dalziel Sef faces us. There are none of the subtleties Gaemock always employed."

"What has happened to Gaemock?" Theoll wondered aloud. "It is no matter. Let the rebels diminish their own rank. We have problems of our own with traitors, don't we, Captain Squann?"

"I'll look into it immediately, Baron."

Squann had barely vanished when Theoll sprang up from his paper-strewn desk and went to the ward spell–guarded box behind the tapestry. For the hundredth time, he ran his fingers over the oak lid. It had been tampered with, he saw. A slow smile crossed his thin lips. Anneshoria knew what lay within—and it was all part of his own trap to snare her. The diminutive baron did not care if Squann allied himself with Anneshoria or not.

What had to be done would be accomplished by his own hand.

Theoll spun and went to the far wall. His dagger scraped away mortar to reveal a tiny lever. Prying it free with his dagger tip produced a grating sound. Part of the wall pulled back to reveal a small, dark tube leading into the depths of the castle. Theoll travelled the secret passages of the castle but had only once used this crawlway. It did not pay to advertise all he knew.

As surely as his eyes spied on others, he knew Anneshoria spied on him. Theoll touched the dagger point with his forefinger and decided the weapon was too nicked for use. He threw it across the room and fetched a new, shiny-bladed dirk.

The weapon's gleaming perfection would soon be marred with drying blood.

Theoll sheathed the dirk and dived headfirst into the small tunnel. On hands and knees he made his way quickly through the maze that spiraled ever downward. Only when he came to the dungeon level did he slow down enough to peer through the frequent spy holes in the walls.

A shiver of anticipation passed through him. Anneshoria had brought two soldiers to the dungeons for questioning. He listened to her torturer asking, "Tell us of Theoll's plan. Tell us all you know about the secret niche in the garden wall."

Theoll smiled broadly. Anneshoria *had* penetrated his spell-locked chest! Fake plans showing a hiding place in the castle wall had been part of the trove left for her eyes. The rest told of how he would kill her this morning when they met—just as she planned to kill him, if Squann was to be believed.

A loud shriek of pain echoed through the chamber. The soldier had died denying any complicity in Theoll's assassination scheme. Theoll felt a pang of guilt for the man's death; he had been innocent. But in Castle Porotane everyone took the risk of becoming involved in plotting. The innocent, most of all, became embroiled because of their naivete.

Theoll slipped forward into a hollow space behind a torture device. His hand rested on the dirk. Anneshoria ought to be here watching the torture. She always sat on a special chair back far enough to prevent blood from spattering on her fine gowns. The chair back had been made specially to Theoll's specification. When she sat with her back to a wall, secure that the chair was constructed of heavy wood, he would strike. The blade would slip through the thin false back in a single stroke.

Anneshoria would die in the torture chamber. It might be long minutes—even hours—before anyone discovered it. And who escaped from the dungeon? Her guards had supplanted those of the late Archbishop Nosto. Only a traitor in her own rank could perform such a feat of murderous magic.

Theoll peered through tiny eyeslits in the device. He frowned when he failed to see her head outlined by grim flame leaping on the torturer's brazier.

Did she know? Had Squann alerted her? No, no, it was impossible. This scheme had never been put to paper. No one save Theoll knew the details. He had done it all himself.

Where was the slut?

Theoll pushed open the compartment lid and dared a quick glance into the dungeon. The second soldier's life swung on a thin cable, and the torturer methodically sawed at it. The burly torturer and the sweaty, bloody, naked soldier he took in with one look. Nowhere was Anneshoria to be seen.

His plan had failed!

Theoll wanted to shout, to strike out, to kill. He contained his destructive impulses. With the well-muscled torturer and his many assistants nearby, anything other than a silent retreat would be self-destructive. Theoll crept back into the narrow tubelike tunnel and sat, legs crossed and mind racing.

Something had gone wrong. Anneshoria never missed her amusements in the torture chamber. She was as bad as Archbishop Nosto had been on this point. Theoll's mind turned from the woman's absence to the reasons that might cause it.

A slow smile replaced the worried frown. The only thing that would draw her away from a particularly toothsome torture session would be— Theoll's death!

The Baron scampered up the tunnel and got into the upper levels. He turned and twisted and forced himself past tight-fitting blocks and came out in more familiar ways. He dusted off his filthy clothing, then forgot about it entirely. He heard Anneshoria and Squann arguing.

Pressing his eye to the spy hole in Squann's quarters, he saw the commander of the guard and Lady Anneshoria.

". . . on the battlements, I swear it, lady!" protested Squann.

"You lie. You play at his game, not mine. You lured me here to kill me. You are in his pay, after all I have given you! After all you have meant to me!"

Theoll smirked. He knew what she had given the captain. He had watched enough times.

"So be it!" Squann reached under the bed and drew his sword. Theoll wanted to cry out and warn the captain; he held his tongue. Fighting Anneshoria in this manner would never work. He was startled that Squann did not realize this—and he was even more surprised that Squann supported him over the lovely lady.

Squann launched a decent attack that would have spitted any other unarmed woman. Anneshoria moved with the speed of a striking snake

and danced back. Theoll watched her fumble with
a large ring and twist off a jewel. She held the ring
to her mouth, her pink tongue darting out to sample the white powder within the tiny compartment revealed.

She had moved with the speed of a viper
before. Now her reactions were blinding. The drug
she had taken speeded up movement tenfold. Try
as he might, Squann found it impossible to do
more than put a single slice in the woman's shoulder.

Theoll knew the drug wore off quickly; Anneshoria made the most of the brief acceleration. A
small dagger hardly longer than her middle finger
came from her bodice. She danced inward, past
Squann's flailing, slow thrust and drove the point
into the man's belly.

Squann gasped and folded over, clutching his
guts.

"You will be dead soon enough, fool," Anneshoria said. "The point was poisoned against your
treachery."

Squann peered up at her with glazed eyes. "I
wanted only for Porotane to be united. Too much
war. Too much." He gasped and dropped to his
knees. Theoll felt a pang of sorrow for the man he
had underestimated. Squann had seen the true
ruler of Porotane in him and had tried to eliminate Anneshoria. Theoll realized that he ought to
have trusted the captain. Anneshoria would not
have been diverted from the torture chamber this
night if he had let the man know his plans.

Theoll discarded such a chimerical notion. He
dared not trust Squann, even now as the man died.
Events had forged this course of events and they
must now run their course.

"Where is he?" demanded Anneshoria. "I came here to kill that little whoreson and I will! I will not spend another night sharing the throne with him!"

"He . . . on the battlements. The northern tower looking out over the rebel front." Squann began writhing on the floor in obvious pain. Only an incoherent gagging sound came from his mouth now.

"Very well. I will see him dead on the battlements." Anneshoria jerked her gown away from Squann's feebly clutching fingers and left.

Theoll watched her walk carefully. A slight falter came to her step. The drug had taken its toll. Although it imparted fantastic speed for a few seconds, it left the user drained. He had heard of the drug but had never found any magician able to concoct it. He wondered at Anneshoria's contacts in obtaining such a valuable spell-laced drug.

Theoll used the tip of the dirk he had intended to drive into Anneshoria's back to force open a small portal into Squann's chambers. The guard captain moaned softly and opened his eyes.

"Baron?" he croaked.

"I listened at the wall," said Theoll. "I believe I know the nature of Anneshoria's poison. Be still and we shall see if it can be countered. I have some small knowledge in such matters." He did not tell Squann that he had systematically poisoned Duke Freow and had made a careful study of all possible deadly drugs.

Theoll went through Squann's quarters until he found spare fire liquid for the table lamp. He poured a generous portion onto the wound, then ignited it. Squann screeched in pain.

"Endure, Captain," ordered the baron. "This is for the best. In this you must trust me."

Squann's face turned deathly pale and his eyes remained clamped firmly shut. His twitchings slowed and he lay as still as he could.

"Good." Theoll looked at the large ring on his own thumb and considered the risks in giving Squann the countering agent hidden within. Anneshoria had shown herself to be adept at the use of poisons. Theoll might need this antidote.

Captain Squann had shown himself to be loyal. Theoll realized the need for allies in the coming battle for supremacy within the castle walls. He knelt and forced open Squann's mouth. He opened his ring and knocked a few grains of the yellow powder onto the officer's tongue. Blisters appeared where each grin touched moist flesh. Theoll clamped the mouth firmly shut as Squann went into convulsions.

"Relax. Trust me. This is the antidote. The fire burned away part of her poison at the wound. This attacks the rest of Anneshoria's poison in your body."

Squann slowly relaxed and his eyes opened, the glaze gone.

"You'll live. I'll send the chirurgeon to tend you."

"Baron, I sent her to the battlements."

"I heard. I had intended to eliminate her in the dungeon, but I have no reason to shun the towers."

"Take guards. She is dangerous."

"Rest. I will return when I have finished with her."

Theoll left through the door into the outer corridor. Finding a chirurgeon he could trust at

this time of night would take too long. Squann
might be weak now but the danger had passed.
The guard commander had shown himself to be
strong and brave; a few more hours of pain would
not do him irreparable harm.

Theoll had an assassination to complete.

As his short legs took him even higher in the
castle and onto the exposed battlements, his mind
worked out a different plan. Anneshoria expected
to find him—he would hunt her down. Everything
she intended to do, he would do first. The element
of surprise would be his.

He smiled wickedly. He hoped she tried to use
her drug again. His reading had shown that two
uses within the circuit of the sun left the user a
mindless husk.

Cold wind blew into his face and pulled lank,
dark hair away from his forehead. He had not realized until this moment how much he perspired.
He did not fear Anneshoria, he told himself over
and over.

Theoll was not sure if he lied to himself on
this point. After Lorens had vanished to hunt the
Demon Crown and Archbishop Nosto had been
killed, the woman had risen to power quickly by
skillfully manipulating the other nobles. Theoll
had been unable to use her to further his own
goals and had agreed to the ridiculous division of
power.

Two sitting simultaneously on the throne? Absurd!

The snap of fabric in the strong wind alerted
him to her presence. She moved in shadows ahead
of him, stalking him, thinking that Squann had
spoken the truth in his death throes.

Anneshoria might be expert at stalking in the

boudoir; out here she proved herself a rank amateur. Theoll closed the distance between them quickly and silently.

Stars shone down from the crystal-clear night sky and provided enough illumination for Theoll to see the woman's face. It was drawn as if she experienced considerable strain. For the first time, Theoll let confidence rise within his breast. She feared him!

The dirk came into his hand. Two quick steps closed the distance between them. With his weaker left hand, Theoll reached out and grabbed a handful of the woman's hair. He jerked hard, snapping her head back and forcing her off balance.

"You thought to kill me, lovely Anneshoria. How foolish of you." He lashed out with his dirk, trying to slit her taut throat. The woman twisted around and lowered her chin in time to take the edge of the knife along her cheek. Dark blood spurted in the moonlight, but Theoll saw instantly that this was not a killing stroke. It would leave her disfigured, but he did not want her beauty marred.

He wanted her dead!

She snapped at his wrist, like a caged animal. Theoll pulled back, dagger ready for a second thrust. Anneshoria slipped free, kicking and screaming for the guard. Theoll lunged and missed—and almost died.

Anneshoria grabbed the back of his cloak and tried to heave him over the battlements to the ground below. For a brief instant, Theoll hung suspended, staring out and down.

Below stretched the deadly brambles that protected the lower portions of the castle from ground attack. And beyond? He saw the glint of silvered moonlight off battered armor as the rebel troops changed positions. His mind worked on a dozen items simultaneously. The rebels prepared for a dawn attack. He had to devise a counterplan or the castle might fall.

Fall. Theoll stared back at the brambles so far below and knew fear. He shrieked and lashed out once more with the dagger. The tip caught the woman's hand and opened a deep gash that sent black blood pouring over him.

She tried again to boost him up and over the stone crenellation but her own blood robbed her of purchase on his clothing. Cursing, Anneshoria backed off to launch a new attack.

This time Theoll was ready for her. She gave voice to a battle cry and rushed him. He dipped under the outstretched arms, got his hands on her waist, and heaved.

"Theoll, wait, no!" she pleaded. They had reversed positions. Where he had hung suspended over the edge of the battlements the woman now struggled. "We can come to an agreement. I will go to the western provinces. I will be content with ruling a maritime—"

His dirk moved upward along her belly, but he did not drive the blade into her softness. He let her feel the deadly steel point, to know true fear.

"Theoll!"

"Good-bye, Anneshoria." He dropped the dagger with a loud, ringing clatter to the stone walkway. She relaxed, thinking he had relented and would allow her to go into exile.

Theoll's muscles bunched as he heaved her up and over the side. Anneshoria cartwheeled through the air to her death below, screaming as she fell.

Theoll retrieved his fallen dirk and put it in his belt. Only then did he look.

A contorted body hung on the brambles below, the foot-long thorns piercing the tender, unmoving body. Theoll stood and stared, drained of all emotion. Then he turned and went down the winding stairs to find a chirurgeon for Captain Squann. If the rebels attacked at dawn, he needed an able leader to mount the defense.

A good king never wasted resources.

King Theoll, he said to himself. *King* Theoll!

CHAPTER ELEVEN

"We must not delay getting into the castle, Majesty," cautioned the lieutenant. "The rebel patrols are everywhere. They form their ranks for a dawn attack. We must not be caught outside."

"You mean we should get inside the castle to regain the throne," said Lorens. His dark eyes scanned the edge of the forest for the sign that Vered and the Demon Crown had arrived. Losing the castle to the rebels meant nothing if he could recover his magical crown. Nothing but this mattered. Nothing. *Nothing!*

"We will meet opposition."

"Doubtful." Lorens chuckled. "I put an impostor on the throne in my place. They believe I have never left the castle. The fools believe I still rule!"

The lieutenant said nothing. Lorens faced the

man and studied him. Sparks of the growing darkness within his soul rose and for a brief instant he saw with more than eyes.

"You think they dared try to depose me? Impossible! I took too many precautions."

"It is dangerous in our exposed position. We have too few men left to properly defend you, Majesty. If we were inside the castle, we could call on the entire army for protection."

Lorens barely listened. The secret entry to the castle lay less than an hour's walk away. They could be inside long before Dalziel Sef launched his morning offensive. What Lorens needed above all else was the Demon Crown. If that cowardly traitor Pandasso hadn't lied, the other thief would bring it directly to his hand.

"There!" he cried when he spotted the one long flash and the two short ones. "Get a lantern. Quickly, fool, a lantern!"

"We don't have any, Majesty. And I advise against showing light. The rebels . . ."

"May the demons take all the rebels!" Lorens reeled as blackness swelled around him and the voices within his head began their incessant shrill howling. He blinked and saw a red-glowing land of jagged black rocks and torments beyond his imaginings. As suddenly as it appeared, it vanished—but the stench of death and decay lingering caused his nostrils to flare.

"If you must signal," spoke up a soldier, "we can use the campfire and this shiny bit of metal."

The lieutenant turned and knocked the soldier back. "Showing our position means death!"

Lorens paid them no attention. He drew a short dagger and walked to the banked campfire. He positioned himself and turned the silver blade in such a way that he reflected back two short flashes and a long—the combination Pandasso had told him. No matter what signal came, send back the reverse.

A long and a short. Lorens sent a short and a long.

"Majesty, this is a dangerous game to play."

Lorens spun on the lieutenant, dagger in hand. He jerked and sent the blade up under the officer's lowest rib and into his heart. The lieutenant convulsed once, then slipped silently to the ground.

"You." Lorens pointed to the soldier who had offered the reflecting metal to him. "Take his rank. You are now lieutenant of my personal guard."

Lorens turned back to study the dark terrain between the edge of the forest and his position on the low rise. A ravine afforded the best spot for ambush. "There," he told the soldier struggling to accept his new rank. "A lone man will ride through that ravine in a few minutes. I want him and what he carries."

"Should we take him alive, Majesty?" the new lieutenant asked.

"Yes!" Lorens' command came out a snake's hiss. He dared not lose the crown again. Vered might have hidden it. Torture would loosen his lips, if he had secreted the crown elsewhere.

The newly commissioned officer rushed off to obey. When he returned with half the force, Lorens stopped him. "These are the ones you have chosen?"

"They are the best of those remaining, Majesty."

"Good. I will command them. You are to remain in camp and take my sister and the ancient thief into custody."

"What of your brother-in-law?"

"Dear Bane will be my honored guest. Chains for the other two, royal treatment for my new ally." With that, Lorens motioned the lieutenant off his horse and got up in his place. This mission was too important to trust to a green officer and one who would probably be put to death soon for incompetence.

It was so hard finding good officers.

Lorens held back the demonic cackling that rose to his lips. For a brief, sobering instant, the red-lit land of death and pain appeared in front of him. Demons cavorted and pointed. Lorens shook off the vision. He was going to recover the Demon Crown. He could deal with the demonic presence later.

The ravine provided better cover than he'd dared hope for. Lorens positioned his men and sat quietly, waiting for Vered and the crown. In less than ten minutes he heard the clicking of a horse's hooves against the rocky ground. The dark figure that rose on the far bank of the ravine made Lorens catch his breath.

The green glow from the Demon Crown was visible even through the carrying bag and the crystal case holding it. Lorens wiped sweat from his upper lip. Did he truly see it or did he *see* it? Whichever it was, Lorens sensed victory close at hand.

He stood, hand on his dagger. There would be no need to let this miserable worm live. He had the crown with him.

Vered rode down the steep embankment. In the instant his horse struggled to keep its footing,

Lorens' guard attacked. The horse neighed loudly as a long pike was thrust in front of its hooves. The horse crashed to its knees and sent rider and crown into the air.

By the time Vered had recovered his breath, he stared up into Lorens' smirking face.

"We meet again, you and I. Give me the crown."

Vered tried to kick Lorens' legs from under him. He failed. Lorens dropped to one knee and pressed his dagger against Vered's throat.

"The crown," repeated Lorens.

Vered reached slowly for the rucksack containing the crown and its case. He opened the flap and revealed the crown. Seeing the Demon Crown again, Lorens forgot everything. Like a greedy youngling given a new toy, he grabbed for the crown with both hands. Vered tried to wiggle free but the guards surrounded him.

"It will destroy you if you put it on again," he warned Lorens.

The wizard-king did not hear him. Hands trembling, he lifted the crown and gently placed it on his brow. Lorens jerked stiffly erect and his eyes glazed over. The crown changed from the verdant, lush, alive hues it had assumed when Lokenna wore it to the all-too-familiar corroded copper green bespeaking decay and death.

"It is Sef who mounts the attack against the castle," Lorens said. He turned toward Castle Porotane. His face hardened. "They killed my double. They killed Nosto. Anneshoria and Theoll now rule—no, wait. Theoll just murdered Anneshoria. Theoll thinks to usurp my power. The sniveling whoreson!"

Lorens spun about and stormed off.

"Majesty, what of this one?" called a soldier with a sword point at Vered's throat. He received no answer from the king, but the lieutenant remembered his orders.

"Never mind him. We ride straight for the castle."

Vered did not question why Lorens had ordered his life preserved for the moment, but he doubted it meant he would die of old age. The question foremost in his mind was the fate of Santon and Lokenna. Nothing would make Santon reveal the signal; he would die first. But what had Lorens done to his sister?

The guards dragged Vered back to the temporary campsite. Another small knot of soldiers told Vered where Santon and Lokenna were. He was shoved against his friend; they went down in a pile.

"Vered, they caught you!" Santon moaned at the disaster that had befallen them.

"The crown. Tell us, Vered. What of it?" Lokenna's fear spread through Vered like wildfire.

"You didn't betray me? But how did he know? Does Lorens still retain the power given him by the crown?"

"No, impossible. But he has the crown now. I saw him ride past. He didn't even look in our direction," said Santon.

"Why bother? He can see anywhere in the kingdom using the magic of the crown. Eyes and ears are feeble in comparison. But I rode into a trap. How did he know?"

Lokenna's face went pale. "My husband. He must have overheard and betrayed us to Lorens."

"But why? This means our death—*all* our deaths." Vered grunted when a soldier poked him with a lance. They moved slowly toward the castle and its towering walls.

They spoke softly as they were herded forward. Santon said, "He and Lokenna are . . . drifting apart."

"Sailing apart is more like it," said Vered. "She has become a queen and left him a poor innkeeper."

"But he loved me!" protested Lokenna, still shocked. "How could Bane turn me over to certain death?"

"Where is he?" asked Vered. "Do you think Lorens has already killed him?"

"Pandasso lives," came the new lieutenant's voice from behind. The officer poked them again with a sword to keep them walking briskly. "He thought to barter with King Lorens."

"The crown for a return to the way it was in Fron," guessed Santon.

"No, not even Bane is that stupid," said Lokenna.

The derisive snort from the young lieutenant contradicted the woman's claim.

"I came through heavy rebel troop emplacements," said Vered. "We are going into the teeth of a new storm."

The lieutenant grunted and prodded harder in way of an answer. Vered was not to be denied his chance to talk. To Santon he said, "There is no way the castle can survive the force Dalziel Sef has mustered. Even if the political will is there, the castle must fall this time."

Santon explained briefly what he had learned of the conditions within Castle Porotane. Nothing his friend said made Vered feel any better.

"I came so far with the crown and not once did I so much as touch it," he said.

"I must know," said Lokenna. "How did you follow us? We saw no hint of you in Ionia's tunnel or on the river."

Vered laughed at this. "I had help. Someone showed me the way through the mountains. It was not easy, but I survived and actually came out below you on the river. I might have arrived here before you."

"Help?" Santon's voice almost cracked with the strain. He knew Vered would not trust any casual meeting with strangers in the Yorral Mountains. "Did Alarice's phantom aid you?"

Vered nodded. "She is drawn by the power in the crown. She sensed my weakness and gave me the will to resist its lure."

Lokenna looked from man to man, not sure if they made fun of her. Their solemn expressions and the way Santon turned away and stared forward fixedly assured her that this was no mere jape on their parts.

"Can we rely on her aid inside the castle?" she asked in a whisper.

Vered shook his head. "She told me that Lorens' power repels her. She is a wizard—but she is also a phantom. Her control over things living is diminishing."

A sudden lightning bolt arched across the vault of the clear nighttime sky. Everyone in the small party looked up in surprise.

"Where is the storm cloud that generated *that*?" Santon wondered aloud.

"It builds over the Castle of the Winds," said Vered. "Alarice fears the Wizard of Storms and his meddling in the kingdom's affairs."

"It's raining from a clear sky. How is this possible?" marvelled Lokenna.

They trotted toward the thick brambles surrounding the castle and, at the officer's goading, pushed aside a wall of thorns to reveal a small highway through the thicket. Lorens dismounted and rushed ahead, the glow from the Demon Crown lighting their way.

"See how it possesses him totally? He is its slave, not its master." Vered hesitated before entering the bramble tunnel. With Lorens ahead and the soldiers behind, their chance of escape would be diminished. A hard blow to the back of his head sent him stumbling forward.

"Move along now," came the cold command. "You've got a tryst with a torturer in the dungeons."

"I would go happily to my death," said Santon, "if I could have only a moment alone with Pandasso."

"I join you in that fond wish," said Vered. Rain pelted down from the empty sky, blown down from storms raging over the northern Uvain Plateau. He jumped again when a clap of thunder rolled across the kingdom. It sounded to him as if the reclusive wizard hidden away in his mountains fastness had just declared war.

"We'll never see our way free of this," he grumbled. "Lorens' soldiers have us bound for the dungeon, Sef attacks at dawn, and the Wizard of Storms sends his own weapons against the lot of us. Even if we escape, we'd likely be frozen in his blizzards or beaten to death by his wind or drowned by his floods."

"That's the Vered I know and love," said Santon. "Always looking on the bright side."

"What's worse, my tunic is getting ripped apart by these damnable thorns!"

They came to the castle's stone wall and paralleled it for half a mile. Neither had seen this entry point. A large gate yawned wide and dark before them. The soldiers crowded them through and into a small courtyard Vered identified as being near the southwestern corner of the castle.

When they were forced together in a tight knot by the soldiers, Bane Pandasso rode in. From his precarious perch on horseback he stared down at them. His eyes had turned to saucers and his hands trembled.

"Lokenna, I never meant for this to happen. I wanted only for it to be the way it was between us. The inn. The—"

"Silence," snapped the lieutenant. "I have no orders concerning you. The others go straight to the dungeons."

Pandasso turned and swung awkwardly, trying to hit the lieutenant. The officer ducked easily and used the flat of his sword to knock Pandasso to the ground.

"Put him in with them," the new officer ordered his squad.

"But King Lorens said he was to be treated as an honored guest."

"Go tell Lorens, then," snapped the lieutenant. "Very well," he continued when he saw that no one in this small command had the nerve. "Get the four of them to the dungeons." A wicked smile crossed the man's lips. "And put them all in the same cell." He saluted Santon and said, "I have no great love for traitors, either."

* * *

Lorens erupted into the main courtyard and looked around wildly. Only a few patrolling sentries saw his dramatic entrance. Hurried whispers passed among them and finally one daring guard rushed off to find the commander of the guard and report this unseemly entrance of a man they had thought dead.

Lorens settled down and used the power of the crown to shift his senses through the castle, examining it room by room, listening and watching and learning. He trembled with rage by the time he spied the frantic guard helping Captain Squann down the corridor and out into the courtyard.

"Squann, where is Theoll?"

"Majesty," the captain said, almost doubled over from his injury. "He and Lady Anneshoria—"

"I know," cut in Lorens. "I know about that. Where lies Baron Theoll's loyalty? To himself or to me?"

Captain Squann straightened painfully. "I am sure he will greet your return. We thought you had died."

"Liar! You saw my double assassinated. You knew it was not I who died!"

"Majesty!" the officer protested. "How could I have known? The double was too good. Until this moment, I thought you had perished and with you the power of the crown." The captain's eyes fixed on the blazing ring of green-glowing gold circling Lorens' head.

"I will deal with you later. First, I must find Theoll." Lorens pivoted and faced the eastern portion of the courtyard. "There, He is there, trying to ascend the throne and take the power and title that belongs to *me*. How dare he!"

Lorens trembled as he felt power welling up within. He tried to form the spell that would cause Theoll's guts to erupt from every orifice in his body. What had worked against the rebel soldiers now failed him, even with the augmenting power from the Demon Crown.

To cover his frustration, Lorens shouted, "I'll kill him with my bare hands!" He ignored the sudden downpour of rain and snow from the clear sky; his attention fixed totally on Baron Theoll.

Lorens saw the castle grapevine at work. Theoll learned of his return almost as quickly and surely as if he had used the Demon Crown. The baron blanched and ran. Lorens watched—*saw*—his every move using the crown's power. Theoll darted down one hallway and up another, finding back staircases and pushing through dormitories where soldiers slept noisily. No matter where he ran, Lorens followed magically.

Theoll fearfully looked up and down a broad corridor before opening a secret carved wood panel and slipping into the myriad ways built between walls. Even the thick stone did not prevent Lorens from seeing where Theoll ran.

Step firm and face cold as his anger grew, Lorens began to close the distance between them. Theoll used the secret passages that had given him power. Lorens relied on the ultimate magic in the Demon Crown.

Lorens came to the throne room. At one end of the immense audience chamber rose the dais holding the throne that so many coveted. He stared at it, as if seeing it for the first time. Since his father King Lamost had reigned from that throne, a usurper, a double, Theoll, and Anneshoria had occupied it. Their rule had been brief.

Lorens would rule for a thousand years!

The power erupting from sources found by the crown, he turned and laid his hands on a blank stone wall. Fingers glowing with an ugly green light, he pulled back suddenly. The wall collapsed and revealed a cowering Theoll.

"You thought to depose me, Baron. I cannot tolerate that."

"I only meant to hold the throne as regent. Majesty. I meant you no harm."

"Liar!" raged Lorens.

Theoll saw death in Lorens' eyes and glowing touch. He stood and stared up at the magic-possessed wizard-king. Fear evaporated in the face of certain death.

"I wanted the throne," Theoll said defiantly. "And the brief time between Freow's death and your return I governed Porotane well. I would do it again!"

Theoll lunged, dirk gleaming in the greenish glow cast by Lorens' hands and the Demon Crown.

The spell conjured by Lorens caught the small baron and threw him high into the air. Theoll crashed to the floor, burned by the magical fires and crushed by the height of his fall. Rebellion still flickered in his dying eyes.

"You mock me. You, you little worm!" Lorens launched a burst of magic so intense it burned the flesh from the left side of Theoll's body. The monarch struggled to create the spell that would make the baron explode. That spell eluded him again.

"I would make a better king," sobbed out Theoll. The baron clawed his way up the steps to the throne. Before Lorens could cross the room and drive the dagger deep into his heart, Theoll sat on the throne.

For the span of a heartbeat he was King of Porotane.

CHAPTER TWELVE

"Don't kill me. Please don't!" begged Bane Pandasso. His eyes had turned wide with fear when the cell door slammed behind them. Birtle Santon and Vered glared at the man. Lokenna stood to one side, not willing to interfere if the two adventurers decided to strangle her husband, as they had promised.

"You betrayed me—us!" roared Vered. "I don't lose my temper often. I am losing it now!"

"Wait, Vered," cautioned Santon. "This will do us no good."

"Killing this slug? It'll make me feel better at being tossed in this stinking dungeon. *That's* what good it will do."

"Lorens is watching with the crown," said Lokenna. "I feel the blackness about it. It . . . it

117

tickles—or burns. It is difficult to describe its vile magic."

"Then let him see what becomes of his toadies."

Santon grabbed Vered's arm and held the younger man back. "Did it ever occur to you that this is exactly what Lorens wants? He'd love nothing better than to see us rip one another apart in our anger."

"Let it be *his* blood that flows." Vered spat at Pandasso.

"I did not mean this to happen. I only wanted life to return to the way it was before you came to Fron." The man's bulky belly rolled to and fro as he talked. "If anyone's to blame, it's the pair of you!"

"You betrayed us to my brother," said Lokenna. "Even one as naive as you, Bane, ought to have known what that meant."

"Lorens *enjoys* wearing the crown," Vered said coldly, his anger beginning to fade. "Or hadn't you noticed?"

"How was I to know?" Pandasso wiped at the tears forming in his eyes. "Do you think an innkeeper knows of such things? Or an innkeeper's wife?" He spun on Lokenna. "What do you mean calling me 'naive'?"

"You are, my husband."

"And you, the wife of a simple innkeeper, have somehow gained the wisdom of the world? Pah!" Pandasso spat and moved from the trio, hunkering down in a corner of the straw-littered stone cell.

"I have," Lokenna said softly. "The Demon Crown educates its wearer quickly."

"But it hasn't taken control of you." Santon

formed the words as a statement, but he almost turned it into a question. Lokenna was vastly different from the woman they had met, and the crown had been the only instrument capable of such change.

"The crown does not force change. It allows it. I lack the proper words to make you understand. If there is weakness, it destroys you through them, but if you use your strength with the crown, you become invincible!"

"Lorens' problem is ambition," said Santon. "He served as Patrin's apprentice for too long. He never learned to handle power because his master failed to train him in its use. Given this boundless magical power, he runs wild."

"There is that," said Lokenna, "but he is also weak and abuses what he has. The crown makes it seem as if it caused the change." She frowned. "It does something more, too. There were hints."

"These were the matters you wished to discuss with Lorens?" asked Vered, who paced the cell like an animal. He rattled the bars in the tiny door window and found no weakness.

"I received hints of a door . . . opening. The door overlooked a perilous land populated with hideous creatures."

"Demons?"

"Yes, perhaps. I don't know." Lokenna turned and leaned against the wall, her head bowed. "It matters naught. He will kill us. He has the crown."

"In case you missed it, we're under siege," said Santon. "The rebel army is going to keep him busy. Knowing where they place the troops, where they attack, where their weaknesses lie, does nothing if Lorens cannot mobilize the castle's defenses."

"Theoll will have tried to regain the throne. He tasted power once after Duke Freow died. He wants it permanently."

"And I am sure others, such as this Lady Anneshoria the guardsmen mentioned on the way down to these fine quarters, see themselves as ruler." Vered peered through the bars, then wiggled his hand down the front of the metal door trying to find the lock. He gave up when cramps caused his arm to twitch.

"Do you think the rebels will win?" asked Lokenna. "I noticed one in particular while using the crown. He seemed a decent sort."

"A decent rebel? Pah! Goes to show how much you've to learn," cut in Pandasso. "They burned my inn. They destroyed your home. *That's* how decent they are!"

"That was Dalziel Sef," she said. "No, another caught my attention. Efran Gaemock."

"Lord Dews' brother," said Santon. "His name is unfamiliar."

"He's supposed to have died years ago," said Vered. "Or perhaps he turned tail and ran."

"He served as jester," said Lokenna. "In the court of the duke."

"Efran Gaemock was Harhar?" Santon and Vered exchanged bemused glances. Santon grinned crookedly. "I always thought more lay behind those mad acts of his than need to make others jolly."

"Why did he have truck with Duke Freow?" asked Vered. "Why not go along with Theoll's scheme to assassinate him?"

"He and Dews Gaemock parted on their desire for stablility in the kingdom," she said. "Efran wanted one of royal blood on the throne and Dews wanted only change."

"Both have their wish now," Vered said, grumbling. He dropped to his knees and examined the lock carefully. From inside the lining of his once-fine tunic he took a slender piece of springy metal. He worked it into the lock and sat patiently, working it about inside the mechanism.

"Can he get us free?" Lokenna asked.

"If anyone can, Vered is our man. He's quite good at this."

Lokenna stared, but Santon saw that she did not watch Vered. Her thoughts drifted elsewhere. She said suddenly, "We need an ally. Against Lorens we have no chance. He is too powerful—and he knows how to use the crown."

"The crown is using him. Don't care what you say," Vered said as he worked at the lock. "You want us to join up with Harhar?"

"Efran?" The woman smiled mysteriously. Santon wondered what thoughts ran through her mind. They were completely closed to him as he studied her face. "No, he lacks the power. We must find another."

"Who can possibly oppose Lorens?" asked Santon. The answer came to him before Lokenna spoke.

"The Wizard of Storms. He is all-powerful while he remains within his Castle of the Winds."

"You mean he cannot leave or he loses his power? No one's ever even hinted at that," exclaimed Santon.

"I don't know how I know it. My senses spread out across Porotane and I touched on many bits of information. But I do know this. He can aid us. The storms he sends cloud Lorens' power—and the wizard commands an army more powerful than any of flesh and blood."

"There!" called Vered. He drew the steel strip from the lock and pushed open the cell door. "Let's go find our wizard."

"You agree we should ally ourselves with him?" Santon asked, startled at his friend's easy acceptance. Vered had never shown any trust of any wizard.

"If the Wizard of Storms is across Porotane, across the Uvain Plateau, and high in the Yorral Mountains, I'm all for seeking him out. I just want to be free of this stinking prison!"

Vered stepped out of the cell and screeched in pain. Santon bulled his way forward and kicked hard at the metal door. It groaned as it swung on its hinges—and the abrupt exit saved Vered from a sword thrust by a jailer.

"Where did he come from?" wondered Vered as he got his feet under him and danced away from the armed man.

Santon's meaty fist crashed into the side of the jailer's head, knocking the man to the floor. Vered pounced like a hunting cat and grabbed away the sword. A single quick lunge ended this threat to their freedom.

"I know where he came from," Lokenna said from inside the cell.

"Another insight from using the crown?" taunted Vered.

"He came with the rest of the squad."

Santon and Vered spun. Facing them were six armed and armored soldiers ready for a fight.

"Here!" called Vered, tossing the nearest soldier the sword he'd captured. The soldier reacted as Vered had hoped. He grabbed for the sword hilt. As he moved out of position, Vered dived low and caught the guardsman just above the knees, bowling him over.

Santon lost track of what happened then. A soldier taller and burlier than he bellowed and charged. Santon's good hand caught the soldier's thick wrist and forced the mace away. The soldier's left hand drove hard into Santon's exposed midriff.

The air erupted from Santon's lungs and he sank to the cold stone floor, gasping for breath. He was aware of Bane Pandasso rushing past him. A single blow from the huge soldier sent Pandasso crashing back into the cell.

By the time his vision cleared and his lungs did not protest air seeping in and out, Santon saw that they were lost. More than a dozen alert guards crowded around, weapons drawn and ready to kill. It took him several seconds to realize that Vered was nowhere to be seen. Hope sprang up inside.

"Don't worry about your friend," the big guardsman said, peering down at Santon. "He cannot get far."

"Even if he does escape us, he'll never run far enough to get away from King Lorens," boasted another.

With a sinking sensation, Santon knew how true this was. A booted foot cut off his ruminations on the subject and drove him back into the cell.

"Oow," moaned Pandasso, nursing his face. Blood flowed freely from his broken nose and split lip. Santon wasn't sure if this didn't improve the piggish man's appearance.

"Are you hurt?" asked Lokenna.

For an instant Santon thought the woman spoke to her husband. Lokenna ignored Pandasso's moanings and had knelt nearby. Santon nodded. "I'll live—at least until they see fit to execute us."

"Vered got away," she said.

"There is still a chance, then," he said, but he doubted it. Vered was a single light against the darkness gathering around them. The entire squad of guards had stayed on duty outside. And what the one soldier said rang all too true. Whenever Lorens saw fit, he could use the Demon Crown to examine every niche in the castle and find Vered. The wizard-king need not leave the safety of the throne room.

"I tried to help," moaned Pandasso. "They were too well armed for me to do anything."

Santon said nothing. Pandasso's attack had been ineffectual. Santon found Lokenna's reactions more interesting. She ignored her husband totally and ran light, probing fingers over the spot where the guardsman's fist had struck him in the chest.

"Bruised ribs," she said, not telling Santon anything he did not already know. "But there is nothing broken."

"It takes more than that to stop me," he boasted. A moment of giddiness passed when he heaved himself to his feet. He peered out and saw even more guards entering the cell block. Even if Vered recruited half the rebel army, there would be no chance of escaping this cordon of steel unscathed.

"What's wrong?" Lokenna asked.

"Your brother might have remembered that there is no need to keep us around," Santon said truthfully. He recognized an execution detail when he saw it. The sight of the commander of the castle guard personally in charge meant their deaths had been ordered.

Santon watched curiously as Captain Squann dismissed most of the men present and positioned the few remaining at the entrance into the dungeons, well away from the cell. Hope flared until the commander spoke.

"Your deaths have been ordered by King Lorens," Squann said loudly.

"It is as I suspected," said Lokenna. Tears welled at the corners of her eyes, but it was her husband who took the sentence the worst. Wracking sobs shook Pandasso's bulky body.

"When?" asked Santon. He had lived on the edge of life overlong. He had known for some time that only luck kept him alive. Now, at least, he would join Alarice in her phantom wanderings across Porotane. Santon did not think that Lorens would allow a proper burial for enemies of their magnitude.

"Keep protesting loudly," whispered Squann. "I am here to release you, but the others do not know."

"What treachery is this? Do you hope to instill hope in us, then dash it to make the torture worse?" Santon studied Squann's pain-etched face and again dared hope.

"I have been ordered to kill you."

"Becoming a traitor to your kind is preferable?" asked Lokenna.

"He cannot be my kind. He is cruel. I . . . I thought Baron Theoll might be able to unite the kingdom and stop this war. I was wrong."

"Lorens might be listening to us. You place

yourself in jeopardy even speaking to us in this way," warned Santon.

"I know. It matters little to me." Sweat beaded on Squann's face. He pulled back his shoulders and winced. "I may be dying. Theoll tried to save me from a poisoned blade, but I fear his magic remedies failed."

"You do this to strike back at Lorens?"

"I do this in the hope that you will be able to bring peace to Porotane." Squann looked over his shoulder, then said in a voice so low that Santon almost failed to hear it. "You must not attempt to escape. Only then can I justify the minimum number of guards."

"What is your plan?"

"There is a secret way from the castle." Santon almost laughed at this. Alarice had known of one and revealed it to him and Vered. Lorens had reentered the castle though another secret door. Did Squann know a third way? Castle Porotane leaked secret passages in and out.

"We agree. Do you understand, Pandasso? We can get out of this with whole skins if you obey. Do you understand?" Santon kicked at Pandasso, who cowered in a corner.

"I'll go. Just don't harm me."

"It means all our lives if you disobey the captain."

Santon and Lokenna exchanged glances. Her eyes were unreadable, but Santon hoped she could control her husband's cowardice. Squann had no reason to lie to them. Lorens had them completely under his power and the giving of hope, then dashing it through a cruel twist did not seem his style of torture.

"Out, prisoners," ordered Squann in a loud

voice. The cell door swung back. The guardsmen turned and drew their weapons, instantly wary. Squann signalled them to proceed. "They won't try to escape. They are resigned to their fate."

"Never seen a prisoner going to his death who was resigned to it, Captain," said one.

"Ruvary, go on ahead and make sure the strangling posts are ready in the courtyard," Squann ordered. The soldier who had spoken started to protest, then turned and left.

Squann walked boldly forward toward the three remaining guards. "You, check the corridors to be certain no one obstructs our progress. You two, follow along behind to make sure they don't dally on their way to execution."

As one turned, Squann drew his dagger and swung the handle down hard on the soldier's head. A sick crunch told of a crushed skull. The other guard turned and for an instant ignored Santon. Santon's powerful right arm circled the man's throat in an unbreakable hold.

"Should I finish him?" asked Santon. A curt nod from Squann spelled the guardsman's death. Santon jerked and broke his neck, then cast him aside.

"Hurry. We have little time before Ruvary wonders what's become of us. He's loyal to Lorens."

"You mean he's after your job."

For the first time Squann smiled. "In other circumstances, I could like you. You understand what happens within these walls."

"I was here long enough to see how you people live," said Santon. He started after Squann, then stopped. "Wait. Vered! We've got to find him!"

"The one who tried to escape earlier?" Squann shook his head. "There is no time. Ruvary is suspicious of me. We dare not waste an instant reaching the tunnel."

"Vered might have already gotten free," said Lokenna.

Santon hesitated. He did not like the idea of abandoning his friend. The clank of heavily armed soldiers patrolling the corridor spurred him into action he did not like.

"Let's get out of here. If we're caught, we're no good to Vered."

"He might have escaped. He remains free, at least," Squann assured him.

They went through the dungeons and up stairs clogged with cobwebs and bold vermin larger than Santon's hand. They came to a small arch that had been sealed years ago.

"This is the spot. Begin pulling down the blocks," ordered Squann. He tossed his dagger to Santon and turned to drag his sword blade along the lines of crumbling mortar.

Santon balanced the dagger in hand for a moment, considering again the chance that this was a complicated trap set by Lorens. Again he had to assume that Squann had nothing to gain by such a charade—and neither did Lorens. The wizard-king took his amusement from other sources.

"Where does this lead?" Santon asked, pushing a block through into the tunnel beyond. Fetid air gusted into his face and bespoke long years of entombment.

"I don't know. I came across it on an ancient map of the castle."

"What became of the map?" asked Lokenna.

"I destroyed it. There's no reason to let others

know of this." Squann grunted as he lifted down a block. His face had grown increasingly pale, but he motioned Lokenna away when she went to aid him. "There's no time. We must get away from the castle. It matters naught if Lorens can see us unless he has the power to reach us."

Santon started to tell the captain about the king's magic spells that had exploded the rebel troops into sausage, but Lokenna shook her head and silenced him.

"Get into the tunnel," urged Squann.

"It's dark in there. And I see red eyes staring out. There's vermin inside bigger'n me!" Pandasso backed away. "You can't make me go in there. I went through that damned tunnel in the mountain. But I won't go here."

"Go or stay and die," said Santon. He had no time for the man's fears. He saw that Lokenna agreed. She stepped over the fallen blocks and went into the tunnel.

"We need a torch to see," she called back.

"There's nothing around here," said Squann. "We dare not find one, either. I hear them searching for us."

Santon cocked his head to one side and strained. From the dungeon came sounds of pursuit. Ruvary had returned and found their handiwork. Two dead guards—and Squann missing. An ambitious man would see his chance and seize it. No matter what happened, Ruvary would have Squann's rank afterward.

"I'll lead the way. My night vision's good," said Santon. "Squann, bring up the rear."

"What about me?" cried Pandasso. "You can't leave me here to die. They want to kill me!"

"Tunnel or death—you choose." Santon

ducked his head and entered the tunnel, squeezing past Lokenna. He heard Pandasso sobbing as he swallowed his fears and entered the tunnel. Proceeding cautiously, Santon checked the floor for sudden pits or deadfalls. The musty odor increased as he walked, however, and he decided that any mechanical traps laid in this corridor had long ago fallen apart. All they needed to worry about was behind them.

"You coming, Squann?" he called back.

"Go on," gasped out the commander of the guard. "I . . . the poison works faster at my guts. Get away. Do what you can."

His voice cut off suddenly and was replaced by the clash of steel against steel.

"We have only minutes before Ruvary follows," said Lokenna.

"Longer," said Santon. "Squann is dying but he has heart. Ruvary won't find him an easy target."

Santon plunged on into the inky tunnel, worrying about what lay ahead and behind—and most of all about Vered's fate.

CHAPTER THIRTEEN

Lightning danced along the chipped stone battlements of Castle Porotane. The vivid purple and green discharges blew away shards of stone and made walking patrol impossible. The guards protested to their officers, who dared not carry the complaints further, fearing what King Lorens might say. Along with the lightning came intense rain and a wind so strong that it ripped away the wizard-king's banner and sent it fluttering into the night.

"Bring the traitor up here," ordered Ruvary. The soldier hesitated; Ruvary did not. He struck the soldier squarely on the side of his head, sending the man tumbling down a flight of stone steps. "When I give an order, you will obey it without question. The next time you think to disobey, you die!"

He had to shout to make himself heard over the intense storm boiling around the castle walls. Ruvary settled down to stare into the turmoil, wondering if he had properly chosen his road to power. Supporting a demented soul like Lorens might mean death if a powerful enough wizard opposed him.

But Ruvary had yet to decide if this storm was the product of magical opposition or the result of a spell conjured by Lorens himself. If the wizard-king brought on such a potent defense of his castle, it would never do abandoning him—betraying him.

Ruvary had been tempted to join Squann in the secret tunnel and escape. Ambition burned too brightly within him for that, though. The idea of bringing to justice such a traitor in the ranks of King Lorens' guard assured him of a secure post.

"As secure as I can get," he muttered to himself. The gusts of wind drowned out his mumbled words and insured that no one overheard. In spite of this isolation caused by the elements, Ruvary looked around guiltily. Lorens knew everything. They said the Demon Crown gave these powers, but Ruvary cared little for such speculation. That the king knew anything was proof enough that he had cast his lot with the winning side.

"May the demons take all rebels!" he shouted in the teeth of the storm. As if answering, a jagged bolt edged down from the sky and blew apart the landing above him. Ruvary threw up his arm to protect his face from flying fragments.

Doubt assailed him again. Did Lorens conjure this storm to protect the castle from the rebel forces or did another, more powerful wizard send it as a screen for the rebel attack?

"Captain, here he is," came a frightened voice. Ruvary turned to see two guards supporting Squann. His predecessor as commander of the guard twitched feebly. One eye came open and peered at him, but Ruvary did not care about Squann's condition.

"Take him to the battlements."

"But the storm!" protested the one who had given him trouble before. This time Ruvary lashed out with his heavy boot. The man lost his balance and tumbled backward down the stone steps. Halfway down the flight bright red spots began to appear. By the time the soldier landed, neck broken and face destroyed, at the foot of the stairs, his blood colored every worn step.

"Take the traitor to the battlements," Ruvary ordered again. This time fear of his punishment outweighed fear of the storm. They dragged a limp Squann to the walkway.

"Over there. Put him by the pole that supported the banner." Ruvary felt uneasiness growing. He stripped off his metal armor and cast it down the steps. He did not allow his men to follow his lead in this. If a lightning bolt came down from above, let it seek out his underlings. They existed only to serve him—and to die, if necessary.

"Ruvary," croaked Squann. "This does no good. I am dying. Poison. Anneshoria poisoned me with a blade."

"You allowed the prisoners to escape. No," said Ruvary, enjoying this moment of superiority to the utmost. "You didn't *allow* the prisoners to escape. You *helped* them."

"The kingdom." Squann's next words vanished in the sonic assault from the thunder. "We must stop the war. It is destroying us all."

"You sell out to rebels? That is your way of ending the fighting? You should have obeyed our liege lord. Only by following King Lorens can we unite Porotane." Ruvary looked around self-consciously, wondering if his noble speech went unheeded by his monarch. He had no hint to the effect of his words, either on king or storm.

"Captain, the storm worsens," protested a soldier. The lightning blast limned him and turned him into something less than human. For a brief instant, Ruvary thought the flesh had been stripped from the guardsman's body and only his skeleton was left. He blinked and wiped the rain from his eyes. A chill worked down from the Yorral Mountains and threatened to turn this cold rain into sleet.

"Tie his hands to the pulley," he ordered. Ruvary watched as Squann was bound to the flagstaff. "Raise him."

The soldiers exchanged glances, then hastened to obey. The thunder deafened them; it also drowned out Squann's cries of pain as they jerked him slowly upward on the staff. The wind caught his thrashing body and pulled him away. Ruvary wondered if he could estimate the wind's velocity by the angle Squann's body made with the flagpole.

Such a notion vanished when the very heavens opened with a powerful jagged sword thrust of lightning that ripped asunder clouds and terminated on Squann's torso. A cascade of burned offal rained down. Again Ruvary tried to protect his eyes but the afterimages remained—and they frightened him.

He did not see yellow and blue dots dancing

merrily. He saw demons cavorting as they feasted on Squann's cremated flesh.

"Down. Get out of the storm. Now!" Ruvary was first down the stairs. He heard the others behind him, but he dared not turn to see if they were uninjured. The image of the demons had burned itself into his brain as surely as the energy bolt had seared Squann's body. Ruvary slipped and almost fell when he came to the foot of the stairs; he had forgotten the pool of blood left by the other unfortunate soldier.

Boots leaving bloody prints, Ruvary went to report the traitor's execution to King Lorens.

"I cannot see. I cannot feel. I am blind and deaf. Who puts me into this black existence?" Lorens paced back and forth, wailing piteously and struggling to set the crown more firmly on his head. No matter how he twisted or turned it, no images from afar appeared.

"Calmness. I must not panic. Why doesn't the Demon Crown work? What have I done wrong? What? A spell? *What?*" He spun in fright when a strong rapping sounded at the door to his chambers. "Who is it?" he called.

"Captain Ruvary reporting, Majesty."

"Enter and be damned."

Ruvary came through the door more timidly than his knock had intimated. Lorens took some small pleasure in being able to frighten an underling. Not a year ago, Ruvary would have terrified him, a poor apprentice wizard never straying far from his master. Now the powerful soldier feared him!

"Majesty, the traitor has been put to death. On the battlements."

"Yes, yes, I know," Lorens said. "I watched." He kept the panic from rising in his voice. Anything within the castle appeared perfectly to the magic of the crown. Nothing beyond the boundaries of Castle Porotane could be spied upon. He was blind and deaf when he needed his power most. What caused this blackness?

Who caused it?

"Do you think the rebels will attack in the storm, Majesty?"

"They are fools if they do. Dalziel Sef might consider it a bold stroke, though."

"Gaemock is not their commander?"

"I could not locate Gaemock." Lorens bit his tongue to keep from revealing more of his weakness. He had concentrated on Sef's troop placements, his weaknesses and his strengths. Of Dews Gaemock he had not seen a trace. If the rebel leader plotted elsewhere in Porotane, such a move had been hidden by the sudden storm.

"Do we prepare to repel or do we mount an offensive of our own and sally forth?" Ruvary shifted restlessly from foot to foot while trying not to seem nervous in the presence of his liege. "I need to know so that I can prepare the formations and have the horses saddled and ready by dawn."

"Attack or defend," mused Lorens. He tried to remember what he could about the rebel position. "Ask Squann. He knows such things."

"Sire, Squann is dead. You witnessed his execution for treason against you."

"What? Yes, of course, I knew that. Yes." The winter cold that had crept into the castle didn't matter; Lorens experienced a sudden fever. His hold on the soldiers seemed tenuous. He dared not let this ambitious whoreson take over. Squann had tried to do that. Squann had died. He remembered that now. He could kill Ruvary, too. Yes, that was what he had to do. But later. After the rebels were defeated.

He smiled crookedly. Ruvary might die a hero in battle. That would solve the problem of another ruthless, relentless soldier trying to usurp power as Baron Theoll had done.

"Defense is out of the question. Dalziel Sef will never launch a direct attack. He will attempt to lay siege to the castle. The early winter favors him, diminishing our stores more quickly."

"Then we attack?" Ruvary sounded uncertain of this approach.

"I know the precise location of every cavalry unit Sef has in the field. Is that not good enough for you to defeat him?"

"He is entrenched on the upper slopes."

"They are not slopes. They are hills. Less!"

Ruvary started to speak but Lorens' mood quieted him. The king did not have to charge up a fortified slope wreathed in falling snow; his men might have to in the morning.

"You worry needlessly, Ruvary." Lorens regained his confidence. Sef would not move his troops in this storm. His position would be unchanged from the last scrying with the crown. "I will show you their troop concentrations, their weaknesses, how you will attack and win."

Lorens pulled out a map of the surrounding countryside and began marking the positions for his new field commander. By the time he left, Ruvary's confidence had soared.

Lorens watched the officer leave, sure of his victory. The longer Lorens thought about it, the less certain he became that he properly remembered the images he had seen. He spent the remainder of the night listening to the storm and worrying.

Why wouldn't the Demon Crown function?

"The storm is lifting, Majesty. Thank you."

Lorens looked at his new captain and almost asked what he meant. Lorens held his tongue in time. It would not do to admit that he had not been the author of the prodigious storm that had hammered away at the castle walls all night.

"You will ride directly to glorious victory. Nothing can stop you. Go now!"

The heavy castle gates cranked open and the line of mounted soldiers stirred in anticipation of the coming battle. When the gates had opened enough to allow a double column through, Ruvary gave the command and they raced out to meet the rebels.

Lorens walked up to the battlements and stared across the countryside to where the major battle would occur. The storm had left the land damp and the sky cloudless and blue. The uneasiness he had felt at being in the storm and blinded by it evaporated when he saw how proud and strong his troops looked. They rode into battle at his order. And they would triumph this day for his glory!

The Demon Crown warmed to his touch and glowed its familiar off-hue green. He closed his eyes, then slowly opened them and both saw and *saw*. Sef had not repositioned his troops during the storm. Everything he had told Ruvary remained true. There was no way he could lose if his soldiers fought valiantly!

Using the magic given him by the crown, Lorens relished the sight of blood flowing as the front of his assault force met the outer fringes of the rebel defense. The enemy drew back, then turned and ran in complete rout. His forces pushed on, the double column splitting, one half going to the east and the other plunging westward.

The rebels to the east had the chance to escape into the farmlands. His cavalry spent needless time tracking down the fleeing cowards. The true battle occurred to the west where his soldiers pinned the rebels into a fork in the river. If Sef were to escape, he would have to cross the River Ty.

Lorens watched and saw that the rebel leader could not do it. He had made no provision for escape, thinking his position secure. That cost Sef the battle. The rebel fought well enough, Lorens *saw*; but to no avail. He had lost the high ground, he could not flee across the river without boats, and the river effectively hemmed him in.

He had to fight like a cornered rat or die.

Lorens laughed aloud, the sound that of a madman. Sef had no choice. He would die even if he fought!

"Squire!" the wizard-king bellowed. "Prepare my steed. I will ride to the scene of battle and personally lead my troops."

The frightened squire hurried to obey. Lorens flicked the hem of his cape up and dangled it over his left arm. Head high, crown giving him minute by minute intelligence about the fight, he went to the courtyard, allowed the squire to help him mount, and then rode quickly for the front lines.

Lorens marvelled at the change that had come about in him. While under Patrin's tutelage, he had feared all things beyond the ordinary. Now he rode through the rebel-infested countryside to take his place at the front of troops fighting a desperate enemy. Courage came with the Demon Crown.

Lorens also knew that there was no one along the road to waylay him. A quick survey using the crown had shown only barren land denuded by troops and the ice-storm of the night before.

He sucked in a lungful of crisp, cold air and rode with head held high, as befitted a conqueror. He had led his men to conquest over the rebels. He had vanquished them. Duke Freow had failed. Theoll had made a botch of it. No one else in Porotane could have succeeded.

"Majesty, you shouldn't be here," came Ruvary's harsh words. "It is too dangerous in the field. They fight with the savagery of a force twice their size."

"You attack in the wrong spot, fool," snapped Lorens. He knew the source of his commander's irritation. The rebels held back his troops, true, but Ruvary did not want the soldiers seeing their king leading. He wished to snatch away all the glory for this victory.

"You!" bellowed Lorens. He signalled to a sergeant leading a small company of lancers directly up the hill and into Sef's main force. "March to the west, then cut north and attack their flank. They will collapse totally."

"Majesty, we have few enough troops. To divide—"

"Silence, worm! Obey or die!" Spittle ran down Lorens' chin. Only the wind turning it icy caused him to notice. He swiped at it and adjusted the crown on his head. Black powers welled up within him. He swallowed hard when he saw the peculiar red-lit land peopled by the grotesque dancing figures of demons. Using the magic power locked within the Demon Crown, he directed his senses deeper into his new and daunting world rather than denying its existence.

No, came a booming voice that caused his bones to quake. *Not yet. Your time for this world will come. But not now.*

Lorens wobbled and almost fell from the saddle. Only a gust of frigid wind that brought him to his senses saved him from embarrassment in front of his men.

"You obey or you die." Lorens used the blackness and the denial of his power to form a spell that quickly grew beyond his control.

Lorens recoiled in horror as the swirling terror he created spun and stalked up the hill toward the rebel forces. One rebel, braver than his comrades or less fleet of foot, vanished into the whirling magical pillar. His shrieks of agony were blotted out almost instantly. Left behind was only the memory of the man.

The tornado dissipated but its dire effect on his troops remained. The frightened sergeant ordered his men around the hill in the flanking maneuver, as his wizard-king ordered. "Captain Ruvary be damned," Lorens *heard* the sergeant say. "All he can do is flay me alive. The king can do *that!*"

The sense of power mounted in Lorens. He turned to Ruvary and smirked. Once he would have been frightened of the powerful soldier with the steel sword and battered shield. No longer. He had found a power transcending anything a mortal could command.

"Dalziel Sef," he said suddenly. "The rebel leader is escaping across the river. He has found a small boat. After him, fool. Don't let him escape!"

Lorens threw caution to the winds and rode directly up the hill into the concentrated might of the rebel forces. Following so closely after the cyclonic death he had sent broke the will of the rebels. They threw down their weapons and fled screaming.

King Lorens was first atop the hill where the rebels had been strongest. He watched, eyes sufficing, as the lancers caught the retreat on the tips of their weapons. Nowhere did a rebel remain with defiance in his heart. All knew fear.

All feared Lorens!

"There," he called to Ruvary. "That small boat making its way across the river. Stop it!"

Two men rowed frantically in the tiny boat to get Dalziel Sef away safely. Lorens tried once more to tap the power that had brought the cyclone into existence. As before, he found only impenetrable darkness that defied his attempts to use another spell. He could do nothing but use the Demon Crown to watch Sef flee.

"Archers. Get archers here. Shoot him out of the water. He must not reach the other side alive!"

The archers tried, but Dalziel Sef had gone beyond their range. The swift current of the snow-fed river carried the tiny boat along quicker than usual for this time of year. But even if it hadn't, Sef's escape would have been assured. His head start was too great.

"All the rebels have surrendered, Majesty," Ruvary reported. "Where do you wish them imprisoned? There's a small village, long deserted, not a half day's travel from here."

Lorens brushed off the suggestion. "Kill them. Kill them all."

"But, Majesty, I recommend—"

Lorens swung on his officer, grabbed the man's tunic and pulled him close. Bowing his head allowed the crown to touch Ruvary's forehead. The office gasped and died instantly from the brief contact. Lorens jerked and threw the body to the ground.

"Let him rot. No one is to touch his foul body," Lorens called out. "Let him remain a symbol to all those who would disobey or question my command!"

A hush fell over the conquering army. Lorens smiled crookedly. He had established complete dominance. He waited for the slaughter of the captured rebels to begin before turning slowly to survey his new kingdom, a kingdom unified under his control.

Only when he stared across at the uplift of the Uvain Plateau did he hesitate. Fierce storms clawed along the buttes leading up to the plateau—and the Demon Crown's power faltered again.

He could not see anything on the Uvain Plateau . . . except for a castle perched high on a pinnacle.

CHAPTER FOURTEEN

"Light!" exclaimed Birtle Santon. "I see light ahead."

"How long have we been in this demon-haunted tunnel?" asked Pandasso. He pressed close to Santon, making the adventurer move more quickly to avoid his touch. He could not forget that Pandasso had betrayed Vered to Lorens. Nothing in the man's behavior since had worked in his favor, either.

"Long enough for there to be light outside," said Santon. Then he frowned. The light had vanished. Pandasso ran full into him again. Santon winced as his withered arm scraped the rocky tunnel wall. He wished he still carried the glass shield Alarice had given him. That device had proven useful, not only in saving his life in battle but for protecting his weak arm. It would have been a true boon in this tunnel when the only guidance he had had was a hand along the wall and his sense of direction.

"I hear a storm. Thunder." Lokenna moved to join them. He did not mind her presence. If he had been able to see in the pitch-blackness of the escape tunnel, he would have killed Pandasso and left his body for the vermin.

"There!" he cried. "Light again."

"It's lightning," Lokenna said. "The brilliance shines against rock and reflects into the tunnel."

"It lasts so long. The storm must be incredible. We might be better off in the tunnel until it blows away," suggested Pandasso.

Santon shook his head, then realized they could not see except in the flashes. "We leave immediately upon finding the exit. I don't know why Ruvary didn't pursue us. He might have been too interested in showing off what a traitor Squann was, but the tunnel is open behind us and a squad with a torch can cover the distance in a matter of minutes."

"I don't like the tunnel, but getting wet would be even worse," complained Pandasso.

"Birtle is right," said Lokenna. "It is dangerous remaining in the tunnel. We are captives limited to travel in only two directions—one, if you consider that we dare not return to the castle."

Santon continued his cautious advance until he came to the tumble of stones blocking the exit. He began pushing the rocks away with his good arm. Lokenna joined him. Only when he saw his wife struggling with the huge chunks of stone did Pandasso lend a hand. In a short while they had cleared a crawl space large enough even for Santon's broad shoulders and Pandasso's girth.

"It's been many years since this tunnel was used," said Santon, looking over the stone. "Let's hope the rebels don't have a guard posted outside to watch."

"They don't," Lokenna said positively. "There is no feel of human presence."

Santon peered at her but the woman's face was still cloaked in shadow. Even the purple flashes of lightning outside failed to show her expression. He wondered if she had become infected with the evil carried by the Demon Crown or if this was a knack she'd always possessed.

"Birtle, you worry so," she said, putting a gentle hand on his shoulder. "The crown has awakened much in me, but it has not harmed me. Truly, it hasn't."

"Wait here while I scout and see where we've come out." Santon wiggled through the hole and tumbled out into a raging storm. Wind caught at flesh and chilled him. Rain mixed with snow battered his face. He tucked his bad arm into his belt to keep it from blowing wildly in the gusty winds.

For a minute, he sat hunched over, squinting into the night. The storm gave occasional glimpses of a surreal land populated by creatures from a demented nightmare. Santon slowly recognized those creatures as trees blown over by the storm, rocks strangely limned by the lightning, naturally occurring formations in the land itself. In the distance he heard the gurgling passage of the River Ty and knew his sense of direction had been accurate. The tunnel had twisted around but had eventually headed due east. He walked slowly to a rise and peered into the night. The ice floe–racked river lay a bowshot away—a perfect escape route for any wishing to flee Porotane.

Santon turned and looked back at the castle. The wind and rain chilled his body. The sight of Castle Porotane locked in the grip of the storm chilled his soul. That could not be a naturally occurring storm. The sharp delineation between calm and storm showed that. It was as if a wizard had positioned the storm to strike only at the castle and those within it.

"The Wizard of Storms shows his power," Lokenna said at Santon's elbow. He jumped. He had not heard her approach.

"I thought you were going to stay in the tunnel until I scouted the countryside."

"There is no danger to us. Not when the Wizard of Storms directs his full wrath against my poor brother." The woman tossed back her head. The wind caught her hair and sent it rippling in a long banner. Rain dotted her face and turned Lokenna into a being more than human. She looked at Santon and saw his expression. She smiled and it was the smile of a goddess.

The night had turned infinitely colder for him.

"I hurt my leg. Help me!" came Pandasso's whining voice. "I can't walk. You'll have to carry me."

"Walk or we throw you into the river," Santon said. "I'm in no condition to carry you and your wife's not strong enough." Santon continued to grumble, saying under his breath, "A full team of draft horses might not be strong enough, you giant fat oaf."

An explosion knocked them flat. Santon shook himself and dared to look at the castle. A jagged bolt of purple and green lightning unlike anything he'd ever seen had smashed the uppermost castle turret. He blinked. He thought he saw a body fastened to the flagpole being whipped about by the storm.

"The Wizard of Storms shows his distaste for Lorens this night," Lokenna said. "Come. Let's see if we can't convince him to join us against my brother."

"We're going all the way to the Uvain Plateau?" protested Pandasso. "My leg's turning game. Can't walk that much. It's too far!"

"Then stay." Santon helped Lokenna to her feet and started walking in the direction of the rebel force. He would have preferred skirting their encampment but time pressed in on him like a weight. The Uvain Plateau lay a hundred miles to the northwest and, once on the plateau, reaching the Castle of the Winds meant another two hundred miles of travel. If they had to fight the wizard's storms every second of the way, they might never get there.

"I sense your uncertainty in asking help from the Wizard of Storms," said Lokenna. "I do not like the idea of entreating a wizard of such power to help us, but Lorens and the Demon Crown are too strong to oppose in any other way."

"The rebels will deal with him. What good does the crown do him if he has no followers?" Pandasso hiked along behind them showing no sign of an injury.

"The power lies within, not in his soldiers," said Lokenna. "He can cause great woe if he uses the power of the crown for his own gain."

Santon fell silent. He remembered how Lorens had exploded the rebel troops when they had landed at the royal docks. Such magical power had not been present when they'd found the frightened apprentice wizard in the Desert of Sazan. The crown had greatly augmented his power and had turned him into a vicious, mad killer.

Santon looked over his shoulder at the castle, wondering at Vered's fate. He held back the tide of guilt mounting within but at great emotional cost. He stopped and stared. The huge flashes of lightning lit the landscape in a continuous, if flickering, display brighter than day. At the bramble barrier, near the spot Alarice had shown them, Santon saw movement. He strained and saw four figures emerging from the tunnel of thorns.

"Lokenna, can you make out who that is?"

She shook her head. "Not at this distance. If I wore the Demon Crown, it would be simple. But now?" She again indicated silently that she could make out no details of the four.

Hope flared. Vered knew only the secret ways in and out of the castle shown them by Alarice and Lorens. The tunnel had been discovered by Squann and would be unknown to Vered.

"We should wait. He might find us. That might be Vered."

"Who're the other three? Friends? More'n likely, he's traded us for his own hide."

"Spoken by one who knows true treachery," said Santon, his shoulder muscles bunching tightly. His hand clamped so firmly around the hilt of the dagger that his knuckles turned white and the veins stood out in bold relief.

"We are surrounded by the rebel army," Lokenna pointed out. "Is this the place to wait to see if that is your friend?"

The four emerging from the secret tunnel through the brambles mounted horses and rode at an angle from the castle. Wherever they went, it would require considerable hiking for Santon to catch up.

His guts churned with indecision. He had no reason to believe that any of the riders was Vered. He only hoped that his friend had eluded Ruvary's guardsmen and had escaped the castle walls. The notion that Vered had perished trying to rescue them, when they had already won free of the castle, pained Santon the most.

"We need horses," he said, still watching the riders battle their way through the storm. "Even if none of them is Vered, we need horses to reach the Uvain Plateau. I have no desire to walk all the way—and listen to *his* complaints."

Lokenna's eyes locked with Santon's and silent agreement passed between them. He found himself liking the woman more by the minute. She displayed courage and good sense, but the feelings he held for Alarice were not replaced by those for Lokenna. He admired Lokenna; he could never love her. She held herself apart, aloof, as if she were a spectator to all that happened around her rather than a participant.

Santon glared at the woman's husband. Bane Pandasso would never merit even grudging respect from him. Santon gestured for them to continue their slow march through the rain. The mud sucked at his boots and made walking a trial. Before they had gone a mile, Santon's feet had turned to lumps of ice and he knew he would be unable to continue much longer.

They needed food, shelter, fire—and horses.

"The rebel lines must be ahead," he said. He stared at the way the hillside had been torn up by scores of horses. Even the drenching rain had not been able to mask this spoor. "I'll see what I can find."

"See what you can steal, you mean," grumbled Pandasso.

"So you want to dance into the rebel camp and ask them nicely to give us what we need? How far will that get us?"

"Didn't mean nothing by it."

Santon tried to tell himself not to get angry at Pandasso, but he refused to take his own advice. He could not forget the man's continual whining—and past treachery. Even if Pandasso had betrayed Vered and the crown to Lorens for what seemed a good reason, Santon could never forgive him. They had lost the only bargaining lever they had with the wizard-king by that simple treason.

"Do you want me to go with you?" asked Lokenna. He saw that she meant what she said. She *would* accompany him, if he thought it would help. How unlike her husband Lokenna was.

"I'm safer alone. Wait a while. If I'm not back by sunrise, you go on toward the plateau. You don't want to be caught between rebels and the castle. Better to be behind their lines where they are less apt to keep a sharp lookout."

Seeing that Lokenna agreed with his reasoning, Santon walked off into the storm-cloaked night. A dozen paces placed him in his own world, cut off from everyone else. Santon used his good hand to wipe the rain from his eyes, then bent over and advanced cautiously.

His hunting sense worked for him again. He would have stumbled across a small sentry post if he had continued walking. He dropped into the freezing mud and wiggled on his belly, ignoring the filth. A moment's thought about Vered and how his friend would have been complaining about ruining his fine clothes passed. Santon concentrated on the guards in the post.

He counted five in a crude lean-to. Two slept, one snoring noisily. The other three huddled around a guttering fire continually assaulted by rain and the occasional snowflake.

"Freezing our arses off and for what?" groused one. "We sit and wait when Sef knows that nothing will happen. Not in this demon-cursed weather."

The other two concurred. Santon made his way around the camp, careful not to make too much noise. The wind and rain and snoring drowned out any stray sounds he may have made. He got to the rude corral where they had penned their horses. Under a tiny shelter of limbs he found their tack.

Santon wasted no time. The sky would begin turning pearly with dawn soon—if the storm allowed such light to show. He got a bridle and saddle from the shelter and outfitted the largest horse. Two more trips saw two more animals ready for travel. They whinnied loudly, but the storm prevented the miserable rebel sentries from hearing. Santon felt sorry for them. When their superiors learned that they had allowed a thief to make off with three horses—why not all five?—they would be disciplined severely.

The thought of spare horses appealed to Santon. He readied a fourth and a fifth. In this way they could ride and allow two horses to rest. Lokenna was so light her horse might not need respite, but Santon and Pandasso both weighed down any animal with their bulk.

Santon vaulted into the saddle and led the other four saddled horses from the corral. The rain lessened, then stopped. He urged the animals to greater speed. The sudden lightning of the sky told him that dawn would soon break over the Iron Range.

"Birtle, we're so glad you came back. There is trouble in the castle." Lokenna was beside herself with worry.

He stood in the stirrups and stared at the castle. The storm had disappeared quickly, again betraying its magical origin. The main gate of the castle caught his attention.

"Lorens launches an assault on the rebel line. We've got to be away quickly!"

"The storm blinded him. I felt him trying to use the crown and failing, but with the magic storm past, he can see everything."

Santon helped Lokenna into the saddle, wheeled his steed about, and put his heels to the heaving flanks.

"We're riding into the rebel camp!" cried Pandasso. "We cannot go there. They'll kill us!"

Santon hunched over his horse's neck and spurred the horse on. The two spare animals raced along easily behind. He heard Lokenna's horse and knew they would survive. Of Pandasso's complaints he heard nothing. His plan would get them safely through the rebel ranks and to the plains beyond.

With luck, they would ride unmolested. With luck.

"Halt!" came the challenge. "Who goes there?"

"Messengers for Dalziel Sef. There's cavalry

from the castle on the road. Lorens has launched a full attack. Spread the word!"

The effect exceeded Santon's wildest hope. The rebel guards vanished as they rushed to spread the word and awaken the sleeping camp. They had planned on siege, not defense.

Through the center of the camp rode Santon, Lokenna, and Pandasso. As they went, Santon called out his warning. He had no real love for Dalziel Sef, but his sympathies lay more with the rebel, in spite of all he had done to Fron and other villages, than with Lorens.

Sef showed cruel ambition—Lorens wore the Demon Crown. That made the wizard-king the more dangerous.

Even as he rode, Santon saw the type of soldier Sef had recruited. For the men, he felt a pang of sorrow. They were poorly equipped and did not react to this dire threat in a trained and military fashion. Most would die if Lorens' field commander kept a tight control over his own troops.

The damned civil war had raged far too long. Santon prayed that Lokenna was right and that some alliance with the Wizard of Storms could be forged.

Santon reached the northernmost limits of the rebel camp, his voice hoarse from shouting the warnings. He heard the first clash of steel against steel. Lorens's soldiers had advanced quickly to engage the rebels this soon after leaving Castle Porotane. Santon had no stomach for staying and lending his single strong arm to the fight.

"Santon!" came Lokenna's cry. "To the left. Lorens' men!"

He had no idea how they had penetrated this far through the rebel line in such a short time.

Two armed and armored riders urged their horses on to cut off his escape. Santon cursed his stupidity. When he had sneaked into the rebel sentry post he should have stolen more than tack. The dagger Squann had given him remained his only weapon.

"Keep riding, Lokenna. I'll slow them down." He tossed the reins of the two spare horses to Pandasso. The man had the good sense not to let them drop. With his wife, Pandasso rode on as hard as he could. Lather already flecked the sides of his straining horse.

Santon hoped the animal wouldn't die of exhaustion. When he spun about to face the two royalist soldiers, he hoped he wouldn't die. The dagger seemed an even more pitiful weapon now that he faced one rider with a lance and the other with a battle-ax.

He gauged his chances, then spurred hard so that he rode between the two. At the last possible instant he jerked on the reins and dodged to the left, effectively cutting off the rider with the ax and engaging the lancer from his weak side. The soldier fought to lift his weapon and get it to his left.

Santon ducked under the descending shaft and backhanded the rider, knocking him from his saddle.

With one foe down, Santon kept riding, heading for a stand of trees where a rider with an ax would be at a disadvantage. He veered to the right and for an instant vanished directly behind the rider, who struggled to get his galloping horse turned for the pursuit.

Santon grunted as a tree limb flashed past at head level. He kicked free of his stirrups and used his powerful left arm to swing like an ape. A sudden heave got him onto the limb. Panting, he lay flat and waited for the soldier to follow his trail.

So intent was the soldier on the hoof marks in the muddy ground that he failed to look up. Santon slipped off the limb and looped his arm around the rider's throat. A spiked gorget cut into Santon's arm, but he cared less for strangling the soldier than he did with unseating him. They crashed to the ground, the armor putting the fallen soldier at a disadvantage.

Santon used his dagger, driving the sharp point into an exposed armpit. The soldier died instantly.

He sank to his knees and unfastened the ax from the soldier's wrist and put it around his own. He still railed against the loss of his glass shield but having an ax once more made him feel complete.

Santon got his horse and spent a few minutes rounding up the other two horses. He checked them for trail rations and found little. Lorens expected this attack to be a quick one. From the decreasing sounds of battle, Santon guessed that Lorens' bold attack had crushed the rebels' spirit.

He headed north and west and found the fresh trail left by Lokenna and Pandasso. Within an hour he had overtaken them. Within two they had left the battleground far behind.

But Birtle Santon kept looking over his shoulder, sure that someone watched their flight.

CHAPTER FIFTEEN

Vered moaned as he rubbed his bruised ribs. He had rolled into the guardsman and used his rib cage as a battering ram—but it had been worth the minor injury. The guards had fallen and spent too much time stumbling over one another to catch him. He didn't like leaving Santon and the others in the cell, but their main hope of rescue lay with him if he stayed free.

He dashed to the door leading from the dungeon and found it open—but nonetheless closed to him. An entire squad of guardsmen rattled and clanked down the stairs in front of him.

Vered spun and looked for somewhere to hide. He shuddered when he saw a torture cabinet door propped open. He ducked into the coffinlike device and pulled the lid shut. He almost screamed in horror when it locked into place.

The click of the lid shutting echoed and drowned out the pounding of the soldiers just a few feet away.

Vered struggled violently and found himself falling backward. He banged his head against a low stone ceiling. For a few seconds he simply lay stunned, wondering what he had gotten himself into. Then a slow smile crossed his lips. The torture cabinet had a false back—he had blundered into a secret passageway.

He got to his hands and knees and peered at the dirt under him. Someone had been here recently if he judged the footprints properly. Vered turned his attention back to the torture cabinet. Spy holes gave a good view of the dungeon; his heart leaped to his throat when he saw the guards pushing Santon and the others back into their cell. Even worse, the squad did not depart. They stayed on duty, posted in such a way that he couldn't hope to overcome one without two others seeing.

Vered decided to explore the secret passage rather than waiting for the guards to become lax and trying to pry open the coffin lid. He felt naked without a decent weapon to hold—and his clothing hung in tatters. He wondered if a bath and a new tunic and breeches might not be available before he tackled the job of rescuing Santon.

He crawled along the dirty passage, bumping his head often on the low ceiling. Whoever had passed this way had been much smaller—Vered wondered if it hadn't been Baron Theoll. The small noble had tried spying on him and Santon from a similar secret passage. They had nearly poked out the baron's eye.

The first exit was blocked. Vered moved on, following the spoor left by the previous traveller in these secret ways. When he emerged from the wall, Vered found himself in a familiar section of the castle. He smiled and turned toward his and Santon's old quarters.

Vered pressed his ear against the door and listened hard. The room had been occupied the last time they had checked. No interesting sounds came from within; Vered entered.

"Ah, a wardrobe still fit for the likes of a master thief." He threw open the wardrobe door and selected carefully. The clothing he had abandoned so many weeks ago still hung neatly in the cabinet. Vered decided a bath was out of the question, even if it did mean putting on decent clothing over a filthy skin. He preened in front of a full-length polished sheet of metal, then began searching the room in earnest for a weapon.

He found nothing. Cursing, he slipped from the room and made his way up the stairs at the end of the corridor to a small armory where he found his glass sword, Santon's glass shield, and enough other weaponry to hold off a small army. Vered gathered what he could and returned to his former quarters.

He dumped his treasure trove onto the floor and began sorting through it. He slipped four daggers into the folds of his clothing. Being caught unarmed did not appeal to him. He hefted the glass sword Alarice had given him and admired the way it fit his hand.

"Such a fine weapon. She forged well in glass." Vered started to thrust it through his belt when he heard the rattle of soldiers' gear in the hallway. He dropped the sword onto Santon's shield and shoved them under a pile of blankets just as the door burst open.

Vered used both hands to brush back his brown hair. In his most commanding voice, he demanded, "What is this? Do you always break into a lord's quarters in this scurvy manner?"

"Lord?" The soldier backed off. "Pardon. We search for a prisoner who has escaped from the dungeons."

"Do I look like any such prisoner? Begone!" Vered heaved a sigh when the soldier backed out and closed the door, still muttering apologies. The proper arrogance often carried the day.

He opened the door a crack and peered into the corridor. Satisfied, he slipped out—and froze.

A half-dozen swords pressed into his body.

"This is the one," came a cold voice. "Take him back to the dungeon and keep him separate from the others. Ruvary will interrogate him personally in the morning."

Vered struggled and held his arms high as he allowed them to prod him back down the steep flight of stone steps to the dungeon. His escape hadn't been as successful as he had hoped, but they had forgotten to search him.

The metal door to the cell clanged shut—and Vered still carried four daggers hidden on him. He would have to put them to good use. How, he couldn't say, but he would find a way. He always did.

"This solves one thorny problem, brother," said Dews Gaemock. "We no longer have to worry about Dalziel Sef."

Efran Gaemock stared down the river at the small boat working its way upstream against the heavy current and ice floes. He did not share his brother's confidence that Sef was soundly defeated:

"He's lost most of the army—*our* army," said Efran. "Does that make him impotent?"

"Hardly," said Dews. "But he no longer poses a threat to my command. Those who still rally against Lorens have only one banner to follow—mine."

Efran remained unconvinced. "Let's hear what he has to say. I cannot believe he was foolish enough to attack the castle."

"The scout reported it."

"We lack Lorens' information-gathering ability," said Efran. "I mistrust our source this time."

Dalziel Sef climbed from the boat and limped toward them. "Lords!" he greeted loudly. "Thank you for your hospitality!"

"Damn him," muttered Efran. "He begs sanctuary and we dare not betray the old customs, not when we need every man possible to replace the army he's lost."

"You worry too much about details, Efran." Dews Gaemock strode forward and extended his hand to Sef. "You've caused quite a stir with your attack," he greeted the rebel.

"My attack?" Sef shook his head and settled down into a proffered camp chair. He warmed his hands in front of the small fire and helped himself to some of the porridge gently boiling in a pot. He made a wry face as he burned his tongue on the hot food. Only then did he say, "Lorens attacked me. His troops came gushing out of the castle like a bucket with a hole in the bottom. We had scant warning he'd try such a bold move."

"He sees your every soldier. He listens in on your counsel. He can use the crown at every instant of the day. Why shouldn't he know his attack would succeed?" asked Efran.

"Your brother wasn't there, Dews. He cannot know of the storm."

"Speak directly to me or to no one!" raged Efran. He whipped out a slender knife and held it under Sef's nose.

The rebel leader looked at his reflection in the blade and said to Dews, "The storm was not natural. A wizard of great power conjured it. I think it was Lorens. He used it to shield his movement from my scouts."

Efran drew the blade back swiftly; a lock of Sef's hair fell, got caught in a gust of wind, and drifted away. Sef appeared not to have noticed. He turned back to his porridge, blowing on it until it cooled enough to eat.

"Good food," he said, wolfing it down. "We've been on the damned river for four days. Mostly eating raw fish. Hate fish. This is very good."

"You don't deny he caught your men sleeping?" asked Efran.

"Your brother's opinion of my talents as a commander are small. I tell you, Lorens sent the storm to hide his movement. We had no idea that an attack was planned. When he was alive, Duke Freow had been content to let us lay siege to the castle for months and months. Who'd think Lorens would attack us?"

"Lorens is mad," said Dews. "But in his madness he has outwitted you."

"A minor setback, nothing more," insisted Dalziel Sef as he helped himself to more porridge.

"How many of your men survived?" asked Efran. "We've heard conflicting numbers." For the first time, Sef stared directly at Efran, his eyes bleak.

"Few. Less than a hundred at a guess."

"What?" Neither Dews nor Efran believed this. "But you had over a thousand!"

"He gave no quarter. Any who were not killed outright were captured and slaughtered like sheep. I managed to escape through a quirk of fate. Some fool came riding through camp bellowing that we were under attack. My aides got me to the river and a boat."

"You left your army and fled like a craven." Efran Gaemock's anger mounted. Not only had Dalziel Sef usurped much of the rebel forces, he had turned tail and run at the instant his leadership was needed most.

"Would it have served any purpose for me to have died there, too?"

"Efran," warned Dews. "Do not harm him. We have need of every sword now—even his."

"Especially mine," corrected Sef. "I have survived Lorens' attack. Only I know his style of command in the field."

"He personally led his men?" Efran hardly believed this revelation.

"He ordered his archers to fire when I had barely begun rowing across the river. I'd know him anywhere—him and the glowing Demon Crown."

"This is worse than I thought," said Dews, scratching his chin. "As long as Lorens let his field commander lead the army, the royalists held back. Seeing their monarch in front of his troops might rally the peasants who were undecided."

"We might have difficulty getting supplies," summed up Efran. He stared at Dalziel Sef, with his cracked and yellowed teeth and wondered what went through the man's mind. He had almost single-handedly lost the war for them. A thousand men dead! He and Dews together led fewer than five hundred.

"We can bring together enough of an army to give him second thoughts on sallying forth into the countryside," said Sef. "A few bands of men along the roads will keep Lorens from travelling freely."

"We need to regroup. This is a major setback." Dews paced as he thought of a dozen different courses to pursue. Efran stared at Sef, trying to decipher the man's nonchalance.

It seemed as if this major defeat meant nothing to Sef. Efran saw the rebel cause dying, unless they were clever and bold. Lorens had not only destroyed most of their fighting force, he had swayed the populace to his side. When the royalists were penned in Castle Porotane, the peasants gave freely to the rebels without fear of reprisal.

That ended with Sef's crushing defeat. Lorens' troops could collect punitive taxes and burn out any farmer thought to be aiding the rebels. If Lorens had ordered the deaths of all rebels who surrendered, he had established the rules for the rest of the conflict.

No quarter asked or given.

Efran Gaemock shuddered. He had played at being court jester for two years trying to avoid such a war. Those following Lorens were not necessarily evil. Fear of the Demon Crown forced many to follow when they would otherwise resist. Now pardon for them was out of the question. Efran cursed again under his breath.

"We return to the oxbow above the castle,"

he heard Sef say. "We establish a camp and from there we spread out slowly. We need to establish our presence once more."

"A good plan," said Dews. "If we force the soldiers back into the castle and prevent them from establishing permanent bases in the countryside, we can triumph yet!"

Efran knew that his brother worked himself up into a frenzy before presenting this plan to the troops. He needed to be completely sure of himself and success or it would communicate to those listening—and doubt would cause even more the remaining five hundred to slip off into the night. With five hundred, they stood a chance, small but possible. With less, the rebellion against the royalists died on the spot.

"We must move downriver quickly," decided Dews. "The longer we allow Lorens to roam unopposed, even near the castle, the more difficult it will be to win."

Efran tacitly agreed. He sat, arms crossed and eyes fixed on Dalziel Sef. The other rebel leader had plans of his own. But what? Efran could not decide, but he would watch carefully. The years spent amid Castle Porotane's political maneuverings had not been wasted on him.

"Lorens should have interdicted travel on the river by now," observed Dews. "We've been able to set up camp so that he cannot pry us loose from our position."

"Unless we try another attack on the castle," said Efran. He stood on the rise peering down into the misty distance. Castle Porotane lay beyond the field of vision, obscured by distance and a feeble gray fog that had crept over the land.

"We can't attack. With luck we can accumulate and train enough men to lay siege to the castle again in the spring."

"We can certainly burn the crops to prevent supplies from reaching the castle," said Efran. He spoke of sieges and long-term plans but his mind turned over more immediate problems. Dalziel Sef had been too well behaved since the defeat. His words were conciliatory and his suggestions cautious. That did not match the personality of the man Efran had come to know.

All that he knew for sure was that the defeat had not broken Sef's will. The arrogance he had shown before when he had seized control of the forces in the Yorral Mountains remained.

"Dews?"

"What is it, brother?" Dews Gaemock pored over a map, drawing small arrows to show where raiding parties would best be used.

"We must not allow Sef to continue in a position of command. Send him to the western provinces to recruit a new army. Get him north to Claymore Pass."

"That is a poor idea," said Dews. "Remember the treaty he tried to sign with Ionia? If we hadn't discovered his perfidy and sent our own ambassador, he and Ionia would have seized the pass and mountains for their personal domains."

"My point is not lost on you, then," said Efran. "I do not trust him. Something more than obedience stirs in his wormy brain."

"He is courageous and skilled, in spite of the defeat he suffered."

"*We* suffered," Efran corrected. "His loss put the entire rebellion into jeopardy."

"We need all the skilled warriors we can find."

Efran clasped his hands behind his back and started to pace, his mind racing. The clatter of hooves brought him out of his reverie. He stopped and watched as a company of cavalry rode down a draw and vanished into the cold fog.

"Dews, where are they going?"

"Who?"

"An entire company is a horse. Where have you sent them? This is too large a group to commit. We'd agreed on that."

"I've sent no one anywhere. I ordered our sappers to fortify the roads leading to our camp and to do what they can to insure a good water supply. Perhaps you saw them leading a company of workers."

"These were armed cavalry." Efran spun and stalked off down the hill, found a checkpoint deserted, and proceeded angrily to find the company commander.

The bivouac was deserted. Campfires had been recently snuffed out. Only wispy columns of smoke rose to show that any soldiers had been here. Efran spun at a sound. Dews stood behind him, eyes wide.

"Where did they go?" Dews asked.

"We had regiment strength scattered about. Do any remain under our command?" asked Efran.

They raced back up the hill to their command post, alerted aides, and mounted, riding hard to find their field officers.

Most had left. Those that remained knew nothing.

Efran pointed and cried, "There! You! Stop!"

A solitary soldier struggled with a pack and

weapons. His left leg dragged slightly, making travel difficult.

"Yes, Lord Efran?"

"Where are your comrades? Where are you going?"

"Why, as you ordered. We're en route to the staging area."

"Staging area for what?" asked Dews, his voice cracking with strain.

"For the attack on the castle. Lord Dalziel leads it at dawn."

Efran and Dews exchanged horrified looks. "May the demons take him for all eternity!" exclaimed Efran. "He's doing the same thing again! The fool!"

They spent the next hour taking inventory of their supplies and the number of troops left them. Of five hundred, only one hundred remained—the one hundred closest to their command post. Dalziel Sef had cleverly taken only those at a distance to prevent the Gaemocks from knowing the full perfidy of his plan.

"Assemble the men immediately," Efran ordered. "We march after Sef. With luck, we can stop him. Without it, we might be able to rescue a few survivors."

He and Dews worked frantically to rally their remaining men. Of the hundred left them by Sef, fewer than eighty followed. Efran did not blame the deserters. When leaders had a falling out, the troops suffered—and died.

They marched hard all night and arrived behind Dalziel Sef's scattered lines to see that Lorens and the Demon Crown had again stolen victory from the rebel.

"He's allowed his ranks to be split by cavalry.

Less than two hundred on one side and ... how many on the other, Efran? I cannot see well through the fog."

Efran checked with a scout. "Fewer than a hundred. The battle has only just begun and already he has lost more than a quarter of his total force."

"If we commit, we can save the smaller group." Dews looked at his brother, his expression grim. "Should we risk eighty to save an equal number? None might survive."

"What choice do we have? If we are crushed again, the rebellion is over for good. No one will follow you or me or any leader other than King Lorens."

"Then we attack." No confidence rang in Dews Gaemock's words.

"Death to the royalists!" shouted Efran. "No quarter! No quarter!" He put spurs to his horse and drew his sword, leading the all-out assault. Anything less would doom them all.

Even this drastic attack might prove too weak. If so, he would die with his men.

CHAPTER SIXTEEN

Birtle Santon pulled up the wool scarf and tried to keep the snow from getting onto his cheeks. They had already frozen—or so it felt. Dancing needles on his face kept him aware of continued life. Everything else assured Santon that he had long since died.

His body aches had gone away. The tingling in his fingers and toes had ceased. Even the nagging pain in his arse from being overlong in the saddle had vanished. His entire body, save for the incipient frostbite in his cheeks, had deserted him.

"We must rest," came Lokenna's plea. "To go on in this storm is madness."

"We have no choice," said Santon. His voice rang hollow and strange in his cold ears. It was as if another spoke. His mind floated free and looked back on his useless, frozen body. "There's no shelter, and without it we die."

"We die if we continue," argued Lokenna.

From Bane Pandasso there came only muffled grunts and peculiar whistles. He had long since ceased complaining and rode with his head bowed, more dead than alive.

"The storms shouldn't have been this vicious this early," Santon might speak the words but fact made a liar. They had ridden steadily and well across the plains to the ochre buttes lifting to the Uvain Plateau. Once they crossed the upper lip of the plateau the first freezing rainstorm struck.

Cold water had smashed into their faces; the rain froze on their faces and bodies almost instantly in the gusty, bitter winds coming down from the north. Santon had found a small cave along the plateau rim. For two days they had waited for the storm to lessen in intensity. Santon lied to himself for a third day that no blizzard could maintain such ferocity. On the fourth day it became apparent that no cessation would occur.

They had journeyed on, daring the elements.

That dare had become a curse. Santon knew the storm was not born from the natural actions of wind and wave. Only the Wizard of Storms' magic could produce such unrelenting cold and impossible tenacity. As effectively as if he'd stationed a thousand soldiers to guard the road to the Castle of the Winds, the cunning wizard defended himself with snow and fierce gale.

"Birtle," the woman said sharply. "We cannot go on like this. *I* cannot ride another instant." She reined in and stood, her horses shaking from the intense cold.

"Where do we camp?"

Lokenna had no answer. The flat plateau provided scant windbreak. The land had been farmed in such a way as to reduce elevations. The wine-growing regions that Vered cherished so for their alcoholic products had been devastated by the preternatural cold, stripping even vegetation from the ground.

"Fire," croaked out Pandasso. "There. Fire."

For a moment Santon thought Pandasso wanted only to start a fire. Then he saw the man painfully lifting a frozen hand to point. A desultory column of smoke rose, seemingly from the middle of a field as flat as the land over which they rode. Santon stood in the stirrups and tried to see the source of the smoke.

It might have been steam naturally occurring or it could have been due to a man-made fire. The former would save them. The latter might pose as much danger as freezing. The Uvain Plateau had been beleaguered by brigands for as long as Santon could remember. The civil war in lower Porotane had sapped the will of the monarch to patrol this section properly, and the rebels encouraged any breakdown in civil authority in nearby towns.

The result after twenty years of civil war had been to turn the plateau into a welter of small fiefdoms, each ruled by a brigand warlord. No visitors from lower Porotane were welcome. In this winter weather, Santon thought that *any* visitor threatening to take away heat and food from a local would be killed on sight.

"We ride to the fire," Lokenna said. "I know your objections. What matters it if we freeze into statues waiting for spring before rot sets in or we die with hot steel in our guts? That, at least, would warm us for an instant before we died." She turned her protesting horse toward the column of smoke. Pandasso followed.

Santon tried again in vain to identify the source of the smoke. He snapped the reins and got his horse moving after Lokenna. She had a point. Dying in one fashion as opposed to another meant little.

A hundred yards away, Santon saw a deep crevice cutting through the fertile farmland. That explained why he had been unable to see the source of the smoke—and smoke it was. Tiny embers rose and flared at ground level before turning to soot and ash. Only gray smoke rose above the ground.

"Can you see who lit the fire?" asked Santon, peering over the edge of the rim. Below he saw the campfire in the center of a tiny bivouac.

"No one," said Lokenna. She blinked her eyes. The eyelashes had frosted over and turned them into long snowflakes. This decided Santon. Brigand camp or not, they had to have shelter soon or die. This deep ravine gave it. They would never be able to fight for the right to stay, but even a hint of warmth might do wonders to restore feeling in their limbs.

"There. A way down. A narrow path. Can the horses stay on it?" Santon pointed to the rocky ledge hardly wider than his shoulders.

Lokenna said nothing. She dismounted and led her horse down. It stumbled and found footing difficult on the rock-strewn path but the escape from the cutting wind gave both animal and woman incentive to continue. Pandasso and a spare horse followed. Santon and the remaining spare animal brought up the rear.

By the time he reached the bottom of the ravine, Santon again felt pain throughout his body. The dancing needles had left his cheeks and now applied themselves to his hands and legs and any other portion of his anatomy that had begun to freeze.

"The fire is untended. What happened to the men who started it?" wondered Lokenna. She rubbed her hands together as she bent over the campfire. Santon threw on fresh wood and caused huge gouts of flame to leap skyward. The intense heat drove him backward. He knew how dangerous it was to thaw out quickly.

He skirted the camp, studying the blankets and other gear left behind. It seemed that the former residents had simply evaporated like the snowflakes falling into the column of rising hot air from the fire. Santon dragged out several of the blankets and gave them to Lokenna and Pandasso, then put one around his own shoulders. They had arrived on the plateau ill-equipped for the storms. With this camp's equipment, they'd stand a much better chance when they continued.

"I don't see any sign of them," Santon answered after a ten-minute pause. His teeth no longer threatened to chatter uncontrollably. "It is as if our unwitting hosts simply got up and left."

"I don't like it," said Pandasso. "It's not natural for men to leave like that. Not in foul weather like this."

"For once he said something I can agree with," said Santon. "The fire had not burned down. Whoever started it couldn't have been gone longer than fifteen minutes before we arrived."

"Perhaps longer," Lokenna said thoughtfully, "but where are they? We would have seen them if they'd departed in the last half hour. It took us some time to reach the edge of the ravine and at least fifteen minutes to come down."

Santon's green eyes scanned the sides of the rocky ravine for sign of ambush. No caves providing convenient hiding spots were evident. The question nagging at Santon was simple: Why leave camp, even if the former residents had intended an ambush?

Lokenna fixed their first decent meal since arriving on the Uvain Plateau from provender left by those now departed. The food rumbling in his belly, his arms and legs again working as well as they ever had, Santon went exploring. He didn't like what he found. Footprints went fewer than a dozen paces—then nothing.

It was as if the men who had been here simply evaporated.

"They must have been brigands. Look at this!" Bane Pandasso spilled out a bag filled with silver coins. In different times, Santon would have been interested. Now the piles of silver coin meant nothing. He wanted to tell Pandasso to stop weighing himself down with the useless coins he eagerly stuffed into his own pouch. Food mattered more than inert metal. Even if they encountered a farmer with grain or fresh meat, he would be unlikely to trade it for silver.

Food, not silver, meant survival in this unnatural winter.

"A storm is forming directly overhead," observed Santon. He watched uneasily as the lead-bellied clouds flowed past, giving him the impression that they stood still and he moved. He blinked hard and the illusion vanished.

But seeing more clearly did nothing for his peace of mind. Wispy tendrils of cloud formed on the underside. He and Vered had seen this before in the Yorral Mountains.

"The Wizard of Storms sent warriors from the sky in a similar fashion," he told Lokenna. "Why would he destroy an entire camp of brigands using his magical warriors?"

"My impression of him is sketchy and distorted," she admitted. "But there seems to be an overriding need for solitude. He can never achieve that when Lorens wears the Demon Crown."

Lokenna's eyes locked with Santon's. "The Wizard of Storms has brought all this down on our necks because he wants to be alone?" he asked.

"Who can say what a wizard's motives might be? I can think of stranger ones." She shuddered, and it wasn't from the cold. "My brother sought power through the crown. Now he seeks total domination of all Porotane."

"He's about got it," said Pandasso.

"No thanks to you," snapped Santon. He could not forget the man's betrayal, but he cut off this futile argument. What Pandasso had done was past—for better or for worse. Vered had not shown up and Santon could only assume his friend had perished.

"Take heart," came a soft whisper of wind that formed words next to his ear. Santon jerked upright, whirling around. A patch of gauzy white fog blew apart at his sudden movement.

"What's wrong, Birtle?" Lokenna asked.

"Nothing," he said. Santon started walking, carefully avoiding the drifting fog. In a low voice he called, "Alarice? Is that you?"

"My phantom, dear Birtle. Wait! Stop! You must not seek me. I find it hard to remain here."

"Show yourself. Please! You appeared to Vered."

"He still lives. Do not despair."

"Alarice!"

He called after the wind. The white fog he thought was her phantom drifted apart and blew damply across his face, leaving a thin film of moisture. He wiped away the droplets that intermixed with his tears.

"Birtle, are you all right?" came Lokenna's worried cry.

"I am. We must leave immediately." He looked upward and saw the tendrils from the clouds dipping ever lower. In a few minutes the cloud tails would sweep along the bottom of the ravine. He remembered all too well the power of the Wizard of Storms' magical defenders. The cloud warriors had decimated the ranks of Lorens' soldiers with little effort. What had driven them away, he could not say.

Whatever it was—the wizard's whim or Lorens' magic—it lay beyond his call.

"Get on your horses. We leave *now!*"

He vaulted into the saddle. His horse protested. He patted the mare's neck and tried to soothe the tired and frightened animal. "We must race the wind, you and I," he told her quietly. "We will not get a second chance."

The whites showed around the horse's fearful eyes. She tossed her head and looked at the long streamers of cloud that came from above.

"The clouds turn into warriors," marvelled Pandasso. "Look at them!"

"Those are what killed the brigands who camped here. We will follow them as phantoms unless we get out of this trap." Santon herded Lokenna before him and decided that Pandasso might finally serve a useful purpose by remaining behind as living decoy. When the first of the cloud warriors took form and reached out a vaporous hand in the man's direction, Pandasso let out a shriek of pure terror and frantically spurred his horse after Santon.

The trip up the side of the ravine took no longer than the journey down, yet Santon aged a hundred years. The cloud warriors lacked mobility. In the bottom of the ravine they reigned supreme but lacked the power to follow up the steeply winding trail.

Panting with exhaustion, the horses heaved themselves over the rim of the ravine and once more entered the full-blown snowstorm. To Santon it came as a breath of fresh air. The warmth of the ravine vanished, but he felt a freedom that had been lacking below.

"The clouds! They bring us more magic warriors," Pandasso shouted over the howling wind.

Santon saw the growing danger even as Pandasso spoke. New pillars of mist descended and solidified into warriors twice the height of a man. With footsteps that left behind frozen patches, the cloud warriors advanced on them.

"What can we do?" asked Lokenna.

"Unless your talents match those of your brother, all we can do is flee."

"I am untrained as a wizard. I know only what was revealed to me by the crown."

"Then we ride!"

Visibility limited, Santon chose the easiest path he could. They rode along the gentle contours of the land but the very flatness prevented him from finding adequate hiding places. The cloud warriors might not be able to climb steep ravine walls—but on this part of the Uvain Plateau they walked unhindered by anything larger than a fist-sized rock.

"They're catching up," wheezed Pandasso, still at the rear. The horse he led stumbled and fell.

Santon looked back in time to see one immense cloud warrior lift a bulbous hand and point a stubby finger in the fallen animal's direction. A shaft lanced forth. At first Santon thought it rivalled the lightning still dancing in the clouds above. Then he saw that the white shaft reflected light rather than produced it.

"Ice. The cloud warrior threw a spear of ice at the horse." Santon swallowed hard when he saw the massive ice lance pinning the horse to the rocky ground. The animal kicked feebly but life slowly drained from its dying body.

The nearest cloud warrior lifted a hand and made a sweeping motion. Hail pelted down on Santon with such force that he felt his skin bruising, even through the heavy layers of cloak and blanket circling his shoulders. One hailstone caught him a glancing blow on the side of the head. He wobbled and would have fallen from his horse if Lokenna hadn't reached across to steady him.

"There," she said. "Veer to the left."

Santon, dazed, did as he was ordered. He fell from horseback when the reins were yanked from his hand and the horse dug in all four feet to come to a skidding halt.

He lay on his back, staring up at the underbelly of the storm cloud spawning the magical warriors. Santon watched the cloud drift back in the direction they'd ridden from. He came up to his knees, then got to his feet ready to fight.

"They're ignoring us," he said in awe. "Lokenna! You used a spell to confuse them!"

"No, Birtle, I did no such thing. I saw a horse and rider through the fog and snow. By swerving from our course, the other acted as decoy. The cloud warriors are powerful but slow to react."

"You sent another to death to save us?"

"What choice was there?"

Santon dashed into the fog until he got a better look at the portion of farmland that had become a fierce battlefield. Not one or two riders had drawn the attention of the cloud warriors but a full dozen. From the way they fought, Santon knew they were not simple farmers.

Arrows arched into the cloud warriors and received answering shafts of pure ice. Swords flashed and tried to sever cloudy tendons. In return came monstrous fists laden with hail and searing lightning.

The fight was uneven and ended swiftly.

"Brigands," Lokenna said from beside him. "The Wizard of Storms seeks out brigands and methodically slays them."

"Why? I mean, the brigands are a menace to everyone on the plateau, but what does it matter to a powerful wizard? He is secure in his fine castle."

"Is he?" asked Lokenna. "The brigands are a

symptom of the problem in Porotane. The Demon Crown is the cause of the trouble."

"But the brigands have nothing to do with Lorens. I don't understand."

"The Wizard of Storms desires only solitude for his research. The civil war disrupts the kingdom for a score of years, but this affects him little," said Lokenna.

"It passed by him—until Vered and I returned from the Desert of Sazan with your brother and the Demon Crown."

"The crown disturbs the Wizard of Storms," she said. "He wants it sent back into oblivion, and if he cannot do that, and I think it likely his powers are not that great, he will kill Lorens."

"Our goals are similar."

"Not so," said Lokenna. "I have no love for Lorens, but he is my brother. I will not see him dead without purpose."

"Can you imagine him handing over the crown—or putting it aside?"

"No," she said in a small voice. "But he is all the family I have."

Santon looked back at her husband. Bane Pandasso cowered near the horses. Fate had dealt with Lokenna cruelly. A crazed tyrant for a brother and a craven for a husband.

"Can we use this need on the wizard's part to enlist his aid?"

"I have believed that for some time. We must reach the Castle of the Winds soon." Lokenna looked at the clouds and the warriors dropping to earth from them. "We have little chance of escaping the Wizard of Storms' minions."

"I wish Vered were here to enjoy this bit of

irony," Santon said. "The very one we seek to align ourselves with wants us dead."

"For all that, you sound cheerful," she said.

Santon smiled and indicated that the woman should mount and ride. How could he feel too sad when Alarice had told him that Vered still lived.

His momentary cheerfulness vanished when the storm lifted and he saw the Castle of the Winds perched high atop a rocky spire wreathed in fluffy white clouds.

CHAPTER SEVENTEEN

"Fight, damn your eyes!" shouted Efran Gaemock. His cry rallied the small band of weary,
frightened men in front of him. They doubled their
efforts, firmed their attack line, and then surged
forward. Lorens' soldiers were taken aback by
such ferocity. The rebels under Dalziel Sef had retreated quickly.

Not so this band of berserkers. And of them
Efran proved the fiercest. Ignoring a dozen cuts
to his arms and legs and one large gash across his
cheek, he always attacked and never retreated.
Left and right he cut with his sword until he
seemed to be a magical creation rather than human. When the blade became dull from cutting
into bone and bouncing off armor, he cast it aside
and picked up a fallen weapon. With this new
sword he continued his battle until he stood alone.

"They're running like whipped dogs," he heard someone nearby say. For the first time since he had entered battle, he saw—really *saw*—what they faced.

Lorens had used the Demon Crown well to find the weaknesses in Dalziel Sef's troop deployment. The cavalry attack from the castle had split the rebel force and doomed the larger portion to annihilation. To his immense surprise, Efran saw that most of the smaller group had survived and managed to fight back effectively.

"Attack Lorens' flank," Efran heard ring over the battlefield. His brother sat on a massive black stallion—not the horse he had ridden into battle. From this majestic perch Dews Gaemock formed a new attack against the rear and weaker side of Lorens' now struggling, demoralized forces. If they had succeeded in keeping the rebel troops split, their earlier slaughter would have been duplicated, but this small rebel victory had doomed Lorens.

Efran's thrill of victory faded when he saw that he had rescued the eighty men—and lost the two hundred. Fewer than one hundred and fifty would survive this day in spite of their valiant fighting. The rebels, because of Sef, had gone from fifteen hundred to one-tenth that number in the span of a few days. Years of careful campaigning and building vanished because of one man's ambition.

"Dews!" he called. Efran waved his bloody sword and reflected light from its silvery blade to catch his brother's attention. When he did, he signalled for immediate retreat. Dews nodded, passed the order to his lieutenants, then jerked on the reins of his captured horse and vanished down the other side of the hill.

Efran began gathering those around him and slowly disengaging. Lorens' soldiers had been taken by surprise and retreated when given the chance.

That gave Efran's small band the opportunity to flee for the dubious safety of their base camp.

Efran supervised the pickup of wounded and the retrieval of what supplies they could.

"No!" he shouted when he saw a rebel start to cut the hroat of a fallen soldier dressed in the uniform of Lorens' personal guard. "Let him be."

"He's one of *them*," the bloodied rebel protested.

"We can't take him prisoner. We let him be."

"If it had been the other way, he'd've killed us! Lorens ordered no prisoners left alive."

Efran looked down at the frightened soldier. One of the man's legs had been broken when a horse fell on him. "Take this back to your comrades. We do not slaughter helpless men and women. Think on who you would rather follow in the next battle."

Efran grabbed the rebel's shoulder and pushed him on.

"Wait!"

Efran turned back to the fallen soldier, his eyes bleak.

"Take me with you. I surrender. I don't want to go back to the castle. They . . . he'll order me executed."

"What?"

"King Lorens said that we either died on the field or walked back as victors. He'll have me killed as a failure." The soldier's plaintive tone told Efran that he spoke the truth.

To the rebel who had been intent on slicing the man's throat, Efran said, "See? We may not be superior in numbers but we soar above them in spirit."

The rebel grumbled and went to the stricken soldier. The soldier recoiled, then saw that he was being helped up. He turned pale and wobbled on his broken leg until the rebel hoisted him onto his back and started back to their camp with the injured man.

Efran smiled wanly. They had won a recruit this day. When the soldier healed, he would fight with twice the strength—and for the rebel cause. They would need many more such conversions, though, if they were to triumph.

Efran caught a horse to replace the one that had been cut from under him by a barrage of arrows. He rubbed his wounded calf; an arrow had passed through the fleshy part and embedded itself in his horse. He swung up into the saddle and wheeled about to get a better idea of their position.

His heart turned to ice. Sef had positioned well enough but had not considered Lorens' perfect intelligence-gathering. As a result, they would have to hasten their departure from the battlefield before Lorens turned the crown on them and saw how battered they really were. A quick thrust with a company of fresh cavalry and the rebellion would be crushed for all time.

"Dews," he shouted. "Can you keep them moving back to the river?"

"I must," his brother answered. Dews seemed unscathed by the battle but his paleness told of shock. Efran rode closer and saw the entire left side of his brother's tunic had blossomed with a bloodstain. Dews was losing blood by the bucket.

"Retreat, get them into barges and away downriver. Lorens might keep his troops close to the castle to consolidate his position. He won't come for us until spring."

"Yes, that is so." Dews leaned forward, winced at the pain, then said, "I ask a boon of you, brother:" Their eyes met.

"I'm searching for him. He won't escape. I promise it."

"Good. We'll wait at the river. Join us quickly. There may not be time, if Lorens is in control."

Efran Gaemock turned his horse and rode quickly in the direction of the battlefield. Fog drifted through the wooded area. Already he heard the soft moans of phantoms escaping their mortal bodies. How many would remain phantoms, haunting this bloody patch of Porotane's once-fertile farmland? Too many, he decided. And it was all one man's fault.

Efran helped a few rebels orient themselves and begin the slow journey back to their camp. Many would die on the way but the few who would survive needed what he had to offer.

He found Dalziel Sef sooner than he'd dared hope. The other rebel leader sat with his back against a tree, his leg twisted under him.

"Efran! You've come for me. Hurry, I hear Lorens' men coming. They hunt out all the wounded and cut their throats—even their own!"

"Lorens considers it a sign of weakness to be injured in battle. I spoke with one of his soldiers." Efran stared at the man responsible for single-handedly destroying the rebel army.

"Help me, man. Don't just sit there on your fine steed." Sef cocked his head to one side and studied the animal. "You steal well. Your other horse was hardly worthy of a rebel lord and general."

"This one seems strong and ready to run all day."

"Then help me up and we'll be on our way."

"Help you I will." Efran dismounted and went to Sef's dead horse. He cut a length of leather harness loose and fashioned a loop. He tossed it over Sef's head and got it about the man's armpits.

"What are you doing?" Sef demanded.

"You're wounded. I wouldn't want you to be left behind."

"I can ride. It's only my leg that's injured. Now help me up!"

Efran fastened the leather thong to the saddle horn. He put his heels into the horse's flanks and took off at a trot, dragging a screaming Dalziel Sef behind. He did not seek out the rockiest areas to drag the rebel over, but he considered it. Rather, Efran chose the fastest route to the river where his brother and the remnants of their once-proud army waited.

"Damn you!" sobbed Sef when Efran finally reined back and came to a halt. "I'm all broken up inside." He spat blood and coughed. Pink froth showed at his lips. Efran thought Sef had a punctured lung, possibly from a broken rib.

Efran ignored Dalziel Sef and went to where Dews lay. His brother's condition had worsened. The paleness bordered on death itself, but the first words he spoke were what Efran expected. "Did you find him?"

"I'll bring him before you for judgment."

Efran tugged hard on the leather harness around Sef's body. Two others had to help him stand. They supported Sef before Dews Gaemock's litter.

"You are a fool," Dews said. "You have cost us years of careful work and turned hope into pain and fear."

"Who are you to say what I've done?" Dalziel Sef spat blood and coughed again. "You dared nothing! I almost won the castle after all your tedious years of laying siege. You are a coward, a weakling!"

"Tie him onto a horse and send him to Lorens," suggested a rebel at the edge of the assembled crowd.

"Hang him!" yelled another. Still another demanded torture.

"You hear the will of those you betrayed," Dews said. "I agree with their judgment in this. Execution!"

Dews rose painfully from the litter, a small dagger in his hand. A sudden flash of steel in the sunlight and then a tiny gasp marked Dalziel Sef's passing.

Efran wished he felt something. Elation. Revenge satisfied. Something. Nothing but a dark and abiding hollowness grew within him. He silently helped his brother onto a barge.

They had a long ways to travel before finding a safe encampment for the winter.

CHAPTER EIGHTEEN

"We can't go around them," said Birtle Santon. He studied the marching pillars of lightning-filled mist and saw nothing but death ahead. They had ridden through the storms and nearly frozen to death over the past week. But they had survived— somehow. Now that they had come to the base of the pinnacle holding the Castle of the Winds, he saw how futile their perilous journey had been.

"He uses the cloud warriors well," said Lokenna.

"There's only the one path to the summit," said Pandasso. "Let's forget this madness and go back to Fron. We can rebuild the inn and . . ." His voice trailed off when he realized that neither his wife nor Santon listened. Both drew small maps in the snow as they tried to figure out ways around the towering cloud warriors.

"We might lure them away," said Lokenna.

"Too risky," Santon told her. "We cannot see past this turning in the road. Others might stand sentry beyond. We sneak by these and we might find ourselves trapped, magical beings ahead and behind."

"I wish I had the crown," she said wistfully. "I could see what lies ahead for us."

"The road is not well kept. The horses will have a difficult time, even if we do get around the cloud warriors." Santon looked at the three horses, now half-starved and at the point of exhaustion. The other two horses had perished along the way. Santon wondered if they weren't the lucky ones. The Uvain Plateau emphatically ended at this spot. The pinnacle was sharp and jutted upward as if it could gouge out a piece of the sky. To follow that road winding around the peak meant a major expedition.

Santon was not sure any of them had the strength left for such a steep and treacherous climb. To fight the magical warriors made it all the more difficult.

"We can't sneak by. The Wizard of Storms would not post them here if they were deaf and blind."

"They might use other senses. After all," said Lokenna, "they are nothing but fog."

"Fog and magic," grumbled Pandasso.

"We might be going at this in the wrong way," said Santon, his mind racing in new directions. "Why do we assume that the wizard wouldn't be glad to see us? His magical minions have had innumerable chances to kill us these past few weeks."

"They seek out brigands," said Lokenna.

"They might ignore peasants—and we might seem so to them."

"*I* am nothing more than a humble inn-keeper," said Pandasso. "I want to return to my village and ply my trade."

"What would we do if we did confront the wizard?" asked Santon. "We kill ourselves trying to get past his guards and then what? Does he reach out and send a lightning bolt into our mouths for daring to speak to him? What do we gain by that?"

"You have a point," admitted Lokenna. She stood and faced the nearest cloud warrior. The towering being of gray mist and burning red eyes turned slowly, as if not knowing who disturbed its sentry duty. A foggy hand lifted. Purple and green lightning arced between the fingers.

"We've come to see the Wizard of Storms," called out Santon, standing next to Lokenna. Bane Pandasso cowered behind a large boulder, not daring to show himself. "We have come far to see him—past brigand and royalist soldier alike."

"I am Lokenna, daughter of Lamost," the woman said. "My brother wears the Demon Crown."

The words caused thunder to rumble deep within the cloud warrior. Above scudded new storm clouds with underbellies of steel gray. They swirled and took shape overhead, trailing wisps of cloud stuff. New warriors dropped to the ground and formed a rank beside the guards already on duty.

"What do we do?" asked Santon.

Lokenna shrugged. "I have no idea. We can always die, if the Wizard of Storms refuses to see us."

"Th-they're coming for us!" Pandasso began scuttling away. Santon grabbed the man with his powerful left hand and jerked him to his feet.

"We stand together," Santon said coldly, but inside he quaked as badly as Pandasso did outwardly.

"I wish I knew a spell to utter," said Lokenna.

"Look. The warriors are . . . dissolving." Santon took a step forward to get a better view of the strange transformation taking place. The cloud warriors bent over, touching one another and forming an arch. The vague human forms turned into less animate walls.

"They still pulse as if life flowed in their veins," said Lokenna.

"Lightning still flashes and snow falls," Santon said, "but they've formed a tunnel for us."

"He wants us to meet with him. He wants us to go up the road to the Castle of the Winds!"

"No, not me. I'm not going—" Pandasso's protests were cut short when Santon heaved. Muscles rippled and sent the innkeeper stumbling forward into the cloudy arch. Pandasso screamed as lightning bolts speared down and collided with his outstretched hands. He bowed his back and continued to scream. Lightning touched his face and legs and bathed his entire body in an eerie purple and green glow.

Then Bane Pandasso disappeared.

"He was blasted into nothingness!" exclaimed Santon.

"No, Birtle, no, he wasn't." Lokenna walked forward with more confidence than Santon felt. She stood, arms aloft. Eye-searing flashes lanced toward her; Lokenna vanished.

Santon had to decide between turning to flee

like a craven or discovering Lokenna's fate. He walked forward, heart hammering fiercely in his chest. The darkness within the arch of clouds made him think that eternal night had fallen. Like the two before him, he raised his arms. His good one he held directly over his head. His withered arm rose only to shoulder level.

He swallowed hard when he saw the vivid, crackling magical energies mounting within the foggy walls of the tunnel. Then he screamed as the lightning reached down and touched his body. Every nerve within him shrieked in protest. Santon took an involuntary step forward and fell to one knee.

"Where . . ." He looked around in surprise. He knew he had to be dead, but this place resembled no hell he had ever heard described.

He stood in the center of a round room with comfortable furniture strewn about haphazardly. Santon ignored this. His full attention focused on the small rainstorms gathered at the walls. Each seemed a miniature of a full-fledged cousin outside. Rain pelted down to the floor and tiny lightnings crashed and crackled—and each time a discharge occurred, a window opened.

"Yes," said Lokenna. "He is able to look out over Porotane through the magic of his storms."

"Why else call me the Wizard of Storms?" asked a straight-backed, leathery, balding man. He pushed up baggy sleeves and revealed thin arms covered with burns and scars. When he saw Santon's frown, he said, "Every apprentice learns to cast spells." He laughed. "He also learns what *not* to do. These are my reminders."

Santon had believed the Wizard of Storms to

be all-powerful and even godlike. The man before him was just . . . a man.

"You seem disappointed." He turned and pointed a gnarled finger. The nimbus of magic around the finger formed a solid green rod that speared deep within the cloud on the southern wall.

"Efran!" cried Lokenna.

"Ah, you know the rebel. And his brother, too. Dews Gaemock is sorely wounded."

"By Lorens?"

"Indirectly," said the Wizard of Storms. "The direct cause was treachery by this one." The scene shifted slightly and showed Dalziel Sef's body strung up by its heels in a tree. Every gust of wind caused the corpse to sway like a clock pendulum. "His ambition proved stronger than the flesh of the rebel soldiers."

"What of Lorens?" asked Santon. "Can you show us the castle?"

"You want to know what has become of your friend Vered."

Santon blanched. This seemingly simple old man was truly a wizard.

"See what happens when I cast my scrying spell in that direction!"

Santon threw up his good arm to protect his eyes. Searing light burst forth from the tiny storm cloud. An instant later scalding water cascaded over him.

"The Demon Crown blocks my magic, even as mine blocks its power. I do not like this. Things were ever so peaceful when Alarice hid the crown and none dared wear it."

"You bring your storms to bedevil us," protested Pandasso.

The wizard glared at him. "I play with the elements. I enjoy fashioning works of kinetic art. Who else uses nature itself as a canvas? No one! Is there any soul in Porotane who claims to make music as potent as mine? Nowhere does anyone make such a false boast."

He threw back his sleeves and produced a crashing drumbeat of thunder punctuated by lightning and the boiling of clouds. "See? Hear? Feel? I produce art stimulating more than one sense. And now Lorens threatens my existence. I find this intolerable, just as I did when Waellkin donned that damnable crown."

"Why did you bring us here?" asked Pandasso.

"I? I did not *bring* you here. You came of your own will. Did I force you to ride across Porotane, across the Uvain Plateau? No! You are intruders on my serenity and as such will be destroyed." The Wizard of Storms pushed back his baggy sleeves again.

"Save the boasts and lies for another," cut in Lokenna.

"You do not think I can destroy you with a pass of my hand?"

"Of course you can—but you won't. You *allowed* us to come, even if you did not bring us here. Your cloud warriors could have slain us rather than the brigands."

"You fought well against my magic," admitted the Wizard of Storms.

"We need one another," the woman said.

"What? I? I am the most powerful wizard in the world! What do I need of you?"

"I can control the Demon Crown. My brother blots out your view. He ruins a masterpiece," Lokenna said shrewdly. "I can control the crown. Kill Lorens and the crown will destroy the world."

"You know." The Wizard of Storms sat down heavily and stared at her. "But you would. You wore the crown and saw what evil your brother has unwittingly unleashed."

"He is weak. I needed to know more about the danger, but he refused to tell me."

"What danger?" demanded Santon. "What are you talking about?"

"Lorens has fallen into a trap set by the demon Kalob three centuries ago. He is narrowing the gap between our worlds. The demons will pour through if my brother does not work to stop it."

"He won't," said Santon.

"He can't," corrected the Wizard of Storms. "He is untrained in the use of power. I warned Patrin about such things, but he'd never listen to me. Willful child."

"Patrin was your son?"

"Everyone is entitled to an indiscretion now and then," said the Wizard of Storms, shrugging.

"We need each other," repeated Lokenna. "We can work together. We want the same thing— peace in Porotane."

"You will guarantee the Demon Crown is rendered impotent after the removal of your brother from the throne?"

"No. I do guarantee that it will never interfere with your artistic creation."

"Impossible. The crown must be destroyed."

"It is a legacy of the realm. It cannot be."

Santon sat back in awe and listened to the argument. Lokenna pleaded their case well. He saw the Wizard of Storms weakening in his resolve to destroy the Demon Crown. As the wizard slowly came over to Lokenna's side, the storm clouds around the room lightened to fluffy white.

"It's agreed. I want nothing to do with your petty rulings after this is resolved."

"A temporary alliance, then," said Lokenna.

Birtle Santon wondered which one lied. From their expressions, he guessed both were. This conflict of magic would not end with Lorens' death.

CHAPTER NINETEEN

Vered sat in the center of the cell trying to knock off the largest pieces of dirt soiling his finery. His trip to his old quarters had given him fresh clothing, for all the good that had accomplished. The dungeon was a filthy place and not the environment for maintaining a decent appearance. As he rubbed the dirt from his tunic, his sharp ears pricked up for any sound of guards.

He heard nothing. He continued brushing himself off and straightening the wrinkles in his tight vermilion and cobalt breeches. As he worked, his nimble fingers touched on the four daggers he had hidden before Ruvary's guards caught him. All were in place.

He went to the cell door and peered through the heavily barred grate. The dungeon was unnaturally devoid of activity. The guards had vanished and even the moans from tortured prisoners had died down. He shuddered. The other prisoners might have been put to death on Lorens' order. The wizard-king had shown no mercy for those less fortunate—or any who opposed him.

Vered touched the skin at his neck, wondering why the guardsmen hadn't simply slit his throat.

"They didn't, and that's my bit of luck." He dropped to his knees and examined the lock on this cell. His heart sank. The keyhole controlling an intricate lock, such as had been on his prior cell, gaped wide open. He thrust his finger through the hole and wiggled it.

The lock had been removed in favor of a heavy exterior locking bar.

Vered scowled. The other lock had fallen easily to his skill. This was another matter. He pulled out the dagger with the thinnest, longest blade and tried working it between doorjamb and door. It refused to enter the cramped space. He had to reach the drop bar outside or he would never be able to escape.

Vered thrust his arm out the small grate, winced as metal cut into his flesh, then tried to grasp the bar and lift it. His fingers curled just under the bar. Grunting with effort and pain, he got his fingertips securely under the heavy bar and heaved with all his strength.

The bar didn't budge.

"Won't do no good," came a voice from the next cell. "They got a cotter pin shoved through it. Takes more'n you got to get it free. Takes two good hands—from the outside."

"Hello there," called Vered, pressing close to

the grate in a vain attempt to see his fellow prisoner. "How is your door locked?"

"Got one of them fancy-ass locks on it. No way I can open it. Might as well have a bar like on yours, for all the good it does."

Vered cursed. If he had been in the other cell, he would be free in a flash. Sooner! The strongest lock made could not withstand his knowledgeable assault. And he was trapped in a cell with such a simple bar mechanism!

"Is there any way you could lift the bar on my cell door?" he asked.

"No way," came the answer. "There'd be nothing in it for me, even if I could."

"Nonsense," said Vered, wanting an ally, no matter who it might be. "We are in the dungeon together. That makes us comrades-in-arms."

"Comrades-in-prison is more like it," the other man said sarcastically.

Vered paced the cell, examining every corner. The wall around the door had been reinforced with a steel plate. Scraping through it would be impossible, even with his daggers. The back wall dripped cold water. When he pressed his ear to it he heard a loud rushing noise.

"There's water behind the back wall," his fellow prisoner called, as if he knew what Vered considered. "Supplies the whole damn castle, it does. Comes off an underground channel from the River Ty. That's why the rebels were never able to pry Freow loose with their sieges. The castle's got all the water it can use."

Vered laughed. "The rebels had intended to damn up the river to prevent the castle from getting water. That wouldn't have given them much of an edge, would it?"

"Don't reckon I can say. Been down here too long to know such things. That Dews Gaemock you're talkin' about?"

Vered's fingers probed the far wall. He used the handle of his dagger to tap the stone blocks. The solid sound worried him. To his fellow prisoner, he called out, "Am I in the end cell?"

"Last in the block, aye. You might tunnel out in the far direction from my cell, but you'd have to move a powerful lot of dirt."

Vered instantly discarded such a notion. Even if the guards failed to see the hole and the growing pile of dirt that would accumulate, such a tunneling operation would take considerable effort and would end up with him dirtier than a pig in a wallow.

"I'm going to take out a block or two in the wall between us."

"You that anxious for company?" asked the other prisoner. "I been down here well nigh two years. You haven't been in your cell for two hours."

Vered began working at the crumbling mortar between the blocks, gouging it out. "I can open the lock on your door and we can both get out of here."

"What makes you think I want out? This might be my idea of cozy."

"If you like it so much, I'll let myself out, then lock you in when I leave."

"No!" From the distress in the man's voice, Vered knew that isolation had worked on him overlong. "I don't want to stay here. I never meant to call Duke Freow a great fat cow. I'd apologize but one guard who talks to me on occasion says that the duke is dead."

"Baron Theoll poisoned him."

"I'll apologize to the baron. I want out!"

"Theoll's dead. Lorens killed him."

"Who's Lorens? Never mind. You can tell me when you get through the wall."

Vered worked steadily for hours, resting for a few minutes to get the cramps from his hands, then applying himself diligently to the task. One block slid through and crashed into the other cell. A grimy face with wild eyes and a thick, matted beard appeared.

"You are human. You're not a demon. I worried about that. Letting a demon into the cell might be my death."

"Help me get the next block free." Vered started to offer the use of a second dagger but he could hear Birtle Santon's voice warning him about his incautious ways. For the few minutes' work it might save, it did not seem prudent putting a weapon in the other man's hands.

He continued scraping at the mortar until a second block fell free. A third followed quickly. Vered scrambled through the tiny opening and brushed himself off.

"You're a weird-looking duck, aren't you?" the other said.

"High fashion dictates such a color match, though I am less partial to vermilion than I am to, say, a deeper, richer color. A wine red, mayhaps."

"What?"

"My clothes." Vered snorted in disgust. "Never mind. Let me get that cell door open. Shouldn't take long. I opened the last one with a lock in less than a minute."

Vered dropped to his knees and examined the sturdy lock. A slow smile crossed his lips. This lock was the twin of the other. He had already probed its depths and knew its secrets. Opening it with the tip of the dagger would be simple.

He began digging about inside when the man crouched behind him hissed like a stepped-on snake and said, "Stop. Listen. A guard's coming. You can't be caught. They'll put us both to death if they see you!"

The man grabbed Vered from behind and shoved him forward against the door. Vered grunted, the hilt of the dagger buried into his belly. Vered struggled and turned. The other prisoner attempted to reach around and pull the dagger from the locking mechanism.

Vered grabbed the other's wrist to stop him. They struggled, Vered falling back when the man showed surprising strength for one who have been imprisoned for two years.

The metallic tearing noise that resulted when the dagger broke off inside the lock hit Vered harder than the dagger hilt had. His stomach turned over.

"You fool!" he shouted. "You broke it off!"

"Silence. The guards!"

Vered shoved his face against the cell door's small grating and peered out. The dungeon remained as empty as before—but he did hear shouts and the clanking of arms and armor.

"The soldiers are running about on the levels above the dungeon. There aren't any guards stationed here." He almost added "you fool" but knew it would do no good. The damage had been done.

Vered dropped once more to his knees and looked into the keyhole. Not only had the tumblers been ruined, but also the dagger's point had lodged firmly in the cylinder.

"What are you waiting for? Open the door!"

"I can't," said Vered. "This door is sealed as surely as the one in the other cell—more. Not even a key can open this lock. The door is permanently sealed."

He sat down heavily, back against the cold metal door as he glared at his fellow prisoner. He still had three good daggers. One could be put to good use on this fool's throat.

CHAPTER TWENTY

"I hate him! How dare he do that to my most masterful creation!" The Wizard of Storms clapped his hands together and produced a tornado that danced and hopped and slowly made its way to the rain cloud on the southern wall of the turret. The scrying cloud had darkened and the lightning had faded from it while the wizard had spied on Castle Porotane. The tornado whirred about its axis and disrupted the rain cloud, sending filmy tendrils of fog in all directions.

"Could he see us?" asked Lokenna.

"No, of course not. Lorens lacks such power, but he blocked my scrying spell."

"Did he—or was it the Demon Crown?" Santon had seen too much magic to be awed by this new spell woven by the Wizard of Storms. The tornado continued to kick up dust and debris from the turret floor. The scrying cloud had not reappeared and Santon doubted that it would. The small window in the center had shown the castle and the guardsmen walking their patrols along the battlements. The spell had carried them farther into the castle and then—words failed Santon.

The edges of the storm had turned green. He shivered at the memory of that peculiar color. The Demon Crown had glowed the same ugly hue when Lorens had worn it. He had become too accustomed to the softer, more cheerful green the crown emitted from Lokenna's brow. Being reminded of the darker side of the magical device's power chilled him.

"My best scrying spell and he ruins it, just as he's ruined so many of my finer pieces. Look," demanded the Wizard of Storms. "Isn't that the finest storm you have ever seen or heard?"

Through the scrying cloud dripping rain on the floor at the north section of the room Santon saw layered clouds interchanging lightning bolts of varying color. Purples and greens and vivid blue-whites dazzled the eye, but most beguiling was the sound.

Rumbles of thunder came in bass and were countered by higher pitched echoes off canyon walls. The entire range of the Yorrals became the Wizard of Storms' drum.

Santon had to admit that the primal, gut-stirring roll of thunder produced strange emotions within him. Not anger, he decided. Perhaps sadness. Even as he tried to identify the emotion, the timbre of the sound changed and his spirits lifted. Blue sky shone through the clouds and a double rainbow formed. Santon choked back an exclamation of joy and tears welled in his eyes.

"He ruins *that*," complained the wizard. "He puts on the damnable crown and blackness oozes out like pus from some vile creature's wound and destroys the spells I weave. I won't stand for it!"

"You cannot look into the castle?" asked Santon. "Not at all?"

"No." The curt answer told Santon far more than he wanted to know. For all his skill and power, the Wizard of Storms stood helpless before the Demon Crown.

"We can do nothing against my brother," said Lokenna. "Santon has tried. I have tried. The rebels have tried."

She paused. The Wizard of Storms picked up what had become a litany of failure. "And I have failed," the wizard admitted glumly.

"Separately we fail. Together we might succeed. Isn't that why you allowed us here?" she asked.

"A truce between us might prove helpful." The wizard stroked over his white-stubbled chin with his gnarled fingers. He snapped the joints and nodded briskly. "I had been drifting along such a path. Your presence has confirmed my intuition."

"Efran Gaemock will be needed, too," said Lokenna.

Santon turned slowly and stared at the woman. Something about the tone she used told that her interest in Efran Gaemock transcended the military alliance against her brother. A certain breathlessness, Santon decided. He looked from the woman to her husband. Bane Pandasso had not noticed the excitement in his wife's voice.

"He is being summoned now," said the wizard.

"It will take a week or more for him to cross

lower Porotane and even if you do not hinder him with your storms on the Uvain Plateau, the trip is a long one. Can we afford to wait?" asked Santon.

The Wizard of Storms smirked. "Your dealings with those such as myself is limited. When a wizard desires something—or someone—it is easily obtained." He pointed to the scrying cloud dripping on the floor to the southeast.

"You've conjured a storm over the rebel camp," said Pandasso. "You send your rain on his head?"

"I send my cloud warriors for him. Look!"

Santon swallowed hard when he saw the filmy tendrils dipping toward the ground, dragging along, and then breaking off to form ten-foot-high soldiers of fog and lightning. The consternation in the rebel camp spread. A few tried to fight the magical warriors. They were brushed aside. The cloud warriors strode across the campground, their footprints drowning fires and their lightest touch giving death.

"Why not send them against Lorens? He cannot stand against such potent magic," Pandasso said, gawking at the cloud warriors' slow progress.

"He finally says something of worth," agreed Santon. "Why can't you send your legions against Lorens?"

The wizard's concentration faltered for a moment and the cloud warriors ceased their hunt for Efran Gaemock. In that instant Santon knew the answer. The Wizard of Storms might control one or two of the mighty magical warriors, but he lacked the ability to command the hundreds—thousands!—that he conjured. The Wizard of Storms could order them to march and march they would, but individual combat for each of his myriad lay beyond his skill.

"There," came Lokenna's excited voice. "There's Efran."

"So it is." The wizard made a small beckoning motion. A cloud warrior bent over and scooped up the struggling rebel leader. Efran fought against mist but was held by fingers stronger than steel bands. Another gesture from the wizard caused the cloud above to dip low.

As if being sucked aloft, cloud warrior and Efran Gaemock vanished into the storm.

"Gaemock will arrive shortly," said the wizard. He slumped into a comfortable chair, exhausted by his effort. Santon saw in this another reason the wizard had not sent his vaporous legions against Lorens. The strain of maintaining his magic must be immense.

"Can I get you anything?" asked Lokenna.

"Ah, the old habits die hard, don't they?" said the Wizard of Storms, smiling gently. Santon thought he looked like any other weary traveller in that instant, seeing a pretty barmaid.

Lokenna grinned sheepishly. "They do."

"I am Kaga'kalb," the Wizard of Storms said unexpectedly.

Santon stared at the wizard. For a sorceror to reveal his personal name meant that a large measure of control had been relinquished. The best and most effective spells were those naming the victim. Some wizards such as Patrin boasted that they were too powerful to worry about such secrecy, but Santon knew that inwardly they feared this personal revelation. When Alarice had revealed her name, Santon had known the complete trust this involved.

Of those in the room, only Pandasso did not seem to know the import of Kaga'kalb's revelation.

"We can share some food. It is not much, but these days I have little appetite. Lorens upsets my work too much." Kaga'kalb made a pass with his hand and mumbled a spell. Small storms appeared above glasses. The rain pelting down proved to be red. Santon sampled his filled glass and discovered the cloud had brought wine. Meat and cheese arrived in a more conventional manner; wind blew open doors and a wheeled cart laden with the food skidded across the room.

"Excuse my little displays of magic. I seldom have anyone to show off for," Kaga'kalb said. "I content myself with the beauty of the elements. The white of snow is such a lovely medium to work with, but I must admit I prefer the greens of spring. But then, each season carries its own secrets and beauties, doesn't it?"

A clap of thunder drowned out Santon's reply. Following the peal came loud cursing and a clattering on steps leading from the turret roof.

"Gaemock has arrived," said Kaga'kalb.

The rebel leader stumbled into the room. For a heart-stopping instant Santon feared that the man had died and only his phantom had come. Efran Gaemock was coated from head to toe in frosty white.

"He's frozen!" exclaimed Lokenna. She rushed to the man and threw her crude blanket-cloak around his shoulders.

"My, I forgot how cold it gets within a cloud. Do accept my abject apologies, Efran," said the Wizard of Storms.

"What is this place? Have I died?"

"You'll be fine," Lokenna assured him. "Rest for a while, and then we can talk. We are offering an alliance against my brother."

"Your brother? Lorens?" The rebel leader wiped melting ice from his eyebrows and studied her closely. "I see a resemblance. You . . . you're his twin! The one the Glass Warrior sent the two adventurers after!"

"And I recognize you as the jester Harhar," spoke up Santon.

"A disguise that proved of little use, it seems. How did you fare after you escaped the castle?"

"There'll be time enough for such gossip later," Lokenna said sternly. "You must get out of those frozen clothes and rest." She looked over her shoulder at Kaga'kalb. The wizard gestured toward a staircase leading down.

"Choose any room," he said. "I never have guests, so none are in use." He spread his hands out in front of him and made a motion encompassing the turret room. "This is my primary residence."

"You're the leader of the rebel army?" asked Bane Pandasso.

"What there is left of it."

"You didn't destroy Fron, did you?" Pandasso glared at Efran, as if challenging him to admit that he had.

"Dalziel Sef was responsible for many misadventures my brother and I never authorized. He has paid the final price for his indiscretions."

"You mean he's dead?"

Efran nodded.

"I'll help him down," the innkeeper offered. "You two make what plans you need with the wizard."

Efran looked at Kaga'kalb, who said, "He is right. A few hours will not matter. I apologize for not realizing that you would be in such a sorry condition as a result of my cloudy transportation."

"You're the Wizard of Storms."

"Kaga'kalb," supplied Pandasso.

Santon was pleased to see that this naming impressed Efran Gaemock, too. The rebel leader he had known as Harhar the court jester understood the trust involved.

"Help me to my quarters. We can talk soon." Efran cocked his head to one side and looked from Kaga'kalb to Lokenna as he added, "Alliance?"

"Yes," she said simply.

Pandasso put his arm around Efran's waist and helped him down the steps. Santon watched them depart, wondering at the innkeeper's sudden helpfulness. He turned back to the old wizard, but Kaga'kalb had summoned a new storm cloud and sat with his head wreathed by its miniature turbulence.

He silently ate of the meat and cheese and enjoyed the wine. No matter how he drank, the rain cloud kept it filled. This innovation would have appealed greatly to Vered, he thought.

To Vered.

Birtle Santon's mood turned morose once more. What had happened to his friend? Even Kaga'kalb's sorcery could not reveal that fate as long as Lorens wore the crown.

CHAPTER TWENTY-ONE

The wizard-king clapped his hands over his ears to shut out the shrieks of pain. It didn't help. Lorens hesitantly opened his closed eyes and saw—nothing. His audience chamber was empty.

The moans and sobs of pain grew louder.

"Stop it, stop it!" Tears rolled down his cheeks as he tried to lift the Demon Crown from his head. It weighed a ton. Fire burned his fingers. It had somehow become fastened to his head. Millions of excuses flashed through his mind. Even as Lorens knew that all were lies, he stopped his attempt to remove the crown.

He sagged as he listened to the tormented souls crying out for surcease. Lorens blinked when the peculiar red-lit world of black rock and dancing figures again appeared in front of him. This time he felt intense heat radiating from the world as sluggish lava flows attacked the floor in front of his dais.

You are the chosen one, came the rasping voice he had grown to fear.

"Who are you?" Lorens cried aloud. The voice had not come from his chamber; it still echoed in the dusty corners of his mind.

Laughter mocked him. *You ask the wrong question, my king. What am I is the true question!*

"Stop," Lorens pleaded. A gust of hot wind seared his face and ripped at the flesh on the backs of his hands. He looked up and saw . . . damnation.

You only now get an inkling, my king? How strange. Even Waellkin, fool that he was, understood better what my purpose was in giving you mortals the Demon Crown.

"You're Kalob!"

I am Kalob and Prebeal and Septhion and Tabros and none of them. I am all, I am none.

"I don't understand."

Oh, my king, you do understand. The laughter threatened to drive Lorens totally mad.

He jumped to his feet and tottered on the edge of the platform. The sea of molten rock threatened him with instant and fiery death. Lorens hesitated, then jumped. He cried bitter tears when he landed squarely in the center of his audience chamber. Only cold stone lay under him. No lava burned away his flesh to rid him of the voices. Life continued in his tormented body, even if the door into the strangely terrifying world had shut.

"Majesty, are you hurt?" came a worried voice.

"Curse you!" Lorens shrieked. "Bring me the spies. The prisoners. Get them here at once!"

"Which ones, Majesty?"

"The spies in the barracks. The ones who tried to desert to the accursed rebels!"

"Oh, those." The squire swallowed hard and backed from the chamber. Lorens sat on the cold stone floor, fingers hesitantly probing in a vain effort to locate the sea of melted rock he had seen. In the distance he heard the squire's footsteps disappearing, then the clank of armed men returning.

Lorens picked himself up and dusted off his clothing the best he could. He had not changed his tunic in a week and his breeches had become stuck to his body with filth. He hardly noticed as he turned to study himself in a full-length polished metal mirror.

The image in the mirror wavered. Lorens saw a tall, handsome, well-groomed man worthy of being king. No fear showed on the face. Even as he began to smile, knowing that he was in command, that his destiny was to rule Porotane, the image changed and was replaced by that of a leering demon.

Lorens spun, hand going to a sheathed dagger. No one stood behind him. He was still alone in the audience chamber—but the ghastly laughter again rattled about inside his head, for only him to hear.

A sudden noise from his right caused him to swing around, dagger drawn. The guardsmen he had summoned herded the four prisoners to a spot in front of his throne.

"You are traitors," he snarled. "You are all traitors. You sought to abandon me and tell my secrets to Gaemock. Don't deny it! I see everything. With this"—he tapped the green-glowing

Demon Crown on his head—"I *know* everything. You will be executed!"

"Majesty, we have done nothing except serve you. There was talk of revolt in our ranks. *We* put down the mass desertion! We should be commended, not condemned."

"Liar. You think I cannot *see* what goes on in my own castle. I can *see* and *hear* anywhere in the kingdom!"

Lorens flopped bonelessly to the floor and let his senses cast forth like a hunting cat. He raced over the rolling hills of lower Porotane, to the up-thrusting ochre cliffs that marked the beginning of the Uvain Plateau and onto the flatness of that grape-growing country.

The wizard-king cried in frustration when the storms began to form around his far-reaching magical senses. In seconds rain obscured his vision and thunder deafened him.

Your enemies do this to you, came the voice he loathed and feared. *You cannot allow the Wizard of Storms to block your magic. These soldiers are his spies. Slay them now!*

"Y-you are spies for the Wizard of Storms," Lorens gasped out. Half his mind still rolled along the ochre buttes. He had increasing difficulty collecting his wits after each of the magically thwarted outings. "You work for the Wizard of Storms."

"We know nothing of . . . aieee!" The leader who had started to protest bent double and clutched at his belly. The audience chamber turned suddenly silent. Then tiny popping and sizzling sounds echoed throughout. The soldier dropped to his knees, hands still at his belly. His lips moved but only pink froth came out.

He toppled to his side, his stomach gone and the cavity turned to smoking charcoal.

"I ... I punish my enemies," said Lorens. Sweat ran down his face. He had done this. He had executed the traitor—but how? He did not know the spell. It had just ... happened.

"Mercy. Have mercy on us, Majesty!" pleaded another.

Lorens lifted a shaking hand and pointed it at the man. "I do not like cowards who beg for their lives."

The soldier's head exploded in a bloody shower that caused the battle-hardened guardsmen to flinch.

Lorens stared at his magical handiwork in shocked silence. Deep within his skull came the soothing words, *You do well. Your skills as a wizard grow daily. There is much to be proud of.*

"There is?" he asked aloud.

"Majesty? What did you say?" asked the boldest of the guardsmen.

Do not let the other traitors escape your vengeance. Make examples of them so that others will know your wrath!

"Th-these two are to be ... executed." Lorens stood up and touched the Demon Crown. Reassuring warmth flooded through him. Confidence returned and the voices in his head fell silent. "They are to be publicly executed. Everyone in the castle will watch or know my wrath!"

"Majesty, at once! We will get the executioner!"

Lorens motioned the guardsmen from the chamber. He took some delight in seeing that they were as fearful as the two condemned prisoners.

He would maintain discipline in the ranks if he had to kill them all!

"I don't need them. I am more powerful than any rebel army. Let the Wizard of Storms come down from his mountain. He cannot stop me. I am Lorens, King of Porotane!"

In the courtyard he heard the trumpets sound the call for all to assemble. The crowd noises rose, then fell as the two traitors were executed. Lorens did not go to the window to watch. He had no need of mere eyes.

He used the Demon Crown.

Faint laughter welled up deep within his mind, laughter that had been denied release for three hundred years.

CHAPTER TWENTY-TWO

"How long can he stay like this?" Santon asked nervously. He wanted to shake Kaga'kalb and see if he could rouse the wizard from his deep trance, yet he feared the consequences. The clouds that orbited his head produced no rain, but the lightning was intense for such small puffs of mist.

"I am no wizard. I cannot say, but he does not seem to be in any danger," said Lokenna. Her eyes kept straying to the staircase leading down to Efran Gaemock's quarters. Santon wondered at her interest in the rebel. While he and Vered had been in Lorens' good graces after giving him the Demon Crown and installing him on the throne, he had come to like the court jester—Efran. He had seen more in the comically wild gyrations and reckless talk than any of those who schemed and killed within the castle walls.

"Why does the storm cloud stay over his head?" Santon asked, pulling his attention away from idle speculation and back to the matters at hand. His mind turned over the possibilities. "If the storms along the walls allow him to see at great distances, mayhap this storm is for scrying closer at hand."

Santon fell silent, realizing that he put words to his own private thoughts. His curiosity would not be assuaged until he learned what business Bane Pandasso had with the rebel lord. That Pandasso had something important to say had been apparent from his attitude. The innkeeper would not last a single day in the machinations of a royal court; his every emotion played on his brutish face.

"He's had time enough to rest from his trip," said Lokenna. "I'll see how Lord Efran fares."

"There is no need," spoke up Kaga'kalb. "I hear his boots on the steps now."

Santon wondered at this. It took his keen ears several long seconds before he heard Efran and Pandasso returning. The rebel had donned dry clothing and a fur-lined cape to ward off the worst of Kaga'kalb's elemental masterpieces raging outside.

"Do you agree to an alliance, Efran?" asked Kaga'kalb.

"What are we each to gain from this? You are a wizard. If we join forces and defeat Lorens—Lokenna's brother"—he bowed in the woman's direction and received a bright smile in return—"how do the oppressed people of Porotane benefit? Are we exchanging one wizard's rule for another's?"

"Kaga'kalb cannot wear the Demon Crown," said Santon. "Only Lokenna can."

"Then there is a new element introduced. Are we substituting one tyrant for another?"

"You're talking about my wife!" protested Pandasso.

"You know my part in getting Lorens onto the throne," said Santon, feeling the weight of forging the alliance resting heavily on him. He was no diplomat but knew he had to convince all parties that defeating Lorens was in their best interests now and later.

Then he had to convince himself. He had seen how the crown had changed Lorens. Lokenna had worn it and not been perverted, but what would a year of exposure do to her?

"Aye, that I do. You're responsible for the condition of our proud kingdom."

"That's a bit harsh on Birtle," defended Lokenna.

"But true, my queen," Santon said before Efran could argue. "Kaga'kalb has no desire to leave his Castle of the Winds. He wants only to work his magic and create his natural art with the storms. Is that not so?"

The Wizard of Storms nodded.

"And," Santon rushed on, "you want peace. Lokenna can give it by uniting the warring factions. Those royalists who have fought so long will follow no one but a monarch wearing the crown."

"I want only what is best for Porotane," said Efran.

"This can work," insisted Santon. "Kaga'kalb is left alone—and leaves the ruling of Porotane to Lokenna."

"She *is* of the royal blood," said Efran, rubbing his chin. "I entered the castle as jester two years ago in hope of installing a member of the family on the throne. That is where I parted company with my brother Dews."

"He is sorely wounded," said Kaga'kalb. "You are the one who must decide for the rebel army."

Efran snorted. "There is no army. Not much, at any rate after Lorens was finished with us."

"Dalziel Sef betrayed you," said Lokenna, softening the sting of the self-criticism Efran had administered.

"We all gain—if we defeat Lorens," said Santon.

"What of you?" asked Pandasso. "You argue well, but what do you gain from this?"

"Aye, you have the look of a thief about you. Even after I learned of your alliance with the Glass Warrior, I wondered how you became embroiled in this."

"Politics is usually the farthest thing from my mind," said Santon, "but Lorens holds my friend in his dungeons. I want him freed."

Santon was acutely aware of the look that went around the room between Lokenna, Efran, and Kaga'kalb. They knew he had scant chance of seeing his friend alive again, but he had to believe. Alarice had told him that Vered lived. Her phantom would not lie to him. Ever.

Even if she had not come to him, hope would have stirred within him.

"We all stand to gain what we hold dearest." Efran glared at Pandasso in a manner that startled Santon. What had happened between the two men? Before he could speak, Efran went on. "Then we should prepare for the assault on Castle Porotane as soon as possible. If you can return me to my camp, I can begin assembling my army. By spring we can—"

"No." Kaga'kalb's single word caused a heavy silence to fall on the room. Even the minor thunderings in his scrying clouds died.

"But we . . ." Santon's voice trailed off when he saw the utter determination written on the wizard's face.

"We fight now. We can go to the rebel camp, if you need to assemble your troops there, but they will hardly be needed if we can destroy Lorens."

"They are needed," insisted Lokenna. "The castle forces must be committed, separated from Lorens. That will give us the best chance of defeating him. Kaga'kalb might not be able to summon many of his cloud warriors—human ones will be needed to bear the brunt of the battle."

"Very well." Kaga'kalb motioned for them to go to the roof of the turret. They silently filed up the stairs. Santon pulled his rude cloak tighter around him when the fierce, bitter cold winds clawed at him. Kaga'kalb herded them into a small circle, then lifted his arms.

Santon tried to scream, but the words jumbled in his throat. He felt impossibly strong hands lift him, yet those hands were composed of fog. Winds buffeted him and snow pelted his face. Lightning of unbelievable intensity crashed around him as he tumbled and fell head over heels.

His arm and legs became numb with the cold. Frost formed on his eyelashes and threatened to freeze his eyelids shut.

At the instant he thought he would surely die, he stumbled and dropped to one knee on the muddy banks of the River Ty. The distance that had taken them weeks to travel on horseback had been traversed in Kaga'kalb's storm in the wink of an eye.

"Assemble your troops. Get them into the field," ordered Kaga'kalb. "And hurry. I . . . I do not like being exposed like this."

"What do you mean?" asked Santon.

The wizard tensed, then seemed resigned. "I have given you my name. I might as well bare my final secret. The storms I have created are all I can do unless I return to my Castle of the Winds."

"You mean you can't summon *any* of the cloud warriors unless you're in your castle?" asked Lokenna.

"From these storms, I can—a little. I cannot conjure new storms. My powers are severely limited."

"Then return to the Castle of the Winds," said Efran. "Let us prepare on this front. We will need all your skills, all your spells."

Lokenna held up her hand. "Wait," she said in a choked voice. "He knows. My brother knows we are here."

"The crown has betrayed our presence," said Santon. He knew, though, that it required no great spell for Lorens to detect their arrival. The prodigious thunderhead rising above them marked something unusual. He hoped that Kaga'kalb had conjured enough in the way of storms.

"Send the soldiers out," ordered Efran. "Use the ambush tactic we discussed." His lieutenant looked skeptical, then rushed off to obey. Santon's heart froze when he saw how few rebels rode out to engage Lorens' troops.

"Only a hundred are left in fighting prime," said Efran. "We will keep them from retreating unscathed, if only they are overzealous in attack."

"You intend to hide and take their riders off the perimeter of their force?" Santon knew that a direct confrontation would destroy the rebel army. Lorens could afford a two-for-one or even a five-for-one loss and still emerge victorious on the ground.

"Aye," said Lokenna, again seeming to have accurately read his thoughts. "The true battle occurs above us."

"I cannot see Lorens. The crown obscures him and those around him, but it will not matter. I will show him magic!" Kaga'kalb thrust his arms upward and made gestures as if trying to grab the clouds between his fingers. A purple nimbus of energy formed around him, then arched up to the thunder cloud in a blinding flash.

"What can I do?" asked Santon, feeling useless.

"There is nothing either of us can do," said Lokenna. "We must let Kaga'kalb and Efran carry the battle to Lorens. Afterward, *then* it will be our time."

Santon paced restlessly, trying to keep the snow and rain from running down his neck. The wind came up in powerful gales, then died as the power was redirected toward Lorens' troops. Through the ebb and flow of the storm, Santon saw Bane Pandasso arguing with Efran.

He edged closer. The rebel leader showed obvious distress at what the man said.

"We can do it, I tell you. It's for the best. He would never harm his sister—or the one who ends this madness!"

Efran Gaemock cried something that vanished in a clap of thunder and pushed Pandasso away angrily. The rebel spun and stalked off, every muscle tense. Pandasso waved a fist at him. When he saw that Efran had vanished into a small tent, the innkeeper looked about. The set of his body warned Santon that Pandasso sought a fight.

He ducked behind a tree and waited for Pandasso, intending to follow him and see what the man did next. The pounding of a horse's hooves startled him. Pandasso rode past his place of concealment, a sword in hand and a look of grim determination on his face.

Santon blinked in surprise. He shook his head in wonder and returned to the low hill where Kaga'kalb mustered his elemental magics for the assault. Lokenna stood to one side, ready to aid the wizard should he require it.

"Lokenna," Santon shouted over the din. "I owe you an apology—and to your husband."

"What? What are you saying?" She turned to him, eyes wide.

"I just saw Pandasso riding out to join the rebels. I misjudged him. I'd thought him a coward."

The sudden cessation of lightning and thunder struck Santon harder than any body blow. One instant there had been peals of thunder and eye-searing aerial discharges. The silence made him feel as if he had become deaf and blind.

Kaga'kalb's cry of outrage put those ideas to rest. "What has that craven done now?"

"Pandasso?" asked Santon, confused. "I was apologizing to Lokenna for thinking her husband was a coward."

The flush of anger that rose on Kaga'kalb's

weathered face cut off any further words. The
Wizard of Storms said fiercely, "He will *not* betray you again. I swear it!"

"Wait, what are you saying?" Lokenna
clutched at the wizard's sleeve. He jerked free. "I
demand to know. He is my husband! What has
Bane done now?"

Kaga'kalb clapped his hands. The small cloud
that Santon had seen in the Castle of the Winds
again formed around the wizard's head. This time
the swirling mist expanded to include both Lokenna and him. Santon staggered. Only Lokenna's
strong hand steadied him. He expected to see
nothing but gray fog.

The world opened for him. Every sense sharpened. He saw. He truly *saw* and realized what al-
lure the Demon Crown had. His ears heard and
heard. By turning slowly, he was able to witness
events happening within a few hundred yards.

"The scrying spells operate at great distance.
This works only for a short way. You see the darkness where Lorens—the Demon Crown—blocks
the magic."

Santon saw tiny darting black motes in the
direction of the castle. Of Castle Porotane or its
inhabitants he saw nothing.

"There he is," said Kaga'kalb. The anger had
not died in his voice.

"Bane," Lokenna said in a choked voice.
"What have you done?"

"Nothing. He tried to get Efran to turn traitor
and sell out to Lorens. Efran refused."

"Why didn't Efran say anything . . ." Santon's
objection drifted away. He knew the answer. He
had seen the look in the rebel's eyes—and it had
matched that in Lokenna's.

"He rides to betray us to Lorens, thinking the tyrant will return all things to the way they were. The unutterable fool!"

"Kaga'kalb, no!" Lokenna tried to stop him but the spell had already formed on the wizard's lips.

A lance of lightning caught Bane Pandasso's sword tip. For an instant the man stiffened—then he simply vanished. No trace remained of rider or horse.

"You didn't have to do that," sobbed Lokenna. "He was my husband."

"He was a demon-cursed fool and a traitor. And a coward. Only you can know what else he was—or wasn't." Kaga'kalb spun around and the scrying cloud vanished.

Again came the eerie silence. Santon stood, feeling helpless in the face of such power and heartache. The crescendo of thunder drove him to his knees. He had no idea where the lightning stroke touched down, nor did he care. Such magic sickened him. Better to die of a clean sword thrust. At least that way you saw your killer.

"Lokenna!" he called, seeing the woman rushing off. He got to his feet and followed her. He overtook the woman outside Efran's tent. "Where are you going?"

"I cannot stay. Not after he . . . he killed Bane!"

"Your husband tried to betray us. Lorens can't see the rebels any more than Kaga'kalb can see into the castle. Magic protects both sides. If he had given Lorens our exact numbers and location, your brother would have killed us all!"

"He was my husband. Why did I ever leave Fron? I should have listened."

"Was he good to you?"

"As good as he could be. In Fron everything was simple. The inn required no great work, and that suited Bane. Me, too."

"It wasn't my fault that you were born to wear the Demon Crown."

"It was your fault you found me!" the woman flared.

"No," came a whispering voice. "Destiny treats us all poorly. We must do what we can—what we must."

"Alarice!" cried Santon. He stepped forward and reached out. His hand passed through the misty patch that was the Glass Warrior's elusive phantom.

"You have done well, Birtle, my love. Now you must show even more courage. Vered still lives—or so I believe. The crown dims what vision remains with me."

"Alarice, I . . ." The phantom passed through him and now faced Lokenna.

"Your husband died because he could not accept change. You will die, also, unless you realize your true position in the kingdom. Be strong, Lokenna."

"This phantom is the Glass Warrior?" asked Lokenna. She reached out. For an instant the mist firmed into a warm human hand that squeezed hers. Then the phantom drifted apart on a small gust of wind from the storm raging above.

Santon stared into the light snow falling all around to catch some small glimpse of Alarice, but she had gone.

From inside the tent came Efran's voice. "You are sure? There is no doubt?"

Santon went around to the front flap and saw that a messenger had arrived. He feared the worst, even though Pandasso's traitorous mission had been cut short by the wizard's spell.

"We've done it!" The rebel leader pushed through the flap and caught Lokenna up in his arms and spun her around. Almost guiltily he put her down and smiled. "Sorry. I couldn't help myself. We caught Lorens' personal guard in the woods. They were overconfident, as I'd hoped. With Kaga'kalb's storm giving us magical cover, we attacked from ambush. We routed them!"

"You defeated them totally?" asked Santon.

"Not that, but we are giving chase. The wizard's storms cut them off from easy retreat. We pursue—cautiously. If we can meet them on our terms in battle just once more, we can crush them."

"What other force does Lorens command?"

"That I don't know, but to send his personal guard tells me that he is not as well armed as we'd thought."

Santon considered this and agreed with Efran. A monarch as insecure as Lorens, even with the Demon Crown, would keep his most highly trained and trusted guardsmen to protect him. If he'd had another regiment, he would have sent it into the field. Even if he had one and did not consider it well enough trained, he would have fielded it.

To be left in the castle with possibly mutinous troops while his personal guard fought and died in the field would be a situation Lorens would avoid at all costs.

"We have him!" cried Efran. "We can push through the remnants of their force and take the castle!"

Santon looked to the south and west. Kaga'kalb's storms hammered at the castle's battlements but did little damage. Lorens was a wizard in his own right—and he still wore the Demon Crown.

What evil power had that accursed crown unleashed in the untrained wizard-king?

CHAPTER TWENTY-THREE

Vered's hands shook uncontrollably. He licked at his dried, cracked lips and tried to remember the last time he'd had a good drink of clear, clean water. He couldn't. The deep rumbling that had bothered him so when it had started he now ignored—it was his belly complaining about the lack of food.

"How long has it been?" he asked his fellow prisoner. The skeletal prisoner slept fitfully at the far side of the cell. Even when awake, he showed little sign of intelligence now.

Vered answered his own question. "Too long. What's happened to the jailers? Do they think to starve us to death?" The rattling and creaking in the castle told him that the guards had been drawn away from such futile work as guarding and feeding prisoners in the dungeons and put to defense on the castle battlements. He knew a huge battle raged above—but who attacked? And who won?

Vered hoped that Santon and Lokenna had not forgotten him. He went to the wall holding back the underground river and began licking at the damp stone. He had considered working free a tiny bit of mortar to let the river water flow through, but he remembered what had happened when he was a small child playing along the coast.

His village had built dikes to reclaim part of the western ocean. One hot summer afternoon he had idly worked a long steel rod into the dike, not knowing or caring what would happen. The first trickle had amused him. When he could not stop it, he had been concerned but not frightened. When huge chunks of the dike began cracking away and the sea threatened to inundate the entire lowland farm, he had rushed off for help.

Only a few acres had been lost back to the sea—but the lesson had stayed with him. Vered knew that he would drown in the cell before the pressure of the water burst open the cell door.

Tongue raw from the rock but his thirst quenched momentarily, he went back to the front of the cell. He had pulled down most of the stone blocks and found only steel plate. In the other prisoner's cell—he had never learned the suspicious man's name—the steel plate had been even thicker. To the rear of the cell ran the underground tributary to River Ty and to the far end of the cell he had found only solid rock. That left the other wall, the far wall in the distant cell.

A half-dozen heavy stone blocks had been pulled free before Vered had given up. It seemed too thick and he grew increasingly weak from lack of food.

He lay on his belly, the third of his four daggers dragging around the flagstone to pry it loose. Vered cursed the loss of his first dagger; its point permanently jammed the lock on the other door. His second dagger had worn down to a nub from working through so many miles of mortar and block.

The third dagger bent at crazy angles as he used it. He knew it would break soon. Vered rolled onto his back and closed his eyes to rest. He should save the final dagger for a quick end.

"I refuse to die of starvation. May all the demons take you for this, Lorens!"

"We are already demon food," said the other prisoner. He propped himself up on an elbow and stared at Vered, his eyes glazed over and unfocused. "This Lorens you curse so. What is he like?"

"He's the kind of ruler who would put a prisoner into a cell and then starve him to death," said Vered. Changing the subject, he asked, "Did you ever make any attempt to escape?"

"Once, then I reconsidered my plight. They tortured others who tried. Me, they left alone. I never questioned that."

"The ship with the smallest sail takes the longest to arrive," said Vered.

"How's that? You from the coast?"

"The ones they tortured are out of their misery," explained Vered. "You evaded death for this."

"Slow death instead of quick," the man said, as if the concept had never occurred to him.

"Haven't seen any guardsman lately, have you? I had a dream."

Vered didn't want to hear about it. He began scraping away again at the flooring. Getting the dagger tip under the large, flat block, he heaved. The knife blade snapped off but he exposed the hard dirt beneath. Hope returned. He drew the fourth dagger and began scratching at the packed dirt.

"What good's it going to do to tunnel under the steel plate?" asked the other man. "You'll still have to tunnel up through the stone floor outside."

"Gravity will work for me then. A small chamber is easy to cut in dirt. A bit of sawing at the block and it falls into the chamber and we can climb out."

"You can climb out," said the other. "I am too weak."

Vered refused to let hope die. He felt as weak as the other prisoner sounded. It had been almost a week since their last meal. Dining off his boots had not helped much, but it had provided bulk for his stomach to work on. Beyond this, he'd eaten nothing.

He lay flat on his stomach, thinking rather than working. What the other man said might be true. In his debilitated condition it might not be possible to perform the ambitious tunneling required for escape.

And what then? What if he managed to get free and into the dungeon proper? He was too weak to engage a soldier in combat. Vered wasn't sure that he could even wield his dagger properly from ambush. How was he to get free of the castle and past the rebel lines to rejoin Santon?

He rested his forehead on the cool stone and thought back on his days with Birtle Santon. Life in the village had been brutal. Soldiers and rebels alike had burned and massacred constantly. Santon had taken him, a young and clumsy thief, away from that and shown him the vastness and beauty of Porotane.

He owed the older man much—his life and more. Who could put a price on the friendship they had shared over the years?

"I can get the blocks removed and begin tunneling under," he said more to himself than to the other prisoner, who again had fallen into a half coma. "I can *start* the tunnel, then pull out a block and let in the river. Let the water cut the rest of the tunnel. It would push away the stone flooring with ease."

He began to dig with more determination now that a plan had formed in his feverish mind. Vered worried if he would be able to survive the time between the cell filling and the water finishing the tunnel under the steel wall.

"I can hold my breath long enough," he mumbled. "And if I can't, it might be just as well. I've always travelled with a full sail—and a big one!"

The only sounds in the cell came from the knife blade scraping on dirt and the distant trumpets and noises of battle.

CHAPTER TWENTY-FOUR

"Look at them run," crowed Efran Gaemock. "They run like cravens!"

"No," said Santon. He had no wish to defend those soldiers who had cast their lot with Lorens, but he felt obligated to point out what no one else wanted to. "They are not cowards. They run because they lack leadership. Where are the officers?"

"We cut them down first. We had to," said Efran. He watched as the squads broke into pairs of men and the pairs split into single soldiers seeking escape. "I see what you mean, though. They have no spirit, no need to fight."

"Consider how many surrender—and what they say. Two surrendered to me," said Lokenna, still somewhat startled at this. "They begged me not to kill them."

"Lorens has taken to executing his own troops if he feels they have not lived up to his expectations. I spoke with one prisoner," said Santon. "They had orders to take no prisoners and had been told we did the same."

"They came into the field thinking they would roll over us as easily as they did before," said Efran. "If only Dews could see this with his own eyes."

"Hearing it from you will be as good," Lokenna said, her hand on Efran's arm. Santon noticed how the rebel leader moved closer to her without seeming to move at all.

"I still cannot penetrate the castle with my spells. The Demon Crown blocks me. It . . . I feel more. My head. *My head!*" Kaga'kalb shrieked and clutched at his temples. Santon grabbed him with his good arm to keep the wizard from falling face forward into a snowbank.

"What's happening?" asked Efran.

The peculiar expression on Lokenna's face told Santon that the woman knew. She turned slowly, as if in a trance. Facing the castle, a look of utter horror began to spread over her lovely face.

"My brother has released a demon. Demons! The crown has somehow opened the door and demons flood into our world!"

"But they were banished," protested Efran. "King Waellkin accepted the crown as proof of their—" The look of horror spread over him, too, as he realized the depths of Lorens' perfidy.

"Lorens has invited them back to this world— to Porotane? He has unleashed the plague of demons upon us again?" Even Birtle Santon, who had come to believe the worst of Lokenna's brother, found this outrageous and frightening.

"He had no choice. He . . . he did not know what he was doing. The crown has perverted him. The lure of power made him believe he was invincible. When his scouts reported back that we had routed his personal guard, he accepted the demons' offer of aid."

"What can we do to stop them?" Santon had fought the best and won, even though he had but one good arm. In a fight such as this, he felt totally helpless.

"Let me up." Kaga'kalb struggled and got to his knees. The wizard's face was haggard and drawn. Santon saw that he had aged a hundred years—more—since this battle of magics had started. "I am not done. They cut me off from my Castle of Winds but I will show them. I know their secret. I advised Waellkin not to take the crown, but I know their secret."

"What?" Efran, Lokenna, and Santon chorused.

"There might seen to be legions of demons, but if you defeat one, they are all defeated."

"You mean there's really only one of them?" asked Santon. He preferred simpler fights. Man against man; ax against steel sword; that was his kind of battle.

"Whether there is only one or many matters naught," said Kaga'kalb. "All we need do is defeat one and the rest vanish. Then we must close the door through which Lorens has invited them!"

"How do you fight a demon?" asked Efran.

Kaga'kalb got to his feet. "Magic. They block me from the center of my power, but they underestimate me. I am still strong. I will drive them back to where they come from!"

Thunder rolled across Porotane in response

to the wizard's battle cry. Kaga'kalb threw back his sleeves and brought down bolt after vivid lightning bolt until the earth turned molten and flowed. Winds came up and blew the superheated liquid away.

Revealed in the center of this cauldron of molten rock stood a smirking demon.

"So, Wizard of Storms, you again oppose us."

"Again I will send you back!" Kaga'kalb clapped his hands. An ice storm of bone-chilling severity blew across the land and swirled around the demon. The demon struggled and fought, but his movements slowed. Kaga'kalb brought down freezing rain, then whipped up a tornado. The ice accumulated faster around the demon, turning him into a statue of gleaming white and blue ice.

Within the cold sheath Santon saw the malevolent dark eyes, the ruddy pallor of the creature's face, the sharp, angular bones that threatened to rupture skin, the emaciated body—and always he returned to those haunting, dark eyes.

"Do not gaze into his eyes," warned Kaga'kalb. "They will steal your will."

"Kill him," muttered Santon, captivated by those infinitely evil eyes. "I have to kill him." He hefted an ax he had taken from the rebel camp and advanced on the ice-encrusted demon.

"Wait, no, Santon, stop!" He heard Efran's warnings. Lokenna's joined the rebel leader's. Even when the Wizard of Storms barked out a command to halt, Santon could not. He had to kill the demon. He had to stop this magical invasion and return Porotane to humanity.

The muscles on his powerful arm knotted with the effort of bringing the heavy ax back and driving it directly for the demon's skull. One swift, powerful stroke would end this invasion.

The ax struck the ice. The explosion caught Santon up in an invisible and supremely powerful hand and cast him backward through the air. He landed in a snowbank, the air gusting from his lungs.

The cold, the gasping for breath, the sight before him, all broke the spell the demon had cast on him.

The demon lifted spindly arms and flexed wiry muscles. The sneer curling his black lips mocked not only Santon but all humanity. "Weakling. I played on your basest desires. I have no fear of this Wizard of Storms. His petty spells cannot harm me. I toy with him!"

Santon rolled from the snowbank, got to his feet and charged, his ax already coming around in a vicious circle that would end with the ax blade sinking deep into the demon's sunken chest.

The shock that rolled along the blade, along the haft, up his arm and to his powerful shoulder rattled Santon's senses. He staggered away, staring numbly at the ax. The edge had shattered against the demon's rib cage.

"You cannot harm me. No mortal can!"

Laughing, the demon plucked the ax from Santon's feeble grasp. He hefted it, then laughed even harder as he cast the ax in Kaga'kalb's direction. The wizard sidestepped the spinning blade.

"You are nimble for an old man," complimented the demon.

Santon turned and saw the demon's trick. The heavy ax had missed Kaga'kalb—but it swung in a wide circle and now returned of its own volition, the heavy blade coming directly for the back of the wizard's skull.

Even before Santon could shout a warning, a lightning bolt crashed down from above and destroyed the ax.

"I *am* nimble, Kalob."

"You misname me. I am not Kalob. I am another." The denial rang false in Santon's ears.

"Kalob will do as a name." Kaga'kalb began an assault of the elements so fierce that Santon struggled to get up the slope and back to where the wizard, Efran, and Lokenna stood. Lightning even more intense, winds of hurricane force, tornadoes swirling in tight circles and sucking up everything in their center, rain and snow and even dust tore at the demon. The ground around him bubbled and boiled and froze and spun as Kaga'kalb varied the type of elemental assault.

During it, Santon closed his eyes and listened. An order came through the Wizard of Storms' attack. It was as if he heard music. Soft here, louder there. Building to a crescendo, then slipping away into a more soothing beat. Kaga'kalb created a natural symphony of death to destroy Kalob.

"He . . . he tries to escape. I must maintain this level of attack to pin him here. Go," urged Kaga'kalb. "Go before I tire. Get the Demon Crown away from Lorens. It is our only hope."

"What?" Santon turned to Lokenna. "Do you know what to do with it if we can wrest it from your brother?"

"I think so. The few times I wore it gave me great insight into its use—and misuse. I know nothing of how Lorens brought the demons here, and I do not know if I can drive them back. But I must try!"

Santon looked from the maelstrom where Kalob was pinned by the elemental forces commanded by Kaga'kalb to the castle. "We ought to try getting in now," he said. "Lorens will be blinded by so much magic. It'll worry him, infuriate him. We have to take advantage of his confusion and fear."

"Wait here. I'll bring horses." Efran Gaemock rushed off. Lokenna turned to say something but he had already gone.

"There is no need for him to go with us," she said, her face lined with concern. "We can do this alone." Lokenna turned and looked into Santon's green eyes. "*I* can do it by myself. There is no reason for either of you to endanger your lives."

"You love him, don't you?" he asked.

She nodded her head slightly. "When I wore the crown the first time, I spied on him. For hours I watched and listened and he never knew." She bowed her head. "I am so ashamed of myself. I was *glad* that Bane had died."

"Glad or relieved?" asked Santon. "There is a difference."

"Relieved. My choices are not easier, but—it does not matter," she said abruptly. "We have much to do. If I fail, my feelings for Efran mean nothing." She laughed weakly. "I dare hope too much. He cannot even like me. My brother has visited upon Porotane the worst plague since the days of King Waellkin. And . . ." Her face hardened.

"And what?" Santon demanded.

"Kaga'kalb is unable to summon his cloud warriors. I sense his dismay. His storms are all he can muster. His nearness to the crown robs him of his most potent weapons."

To this Santon said nothing. Matters became increasingly complex. He had seen how Efran looked at her when she was not aware of his interest. Still, Lokenna was right about them having much to do, and it was all dangerous. Their love lives could be straightened out afterward.

If there was an afterward for any of them.

"You do not have to go, Birtle. It is too risky."

"Vered's alive in the castle. Alarice believes this, and so must I."

Before she could answer, Efran rode up leading two horses. He tossed the reins down to Santon and Lokenna. "We must ride like the wind. We dare not hope he can maintain this level of exertion long."

Santon saw that Efran was right. Kaga'kalb weakened visibly, yet any less effort on the wizard's part would release Kalob from the pen of wind and fire that held him.

Santon clumsily mounted, rubbed his withered arm, and flexed his good hand. The cold had begun to take its toll on his joints, yet he wished he had the security of the battle-ax on a leather thong weighing down his wrist again. There was no time to replace the ax; they had to ride directly to the castle.

"I know a way in," said Efran. "From my days as jester, I poked into every passageway until I found all Baron Theoll's secret tunnels and spy holes."

Santon had to chuckle as they rode. Again he entered Castle Porotane and it was not by the main gate. He would learn every secret tunnel into the place before he used the way most entered.

"The brambles," said Lokenna. "They can hold back any attacking army." She studied the thorny tangle. "I see why my brother is so frightened of Kaga'kalb. The cloud warriors could pass through unharmed."

"Or descend from the sky. Or even be formed within the castle, if Kaga'kalb could see where to cast the appropriate spell," said Efran. "I have given him a map showing the layout of the castle, but he said he needs his scrying spell to work before he can send his magical warriors."

Santon and Lokenna exchanged glances. Kaga'kalb lied to Efran to bolster his spirit. There would be no cloud warriors. Santon settled down and watched closely for patrols as they rode. He saw none, even on the castle's battlements. If he had not known better, he would have thought Castle Porotane to be deserted. They dismounted when they came to a particularly heavy patch in the bramble wall.

"Here?" asked Lokenna. "There's no way to crawl through without being cut to pieces."

"Therein lies the beauty of this tunnel," said Efran. He poked around for a few minutes until he found what he sought. A loud *click*! sounded and he worked to push away a heavy door covered with camouflaging brambles. "Inside and hurry. It is not far to the innermost courtyard, but I do not want our king spying on us."

"What does it matter where we are when he sees us?" asked Santon. "With the crown, walls— or tunnels—mean nothing." He remembered the brief glimpse through the magics of Kaga'kalb's scrying spell. To *see* and *hear* like that all the time would be a boon second to none!

"This tunnel is equipped with special . . . traps. It has floodgates built in near the castle proper. Should we be seen while in the tunnel, those gates can be opened." Efran took a deep breath and exhaled, sending silvery plumes into the frigid air. "We would be drowned like rats in the bilge of a barge."

"A cheerful notion," said Santon, diving into the hole. The darkness stopped him. He felt as if he had walked into a midnight black curtain. His eyes adapted to the darkness and he saw faint pin-points of light along the roof.

"Special holes cut through to provide guid-ance, but be careful," warned Efran. "If you see a red light, stop and let me know. That marks a spe-cial deadfall that must be skirted."

Santon walked slowly, carefully picking his way in the muddy tunnel. He followed the twin-kling pinpoints of light until he came to a red one. He called out the warning.

"Turn to your right and walk forward two paces," ordered Efran. "We're following. Now turn left and continue. That should avoid the trip-wire."

"What would it trigger?"

"Who can say?" answered Efran. "I have been down this tunnel only once, and that was from the other direction. On rare occasions, I slipped away from the castle to meet with my brother to see how the war progressed."

"I see a brighter light," interrupted Santon. "What does that mean?"

"It means we have come to the end—and now the real danger confronts us." Efran and Lokenna pressed close as Santon made his way up a slip-pery ramp to a stone door. He slipped his hand through the rusty metal ring and heaved. The door opened slowly and silently. Efran slid past, hand on his sword.

"It's safe. No one in sight."

Santon hung back a pace and let Efran and Lokenna precede him. When they reached the courtyard, he motioned for them to stop.

"What is it, Birtle?" asked Lokenna. Her face was pale and drawn but he thought she held up well to the danger. "My brother is . . . in the throne room," she finished. "I can *feel* his evil presence. The blackness fluttering around him is like a veil."

"I can do nothing against such magic," Santon said. "I want to seek out Vered. With another sword and his quick wit, perhaps we stand a better chance of defeating Lorens."

"Lorens is leaving the throne room," said Lokenna. She turned as if she watched him. "He is climbing stairs, going to the battlements." Lokenna stepped out into the courtyard, oblivious to the cold rain against her upturned face. "There. He is there."

Santon saw nothing where she pointed; the storm clouds obscured vision beyond a few score of yards.

Efran Gaemock looked from Lokenna to the hidden Lorens and back to Santon. "Go, find your friend. I remember Vered with fondness. I wish you both well." He clapped Santon on the shoulder.

"I'm not abandoning you—*we're* not," he said, speaking for Vered, too. "We'll join you when we can."

"Hurry," said Lokenna. "Kaga'kalb weakens and Kalob is fighting his way free of the storm prison. We must get to Lorens quickly. Only the crown can drive Kalob back into his netherworld." She started off, not waiting to see if Efran or Santon followed.

"Luck," Santon told Efran, "and save some of the good times for us. We'll be there. I promise."

Efran Gaemock squeezed Santon's shoulder in a comradely grip and then hastened after Lokenna. Santon stood in the cold, driving rain and wondered if he had lost his mind. Vered might be dead; hunting for him would take time and endanger Lokenna's chances of besting her brother. They ought to remain together.

Santon watched Efran and Lokenna vanish into the castle. He turned and ran for the door leading to the dungeons. Bare-handed he would fight his way to the torture chambers and get his friend out. *Then* they would help Lokenna against her brother.

To Santon's surprise, he encountered no guards as he spiraled down the stone staircase to the dungeon. The heavy metal grating barring entry into the cell block was easily opened. A departing guard had carelessly tossed aside the key. Santon jerked open the grating and dashed into the dungeon.

Silence greeted him. He peered in one cell after another and saw the same sight. Bodies. Decaying humans. Emaciated corpses. The prisoners had starved to death. Hope died with each cell and left only drifting gauzy white phantoms.

He came to the end of the cell block and peered in the small grate. An obviously dead prisoner sprawled in the back, but Santon's attention came to the hole through the wall into the next cell. He rushed to this door and peered in.

Empty.

He fumbled with his key ring and then saw it wasn't necessary. This door was barred, a heavy pin holding the locking bar in place. He jerked free the cotter pin and drew the bar.

Santon stepped into the cell and yelled as he fell into a hole. He turned in the hole and looked back through the open door in time to see the flagstone in the floor rising. He jerked his right hand in an instinctive motion designed to get his ax into hand.

No ax. No weapon. He struggled to get free of the pit.

The flagstone slid back and a head poked through. "You've picked a fine time to open the door for me," said Vered.

Santon leaned against the cell door and shook his head. Alarice had been right. Vered was a survivor.

All they had to do now was survive the battle with Lorens and the Demon Crown.

CHAPTER TWENTY-FIVE

"Are you going to help me up? I am so giddy I can barely stand." Vered crawled onto the cold stone floor and held out his hand for Santon to give him a boost. Santon's meaty hand closed around Vered's thinner one and heaved. Vered shot to his feet. "There. That's better. Except for my finery. All ruined." He made a futile brushing motion to dislodge the worst of the caked dirt.

"You hardly needed me. You were already out of the cell."

"It took you so long getting here, I decided not to wait." Vered wobbled. Santon had to support him.

"You appear a bit the worse for the lesson in patience."

"Food stopped coming . . . a while ago."

"I noticed its effect on the other prisoners."

The stark silence in the dungeon emphasized Santon's epitaph for the others. "How did you survive?"

"I was stronger. They had just put me in when the food stopped." Vered looked at his bare feet. "I need new boots."

"Easily done. There is a rack of guards' clothing. They had to change after torture."

"Bloodstains are difficult to conceal when you must attend state dinners," agreed Vered. He walked on unsteady feet to the small wardrobe Santon had pointed out. He found a pair of boots that almost fit. He stuffed in a few rags to make up the difference.

"Food is what you need."

"I need more than that," said Vered, a twinkle in his eye. "And so do you." In a conspiratorial whisper he said, "I know where to find your shield and the sword Alarice gave me."

"Where?" barked Santon. He calmed. "I'm sorry. Food for you, first."

"Not much. It would make me sick. Let me build up slowly. Then I'll demand a full banquet."

Together they left the dungeon and made their way to the deserted kitchens. Food was scarce; Vered got his wish not to be overfed. Santon's belly rumbled from lack of food, too, but he let his friend eat what he wanted before sampling of the moldy bread and tough, wormy meat.

"Lorens always did know how to set a fine table," remarked Vered as he finished off the last of the bread. He spat out a gristle and rubbed his stomach. "It'll take a few minutes for the food to give me strength. Remember our old quarters?"

"The shield is there?"

"Aye, and my sword. Look under the pile of

blankets near the bed. And while you are rummaging about up there, bring me back another change of clothing. These rags simply will not do if I am to appear before a king."

"Keep eating," Santon said. "You need to fill out that form. You always were a trifle on the skinny side, even if you did eat like a team of mules."

"If I eat any more, I might explode." Vered poked at the maggot-infested meat. "Then again, if I don't eat it, it might decide to eat me."

Santon left and hurried through the corridors, wondering where the castle residents had gone. The entire time he had been inside he had seen no one. Even by straining, he had been unable to hear anything more than the crash and rumble of Kaga'kalb's storms.

The thought of Lokenna and Efran facing Lorens alone added speed to his journey. He raced along the empty halls until he found their old quarters. Inside the room, he dived and slid on his belly to look under the blankets. He gusted a sigh of relief. Ax and glass shield supported Vered's sword. He drew out the bundle and carefully fastened the shield onto his withered arm until he could maneuver it as he had in the past. His ax felt good in his grip once more.

With Vered's sword thrust through his belt and an armful of clothing snatched from the wardrobe, he returned to the kitchens.

"What was that hideous sound?" he asked.

"I belched. I'm not tolerating this so-called food very well." Vered belched again and wiped his mouth with the back of his hand. "Starvation might prove a more humane death than what this is doing." He stood and came to the door. Santon noted the familiar spring in his friend's step. He would be weak when it came to a fight, but his condition had improved greatly from the tainted food.

"Ah, my precious sword. And you have your shield," said Vered. "Let's not dally. Let me get into the clothing you fetched—your color sense is abominable, dear friend—and we shall be off to do . . . what?"

Santon tersely explained the situation as Vered changed his clothes. "Kaga'kalb cannot hold Kalob prisoner much longer. When he weakens, the demon will be free again."

"So Lorens let the demons back into Porotane." Vered shook his head. "I never thought he showed any common sense. Too much power too soon and you sell out to the netherworld. It's an old and sorry story."

"You'd have done the same thing. I saw how the Demon Crown affected you."

"Of course I would. I admit to avarice and a fine lust for power. I've never pretended otherwise. Now where is the battle taking place? I've seen no one around here."

"I encountered no one in the upper corridors, either," said Santon. "I find it strange."

"Has Lorens slain everyone?"

"It is possible, but he would have left bodies littered all around—or he would have stored the prisoners in the dungeons."

"There's only one solution to this small riddle. Let's ask the whoreson ourselves!" Vered pushed past Santon and went back into the courtyard.

"There," said Santon. "There's where Lokenna said her brother had gone."

"You can see through this storm? Snow, fog, rain, what isn't falling on our heads?" Even as he spoke, a clap of thunder sounded and a vibrant bolt of lightning lashed through the clouds to the uppermost turret.

"There's Lorens."

Santon and Vered made their way through the empty passageways and to the throne room. Lorens' audience chamber contained a few bodies, some blown apart from the inside and others that had perished from severe sword wounds.

"Unless I misinterpret this," said Vered, "Lorens has survived a castle revolt. Those poor wights with the blown-out guts tried to seize power. The ones with the swords defended—until Lorens made his wishes in the matter known magically."

"He killed them all," said Santon.

"The crown did it."

They silently left the audience chamber and found the spiraling stone stairs that led to the upper levels. From here they heard the raging storm outside. Snow piled up at the end of a corridor, blown from above.

"What an invitation," muttered Santon. "They've left the door open for us."

Vered pulled his cloak tighter around him. He still shivered. With a small flourish, he drew his sword and waved it about. "Standing here does nothing to help Lokenna and Efran." Vered looked at his friend. "Is Efran as clever and witty as he was when he pretended to be a jester?"

Santon didn't bother answering. He made certain his glass shield rested easily on his arm, flipped the battle ax into his grip, then advanced. The biting wind cut at his face and arms, but he left the warmth of the castle and ventured onto the battlements.

Behind him he heard Vered panting and puffing with exertion. The man had yet to recover his full strength—Santon knew it would take days before that happened. It was their destiny that they were thrust into the fight before either was ready.

Birtle Santon swallowed hard and wondered if he would ever have been ready. The sight before him told the answer.

Lorens stood on the highest point in the tallest tower, his arms outthrust as if daring Kaga'kalb to bring down his lightning bolts. The Wizard of Storms did just that. Santon lifted his shield to protect his eyes when the prodigious blue-white bolt struck Lorens. The wizard-king staggered, but other than this small indication of weakness showed no injury.

The Demon Crown had drained the brutal thrust of Kaga'kalb's energy.

"Where are Lokenna and Efran?" asked Vered.

"I don't see them."

"Then we should press on. We can't let Lorens stare at the scenery overlong. He might get to enjoy it too much to stop."

They started forward, the cold wind buffeting them. They hadn't advanced ten paces when Santon sensed movement to one side. He spun, his shield coming up to protect his head. A heavy cudgel landed and drove him to his knees. As in prior fights, when one was attacked, the other countered.

Vered came around the side with a long lunge that spitted Santon's opponent neatly. The glass tip entered the guardman's armpit far enough to kill with the single thrust. Vered recovered and let Santon stand in time to deflect a sword attack.

"Lorens' personal guard," muttered Vered.

"Green soldiers. Efran routed the personal guard outside the castle walls."

"Why didn't you say so? These younglings will fall quickly to a master swordsman such as myself!" Vered launched a flurry of thrusts, ripostes, and parries. Santon joined him, knowing that his friend's strength would soon fade in the face of such opposition.

Vered drove one guardsman over the battlements to his death. Santon used his shield to catch another under the chin; the soldier's head snapped back and made a crack so loud they heard it over the thunder. A third guardsman tumbled to the inner courtyard when Santon's ax bit deeply into his thigh.

"This is all Lorens has left to protect him? How absurd. We can fight them all day long!"

Santon saw that Vered boasted. This minor skirmish had drained him of strength. Vered stumbled as they made their way forward. When they reached Lorens, Vered would be unable to lift even his light glass sword.

"Guard my back. Here come two more!" Santon rushed the guardsmen rather than letting them choose the battleground. He upended one and sent him tumbling over the stone battlement. He heard the poor wight's screams of agony as he was impaled on the thorny brambles outside the castle wall. The second soldier fought more cautiously, avoiding direct blows from Santon's mighty ax and turning to keep Santon's shield out of position.

"You, soldier," called Santon, his voice

sounding faint and distant in the storm. "We have no quarrel with you. Is that the man you want as king? Up there?"

The guardsman cast a quick glance over his shoulder. Santon stepped back, both to give the young man a chance to study his liege lord and to rest. The cold robbed him of vitality faster than he would have liked. He worried at what this fight in the frigid wind did to Vered if he felt this drained himself.

Lorens shrieked and ranted and made gestures in the direction of the rebel camp. Santon did not know if the Demon Crown allowed the wizard-king to seek Kaga'kalb or if Lorens merely vented his wrath in the most convenient way. The expression on his face defied description. He had once been a handsome enough youth. The lines furrowed into his leather-skinned forehead were those of someone carrying the burdens of the world. His hair had turned white, either from frost or strain. Most telling of all was his frame. He had been well muscled when they had arrived in Porotane.

He now stood as gaunt as a demon, his cheekbones protruding and his eyes dark pits. Lorens shook all over as magical spells tumbled from his lips.

"Is *he* your monarch?" repeated Santon.

The young soldier looked back. "He has killed my friends. He has destroyed most of the people within the castle walls. He has done what the rebels were unable to do in twenty years of fighting."

The soldier lowered his sword and waited. Santon turned, putting his back to the battlements and motioning the man by. The soldier cast his sword into the courtyard and then rushed past Santon and Vered, obviously glad to put this to an end.

"So much for inspiring loyalty," said Vered, watching the young man descend the icy stone steps and vanish into the castle.

Santon wasn't listening. He stared at Lorens, wondering if any shred of humanity remained in that fragile-appearing husk. It didn't look like it.

He and Vered made their way to the steps leading to the platform where Lorens muttered his spells. The wizard-king's attention was focused elsewhere. He took no notice of them.

"Can we kill him this easily?" Santon said, his voice a whisper.

"Trying is the only way to find out." Vered wiped the snow from his eyebrows and gripped the hilt of his sword so hard his knuckles turned white with strain.

"Wait!"

They spun, ready to fight. Lokenna motioned them away. She had taken refuge in a small guard post at the base of the tower.

"Birtle, Vered, please!"

Santon backed from the steps leading to Lorens. The king remained oblivious to their presence. Attacking him now might be their best opportunity for victory. Even knowing this, he motioned Vered to join Lokenna, then ducked into the guard post.

The small room was crowded with two. With four it made for a closeness Santon didn't want. Efran hunched over, holding his side. A bright red stain showed where a heavy sword blade had slashed through his light armor.

"He will be all right," said Lokenna. The look on her face assured Santon that she did not speak simply to bolster Efran's spirits. She truly thought he would live. "We must wait before we go after my brother. The crown gives him power beyond belief."

"Can Kaga'kalb wear him down?" asked Santon. "That *is* what you're waiting for?"

The stricken look on the woman's face gave Santon his first hint that the battle of magics did not go well. Without his cloud warriors, Kaga'kalb had to rely solely on his storm-bringing ability—and this was limited by nearness to the Demon Crown.

"There is so little I can do. Kaga'kalb must carry on the fight while I stand and watch. The last of Lorens' guard is gone. Beyond this . . ."

Vered poked his head outside into the storm and held up a hand to shield his eyes from the rain. He ducked back in and said, "Lorens shows no sign of weakening. If anything, he seems to be turning aside the worst of the storm."

"What can we do?" asked Santon.

"I . . . I don't know. When we came up here, I thought I could deal with my brother."

"He'd never listen," cut in Efran. "He is crazed with the crown's power. Trying to reason with him was foolish on our part."

"He killed almost everyone within the castle," Lokenna said in a choked voice. "I hadn't known that until we . . . until we came across the rooms where the bodies are stacked."

Efran moaned, then bit his lower lip to keep from crying out again. Santon knew that they could not remain here indefinitely. Efran needed help desperately. Vered was still weak from starvation. Kaga'kalb's power waned as the spell battle raged on. The fight had to be carried directly to Lorens.

"Santon, where are you going?" asked Vered. Santon pushed his friend back and stepped into the storm. In front of him moved a patch of fog that flowed and took shape.

"Alarice?" he asked, not daring to hope.

"The demon comes. Lorens has worn down Kaga'kalb. You must act now, dear Birtle. Do it now or all is lost!"

Lightning flared across the sky and drove away Alarice's phantom. Santon gave the leather thong on his wrist a quick jerk and brought the ax to fighting position. He went to the stone steps and started up. He hesitated when he felt a presence behind him.

"Vered, don't," he said, then stopped. With Vered was Lokenna and Efran—and behind them wavered a phantom.

"We all go or none do," said Vered. "It is only fair. Why should it be any different from the way it's always been?"

Lokenna nodded her agreement. Efran hefted his sword and held his ribs, anxious to engage. Behind them Santon saw Alarice's face with its gentle smile. He turned and raced up the stone steps.

The turret had protected him from the worst of the wind. When he got to the top, storm winds buffeted him from all directions. Santon wavered for a moment, then plunged ahead, ignoring cold and snow and wind. Lorens and the Demon Crown became the center of his universe.

With a bull-throated war cry, Santon swung his ax directly at Lorens' throat. The heavy blade struck its target—and rebounded. Santon yelped in surprise as the shock worked its way back along his arm and into his shoulder.

Fighting instinct saved him. He threw up the glass shield as if to ward off a blow. Energies beyond any mere steel blade boiled on the rounded shield's surface. Santon swung again, hunkered down behind the shield. This time he aimed at Lorens' legs.

The impact again knocked him back. It also brought Lorens to his knees.

"Who dares attack me in this manner?" The voice came from Lorens' mouth but the hollow, ringing quality to it was not human.

"You are Kalob, not Lorens," accused Santon.

Ghastly, shrill laughter drowned out the thunder. "Kalob is my ally. I have allowed him to enter this world again. He fights the traitor Kaga'kalb."

"You know his name!" Lokenna gasped.

"The Demon Crown reveals all to me!" Again Lorens laughed. This time Vered and Efran attacked him, one from each side. Efran's steel sword failed to injure the wizard-king, but Vered's glass blade dug deeply into Lorens' side. Black blood trickled out of the wound.

"He's not human," muttered Efran. "He has become a demon, too!"

The three men attacked simultaneously, but failed to penetrate the ring of Lorens' spells. Whatever magic he used now proved effective and kept them at bay.

"I know this spell," Lokenna said in a small voice. "Attack him again. *Now!*"

The three men reacted as one. Vered swung at the man's eyes. Santon's ax drove deep into Lorens' right thigh and produced a new artesian well of the inky blood. Efran lunged directly for the wizard-king's heart. All three felt their weapons strike and wound.

Lorens screamed in pain, clawing at his injured eyes, hobbling on his leg, and geysering blood from a ruptured heart.

"No man can survive those injuries," marvelled Vered. "He cannot be human!"

"Human or not, he dies!" Santon stood over Lorens, ax raised for the killing blow. As powerful as the downward blow was, the hand grabbing his wrist and lifting him off the turret was stronger. Santon struggled in the impossibly strong grip, twisting to see his attacker.

"Kalob!" he gasped.

"Kaga'kalb fights himself." The demon sneered, black lips pulled away from bloody fangs. "I have escaped his traps. I stopped him from conjuring his cloud warriors. Now I must rescue my puppet. Lorens has allowed me back into this world. He will serve me well when the new order is established."

Santon kicked and fought but could not free himself from the demon's grip. Both Vered and Efran had collapsed on the turret, exhausted from the fight with Lorens—or under Kalob's spell.

Only Lokenna remained on her feet. Beside her glowed the patch of mist that was Alarice.

"There is a way of forcing you back," Lokenna said in a voice unlike her own. Santon ceased his struggles for a moment and stared at her. She had reached out. Alarice's phantom sent out a glowing tendril that rested on Lokenna's palm. "I know what it is. When I wore the crown, I knew it. My brother knows, also, but he is too weak."

"*You* are weak, bitch!" roared Kalob. With a contemptuous gesture, he threw Santon across the turret roof. Santon skidded and managed to keep from falling to his death below at the last instant by clutching at Vered's leg. Vered twitched weakly and moaned. He showed no other sign of life.

'There is a different power, one I can use," Lokenna said. "I have always known it—all my life."

"You fear it, bitch. You cannot use it because you are weak!"

"I could not use it because I lacked the power, not the will!" Lokenna spun and reached out to take the Demon Crown from her brother's head. Lorens jerked away.

Santon saw that Lokenna needed the crown if Kalob was to be forced back into his netherworld. Santon rolled and swung the edge of the glass shield at the back of Lorens' neck. The impact knocked the wizard-king's head forward. In a smooth motion, Lokenna snared the falling crown and held it.

The transition from ugly, corrupt green to the verdant emerald came abruptly. Kalob roared in anger as Lokenna put the crown on her head and began muttering the spells that would break the demon's power.

Kalob fought. He reached out with his spindly arms and skeletal hand and caught Santon by the throat. He lifted and held the struggling man over the edge of the turret.

"Give Lorens the crown or I drop this feeble worm!"

"You cannot open your hand," Lokenna said. Santon gagged as the demon's fingers tightened on his throat. His feet kicked above a drop of two hundred feet—and hidden below in the swirling clouds lay the treacherous brambles. The six-inch-long thorns would kill him, even if the fall did not.

"Bitch! Do not oppose me in this. Return the crown. Now! Do it now!"

Lokenna stood for a few seconds, bathed in the vivid green glow of the Demon Crown.

"Release him," she ordered.

Santon felt the demon's claws opening. He grabbed for the spindly arm; he had no desire to die, but if he did, he would take Kalob with him.

The demon discarded him as if he were a piece of offal. Santon screamed as he fell away from the turret, tumbling over and over, falling to his death.

The wind he had hated for so long cut against his face, caught at his clothing—lifted him. Like some ungainly bird, Santon flew on the powerful currents. He swooped low over the deadly brambles and blasted upward into the sky. Clouds drifted under him and supported him with their misty substance. Lightning flared around him, lighting his way through the rain and snow and dust.

As light as a feather, the winds put him down in the edge of the turret again. The sight of the human returned from certain death shocked Kalob. He tried to utter a spell, to finish the job he had begun, but Lokenna's voice cut deeper than any blade.

"Your legs are numb. Your vision fades. Kalob, your senses are being taken from you. Blind, deaf, without feeling, you are slipping away. There is no taste or odor in this world. Only yourself, only you, and you are growing weaker."

"You cannot do this to me! I beg you! You have no idea how terrible it is in my world!"

Lokenna stepped forward. The crown sat on her head and drew every lightning strike. She was not the target of destruction; she was the center of power. As she moved, her lips worked on the spells needed to banish the demon.

Kalob shrank in size. The fragility of his body increased. Santon moved forward and used the edge of his shield against the demon's neck. Kalob's head flew into the storm. Lokenna pointed and a bolt of lightning vaporized the skull. She reached out and lightly touched the still-wiggling body. It tumbled off the turret.

Santon saw it vanish as if it were mist evaporating in the morning sun.

"He is banished," Lokenna said. "The gateway opened by my brother is closed—and will remain so."

Santon sank to his knees, thankful for the respite. He started to speak and then saw the determination on the woman's face.

"Lokenna, no, let me!"

Santon's warning came too late. Lokenna went to her brother, who hopped on one leg. As she had done with Kalob, she reached out and gently shoved. Lorens shrieked as he lost his balance and tumbled backward off the turret.

Santon fell belly down and peered over the brink. No bolt of lightning vaporized Lorens. His body cut a tunnel through the clouds. Santon got a long look at the wizard-king's twisted body impaled on the deadly thorns before the storm closed the pathway to death.

"There is no need to worry about me, dear Birtle," she said, touching his cheek. "He was my brother, my twin, but he was also venal and . . .

evil." She straightened. "As my relative, it was my duty to do what had to be done."

Lokenna turned from Santon, then fainted, falling face forward. He tried to catch her and only partially broke her fall. He lay beside her on the turret, too weak to move. Above, the storm began to abate. Within minutes blue sky arched above and soft, almost springlike winds blew.

Santon remembered the rainbow before passing out.

CHAPTER TWENTY-SIX

Vered stretched and leaned back in the cushioned chair, hiking his feet to the table in front of him. He took a morsel of bread and carefully ate it as he stared out the slit window in the room. Behind him Birtle Santon moaned softly.

"Are you awake, Santon?" he called.

"Awake? What?" The man came fully awake, hand reaching for his ax. Santon groaned again and got out of bed. Standing beside Vered, he said, "You're looking plump. You must have been gorging yourself to put on so much weight in . . ." His voice trailed off. Outside the trees tried to put on leaves and the grass had turned green once more. The snows had gone and the day looked like a perfect spring.

"No, you've not slept *that* long. But three days is a long time."

"Three days!"

"A little over. Much has happened while you've been dreaming away your life."

Santon grabbed Vered's shoulders and spun the man around. "Tell me what's happened."

"First of all, you seem well enough after your sleep. Have some food. Nothing wormy in this scrumptious food. Efran sent for his brother and the peasants robbed their winter larder to provide decent food for the conquering heroes—that's us."

"Winter?" Santon went to the window and felt warm breeze against his skin. Tears came to his eyes. He had not thought to ever see spring again.

"It *is* winter, but this is Kaga'kalb's coronation gift to Lokenna."

"Is he in the castle?"

"He returned immediately to his Castle of the Winds. He was even more drained than you, but Efran and Lokenna would not let him go until they'd forged a strong treaty. He can create his masterpieces of clouds and his symphonies of thunder and lightning as long as he does it in the Yorral Mountains. No more of this perpetual winter, even though we are barely into autumn."

"Then we will see winter again?"

"Soon, he said. But it will be natural and not the product of his magic. This unusual warmth is a reaction to the magic he used to defeat Lorens and the demon."

"They are gone?"

Vered shuddered. "Lokenna has the way of a queen about her. She refuses to allow her brother's body to be taken down from the thorns. He's to remain until the crows pick his skeleton clean. Then she's decreed that his bones be broken and sent to every corner of Porotane and put on display."

"The crown?" Santon was hesitant to even suggest that the Demon Crown also corrupted her.

"No. She considers this justice for what he had done to Porotane." Vered shrugged. "Mayhap she is right. The peasants seem to enjoy the thought of looking on the tyrant's bones and spitting on them. But then you know how peasants are."

"How can I have slept through all this?"

"You were exhausted by the battle. You of all, save for Lokenna and Kaga'kalb and perhaps Efran and myself, expended the most to save Porotane." Vered popped another choice tidbit into his mouth and chewed contentedly.

"Then all is well in the castle?"

"As smooth as silk," said Vered. "The formal coronation is slated for this afternoon. Most of the principals have recovered from the battle. Lokenna thought it was a reasonable time. She dares not wait too long or the kingdom will fall apart again and the petty warlords will stir up armies in opposition."

"What of the Gaemocks?"

Vered laughed. "She has them firmly on her side." Vered laughed even louder. "With Efran, she has more than this. She has him firmly in her bed."

"From the looks he gave her when they were together, he is not complaining," said Santon.

"Far from it. The court jester has now become the court favorite. It would not surprise me if she decides to make him more than consort. He is a valuable resource at this court. And if things do get dull, he can always cut a caper or two and liven them up. I suspect life will soon enough become dull here."

"He knows the politics of rule," agreed Santon. "And his brother? What of Dews' ambition for the throne?"

"He is a strange breed of man, that Dews Gaemock. He always avowed that he had no desire to sit on the throne, that he opposed Duke Freow simply because he wanted to see someone competent ruling the kingdom—and not necessarily himself."

"So he has bowed out?"

"Hardly. Lokenna would be suspicious of him if he had not exacted some post from her. He is now Marshal of Armies entrusted with maintaining order throughout the kingdom."

"In certain ways, this is a more powerful position than monarch. He collects taxes."

"He collects taxes and maintains the army against brigands, but Lokenna need have no fear of perfidy when he's off in the provinces. She still wears the Demon Crown."

The information worried Santon. Lorens had not been the evil fiend when he first donned the crown. He had been weak and from that weakness came the evil. The Demon Crown was a potent symbol, a magical relic of immense power. The potential for abuse and destruction was also great.

"Lokenna," said Santon, "uses the crown in a fashion different from Lorens. Therein lies the safety of the kingdom."

"She can still see or hear—spy on!—anyone anywhere she pleases. Except in the Castle of the Winds. That was part of the agreement between her and Kaga'kalb."

"His magic prevents such use, anyway," said

Santon. "No, she does more than spy. She looks into a person's soul and ferrets out emotion." He remembered the times she had seemed to read his thoughts—and she had not even been wearing the crown.

"I'm not certain I want a ruler who can do that. There is blackness lurking within that I refuse to face. Why should someone else know what I cannot about myself?" Vered's words hung heavy but his attitude dispelled any gloom.

"Will you stop eating for a moment?"

"Why? I am still famished. The time in the prison was awful—and be sure to remind me to always buy a high quality of boot. The leather in my old ones was well nigh inedible."

Santon stared into the countryside and saw a steady stream of people coming into the castle for the coronation. He asked Vered, "When is Lokenna to be installed as queen?"

"Soon. Get yourself into what rags you wish to be seen in publicly. Myself, I feel quite comfortable in these old things." Vered stood and pirouetted to show off his finery. Santon noticed the tunic and breeches less than he did the gleaming daggers Vered had hidden away in the folds.

"Expecting a new war to break out?"

"They saved me once. Call me superstitious. I intend to always carry four daggers with me. And my glass sword, of course." He tapped the hilt. Santon shook his head and went to dress. To his surprise the wardrobes overflowed with clothing that fit him as if tailor-made.

"I've had to do something to occupy my time. Choosing suitable clothing for you gave me some small respite from boredom."

Santon thanked him and stood before the polished metal sheet to study himself. He cut a fine figure, he decided, even though he would never tell Vered. His friend carried the "better things in life" to extremes. Santon preferred to be astride a strong horse with the stars above. Even a wind in the face as he rode would not be amiss.

"Hurry, Santon. The ceremonies begin without us."

Santon hitched up the glass shield and slung his ax in a belt loop. Crowning or not, he, like Vered, did not feel comfortable without weapons. They made their way down the back ways of the castle and came into the throne room through a side door.

"Isn't she lovely?" whispered Vered.

"Aye, she is. A regal bearing for a true queen." A catch came to Santon's voice when Lokenna took the Demon Crown from a plush pillow and placed the gold circlet on her head. A hush fell over the assemblage as the crown turned a light green, then began to shine with a clear, pure emerald light.

Santon let out pent-up breath he hadn't known he was holding. He had feared the crown would be the same ugly color it had been on Lorens' brow.

"Can you hear what she's saying?" asked Vered.

"Not well. She's thanking everyone. Kaga'kalb. Something about the alliance with the Wizard of Storms, blah, blah, blah. Dews Gaemock is Marshal of Armies." Santon smiled. "Your rumormongering is accurate, it seems."

"I hear something about Efran. Surely she is not appointing him court jester?"

"Nor consort. They've announced an alliance

more binding. This is a coronation and a wedding."

"A better choice than Bane Pandasso. She has learned quality in men, though why she chose him over me is something I will never understand."

Santon looked around the large chamber and saw the rapt faces. Rebel soldiers stood next to royalists. Peasants mingled with the few nobles remaining in the kingdom. There would be much rebuilding. New orders of nobility awarded, a settling into peace that might stretch for years.

Porotane needed the healing. The civil war had been too destructive for too long.

"Do you feel it, too?" asked Vered.

"What?"

"Sadness. It is over."

Santon considered, then nodded. "There is one item that remains to be done."

"I have no wish to stay in the castle and have them force baronies or even duchies on me. You know how I loathe it when beautiful women fawn on me and thrust riches into my hands."

"I've noticed," said Santon. "Shall we do what must be done?"

"Of course."

Long before Lokenna, Queen of Porotane, came to their names on the lists of nobility, Birtle Santon and Vered had departed the castle.

One last obligation had to be met.

CHAPTER TWENTY-SEVEN

The dust storm cut at their faces and hands and forced Santon and Vered to stop too often. Even worse than the biting dust was the freezing cold.

"I thought deserts were supposed to be hot. This is terrible." Vered huddled behind his horse in a vain attempt to find shelter from the storm raging across the Desert of Sazan.

"It's winter. There's nothing to keep the heat in. Do you see anything but rocks and sand?"

"It wasn't much warmer in the Iron Range when we came through the passes. Won't this ever get any better?"

"Not until summer. Then the heat will fry your brains inside your skull."

"I remember all too well," Vered said glumly. "I think that's already happened. There's no other reason for us to be out here exposing our precious bodies to the elements.''

They had left Castle Porotane, taking horses and supplies for their long journey. Not bothering to consult with Lokenna had speeded them on their way. As Santon pointed out, the new ruler of Porotane could find them easily if she desired. All she had to do was don the Demon Crown and *look* for them.

The black, angular peaks of the Iron Range had brought fierce winter storms and bands of brigands who had not heard of the new law in the land. Each group they eluded or outfought reminded them that Dews Gaemock would not tolerate such thievery—but bringing law to this portion of the kingdom would take months or even years.

The Inquisitor had finally risen at their backs and the barren Desert of Sazan stretched before them.

"How are we going to find it?" demanded Vered. "I can't see ten paces in this dust."

"We'll find a way. We must."

Vered grumbled a bit, then said, "We owe her much. It's a pity her phantom cannot aid us now." No phantom could locate the body from which it came. No one had been able to give a reasonable explanation; Santon and Vered had aided more than one phantom in Claymore Pass and other battlegrounds to find eternal rest. For Alarice they could perform the same service.

Without her, Porotane would not have a decent queen on the throne and peace for the first time in over twenty years.

"Patrin's City of Stolen Dreams was near this spot," said Santon.

"How can you tell?"

"I've not lost my tracking sense. We found it before, when Alarice led us here. I can always retrace my steps."

"I've heard of birds being able to perform such a feat," muttered Vered, pulling his cloak up to protect his nose and mouth. He took a step forward and stumbled over something buried in the sand.

"What's that?" Santon pounced on the broken pot.

"It looks like one of Patrin's dream jars. Do you think it remained when his entire city just . . . vanished."

"It might have. If so, that means she is near— her remains are near," he corrected, his voice choked with emotion. Vered rested a reassuring hand on his friend's shoulder.

"There is much desert to search and the sands will have drifted over her," said Vered as gently as possible. "It might be the work of a lifetime finding her skeleton. This storm makes it even more difficult to do."

"I'll do it."

"We'll do it," said Vered.

They began their hunt until both dropped to the ground in exhaustion.

"It's so cold and the demon-damned wind never stops," said Vered. "How can we be sure that we're not simply searching the same spot over and over? I'm so turned around, I cannot tell where I am."

"We've been . . ." Santon's voice trailed off as the wind died. In the distance he saw huge pillars of cloud rising to form black anvilheads. Lightning crashed within the clouds.

"Those look exactly like the storms Kaga'kalb conjured," said Vered.

"Quiet. Listen!"

"Music!"

"The thunder. It . . . it's a song!" Santon stood and made his way to the top of a sand dune. From here he was able to get an unobstructed view of the two towering columns of lightning-filled storm.

"The winds still rage except down the corridor," said Vered. "Do you think Kaga'kalb is aiding us?"

"He is," came Alarice's faint voice. "I cannot help you to help me. But Kaga'kalb can—and so is Lokenna."

"Lokenna?"

"The Demon Crown. She can see anything no matter where it is!"

Santon said, "The cloud warriors—look. Kaga'kalb sends one toward us."

"Lokenna guides it, Kaga'kalb sends it," came Alarice's voice, hardly more than a whisper in the desert.

"I see no remains of Patrin's city," said Vered, "but the cloud warrior must. He's stopped and is pointing."

Santon rushed forward, Vered following. They approached the cloud warrior cautiously. The huge, nebulous figure pointed to a spot in the desert. Santon dropped to his knees and began digging frantically with his good hand. Vered took the shield from his friend's left arm and used it as a giant scoop to move even more sand.

"A skeleton," Santon announced. He gingerly pushed away the sand until the entire body was revealed. "The ants have stripped off the flesh and there is no clothing left—the elements have done them in. How can we know this is Alarice's body?"

"By this," said Vered. He had continued to dig and had found a long glass sword. He held it up so that it gleamed in the bright sunlight and reflected a beam down to a rocky outjutting.

"There," said Santon, pointing to the rock the light beam selected. "We'll entomb her there."

"That's a major undertaking. It's solid rock. How can we—"

Vered and Santon were blown backward by the lightning bolt that struck the rock prominence and burned a cavity in it.

"Kaga'kalb," saluted Vered. He flourished the long glass sword in the direction of the distant Castle of the Winds. "Thank you."

They carried the bones and put them into the crypt. Santon took the glass sword from Vered and gently laid it across Alarice's skeleton. The Glass Warrior had found her final resting place.

"Rest in peace, my love," he said.

"Thank you, dear Birtle," came the phantom whisper.

Santon and Vered stepped back when the cloud warrior motioned them away. Another bolt from the twin storms at the edge of the desert fused the stone over Alarice's remains. Santon quietly recited the ceremony that would lay Alarice to rest for all eternity.

As he finished a cold wind blew choking dust in his face.

"Kaga'kalb has done what he can," said Vered. "We again have miserable winter storms in this miserable desert to plague us. Let us find somewhere cozy and warm to spend the winter. You mentioned an hospitable town to the south?"

"Let's see what we can find," said Santon. "It's been too many years since I've been in that direction. Porotane holds no real challenge for us."

Vered mounted and began singing a bawdy ballad he had learned in a western province seaport tavern. Birtle Santon did not listen to the off-key song. In his ear he heard the faint whispers of his lover.

Then they were gone.

He joined in Vered's song and did not look back.